THE
STRANGER

THE LABYRINTHS OF ECHO: BOOK ONE

THE
STRANGER

MAX FREI

Translated from the Russian by Polly Gannon

THE OVERLOOOK PRESS
New York

This edition first published in the United States in 2009 by

The Overlook Press, Peter Mayer Publishers, Inc.
141 Wooster Street
New York, NY 10012
www.overlookpress.com

Cataloging-in-Publication Data is available from the Library of Congress

Book design and type formatting by Bernard Schleifer
Manufactured in the United States of America
ISBN 978-1-59020-065-0
FIRST EDITION
1 3 5 7 9 10 8 6 4 2

CONTENTS

CHAPTER ONE

DEBUT IN ECHO

Y OU NEVER KNOW WHEN YOU'LL LUCK OUT. TAKE IT FROM ONE WHO knows. For the first twenty-nine years of my life, I was a classic loser. People tend to seek (and find) all manner of excuses for their bad luck; I didn't even have to look.

From earliest childhood I couldn't sleep at night. As soon as morning rolled around, though, I slept like a lamb. And as everyone knows, this is exactly the time when they hand out the lucky tickets. Each morning at dawn, fiery letters spanned the horizon spelling out the most unfair of all possible proverbs, "The early bird catches the worm." Don't tell me you haven't noticed!

The horror of my childhood was waiting, night after night, for the moment when my mother would tell me, "Sleep tight—don't let the bedbugs bite." Time seemed to drop its anchor under my blanket; endless hours were eaten away by my vain attempts to fall asleep. To be sure, there are also happy memories, of the sense of freedom that descends upon you when everyone else is asleep (provided, of course, that you learn to move around quietly and cover the traces of your secret activities).

But most tormenting of all was to be woken up in the morning right after I had finally dozed off. This was what made me despise kindergarten, and eventually all my years at school. True, I did get assigned to the afternoon shift two years in a row. For those two years, I was nearly an A student. That was my final (and only) brush with glory as a star pupil—until I met Sir. Juffin Hully, of course.

With time, not surprisingly, the habit that prevented me from merging harmoniously with polite society became more firmly entrenched. At the very moment when I was absolutely convinced that an inveterate night owl like me would never shine in a world ruled by larks, I met him. Sir Juffin Hully.

With a wave of his hand he put me at the maximum possible distance from home, and I found a job that corresponded absolutely to my abilities and ambitions: I became the Nocturnal Representative of the Most Venerable Head of the Minor Secret Investigative Force of the city of Echo.

❋

The story of how I came to occupy this position is so curious that it deserves a space of its own. For the time being, I will limit myself to a brief account of those distant events.

I should begin by saying, I suppose, that dreaming has always constituted an important part of my existence. Waking up from a nightmare, I was always certain deep down that my life was truly in grave danger. Falling in love with a girl from a dream could easily make me break up with my real-life girlfriend (in my youth, my heart couldn't accommodate more than one passion at a time). If I read a book in a dream, I would quote from that book to my friends as if I had read it in real life. And once, after I had a dream about a trip to Paris, I felt no compunction about claiming that I had actually been there. It wasn't that I was liar; I simply didn't see, nor did I understand, nor even feel, the difference.

❋

I should add that I met Sir Juffin Hully in my dreams. Little by little, you could say, we became acquainted.

Sir Juffin could easily be taken for Rutger Hauer's older brother. (If your imagination stretches that far, try to augment his striking image with a pair of light, slightly slanting eyes.) This effervescent gentleman, with the mannerisms and flair of an emperor of the Orient or a ringmaster in a circus, immediately won the heart of the boy I once was, the boy I remember still.

In one of my dreams we began nodding hello to each another. Soon we would chat about the weather, like regulars in a café. Such superficial banter continued for several years, when out of the blue Sir Juffin offered to help me find employment.

He announced that I had, as he put it, an extraordinary bent for magic, which I simply had to develop if I didn't want to spend the rest of my life in an asylum. He then offered his services as a coach, employer, and considerate uncle, all rolled into one. This absurd announcement was nevertheless very attractive, considering that until then I hadn't discovered a single latent talent in myself. Even in my dreams I realized that no matter how you looked at it, my career wasn't going anywhere. Sir Juffin, inspired by my apparent willingness, plucked me out of reality like a dumpling from a bowl of soup. Up until then, I was certain that I had been a victim of my own imagination—how strange we humans are, when all is said and done!

※

I will, I think, postpone the saga of my very first journey between worlds—if only because I remembered almost nothing during the earliest days of my sojourn on Echo. In fact, I couldn't make sense of anything that had happened. Quite frankly, I suspected that it was all a protracted dream, if not a convoluted hallucination. I tried not to analyze the situation, but to concentrate on solving the problems at hand, since there seemed to be plenty of them. For a start, I had to undergo an intensive period of adaptation to my new life, for I had arrived in this World far less prepared than an ordinary newborn. From the first moments of their lives babies squall and dirty their diapers without disrupting the local traditions. But from the very first I did everything all wrong. I had to sweat like a horse before I could even pass for the village idiot.

※

When I found myself in the home of Sir Juffin Hully for the first time, he was absent from the premises. Indeed, being the Most Venerable Head of the Minor Secret Investigative Force of the Capital of the Unified Kingdom was a busy job, and my protector had been detained somewhere.

The Head Butler, Kimpa, who had strict instructions from his master to give me the red-carpet treatment, was somewhat perplexed. Until now he had welcomed only respectable people to the house.

I began my new life with a question: where to find the bathroom. Even this turned out to be a faux pas. Every citizen of the Unified

Kingdom older than two knows that the bathroom facilities of every dwelling occupy the basement and are reached by a special staircase.

And my attire! Jeans, a sweater, a vest made of thick un-dyed leather, and heavy blunt-nosed boots, all succeeded in shocking the old gentleman, usually as unflappable as an Indian chieftain. He looked me up and down from head to foot for ten seconds at least. Sir Juffin swears that Kimpa hadn't fixed his stare on anyone for so long since the day of his wedding, two hundred years before, to the now-departed Mrs. Kimpa. The result of this inspection was that he suggested I change my clothes. I didn't object—I simply couldn't disappoint the expectations of the old fellow with ruffled feathers.

What happened next was painfully awkward. I was given a pile of colored fabric. I bunched up these masses of formless material in my hands, damp from agitation, and blinked my eyes wildly. Luckily, Mr. Kimpa had led a long and undoubtedly colorful life. In his time he had seen many wonders, not excluding cretins like me who lacked the most rudimentary of skills. So as not to bring shame upon the good name of his "Most Venerable Master" (as he called Sir Juffin), Kimpa set to work. In ten minutes, I looked fairly presentable from the point of view of any local resident of Echo; though, in my own humble opinion, I looked and felt extremely clumsy. When I was convinced that all these drapes and folds wouldn't inhibit my movements, and wouldn't tumble to the floor when I took a step or two, I regained my composure.

We then undertook the next test of my nerves: dinner. In a noble gesture, Kimpa deigned to keep me company at the meal. The time was thus put to good use. Before tasting each of the dishes, I would observe the performance of my teacher. After I had scrutinized the spectacle, I attempted to put the accumulated wisdom into action; that is, I dispatched toward my mouth the corresponding utensils filled with the necessary ingredients. I even went so far as to copy the expressions on his face, just in case.

At last I was left to my own devices, and was advised to take a look around the house and gardens. This I gladly did, in the company of Chuff, a charming creature who looked like a shaggy bulldog. Chuff was my guide. Without him I would most likely have gone astray in the huge, half-empty house, and been unable to find the door that led into the dense, overgrown garden. When I reached it I lay down in the grass and finally relaxed.

At sundown the elderly butler marched ceremoniously to a

diminutive, elegant shed at the end of the garden. He soon emerged from it on a small wonder of technology, which, to judge from its appearance, could only be propelled by a team of horses. Nevertheless, it moved forward on horsepower of its own. Kimpa maneuvered this contraption with a speed that, it seemed to me, corresponded to his age. (Later I learned that at one point in his long life Kimpa had been a race-car driver, and the speed at which he drove the *amobiler*—this was the name of the peculiar vehicle—was the maximum of its capacity.)

Kimpa was not alone when he returned: my old friend, denizen of my wondrous dreams, Sir Juffin Hully himself, was enthroned on the soft cushions of this motorized carriage.

Only then did I realize that everything that had happened had, indeed, happened. I rose to greet him, and in the same movement dropped to my knees in the grass, rubbing my eyes, my mouth hanging open in wonder. When my vision returned, I saw two smiling Sir Juffins coming toward me. With an intense effort of will, I merged them into one, pulled myself up on my feet, and even managed to close my jaw. This may have been the most courageous act of my life.

"That's all right, Max," Sir Juffin Hully said soothingly. "I'm not quite myself, either, and I have a tad bit more experience in these matters. I'm glad to finally make your acquaintance, body and soul!" After these words he covered his eyes with his left hand and announced solemnly: "I see you as though in a waking dream!" Then he removed his hand from his eyes and winked at me.

"This is how we make someone's acquaintance, Sir Max. Repeat after me."

I did as I was told. It turned out that my performance was "not bad for a start," after which I had to repeat the whole thing about seventeen times. I felt like the dull-witted heir to a throne, for whom they finally must enlist the help of an accomplished mentor in good manners.

Alas, the training in local etiquette didn't stop there. The fact is that Echo, from time immemorial, has been inhabited by magicians. I suspect that all Echo natives are magicians, to some degree. Luckily, exactly one-hundred fifteen years before my arrival here, the ancient rivalry between the innumerable Orders of Magicians ended in the triumph of the Order of the Seven-Leaf Clover and King Gurig VII. Since then, citizens of Echo are permitted to indulge in only the simplest kinds of magic, mainly of a medicinal or culinary nature. For instance, magic is used in the preparation of *kamra*, a substance that serves as the local alternative to tea or coffee, and is intolerably bitter without some magic to ease the effect. A touch of magic is also useful for warding off grease from plates—a groundbreaking achievement, in my opinion!

※

So I simply can't describe the sincere gratitude I feel for the Order of the Seven-Leaf Clover. Thanks to their scheming intrigues that determined the course of history, I didn't have to learn, say, the two-hundred thirty-fourth degree of White Magic—which experts consider to be the apex of human capability. I decided that as far as I was concerned, the officially permitted tricks were the limit of my meager abilities. In a sense, I am a virtuoso-invalid, not unlike the legless British flying ace, Douglas Bader. Sir Juffin insists, by the way, that my greatest virtue is that I belong to the world of wizardry, albeit not that I know how to cope with it . . .

On the evening of the first day of my new life, I stood before the mirror in the bedroom assigned to me and studied my reflection. I was wrapped up like a mannequin in the thin folds of the *skaba*, a long roomy tunic, and the heavy folds of the *looxi*, an overgarment that resembled a delightful compromise between a long raincoat and a poncho. The extravagant turban, strange as it may seem, looked very becoming on me. Maybe in this guise it was easier to preserve my equilibrium while straining to grasp just what was happening to me, for that guy in the mirror could be just about anybody in the world—except a close acquaintance of mine by the name of Max.

Chuff came up and began yapping and nudging my knee with his nose. *You're big and kind!* I suddenly thought, in a voice not my own. Then I realized that the thought was not mine, but his. The intelligent dog became my first teacher of Silent Speech in this World. If I am even mildly adept at White Magic of the Fourth Degree, which includes this kind of communication, I would kindly ask you to direct all compliments toward this remarkable canine.

※

The days reeled quickly by. I slept away the mornings. Toward evening I got up, dressed, ate, and then hovered around Kimpa with endless questions and observations. Luckily, I was never troubled by any linguistic barriers between myself and the other residents of the Unified Kingdom—why, I don't know to this day. All I found it necessary to do was master the local pronunciation and take note of a few new idioms, but that was just a matter of time.

My training progressed under the gentle but rigorous supervision of Kimpa, who had been entrusted with the task of making a "true gentleman out of this barbarian, born on the border of the County Vook and the Barren Lands." Such was the "legend" of my origins for Kimpa and all the others.

It was a very cleverly concocted legend, as I now know: a true masterpiece on the part of Sir Juffin Hully, in the genre of improvised falsification. See, County Vook is the part of the Unified Kingdom most distant from Echo. These Borderlands are sparsely populated plains that gently merge into the endless, inhospitable expanses of the Barren Lands, which are not under the domain of the Unified Kingdom. Almost no one from the capital had ever been there, as there was no point in taking such a trip, one that was not without danger. Those who dwell there—the good half of whom (according to Sir Juffin) were ignorant nomads, and the rest, runaway rebel magicians—don't lavish their praises on the capital, either.

"However quirky you may seem," Sir Juffin Hully mused, rocking cozily in his favorite chair, "you won't have to make any excuses for yourself. Your origins are the best explanation for anything that constitutes a blunder in the eyes of the local snobs. Take it from me: I myself arrived in the capital from Kettari, a small town in the county of Shimara. That was long ago, but they're still expecting outlandish pranks from me. I sometimes think they feel affronted that I behave with such aplomb."

"Excellent, Sir Juffin! Then I'll go ahead and start acting like one right here and now!" With that I did what I had been longing to do—I snatched up a tiny warm tart from my plate, without the aid of the miniature hook that looked more like an instrument of torture from a dentist's arsenal than silverware. Sir Juffin smiled indulgently.

"You'll make a first-class barbarian, Max. I don't doubt it for a minute."

"That doesn't bother me in the least," I said with my mouth full. "You see, Juffin, all my life I've been absolutely certain that I'm fine just as I am, and that I'm immune to the consequences of a bad reputation. That is to say, I have too much self-love to trouble myself with the torments of self-doubt and the search for self-affirmation, if you know what I mean."

"But you're a true philosopher!"

Sir Juffin Hully seemed to be quite satisfied with me.

✷

Let me return to describing my studies. My passion for the printed word had never been as useful to me as it was during those first days. At night I devoured books by the dozens from Sir Juffin's library. I learned about my new surroundings, at the same time grasping the idiosyncrasies of the locals and cramming my head full of colorful turns of phrase. Chuff tagged along at my heels and was fully engaged in my schooling for he gave me lessons in Silent Speech. Evenings (the middle of the day, by my personal clock), I reported to Sir Juffin. He kept me company at dinner and unobtrusively monitored all aspects of my progress. An hour or two later, Sir Juffin would disappear into his bedroom and I would move on to the library.

✷

One evening, roughly two weeks after my abrupt arrival in Echo, Sir Juffin announced that I now fully resembled an ordinary person, and thus deserved a reward.

"Today we're dining in the *Glutton*, Max! I've been looking forward to this moment."

"Dining where?"

"The *Glutton Bunba*, the most elegant mangy dive of them all: hot pâtés, the best kamra in Echo, the splendid Madam Zizinda, and not a single sourpuss to be seen at this hour of day."

"What do you mean, not a single sourpuss?"

"Actually, not a single unpleasant face of any kind—but you know this place better than most Echoers!"

"How's that?"

"You'll see. Put on your shoes and let's go. I'm as hungry as an armless thief."

And so for the first time I changed from my house slippers into tall moccasins that aspired to look like real boots. I also had a driver's test—ha! As if that was anything to worry about! Having mastered the rusty heap that had belonged to my cousin, and even inherited it when he hit the big time and treated himself to some swanky new wheels, driving the amobiler didn't pose any problem for me. Several days before, Kimpa had demonstrated for me the simple steps of operating the car, carried out with the help of a single lever. After a short ride in my company, he announced, "You're going to be fine," and left. Now Juffin was admiring my professionalism, saying: "Take it easy, young man! Life's short enough as it is!" After a few minutes he added: "Too bad I don't need a chauffeur. I'd hire you in a minute." I swelled with pride right then and there.

Driving did not distract me from my first real encounter with Echo. First we threaded our way through narrow lanes weaving through the magnificent gardens of the Left Bank. Each yard was illumined in keeping with the taste of its owner, so we rode through bright dappled patches of color, yellow, pink, green, and lilac. I had often admired the nighttime gardens of the Left Bank from the roof of our house, but floating from one lush lake of color to another—it was something else entirely!

Then we entered what appeared to be a broad avenue lined with the bright little lights of stores still open. It turned out though that I hadn't understood a thing about this particular urban landscape. This wasn't an avenue, but rather, Echo Crest, one of the many bridges that connected the Left Bank with the Right. The waters of a river declared the finest in the Unified Kingdom, the Xuron, sparkled in the spaces between buildings. Halfway across the bridge I even slowed down, struck by the splendor of the view on both sides. To my right, on a large island in the middle of the river, was Rulx Castle, the royal residence, glittering with all the hues of a rainbow, while on the left another island gleamed with a steady sapphire light.

"That's Xolomi, Max. The Xolomi prison is there. A splendid little place!"

"Splendid?"

"From the point of view of the Head of the Minor Secret Investigative Force, such as I am, if you will remember, it is the most exquisite place in the World!" Juffin gave a short snort.

"Oh, I forgot who I was contending with . . ."

I glanced at Juffin. He twisted his face into an evil grimace, winked, and we both burst into laughter.

After we composed ourselves, we continued on our way until there it was, the Right Bank. Juffin began issuing abrupt commands: "Right, right, now to the left!" in response to which I assumed the dignified bearing of an army chauffeur, though where that particular bent came from I have no idea. A bit farther and we were on the Street of the Copper Pots.

"Over there is our House by the Bridge," Juffin remarked, waving his hand toward the orange mist under some street lights. "But your visit there is yet to come. As for now—stop! We're here."

I halted the amobiler and stepped onto the mosaic sidewalk of the Right Bank for the first time. Oh, was it really the first time? But I suppressed the dangerous dizziness, nipped it square in the bud, and passed over the threshold of the *Glutton Bunba Inn*. Of course—it was the pub from my dreams, the very place I had met Sir Juffin Hully and frivolously accepted the strangest job offer anyone could ever imagine!

Without even thinking, I walked over to the familiar spot between the bar and a window onto the yard. A plump brunette smiled at me as though I was an old customer (this was Madam Zizinda herself, granddaughter of the original glutton named Bunba). But why "as though"? I was, indeed, an old, a very old, customer.

"This is my favorite little spot," Juffin announced. "I'll tell you a basic principle for choosing future colleagues. If they like the same food and, in particular, the same table you like, psychological compatibility with the team is guaranteed."

Madam Zizinda, in the meantime, had placed pots with hot pâté on our table. As for the other events of the evening that followed, someday I will commit them to paper, when I sit down to write my tourist guidebook: *The Finest Taverns of the City of Echo*.

❀

My second foray into society took place two days later. Sir Juffin returned home very early, even before dusk. I was just about to have breakfast.

"Tonight is your debut performance, Max!" Juffin declared, confiscating my mug of kamra without waiting for Kimpa to pour him his own. "We're going to test your progress on my favorite neighbor. If old Makluk still says hello to me after our visit, we may conclude that you are ready for independence. In my view, you can already manage very well on your own. But I'm not being objective: I'm too eager to put you to work."

"But just think, Juffin; he's your neighbor! You'll have to live with him afterward."

"Makluk is kind and inoffensive. Moreover, he's practically a hermit. He found society so unbearably cloying while he was the Long Arm for the Elimination of Irksome Misunderstandings at the Royal Court that now he can endure the company only of me and a few elderly chatterbox widowers—and that very seldom."

"Are you a widower?"

"Yes, more than thirty years now; so it's not a forbidden topic. For the first twenty years or so, though, I preferred not to talk about it. We marry at a ripe age, and, generally (we hope), for a long time. But we are accustomed to suppose that fate is wiser than the heart, so don't fret!"

And so that I would fret as little as possible, he seized the second mug of kamra, which, I must admit, I had wanted very much myself.

※

We arrayed ourselves in formal dress and set off to pay our visit. Fortunately, visiting costume differed from everyday dress only in its richness of hue and ornament, and not in its cut, to which I had already grown accustomed. I was on my way to an exam, and my heart leapt about in my chest, looking for the shortest route to my heels.

"Max, what's with the serious face?" Juffin asked in a knowing tone. He always could tell what I was feeling; I supposed that for him, my emotional state was like the headline on the front page of a tabloid: utter nonsense, but written in boldface type that makes glasses superfluous.

"I'm getting into the role," I improvised. "Any barbarian from the Borderlands would be nervous before meeting someone who had gotten cuffs on the ear from His Royal Highness all his life."

"Ingenuity, B; erudition D-plus: 'Barbarians from the Borderlands,' as you phrase it, are supercilious, proud, and ignorant. They scoff at our public servants and officials in the capital. Intuition, A-plus! How else could you have guessed that once, under the reign of Gurig, Sir Makluk really did earn a royal box on the ears when he trod on the hem of the royal robe?"

"To be honest, I was trying to joke, not playing a guessing game."

"That's what I meant when I mentioned intuition. Just like that, apropos of nothing, you let something slip, and it's right on the nose!"

"Okay, suppose I am a prodigy. Also, according to your legend, I'm a barbarian who has serious intentions of settling down in Echo and embarking on a career. So I must be somewhat different from my ignorant but proud countrymen. And when a person wears a veneer of studied hauteur, shyness is usually lurking underneath. I know: I'm the same way. Do you take back your D-plus?"

"All right, you've convinced me. I'll take back the 'D,' and you can keep the 'plus.'"

We crossed our garden and entered the neighbor's through a side gate. Then we were at the front door, with an inscription that read "Here lives Sir Makluk. Are you sure you've come to the right place?" I laughed halfheartedly, as I was not at all sure. On the other hand, Sir Juffin had enough conviction for both of us.

The door opened silently, and four servants in identical gray uniforms invited us in chorus to enter. A quartet that was nothing if not professional; I had to hand it to them.

And so began that for which I was not prepared; but then, Juffin claims that no one is ever prepared for a reception by Sir Makluk, except inveterate society lions—the most important and useless creatures in the world.

A horde of strapping young fellows advanced ominously upon us from the corner, with two palanquins atilt. At the same time, the servants in gray handed us each a pile of multihued rags of ambiguous purpose. There was only one thing for me to do: watch Juffin and try to mimic all his actions.

First I had to take off the looxi, without which I felt somewhat naked: the thin skaba that gave my body a high-definition contour did not at the moment seem appropriate dress for appearing in public. Then I began studying the garments I had been given and determined it wasn't a pile of varied rags, but a one-piece construction—a large crescent made of thick fabric, with enormous patch pockets. The inner edge of the crescent was adorned with a kind of necklace made from bright scraps of sheer material. I stared at Sir Juffin. My only guide through the labyrinth of good manners donned his crescent with a careless gesture like it was a baby's bib. Shuddering, I repeated his performance. The band of butlers remained expressionless. Juffin wasn't putting on an act for me, apparently; we were doing just what was expected of us.

When we were finally appropriately decked out, the fellows with the palanquins went down on their knees before us. Sir Juffin mounted the contraption and reclined gracefully upon it. I gulped and clambered onto my own glorified stretcher in turn. We were carried along in this way for quite some time, gazing down deserted corridors as broad as streets as we progressed. The sheer spaciousness of Sir

Makluk's dwelling made an indelible impression on me, and judging by the outside of the house, you'd never have known—it appeared to be just an ordinary house of modest dimensions.

Finally we arrived at a large hall, half-empty, like all the rooms in the only house in Echo with which I was acquainted. But the similarity to Sir Juffin's interiors stopped there. Instead of a normal dining table and comfortable armchairs, my eyes beheld something quite extraordinary.

A narrow and seemingly endless oval table cut through the length of the room. Its centerpiece was a fountain, surrounded by a thick paling of low podiums. On one of the podiums was a palanquin that resembled those in which we had just had the distinct pleasure of arriving. A lively-looking gray-haired old man, who didn't appear in the least like a grandee, peered out of the palanquin. This was Sir Makluk, our hospitable host. When he saw me he covered his eyes with his hand and greeted me:

"I see you as though in a waking dream!"

I reciprocated his gesture: Juffin and I had gone through this one. Then the little old man held out his hand to Juffin, doing this with such ardent warmth that he nearly tumbled off the podium, together with his dubious means of transportation.

"Hide the food, here comes Sir Hully the Hun!" he exclaimed gleefully. I readily concluded that this was an official form of greeting, and stored it away for future reference. It turned out I was mistaken, however: the host was in the mood for joking. I was more than a little insulted. I tried to grin and bear it, but, come what may, one's emotional health is more important than emotional equilibrium. Did you wish to spend the weekend in the company of Mad Max, dear Juffin? Well, that's just what's in store for you! Here goes nothing . . .

But nothing came of it, for again I was thrown into a state of bewilderment when a very young creature of indeterminate sex came up to me. To distinguish a girl from a boy here, you need a keen eye and a great deal of experience, since they dress identically, and the hair of both sexes is allowed to grow as it will and then bound up, so that it doesn't get in the way. The child was holding a basket with appetizing little bread rolls, which I had already grown fond of while devouring the breakfasts prepared by Kimpa. As fate would have it, I was the first stop for the little peddler of delicacies. No one was there to save me, as Juffin had been steered to the other end of the room to join the hospitable host. I helped myself silently to one bread roll. The little creature seemed surprised, but quickly slipped away. When it took the offerings to the gentlemen who had more experience in such matters than I, I realized what had caused the reaction—my very modesty and restraint! Juffin, and Sir Makluk, following suit, began raking up bread rolls by the handfuls and stuffing them into the roomy pockets of their "bibs." It looked like I was going to starve.

In the meantime, my stretcher-bearers had begun shifting their feet, as though they couldn't figure out where to deposit me. Judging by their blank faces, I was supposed to make this decision myself.

Raise your thumb, resounded someone else's thought through my poor brain, *and they'll start walking. When you want to stop, show them your fist.*

Thank you, Juffin, I answered, trying with all my might to address my mute message with maximum accuracy to its destination. *You just about saved my life. I wish you always would!*

Excellent. You're getting the hang of Silent Speech, he declared happily.

I carried out the first part of his instructions and found myself floating in the direction of my dinner companions. When I was close enough to observe their actions, I threatened the bearers with my fist; they stopped, and raised me up onto a podium. I sighed with relief; finally, I had a moment to catch my breath.

Altogether, we journeyed around the table several times. The system was as follows: opposite every podium stood one dish. Having tasted it and wiped your mouth with one of the bright scraps that decorated the "bib," the idea was to raise your thumb and travel around the table at a leisurely pace. When you came upon a dish that aroused the interest of the taste-buds, you were supposed to drop anchor for a spell.

For the first half-hour I was still rather timid, and stayed put even when the food in front of me did not deserve such a lengthy pause. Finally, with a "what the hey," I got into the swing of things. I tasted everything there was to taste, some things more than once. After downing some "Jubatic Juice," the local firewater, with its unassuming, yet somehow fitting name, I even ventured to join in the conversation of the old friends—and judging from Sir Makluk's jovial demeanor, not without some success.

In short, the dinner went off without any untoward surprises.

�

As soon as we left Sir Makluk's, I could no longer constrain my curiosity.

"Well, how did it go? You discussed me with your neighbor, didn't you? Of course, Silent Speech allows you to do that in your victim's presence—"

"My fabrication unraveled completely!" Sir Juffin said, grinning with fiendish pleasure. He paused dramatically, during which time I berated myself for being a miserable, dull-witted imbecile. Then he rescued me from my despair: "The old man kept trying to weasel out of me where I had dug up such well-mannered specimen of barbarian! Much more, and he would have offered you a position at court."

"Oh no! What will happen now?"

"Nothing much. In a week or two we'll find you an apartment and furnish it according to your inclinations, after which I'll get you off my back and you'll get down to work. For the time being, you still have a few lessons left with me."

"What kinds of lessons?"

"Very interesting ones. Don't worry, the lessons in dining etiquette are over. It's time to get down to business. At long last, I've acquired an assistant who has a distinct proclivity for Invisible Magic. You'll be surprised to discover how easily it comes to you."

"Wherever did you get the idea that I—?"

"Whenever did you stop trusting me?"

"The moment we stepped inside the home of your neighbor Sir Makluk! You never warned me about the palanquins and all the rest. I nearly died right there on the spot!"

"But you didn't!" Sir Juffin Hully said. "Who would have thought!"

That night I not only retired to bed long before dawn, but slept like a log, to the great surprise of little Chuff. He already took it for granted that life only starts to get really interesting after midnight.

✤

The next two days were busy and pleasant. During the day I read old newspaper files from the *Royal Voice* and *Echo Hustle and Bustle*. Sir Juffin had immodestly marked all the enthusiastic articles that had to do with the affairs of the Secret Investigative Force.

This made for far more exciting reading than the most piquant literature. It was the first time I had read newspapers in which dull announcements about the misuse of forbidden magic far exceeded stories about everyday murder, revenge, and extortion—though such things happen here, too, of course. I quickly learned the names of my future colleagues: Sir Melifaro (for some reason his first name was never mentioned), Sir Kofa Yox, Sir Shurf Lonli-Lokli, Lady Melamori Blimm, and Sir Lookfi Pence. They pretty much made up the entire Minor Secret Investigative Force—and a fairly diminutive one it was.

Here in Echo, photography had still not been discovered, and portrait artists would not condescend to squander their talents on newspapers. Thus, I put my imagination to work, summoning up portraits of them in my head. (Whatever Sir Juffin might have said about my intuition, it turned out that I hadn't guessed right a single time!)

At sunset, I took the amobiler and set off for the Right Bank. I got out and meandered along mosaic-laden sidewalks, gazing this way and that, made brief stops at cozy inns, and got a feel for the topography. Indeed, what kind of figure would I cut as a Nocturnal Representative of the Venerable Head of the Minor Secret Investigative Force if I couldn't even track down the street where my own department was located? It turned out to be fairly easy, however. I've never heard of a wolf getting lost in the woods, even if they're not the woods in which he was born. I suspect the existence of some as-yet-undiscovered "urban instinct," whereby if you can navigate one city, you won't feel daunted by any other metropolis.

Then I was on my way home. As it had ever been in my life, nighttime still proved to be the most enchanting time of day. Sir Juffin, by his own admission, had had a temporary quarrel with his blanket. After dinner, he didn't retire, but steered me into his study, where we undertook to "meditate on the memory of things." This aspect of Invisible Magic, the most abstract and obscure science of this World, was the simplest and most indispensable one for my future profession.

There are few in the World who have any inkling of its existence. A knack for Invisible Magic, as far as I understand it, is in no way linked to the wondrous qualities of the Heart of the World. Indeed, this talent had been discovered in me, an alien. Sir Juffin himself, the undisputed expert in this area, hails from Kettari, a small town in the county of Shimara. The residents of that place lag significantly behind residents of the capital when it comes to knowing how to enhance their lives by means of magic.

But back to the lessons. I discovered very quickly that if you let your eyes rest on an inanimate object with a "special gaze" (I don't know how else to describe it), the object would reveal its past to the observer—that is to say, events that happened in its presence. Sometimes these events were quite horrific, as I learned after an encounter with a pin for a looxi that had belonged long ago to a member of the Order of the Icy Hand, one of the most sinister and wicked of the ancient orders of magic. The pin showed us the rite of passage into the Order: a frenzied, exultant bear of a fellow voluntarily hacked off his left hand from his arm, after which a handsome, spry old fellow in a shiny turban (the Grand Master of the Order, as Juffin informed me) launched into some bizarre, incomprehensible fumblings with the amputated piece of anatomy. During the finale, the hand was presented to its former owner in the center of a glittering ice crystal. It turned my stomach.

Juffin explained that as a result of this procedure the fresh-baked invalid had gained an eternal inner fountain of marvelous youthful energy, and his missing digits would become a kind of "supersponge" that provided him with the powers indispensable to that occupation.

"Does he really need that?" I asked in naïve wonder.

"People will do strange things to sate their hunger for power and glory," Juffin replied with a shrug. "You and I are lucky. We live in a much more moderate age. The opposition is complaining about the tyranny of the King and the Order of the Seven-Leaf Clover, yet they forget the true tyranny of several dozen omnipotent orders of magic, of which almost none has ever chosen the path of rejecting vice and ambition altogether."

"Why didn't they tear the World to shreds?"

"They almost did, Max. They almost did . . . But we'll have time to talk about that later. This is the night when you to begin your studies in earnest. So, grab that cup there . . ."

❋

This was all too good to be able to last for very long. The idyll was shattered on the evening of the third day, when Kimpa announced the arrival of Sir Makluk.

"Strange," Juffin said. "In the ten years we have been neighbors this is the first time Makluk has ever honored me with a visit. And so casually! Too casually, by far. My heart fears that there is some business to take care of."

Little did he know how right he was.

"I'm afraid circumstances force me to request a service of you!" Makluk exclaimed, still standing in the threshold, holding one hand to his chest, and gesticulating wildly with the other. "I beg your pardon, Sir Hully, but I am in great need of your help and advice."

They exchanged a long, meaningful glance; the old fellow had switched to Silent Speech. A moment later, Juffin frowned, and Sir Makluk shrugged, looking a bit shamefaced.

"Let's go," Juffin said abruptly, and stood up. "And you, Max, come with us. Don't bother to dress up. This is business."

For the first time I was witnessing Juffin Hully on the job—or, more precisely, on the verge of one. The speed at which he crossed the garden exceeded in all likelihood the cruising speed of the amobiler. I automatically undertook to pacify Sir Makluk, who clearly felt a bit unmoored without the four heavyweights who carried his palanquin. We reached the finish without breaking any records—but also without doing any damage to his weak knees. Along the way, Sir Makluk took advantage of the opportunity to confide in the "Gentle Barbarian." He seemed to need to get it off his chest.

"I have—or, rather, had—a servant named Krops Kooly, a good lad. I had even planned to secure a place for him at court in fifteen or twenty years, when he had some experience under his belt . . . But I digress. A few days ago, he disappeared. Disappeared—just like that. He had a sweetheart on the Right Bank. Naturally, his colleagues decided that since you're only young once, they wouldn't make a fuss about it. You know, simple people are also capable of noble discretion . . . His disappearance was reported to me only today. My cook ran into his girlfriend at Linus Market, and the girl asked him why Krops hadn't been to see her in so long—didn't they allow him any Days of Freedom from his professional commitments? Then everyone began to panic. How could Krops just up and leave? Where had he gone, and why? About an hour and a half ago, Maddi and Shuvish went to clean the room of my late cousin, Sir Makluk-Olli, as they always did at that time. Yes, Sir Max, I had a cousin, a big bore, I'll have you know. It even took him ten years to die. He finally decided to go at the beginning of the year, soon after the Day of Foreign Gods. Yes . . . and in there, in the room of my late cousin Olli, they found poor Mr. Kooly; and in what condition!"

Sir Makluk shivered visibly, as if to say that he had never expected such antics from poor Krops Kooly, even posthumously.

In the meantime, we had arrived at a small door—the backdoor of Sir Makluk's luxurious living quarters. The old fellow had grown somewhat calmer after relating the recent events. Silent Speech is all well and good, but it's not for nothing that psychotherapists make their patients talk out loud.

Without wasting time to call for a palanquin, we made our way into the late Sir Olli's bedroom. Almost half the room was taken up by a soft floor. Here in Echo this is the way beds are constructed. A few tiny marquetry tables were scattered haphazardly around the giant lair. One wall was an enormous window onto the garden. On the opposite wall there was an ancient mirror with a small vanity table to the side.

It would have been preferable if this had about summed things up, but there was another element of the room's interior. On the floor, between the mirror and the window, lay a corpse, a dead body that resembled, more than anything else, slobbery chewing gum. The spectacle was not even grisly; it was, rather, awkward, even absurd.

Somehow, it didn't fit my notions of a crime victim—no streams of blood, spattered brains, no icy gaze of a dead man. Just some sorry, rubbery ABC gum.

I didn't see Juffin at first. He had retreated to the farthest corner of the room. His slanting eyes shone phosphorescent in the dusk. When he saw us, he abandoned his post and came up to us with a deeply troubled expression.

"For the time being, two pieces of bad news; I daresay more will follow. First, this is no ordinary murder. You don't end up with someone looking like that with your bare hands alone. Second, I've not discovered any signs of Forbidden Magic. I'm very suspicious of the mirror, as it seems to be too close to the body. This looks like a case of Black Magic of the Second Degree; the Third Degree, at most. And, it already happened long ago." In his hands Juffin was pensively rotating a pipe with a built-in gauge, which conveyed precise information about the degree of magic that it detected. Now the arrow pointed to the number "2" on the black half of the round dial. Sometimes it shuddered visibly, trying to crawl up to "3"; but the kind of magic locked in the ancient mirror wasn't strong enough for that.

"My advice to you, neighbor, is to go get some rest. Just, tell your vassals that Max and I will still snoop around here. Have them assist us in the investigation."

"Sir Hully, are you sure I can't help you?"

"I'm positive," Juffin sighed. "It's possible that your people can—so give them your orders, and retire to bed. Whatever has happened, it's no reason to neglect your own health."

"Thank you," the old man said, drawing his lips into a troubled smile. "I've truly had all I can handle for one day."

Sir Makluk turned toward the door with an expression of relief. At the threshold he met someone who looked to be the same age as he, though a very colorful character. The face of the stranger resembled that of some Grand Inquisitor—putting him under the gray turban of a servant that he wore was an inexcusable waste. But I wasn't the one who made this World, and I was certainly in no position to change the way things are.

"Dear Govins," Sir Makluk said, addressing the "Grand Inquisitor." "Be so kind as to assist these superb gentlemen in all their efforts. This is our neighbor, Sir Juffin Hully, and he—"

"How could I, an inveterate reader of the *Echo Hustle and Bustle,* not know Sir Most Venerable Head?" A servile smile spread over the Inquisitor's face.

"Splendid," Sir Makluk, said almost in a whisper. "Govins will take care of everything. He's still stronger than I am, though he fussed over me in the blessed days when I was too small to sneak a little bowl of jam from the kitchen."

On that sentimental note, Sir Makluk was hoisted onto the palanquin by the eager stretcher-bearers and borne away to his bedchamber.

"If you don't mind, I'll have a few words with you in a minute. I hope in your wisdom you'll agree that our first acquaintance could have taken place in more . . . er . . . less messy circumstances!" Juffin said to Govins, smiling with irresistible aplomb.

"The small parlor, the best kamra in the capital, and your humble servant await you whenever you wish." With these words, the elderly gentleman seemed to dissolve into the half-gloom of the corridor.

We were left by ourselves, not counting the chewed up fellow on the floor, and he didn't really count any more.

"Max," Juffin said, turning to me, his *joie de vivre* suddenly snuffed out. "There's another bit of bad news. Not a single thing in this room wants to reveal the past. They—how should I put it to you . . . No, let's try it again, together! You'll see what I mean."

And try we did, concentrating our attention on a round box with balsam soap, randomly selected from the dressing table. Nothing! More to the point, worse than nothing. I was suddenly stricken with a fright, the kind you feel in a nightmare when your feet are planted to the ground and they are creeping upon you out of the darkness. My nerves gave out; I let go of the box. At almost the same time, Juffin's fingers released it, and the box fell to the floor. It bounced rather awkwardly, turned over on its side, and instead of rolling in the direction of the window, it seemed to try to slip into the corridor. Halfway there, it stopped short, clattered plaintively, and made a comical little leap. We stared at it spellbound.

"You were right, Sir Juffin," I said, whispering for some reason. "The things are silent, and they're . . . *scared*!"

"What are they afraid of, is what I'd like to know! It is possible to find out—but for that we need magic of at least the hundredth degree. But in this case—"

"Wait, what degree was that?"

"You heard right! Come along, let's have a talk with the leader of the local serfs and his underlings. What else can we do?"

Mr. Govins was waiting for us in the "small parlor" (which was actually just slightly smaller than your average football field). Mugs of kamra were steaming on a miniscule table. Juffin relaxed ever so slightly.

"I must know everything concerning these premises, Govins. And I mean *everything*! Facts, rumors, tall tales. And, preferably, first hand."

"I am the oldest resident of this house," the old man began pompously, then broke into a disarming smile. "Wherever you might turn, I'm the oldest! Well, in Echo there are a few old stumps that are even more ancient than I am. I assure you, Sir Venerable Head, it's a very ordinary chamber. No wonders or miracles—whether permitted or outlawed. For as long as I can remember, that has always been someone's bedroom. At times, it was occupied, at times it stood empty. But no one ever complained about family ghosts. Moreover, before Sir Makluk-Olli, no one had ever died there. And even he lived five years longer than he was expected to."

"How did he die?"

"There were a number of causes. He had been ailing since childhood. A weak heart, delicate digestion, nerves. And about ten years ago, he lost the Spark."

"Sinning Magicians! Do you mean that?"

"Absolutely. But he had amazing tenacity of spirit. For you know, of course, that people without the Spark seldom hold out longer than a year. Sir Olli was told that if he remained immobile and refused to take food he would live another five years or so, provided there was a good Seer in attendance on him. For ten years, he didn't leave his room. He fasted, hired a dozen mad but powerful old crones who guarded his shadow in voluntary confinement with him all those years . . . As you see, Olli established a kind of record. But the old crones did their spells at their own homes, so in Olli's bedchamber nothing out of the ordinary went on."

Sir Juffin didn't neglect to send me a Silent Message: *To lose the Spark means to lose the ability to protect oneself from whatever might happen. Even ordinary food may be poisonous for the unlucky person, and a common cold can kill him in a few hours. And that the crones guarded his shadow . . . well, it's quite complicated. I'll explain later!*

"Old Sir Makluk-Olli led the quietest of lives. A year before his death he gave one sign of life when he threw a washbowl at Maddi, who was waiting on him that day. The water he had drawn was a tad warmer than it ought to have been. I gave Maddi compensation for the blow, but even without the money he wouldn't have kicked up a fuss. Sir Olli made a pitiful spectacle. The servants never made any more mistakes like that. As for Sir Olli, he didn't get up to any mischief again, and nothing unusual, it would seem, ever occurred . . ."

Juffin frowned.

"Don't hide anything from me, old man. I admire your loyalty to the house, but I'm the one who helped Sir Makluk hush up the unpleasantness half a year ago, when that young fellow from Gazhin cut his own throat. So do give me some balm to ease my aching heart: did that happen in the bedchamber?"

Govins nodded.

If you think that Govins' confession solves the case, you're mistaken, Juffin said soundlessly, with a wink in my direction. *It only confuses the matter, though, further down the line . . . This all smacks of magic from the time of the Ancient Orders, but the blasted magic gauge, a hole in the heavens above it . . . Then again, that's what makes life worth living: you never know what to expect!*

He turned to Govins.

"I want to see: the person who first discovered the poor blighter today, the person who discovered the bloody fountain last time, the crones hired by Sir Olli, and a mug of your excellent kamra for everyone present. Oh, and just to be sure, ask the unhappy victim of domestic tyranny to come, as well. The one who was wounded by the washbowl."

Govins nodded. A middle-aged man in gray with a proud bearing appeared at the door carrying a tray of mugs. This was Mr. Maddi himself, victim of the erstwhile fury of Sir Makluk-Olli; and, as if by design, the primary witness of today's crime. That's true organizational genius! Take note, gentlemen—one person entered the room, and three of five requests had already been carried out!

Maddi was burning with embarrassment, but good bearing never served a man amiss. Eyes cast down, he reported without undue circumlocutions that this evening he had entered the room first, looked out the window at the sunset, then looked down to see something one couldn't miss. He quickly realized that it was best not to touch *it* and instead to send for Mr. Govins. Which he did.

"I asked Shuvish to stay in the corridor. He's still too young to see the likes of that," Maddi said, hesitating, as though he might have overstepped his bounds.

"You didn't hear any noise?"

"The bedchamber was soundproofed, Sir Olli ordered that it be made so. What I mean is, even if you were screaming fit to burst, no one would hear. Nor would *you* hear any noise, naturally."

"Fine. That all makes sense. But what was this fight you had with Sir Olli? They say he really let you have it."

"No fight, Sir Venerable Head. A sick man doesn't want to die; he's unhappy about everything. He always explained to me how he wanted the water for his bath. But then the next day he wanted the water to be another way altogether. Every time I went and did as he ordered, but one day Sir Olli got mad and threw the washbowl at me. And you should've seen the man throw! He never should have died," Maddi let out a low whistle of admiration.

I was sure that if he had been a basketball coach, he would have tried to recruit Sir Olli onto his team without a second thought.

"The bowl hit me straight in the face, the edge gouging my eyebrow. It started to bleed, and like an imbecile, I tried to turn away, and crashed into the mirror with all my might. Luckily, it was a sturdy thing. Old craftsmanship! I was soaking wet, my face covered in blood, the mirror all bloodied up, too. Sir Olli panicked, he thought he had killed me. Raised quite a commotion. And when I washed my face, it turned out that it was nothing at all—a scratch half a finger's length long. It didn't even leave a scar! It never entered my head to complain—you can't let yourself get insulted by an old man. He didn't even have the Spark anymore; he was all but dead already—and I'm still strong and kicking. I can grin and bear it."

"Fine, fine, my friend. That's all we needed to know. Don't worry—you did just what you were supposed to do."

Maddi was dismissed, and went off to contemplate his dreams—and simple and innocent dreams they were, of that I'm certain. Sir Juffin glanced at Govins questioningly.

"The crones have been sent for. I hope they'll all be found. They have the same sort of nomadic profession that you have. For the time being, I may be able to assist you myself, since the death of Nattis, that unfortunate young man, took place right under my nose."

"That's news to me! How did you manage that?"

"Such was the order of things. The boy was my ward. You see, Nattis wasn't a servant in the house. An ordinary servant, that is. Two years ago he came to Echo from Gazhin. He arrived with a note from his grandfather, one of my oldest friends. The old man wrote that his grandson was an orphan, and was still wet behind the ears. The kind of knowledge he could pick up in Gazhin wasn't much use here in Echo. But the boy was quick-witted—that was plain as day. My friend asked me to help his grandson in any way I could. Sir Makluk promised to give him the highest recommendation. He even intended to set him up with someone at the Court. You understand, it's a real privilege to be offered a place at Court! But in the interim, I taught him to the best of my abilities. Believe me, I had just as much reason to praise him when he was still alive. Occasionally we gave him a Day of Freedom from Some Chores. On those days he wasn't free to go off on his own, as he was on ordinary Days of Freedom, but stayed home. He was relieved of his duties, however, and was expected to live the life of a gentleman."

At this point, I couldn't repress a sigh of sympathy. Poor guy!

Govins interpreted my sigh in his own way, shook his head sadly, and continued: "What I mean is that if you wish to go far in life, you need know not only how to work, but also how to give orders. On those days, Nattis got up in the morning, called for a servant, bathed and groomed himself, dressed like a gentleman, ate like a gentleman, read the newspaper. Then he would go for a walk on the Right Bank, and there he also did his best to look like a young gentleman of the capital rather than a young upstart from Gazhin. And on those days he was permitted to use Sir Olli's bedchamber—the poor bloke had just died when Nattis arrived and began his apprenticeship. The fellow would sleep in that bedroom, and in the morning would call for a servant—and the servant was me! The idea was not only to put on a charade, but to be able to observe all his shortcomings and mistakes, and so to correct them. In short, on those days I was inseparable from the lad, and this was both instructive and pleasant . . . So on that fateful morning, I answered his summons, as usual. I brought in the bath water. Of course, this was only a ceremonial ritual—there is a bathroom attached to the bedchamber. But a real gentleman begins his morning by demanding his rightful portion of warm water for a bath!"

At this point in the narrative I became a bit glum. I'd never become a "real gentleman"; and Sir Juffin wouldn't either, I'm afraid. The finicky Sir Govins, in the meantime, went on with his story: "Nattis washed and went into the bathroom to shave. But the poor lad remembered all of a sudden how I had scolded him for this. As long as you're god-knows-who, whether you shave in the bathroom or don't bother to shave at all is no one's business but your own. But if you're a gentleman, you must shave in front of a proper looking glass! It turned out that my efforts hadn't been for nought. The young chap came back into the room and very contritely requested a shaving kit. I feigned not to hear. Then he drew himself up, his eyes sparking—and I was there with the shaving kit and a towel, on the double! And then—how it could have happened, my mind simply cannot fathom. That a hale and hearty young fellow could cut his throat with a razor in a split second! I was standing a few steps away from him, as is the custom, with a towel and some balsam soap; but I had no time to do anything. I didn't even realize what had happened . . . and what happened afterward! Well, you know as well as I do, if you've been trying to hush up this sorry affair."

"You're a wonderful raconteur, Mr. Govins!" Juffin nodded approvingly. "So I will with great satisfaction hear the ending of the story from your lips. I was, of course, very busy during those days. All I could manage to do (and it was enough for me!) was to pick up the 'suicide file' from the department of General Boboota Box, whose subordinates so pestered everyone in this house. I had no time to delve into the matter more deeply."

The door opened, and fresh kamra was served to us. Govins cleared his throat, and resumed speaking. "There's really nothing more to add. Of course, Sir Malkuk informed the House by the Bridge about what had happened. It was a straightforward case, so they sent it to General Box, Head of Public Order. Then his subordinates inundated our house—"

"Listen, Govins, maybe you can tell me. Did they check the level of magic present in the room?"

"It never even occurred to them. At first they thought it was all clear and simple: the man was drunk. When I told them that Nattis had never once been drunk in his whole short life, they decided again that it was all clear and simple: I had killed him. And then they just disappeared. As I understand, now, Sir Venerable Head, through your intercession."

"How typical that is of Boboota's boys," Juffin groaned, clasping his hand to his forehead. "Sinning Magicians, how very typical!"

Our interlocutor remained tactfully silent.

Just then, three of the twelve wise crones arrived. It was revealed that six more of them were keeping watch over patients, two were simply nowhere to be found, and one old woman, according to the messenger, refused point-blank to return to "that black house." She's gone off her rocker, poor thing, I thought compassionately.

Juffin thought for a moment, then ordered all three of them at once to come in. I received a silent explanation about this from him: *When you want to interrogate several women, it's best to question them all together. Each of them will try so hard to outdo the other that they will end up telling you more than they intended. The only problem is trying not to lose your mind in the hubbub!*

And so the ladies entered the parlor and seated themselves ceremoniously at the table. The eldest was called Mallis. The two others, by no means young, were Tisa and Retani. I grew a bit sad. For the first time I was in the company of otherworldly ladies, and just my luck—the youngest of them was pushing 300!

Juffin's behavior deserves separate commentary. First, he sculpted his face into the gloomiest frown that you can imagine. Then, in addition to the mournful expression of his physiognomy, the grannies were fated to witness him cover his eyes with the palm of his hand in a pathetic gesture, and further to hear the emotionally burdened recitative of his initial greeting. His intonations were wracked with a wailing of the spirit, more akin to the cadences of tragic drama than an interrogation. The order of his words and sentences started slipping around in the most peculiar way. Of course, in Echo one must address wisewomen with due respect and solemnity, as one would be expected to address a university professor in my homeland. In my opinion, however, Mr. Venerable Head went a little overboard. But my opinion would hardly have interested any of those present, which is why I modestly lowered my eyes and kept my mouth shut. Actually, I returned to my kamra, which I had clearly drunk too much of already, since it was there for the taking.

"Excuse my haste and the inconvenience I may have caused you, my wise ladies," Juffin declaimed with lofty precision. "But without judicious counsel, my life has no meaning or purpose. I have heard that your wondrous powers were able to extend the measure of life of an inhabitant of this house, one who had lost the Spark, to a most remarkable degree."

"Ah, yes; Olli, one of the young Makluks," Tisa replied knowingly.

One of the *young* Makluks? I must admit, I thought the old woman had gotten it all wrong, but Juffin nodded right back at her. Then again, she had most likely known their common grandfather. (Later I found out that the crones were far older than I could ever have imagined. Here in Echo, the lifespan of an ordinary person is three hundred years, and greater longevity is a matter of personal stamina. So in their line of work, at the age of five hundred you're still a spring chicken!)

"Olli was very strong," Lady Mallis announced. "And if you think about the fact that the twelve strongest ladies in Echo guarded his shadow, you will understand that his life was too short by far! We, of course, thought that the Spark would return to him. In days long ago, that happened often, though you young ones don't believe it. Young Olli didn't believe it, either; but that wasn't necessary. He still had a chance to get back the Spark!"

"I've never heard the likes of it, my Lady!" Juffin declared, his curiosity piqued. (Later he admitted to me that he had lied—"just to liven up the conversation.") "I thought the poor fellow had lived surprisingly long, but it turns out that he died before he should have!"

"No one dies too early or too late; everyone dies in his own time. But you, a Kettari man, should know that! You look into the darkness, don't you? But it wasn't our fault that Olli died."

"Of course, I have never had any doubt on that score, my Lady!"

"You doubt everything, you sly old fox. And that's as it should be. I can tell you one thing—we don't know why Olli died. And we should know. We need to know."

"Braba knows, but won't tell," Lady Tisa broke in. "That's why she refused to come to the house of the Makluks. And she won't come. But there's no need for this. Retari visited her the day after Olli's death. Tell them, Retari! We never asked you about it, because we had other worries. But now, it seems the Kettarian has only one worry—to find out why Braba is afraid to come here. And until he finds out, he's not going to give us a moment's peace."

Silence reigned. Then Juffin bowed graciously to Lady Tisa.

"You read my heart like an open book, my Lady!"

The old wisewoman smiled coquettishly at Juffin and winked. After this interlude of gallantry, everyone present stared intently at Lady Retari.

"Braba doesn't understand a thing herself, but she's mortally afraid. She hasn't been able to work since then, so fearful is she—like a young girl. She says someone lured away Ollie's shadow and nearly snatched her own. We were all sure that his shadow had departed on its own. We didn't know why; but it departed. Quickly—like a woman who doesn't want to give her love. But Braba says someone lured it away. Someone she couldn't discern. But she was so frightened that we decided, why bother asking? You can't get the shadow back. Why take on someone else's fear?" and Lady Retari fell silent, at least a year, it seemed.

The witches sipped kamra in the stillness and crunched their cookies daintily. Sir Juffin meditated. Mr. Govins was portentously silent. I gazed at this quaint group of people in innocent admiration. Without warning, however, I felt the air in the room had grown so thick that it was impossible to breathe. Something horrible and disgusting entered for a moment, then instantly retreated, not touching anyone in the room except myself. And even I hadn't time to realize what was happening; but a viscous lump of absolute terror penetrated my lungs when I breathed in as the shadow of some vile enigma encroached upon me, and then to my great relief disappeared as abruptly as it had come. It was probably "someone else's fear," as the old crone had just mentioned; but at the time I considered the episode to be a groundless mood shift—something very familiar to me. I didn't even consider sharing this silly inner anxiety with Sir Juffin.

Later, I understood that I had been imprudently reticent. Those "silly inner anxieties" were an extremely important part of my future occupation, for it is the sacred duty of an employee of the Secret Force to report every vague presentiment, nightmare, skip of a heartbeat, or other spiritual tremor (though analysis of the situation and other deductions you can and ought keep to yourself). At the time, though, I just tried to forget about this unpleasant lump of someone else's fear. My efforts met with almost immediate success.

"I know how a shadow departs," Juffin finally announced. "Tell me wise Ladies, did none of you except Braba really sense that something was amiss?"

"We all sensed it," Lady Mallis said. "Sensed it—and that was that. None of us knows what it was we sensed. We can't always say what it is. It's too strenuous a task for us, and it will be for you, though you peer into the darkness much more often than we do. And the lad there won't be any help, either."

I suddenly realized with horror that the old woman had focused her undivided attention on me.

"'Tis a secret, Sir. Just someone else's bad secret," Lady Tisa said, saving me. "None of us likes it. We didn't wish to talk about it, for it's pointless to talk about what you don't know. But when you're in the company of two gentlemen whose fate it is to peer into the darkness—well, we decided to tell all, though it won't be of any benefit to you."

And the three old crones, with the gracefulness of young felines, disappeared through the door.

Juffin! I started badgering him with my Silent Speech as soon as they were gone. *What was that business about "two gentlemen peering into the darkness"? What did that mean?*

Don't concern yourself with nonsense. That's just how these ladies see you and me. They know precious little about Invisible Magic; that's why they imagine it to be "darkness." It's simpler for them that way. In general, you shouldn't attach too much importance to what they say. Those old wisewomen aren't too bad in practical matters—but in matters of theory, they're no great shakes.

And with that Sir Juffin Hully stood up from the table.

"We're leaving, Govins. We've got to do some thinking. Tell the master that he need not send anyone to the House by the Bridge. I'll take care of all that myself. In the morning I'll send you written permission allowing you to bury the poor fellow. But I can't promise that everything else can be taken care of as quickly as the bothersome paperwork. You'll just have wait it out, and moreover, I'll be very busy in the next few days. And make sure no one hangs around in that bedchamber. Let it remain untidy, for Magicians' sake! If I don't show up for a time, Sir Makluk shouldn't worry; I won't forget about this matter, even if I wish I could . . . but if—"

"Yes, Sir. If something happens?"

"Let's just hope nothing does. Better not go in there, all the same. See to it, dear Govins."

"You can rely on me, Sir Venerable Head."

"Wonderful. Sir Max, are you still alive? And you haven't turned into a jug of kamra? Because that stuff can do that to you, you know . . ."

"Juffin, may I go into the room one last time?"

He raised his brow in surprise.

"Of course, although . . . all right, we'll go together."

We entered the twilit bedchamber. Everything was quiet and tranquil. The needle on Sir Juffin's pipe jerked, and began again to seek a compromise between the "2" and the "3." But that wasn't why I wanted to return. Looking around, I immediately found the box with balsam soap that we unsuccessfully tried to charm earlier in the evening. It was still lying on the floor, halfway to the corridor. I lifted the box and put it in the pocket of my looxi, praise to the skies, an opportunity furnished by the local fashion.

I looked at Juffin guiltily. He chuckled. Never mind, Juffin would be none the worse for it; and he certainly deserved some light entertainment.

"What do you need that thing for, Max?" Juffin asked, when we had gone out into the garden and were traipsing toward home. "Do you always clean up the premises when you've been on a visit? Why did you rob my neighbor—'fess up!"

"You'll laugh . . . you're already laughing, Magicians be with you! But you saw yourself how scared it was! I just couldn't abandon it there."

"A box? You're talking about a box?"

"Yes, the box. Why? I felt its fear, I saw it try to roll away, and if things can remember the past, it means that they are sentient, they are able to perceive and feel. That means they live their own inscrutable lives, doesn't it? In that case, what's the difference whether one rescues a damsel in distress or a box?"

Juffin burst out laughing. "I suppose it's a matter of taste, of course! What an imagination you have, young man! Good going! I've lived a long time on this earth, but I've never taken part in the rescue of a box!"

He teased me until we reached the gate, then grew suddenly serious.

"Max, you're a genius! Fantastic! I'm not sure about the inscrutable lives of boxes, but if you remove it from a zone of fear . . . Sinning Magicians! You're absolutely right, Max! Of course we may be able to charm at home! Not right away, of course, but perhaps it may remember something, your sweet little thing. You thief you! And the old crone can eat her skaba! As if you and I can't solve this case together! We've had harder nuts to crack, and we managed."

I decided to take advantage of the fortuitous moment and inquire cautiously: "But still—what do you think they meant when they were talking about the darkness we peer into? That all makes me a bit uneasy."

"And you should be uneasy about it," Juffin snapped. "It's completely understandable. Remember how you got here?"

"I do," I murmured. "But I try not to think about it."

"Very well. You'll have plenty of time to think. But you have to agree, it doesn't happen to everyone—to flit from one world to another, with all your wits about you and your body in one piece! You and I are the kind that happens to—and that's not all that happens to us. The old crones practice magic, but not like everyone else here—once a year in their own kitchens. They practice very long and hard. You might say it's the only thing they do. And experience tells them there's something not quite right about us. That 'not quite right' is what they call 'darkness.' Understand?"

"Not really," I admitted.

"Okay, let me put it this way, then. Are you sometimes scared, or happy, just like that, out of the blue, apropos of nothing? You hurry out on some stupid errand, and suddenly you feel a thrill of improbable, intense, boundless joy? Or it happens that everything seems to be in its rightful place, your beloved is sleeping sweetly next to you, you're young and full of as much energy as a puppy—and suddenly you feel you are suspended in emptiness, and a leaden sorrow clamps down on your heart, as though you were dead. Not only that, but as though you had *never been alive*. And sometimes you look at yourself in the mirror, and you can't remember who that chap is, or why he's there at all. Then your own reflection turns around and walks away, and you watch silently as it retreats. You don't have to say anything. I already know that this happens to you from time to time. The same thing happens to me, Max; only I've had enough time to get used to it. It happens because something ineffable is reaching for us— we never know where and when it will show up and start tugging on our sleeve. The fact is, you and I have a talent for a strange craft that no one really understands. And, frankly, I can't tell you anything about it that makes any sense. You know, it's not customary to talk about this aloud. And it's dangerous. Things like this should stay secret. There is one person here in Echo who understands more than we do about these things. You'll meet him at some point. But until then—nary a word. Agreed?"

"Who am I going to talk to, I wonder, besides you? Chuff?"

"Well, yes—you can talk to Chuff, of course. And to me. But soon you'll embark on a much stormier existence."

"You're always threatening that . . ."

"Wasn't tonight enough proof for you? I would be glad to take you with me to the House by the Bridge, but things move slowly in Echo. I submitted the request for your appointment to the Court . . . yes, the day after our trip to the *Glutton*. As all matters in my department are decided with maximum efficiency and promptness, everything should be settled within two or three dozen days."

"You call that 'maximum efficiency and promptness'?"

"Yes, and so must you."

Then we were home. Juffin went to his room, and I stayed behind, alone, just the time to think about the darkness into which I was peering. Those dames had given me a scare! And then Juffin, with his lecture about the secret reasons behind the jumps and starts in my moods . . . arghhh!

When I was in my own room, I pulled out the salvaged "box-in-distress" from the pocket of my looxi. Take it easy, sweetheart, Uncle Max may not be all there, but he's kind and good! He'll protect you from all misfortune; he's just going to peer into the darkness . . . But at the very moment of the deepest flowering of my honestly acquired phobia, a warm clump of fur jumped out this very darkness: *Max sad—don't be sad!* My little friend Chuff wagged his stumpy tail so violently that the devilish darkness scattered into little bits. I relaxed, banished from my mind the paranoid murmurings of the matronly sirens, and Chuff and I went to the living room to find something to eat while we read the evening news.

As it turned out, I didn't go to sleep before dawn that day. I waited for Juffin to talk over the events of the evening one more time over a mug of kamra. I must admit, I expected that from that moment on, Sir Juffin would be wracking his brains over the mysterious murder. In other words, like good old Sherlock Holmes, or the equally old and good Commissioner Maigret, he would suck on his pipe for hours on end, and wander about at the scene of the crime. And at the end of yet another sleepless night, and not without my help, he would crack the case of the "ABC Gum Corpse." Then everyone dances with delight.

I was sorely disappointed. Our morning conference lasted all of twenty minutes. The entire time, Sir Juffin speculated about my lonely future—that is, how I would survive the next three days without him. It turned out that the time for his annual friendly visit to the Royal Court had rolled around, and as this joyful occasion is granted by King only a few times a year, he was generally in no hurry to release his charming vassal. On average, according to Sir Juffin's calculations, these forced circumstances lasted about three or four days. Then the cries of distress of his subjects, abandoned temporarily to the caprices of fate, would force the monarch to loosen his embrace and return his captive to the World again.

I must say, I understand His Majesty. In the literature of the Unified Kingdom, the detective novel does not seem to exist at all, and newspaper articles and dry accounts of the courtiers about all the *other* courtiers cannot compete with the juicy worldly gossip of Sir Juffin Hully, Venerable Head of all that transpires.

For my part, I coped fairly well with the loneliness. I walked a lot, gazed at passersby, learned the names of streets. At the same time I inquired about the prices of houses for lease. I was very particular about my choice of a future home. I wanted it to be close to the Street of the Copper Pots, at the end of which stood the House by the Bridge, the residence of the Headquarters of Perfect Public Order. At night I "did my homework"—again and again I grilled the objects of material culture about their past. It was pleasant to realize that I could already perform these tricks without Juffin's guidance. Objects were increasingly willing to share their memories with me. Only the box from the bedchamber of the late Sir Makluk-Olli held its tongue with the obstinacy of a partisan of the Resistance, we observed no more outbursts of uncontrollable fear in it. Thank goodness for that!

Late on the evening of the fourth day, Sir Juffin Hully returned, laden with royal gifts, fresh news (to me all quite abstract), and problems from work that had accumulated in his absence. In short, neither that evening, nor the next, did we return to the subject of the Mysterious Murder in the Empty Room.

Eventually, life began to resume its normal pattern. Juffin started coming home earlier. We took up our leisurely dinner discussions again, and even our evening seminars. Two weeks had passed since the event of the murder in Sir Makluk's house. That is to say, two weeks by my count—the locals don't divide the year into weeks and months. They count days by dozens, and define their temporal coordinates very laconically—around such and such a day in about such and such a year. That's all. So if we use the local method of calculating time, more than a dozen days had passed since our nocturnal visit to our neighbor's house. This was too long to sustain the flame of my curiosity: it sparks like lightning, but it dies just as quickly if it finds no immediate sustenance.

Oh, if only the balsam-filled box that I rescued had begun to talk before I forgot about it and turned my attention to more garrulous objects! Then Sir Juffin gradually began to teach me more captivating things. Who knows how humdrum this silly matter could have ended up, had it not been for my own amnesia?

Somehow or other, the next sign of a fast-approaching tempest caught up with me early in the evening of what had otherwise been a delightful day. I was enjoying the masterpieces of the ancient poetry of Uguland, having dared for the first time to drag the weighty folio out of the dust of the library into the garden. I scrambled onto the branch of a spreading Vaxari tree, a wonderful variety of tree exceptionally well-suited for climbing by men of middle age who have fallen back into the habits of childhood.

From this vantage point, I noticed a man in gray hurrying over to our grounds from the direction of Sir Makluk's house. I remembered immediately the circumstances of our prior visit, and decided to go inside the house just in case. Sir Juffin had still not returned, and I was determined to hear the news firsthand. I descended the tree too slowly for my own taste; but all the same I crossed the threshold before Sir Makluk's servant reached the home stretch—the path of transparent colored pebbles that led up to the house.

In the hall I ran into Kimpa, who was already hurrying to admit the visitor. As soon as the door was opened, I declared:

"Sir Juffin Hully isn't here at the moment, so I'm the one to talk to!"

Sir Makluk's emissary was somewhat nonplussed, perhaps because at that time I still hadn't gotten rid of the accent that so grated on the ears of the capital-dwellers. But my debonair appearance and delib-

erate manner, and maybe a sign from old man Kimpa that went
unnoticed by me, had the desired effect.

"Sir Makluk requests that I inform Sir Venerable Head that old
Govins has disappeared. In fact, no one has seen him since morning,
something which hasn't happened in more than 90 years! In addition,
Sir Makluk commanded me to report that he is troubled by dark
forebodings."

I dismissed the emissary with a stern nod of my head. There
were no two ways about it: I had to alert Juffin immediately. I had
had no experience with this kind of situation until that moment,
and while it isn't so hard to use Silent Speech when your interlocutor is sitting right next to you, communicating with him when his
whereabouts are unknown is an entirely different game. Sir Juffin
had once tried to convince me that it didn't make any difference. If
it had worked once, the next time it would work just as easily. I was
of another opinion, but perhaps I just lacked the experience or
imagination.

Of course, I could have asked Kimpa's help. There were no obstacles to this—it was not classified information, and my own ambition
wouldn't have stood in the way.

The truth is, it just didn't occur to me to turn to Kimpa. And
Kimpa, the most tactful of servants, wouldn't have dared interfere in
my affairs.

And so I tried to establish contact with Sir Juffin. Within the
space of three minutes, I was wet with perspiration, disheveled, and
on the verge of despair. It wasn't working! I felt I was pinned up
against a wall. That's a short route to the conclusion that you're a
worthless nothing.

When I had given up all but the faintest of hopes, I tried one last
time. And suddenly—it worked! I made the connection with Sir
Juffin, though I can't imagine how.

Juffin had summed up the situation in no time. *What gives, Max?*

He had tried many times in the past, always unsuccessfully, to
challenge me to this metaphysical problem for "the advanced learner."
So he had reached a corresponding conclusion—"If this blockhead
has finally managed to get through to me, the circumstances that
prompted it must be dire, indeed!"

I gathered my wits about me and tried to explain it all in a single
thought.

Good, Max. I'm on my way. Juffin was almost curt—generously sparing my depleted energies.

Having done my part, I sighed with relief and went to change—I hadn't sweated like that in a blue moon! Kimpa looked at me with indulgence, but he tactfully refrained from making any remarks, God bless him!

By the time Juffin had arrived, I was completely ready—but still I neglected our "witness number one": the little box with balsam. I would probably have remembered it with time, but Juffin wasn't alone when he arrived and I got distracted. He was with his second-in-command, Sir Melifaro, and believe me, meeting this gentleman is like being at the epicenter of an earthquake that registers 5 to 6 on the Richter scale. Sir Melifaro is not only the Diurnal Representative of the Head of the Minor Secret Investigative Force—he is the main traveling show of Echo. I'm sure you could get people to pay to see him. I'd buy a ticket myself once every dozen days if I weren't forced to have this pleasure on a daily basis free of charge, as a bonus for good work.

On that day, though, I still didn't know what was in store for me.

Into the living room rushed a handsome, dark-haired fellow— judging by appearances, of the same age as me. He was a "type" that was much coveted in postwar Hollywood, the kind that was recruited to play the "good" boxer or detective. However, the stranger's attire made an even stronger impression on me than his face. Underneath his bright red looxi, an emerald-green skaba was just visible. His head was piled high with an orange turban, and bright yellow boots the color of egg yolk adorned his feet. I'm sure that if the daily costume of Echo-dwellers consisted of a hundred pieces, this clotheshorse would have chosen for himself every imaginable color and shade. But social custom did not yet permit him to blossom in his full glory.

The newcomer flashed his dark eyes, and raised his eyebrows so high that they disappeared under his turban. He covered his face with his hands in a theatrical gesture, and wailed, "I see you as in a waking dream, O marvelous barbarian, and I fear that your image will haunt me in my nightmares!" Then he turned a complete pirouette on the shaggy carpet, as though it were made of ice, and collapsed into an armchair, groaning from the exertion. After that, he froze as still as death (he even seemed to stop breathing), and studied me with a penetrating gaze, unexpectedly serious and somehow empty, completely at odds with his recent acrobatics.

I realized I had to greet him in some manner, too, so I covered my eyes with the palm of my hand, as one is supposed to do. But all I could utter was: "Okay."

Melifaro grinned and unexpectedly (as everything he did was unexpected) winked at me.

"You, Sir Max, are quite a guy! The future nocturnal backside of our 'Venerable Head.' Don't worry, I'm his diurnal backside, have been for sixteen years now. A person gets used to everything, you know."

"It's just a matter of time before the reputation of our office is toppled once and for all in the eyes of Sir Max!" Juffin hurried to intervene. "All my labors will turn to dust. He'll realize that I'm a humble director of a Refuge for the Mad and rush back to the Barren Lands, suddenly seeing the advantages of life in the fresh air."

I blinked helplessly.

"Was that everything you knew?" Juffin asked me. "No more news?"

"That wasn't enough for you?"

"Of course it wasn't, old chap!" Melifaro retorted. "They failed to tell you where the fellow disappeared to, what happened to him, and who's to blame in all of this. And they didn't take the trouble to bring the criminal to justice. So now we have to do their work for them!"

"Melifaro! Sir Max has already figured out that you're the wittiest, the most irresistible, and the most magnificent of them all. He is beside himself with joy, having discovered the very source of the glory and might of the Unified Kingdom. And now we're going to get down to work," Sir Juffin commanded, somehow very calmly and tenderly. Melifaro snorted, then started issuing instructions.

"Max, you're coming with us. Three is a crowd. I signed an order granting Sir Lonli-Lokli and his magic hands five Days of Freedom from Chores, and he wisely left town yesterday morning. Melamori is relieved of duty, as her influential daddykins missed her. And Sir Kofa Yox is keeping watch at our Pleasure Factory by the Bridge, instead of methodically chewing a steak in some *Sated Skeleton* or other, the poor bloke. But we ourselves will have a little snack, otherwise Sir Melifaro will lose the ability to think once and for all. And you are always up for that, as far as I've been able to find out, aren't you?"

We snacked abundantly, but in great haste. Sir Melifaro, by the way, attempted to make it into the Guinness Book of Records in that category of strapping fellows who consume sources of nourishment in huge quantities before you could say Jack Robinson.

All the while, he regaled us with questions, asking me whether it was difficult to get along without sun-cured horsemeat, and asking Sir Juffin whether it might be possible to get a sandwich with the meat of some pickled mutinous Magician or other. (I was able to appreciate this joke only later, when Sir Kofa Yox gave me a comprehensive lecture about the most enduring urban legends.)

We walked over to Sir Makluk's house in silence. Sir Juffin was thinking troubled thoughts, Melifaro whistled a tune absently, and I waited expectantly for my first slice of true adventure. I'll say right off that I got much more than I had bargained for.

The usual man in gray admitted us at a small side door. I immediately felt ill at ease—not so much frightened as sad and disgusted. I had experienced something like this before, in those rare cases when I had to visit my grandmother. In that hospital there had been a special ward for the terminally ill and dying. Sweet little place . . .

Juffin cast a warning glance at me. *Max, do you notice it, too?*

"What is it?" I asked aloud, confused. Melifaro turned away in amazement, but said nothing.

Juffin preferred Silent Speech. *It's the smell of a foul death. I've come across this before. None of this bodes any good.* He then continued out loud.

"All right, let's go into the bedchamber. My heart tells me that the old man couldn't resist and popped in this morning to tidy up. Melifaro, today you'll take Lonli-Lokli's place."

"I won't be able to pull it off. I can't puff out my chest like he does."

"Never mind. You don't have to, just throw yourself into the scorching fire; that's all there is to it. According to instructions, I can't subject you to the risk of being deprived of my company. And Sir Max doesn't have a clue about what to do after you enter the room."

"So in that case, you won't miss me, will you? I know, I know, you got sick of me a long time ago. Maybe you can just kick me out of the service and you'll have a clean conscience? Think about it before it's too late!" Sir Melifaro said with a smirk.

"Yes, you see, I'm planning to take your place," I explained.

"And for your boss, it's easier just to kill someone than to offend him without cause. So—"

"Well, fine," Melifaro replied with a sigh of resignation. "Of course, otherwise why would he have fed me? He was granting me my last wish."

"Gentlemen, could you perhaps be so kind as to shut up?" said Juffin.

We bit our tongues and fell in step behind our stern leader until he halted by the door to the bedchamber.

"It's here, Melifaro. Welcome."

Melifaro didn't try to pull any stunts in the tradition of a brave storm-trooper from the movies. He simply opened the door and entered the empty chamber. The epicenter of the "smell of a foul death" was right here—judging by how unwell I felt. But what must be done, must be done! And so I followed right behind Melifaro.

For a brief moment it seemed to me that I had died many years before. Then I began to feel wracked with a longing for death—a peculiar kind of nostalgia; but a tiny part of the phlegmatic, sensible Max was still alive in me. So I got a grip on myself—or, rather, the sensible kid gathered up all the rest of the Maxes, all howling in a frenzy of morbid longing.

Sir Melifaro, who until that moment had remained blissfully ignorant, was now also on the alert. He mumbled gloomily, "Not the cheeriest place in Echo, Chief. Why did you drag me in here? Bring on the music and the girls!"

Then Sir Juffin spoke in a voice that sounded like it came from someone else:

"Back off, boys! This time my pipe is going off the scales!"

The dial on the pipe was calibrated to detect magic up to the hundredth degree. This should be plenty, as even during the romantic Epoch of Orders, masters who had greater abilities were few and far between. So if the wand was going "off the scales," the magic here must be greater than the hundredth degree—say, the 173rd or 212th. From my perspective, it was all the same at that point.

"What's going—?" Melifaro tried to ask, but Juffin shouted:

"Clear out! On the double!"

In the same instant, he tugged me by the leg, and I crashed onto the floor, just in time to notice Melifaro's legs flying up in a bizarre somersault as he jumped out of the window. Well, almost jumped out. The sound of shattering glass rang out, and shards flew every-where, but Melifaro's flight was broken off abruptly. He slid down onto the floor, turned around, and started walking slowly away from the window.

"Where are you going, you fool! Get out, I say!" Juffin shouted, but without much hope. Even I understood that the fellow wasn't walking of his own accord. I thought I could see a spiderweb, glisten-ing like cold crystal, envelop Melifaro. His face became completely childlike and helpless. He looked at us from someplace far away, from a dark, intoxicated distance. He smiled awkwardly, blissfully. Slowly, he walked toward the source of the web that had ensnared him, toward what had recently been the large, antique mirror.

Juffin raised his hands above his head. It seemed to me that a warm yellow light flared up inside him, and he began to glow like a kerosene lamp. First the spiderweb that enveloped Melifaro became illuminated; then Melifaro himself grew bright. He stopped and turned toward us. Now he'll be all right, I thought. But the warm yel-low glow faded, and died. Melifaro, still smiling his beatific smile, took another step toward the mirror's dark maw.

Juffin bunched himself up into a tight mass and started hissing. The spiderweb shuddered, and several threads broke off with a strange sound that made my stomach churn. In the darkness, the thing we took to be a mirror started to shimmer and shift. Two empty eyes were staring at us, gleaming with the same crystalline chill as the spiderweb. Something that looked like the face of a dead ape materialized around the brilliant, fiery eyes. In the place where mammals usually have a mouth, a gaping, moist darkness appeared, repulsive and yet captivating. The cavernous black hole was framed by what appeared at first to be a beard, but peering closer, I saw with horror that the "beard" was alive. Around the creature's hideous mouth, hairy growths like spider legs wriggled madly, writhing of their own accord. The creature gazed at Melifaro with a cold curiosity; it didn't seem to notice us at all. Melifaro smiled, and said quietly, "You can see that I'm on my way." And he took another step.

Juffin tore off like a whirlwind. Screaming in an unnatural, stran-gled voice, and beating the floor rhythmically with his feet, he crossed the room at a diagonal, then again, and yet again. The rhythm of his stamping and shouting, oddly enough, comforted me. I stared transfixed at this dizzying shamanic frenzy. The spiderweb trembled, then faded and went dark. I watched the mirror creature follow Juffin's every move with its fading gaze.

It's dying, I thought calmly. It was always dead; but now it's dying—how very odd.

Juffin quickened his pace; the pounding of his feet became louder and louder, his cries became a roar that drowned out all my thoughts. His body seemed disproportionately large and dark to me, like a huge shadow, and the walls of the room shone with an azure light. One of the small tables suddenly rose up into the air and dashed toward the mirror, but burst into pieces halfway there. The splinters of wood mixed with the shards of broken glass.

Then I realized that I was falling asleep . . . or dying. If there was one thing I had never had any intention of doing, it was dying in the presence of a dead ape with a hairy mug.

Then, from somewhere in the depths of the room, an enormous candlestick flew out with a shrill whistle. It seemed to be aimed directly at my forehead. I was suddenly possessed with fury. I jerked violently, and the candlestick crashed down, an inch from my head. Then it was all over.

Well, to say that it was "all over" was an exaggeration. But the light, the spiderweb, and even the "smell of a foul death" were gone. The mirror again looked like a mirror—but it didn't reflect anything. Sir Melifaro stood motionless in the center of the room among the domestic ruins. His face was now a sad, lifeless mask. The crystalline spiderweb drooped in dull, stringy, but completely real fibers that looked like spun sugar. Melifaro, poor fellow, was completely wrapped up in the sticky mess. Sir Juffin Hully sat next to me on his haunches and examined my face intently.

"You okay, Max?"

"I don't know. Better than him, anyway," I said, nodding at Melifaro. "What was that?"

"That was magic of the 212th degree, my friend. What did you think of it?"

"What do you think I think!"

"I think it's all very strange. Technically, you should be in the same condition he's in." We both turned around to gaze at the frozen figure of Melifaro.

"Tell me, you did begin to fall asleep, didn't you? What happened next?"

"To be honest, I didn't know whether I was falling asleep or dying. I thought . . . I didn't want to die in the company of that monkey. Dumb, wasn't it? And when the candlestick flew at me, I finally got furious—at the stupid piece of iron, at the monster in the mirror, even at you, for some reason. And I decided, no way, I'm not dying here! And, that's about it."

"Well, you're a piece of work, kid! Until now it was thought to be absolutely impossible; and then he up and gets offended! And refuses to die, to spite all his enemies . . . Funny. But all the same, how do you feel?"

Suddenly I wanted to laugh. Who does he think he is, Doctor Dolittle? But paying attention to my sensations, I realized that I really didn't feel quite right. For example, I understood perfectly what had happened here. I didn't need to question Juffin. I already knew that twice he had tried, unsuccessfully, to conquer the strange power that resided in the mirror. The third time he simply made the world in the room stand stock-still. I even knew *how* he had done this, although I couldn't have repeated it even to myself. I also understood that now it was impossible to destroy the creature in the mirror without harming Melifaro—the spiderweb had bound them together like Siamese twins.

At the same time . . . at the same time I was tormented by other, unrelated, questions. For example, how would Sir Juffin look if I took a splinter of glass from the broken window and dragged it across his cheek? And what would his blood taste like? And . . .

I licked my parched lips.

"Max," Juffin ordered sternly. "Get a grip on yourself, or else you'll crack up. I can help you when we leave this room, but it would be better if you managed on your own. Compared to what you've already done, it's a piece of cake!"

I fumbled around in the basement of my soul in search of the small, sensible fellow who often comes to the rescue during emergencies. It looked like he wasn't home.

Suddenly, I thought of some old B-movie about vampires. The main characters had faces white with greasepaint and mouths unappetizingly smeared with blood—like babies left with a good-for-nothing nanny and jam for breakfast. I imagined myself in that guise: Max, the regular guy, beloved of girls and house pets. At first I felt ashamed; then I burst out laughing. Juffin joined in.

"What an imagination you have, lad! Oh, you kill me!"

"It's not my imagination, I just have a good memory. If only you could see that movie!" I cut myself off abruptly, and asked, "Wait, you read my thoughts, too?"

Juffin, unperturbed, confirmed my suspicions. "Sometimes. If it's necessary for the task at hand."

But by then I wasn't even listening to him. I was consumed again by the desire to take a sip of his blood. One small sip. My stomach knotted up in a spasm of hunger. I couldn't think of anything but the taste of Juffin's blood. Ugh, how vile! I'm getting obsessed!

"Am I losing my mind?"

"Something like that, Max. But it's doing you good, it seems. You know, I think that if you were able to withstand my curse, you can certainly deal with your own madness! I can cure you, so if you're in trouble, let me know. But . . . you know . . ."

I did know. Along with madness came the secret knowledge, which I had so suddenly come to possess. And the circumstances were such that the qualified help of a psychologically unbalanced vampire were far more useful to Sir Juffin than the confused bleating of the normal, ignorant Max. On the other hand, if he accidentally cut his hand, I could . . . again, I started to drool. I feverishly swallowed my bitter saliva, grabbed a shard of glass, and slashed my own palm. Sharp pain, the salty taste of blood—it brought me an unprecedented sense of relief.

"Could you help me up, Juffin. My head's spinning . . ."

He smiled, nodded, and held out his hand. I stood up, wondering how I could have spent my whole life at such dizzying heights. The floor was on the other side of the universe, if anywhere. Leaning on Juffin for support and carefully shuffling my benumbed feet, I moved out into the corridor.

I knew what was in store for us. The powers summoned to life by the curse of my protector had upset the balance of the World. Nothing to write home about, even by the standards of the Left Bank—but on the scale of the house! Any closed space is immediately saturated through and through with this harmony-destroying radiation. We had to "stop life" in the place right away, already gradually losing its contours, to restore order to it. There was no time to spare.

All that happened is still right before my very eyes, though at the same time the memory is vague.

At first we seemed to roam aimlessly through the enormous house. The people in gray tried to run away from us, although some of them snarled at us and bared their teeth.

Sometimes they behaved even more bizarrely. In the large salon with the fountain, where Sir Makluk had received us the first time, two boys executed an intricate ritual dance in complete silence. They gracefully ensnared themselves in what looked like neon streamers. When we approached them, however, we saw with horror that the streamers were their own intestines, which the boys were pensively drawing from their own stomachs. There was no blood—and no pain, either, apparently. The viscera glistened in the twilight of the huge hall, reflected in the streams of water from the fountain.

"There's nothing we can do to save them," Juffin whispered. With a careful gesture he suspended the scene. Now that the curse that stopped the World had been carried out, there was no need to start the whole process all over each time. The curse followed behind Juffin like the train of a garment, and I, in some way, helped him carry it. The only thing to do was to wrap each room as we came to it in the shadow of the curse, forcing people to freeze in the most eccentric poses.

We wandered through the house; our journey seemed to have no end. Sometimes I was beset by the thirst for blood, but I was too preoccupied by warding off the attacks of the frenzied household items hunting us down. More than anything else, I was insulted by the attack of a thick volume of the *Chronicles of Uguland*.

"Hey! I *read* you, you jerk!" I shouted indignantly, fending off the assault of the savage fount of knowledge with a weighty cane with which I had sensibly armed myself at the start of our campaign. Sir Juffin put a stop to this scene, as well.

In one of the rooms I saw my own reflection in a mirror and shuddered. Where had those burning eyes and sunken cheeks come from? When had I become so emaciated and haggard? I had eaten not so very long ago! Actually, from Count Dracula's point of view, I had never eaten anything worthwhile. Ugh! How disgusting! But it wasn't too difficult to keep myself in check. A person grows used to everything. We'll leave it at that.

We roamed through the house. It seemed that was the way it would always be from now on: time had stopped, we had died, and ended up in our individual, honestly earned purgatory. In one of the rooms, we came upon Sir Makluk himself. He was occupied with domestic duties: he was industriously rolling up an enormous bookcase, with all the books inside it. The most amazing thing was that he was already halfway finished. The old man turned to us and asked amiably how we were doing. "Soon everything will be well," Juffin promised, and Sir Makluk froze in the middle of his monstrous labors. Yet another statue in this newly established wax museum. A youth in gray was shuffling around on the threshold, quietly snarling and clapping his hands rhythmically. In a moment, he froze, too.

Then we walked through the empty corridor, and it seemed to me that I was lagging behind ourselves, because for a fraction of a second I observed the backs of *two* heads. One belonged to Sir Juffin, and the other was my own.

"Are you tired, Sir Max?" Juffin asked with a smile.

"Let's get out of here," I replied mechanically.

"Sure. What is there left for us to do here? Get ready. Soon you'll be fine."

"I already feel pretty normal. Everything has passed, except for the nausea."

"That's just hunger. A couple bucketfuls of my blood and it will disappear like magic!"

"Very funny."

"If I didn't laugh I'd retch at the sight of you. Have you looked in the mirror?"

"You think you looked any better when you hissed at the monster in the bedchamber?"

"Yes, I can only imagine. Onward, Max! We both truly deserve a breather."

We went out into the garden. It was already getting dark. The bright round orb of the moon lit up Juffin's weary face; his light eyes shone yellow. The yellow light enveloped me, and I thought stupidly, surprised: Why do people need eyes! Aren't lanterns enough for them? That was my last thought. To be honest, I could have gotten along without that one, too . . .

Then I looked at my wounded hand, and blacked out.

❀

Do you think I came to a week later in a soft bed, holding the hand of a pretty nurse? Think again! You still don't understand what it means to work for Sir Juffin Hully. Do you think he'd let me lie around unconscious? Not he!

They brought me around immediately; true, in a very pleasant way. I found myself slumped against a tree with my mouth full of some amazing potion. Kimpa was kneeling at my side with a cup, which I reached out for eagerly. Another gulp of the reviving liquid was administered to me.

"Yum!" I said. And then demanded, "More!"

"That's enough!" Juffin insisted. "I'm not stingy, but Elixir of Kaxar is the strongest tonic known to our science. Black Magic of the Eighth Degree! But I didn't tell you that."

"And who could I possibly tell? You, I suppose."

"You never know . . . Well, still hankering after a little blood?"

I listened attentively to my body's voice. It wasn't calling out for blood. Then I turned my attention to the other aspects of my existence. Hm, newly acquired wisdom also nowhere in evidence. Although . . .

"Looks like there's still something left from all that happened—though not like back there, of course."

Juffin nodded.

"That shake-up did you good, Max. You never know what's coming. Boy, what a day it was! But all joking aside, Melifaro is in deep trouble."

"Those pathological specimens back at the fountain are in it even deeper."

Sir Juffin waved his hand indifferently.

"It's too late for them already. Helping the others will be as easy as one-two-three. But Melifaro, poor lad, has only a small chance. Let's go home, Sir Max. We'll feast, mourn, and think."

At home, the first thing we did was to consume everything in sight in the kitchen. This revived me even more. The process of meditative mastication stimulates mental activity. My own, at least.

Just before dessert a belated ray of enlightenment visited me. I sat suddenly upright in the armchair, swallowed a piece of something that went down the wrong way, started coughing, and reached for a glass of water. To top off all the other misfortunes and mishaps of the day, I mistook a jug of the strongest Jubatic firewater for regular water, and chugged it down in one burning swig.

Juffin observed me with the interest of a research scientist.

"Whence this sudden passion for alcohol? What's gotten into you?"

"I'm an idiot," I admitted despondently.

Juffin rushed to console me. "Naturally, but don't be so hard on yourself. You have plenty of other abilities."

"I completely forgot about our witness! The little box! I had planned to chat with it at my leisure, but—"

Sir Juffin's face underwent a sudden change.

"I also have plenty of other abilities. And now is just the time to think about them. An inexcusable blunder! *You* had every right to forget about the box—but me! I always suspected that the dimwittedness of Boboota Box was contagious. All the symptoms are there—I'm terribly sick. Go get your treasure and bring it here, Max. Let's see what it can tell us."

I went to my room. One of my slippers was lying on top of my pillow. On top of it, Chuff was dozing peacefully. I gingerly touched his shaggy ruff. Chuff smacked his lips, but didn't wake up. And he was right not to—this was no time for waking up.

I found the little box at the bottom of one of the drawers, and tip-toed back out. My hands trembled slightly, for some reason. I felt a foreboding in my heart. What if it didn't want to talk this time, either? Never mind, Juffin would think of something. He would shake the soul loose from it. I wonder what the soul of a box looks like? I cleared my throat, and the heavy feeling in my chest began to dissipate.

The dessert that goodhearted Kimpa decided to regale the exhausted heroes with exceeded my wildest expectations. This meant that the interrogation of the box was postponed for another quarter of an hour.

Finally, Sir Juffin made his way into the study. I followed behind, squeezing the smooth body of our singular and precious witness in my cold, moist hands. No denying, I was nervous. Something told me the little box was ready to talk to us, and this unnerved me all the more. I had always been fond of horror films, but now I would have been glad to watch *The Muppet Show*. Just for the sake of variety.

This time, the preparations for communicating with the box were far more elaborate than before. Sir Juffin rummaged around for a long time in the drawer where he kept the candles. Finally, he chose one, bluish-white, with an intricate design formed by tiny dark-red smatterings of wax. For five minutes or so he tried to start a fire using some kind of awkward flint stone, the workings of which I couldn't fathom. At long last his efforts met with success. Placing the candle by the far wall, Juffin lay on his stomach in the opposite corner and gestured to me to join him. This I did. The floor in the study was bare and cold; there were no rugs. I thought: perhaps these inconvenient little rituals qualify as a kind of bribe to the "powers of the unknown." Are the "powers of the unknown" really so petty?

Everything was ready. The little box occupied a spot exactly in the middle, between us and the candle. I had to exert very little effort to reach the little box's memory. The box seemed even to have been pining for the opportunity to talk to someone. The "picture show" began with a bang—we just had to watch.

Sometimes my attention wandered. I had never had to perform this feat of concentration for more than an hour at a time in the past. When this happened, Juffin silently handed me a cup of Elixir of Kaxar. Once in a while he also took a nip of the herbal infusion. I don't know whether he really needed it, or was just taking advantage of the situation.

The box, a clever little thing, showed us only what we were really interested in! True, Sir Juffin had often said that objects are inclined to remember first those events in which magic is present. He must have been right. But I liked to think that the little box was very much aware of what we were seeking. They say that we become sincerely attached to someone we help without expecting anything in return. Judging by my involuntary tenderness toward the box pilfered from Makluk's bedchamber, this was certainly the case.

It started with the fracas involving the tub, which the injured party had told us about recently. There was the fragile old man with the handsome, weary face of an ascetic, the capricious expression of a spoiled child frozen on it. Our acquaintance Maddi is holding the washbowl. The old man's little finger dips into the water. His lips curl in displeasure. The servant gets up off his knees, goes toward the door. The face of the sick man, contorted with rage, assumes a kind of demonically cheerful expression . . . he pitches and scores! The washbowl made from the finest china (we must presume) strikes the forehead of the unlucky fellow and smashes to smithereens.

Stunned, blinded by water and a thin stream of his own blood, Maddi executes an agile sideways leap worthy of an Olympic medal—if the Olympic Committee recognized the sideways leap as a full-fledged sport. The fatal mirror lay in the direct path of the poor Maddi, and blocked his flight. Nevertheless, everything turns out all right—no broken noses or missing teeth. No irreparable damage has been done—Maddi just bumps his face against the mirror, smeared it with his blood mixed with the water, and that is all.

Astonished, he turns to Sir Olli. At the sight of his face covered with blood, the fury of the old man turns to fear; the capricious grimace to an expression of shamefaced guilt. Peace negotiations get underway.

None of those involved in the event noticed what we were able to see. About the surface of the old mirror skittered a light ripple, like a sigh. In the places where the unlucky servant's daubs of blood had touched the ancient glass, something began to pulsate and move. In a moment, it was all over. Only the mirror had become slightly darker, and deeper. But who pays attention to things like that? Sir Olli's lips began to form sounds, a timid smile of relief appeared on Maddi's bloodstained face. From behind the door someone's head appeared. End of scene. The gloom thickened in front of us for a moment.

In a few seconds this gloom became the cozy darkness of the bed-chamber. The weak light from a sliver of moon played over the sunken cheeks of Sir Olli. Something woke the old man up. I could tell that he was frightened. I felt his fear with my whole body—his help-lessness and despair. I heard how he tried calling out to the servants; I felt that for the first time in his life something didn't happen when he wished it to; just like today, when I couldn't reach Juffin with my call. But in my case, I just lacked experience, though I had enough strength. Plus, in the end, I did manage to get through. Sir Olli, however, no longer had the strength to use Silent Speech. He was overcome by an icy horror. Something utterly alien and uncanny, which he could neither control nor understand, was in the room with him. For a moment it seemed to me that I saw a tiny object crawling along the old man's cheek. I was seized by a shudder of disgust.

"Max, do you see that tiny vile thing?" Juffin asked in a whisper.

"Yes, I think I do."

"Don't look directly at it. Even better, don't look at it at all. It's a very powerful nasty little thing! The Master of the Mirror can take away your shadow, even now, when it is just a vision. Now I under-stand why old Lady Braba was frightened out of her wits—she's the most gifted Seer in Echo. Not everyone has the strength to discern something like that—thank goodness! Take a sip of the elixir Max; a bit of protection wouldn't hurt you at this point . . . There—the monster is going back into the mirror. In the places where the blood had smudged the mirror, he now has a door. You can look now. Have you ever seen a shadow disappear? Look, look!"

My trembling passed; my fear, as well. I concentrated again, and almost immediately saw the familiar outlines of the bedchamber. A semi-transparent Sir Makluk-Olli, looking younger but deathly scared, stood beside the mirror and looked at the other Sir Makluk-Olli, lying immobile in the bed. The surface of the mirror shuddered. The shadow (apparently, it was a shadow) sobbed helplessly, turned to the mirror, then tried to step back, to no avail. It didn't melt, but seemed to disperse into the air in thousands of little shimmering flames of light. The flames burned out quickly, but I had time to notice that several of them disappeared into the mirror's glassy surface. Five little flames: the exact number of poor Maddi's spots of blood on the mirror.

Then the fear subsided, sharply and absolutely. The darkness of the bedroom became cozy and comforting—although there was now a dead man in the room. After all, death is something natural and predictable, unlike Magic of the 200th and Something Degree, be it black, white, or gray-brown-raspberry colored.

I realized I had stopped distinguishing the outline of our vision. Sir Juffin nudged me with his elbow. The show went on.

It was light again in the bedchamber. I saw a nice-looking young man in a festive bright-orange skaba. That was, of course, the hapless Nattis, the apprentice-courtier, who regrettably had not stayed home in the grand city of Gazhin. The young fellow smiled shyly, revealing the childish dimples in his cheeks. Then he concentrated hard and assumed a comically threatening countenance. Just then, Mr. Govins appeared in the frame—there was no longer any doubt in my mind about his sad fate. The mentor handed the pupil a razor, the handle of which might have inspired a nervous tic in any antique collector. Even I appreciated it.

I became hopelessly distracted and reached for the miracle elixir. Sir Juffin looked at me slightly askance, and not without suspicion.

"Just a drop," I whispered guiltily.

"Never mind me, boy! I'm simply very envious . . . Well, give me a slug, too!"

When my vision returned to me, Nattis had already gotten down to work. He dragged the razor carefully over his cheek, smiling slightly at his own thoughts. The razor gradually crawled closer and closer to the pulsing, bluish vein on his slender boyish neck. Nevertheless, there was nothing unusual about it—it was an ordinary shaving routine.

But the mirror was not sleeping. At a certain moment, several points on its surface shuddered, and the icy horror again gripped my heart, fastened on it like an old Lovelace eyeing the appetizing derrière of a young girl.

Sir Juffin tweaked my chin gently.

"Turn away. Another improper scene. I myself try not to watch things like this. You know, they told me about these kinds of things long ago. And at the end of the story they hinted at the fact that it was better to make peace with such a creature than to struggle against it . . . Mmm, my neighbor has nice furniture, you can't deny it! And yet he looks like such a nice man . . . Well, the boy, of course submitted to its whispering . . . Ah, Max! Now you must look very carefully. I've never seen anything like it! Only, be careful—don't overrate your own strength."

The first thing I saw was a helpless grin on the fellow's face that closely resembled the awkward smile on our unfortunate Melifaro. The dimples froze forever in his cheeks, the smooth left one, and the unshaven right one. And blood, a great deal of blood. Blood poured over the mirror, which shivered in excitement under its spurting. This is how the breath of an inexperienced diver quickens as he struggles to reach the surface. There was no longer any doubt: blood returned life to the mirror, which only seemed to be a mirror, but was really a slumbering door to another, very foul place, to such a vile little place I sensibly averted my eyes and took a deep breath, as I had begun to give in to the nauseating rhythm in a very unpleasant way. Again I peeked cautiously. Nattis, of course, was already lying on the floor; Govins stared at his face, transfixed, and didn't see how the bloody mirror, sated now, shuddered one last time, then grew dark and quiet—for the time being, of course. People crowded into the room. The vision disappeared.

"Juffin," I said quietly. "So you know what this is?"

"I know what there is to know, insofar as it's possible to know at all. This, Max, is a legend, you see. And it's a legend I haven't allowed myself to believe up until now. Well, I mean, whether I believed it or not—that's not the point. I just didn't bother to give it much thought. And lo and behold . . . well, never mind. Look! Now comes the most interesting part."

"I wouldn't mind something slightly more boring, Juffin. I'm feeling sick already."

"What did you expect? Sure it's sickening . . . It's okay, though. After a debut like this, your job in the service will seem like a piece of cake! Things like this don't happen every day, you know. Generally they don't happen at all."

"I hope not. Though I am lucky when it comes to entertainment."

Next episode. We saw how Krops Kooly appeared in the bed-chamber, another nice-looking young fellow with hair the color of an orange—which, by the way, is considered to be an undisputed sign of masculine strength and beauty in Echo. In the case of Krops Kooly, this belief was absolutely justified. There are many attractive people here, I thought suddenly. Many more than where I come from. Although they themselves aren't aware of it, they have completely different esthetic norms. I wonder if I am considered to be attractive here, or a total scarecrow? Or what?

A very relevant question, indeed.

Meanwhile, the redhead went robustly through the motions of tidying the room. What else can you do if someone sends you to clean up a long-empty room, which is nevertheless cleaned up every day? He busied himself in every corner, menacingly waving his feather duster about—the only tool of his trade. Several minutes later it wasn't even worth going through this. The room was in a pristine state. Then young Krops apparently decided that he had earned a rest. He stopped in front of the mirror and studied his face. With his fingers he pulled the corners of his eyes slightly. Then he let them go with a sigh of regret. It seemed that the almond-shaped variety had been tried before many times, and each time he found it more to his liking. Then he examined his nose with a critical air. (Show me a young person of either sex who is satisfied with his or her nose.)

I'm afraid that this trifling dissatisfaction was the last feeling he experienced in this life. The transparent spiderweb was already glistening on his sleeve. In a few seconds the boy ended up in the middle of an almost invisible cocoon. I felt in my stomach the dull relief that gripped the poor fellow—everything became irrevocably simple.

YOU MUST GO THERE! And orange-haired Krops Kooly stepped into the depths of the looking glass. His helpless smile again resembled the expression on the petrified Sir Melifaro.

I turned away when I realized that my feelings coincided unpleasantly with the experiences of young Krops: I already almost felt how I was being consumed; and most disgusting of all, I felt I could easily grow to like it! The decomposing ape face appeared before me. The cavernous orifice of the mouth surrounded by squirming spider legs seemed so calm and inviting, such a desirable haven . . .

I took a bracing gulp of Elixir of Kaxar. Yes, Magic of the Eighth Degree—it's really something! It's devilishly delicious, and all your delusions seem to blow away like a puff of smoke! Since childhood I had been taught that only the bitterest, most foul-tasting concoctions could do you any good—and here I had discovered that it was all poppycock! Good news!

Convinced that my good sense was still in working order, I forced myself to return to the vision. Again, the empty bedchamber, tidy and clean.

"You see, Max?" Juffin's elbow jabbed my long-suffering side. "You see?"

"What?"

"That's exactly it—there is ab-so-lute-ly nothing there! Everything ended right then and there, like it had been switched off. It's no wonder my gauge read only two to three that evening."

It suddenly dawned on me. Evidently, the cheerful adventure in loving memory of Count Dracula really had raised my poor little IQ.

"After it eats, it sleeps . . . right? And nothing happens, because the mirror sleeps with its victims inside. And there's no magic! Right?"

"Right. That's how it fooled us. All our suspicions came to naught with one glance at the indicator on my pipe. Magic usually exists in the object in which it is invested. It either exists or it doesn't. But this monstrous piece of furniture—it's alive. And a living creature is sometimes wont to go off into the world of dreams. When a magus sleeps, all gauges fall silent. Most likely they are going crazy in other worlds, if such gauges were to exist in other worlds. Which, frankly speaking, I doubt. Well, let's go back into the living room, Sir Max."

"You know me—always ready for a snack!"

Sir Juffin got up off the floor, cracked his knuckles, and stretched. I carefully picked up the little box and put it in my pocket. I had always wanted a talisman. Now, it appeared, I had one at last. This one was plenty.

The candle, in the meantime, had burned out. I reached out mechanically to lift the stub up off the floor. There was nothing there. Nothing! By then, I wasn't surprised, and I just filed it away.

We returned to the living room. The sky was growing light behind the window. We had a nice little sit-down, I remarked to myself indifferently. It had been twelve hours since Sir Makluk's messenger arrived! Think of that!

The kamra was exquisite. The imperturbable Kimpa brought us a plate with tiny cookies that melted in the mouth. A sleepy Chuff came out to join us, wagging his tail. Right away, Juffin and I began a silent contest: who could feed Chuff the most cookies? Chuff succeeded in pleasing and amusing both of us, flying through the room like a small, shaggy torpedo. Having eaten his fill, he settled down between us under the table.

"Max," Juffin said, suddenly sad. "Now I'm not sure whether Melifaro has even the slightest chance. We can't just grab him by the scruff of the neck, pull him out of the room, and then bring him to his senses. He already belongs to the mirror, and it's impossible to break those kinds of ties while life is on hold. When the mirror comes to life again, it will demand its victim, and take it anywhere it can get it—even from another world. I could, of course, destroy the monster. Shurf Lonli-Lokli can, too. But I'm not sure that anyone will be able to kill it fast enough to keep Melifaro on this side of life. And I can't let everything remain as it is now. That can't go on indefinitely. I must put an end to the mirror and its ravenous Master. But you can't just destroy anything you want to while the world stands still! To kill the monster, I need to wake him up. And that means sacrificing Melifaro to him after all. You understand that that isn't a sacrifice I'm willing to make. I don't even want to consider the possibility! It's a vicious circle, Max, a vicious circle."

I reached for another cookie absently. I was sad. Before this, it would never even have entered my head that Sir Juffin, a man who had transferred me from one world to another in his spare time (tell me, what could be more improbable!) could grow so despondent and weary. I understood that there were limits to his might. This made me feel lonely and uncomfortable. I crunched my cookie loudly in the quiet room. A vicious circle . . . suddenly, an idea took my breath away. No, it couldn't be as simple as that! If it had been that simple, Sir Juffin would certainly have thought of it himself. And yet . . .

"Juffin!" I called out hoarsely. I stopped, cleared my throat, and began again. "This is probably very stupid—but you said 'a vicious circle.' So, when one mirror is placed opposite another, that's also a vicious circle. I was thinking—maybe if the monster sees its own reflection, they'll want to feast on each other?" I finally plucked up the courage to look Juffin in the eye. He was looking at me, his mouth agape. Then the dam burst.

"Sinning Magicians! Do you have any idea what you've just said, lad? Are you aware of what a unique specimen you are? Tell me honestly!"

I must admit, I never expected such a storm of enthusiasm. The first few seconds I enjoyed the effects of my performance; then I began to feel embarrassed. I hadn't made any shocking discovery. And it wasn't even certain whether it would work, though something told me it would. A similar presentiment seemed to flood Juffin's heart. "It will work—and how, it will work!" he cried jubilantly.

I stood up from the table, stretched, and went over to the window. The beauty of the sunrise could compensate for any sleepless night. I'll tell you, the dawn is much more impressive when it comes as a surprise than when you dread its arrival.

"Go to sleep, Max," Juffin urged me. "I've summoned Lonli-Lokli. He'll be here in a few hours. Sir Shurf and his wonder-working hands. You'll like him. But now you can rest awhile. I'm not going to let this chance slip by, either."

"What do you mean by 'wonder-working hands'?"

"You'll see, Max, you'll see. Sir Lonli-Lokli is our pride and joy. Try not to garble his name—he's a real stickler in the matter of his own moniker . . . and not just that. I can't begin to convey to you the pleasure that's in store. But now—beddie-bye!"

In no mood to protest, I headed for my room. I fell onto the soft floor and wrapped myself in a furry blanket, as happy as I had ever been. I hadn't realized how tired I was until that moment. All the same, something interfered in my bliss. I raised my head with difficulty; I almost had to pry open my eyelids with my fingers. Of course—on the pillow lay a single slipper, left there by a small fetishist named Chuff. The soft tap-tap of paws warned me that the culprit wasn't far. I put the footwear back in its proper place. Then Chuff decided there was room for two on the pillow. I had no objections.

"Wake me up when this handyman Lonli-Lokli shows up, okay?" I asked, turning away from the excessively moist nose.

Chuff gave a conciliatory snuffle. *Max sleeping. Tomorrow guests. Need to get up. Wake him.* The logical deductions of this understanding dog drifted through my brain. And then I wasn't there.

※

Strangely enough, I woke up without any help an hour before I needed to. I felt amazingly well. It was probably the aftereffects of that bracing Elixir of Kaxar. Wonderful stuff!

Chuff wasn't around. He was probably wandering about in the hall, eager not to miss the arrival of Sir Lonli-Lokli so that he could carry out his instructions. For another ten minutes I just lolled around, stretched, and lazily indulged in the morning thoughts that afford real pleasure only when you've have a good night's sleep. Then I got up, washed with enjoyment, and even made myself shave—a man's daily forced labor; only the bearded are truly happy and free. I confess that the bathroom mirror awakened no unpleasant associations in me. It wasn't that I was so thick-skinned; I just *knew* that it was an ordinary mirror. And I had come to know a bit more about things in my midst after my metamorphosis into a vampire the day before. Hm, yet another glorious page in my biography. I'll definitely have something to talk about with girls—if only there were any girls. As for bedtime stories, there's no shortage of those.

I went into the living room. Kimpa materialized by the table, a tray in his hands. Then Chuff appeared, surmising correctly that a good half of the breakfast would be coming his way. I gathered the dog in my arms, settled him on my lap, took my first cup of kamra, opened yesterday's paper, and fished a cigarette from my domestic supply out of my pocket. I hadn't had any luck trying to switch to the local pipe tobacco, the taste of which threatened to cast a pall over my existence. In this sense I am very conservative. It seems that it's far easier for me to change my profession, my place of domicile, and even my perception of reality, than to get used to a new kind of tobacco.

"It's good you didn't remain a vampire, Max!" Juffin said by way of greeting. "Or I wouldn't know what to feed you! I'd say to Kimpa in the morning: 'Please, dear fellow, kamra and some toast for me, and a ladle of blood for Sir Max!' I'd have to exterminate the neighbors one by one, use the privileges of office, cover up the tracks. I wouldn't want to drive away such a clever and useful chap over such paltry nonsense. I just praised you, did you notice?"

"You're just rubbing salt into the wounds!" I smiled, automatically examining the palm that had been hurt yesterday, which I had completely forgotten about. It wasn't hard to forget, since the hand was almost completely healed already. The very faint, thread-like scar, which could pass for an extension of my lifeline, looked like it had been there for a few years already.

Juffin noticed my surprise.

"It's just Black Magic of the Second Degree. That salve isn't half bad! Kimpa rubbed it on your hand yesterday while you were making up your mind whether to return to consciousness. Why are you so surprised?"

"Oh, because of everything."

"That's your right. Oh, look! We're all here."

Sir Lonli-Lokli, whose absence had grieved his colleagues more than me, seemed to have been created with the specific purpose of shaking me down to the soles of my shoes. Me, and no one else, mind you! The indigenous people of Echo will never be able to appreciate the fellow's merits until the Rolling Stones have played this World. Therefore, no one but me will be surprised at the remarkable likeness of Sir Lonli-Lokli to drummer Charlie Watts.

Add to that the stony immobility of his facial muscles; the exceptional height, combined with exceptional leanness, of his physique; wrap the result in the white folds of a looxi; crown him with a turban the color of alpine snow; and top it off with enormous leather gloves adorned with the local version of ancient runes . . . Well, you can imagine my surprise!

On the other hand, the ceremony of introduction to my future colleague unfolded without any deviations from the protocol. Having just finished with the formalities and sat down decorously at the table, Lonli-Lokli consumed his due portion of kamra. I kept waiting for him to draw some drumsticks out from under his armpits; I was on pins and needles in anticipation.

"I've heard all about you, Sir Max!" my new acquaintance exclaimed courteously, turning to me. "In my spare time, I often delve into books, and so I am in no way surprised at your upcoming appointment. Many authoritative sources mention the remarkable traditions of the inhabitants of the Barren Lands, which foster the development of certain magic skills that we, inhabitants of the Heart of the World, are deprived of. Sir Manga Melifaro himself called attention to your countrymen in the third volume of his *Encyclopedia of the World.*"

"Melifaro?" I cried out in astonishment. "You mean to say that that chap also wrote for the *Encyclopedia*? I would never have suspected that!"

"If you mean my colleague, I completely endorse your suspicions. Sir Melifaro hardly has a bent for systematic scholarly labor," Lonli-Lokli agreed. Then he went quiet, not bothering to explain himself.

"Manga Melifaro, the author of the *Encyclopedia of the World,* is the father of the candidate for the position of forever being in your debt," Juffin explained. "If the imminent adventure ends well, I'll make Melifaro promise to present us each with a set. He'll be delighted—the poor man's house is so stuffed with his father's scribblings there's no room to turn around."

"You didn't allow me to finish, gentlemen. I had intended to say that in the third volume of his *Encyclopedia* Sir Manga Melifaro wrote, 'The border area of the Barren Lands is inhabited by the most diverse, sometimes extraordinarily powerful people, and not just wild barbarians, as capital-dwellers are sometimes inclined to believe.' Therefore, I am glad to see you here, Max."

On behalf of all the inhabitants of the Borderlands, I expressed my gratitude to the magnanimous Master Who Snuffs Out Unnecessary Lives. (Such was the official name of the position held by this gentleman, extraordinary in every way.)

※

"The time has come, gentlemen!" Juffin said finally, getting up from the table. "By the way, Sir Shurf, we need to take a mirror with us. The largest one is hanging in the hall. I bought it at the Murky Market, at the very beginning of our Codex Epoch, when antique stores in the Old City weren't yet open and the demand for luxury goods was just starting to grow. Best time to buy. I'm afraid it was the most expensive mirror in the whole Left Bank—I gave a whopping five crowns for it. And now look—ah, the sacrifices one has to make!"

We all went into the hall. The mirror was truly gigantic, and it seemed to me that it was worth every bit of five crowns, though at the time I wasn't very knowledgeable about the local economy.

Well, we've got our work cut out for us! How are we going to haul it over there? I wondered in dismay. Although, with the three of us . . . maybe.

But Juffin had something else in mind.

"Pick it up, Sir Shurf, and let's get a move on!"

I was about to conclude that this ceremonious Sir Lonli-Lokli had a mystical weightlifting gift. That would have come in handy. But the fellow had no intention of lifting a finger to carry it. Instead, he casually ran his hand, encased in its huge glove, over the surface of the mirror from top to bottom. The mirror disappeared—as far as I could tell—into his hand. My jaw dropped.

Jufffin, could you teach me that?

I had enough presence of mind not to shout it out loud, but to use the opportunity for Silent Speech—just in case.

Sure, Juffin replied calmly. *Or Sir Shurf will teach you. Remind me sometime, when we're taking it easy.*

❦

Upon return, Makluk's house resembled a huge, abandoned crypt. Sir Lonli-Lokli, observing official protocol, opened the door and was the first to step over the threshold to the bedchamber. We followed close behind. The room was exactly as we had left it.

At the sight of poor motionless Melifaro, I must admit that my spirits plummeted. How could I have been so certain that I could save the day? What if my idea didn't work? What would that make us, then—murderers? Or just fools? Good question. Rather, a moral dilemma. Bring on the anguish!

Sir Lonli-Lokli took a simpler view of things. "It's a good thing he's silent," said this compassionate man, nodding in Melifaro's direction. "If only he were always like this!"

In his tone there wasn't a trace of spite—it was just a factual observation that he liked Melifaro more when he was quiet than when he was chatty. A purely aesthetic preference. Nothing personal.

Having expressed his opinion, Lonli-Lokli shook his fist vigorously, then opened it up and spread out his hand. The huge mirror
from Juffin's hallway dropped neatly to the floor between the Statue
Melifaro and the secret entrance to another, baneful dimension.

"It's a little crooked," Juffin remarked. "Let's try moving it a bit
to the right, the three of us together."

"Why all together, Sir?" the magnificent Lonli-Lokli asked. "I
can manage on my own." And with stunning carelessness, he shifted
the huge bulk of the mirror with just his left hand. It turned out that
the "mystical weightlifting gift" existed after all. I looked at him and
held my breath in wonder, like a scrawny adolescent looking at a
real-life Hercules.

Juffin looked over the layout critically. Everything was ready: the
reflection of the bedchamber mirror fit snugly into ours, with even a
bit of surplus around the edges. And the most important thing—the
valuable antique of Sir Juffin's completely concealed Melifaro.

The Chief of the Secret Investigative Force threw a parting glance
at his treasure and began issuing commands.

"Get ready, Shurf! Max, get behind my back. Or, better yet, go
stand by the door. You've already done everything you could. Your
job now is to stay alive. I'm serious, Max!"

I took up position by the door. I had no objections to staying
alive.

Sir Lonli-Lokli finally deigned to remove his gloves. Only then did
I realize that what everyone said about Lonli-Lokli's "capable hands"
was not just a pretty expression. My eyes beheld two hands that were
semi-transparent, and shone brilliantly in the midday sun. The long
sharp nails cut through the air, then took refuge under the snow-white
looxi. I blinked my eyes, dumbstruck, unable to express my admiration
in any other way. Then I suddenly remembered—I had seen something
like this, and not so very long ago. Where, I wondered, in a nightmare,
perhaps? Sir Juffin took pity on my poor head and prompted in a whisper, "Remember we were studying the memory of a pin? The ceremonial severing of a hand? The Order of the Icy Hand—remember?"

I remembered, and opened my mouth to ask how the severed
hands had become the hands of our esteemed colleague. But Juffin
had anticipated my question:

"They're gloves. I'll explain later. Now it's time to get down to
work!"

With these words Juffin approached the motionless Melifaro. He stood at a vantage point that allowed him to observe the reflections of both mirrors. Then he stood absolutely still, on tiptoe. I held my breath, waiting.

This time there was no dance. But Juffin's face and stance betrayed an unbelievable tension. Then, suddenly relaxing, Juffin made a slight gesture, as if he were removing a delicate covering from a priceless vase. At almost the same moment, and with all his might, he shoved the poor Melifaro. The body, immobile at first, then bent over convulsively, flew to the other end of the room, and collapsed onto the soft floor that served as a bed. Sir Lonli-Lokli immediately rushed over to him. Hiding his left hand behind his looxi, with his right hand he seemed to be rummaging about the figure of the stunned Melifaro. I realized what he was doing: Lonli-Lokli was destroying the glistening fibers that had enveloped the unlucky fellow. This was no small task; it was like looking for fleas on a stray dog. Sir Juffin stood out of the way, not taking his eyes off the mirror.

"Max!" he shouted all of a sudden. "We're quite a pair! Amazing! It's working! You can take a look—but be careful, even more careful than yesterday."

Not everything was visible from where I stood, but I sensibly decided not to step any closer.

The mirror began to move. The newly awakened mirror-dweller was hungry and cranky; but its double was already stirring to life in the second mirror. The two monstrosities groped toward each other in curious wonder. I stared at the heavy, formless body of the creature, which looked more like the body of a huge, white frog suffering from obesity than anything else. The creature's body was covered in the same disgusting, living hair that surrounded its mouth—dark, moist, drawing me in with a magnetic attraction . . .

I averted my eyes, but the mouth still stayed in the inmost depths of my consciousness. Then I forced myself to remember the bracing taste of Elixir of Kaxar. That helped, but only somewhat. If only a flagon of the potion was within reach!

To rid myself of the hallucination, I boxed my own ears and screamed silently, get a grip on yourself, man! After a few seconds I was so sober and clear-headed that curiosity got the upper hand. I looked again at the mirrors.

The first thing I saw was the silhouette of Lonli-Lokli, hanging over a sticky, mucous-like ball between the two grappling monsters. The powers were evenly matched. The double—I have to give him that—was not to be outdone by its original. The vile little ball rolled along the floor, and I went faint at the thought that it might make a rush for my leg. I didn't even think about the danger, so great was my feeling of revulsion.

Lonli-Lokli's left hand swept upward, slowly and solemnly—it was a strikingly beautiful gesture, laconic and powerful. The tips of his fingers shot out sparks, like sparks from a welder's arc. A shrill scream, undetectable by the human ear, which nevertheless seared my insides, forced me to bend over in pain. Then the scream stopped just as abruptly as it had begun. The creatures erupted into white flames. I thought that these fireworks signaled the successful end of the operation; but then something happened that was completely not of this world. The mirrors themselves actually began to move. The abyss behind the mirror and its reflection attracted each other like magnets. Their collision, I understood, threatened us with unpredictable consequences.

"Max, get down on the floor!" Juffin barked. "NOW!"

I flung myself down, as he had ordered. He himself somersaulted over to the window that had been smashed the day before, then stood stock-still and alert. Sir Lonli-Lokli retreated backwards in one smooth motion, over to Melifaro's body. There he sat on his haunches, clasping his hands prudently in front of him.

A quiet, but clearly hostile rumble started up from the matching depths. The glass in the mirrors buckled and grew convex, like sails billowing in the wind.

It seemed to me that we were in no real danger, for the mirrors had absolutely no interest in us. Instead, each revolting infinity advanced on its copy, until they merged into a kind of rabid Möbius strip, as each tried to swallow the other, just as the Mirror Monsters had just done. When it was finished, a dark, twisted up clump of some dark sticky substance was all that remained.

"Well, Sir Shurf, that last piece was your job, I suppose," Juffin observed with obvious relief.

"Yes, sir. I think so."

Another moment, and nothing was left of the nightmare.

Juffin jumped to his feet. The first thing he did was to go over and examine Melifaro, who was writhing around in the blankets.

"An ordinary faint," he reported cheerfully. "The most common, everyday sort of fainting spell. He should be ashamed of himself! Let's go, Max. Help me put this house in order. And you, Sir Shurf, deliver this priceless piece of meat into the arms of Kimpa. Let Kimpa bring him around, prepare oceans of kamra, and no less than a hundred sandwiches. Scarf down the food as soon as it's served, and we'll come and join you. Come on, Sir Max! Do you realize what has just happened? We did it! Sinning Magicians, we did it!"

Sir Shurf pulled on his thick protective gloves, grabbed up Melifaro, and carried him off under his arm like a rolled-up carpet.

And Juffin and I set out on a new journey through the house as it shrugged off the curse slowly, step by step. The spell of petrifaction that reigned over its dwellers merged into a deep sleep. It was far better this way. Sleep smoothes out the alien grimaces of another world. All would be forgotten; none of the survivors would be marked for the rest of their lives by the curse of the previous night. Tomorrow morning everything in this big house would be almost back to normal. The only thing that remained to do was to bury the unfortunate fellows who had been capering about the hall by the fountain, organize a spring cleaning, and call in a good medicine man to administer a calming herb to all members of the household for the next two dozen days.

It could have been worse. It could have ended very badly, indeed.

We went out into the garden.

"How nice it is out here!" I said with a sigh with relief.

Sir Juffin Hully took the liberty of patting me on the back, which is only allowed to the closest of friends in the Unified Kingdom.

"You turned out to be a wild wind, Sir Max! Much wilder than I expected. And I already had a high opinion of you, you may be quite sure!"

"A 'wild wind'? Why 'wind,' Juffin?"

"That's what we call people who are unpredictable. The kind about whom you never know what they might pull off next, how they'll behave in a fight, what kind of effect magic will have on them—or Jubatic Juice! You never even know how much such a person will eat: one day he'll empty the whole pot, and the next he'll start preaching moderation . . . That was exactly what I needed: a wild wind, a fresh wind from another world. But you turned out to be a real hurricane, Sir Max! Lucky me!"

I was about to feel embarrassed, but then I thought—why should I? I really was pretty good; at least my part in the story of the mirrors. I'll start indulging in modesty once the number of my exploits exceeds one hundred.

※

At home we found not only Lonli-Lokli waiting for us, decorously sipping his kamra, but also Melifaro, pale but quite lively, devouring the sandwiches from a tray resting on his lap. Chuff followed all his motions with great interest. Judging by the crumbs that had collected abundantly around the dog's mouth, Sir Melifaro also had a soft spot in his heart for him.

"It's too bad you saved me," Melifaro said, grinning from ear to ear and bowing to Juffin. "Your pantry is running low with me around!"

"As if that matters! My pantry has long been in need of an airing. By the way, Max is the one you should thank. He was your main rescuer."

"Thank you," Melifaro purred, his mouth full of food. "So you, my fine friend, ate up the frog? And I thought it was our baleful sorcerers who took care of it."

"Shurf and I, of course, worked with our hands," Juffin explained modestly. "But only after Sir Max worked with his head. If it hadn't been for his crazy idea about a second mirror, you would have been someone's sandwich. Do you remember anything at all, you lucky devil?"

"Not a thing. Loki-Lonki described the scenario briefly—but his account lacked picturesque detail. I require a literary description!"

"You'll get your picturesque detail. Chew up, first, or you'll choke!" Sir Juffin said, shaking his head sternly.

"Sir Melifaro, my name is Lonli-Lokli. Please oblige me by learning how to pronounce it. It's high time. There are only ten letters; it's not such a daunting task!"

"That's what I'm saying—Lonki-Lomki!" And Melifaro turned to me abruptly. "So in fact you're my main rescuer? Well, what do you know, Sir Nocturnal Nightmare! I owe you one."

That was the moment of triumph for me. I had been preparing my acceptance speech on the way over.

"Nonsense. Where we live, in the Barren Lands, every beggarly nomad has a mirror like Makluk's in his household. I don't understand why here, in the capital, people make such a big fuss over something so trivial."

Shurf Lonli-Lokli expressed polite surprise. "Really, Sir Max? It's strange that scholars make no mention of this."

"There's nothing strange about it." I snapped, putting on a malevolent leer. "The ones who could have told the story are now forever silent. We have to feed our favorite house-pets somehow!"

Sir Juffin Hully burst out laughing. Melifaro raised his eyebrows in surprise, but realized almost immediately that I was just teasing and let out a guffaw. Lonli-Lokli shrugged indulgently and reached again for his mug.

"Save your strength, gentlemen," Juffin warned. "Today in the *Glutton* a public holiday has been declared: it's Melifaro's resurrection. You do as you wish, but Max and I are going out to carouse. We've earned it! Sir Shurf, you're coming too; and that's an order! Melifaro, you're probably still too weak. You stay here and get better. We'll carouse for you!"

"Me, weak? You can just drive me to the *Glutton*."

"Well, all right. We'll drive you right to the doorstep. But you don't know how Sir Max drives the amobiler! He'll keep you in check—he'll shake the living daylights right out of you!"

"Sir Max? You mean to say you're a real racer?"

"I didn't think so," I said proudly, "but Sir Juffin was very dissatisfied when he came for a spin with me. He kept asking me to slow down, even though I was virtually crawling. Actually, everyone here drives slowly. Why is that I wonder?"

Melifaro leaped out of his chair.

"If that is true, then you're perfect! Why is it that you haven't conquered us yet?"

"The military potential of border-dwellers is extremely low," Sir Lonli-Lokli remarked pedantically. "On the other hand, their intellectual capabilities are without doubt higher than ours. Unlike you, Sir Max learned to pronounce my name on the first try. An impressive debut, wouldn't you say?"

CHAPTER TWO

JUBA CHEBOBARGO AND OTHER NICE FOLKS

"**M**AX, ARE YOU *SURE* YOU'RE GOING TO BE COMFORTABLE here?" asked Juffin. He himself looked rather uncertain. "Or have you not yet come to terms with the fact that the King will be paying for your lodgings now?"

It all seemed quite funny to me: just yesterday the very idea that I could move into this massive empty house made my head spin. Sure, it was only two stories high, with one room on each story; but each room was the size of a small stadium. For some reason, they don't seem to feel the need to economize on space in Echo. Local architecture features only low buildings, two or three stories high, which are, nevertheless, incredibly spacious. The house that I chose on the Street of Old Coins was smaller than its neighbors, which I rather liked about it. Judging by Juffin's expression, however, it seemed I was enchanted to be living in a slum.

"We Border Dwellers are slaves to habit," I said proudly. "If only you could see the yurts we inhabit in the Barren Lands." This secret ethnographic reference was for the benefit of the house's owner, who stood deferentially to the side. After all, you can't very well tell a respectable citizen that the person who wants to rent his house is an émigré from another world. The poor fellow was, of course, delighted by his good fortune, but not enough to let this intriguing information about my origins slip by unnoticed.

"And besides, I made my choice out of a sense of duty. The more wretched my conditions at home, the more time I will spend at work."

"Sounds reasonable, Sir Max. Very well, you can sleep upstairs and entertain guests on the first floor. But where do you propose to keep the help?"

I decided it was time to stand my ground with my boss.

"I don't approve of keeping servants. I can't have strangers walking around in my house—closing books that I leave open, going through my private belongings, stealing my cookies, and looking into my eyes with devotion while waiting for me to give orders. I should pay money for that? No, thank you."

"I see, Sir Max. You're suffering from a bad case of asceticism, complicated by pathological stinginess. How do you plan to spend the money you've saved?"

"I'll collect amobilers. With my driving habits, I'll go through them in no time."

Sir Juffin sighed. For him, forty miles an hour was insufferable recklessness, and perhaps that wasn't too far from the truth. Before my arrival, people in Echo were under the impression that thirty miles per hour was the absolute limit for this cutting-edge miracle of local technology. That was how I first became something of an attraction in those parts.

"You really are an oddball, Sir Max, moving into a house with only three bathing pools!"

Here I had to admit I had slipped up. In Echo, the bathroom is a special place. Having five to six small swimming pools with water of varying temperatures and aromas is considered not a luxury, but the norm. But even that wasn't enough to turn me into a sybarite. In Sir Juffin's house, where there were eleven such baths, I felt that bathing was hard work, and not something to be enjoyed. So I was quite sure that three baths would be more than enough for me.

"I suppose you're right," Sir Juffin said. "What difference does it make where you make your bed at night? Oh, well, it's your life and you can indulge in self-deprivation if you wish. Let's go over to the *Glutton*, Sir Max. It would be great if we made it over there an hour before everyone else."

The amobiler sent by the Ministry of Perfect Public Order was already waiting for us. The owner of the house had us sign the rental papers, and, still unable to believe his luck, disappeared before we could reconsider.

※

We were given a warm welcome at the *Glutton Bunba*, the best pub in Echo. We sat down at our favorite table between the bar (they say it's the longest in the whole city) and the courtyard window. I sat facing the unprepossessing landscape. Sir Juffin sat across from me, with a view of the bar and Madame Zizinda's unbelievable bust thrown into the bargain.

As we had hoped, we were the first to arrive. Today was to be my official introduction to my colleagues, and Sir Juffin traditionally held such meetings at the *Glutton*. The protocol would be somewhat simplified, as I had already become acquainted with two combat units of the Minor Secret Investigative Force. I had met Sir Melifaro, the Diurnal Representative of Sir Juffin Hully, and Sir Shurf Lonli-Lokli, the Master Who Snuffs Out Unnecessary Lives (a delightful little job that fellow has, I must say), when we had to restrain Sir Makluk's berserk mirror. My new acquaintances were more than willing to share the story with listeners over a cup of kamra. Juffin's remarks would only fan the flames of interest.

As a result, I got the reputation of being some sort of superman. That was enjoyable, of course, but it also gave me certain responsibilities to live up to. I was nervous and grateful to Juffin for suggesting we arrive at the *Glutton* before the others. At least I would have a warm seat beneath me before my colleagues arrived, and I might even be in high spirits if someone offered me a glass of Jubatic Juice.

It turned out, however, that Jubatic Juice was not considered the acme of liquid perfection. They brought us some excellent kamra and a jug of aromatic liqueur, the name of which—Tears of Darkness—gave me an uneasy feeling. As I soon found out, though, that this was just a poetic name given to the drink by its ancient inventor, and had nothing to do with its taste.

"Take it easy, Max," said Juffin. "Melifaro and I talked about you at such length, and Sir Lonli-Lokli was so eloquently silent, that the poor fellows are going to show up here draped in protective amulets of every kind."

"Yes, I thought as much . . . Juffin, that old lady at the next table —is she by any chance one of your crew? She seems to be eyeing me suspiciously."

To my surprise, Juffin stared at me with a nearly threatening gaze. I didn't know what to think.

"Why do you say that, Max?"

"I'm sorry. I was just trying to be funny. That sweet lady definitely had her eye on me. She still does."

"You surprise me, Sir Max."

"What do you mean?"

"I mean that tomorrow I'll be wearing protective amulets too, just in case."

Meanwhile, enveloped in the folds of her dark looxi, the sweet lady, who was in fact a large old woman, stood up gracefully from her table and approached us. The woman's face underwent a transformation as she made her way over to us. By the time she arrived at our table, she was an elderly gentleman of ample and squat build. I blinked my eyes, unable to grasp what was going on.

"I see you as in a waking dream, Sir Max," he said politely, covering his eyes with the palm of his hand, as one does upon first being introduced. I automatically returned the gesture.

"I'm glad to speak my name: I am Kofa Yox, Master Eavesdropper. Congratulations, son. You saw right through me."

"But sir, I didn't mean to," I began, embarrassed. "I was just making a joke."

"Right. Next thing you know, you're going to say you're sorry, and that it won't happen again," said Juffin, laughing out loud. "Just look at him, sitting there with a guilty expression. Anyone else would be gloating over it!"

Kofa Yox smiled gently. "That's reassuring. It's great to have at least one humble person working in our organization." He sat down next to Juffin, facing me, and took a sip of kamra.

"This place has the best food in all of Echo, to be sure!" Sir Kofa Yox said, and smiled again. "I have news for both of you. Everyone in the city is talking about the Venerable Head's new Nocturnal Representative—that's you, son. There are two popular versions of the story. The first is that Juffin Hully brought a creature from the World of the Dead to Echo. Is that a look of delight I see, Sir Max? The second version is that the Venerable Head gave a job in the Force to his illegitimate son, whom he had been hiding away since time immemorial. What do you think of that, Juffin?"

"They couldn't come up with anything more interesting than that?" my boss asked with a snort. "Capital City lore seems to thrive on only two topics: forbidden magic and the amorous adventures of my youth. The latter seems to arouse particular interest, because instead of being born in Echo like most normal people, I came here from Kettari. People think that there's nothing to do in the provinces but indulge in daily fits of shameless lust. Yes, Kofa, the King will have to raise your salary. What a job, having to listen to such idle nonsense, day in and day out!"

"It's all right. It annoyed me for the first eighty years, but I got used to it after that. I've worked with Juffin for a long time, Max," said Kofa Yox, giving me another soft paternal smile.

"Before that, Sir Yox was Police General of the Right Bank," said Juffin, "and tried to have me arrested for many years. On several occasions, his efforts nearly succeeded, but in the end, they all fell through. That was during the Epoch of Orders, a long time before the battle for the Code of Krember. In those days, any citizen could perform magic of the fortieth degree on a whim. Can you imagine?"

I shook my head. It was hard to adjust to the fact that people here lived no fewer than three hundred years. As for more prominent persons, who made up the majority of my acquaintances, they managed to extend their existence almost indefinitely.

How old was Kofa, anyway? I wondered. I would have said he was no older than sixty, and a sixty-year-old is a teenager by local standards. Melifaro, for example, who was about my age, I had thought, turned out to be one hundred and fifteen years old. He was born on the very morning that the Code of Krember had been established. In other words, he was born on the first day of the first year of the Code Epoch, something he liked to joke about, though in his heart I believe he was very proud of it. As for Juffin's age, for some reason I was too shy to ask. Or maybe I was afraid of whatever mind-boggling number the answer might be. In any case, at the ripe old age of thirty I cut a strange figure in their midst. At my age they were only children, just learning to read and write.

While I was doing this arithmetic, our numbers had grown. A young man with a disproportionately long, skinny body hidden in a violet looxi stood in the doorway, smiling shyly. Walking toward us, he managed to knock over a stool. He apologized so sweetly to the middle-aged lady sitting near ground zero that she followed the clumsy young man with a tender gaze. The affable creature began talking even before he got to our table, gesticulating as he advanced.

"I am most honored to be able to pay you my respects in person, Sir Max! I have so many things to ask you. I must admit that I have been burning with anticipation for the past few days, if you will forgive my lack of discretion."

"And you are—?" I asked.

The corners of my mouth began to spread into a smile. I felt like a rock star in the embraces of a fan who had been raised by his elderly grandmother, a countess.

"Please forgive me! I am very glad to speak my name. Sir Lookfi Pence, Master Keeper of Knowledge, at your service."

"This little marvel of nature looks after our *buriwoks*, Sir Max," Sir Juffin said. "Or, rather, the buriwoks look after him in their spare time."

My interest in Mr. Pence grew. I had already heard about these clever talking birds endowed with absolute memory. Buriwoks are rare in the Unified Kingdom. They come from the distant shores of Arvarox, but there are several hundred such wonderful creatures at the House by the Bridge. They serve as an archive for the Ministry of Perfect Public Order. The bird's prodigious memory can store thousands of dates, names, and facts. I can certainly imagine that it would be much more interesting to talk to a buriwok than to sift through reams of paper. I was desperate to see one of these amazing birds with my own eyes, so the man who spent all his working days with them seemed to be a useful acquaintance.

"Why are you alone, Sir Lookfi?" asked Juffin, smiling at the Master Keeper of Knowledge, who had already seated himself beside me. One of the edges of his expensive looxi accidentally ended up in a mug of kamra though this was his only mishap for the moment.

Now, having studied his face for a time, I saw that Sir Lookfi was not as young as I'd first thought. Rather, he belonged to that rare breed of men who look like boys until they are old, when all of a sudden they begin to look their own age.

Lookfi smiled and said, "I'm alone, Sir Juffin, because the others stayed behind to discuss a philosophical matter: the question of necessity versus free will."

"Sinning Magicians! What's going on over there?"

"No need for concern, sir. They are trying to come to a decision. After all, someone should stay behind at the Ministry. On the one hand, that is Sir Melifaro's responsibility. He is your Representative, and when you can't be at the House by the Bridge, his presence there is required. He already knows Sir Max, so his presence here as a matter of etiquette would seem unnecessary. On the other hand, as your Deputy and our Senior, he has the right to appoint any substitute he judges to be competent."

Juffin chuckled, and Sir Kofa smiled.

"When I left," Lookfi continued, after absent-mindedly taking a gulp from my glass of Tears of Darkness, "Lady Melamori was saying that of the three of them, she was the only one who had not yet met Sir Max. She said she didn't want to hear any more of their philosophical wrangling, and that she was going to sit in the next room until they finished their idiotic debate. Allow me, if I may, to disagree with her view of the matter. I think the discussion was very interesting, and I believe there is a moral to be learned from it. But I thought it might occur to Sir Melifaro that I am also a member of the Secret Investigative Force. In short, I thought it best to be impolite and leave on my own accord."

"Give that glass back to Sir Max and take your own. There's more in it," Kofa Yox whispered. "Be careful, my boy: what if that's considered a terrible insult among the inhabitants of the Barren Lands? You can't imagine how frightening Sir Max is when he's enraged."

"Oh dear . . ." Sir Lookfi's face expressed both of fear and curiosity at the same time. "Is that true, Sir Max?"

"You're in luck," I said. "According to our traditions, that signifies the beginning of a long and close friendship. To seal this pact, however, I must finish your glass. Besides, it's brimming over!"

Sir Juffin Hully looked at me with almost fatherly pride. Lookfi was radiant:

"You see, Sir Kofa! And you said it was an insult. I have very good intuition, you know. When I was still just a schoolboy, I already . . . Oh, forgive me gentlemen. I get carried away sometimes. My school years are not the most interesting subject for table-talk." He turned to me. "Sir Max, is it true that you will be working alone and only by night? You know, night is the most interesting time of day! I've always envied people who don't feel the need to go to bed as soon as the sun sets. For example, my wife Varisha also believes that real life only begins after nightfall. That's why I almost never get enough sleep." He finished his speech abruptly, looking quite sheepish.

"Don't worry," I said. "Your habits also have their advantages."

"It seems that the idea of responsibility has won in the philosophical debate," Juffin said. "I salute the victors!"

Now I saw a couple, charming in all respects, approaching us. One of the two was the tall, lean Sir Shurf Lonli-Lokli, who resembled Charlie Watts. He was dressed, as usual, all in white. Leaning on his arm was a petite, spry lady, wrapped in an elegant looxi the color of the night sky.

Instead of the broad-shouldered Amazon I had expected as my colleague, she was a celestial creature with the face of Diana Rigg, the English actress who played James Bond's erstwhile girlfriend. I wonder how they feel about office romances here? I made a mental note to ask Juffin about that.

Jokes aside, the lady was indeed lovely. Her eyes twinkled with intelligence and humor. I had always thought those were two sides of the same coin. I sensed with all my body—only recently awakened to all the wonderful possibilities—the power that exuded from this little lady, no less dangerous than that of the phlegmatic Sir Lonli-Lokli, whose deadly hands I had already seen in action.

"I am happy to speak my name: Melamori Blimm, Master of Pursuit of the Fleeing and Hiding," the lady introduced herself quietly. Much to my surprise she seemed visibly nervous. Sinning Magicians, what had they told her about me?

"It gives me joy to hear your name spoken," said I. Not out of a sense of courtesy. I sincerely meant it.

Lonli-Lokli nodded at me politely with the surreptitious pride of an old friend and sat down next to Lookfi Pence. Melamori moved closer, and my head felt giddy from the pungent scent of her perfume.

"Forgive my familiarity, Sir Max, but I decided to come with a gift. Sir Juffin would surely think me a miser if I had done otherwise." With these words she drew out a bottle from the folds of her looxi. "I am sure you have not tried wine of this kind before. I myself have rarely had the pleasure to enjoy it, although my uncle, Kima Blimm, favors me above everyone else in the family."

Handing me the bottle carefully, she sat down on a stool next to Kofa. I examined the bottle.

"You're a lucky man, Sir Max!" Juffin exclaimed. Suddenly he looked two hundred years younger. "That is indeed a rarity. Eternal Dew is a wine from the deepest cellars of the Order of the Seven-Leaf Clover! Kima Blimm, Melamori's uncle, is the Supervisor in Chief of the Order's wines. That's why I hired her. There, there, don't take offense, Lady Melamori! We didn't meet just yesterday. You could very well make a list of Sir Juffin Hully's Worst Jokes and sell it to the *Echo Hustle and Bustle*."

"Well, Sir Max has just met me, and he'll think that I got my job in the Secret Investigative Force because of my relatives," Melamori said, sounding hurt.

"Sir Max knows me too well, my dear. Besides, I suspect he's already sensed your worth. Not even half an hour ago he pointed out Sir Kofa, who came disguised as a lady of grand proportions, and asked me if he wasn't one of the Secret Investigators. Isn't that right, Sir Max?"

Three pairs of eyes fastened themselves upon me. I felt a strong urge to study the contents of my cup.

"You're exaggerating, sir. Suppose that my guess *was* right, just for once . . . All right, I admit that when I saw Lady Melamori, I thought that she must be at least as dangerous as Sir Shurf, that's all," I said, winking at the pouting beauty. "Am I right?"

Melamori smiled like a cat who had eaten a filling meal.

"I think the men I dragged by the collar and threw into Xolomi, or someplace worse, would agree with you, Sir Max," she said, then added with the expression of a sweet little girl, "Still, you do me too much credit. Sir Shurf is an unparalleled killer. Me? I'm still learning. But I am good at manhunting!" Melamori smiled again, showing her sharp little teeth. "And I need only start trailing a man for his luck to turn and his strength to wane," the dangerous lady said, then looked at us quizzically. "Forgive me, I seem to have allowed myself to get carried away!"

"It's quite all right," said Juffin. "You should take advantage of Melifaro's absence while you can, dear girl. At what point do you think he would have interrupted that fiery speech of yours?"

"Right after the second word," said Melamori, and giggled. "That's for sure! Although when Sir Melifaro and I are alone, his gallantry knows no bounds. He lets me say at least five or six words at a time. Can you believe it?"

"No, I can't. Even I am rarely able to accomplish that; and I am the Most Venerable Head! By the way, Shurf, how did you manage to get past him?"

"That was easy. I asked your personal buriwok, Kurush, to quote from the section of the Code that Sir Melifaro received upon being appointed to his job. It clearly stated that—"

"I see," said Juffin, laughing. "There is no need to continue. A hole in the heavens above you both! You're two of a kind!"

Harmony in the Minor Secret Investigative Force, I surmised, was based on the ancient dialectical principle of the unity and struggle of opposites. Temperamental Melifaro and cold-blooded Lonli-Lokli; unpredictable Juffin and steady, reliable Kofa Yox; harmless, gangly Lookfi and the formidable little lady Melamori Blimm. I wonder, which of them I would have to counterbalance? I suppose it would have to be all of them at once. I am, after all, a creature from another world.

In the meantime, everyone's attention seemed to be fixed on the bottle of Eternal Dew.

"May I ask you, Sir Kofa, to divide this luxury between all of us fairly?" My intuition told me that this elderly gentleman was a person one could depend on in such sticky everyday situations.

My generosity won me the heartfelt goodwill of all present. Later, Sir Juffin told me that if I had taken the gift home with me it would have been accepted as a matter of course—they know how to respect the gastronomic weaknesses of others here. But my decision came as a pleasant surprise to the gathering of gourmets.

During the tasting, Lonli-Lokli astonished me yet again. From beneath the snow-white folds of his looxi he produced a wooden cup, darkened with age, and handed it to Sir Kofa. This in itself did not surprise me: I could very well imagine Sir Shurf carrying an ancient family heirloom around with him everywhere he went for just such an occasion. Then I noticed that the cup had no bottom. Sir Kofa paid this no heed and impassively filled the holy chalice with the rare drink. Not a drop spilled from the cup. Juffin understood that I was in urgent need of a brief history lesson.

"Don't look so surprised, Max. In his time, Sir Shurf was a member of the Order of the Holey Cup. He served there as a Fish-Fellow, Keeper of the Order's Aquariums, which had as many holes as this honorable vessel. Members of the Order ate only fish, which they bred in those very aquariums, and washed down their meals with drinks from jugs with holes in the bottom. Isn't that right, my friend?"

Lonli-Lokli nodded gravely, and downed his portion of the drink.

"Before the Troubled Times," Juffin continued, "the Order of the Holey Cup was in good standing with the Order of the Seven-Leaf Clover." This he said with a respectfully comic bow in the direction of Lady Melamori. "So it was dissolved on very agreeable terms. Like his other former colleagues, our good Sir Shurf still has special permission to adhere to the ancient traditions of his order. In other words, he may drink from a holey cup. Because he is using forbidden magic, he is obliged to offset the potentially dire consequences of his actions with all his might. This he does every time, although it consumes a great deal of the power he gains from the ritual. Have I left anything out, Sir Lonli-Lokli?"

"You have explained the reasons and consequences of my action in a succinct and informative manner," Lonli-Lokli intoned with a nod. He held the cup in both hands, and his impassive face radiated an intense serenity.

After a tray filled with pots of delicacies and a portion of Eternal Dew had been sent off to poor Melifaro at my insistence, I could be certain that from then on, every one of my colleagues would be willing to die for a smile from me. I wasn't going to be the one to impose that fate on them, though. I smiled a lot that evening, and absolutely free of charge. I managed to maneuver around the thorny ethnographical questions that poured from the curious but trusting Lookfi, to flirt with Lady Melamori, to listen to Sir Kofa, to pronounce Lonli-Lokli's name correctly, and to amuse Juffin. It was amazing! For the first time in my life I was the life of the party, and a significant one at that. When the number of dirty dishes finally exceeded the capabilities of any local dishwasher, we decided to part ways. Sir Kofa Yox kindly deigned to take Melifaro's shift, and in an equally compassionate gesture, Sir Juffin Hully awarded them each an extra Day of Freedom from Chores. Then he extended an invitation to both of them for dinner tomorrow around sunset at the *Glutton*. So it seemed that Melifaro had only gained from missing today's event.

✺

The Ministry of Perfect Public Order had to do without me for one last night. I planned to spend it moving into my new place. The next day, after lunch, I was supposed to report to the House by the Bridge and officially begin my job. Put simply, I had to figure out what was required of me in the course of a few hours, though doubts about my abilities were gradually disappearing.

The family amobiler arrived for Lady Melamori. The fragile, petite Master of Pursuit smiled as we bid each other goodnight and told me quietly that Sir Max was a strange name: a bit too short, but it sounded nice all the same. And off she rolled toward home in truly royal pomp and splendor. Besides the driver, her amobiler boasted two musicians, whose job it was to fulfill the role of a car stereo.

Lookfi and Lonli-Lokli set off for home in the company amobiler. Everyone has the right to do this, though not everyone takes advantage of the privilege. Old Kimpa, Sir Juffin Hully's butler, came to pick us up. Juffin always leaves for home in his own amobiler, which he justifies by saying that the company vehicle makes him feel like he's still at work. In his own amobiler, however, he feels like he's already home. And you'd have to be the last fool on earth to refuse to knock off work a half hour early. I think that makes perfect sense.

On our way back home we sat side by side in silent contentment. When you know what to talk about with someone, it's a sign of mutual sympathy. But when you are moved to be quiet together— well, that's the start of a real friendship.

%

"Should we sit another half hour over some kamra?" asked Juffin. It wasn't really a question, but more a statement of fact on his part, as we stood in the doorway of the house. Little Chuff met us in the foyer, wagging his stubby tail. *Max has come! But he is leaving, going far far away*, the mournful thoughts of the old dog reached me.

"I won't be that far, Chuff!" I said to the dog. "I'd take you with me, but I know you couldn't stand being away from your master. Besides, unlike Kimpa, I don't know how to cook, and I know you have gourmet tastes. I'll come visit you, all right?"

My furry friend sighed and licked his chops. *You'll come visit. For lunch*, he responded with enthusiasm.

Sir Juffin was pleased.

"So you see, everything is taken care of. That a boy, Chuff! A healthy, pragmatic attitude, and no sentiment whatsoever!"

We settled ourselves in comfortable armchairs in the parlor, and Chuff lay down at my feet, allowing himself this slight disloyalty to Juffin in view of the occasion. Kimpa served us kamra and cookies. I enjoyed lighting up my last cigarette, as my reserves had finally run out. My new life was about to begin. I would switch to smoking a pipe or quit smoking altogether. Neither choice seemed particularly appealing, but there were no others in sight.

We exchanged a bit of gossip about my new acquaintances— Juffin's curiosity seemed to know no bounds. Now he wanted to know my opinion: Did I like Kofa? What about Lookfi? And Melamori? Since the topic had come up anyway, I decided to ask about office romances. Were they outlawed by some regulation in the Code of Krember? Because if they were forbidden, Juffin was free to arrest me right then and there for criminal intent.

"I'm not aware that such things are forbidden. A strange idea, really . . . Is it where you come from? Forbidden, I mean?" he asked in surprise.

"No, not really. But having a relationship with someone at work is frowned upon. Although that's all anyone ever does."

"Your World is an odd place, Max! You think one thing, but you do the opposite. We don't 'think' anything. The law stipulates what is required of us, superstition is a matter of inner conviction, traditions attest to our love of habit; but even so, everyone is free to do what he wishes. Go ahead and give it a try, if you feel like it. Although, I don't think it's such a good idea. Lady Melamori is a strange young woman. She's an incurable idealist, and I do believe she enjoys her solitude. Melifaro has been courting her for several years now, without success. She enjoys telling everyone about it; but what good can come of it?"

"Oh, I can just imagine what Melifaro's attentions are like! 'Please be so kind as to remove your splendiferous backside from my presence, dear, for its divine shapeliness is distracting me!'"

Sir Juffin laughed. "You guessed it, Max! You really are clairvoyant!"

"Not at all. It's just that some things go without saying."

"Regardless, Melifaro is a favorite among the ladies. Although he is no redhead; but then again, neither are you! Do as you wish, though I fear your efforts will not meet with success."

"I've never really had any luck with women in my life. Well, at first I was fairly lucky. Then all of a sudden, they all thought they had to get married for some reason. And not to me. It's especially strange, because I almost always fell in love with very smart girls. Even that didn't help matters. I don't see how any intelligent person could seriously want to get married. In any case, I'm used to it."

"Well, if that's how it is, it means you're either the most thick-skinned or the slipperiest son-of-a-werewolf in the entire Unified Kingdom."

"Neither. This is probably another one of those cultural differences. We forget pain quickly, and those who can't at least dull it are apt to inspire pity mixed with incomprehension. Their relatives may also try to persuade them to see a psychoanalyst. I suppose that's because we don't live very long, and spending several years on one sorrow would be a ridiculous extravagance."

"How long do you live?" asked Sir Juffin in surprise.

"About seventy or eighty years. Why do you ask?"

"You die so young? Every one of you?"

"But you see, we're old by that time."

"How old are you, Max?"

"Thirty . . . at least, I will be soon. Perhaps I already am. When is my birthday? I've lost count since I came here."

Sir Juffin became seriously alarmed.

"Still a child! Oh dear! I hope you're not going to die prematurely in forty or fifty years time. Now, let me take a good look at you."

Juffin jumped out of his chair. A second later he was poking my back with his hands, which suddenly became ice-cold and heavy. Then his hands grew hot, and I felt that my mind, which always used to occupy a place somewhere behind my eyes, was shifting, moving down my spine. I could "see" the warm radiance of his coarse palms with my . . . back! Then it ended, just as unexpectedly as it had begun. Sir Juffin returned to his place, thoroughly satisfied with the results of his examination.

"It's all right, boy. You're no different from me, though you may find it hard to believe. That must mean that it isn't your nature, but your lifestyle that determines your life expectancy. Here in the World you can live for well over three hundred years—as long as no one kills you, that is. You had me frightened for a moment there, Sir Max! What kind of place is your homeland anyway? What sort of hellhole did I pull you out of?"

"The World of the Dead, apparently," I said with a rueful laugh. "Your city's taletellers had it almost right. But it's not all that bad. When you've known only one world since childhood, it's inevitable that it all seems natural. When I left home, I didn't regret a thing. I doubt, though, that you'll find many like me. I don't count, anyway, because I was always a dreamer. I suppose I really was a classic loser. Most people would tell you that nothing good could come of dreaming. The life expectancy you have here, on the other hand, could get a lot of folks to switch sides. If you plan to recruit more of my people, keep that in mind."

"As if I needed your countrymen."

"What if another guy makes a habit of seeing you in his dreams?"

"Well, then we'd have to find another vacancy for him. Okay, okay; you're right. I won't make a promise I can't keep."

※

Alas, all things have the idiotic habit of ending at some point. Sir Juffin went to bed and I began to get ready to move.

I was sure that I had almost nothing to pack. Boy was I wrong! My earthly riches consisted of a catastrophically overgrown wardrobe and library. There were also Juffin's gifts and the fruits of my walks about the city, when I had visited all kinds of shops, frittering away the advance I'd received on my salary. As for the library, it included the *Encyclopedia of the World* by Manga Melifaro, kindly given to me by his youngest son. That unwieldy eight-volume set was but a drop in the ocean of my possessions.

Along with all the rest, I packed the outfit I had been wearing on the day I first arrived in Echo. It was highly unlikely that I would ever again need to wear that pair of jeans and a sweater, but I couldn't just throw them out, either. Perhaps I'd get a chance to go home for a visit, if only to pick up some cigarettes. Who knows?

Trips between my bedroom and my new amobiler parked by the gate outside took almost an hour. But even this work was finished eventually. I drove home with my heart beating happily and my head a complete void. "Home." How strange the word sounded to me!

I crossed over the Echo Crest Bridge, full of the inviting lights of shops and bars, still doing a lively trade even at this late hour. Here in Echo people really get the meaning of night life. Maybe that's because even permitted magic allows you to carouse for a night or two without seriously harming your health.

Across the bridge I found myself on the Right Bank. Now my path led straight to the heart of the Old City. I preferred to dwell in its narrow alleyways rather than the wide streets of the New City, Echo's wealthy downtown.

The mosaic sidewalks of the Street of Old Coins had lost almost all of their original color. Still, I preferred the tiny stones of the ancient mosaics to the big bright tiles that covered the new streets. My newly gained experience told me that material objects remember events and can tell us about them. Juffin had taught me to listen to their murmurings, or, rather, the visions they transmit. I had always loved ancient history. I'd have something to do in my spare time, anyway!

My new house was glad to see me. Not long ago I would have thought I was letting my imagination get the better of me. Now I knew that I could trust my vague inklings as much as obvious facts. Well, good; we like each other, my new house and I. It was probably tired of standing empty. The landlord said that the prior inhabitants moved out some forty years ago, and since that time, the only visitors had been the cleaners.

I got out of the amobiler and took my belongings into the parlor. The room was almost empty, as is the custom here in Echo. I've always liked interiors like that, but until now I had never had the opportunity to develop this aesthetic. There was a small table covered entirely by a basket of provisions I had ordered from the *Glutton Bunba*, several comfortable armchairs like the ones Sir Juffin had in his sitting room, and several shelves nestled against the wall. What more does a man need?

I spent the next two hours arranging my books and trinkets on the shelves. After that, I went upstairs to the bedroom. Half the enormous space was taken up by a soft fuzzy floor: no risk of falling out of bed here! Several pillows and fur blankets were heaped together at the far end of the stadium-sized dream-dome. A wardrobe loomed somewhere in the distance, and there I stuffed a pile of colored fabric—my newly acquired clothes. My nostalgia garb—jeans, sweater, and vest—was stashed nearby. There was a little bathroom next to the bedroom that would only be suitable for my morning toilette. The other facilities were in the basement.

My work was done, and I was neither hungry nor sleepy; yet I didn't want to leave the house to take a walk, either. I would gladly have sold my soul to the devil for a single pack of cigarettes.

I sat in the parlor, awkwardly filling my pipe with tobacco and bemoaning my bitter fate. In this hour of sorrow, the only comfort I found was in the view from the window. Just opposite stood an ancient three-story mansion with little triangular windows and a tall peaked roof. As someone who has spent most of his life in high-rise apartment blocks, my heart begins to beat faster at even the slightest patina of age. Here every stone cried out "days of yore!"

After I had my fill of the view, I went up to the bedroom with the third volume of Sir Manga Melifaro's *Encyclopedia* under my arm. The book expounded on my so-called countrymen, the inhabitants of the County Vook and the Barren Lands. Everyone should love his homeland, even an invented one. It's very important to study it— especially in my case, since I was aware of good Lookfi Pence's curiosity and the grilling I expected to get from him. Besides, I found this reading to be dreadfully amusing. Page forty dealt with a certain tribe of nomads from the Barren Lands, who, in an act of unbelievable absent-mindedness, lost their juvenile chief in the steppe. After I reached the part of the chronicle in which these dunderheads put a curse on themselves, I fell asleep and dreamed my own version of this mad tale with a happy ending. Their chief, now an adult, appealed to our Ministry for assistance, and Sir Juffin and I helped the guy track down his poor people. In parting, Sir Lonli-Lokli drew up a clear and concise code of conduct for Tribal Nomad Chiefs in their far-flung workplace.

❊

I woke up before noon, which by my standards is still very early. I spent a long time getting ready: after all, this was my first day on the job. I went downstairs and splashed around in my three bathing pools, one after the other. No matter what they say, three bathtubs are better than one . . . and way better than eleven, with all due respect to the snobs of the capital, headed by Sir Juffin Hully.

The hour had come to open the basket of provisions from the *Glutton*. To my great delight, I found a jug of kamra inside that I could reheat. As for attempting to make the drink myself, thus far I had had to dispose of all the fruits of my experiments. Sir Juffin Hully had suggested using my kamra as a deterrent to especially dangerous criminals. The only thing stopping him was the fact that he feared this method might be considered too ruthless.

So I warmed up the kamra on a miniature brazier (an indispensable feature of any civilized sitting room). It was a lovely morning. Finally I even lit the pipe I'd prepared for myself the evening before. It wasn't so bad after all. Not even the unfamiliar taste of the local tobacco could put a dent in my optimism.

I went to work on foot. I planned to show off my expensive dark, intricately patterned looxi and black turban, which transformed me from your everyday good-looker into a prince. No one in the city besides me seemed to take any notice of this, though. People hurried about their business or stared dreamily into storefront windows in the Old Town. No gapes of wonder, no beautiful damsels eager to throw themselves into my arms in fits of trembling exaltation. So there was one thing that hadn't changed.

I turned onto the Street of Copper Pots. I had just a short way to go before I took my first steps over the threshold of the Secret Door leading to the House by the Bridge. Before that day, I hadn't had the right to enter the Ministry of Perfect Public Order through that door.

Of course, I could have used the visitor's entrance, but I decided against that. There had been nothing for me to do there before, anyway.

A short corridor led to the half of the building occupied by the Minor Secret Investigative Force, the organization that would soon be home to me. The other half of the building belonged to the Echo City Police Department, under the command of General of Public Order Sir Boboota Box, of whom I had never once heard a kind word spoken. I passed an enormous empty reception hall (the courier dozing off on the edge of his chair didn't count) and entered the Hall of Common Labor, to find Lonli-Lokli writing something in an oversized notebook. I was immediately disappointed. Well, whaddayaknow: paperwork, even here! What about those self-inscribing tablets and buriwoks who memorize every word you say?

My worries were premature, though. Sir Shurf Lonli-Lokli kept a personal work diary for his own pleasure. I was not inclined to disturb his bureaucratic serfdom, and went into Juffin's office, which was a relatively small and comfortable room.

Sir Venerable Head was sitting at his desk, choking with laughter, while trying to scold Lady Melamori, who stood frozen before him with the look of a timid schoolgirl.

"Oh, it's you, Sir Max. Your first mission is to go into the city and commit a bestial murder of some sort. The fellows are going mad with boredom. Do you know what the first and only lady of the Secret Investigative Force has been up to? She began shadowing Captain Foofloss, who is deputy, brother-in-law, and brother in arms to General Boboota Box. The poor fool started to get chest pains, and he was consumed by a terrible feeling of dread. For the first time in his life, he started asking himself the fundamental questions of life, and was none the happier for it. Only the quick wit of young Lieutenant Kamshi saved Mr. Foofloss from suicide. They sent him off to an estate to unwind, and Lieutenant Kamshi was obliged to write me an official report. The City Police is held together by people like that. If only Sir Kamshi were in Boboota's place . . . Isn't that hilarious?"

"You seem to think it is," I said. "Don't fight your natural inclinations; you look like you're about to burst!"

Juffin nodded, and heeding my medical advice, gave vent to his laughter. Melamori looked at us almost reprovingly, as though she had broken the law once in a lifetime and we had the temerity to snicker about it.

"Well, what am I to do with you, young lady? Count yourself lucky that Kamshi seems to have taken a fancy to you. Can you imagine the uproar it would have caused if he had been eager to enforce the letter of the law, or had been more concerned about his boss's state of mind?"

"Then we would have proven that Captain Foofloss was a criminal!" Melamori retorted, smiling her irresistible smile. "You'd be the first to enjoy it."

"I assure you, I have enough to enjoy without your help. So this is how it's going to be, Miss. As boredom seems to have addled your brain, you are being sent to Xolomi for three days. There you will help the commandant to study the Secret Archive. I don't know anyone better than you for getting the job done. Keeping secrets is in your blood. You'll feel like a prisoner, as well you should! If anything happens here, I'll send for you. So pray to the Dark Magicians for a bloody crime. Oh yes, and don't forget to bribe Sir Kamshi. A kiss would be cheaper, but I'd advise you to warm him up with something from your Uncle Kima's wine cellars. That way you won't have to make a commitment, and it will certainly surpass even his wildest expectations. Now off to jail you go."

Lady Melamori rolled her eyes in mock martyrdom. "You see, Max? There you have it: the fist of tyranny! Sending me to Xolomi for three days because of an innocent prank!"

"That's what you think!" Juffin said with a caustic chuckle. "The old commandant will treat you like royalty. Have you heard about his chef?"

"Yes, and that's the only reason I haven't poisoned myself right here in your office." Melamori stopped short, and added petulantly, "Forgive me, Sir Juffin, but Foofloss is such an idiot. I couldn't help myself."

"I'm not surprised in the least!" And with that, Juffin started laughing again.

I had little doubt that in the past Melamori Blimm had gotten away with other, less innocent, pranks.

※

Before the lovely criminal was whisked off to Xolomi in one of the company amobilers, she whispered to me quickly, "I'm not always like this." I'd have liked to believe it.

"I am afraid, Sir Max, that today I will have to address you on an official footing," said Juffin, whose manner had become instantly solemn. "Let me first tell you a bit about Kurush."

The story of Lady Melamori's malfeasance had occupied my full attention. Only then did I notice the shaggy owl-like bird, seated on the back of an empty arm chair. The buriwok (and it was definitely a buriwok) deigned to study my personage from on high.

"It's all right, he'll do," the feathered wonder said at long last. As far as I could make out, it was referring to me.

"Thank you, Kurush," I said. I had wanted to joke, but it came out sounding quite serious. Sir Juffin nodded.

"That means a lot coming from him. If you only knew the things he said about the others!"

"What did you say about the others?" I asked the bird.

"That is classified information," Kurush answered stolidly. "And you have business to attend to."

The "business" was that Sir Juffin made me repeat some mumbo-jumbo in an unintelligible language. Apparently, it was a powerful ancient spell that bound me to serve the interests of the crown.

"But I don't feel a thing," I said in confusion, having gotten through the tongue-twisting text with some difficulty.

"You aren't supposed to feel anything. At least, when I said it I didn't feel anything out of the ordinary either. Maybe it's just an old superstition. Then again, perhaps it does work; who knows? Now get ready. I must read you the Employee's Code in Kurush's presence. You don't have to pay too much attention to it; just try to think about something pleasant. The reading will take some time. Kurush will be able to quote from any chapter, if necessary. Isn't that right, dear?" Juffin looked tenderly at the buriwok, who in turn swelled with pride.

I won't take it upon myself to repeat the instructions read to me. In a nutshell, I was told that I should do everything I am supposed to and not do anything that I am not supposed to do. To convey this simple truth, some bored court bureaucrat wasted several sheets of first-rate paper, and Sir Juffin spent more than half an hour reiterating this literary masterpiece. He finished with a sigh of relief. Another sigh escaped me at the same time. Only Kurush seemed to get any pleasure out of the procedure.

"Why do birds as smart as yourself work for humans?" I asked the buriwok. The question had been nagging me for the last half an hour.

"There aren't very many of us here," the bird answered. "It's hard to make a living, but some of us find living with people to be peaceful and interesting. Where there are more of us, we live in isolation and possess great powers. But here there are so many different words, so many stories!"

"That's a good answer, Kurush," Juffin said, smiling affectionately. "Do you understand, Max? They find us amusing!"

After that I was ceremoniously handed my "battle weapon," a miniature dagger that looked more like a manicure accessory than a deadly instrument. There was a gauge in the hilt that signaled the presence of both forbidden and permitted magic. In fact, I had already seen one of these things in action and concluded that it wasn't all that powerful. Well, all the better. It's best not to be under any illusions from the outset.

Having finished with the formalities, we went up to the top floor of the House by the Bridge, where I was introduced to a plump, kindly little man in an orange looxi.

"I am glad to speak my name. I am Sir Qumbra Qurmac, Chief of Great and Minor Awards for the Ministry of Perfect Public Order. I am one of the most personable subjects in the whole of this forbidding place, as I am in charge of awarding prizes and other such pleasant things," said the friendly man, who vaguely resembled a tangerine.

"Sir Qumbra Qurmac is the only official representative of the Royal Court in the Ministry," Juffin added. "So no matter how intensive our efforts, without the weighty backing of Sir Qumbra they would vanish into obscurity."

"Don't believe a word Sir Hully says," the fat man countered, clearly flattered. "He is one person whose opinion is always welcome at court. Still, I do believe, Sir Max, that I was the first one to report your outstanding deeds to the King."

I stared at my boss, dumbfounded. What outstanding deeds? asked my bewildered expression.

"He means the affair with old Makluk's mirror," explained Juffin. "Of course you weren't yet employed in the Ministry, but that makes it all the more of an honor! The Unified Kingdom must celebrate its heroes."

"You, Sir Max, are the first person I recall entering the service with an award already under your belt," said Sir Qumbra Qurmac, and bowed. "And believe me, I have been in the service for many years. I ask that you kindly accept this gift." He gave me a little box made of dark wood. I knew that upon receiving a gift in Echo one is expected inspect it very closely. I tried to open the box, to no avail.

"Max, that is a gift from the King!" Juffin chastised. "You can't open it just like that. I believe white magic of the fourth degree is required. So you'll have to open it at home; casting spells in public places is forbidden. And there is a reason for that: one should enjoy a royal gift in private."

"I'm sorry," I said blushing. "I've never gotten a gift from the King before."

"It's quite all right, Sir Max," Sir Qumbra said consolingly. "Just think of how many employees there are here who know exactly what to do with a gift like that, but have never had the honor of receiving one. I'd say you're in an enviable position."

I thanked the King and his court, and in particular Sir Qurmac, profusely. Then Juffin and I departed.

"You should have told me," I grumbled. "But you enjoy watching my blunders, don't you?"

"Believe me, it's better for everyone that way. What kind of 'barbarian from the borderlands' would you be if you did everything right? Have faith, my boy; conspiracy is a great power, indeed!"

"Yeah, right. Give me a hand with this box, will you? I don't think I can do it myself."

"Don't be so modest. You try first, and if nothing comes of it then I'll give you a hand. Let's lock the door first, though. It's all right, don't worry! Stranger things have taken place in my office."

I put the box on the table and tried to relax, recalling all the things I had been taught. Nothing happened. Ashamed, I made a helpless gesture.

"Sir Max, I am afraid I could be mistaken. Let's see here . . . Yes, all you need is magic of the fourth degree. You know that already; give it another try."

Then I got angry. Angry at the box, angry at the King who had foisted it on me in the first place, angry at Juffin who just didn't want to help . . . Fine, we'll try something different for a change! In my rage, I called for the courier so imperiously that he probably fell off his chair in alarm. I even imagined that I heard the smack as he hit the floor, although that was impossible, of course. A few seconds later, he knocked on the door timorously. Sir Juffin was taken aback.

"What's come over you?"

"I won't be able to get through this without a warm cup of kamra!"

"That's not a bad idea."

The frightened courier, his whole body shaking, left the tray on the edge of the table right underneath my nose and promptly vanished. Juffin stared at the door in bewilderment.

"What was wrong with him? I know they're afraid of me, but not *that* afraid!"

"Not you; it's me he's afraid of. I think I went a little overboard when I summoned him."

"Oh, that's all right, then. They should be afraid of you. You're new here. If you don't frighten them right from the start, you'll end up spending the rest of your days waiting for the lazy fellows to answer your calls. But Max, are you really angry?"

"Yes!" I barked. I drank the mug of kamra in one gulp and hit the table with my pinky finger near the box, just as I had been taught to do. To my astonishment, the box turned to dust. But the small object that was hidden inside fortunately remained intact. I relaxed.

"Uh-oh," I said, "What did I do wrong?"

"Nothing much. You just used magic of the sixth degree instead of the fourth. And black instead of white. And you ruined a nice little trinket to boot. But it could happen to anyone, really. Anyway, all's well that ends well. It's a good thing that my office is sealed off from the other rooms. I can only imagine what a fuss they'd make at the Ministry!" The boss seemed thrilled by my escapade.

"But Juffin, you didn't teach me that, and I wasn't much of a student to begin with. How can that be?"

"Who in the name of Magicians knows, Max. I said it before, and I'll say it again: you're a wild wind! Please limit the area of destruction to this office, and everything will be just fine. Let's see what's inside."

We both stared at the little bundle lying in the pile of ashes. Carefully I unfolded the fine cloth. A pea the color of dark cherry was hidden inside. I rolled it around on the palm of my hand.

"What is it?"

Juffin smiled pensively.

"That, Sir Max, is a myth. Something that doesn't exist. It is a Child of the Crimson Pearl of Gurig VII. The funny thing is that no one, not even the late King himself or his heir who now reigns, has ever seen the 'mother' of this pearl. Her presence in the palace was discovered by a wise old Magician—a good friend of mine, by the way. He decided not to tell anyone the exact location of this miracle. He said he didn't know; but I think he could have come up with something a little more convincing. Her children turn up regularly in all the palace's nooks and crannies. His Majesty gives the 'orphans' to citizens who have proven themselves worthy. I have three of them already. But you got yours very quickly. I'm not saying you don't deserve it, though. You had a rough time of it at my neighbor's house the other day."

"Are they magic pearls?"

"Yes and no. It's clear that they have some power. But what exactly is it? Someday we'll find out; but for the time being, no one has discovered it. You can keep it at home or have the jeweler mount it for you, whatever suits your taste."

"I suppose I'll go for the first option. I never much cared for baubles."

"A typical sentiment for a barbarian, you scourge of couriers, you!" said Juffin with a laugh.

After this I was left to the winds of fate. Juffin left me in charge and headed for the *Glutton Bunba* to have dinner with Melifaro.

"Tell him he owes me one!" I called after my boss as he slipped away. "A whole helicopter of humanitarian aid; and it had better be on him!"

"Humanitarian aid? Is that a hot appetizer?" asked Sir Juffin.

"That just means a whole lot of food at the right moment," I explained.

That night was so uneventful that I was slightly disappointed. Kurush amused me as best he could. The wise bird turned out to be just as much of a night owl as myself. As a kindred spirit, I was obliged to tell the buriwok my life story. But before I did, I made Kurush take a dreadful oath to keep the information confidential and file it under Far More Secret Than Top Secret. The buriwok bore himself like an Indian chieftain, which greatly impressed me.

The following morning began with a visit from Kofa Yox, who arrived before the first light. He, too, often worked at night, since his main job was to listen to the idle talk in Echo's taverns and glean grains of useful information from the idle chitchat. When the Master Eavesdropper showed up at the House by the Bridge most mornings, he would transform his ever-changing countenance into one appropriate to the harsh realities of life. He would share these intriguing facts, and occasional brilliant ideas, with Sir Juffin Hully over a cup of kamra.

"In the city they're saying that you're the King's illegitimate son, my boy!" Kofa Yox greeted me. "My conclusion is that you received a royal honor on your first day at work. Juffin and I even made a bet. He wagered in your favor, and I against. The old fox earned six crowns on your luck and His Highness Gurig VIII's sentimental mood. No matter though, I won several handfuls at dice, so at least I have something to pay him with."

"Where do rumors come from, Sir Kofa?" I was truly curious to know the answer.

"Where *don't* they come from? I suppose the majority of rumors are a combination of leaked information and the astounding imaginations of numerous storytellers. And, of course, the hope that things aren't really as boring as they seem on the surface. I don't know, Max, I just don't know . . ."

"People love to talk," Kurush noted condescendingly.

"Do you know what sorts of things people say about our Most Venerable Head?" Kofa asked. "We start half of those rumors ourselves: the Secret Investigative Force has to inspire superstitious fear in the general populace. Did you know, for example, that Sir Juffin Hully is said to have a ring called the Master of Lies that lets off invisible deadly rays? Anyone who tells a lie in his presence soon dies a painful death. The first version was far more modest. It went something like this: Sir Juffin can tell a liar with the help of a magical object. We owe the story's terrifying details to the common folk."

"What else?" I asked.

"That Juffin eats the dried flesh of rebellious Magicians, whom he holds captive in his basement. One should never look directly into his eyes, or one will lose the Spark forever and pine away. Oh, and of course, Juffin takes the Spark for himself. Hmm, what else . . . That he is immortal; that his parents are two ancient Magicians who modeled our boss out of sand and their own saliva; that he had a twin brother whom he ate; that he becomes a shadow at night, and—"

"Gossiping about me again?" asked the hero of urban folklore, as he fell into his armchair.

"I'm just trying to warn the poor young man," Kofa said and smiled.

"'Poor young man?'" You should see him when he turns into a vampire! So how was the night, hero?"

"Boring," I complained. "Kurush and I chatted and rummaged through the gifts that you and Melifaro have received. Terrible."

"My night was nothing to write home about, either," said Sir Kofa. "Just a few small house robberies in rich neighborhoods. The thieves took the most valuable possessions; but it's a case that even Boboota can solve. The boy is right, it's terrible! Echo, for so long a stronghold of criminal romance, is becoming a provincial swamp."

"That isn't terrible, it's wonderful! It's terrible when things really start hopping here. Go get some rest, Sir Max. Take advantage of the opportunity."

❦

So I set off to get some sleep. When I got near the main doors to the street, I heard a roar coming from outside.

"Bull's tits! You can save that for your own tail end in the latrine!" A powerful bass, sometimes breaking into a shrill falsetto, shook the old walls. "I've been in this cesspit for sixty years, and not one single butt—"

I threw the door open. A bearded goon of impressive stature draped in crimson silk, who looked like a cross between a sumo wrestler and an athlete, was hanging over the frightened driver of the official amobiler of the Ministry of Perfect Public Order.

"Silence!" I barked menacingly. "The Most Venerable Head of the Minor Secret Investigative Force has vowed to smite anyone who dares disturb him! And don't you yell at the coachman; he is in the King's Service!"

I pulled the aged hooligan off the driver and got into the amobiler. I had wanted to walk home, but now I would have to help the driver out: I couldn't just leave him there to be tormented by that bully.

"Bull's tits! So who is this new turd in my cesspit?" It seemed that the gift of speech had returned to the brute.

"You must have had a bit too much to drink, sir." I was having fun. "Your latrine is at your house; *this* is the Ministry of

Perfect Public Order of the capital of the Unified Kingdom. Do yourself a favor and think about that, because there are quite a few angry men around here who didn't arrest anyone last night, and are raring to go. Let's move it!" I said, addressing the driver, and we rode off to the sound of another volley of improvisations on the topic of latrines.

"Thank you, Sir Max," said the old coachman, and bowed to me.

"Why did you let him yell at you like that? The guy looks frightening and all, but you work for the King and Sir Juffin Hully. You're an important person, my friend."

"Sir Boboota Box doesn't usually take things like that into account. He thinks I shouldn't have parked the amobiler so close to the doors; but his own driver parks practically inside the corridor every day!"

"So that was General Boboota Box? Whoa! He's gonna get it!"

The foul-mouthed culprit reminded me of one of my old bosses. I felt an ominous satisfaction. That's it, your time is up; now Sir Max will assign you each a latrine. Such spitefulness does me no honor, but what can I do? I'm a human, not an angel. *This* is who I am.

❦

As soon as I got home I realized I was exhausted. The coziest bed in the Unified Kingdom was at my disposal. As for dreams, I guess you could say that they betrayed me.

Dreams have always been an extremely important part of my life, so a bad dream can throw me into a funk more easily than real misfortune. That morning there was a nightmare in store for me.

I dreamed I couldn't go to sleep, which I guess shouldn't have come as a surprise, considering that I was lying on top of the living room table. I lay there like a hearty lunch, gazing at the windows in the building opposite, that elegant architectural masterpiece of the olden days that I had admired during my first night in the apartment. In my waking hours, I had liked the building. Now it inspired a vague but powerful loathing in me. The gloom behind the triangular windows didn't promise anything good. I knew that the inhabitants had died long ago, and only seemed to be alive. But by themselves they didn't pose any danger.

For some time, nothing happened. I just couldn't move, and I felt very uneasy about that. More than that, I disliked the strong premonition I had that something was about to happen. Something began to approach me from afar. It needed time—and it took it.

This arduous process seemed to drag on an without end. I began to think that it had always been that way, and always would be. But at a certain point I was able to wake myself up.

With a headache, wet and sticky from sweat—the vile companion of nightmares—I was happy. Waking up was so wonderful! I dug around in the closet and found the precious bottle of Elixir of Kaxar. "Take care of this, Max; it should be for special occasions, not every day," Juffin had advised me. But my body was begging for mercy, and I didn't torment myself with doubt, either. Before I had gotten my hands on a bottle of that wonderful remedy, a dream like that could have stripped me of all spiritual strength for weeks. Now, I felt immediate relief, and I hoped that it would last for a while. I smiled at the afternoon sun and went downstairs to enhance the pleasant change I was experiencing with a bath and some good kamra.

In an hour's time I was fully dressed, but it was too early to go to work. I spent some time in the living room with a book on my lap. The view from the window no longer pleased me as it used to; but for some reason I didn't dare turn my back on the scene.

Finally, I had to admit that it was no use. I put aside the third volume of Manga Melifaro's *Encyclopedia* and went out into the street to get a closer look at the house opposite. I got out my brand new dagger and took a look at the gauge on its hilt. The building was innocent as a babe. There were traces of permitted second-degree black magic. Perhaps the owners were making kamra, or trying to remove oil spatterings, which they had every right to do.

But my heart was of a different opinion. "This is a foul place," it thumped anxiously. That invaluable muscle had become a good advisor to me of late. I knew I should heed its judgment; but I wanted something entirely different. I wanted to calm down and go on living. I did my best.

You have to stop listening to scary stories before bedtime, my dear boy! I told myself breezily.

To distract myself, I took my new toy down the block, checking my neighbors' observance of the Code of Krember as I went along. Judging by the gauge, they were law-abiding and singularly devoted to culinary experiments. Black magic of the second degree oozed out of almost all the windows. When after a time the needle began to career dangerously between the permitted two and the highly undesirable three, I looked around. In front of me was a small tavern with the menacing name of *The Sated Skeleton*. The cook there must really love his work, I thought, and decided to stop in for breakfast. *The Glutton Bunba* is, of course, my all-time favorite; but I do like to try new things for a change.

Nightmares or not, I had a good appetite that called for more than my usual humble breakfast rations. At the table next to mine, two local women were discussing a certain Lady Alatan, who had been robbed while she was out shopping; and "those whelps taught her a good lesson!" In my thoughts, I gave my condolences to the hapless lady: I had already met the gentleman whose duty it was to protect her possessions. But even that didn't spoil my appetite.

After breakfast I set off leisurely for work, tracing a concentric circle around the Old Town. There I spent all the money I had in my pocket on completely useless but charming housewares. Where I come from, it is believed that retail therapy can save housewives ground down by routine. I can bear witness to the fact that it also saves certain gallant members of the Secret Force from the vestiges of the previous night's bad dreams.

Weighed down with packages, I arrived at the House by the Bridge only a half hour earlier than I was supposed to.

"Settling into your home, then, are you, O Policeman's Blight?" asked Juffin, as he studied my packages. "You know, Max, Boboota thinks that because you yelled at him, you have the right to do so. He respects you. I believe he is also looking forward to strangling you. Good job, my boy. Tell me the truth, did you really think he was just a run-of-the-mill ruffian?"

"He was being a troublemaker! It's inappropriate for government officials to act like that. I'll have this place cleaned up in no time!" I made a scary face and then admitted, "I've always dreamed of being in a position of power, sir."

"That's good," said Juffin. "Maybe together we could tame him. What's the matter with you, Max? You seem a bit odd today." I was shocked.

"Is it really that noticeable? I thought—"

"It is to me. I hope Boboota hasn't hired a witch. No, he wouldn't do that. He's actually one of the most law-abiding of citizens. He even has his wife do permitted magic at home, and he doesn't lift a finger. So what happened, Max?"

I was glad for the opportunity to get it off my back. Maybe that's why I ended up getting to work early.

"It's nothing really, just a dream I had last night. In my case, though, it's a problem. I had a nightmare, that's all. A disgusting nightmare; nothing really even happened in it but it left me with the most loathsome feeling." And I told him my dream down to the last detail.

"Did you check the house when you woke up?"

"Yeah. Black magic of the second degree. I guess the former tenants brewed kamra. But you know better than I do that sometimes the sensor can be wrong."

"I know; but sealing off a house in such a way that the needle doesn't stay at zero, and shows more or less average readings . . . theoretically, it's possible, but who would be capable of doing that? I certainly wouldn't. No, not even me, boy! I may not be the most powerful wizard in the world, but I am certainly not in the minor leagues. You said that you had an unpleasant reaction?"

"To put in mildly. My heart almost gave out in the madness."

"Well, Max, I'm going to take a little walk around that neighborhood on my way home. I had nothing planned anyway. I even gave my diurnal rep permission to go frolic at his parents' mansion. And Sir Lonli-Lokli returned home an hour earlier than usual, which hasn't happened in several dozen years. Let's go to the *Glutton* for a glass of kamra. Will you look after things here, Kurush? Max will bring back something tasty for you. Maybe later, we can take a stroll down to the Main Archive. I don't know about your kinsmen, but Sir Lookfi Pence would be thrilled. Anyway, my heart tells me that tonight will be even quieter than last night, if that's possible. Let's go, Max."

"Don't forget the treat," Kurush reminded us.

All the while we were at the *Glutton* Sir Juffin was the embodiment of paternal concern. It was amazing—he really showed sympathy for me and my silly problem.

"Whatever it is, Max, you're not the type of kid to get a nightmare from acid indigestion. Sometimes your dreams are unusual. If this happens again, I think you had better spend a few days at my place, at least until we get to the bottom of it."

"Thank you, Juffin. But I don't want to leave my house. All my life I've wanted a house like that, with a bedroom beneath the eaves, a living room downstairs, stairs that creak, and no extra furniture. Now, at last I've found the house I've been looking for. And you know what? Like hell they're going to chase me out of it!"

"So you're going to sleep at home and entertain yourself with a half dozen nightmares every night?"

"I certainly hope not. Maybe it won't happen again. Everyone has nightmares, and they usually don't mean anything at all."

"And what about your chest pains when you went outside? You think that was just a coincidence? A cat has nine lives, but you're no cat."

I jumped in surprise at hearing the old turn of phrase.

"Do you have cats here?"

"Who doesn't!"

"Why haven't I seen one yet?"

"Where could you have seen one? You've never been to the countryside. We don't keep cats at home; they're like cows and sheep."

"That's odd. I guess yours are the wrong sort of cats."

"You mean *yours* are the wrong sort of cats," Juffin retorted. "*Ours* are the rightest sort of cats in the entire Universe!"

❋

Then we parted ways. Juffin Hully set off for a stroll around the Street of Old Coins, and I went to the House by the Bridge to hang out. Kurush got a cream pastry. According to my colleagues, they're his favorite. It turned out that the buriwok was unable to clean the sticky cream off his beak, and I had to run around the office in search of a napkin.

Then I went upstairs and regaled Sir Lookfi Pence and a good hundred or so buriwoks with tales from the Barren Lands, which I'd borrowed from the third volume of *Encyclopedia*. When the long twilight shadows had thickened into night, Sir Lookfi began getting ready to go home, knocking over chairs all the while. That was how I learned that his working day lasts from noon to nightfall. The rest of the time the buriwoks like going about their own business, and it's best not to disturb them. They looked upon dear old Kurush as something of an oddball for spending all his time with humans.

I invited Sir Lookfi for a mug of kamra in my office. He seemed pleased and shy at the same time. He sent a call to his wife, after which he said:

"Varisha has agreed to miss me for another hour. Thank you, Sir Max! I apologize that I didn't accept your invitation immediately.

You see, we're newlyweds and . . ." Embarrassed, the poor fellow got tangled up in the folds of his own looxi. I had to catch him so he wouldn't fall.

"Don't apologize," I said, smiling. "You did just the right thing, my friend."

Once I was back in the office, I called for the courier, who darted in seconds later and looked into my eyes with fawning devotion. I could just see it, the title of a horror movie: *Max, Devourer of Underlings*. Quite a nice ring to it, I thought!

Lookfi sipped his kamra with evident enjoyment, all the while soaking the intricately-patterned hem of his looxi in his cup. I didn't waste any time, and started asking him about the buriwoks. I had already heard Kurush's take on things, and now I wanted to hear the opinion of one of the other parties involved.

"I was offered this job by the buriwoks themselves," said Sir Lookfi. "I don't know why they chose me, but one day, a long time ago—a long *long* time ago—a courier came to my house and brought me an invitation from the House by the Bridge. The birds said that they would find my presence most suitable. They rejected the other candidates out of hand—even the cousin of the King's Advisor. Do you know why, Kurush?"

"I've told you many times—because you can tell us apart."

"Kurush, you're just as much of a joker as Sir Juffin! Who in the world wouldn't be able to tell you apart?"

"I would probably have a hard time telling one buriwok from another," I confessed in perplexity.

"There you have it. I've been telling him the same thing over and over for more than a hundred years, and he still doesn't believe me," Kurush grumbled. "Although, it's true, his memory isn't too bad; for a human, of course."

"I suppose I do have a good memory," said Lookfi. "Yet all my life I thought others were forgetful and *I* was only average."

"He remembers how many feathers each of us has," Kurush told me confidingly.

"No kidding!" I whistled. "If that was the one and only thing you remembered, Lookfi, I would *still* be a dimwit compared to you."

"Don't say that, Sir Max," said Lookfi. "You're not a dimwit at all; you're just a bit absent-minded."

Sinning Magicians, I thought, look who's talking!

Finally, Lookfi took his leave, and Kurush and I were left alone together. I think the buriwok had fallen asleep. I found some newspapers on Juffin's desk; some fresh, and others less recent. It's good to be new in someone else's world: the evening papers are as enthralling as a fantasy novel. The only difference is that you can open the door at any moment you please and go for a walk in this imaginary world.

❁

Sir Kofa Yox arrived again before dawn. He grumpily informed me that there was no news and that none was expected: four more house robberies for the valiant police force to deal with. So boring! That was why he was turning in for the night. I nodded sympathetically, sighed, and became absorbed once more in a copy of the *Echo Hustle and Bustle* dating back to the previous year.

Sir Juffin Hully showed up for work rather early, demanded some kamra, and then stared at me thoughtfully.

"No news yet, Max. I mean no *real* news, at any rate. But I do have one idea. This is what it comes down to. My house is always open to you, you know that. But you were right. Try sleeping at your place for another day or two. If you don't have any more nightmares, great! If you do, though . . . I understand that it isn't pleasant, but there's a chance the plot might start to unfold. Perhaps something interesting will come to light."

"What do *you* think? What should I prepare myself for?"

"Honestly? I think you should prepare for the worst. I didn't like the look of that house from the start. I didn't like it one bit, but there was nothing I could put my finger on. I can't remember anything like this happening before. Maybe my imagination is running away with me out of boredom, but I don't think so. I think we'll dig something up on that house. When Lookfi gets here we'll find out something about the owners. And about the neighbors, as well. About how they feel living there. For the time being, take this." Juffin offered me an unsightly scrap of cloth. "Wrap this around your neck before going to sleep. This will definitely wake you up."

"What? Could it really be that dangerous?"

"Life is full of extremely dangerous things. Most dangerous of all are the things we don't understand. Or things that don't exist at all. All right, let me know when you wake up."

❅

A sense of obligation is not the best kind of sleeping pill. After tossing restlessly from side to side, I surrounded myself with volumes of Manga Melifaro's *Encyclopedia* and began studying its excellent illustrations. I was interested in the local cat species and hoped to find pictures of them. It took me a long time to find them, but at last I was successful. At first glance, these wondrous beasts seemed like ordinary fluffy cats. What was striking about them, though, was their size. These furry short-limbed creatures were no less than three feet in length. Their shoulder height was around a foot and a half. I determined this by comparing the picture of the cat with that of a gentleman in a knitted looxi. Turning to the accompanying text, I learned that the gentleman was none other than a *shepherd*. Reading further I discovered that "the peasant folk of Landaland breed cats for their warm coats." Just like sheep! I was surprised and fascinated. Maybe it's time I got myself a kitten. So what if the snobs from the capital consider them to be petty livestock that should be kept on farms? A barbarian from the Barren Lands, I was certain, would be forgiven more serious eccentricities than that.

Lulled by thoughts of my future status as the first cat-owner of Echo, I finally fell asleep. Alas, it would have been better if my insomnia had continued! The merciful sleep of oblivion quickly dissolved into a clear vision: again, I was lying on the table in the living room, helpless and motionless.

Worst of all, I had lost all sense of myself. Who I was, what I was like, where I was from, where exactly I was just then, what I was doing, say, a year ago, what type of women I preferred, what my friends' names were, where I had lived as a child—I didn't have the answer to any of those questions. Worse yet, I didn't have any questions. My understanding of the world was limited to the sitting room and the triangular windows of the house next door. That, and great fear. Yes, that's how it was: all I knew about the world around me was that it was a terrifying place, and that I felt wretched.

At last, the window of the house began to open slowly. Someone was staring at me from inside the room. Then, in the window, someone's hand appeared briefly. A handful of sand flew out of the darkness, but instead of scattering onto the sidewalk below, it froze in midair like a small golden cloud. Then came another handful of sand,

and another, and another. Now there was much more than just a cloud—a whole pathway was quivering in the sky. It was a short path and I was certain I knew where it led. So, the plot is developing, I thought. Well now, isn't this just dandy? The plot has to unfold . . . Wait, that isn't even my own thought, those are Juffin's words! That's just what he said, word for word.

As soon as I remembered my conversation with Juffin, I remembered who I was, too. That made me feel a bit better. The fear, unfortunately, remained; but it was no longer the sole component of my existence. Now I knew that I was sleeping. And I knew that I wasn't simply sleeping, but sleeping with the purpose of observing the nightmare unfold. I also knew that I needed to wake up just then, but for some reason I couldn't.

Idiot! I forgot to put on that scrap of cloth! I thought in panic. Praise to the Magicians, I suddenly woke up. Lowering my feet down off the table—

Heavens above! So I *did* fall asleep on the living room table and not in the comfortable bed upstairs, surrounded by eight volumes of the *Encyclopedia of the World*. What nonsense! No, it wasn't just nonsense. It looked like a fairly solid storyline for your average B horror movie.

I went upstairs. My knees were trembling. More than anything I was afraid of finding another Max sleeping in my bed. Go figure which one of us was the real one. The bed was empty. With shaking hands I reached for the bottle of Elixir of Kaxar that I'd had the foresight to leave at the head of the bed. I took a gulp, then another. I felt a great deal better. I collapsed onto the bed. Even if I didn't get any sleep, I could rest a bit, at the very least. But I had to get in touch with Juffin. Luckily, I had something to report to him, as well.

I'm awake, Juffin. Things are pretty bad.

Well, if you're awake then all is not lost. Come to the Glutton, *I'll treat you to breakfast. In fact, I have some news for you as well.*

I'll be there in an hour. Over and out.

"Over what?"

Over and out. It means: that's all, this thought-exchange is over.

Over and out, Juffin repeated with delight.

The *Glutton* is a truly magical place. Those walls could make anyone feel right at home. I was describing my adventures and starting to relax. That was more than I could say for Juffin, who looked like someone paying a scheduled visit to the dentist's office.

"So you say that you woke up on the table. That means things are more serious than I thought. I think you should move back to my place for a while. But *I* am going to spend the night in your bed. Maybe I'll dream of some horrible thing as well."

"I have a better idea. How about I sleep at home, and you hold my hand like a kindly nurse?"

"I had a similar idea to begin with, but—"

"But what, Juffin? It's already happening to me, and the plot is unfolding; but if you stay there, you'll have to start watching from the first episode, then the second. We'll lose two days that way."

"That may be, but I don't like the way this whole thing is affecting you. I'm afraid you're still too vulnerable when you're asleep."

"Well, that depends on how you look at it. Because I did remember that it was a dream. And I woke up, even though I forgot to put on that scrap you gave me."

"Oh, but that was very unwise, Max! You can't neglect things like that. By the way, that 'little scrap,' as you call it, is merely the personal kerchief of the Grand Magician of the Order of the Secret Grass."

"Isn't he one of those guys whose dried flesh you partake of daily to strengthen your powers?"

Juffin gave a quick laugh and then scowled again.

"I think you got a little carried away with the Kaxar, Max. Your *joie de vivre* is beginning to frighten me."

"It scares me, too. So, do you agree to sing me a lullaby?"

"I suppose I could try, though I suspect that the presence of a person awake, especially one as notable as me, might hinder events as they develop."

"At least I'll get some sleep. What if we both go to sleep?"

"Yes, I suppose we could try that. Although," Juffin grew more animated, "who says I have to be in the same room? I can watch you without even leaving my office. It's settled, then. I think that's what we should do. But first I'll spend a night at your house, to be on the safe side."

"The house is at your disposal. But I only have three bathing pools, remember? Not even that will dissuade you?"

"What lengths wouldn't one go to for the peaceful well-being of the Unified Kingdom . . . and for one's own well-being, for that matter! I had a bad feeling about that place from the very beginning; I shouldn't have let you move into that doghouse at all!"

"It's all right," I said, trying to comfort my boss. "When I grow up and I'm big and strong, I'll learn to take bribes, and then I'll build a palace for myself on the left bank. What about your news? You said you were going to consult the buriwoks."

"That's what I spent half the day doing. I have some news, and it's rather worrying. It's just too bad that I didn't take on this case a couple of years ago. But if it hadn't been for your dreams, it never would have occurred to me to make a connection between some of the facts that on their own just aren't very interesting. Let's go to the Ministry, so you can hear for yourself."

And we headed straightaway to the Main Archive.

※

"Lookfi, I'd like to listen again to the information that you gathered today."

"Of course, Sir Hully. Good day, Sir Max; you're here early today! They say nothing much has been happening lately."

Lookfi approached one of the buriwoks.

"Please tell us one more time about the Street of Old Coins, Tatoon."

It looked to me like the bird had shrugged, as if to say, "I'd rather not repeat the same trivial story twice, but since it's my job—here we go again." With that, the buriwok began to recite:

"Information regarding owners of real estate as of Day 208 of the Year 115. Street of Old Coins, house #1. Owner: Ms. Xarista Aag. No criminal record. Lives in the countryside. In the year 109 of the Code Epoch, the house was temporarily leased to the Poedra family. Three dozen years' rent was paid up front. In the year 112, Gar Poedra lost the Spark and died. His wife, Pita Poedra, and daughter, Xitta, are known to inhabit the premises to the present day. The daughter still suffers from a childhood illness, but does not seek the assistance of specialists and does not leave the house. They live in a reclusive fashion and do not entertain guests. No criminal record.

"House #2. Owner: Kunk Stifan. Lives in the house with two underage sons. His wife, Trita Stifan, died in the year 107. In the year 110, he was suspected of killing the maid, one Pamma Lorras. He was proven innocent and received compensation for damages. A witch-doctor confirmed that his wife died in her sleep of heart disease. Uses the services of a daytime maid and four tutors for the boys. Does not employ full-time help. He was obliged to leave his position at the Ministry of Big Money due to illness at the beginning of this year.

"House #3. Owner: Rogro Zhil, editor-in-chief of the *Royal Voice* and co-owner of the *Echo Hustle and Bustle*. His detailed dossier is kept in the archives. He currently lives on Ginger Dream Street in the New City. The house on the Street of Old Coins is neither for rent nor for sale, as the owner is in no need of funds."

"His dossier is something of an epic poem," whispered Juffin. "But at the moment that's not what we are interested in. You may enjoy reading it, though, in your spare time. I highly recommend it."

Houses #4, #5, #6 . . . All the stories bore a certain resemblance to one another. The inhabitants of the Street of Old Coins turned out to be the most miserable wretches in all of Echo: they got sick, lost their loved ones, and then they died. No criminal records, no suicides, nothing mysterious. But a whole street full of terminally ill widows and orphans? And in Echo, of all places, where your average witch-doctor was nearly capable of bringing the dead back to life! Talk about coincidence.

"House seven," the bird repeated patiently, "Owner: Tolakan Enn; wife: Feni Enn, no children. In the year 54 of the Code Epoch, the house was left to him by his father, Sir Genelad Enn, the Royal Court's Chief Supplier. Altogether his inheritance was worth a dozen million crowns."

I whistled in surprise. Sir Tolakan was absurdly wealthy. You could live for a week on just one crown—if, of course, you didn't buy large quantities of the expensive nonsense that is displayed in the windows of antique shops.

"No criminal record," the buriwok continued. "They do not socialize. A detailed dossier on these individuals can be found in the archives."

"Amazing, isn't it?" Sir Juffin remarked. "For the last five dozen years already, one unfathomably rich man has been a resident of this wretched slum. Oh, sorry Max, don't get me wrong. I was just quoting public opinion on the matter. Anyway, of all the people on the whole street, he and his wife are the only ones who are neither stricken with illness nor on their deathbeds."

"House eight," the buriwok continued in a monotonous voice. "Owner: Gina Ursil. No criminal record. The house's prior owner, Lea Ursil, Gina's mother, lost the Spark and died in the year 87 of the Codex Epoch. Since then, the house has been empty, as the owner lives in her Estate in Uruland."

"I assume you've already heard the most important bits," said Juffin and sighed. "It goes on and on like this. Empty houses, sick widows, frail widowers, dead parents, and children in weak health. And, finally, your little bachelor pad, which, as we already know, has its own mournful history. Well, thank you Tatoon. I think that will be all for now. I'll ask Kurush for the details."

"What about the pub?" I asked. "The *Sated Skeleton*. I had breakfast over there yesterday. Is it all right?"

"That's the brightest place on your cheery little street. Mind you, people work there and eat there, of course, but they don't sleep there. Even the proprietor, Goppa Talabunn, lives above the *Drunken Skeleton*, one of his other pubs. I think he has about a dozen of them, but the word *skeleton* figures in all their names. Goppa thinks it sounds amusing, and most of his clientele thinks the same."

※

Juffin thanked Lookfi and the buriwoks and we set out for the office. Kurush, as always, was dozing on the back of an armchair.

"Wake up," said Juffin, tenderly ruffling the feathers on the buriwok's soft neck. "We need to get some work done."

Kurush opened his round eyes and said, "Peanuts first."

While the smarty-pants consumed his peanuts, Juffin and I managed to drink down a mug of kamra and even ordered refills.

"I'm ready," Kurush announced finally.

"In that case, start digging through your memory, buddy. We are interested in anything that has to do with Number Seven on the Street of Old Coins. Once you've collected all the material, you may begin reciting it. Sir Max is collecting gossip about his neighbors, so I *do* hope you come up with something worthwhile."

Kurush puffed himself up and then fell silent. I imagined him quietly humming like a small computer. Several minutes later, the buriwok shook his feathers, and began.

"Number Seven on the Street of Old Coins is one of the oldest in Echo. It was built in the year 1140 by a Master Blacksmith, one

Stremmi Broh, and later inherited by his son, Kardu Broh, then by his heiress, Vamira Broh. In 2154, during the Epoch of Orders, Vamira Broh sold the house to the Gusot family. Mener Gusot, known as Grand Magician of the Order of Green Moons was born in the house in 2346. Later the house was presented to him as a gift after his coming of age, and he lived there, cut off from the rest of the world. As everyone knows, in the year 2504, Mener Gusot founded the Order of Green Moons. Until the power of the order became common knowledge, they held their meetings at the Grand Magician's apartment. Number seven on the Street of Old Coins never stood empty. Even after a new residency was built for the Order in 2675, the Grand Magician said that he was involved in 'especially important work' there.

"During the Troubled Times, the Order of Green Moons was one of the first to fall, because it belonged to a number of groups that made no secret of their rivalry with the Order of the Seven-Leaf Clover. Almost all the Order's disciples, novices, and Magicians were killed. The Grand Magician, Mener Gusot, committed suicide in the courtyard of the burning residency of the Order on the 233rd day of the year 3183 of the Epoch of Orders, five years before the beginning of the Code Epoch. It is known that twelve initiates of the movement survived. According to information from the Order of the Seven-Leaf Clover they all left the Unified Kingdom immediately. Information about each of them can be found in the Main Archive and is updated whenever new information becomes available.

"All the late Mener Gusot's property, including the house on the Street of Old Coins, passed into the possession of the King. In the 8th year of the Code Epoch, the house was sold by order of the highest authority to Sir Genelad Enn, Chief Supplier to the Royal Court. In the year 10, Sir Genelad Enn died and Sir Tolakan Enn, Chief Advisor to the Department for the Dispensation of Allowances, and the only son of the deceased, inherited the house. The Estate stood empty until the year 54, when the Enn family moved back from their country home. In the year 55, Sir Tolakan Enn left his position at the Department for the Dispensation of Allowances. Since then, they have lived in a reclusive fashion, employing only day servants. Popular opinion attributes the adoption of such a lifestyle to the extreme stinginess sometimes found in the very wealthy. And give me some more peanuts."

After that imperious demand, Kurush fell silent.

"What a story, Sir Max." Juffin chuckled, gathering peanuts from his various desk drawers. "So, the father gets the house and dies two years later. All is fine while the house stands empty. In 54 an heir moves in. Not even a year goes by and he undergoes a complete personality change. He leaves his job for no apparent reason, dismisses all the help, and becomes one of Echo's most reticent inhabitants. And Lady Feni, the most famous socialite of the first half of the century, doesn't object? His old friends don't get any explanations, believe me, I've checked. There is no solid proof of foul play, however, and when it comes to people's private lives . . . well, even the richest man in the city has the right to keep to himself. Everyone is perplexed by it at first, but then they just forget about it and get on with their business."

"So those two just never leave their house?"

"Well, not exactly; Lady Feni does. She goes out at least once every dozen days or so. And she is just as cold and impenetrable as back in the day when her beauty was the greatest sensation at the royal court. But she makes no visits of any kind. Lady Feni goes shopping. She buys mounds of stuff—sometimes necessary, but for the most part useless. She seems to have set herself the task of acquiring the most extensive range of hodgepodge in the shortest possible time. However, for a woman of her standing, and with the fortune and the amount of free time she has at her disposal, such behavior is completely normal."

"Juffin, you've done a lot of research!"

"Oh Max, I'm afraid I haven't done enough; but it was all I could manage in such a short amount of time. Just thank the Magicians that you can rest at work. Gather your strength and enjoy life. I'm off to your place. I'll try my best to sleep in that slum. A hole in the heavens above you, Max! Just when I thought my days of ascetic adventurism were over . . ."

Sir Juffin left, and I stayed at the House by the Bridge. All night long I tried to go about honorably fulfilling my boss's orders to rest and enjoy life. Not the easiest task in the world, but I did my best.

Morning began, as always, with Sir Kofa's arrival. He looked befuddled. I must add that this expression suited him far better than his usual squeamish grimace of unending boredom.

"The robberies have continued, Max," he reported. "You know, this is starting to get absurd. And absurdity is always unnerving. People are now saying that the robberies are being committed by the same person. But how does this elusive creature manage to visit houses at opposite ends of Echo at the same time? That's what I want to know. And if the perpetrators are indeed different people, then what manner of genius was able to train them so well? And, more important, why? So that even Boboota gets the news that it might be a single criminal gang working together? Right then, son. Tell Juffin to get in touch with me if he gets bored. Of course, these events aren't really interesting, nor are they matters for our department to deal with. But as the saying goes, at night even a skinny woman can seem like a blanket."

"Better a small fish than an empty dish," I translated automatically. "I'll give him your message, Sir Kofa, but I have a feeling Sir Juffin won't be bored today. I found a little job for him to do . . ."

"Oh, to hell with the robberies, then! They can wait for a rainy day. Have fun, Max. I'm planning to stop in at a few more places on my way home, so if you'll excuse me."

I waited around for another half an hour before receiving a message from Juffin. *I'm quite fine, except for the bath that awaits me in your tiny tubs. I'll be out soon, so let's call over to the* Glutton *for breakfast.*

With great enjoyment I took to fussing over our menu. By the time Juffin arrived, our office had all the qualities of a good restaurant: a splendid centerpiece on the table, tempting aromas, and a hungry gourmet exemplified in my person. Sir Venerable Head was satisfied.

"Allow me to report, sir," said Juffin, who parodied a new recruit just returned from his first assignment. "The results of the investigative experiment just conducted prove that: a) there is something inhabiting the house opposite, and b) it is scared of me. Or, alternatively, it is disgusted by me. Or finds me unappetizing. Or it subscribes to the *Echo Hustle and Bustle* and is an admiring and devoted fan. In any case, no one so much as touched a hair on my head. No, it was more amusing than that. At first, I dreamed I was lying on that dinner table of yours; but it lasted for only a second. Then I stopped dreaming. All at once there was nothing. I was free as a bird and I could sleep for as long as I wished! But I wouldn't let myself off the hook. I tried to close in on our mysterious friend myself. He had already surrounded himself with such unassailable defenses that inside that worthy mansion I wasn't able to find anyone except its owners, who were fast asleep. Still, we did find out something new."

"Like what?"

"That this could not possibly be the work of human hand. That is to say, there might have been someone who awoke other, inhuman, forces that are inhabiting the house. As a matter of fact, I suspect that history even preserved that person's name for the curious. Of all the former inhabitants of the house, who but the Grand Magician of the Order of Green Moons could have pulled off such a prank? That doesn't change the fact that you are being harassed by some wretch from another world, though. Pretty exotic, huh?"

"I thought I was the exotic one," I spluttered. "Well, what does it want from me, anyway?"

"What do you think? Yum-yum!" said Juffin, and let out a bloodthirsty chuckle. "In any case, its intentions are unkind, make no mistake! Why else would residents of the neighborhood be kicking the bucket left and right? Let's see, what else do we know about the enemy? Judging from last night, I would say that he acts carefully and is choosy. He wouldn't risk coming up against a serious opponent such as myself. Furthermore, our little friend makes mistakes sometimes, which became quite clear today when he first invaded my dreams and then shamelessly fled. That's comforting. I do not like getting involved with unmitigated evil—it's a lot of bother. No matter how you look at it, Sir Max, the information that we have now is simply not enough. So you're going to have to undergo nightmares for the sake of the cause for another few nights. I'll shut myself up in the office and oversee your adventures from here. But don't you even *think* of going to bed tonight without the protective amulet I was considerate enough to provide you with!"

"You mean that rag?"

"I *mean* the kerchief of the Grand Magician of the Order of Clandestine Weeds. Your frivolousness is killing me! Without that 'rag,' as you so irreverently call it, no one can guarantee that you will ever wake up again. Do you fancy that prospect?"

"Not particularly. I won't forget, Juffin. I can't believe I forgot about it yesterday! Could that unknown beast, hidden in ambush, have caused my absent-mindedness?"

"That could very well be. All the worse, Sir Max, all the worse."

"If you really are going to be looking out for me, then please recite the safety measures to me just before I climb into bed. I'm either becoming absentminded, or the creature is turning me into an idiot."

"You're right. Stranger things have happened. In any case, an extra reminder never hurt anyone. You're not eating enough. Don't let nonsense like this spoil your appetite. Problems come and go, but your belly stays with you. Its needs are sacred."

"I promise I'll be good, sir."

And indeed I was. I devoured a plateful of food, and after wiping my plate clean, I reached for a second helping. Sir Juffin Hully looked at me with the approval of a loving grandmother.

Soon it was time to go back home and see this night's screening of *Nightmare on Elm Street*, starring poor Max. I can't say that I was really looking forward to it. Now I was struck by my own idiotic heroism, under the influence of which I had refused to stay over at Juffin's the other day. It was supposedly in the "interests of our mission," but to tell the truth, it was just plain stubbornness.

Home was cozy, in spite of it all. Rays of sunshine beat through the new chocolate colored curtains I had procured to turn the bright light of day into the warm half-gloom of an underwater grotto. Of course, the main reason for my purchase had been to get rid of the view from the window, which only a few days before had been one of the main arguments in favor of my choosing this place as my home.

I noticed the evidence of Juffin's presence in the living room (an unwashed glass and an empty kamra jug), and in the bedroom (the pillows and blankets had migrated to the far corner of the gigantic bed, and my library at the head of the bed had undergone thorough censorship, with the consequent scattering of all books deemed improper about the room). Following a strange logic of free association, I started thinking about cats. As soon as this is all over and done with, I'm getting a kitten, I promised myself. I tried to settle in more comfortably.

Hey Max, Juffin's call jangled in my head, importunate as the sound of an alarm clock. *Don't forget to put on the scarf!*

Sinning Magicians! I nearly forgot the talisman! How was it possible? I was so frightened there could have been no question of absent-mindedness. I quickly wrapped the protective cloth around my neck.

Looks like you were right, Max. You're able to focus your attention on anything but matters of your own safety. Thoughts about the amulet were blocked, and in a very interesting way, I might add. It's too bad you wouldn't be able to understand my explanation of the matter yet. It seems we've come upon a very curious phenomenon. Perhaps you have some other amulets as well? Just objects that you especially like, or things that calm you down, like a child with his favorite toy. Lie down with things like that arranged from head to toe. They can't do any harm, and who knows what small talismans are capable of? And don't huff and puff so much trying to send me a message! I'm near you all the time in a sense. I see everything and I hear everything. Everything is under control. So just relax. What was it that you said recently? Over and out? Well, that's all. So long!

I tried to think. Amulets. What sorts of amulets could I have? Actually, I do have one thing I could probably use: the balsam box from Sir Makluk's bedroom, which was my very first trophy. I had removed it from the place it had so clearly not wanted to stay, and I had the feeling that the trinket was especially fond of me. So I placed my little friend carefully at the head of the bed.

But what else? Was that all? Except maybe the Child of the Crimson Pearl, which was, after all, a royal gift. It couldn't hurt to have it around. And the third volume of Sir Manga Malifaro's *Encyclopedia of the World*, too. I really had grown used to falling asleep with it, like a child with its teddy bear.

I built an elegant barricade of amulets and touched my neck to make sure that the magic rag was still there. Then I lay down in bed with a distinct feeling of despair. I flipped through a book for a while. Sleep crept into my eyes stealthily and quickly, although at first I was sure that today's experiment might fail due to "technical difficulties." To tell the truth, I usually get insomnia from fear and stress. But not tonight. I felt as though I'd been pumped full of sleeping pills; and I bet that Freddy Kruger next door had seen to it that his patient had no problems with fitful sleep. I must remember to ask Juffin whether that was true, I thought, falling asleep. Then again, why bother. Wasn't it obvious?

This time the nightmare wasn't as horrid. I was conscious of the fact that I was sleeping. I remembered who I was, why I was there, what I was waiting for, and so forth. I didn't feel Juffin's presence, but at least I knew who he was subconsciously.

I lay on my dining room table again, in the usual ostentatious serving-dish pose. The curtains, of course, had been parted by some invisible jerk, so I couldn't escape the lovely view of the ancient palace. My heart tightened in terror, as if an invisible hand was giving me painful intramuscular injections, but for the moment I had the strength to resist. To my great surprise, I even started getting angry. Of course, anger didn't help me in any way; but then again, I didn't know what would happen next. In any case, I latched onto this rage, as it seemed to me to be one of the better alternatives to fear.

Some wretch won't let me get a good night's sleep in my own house, which I pay good money for, for crying out loud! Some foul, loathsome thing is preventing me from getting any rest! And instead of a suspenseful nightmare, I am being subjected to this moronic boredom, I told myself angrily. I did all I could to get myself worked up. And I ended up getting myself worked up with a vengeance.

Good show, Max! Juffin's voice in my head interrupted my furious inner monologue. *Good show, and it's working! Now try to be scared again. Your fright is excellent bait. If you don't show any fear at all, this thing might leave you alone. And we have to lure it out of its foxhole somehow. Be a good boy now, act as if you're giving up.*

It's easy enough to tell someone to "be scared." By then I was ready to go on a rampage and smash everything in sight. On the crest of my own righteous anger, I think I was nearing victory over the horrible stupor that had turned me into the most helpless creature in the universe.

One good thing about this kind of situation is that if you really want to be frightened, then all the scary stories in the world of nightmares are at your disposal. I needed only to focus on the dark triangular window in the house across the street, and the pathway of sand leading from it, and all my anger turned to a fear that was almost panic. By way of experiment, and for my own emotional well-being, as well, I tried to get angry again. It worked! I enjoyed being able to change my own mood at will. Not having to choose the lesser of two evils, but rather having both at my command—that was variety for you!

At last I managed to find a balance between fear and anger: to be frightened, but not to the point of losing all other feeling; to be angry, but to remain conscious of my own helplessness.

Then the hand inside the darkness again threw a fistful of sand, then another, and another. The ghostly path between our windows grew longer. An eternity went by, and a second eternity followed. As a third eternity drew to a close, my heart again tried to refuse to take part in the drama, but I was able to negotiate with it. I could have woken up, but I didn't feel like waiting until tomorrow to see the next episode. If Juffin wanted to get a glimpse of the star in this matinée, I would try to give him the pleasure. I would tolerate as much as I could, and then just a bit more. It was sort of like going to the dentist: the kind of satisfaction you don't want to drag out for too long.

When the edge of the sandy path neared the table with the heap of fear and anger formerly known as Max lying on it, I actually felt relief. The denouement was near.

Sure enough, a dark silhouette appeared in the window and took the first step along the ghostly pathway. Step by step, he drew nearer to me: a middle-aged man with indistinct facial features and empty, shining eyes.

All of a sudden, I realized I was no longer in control of the situation. Not because the whole situation was too ghastly, and not even because the creature was not (and could not be) human. In theory, I was ready for that. But I could already feel some kind of connection between us, and it was a great deal worse than any fear or spiritual turmoil. I not only felt, but saw, how something started pouring out of my body. It wasn't blood; it was some kind of invisible substance. All I knew was that my further existence in any form would be impossible without it.

Something started squeezing my throat. I can't say it was violent, but it was unexpected enough to wake me up. So the "rag," the merits of which Sir Juffin Hully had talked so much about, worked beautifully. And most important of all, it had worked just in the nick of time! One more second, and I'm not sure there would have been any of me left to wake up.

I swung my legs down off the dining room table, unsurprised by anything anymore. The frame of the open window creaked balefully in the wind. I closed the window and shut the curtains with relief. My body hinted, embarrassed, that it felt like fainting dead away. I shook my fist in reply: just you try!

Good morning, Max! Juffin's energetic voice was honey to my tormented senses. *Good show, boy! Good show! Congratulations on reaching the end of this unpleasant adventure. Now we know everything we need to know, so the finale can't be too far away. Take a swig of Elixir of Kaxar as though it's your wedding day, brush off your feathers, and run over to my place. Righto? Over and out.*

All right, I answered, and dragged my feet back into the bedroom. Five minutes later, I went down to the bathroom with a hop, skip, and a jump, restored to life by the most medicinal of all drinks in this World.

Juffin's words about "reaching the end of this unpleasant journey" only now began making sense to me. Did that mean it was over? Could it possibly mean that I would never have to have that terrible nightmare again? Sinning Magicians, what else did a man need to be truly happy!

On my way to work I decided that one thing a man *definitely* needs is a light breakfast at the *Sated Skeleton*. With that, I turned off into the warm half-gloom of the pub. Sir Juffin Hully never required his subordinates to go to work on an empty stomach, even in the line of duty.

❀

There were more people than usual at the House by the Bridge. Sir Lonli-Lokli was crouched on the edge of a chair writing in a thick notebook in a pose so uncomfortable that it was painful even to look at him. Sir Melifaro, who had only just returned from a visit to his parents' estate, leaped out of his office like a genie from a bottle. He crowed that the most famous of illegitimate princes was among us and that he was unspeakably glad to bask in the glow of my fame. I thought that the poor guy had gone nuts until it occurred to me that he was referring to the royal gift that had been given to me three days . . . no, an eternity ago. Nightmares can convince anyone that life is all vanity of vanities and weariness unto death. Shaking my fist at my daytime counterpart, I swore I would "tell Dad," and went to see Juffin.

I found Lady Melamori in his office, looking much too gloomy for a recently released "prisoner."

"Glad you could come so quickly, Max. Our business can wait for an hour. It seems that we have some family matters that need taking care of. I think I should call the others in as well."

"Family matters? What do you mean?" I asked in dismay.

"I've been robbed," Melamori said. "I came home and saw that everything had been turned upside down. All of my jewelry boxes were opened. A hole in the heavens above that thief! I am so upset! When I joined the Secret Investigative Force I was sure that crooks would go three blocks around my house to avoid me."

"What's the problem, my lady?" I asked. "Start tracking the scoundrel and the case will be closed before you know it."

"But there's not a track to be found!" said Melamori. "It's as though everything missing simply picked up and left."

"I've always said that living alone is not the life for a lovely little lady!" announced Sir Melifaro as he entered the office. "If I had been in your bedchamber, nothing like this could have happened, my precious!"

"I'd rather get a dog," said Melamori pursing her lips. "It would guard the house, and eat a whole lot less too. They say that dogs can even understand human speech, which is more than I can say for you."

Lonli-Lokli politely let Sir Kofa enter the room first. Everyone was there except for Lookfi, who, as I understood, was not usually called in on such occasions. Our affairs had little to do with his work at the Main Archive.

"Well, what do you think of the news?" Juffin asked, fixing each of us with a hard gaze. "We've taken a hit! I hope you all agree that Melamori's possessions should be returned immediately! The lady is upset, which does not bode well for our general humor, and the whole city is waiting on pins and needles to witness the retaliatory acts of the Secret Investigative Force. Dear girl, I know that you haven't told anyone anything, but Echo is full of two-bit clairvoyants. Sir Melifaro, I'm assigning this to you. Do whatever you see fit. Max and I have other urgent matters to attend. I'm sorry."

Melifaro immediately seated himself on the arm of Melamori's chair. I noted without any particular pleasure that she buried her nose in his shoulder.

"I need a list of the stolen objects, sweetie," said Melifaro, toying with the ends of his colleague's long bangs.

"Thirty-eight rings, all with the Blimm family crest on the inside. Money . . . I don't know how much there was, I didn't count . . . A lot

of money. A couple thousand crowns maybe . . . In other words, I don't
know. Eight necklaces, also with the family crest on the clasp. In
my family we always engrave precious jewelry. I've always teased my
parents about it. I guess I shouldn't have . . . I think that's about it.
They didn't touch the talismans. Oh, I almost forgot, they also took
the little doll that you gave me on Middle of the Year Day. Remember
Sir Melifaro?"

Melifaro winced.

"Of course I remember. You don't easily forget such huge burns
in your pocket! It was a beautiful toy. Strange that they would have
taken that. It stands to reason they'd want the rest of the stuff. Sir
Juffin, perhaps you'll treat us to some kamra, since we're all here.
Then we can think through this one together and chat. I've been feeling a bit listless in that little village lately. I'm sure that your important business can wait for just another half hour, can't it?"

"Anything can wait for half an hour, except the bodily functions
General Boboota is so fond of discussing! All right, may there be a
sea of kamra brought over from the *Glutton*; only you'll have to
work to deserve it, old boy!"

"Don't I know it! Say Juffin, don't you think it's a bit odd to steal
the smallest and most expensive things in a house, which one can
carry away in the pocket of a looxi, and then grab a doll that's the
size of a three-year-old child as an afterthought? It isn't a worthless
trifle, of course; but in that case, why not take all the dishes, or the
armchair from the living room? As far as I know, they would have
been more valuable than the doll." Melifaro had left his place on the
arm of Melamori's chair and was squatting next to the boss, who was
forced to look down at him from above.

"I knew you'd catch that. You already deserve one portion of
kamra."

"I may have deserved it, but if we are to drink, then let's do it
together! Well, then, Sir Kofa, which of the honorable city policemen
comes first on our White List?"

"Sir Kamshi, but he's not at the Ministry right now. Try to get in
touch with Lieutenant Shixola. He occupies fourth place, and he also
specializes in burglaries."

"All right, I'll be back in just a moment. Anyone who so much as
touches my kamra will choke on it!" With that, Melifaro was gone.

His pace impressed me. If somebody wanted to make a movie

about the great Investigator Sir Melifaro of Echo, they'd have to settle with filming a series of shorts.

"What's this White List?" I asked Sir Kofa. He laughed heartily. Even Lady Melamori let out a giggle.

"Oh Max! That's just a little game of ours. From time to time we make an objective list of a dozen of the brightest members of the Police Force. The ones we'd want to be involved with, should the need arise. In fact, they do have smart people working over there, but with bosses like Boboota and Foofloss the poor fellows will still end up a laughing stock. And making it onto our White List is a great honor for them. They swell with pride if they get listed. For them it's even more important than Royal Gratitude, which Boboota is awarded once a year because of his rank. I see you've caught on!"

I'll say! I couldn't stop laughing, impressed with the clever idea of such a chart. "The Top Twelve" at the House by the Bridge! Extra, extra, read all about it! Get your copy of the new chart!

Even Lonli-Lockli livened up.

"The White List really helps bolster the work ethic over there, Sir Max," he said in an edifying manner.

"Sir Shurf is one of the movers and shakers behind the List," chuckled Juffin. "And here is our kamra!"

The jugs of kamra weren't even visible from behind the mountain of treats that arrived from the *Glutton*. Melifaro reappeared instantly, as if led by his own nose, and he came bearing a pile of self-inscribing tablets. He leapt over the back and into his chair, and was the first to snatch a pastry and pop the whole thing into his mouth. He looked a bit like Kurush: rumpled, smeared with pastry cream, but very happy. He emptied his cup in one gulp and buried himself in a tablet. For a minute and a half—an eternity by his standards—he read, deep in concentration. Then he jumped up for another pastry, and began holding court with his mouth full. A few seconds later his speech became comprehensible for the rest of us.

"Ah-hah! Just as I thought! In every case a doll like that one was stolen. Besides a load of valuables, of course. But the main thing is that dolls feature in each and every list of stolen goods. Unbelievable! Darling, it seems I gave you a rotten apple. And not without reason! Slighted suitors are terrible in their fury. Now, where did I buy that thing? At some stall in Twilight Market. Well, no matter. I'll turn the place upside down when I get there."

"Hold on a minute," said Sir Kofa. "Tell me, what kind of doll was it? What did your doll look like, Melamori?"

"It looked like a redheaded boy of around twenty years old. It looked almost like a real boy; just shorter. Very handsome face. And the hands were made so beautifully. I examined them closely. Long slender fingers—even the palms were lined. It was wearing some foreign attire made of expensive cloth. I can't say I know where it was from. The garment began above waist length and flowed down to the floor. And it had a splendid collar, something like a short looxi. It was even a little bit warm, like a human. I was somewhat afraid of it. I put it in the parlor, although people usually keep gifts like that in their bedrooms."

"Enough said, my girl! There is no need to go to Twilight Market, Melifaro. Eat, take your time. I'll wager there's only one craftsman in all of Echo who does that kind of work: Jubo Chebobargo, the man with the magic hands!" Kofa announced triumphantly.

"Sweet," Juffin purred. "Now all three of you have something to do this evening. And Max and I will take Sir Shurf and go introduce ourselves to . . . Oh, what is it now! A hole in the heavens above you, boy!" This was addressed to a terrified courier who had blundered in to the room without even knocking.

"An evil force is on the loose!" He mumbled breathlessly. "An evil force is on the loose in the Street of Old Coins! It savaged someone already!"

"Oh, I see. *An emergency call*; that's what it is. *An emergency call*," said Juffin impassively, giving him a curt nod. "Run along then, boy. Why are you shaking like a leaf? Haven't you ever seen an evil spirit before? Are you new here?"

The courier nodded feverishly and dissolved into the gloom of the corridor.

"Let's go, boys," said Juffin. "I can't imagine why such a thing would want to savage a human. As far as I know, creatures like that usually prefer other games. If it hadn't been for your appetite, Sir Melifaro, we wouldn't have missed the beginning of the show! Okay, you have your own business to attend to. Cheers!" Then he turned to me. "Don't just sit there. Let's go!"

✼

The whole time we were in the office I had been feeling somewhat sedated, and at that moment I can't say my condition had improved. Nonetheless, I did somehow manage to stand up and drag myself to the amobiler.

More than anything else I wished someone would tell me what was going on. But Juffin made it clear he had no idea himself.

"You see, Max, you kept a firm grip on yourself, and that gave me time to study the beast. I was absolutely certain that it wasn't capable of that—of attacking people in broad daylight . . . By the way, Sir Shurf, keep in mind that there is only one course of action in this situation: destroy it. So you'll be the only one getting your hands dirty. We'll just watch. Is that clear?"

"Yes, sir," Lonli-Lokli said, nodding. His face looked as though he'd just been told to wash the dishes.

"Do you know what was visiting you, Max? The remains of your honorable neighbor: Sir Tolakan Enn himself."

"How's that possible?"

"I think he made a mistake moving into that house. The place is inhabited by a Phetan; it's clear to me now."

"A *Phetan*?"

"A Phetan is a spirit from another world, taught to do specific tasks and sent on a mission here. Even during the Epoch of Orders, the appearance of such beasts was extremely rare, because as they master new skills they become more useful, but also more dangerous. The longer a Phetan lives, the more powerful it becomes. Sooner or later it rebels against the Magician who summoned it, and . . . Most of the time the Phetan will take the body of its master. You see, Phetans miss having a body of their own; and once they get one, they set off in search of food.

"It's not too difficult to destroy a Phetan—you'll see that for yourself very soon—but it's next to impossible to detect its presence. A Phetan surrounds itself with an almost impenetrable protective field. Its main goal is not to attract too much attention. This protective field prevents you from homing in on it. You can't even detect it. Even if you do notice something, you won't be able to recall it later. The Phetan feeds its new body on the energy of sleeping people, and after they wake up—*if* they wake up—they can't remember what happened. We really are lucky, Sir Max. Very lucky! I'll tell you why later; that's another story. There's one thing that still bothers me, though. Since when does a Phetan attack someone who's not asleep? I've never heard of such a thing before. But no matter—we'll figure this thing out."

"But if it flees," I asked, "how are we going to find it?"

"Out of the question, Sir Max, completely out of the question! Not one Phetan can leave the place it inhabits. It's a law of nature. That's exactly why some Magicians involve themselves with Phetans: because you can always escape if you have a head on your shoulders. Sell the house together with its inhabitant, and other people will have to deal with the consequences."

"But how could Lady Feni go out shopping, if—"

"Good question, boy! I think that having two bodies at its disposal, the Phetan could allow one of them to go free from time to time; though not for long, of course. I'm quite certain it was not Lady Feni going out shopping, but a pitiful semblance of the person she once was, programmed to do certain things. It was a diversionary tactic; a good way of maintaining secrecy. And Phetans covet secrecy. Here we are gentlemen, we can get out now."

We got out of the amobiler right in front of my house. The Street of Old Coins was pretty crowded. There were a few policemen, half a dozen housewives, and a crowd of gawkers who had come out of the *Sated Skeleton*. In the center of the circle they formed we found a modestly dressed middle-aged woman whose head was nearly severed from the rest of her body. A basket of nuts lay nearby. The scattered nuts formed a sort of pathway between my house and the Phetan's, as though the invisible sandy bridge from my dream was casting a very real shadow on the earth beneath it.

My observations were interrupted by the voice of Sir Juffin demanding an explanation from the policemen.

"Witnesses say that it was a very little man, sir," said the policeman, perplexed.

"Where are the witnesses?"

A young couple emerged from the crowd of onlookers. They seemed pleasant, and very youthful, probably around sixty years old by local standards. The lady turned out to be more talkative than her companion.

"We were taking a stroll around the city, and we chanced upon this street. It seemed quiet enough; there wasn't anyone around, just one lady with a basket, walking along ahead of us. Then all of a sudden a little man jumped out from behind that house." Here the girl pointed to the ancient architectural masterpiece that I was already so sick of.

"Are you sure he was small?" asked Juffin.

"I'm sure, sir! You can ask Frud here. He was very small, like a baby, or even smaller. But he was dressed like a grownup, all nice and fancy. At first we didn't understand what was going on. We thought that the man recognized the lady and ran up to hug her. Well, he jumped up; because of course how else could he hug her, being so little and all. We thought it was cute. But then the lady fell over, and we got scared. The man jumped up and down on top of her a few more times, and then left."

"Where did he go?"

"He just left . . . Well, he didn't come toward us, praise to the Magicians! Frud wanted to chase after him, but I got scared. Then we started crying for help."

"Thank you my dear. Very good," said Juffin. He then turned to the police officers. "Did you see anyone leaving the house, boys?"

"No, Sir Venerable Head! And we didn't go inside, because—"

"And a very good thing you didn't! Max, Shurf, let's go!"

So we went to pay a visit to my neighbors, a thousand werewolves on their nuptial bed! Inside, the house was dark and very quiet—and very foul, I might add! A massive parlor laden with valuables gave the impression of an odious museum built in the foyer of hell, a collection comprised of belongings stolen from sinners. And I'm not saying that just because I suffered at the hands of the house's owners. The atmosphere of the house was truly disgusting. Even Lonli-Lokli winced squeamishly; and I'm quite sure that doesn't happen often.

For the first time since I arrived in Echo, the oversized spaces annoyed me. It took us several minutes to search the first floor, even though we worked very quickly; to no avail. Our search yielded nothing but a thoroughly rotten mood.

We went upstairs. The second floor was as dark and quiet as the first. Lonli-Lokli stepped onto the staircase that led to the third floor. I followed him with a feeling of certain doom. It would have been so nice to wake up just then, but I couldn't have been more awake.

Hey Max, don't get depressed! Juffin sensed that I was losing heart and magnanimously sent me a call. *No matter what happens, this is work for Shurf; and it's not difficult, either. You and I are just here out of curiosity. It's not the most pleasant outing, but it's nothing more than that. Chin up, my boy!*

I felt a bit better. I even mustered a weak smile and had it sent General Delivery to Sir Juffin.

Finally we were on the top floor of the house. Above it there was nothing but sky.

They were waiting for us—Tolakan and Feni Enn: fabulously wealthy, smitten with love for each other, and happy together till the end of time. But, no, they'd been gone for a long time already. Only the formidable Phetan remained, extending his longevity with the two sequestered bodies.

The beast knew very well that the situation was hopeless, and knew what awaited him. It didn't even try to put up a fight. Suddenly, I got an uneasy feeling. I think I was beginning to sympathize with this unknown beast, who was not even here of its own will; it was merely trying to survive in the only way it knew how. What if some crazy Magician summoned me? And with my talent for getting into trouble, even in my sleep . . . I felt a chill, and shivered.

Five snow-white rays raced toward the motionless couple. Sir Lonli-Lokli's left hand smote the double-bodied beast quickly and efficiently. Painlessly, as well, I hoped.

"Juffin?" I asked in the ringing silence. "Is there anything left of the Enns themselves? A soul, I mean, or whatever the scientific word for that is . . ."

"No one kno— Oh, Max!"

Quick as lightening, he struck the back of my knees, and I collapsed to the floor. As I was falling, I realized there was something wrong with the nape of my neck. I felt a painful incision in the very place where the hair turns into frivolous fluff. Then a cold sensation spread over my neck. I cried out, and then lost consciousness.

After a few seconds of total darkness, I realized I was still alive. A sharp pain in my right knee and chin witnessed to that. The back of my neck was numb, as though from a shot of Novocain. Something warm was dripping down my neck. If that's blood, then it's goodbye to my favorite looxi, I thought darkly.

I felt a hot hand on the back of my neck. It was an extremely pleasant sensation. I relaxed and floated away into a land of tender forgetfulness. But I didn't stay there for long.

When I opened my eyes, I felt better, though far from ideal. My knee and chin admitted that they had been badly mistreated and were on the road to recovery now. But my neck and the back of my head worried me. Sir Juffin Hully looked around fastidiously for something to wipe off his bloodied hands.

"The curtains," I said, surprised at my own falsetto croak. "I doubt the heirs will sue you."

"Good boy, Max! What would I do without you?"

"Drink kamra quietly in your office without a worry or care. What was that, Juffin?"

"It was the comprehensive answer to several theoretical questions that armchair philosophers sometimes feel compelled to examine. See for yourself. Come on, you can turn your head. I've stopped the bleeding, and the wound has closed. And it wasn't such a bad injury to begin with. Your head didn't fall off, anyway. And if it did, I'd sew a new one on you, even better than the last."

"Very funny. So where is this comprehensive answer?"

"Here it is, Sir Max," said sir Lonli-Lokli, and he kneeled down to show me two small objects, which he held in his right, less dangerous hand. It was a figurine broken in half, the figure of a small woman with a trident. The face, though not attractive, was extremely lifelike, and full of a threatening intensity that made it unforgettable. An impressive trinket.

"Sinning Magicians! What is it?"

"One of the masterpieces from the beginning of the Epoch of Orders," he explained. "An amulet to protect the household. And a powerful thing it was. I think the ghost of Lady Feni picked it up randomly at one of those places at the market where prices start at several hundred crowns. As for the craftsman who made the thing— Sinning Magicians, may werewolves bite off his ears!"

"It is striking," I agreed, "And look at the face . . . Was it a magical object?"

"Well, yes. In her time, this damsel protected the house from thieves and other unexpected visitors. And she did a good job of it, too; she was no less fierce than an armed thug. It's all right as long as amulets like that end up in ordinary households of ordinary families. But in a house inhabited by a Phetan, anything can happen to a magical object. This is an age-old truth that is every so often called into question by certain armchair philosophers. The ancient object that attacked you went completely nuts. That's what I call a comprehensive answer to theoretical questions. It was my fault, of course; you can never let your guard down in a place like this. If you and I had just waited a little longer with our conversation, then your neck would've been in much better condition now. Not to mention your morale. Anyway, let's get out of here. The House by the Bridge is a good deal cozier. Or perhaps you want to go home and get some rest, Sir Max? You are injured, after all, and your house is just across the street."

"Oh, right! Sleep is just what I need now, while you stuff your-selves with pastries and make a big fuss about our adventures today. The only way you'll get rid of me is to kill me!"

"Curiosity and gluttony will be the death of you in this job," Juffin said. "Well, then, let's be off."

Lonli-Lokli helped me stand up; but to do this he had to wrap his hand in the cloth of his cape, since he had forgotten his protective gloves in the amobiler. It occurred to me that leaning on the elbow of a fellow like him was probably as dangerous as passing the time by throwing a party at a nuclear power plant. So I tried to make it downstairs without assistance. I made my way down, not exactly bouncing, but energetic nonetheless.

We had just gotten to the amobiler when Juffin's face suddenly looked like he had eaten a whole lemon.

"Dinner's postponed, boys. Melifaro is screaming for help. I think they're in big trouble. And if even Sir Melifaro is complaining, then it must be something serious. The poor fellow didn't even have time to explain himself. He says an evil force is abroad, and it's running amuck. Sounds like fun. So we're heading for the Street of Little Generals. Get behind the wheel, Sir Max! We could use some of your reckless driving right now. As for you, son, get back to the House by the Bridge and read the paper there or something. Come on now, clear out!" said Juffin, and nudged the bewildered driver from the driver's seat.

I took his place, and we were off. Juffin hardly managed to keep up with my driving, shouting "to the left, now right, now left again!" I believe that evening I was able to squeeze sixty miles per hour out of the technological miracle.

Our speed was justified, as the Street of Little Generals was all the way on the western edge of the city; but we made it there in about fifteen minutes. Juffin needn't have taken the trouble to announce that we had arrived. To be honest, I didn't doubt it for a minute.

I can't say that Echo is the quietest place in the world in the evening. Even so, it's unusual for locals to run around in groups of twenty to thirty, dressed only in their underwear and accompanied by their young children and hysterical domestic animals. As far as I know, shrieking so loud that the sound carries above the rooftops is not common, either. But that is precisely what everyone was doing at the moment.

"Juba Chebobargo's house. It's that dirty pink chicken shed over there," said Juffin, pointing.

A barefoot man, whose firm body was only just covered by some pathetic scraps of a ragged tunic, ran out of the building just described to me in such unkind terms. A bright shiny object, too large to be a piece of jewelry, was attached to the hem of the tattered garment. The next instant I noticed that the "object" was alive.

A rat! I thought. Could it really be a rat? Ugh!

I've been afraid of rats since childhood. This common phobia even has a long scientific name, but I can't for the life of me remember what it is.

A moment later I calmed down. I told myself that multicolored rats like that don't exist in nature. The creature known as a rat has to be the same grayish or dun color, no matter what world it's in. Besides, this thing had clearly anthropomorphic features.

"It's a little man!" I shouted happily. "Just a little man! Exactly like the one the girl described!"

The white flame that leaped out of Lonli-Lokli's left hand consumed the little man completely, leaving not even a pile of ashes. The sturdy fellow in the tattered tunic carried on, frightened but completely unhurt, his pale backside flickering mysteriously in the gathering twilight for the benefit of any incidental fans of male striptease.

"Should I stop him?" asked Shurf.

Juffin shook his head. "It's not Juba. Let him run around, there's no harm in that. And what on earth are you so pleased about, Max? Is it something to do with the little man?"

"Not exactly." I felt myself blushing. "I was just glad it wasn't . . . a rat."

"A rat? What's a rat?"

"You don't have rats here?"

"I guess not, unless we call them something else. Let's go see what's going on inside the house. Sir Shurf, you go first; and you, Max, keep your wits about you. Today doesn't seem to be your lucky day."

❦

That day I realized that I truly enjoyed being in the company of Sir Shurf Lonli-Lokli. Shurf was a consummate killer. To be standing so close to death, and yet to be certain it won't touch you, is a unique feeling. It gives you an unfounded but absolute confidence in your own powers. It made my head spin!

In the hallway of the pink chicken coop, my inappropriately buoyant mood hit the skids. Another little tot was smacking his lips and chewing happily as he sat on the stomach of an ample, middle-aged dead man, upon whose innards he was snacking. Lonli-Lokli quickly put an end to this grotesque scene. If it had gone on a second longer, I would have run the risk of parting with the pastries I myself had eaten only a short time before.

"Why, that's Krelo Shir!" Juffin exclaimed, approaching the mutilated body. "What a shame! I never would have thought Juba could afford such an excellent chef. Poor artist my foot!"

We entered the living room. The scene before us deserved to be sculpted in bronze. The heroic Sir Melifaro, in a cloud of fluttering remnants of a turquoise looxi, was ripping apart a writhing, angry little body with his bare hands. A good ten miniature bodies lay motionless, strewn about like a splendid backdrop to this immortal exploit. I couldn't help but laugh. Lonli-Lokli shot out of the room like a bullet.

"Was he really that repelled by my laughter?" I asked Juffin in confusion.

Melifaro brandished the beheaded torso, and grinned at the same time. He was probably imagining how this scene must look to an outsider.

"Oh, no, Max, not at all. I simply sent him to go after the others."

"There're more?"

"No less than a dozen running about. And Mister Juba made a run for it, too. But I wouldn't worry about him. Our friend Melamori doesn't take kindly to men who don't lavish attention on her," Melifaro assured me. "She'll smoke him out wherever he is."

"Just what are these little freaks? Can you tell me, O slayer of trolls?"

"Why do you call them freaks? They're sweet, really; take a look!" Melifaro held out a little head that had been separated from its body. I winced. Then I saw that the head was made out of wood. And the face was truly lovely. Sinning Magicians!"

"Is that a doll? The same one you gave Melamori?"

"The same one, or a different one. It doesn't matter. There were several dozen of the little monsters and they just went mad. When we first arrived they were having a meeting, discussing whether they should kill Juba or swear loyalty to him. He was a sorry sight."

"Let's go, fellows," Juffin said, cutting short our intriguing conversation. "We're no match for Sir Shurf, but we should each try to make ourselves useful, insofar as our humble abilities will allow us. Where, by the way, is good Sir Shixola? Could he possibly have deserted?"

"Just about! No, just joking. He called for a backup, too, and now he's heading up the races on the rooftops, in the company of the city police. I hope they've managed to catch one or two. Patch me up, will you, Juffin? Jokes aside, I don't think I'm in very good shape."

I watched, enchanted, as Sir Juffin Hully stroked Melifaro's arms, which were covered in tooth marks, with the tips of his fingers. Melifaro winced.

"That's nothing; my stomach is in a much worse state."

"Ah-hah!" Sir Juffin's palms darted to the spot where Melifaro's bright yellow tunic was darkening with a maroon stain. "Goodness, my boy! It looks like these beasts are crazy about human bellies! Are you still on your feet? Good show! There you go. You're lucky that these critters can jump so high. A little lower, and even I wouldn't be able to redeem your personal life."

"Werewolves take you, Juffin! That's no occasion for joking!"

"No worse than your jokes. Alright then, let's go."

※

Outside, the apocalypse raged on. A child ran right past me with a shriek. Horrified, I noticed that a tiny figure was prancing right at its heels, emitting a barely audible hissing noise. In the twilight it looked so much like a rat that I had to summon all my courage to perform a deed worthy of renown. Bending over, I grabbed the beast by its fragile leg and, shuddering with fright, smashed the horrid creature on the cobblestones. The doll shattered to bits.

"Is that how you punish disobedient children in the Barren Lands?" asked Melifaro with acerbic admiration. "Let's go look for some more to finish off. Maybe we'll get lucky!"

But lucky we were not. No sooner had we started our excursion around the block when we came upon Sir Lonli-Lokli, who looked tired, but absolutely calm. His snow-white looxi was still flawlessly draped.

"That's that," he announced. "I told the police to start restoring the peace. There are no dolls left."

"Are you sure there are no more of them?" I almost asked, but restrained myself in the nick of time. If Sir Shurf Lonli-Lokli says something, then it must be true. I should have learned that by now.

"Thank you for your expediency, Sir Shurf. I have been dying for some kamra for an hour and a half now," Juffin said, and yawned.

"That is just why I made haste, sir."

If I didn't know Lonli-Lokli better, I would have sworn that he was teasing. We went back to the amobiler, but on the way a familiar operatic growl caught our attention.

"Crap like that should stay in a pig's toilet where it belongs! Bull's tits! You're going in there, and you'll eat your own turds until they stop coming out of your skinny little butt!"

"Boboota's leading the operation?" I asked.

"But of course!" said Juffin. "It's great publicity, restoring the peace and whatnot. Do you really think he'd miss a good opportunity to go wild? Boboota jumps at the chance to wave his sword around. It's his only talent, after all. Praise to the Magicians, have my dreams come true? Looks like one of the little monsters managed to bite him!"

"No, sir," said Lonli-Lokli. "Captain Foofloss arrived along with General Box. Sir Foofloss, as you know, is a very disciplined soldier. If ordered to open fire with a Baboom slingshot, he does it."

Juffin and Melifaro exchanged glances and guffawed.

"Captain Foofloss is the worst marksman under the sun!" Juffin explained through his laughter. "If he aims for the ground right under him, he shoots into the sky."

Then he turned to Lonli-Lokli, "So, what happened?"

"Captain Foofloss' shot ricocheted off the wall and hit General Box. The injury isn't serious, but it's liable to cause him a good deal of discomfort. I mean it will be difficult for him to sit down for a while."

I joined in the mirth with my colleagues.

❋

Finding myself in the driver's seat of the amobiler, I decided that I, too, needed a bit of kamra. So we drove back even faster than we had on our way here. I'd swear the darned jalopy was about to take off flying. If anyone besides me got pleasure out of the ride, it was Melifaro. In any event, I had to promise that I would reveal the secret of speed to him. As if it was a secret!

All of a sudden I thought, I'm one to laugh at Captain Foofloss! I don't even know how to shoot a Baboom! In fact, I don't even know what it is.

Juffin intercepted my inner monologue, and rushed to comfort me. *If you like, we could practice a bit together at the shooting gallery in our free time. But you must keep in mind that we are Secret Investigators, and thus find it beneath our dignity to be involved in such nonsense. And keep your eye on the road, for good-ness' sake!*

It was indeed comforting.

❋

An unusually heartwarming sight awaited us when we returned to the House by the Bridge. We found Melamori lounging upon the table in the Hall of Common Labor. She looked disheveled, but very happy. Her narrow feet, covered in scratches, were clamped around the muscular neck of a sturdy blond young man whose face had gone burgundy for lack of oxygen. He had had no choice but to set-tle into a position so uncomfortable that if I had been the Venerable Head of the Office of Quick Retribution (the Supreme Court, in other words), I would have thought such a punishment to be more than enough.

"He's all yours, Sir Melifaro," the sweet lady twittered. "I've been sitting with him here for an hour already."

"It's your own fault. You could have settled for a less ravishing pose. We would have appreciated you anyway," Juffin grumbled. "Get that fright into Melifaro's office. I can't bear the sight of him. What hands, what talent! And to waste it all churning out those odious monsters. What's up, genius? Were you too broke for a jug of kamra?"

Juba Chebobargo was not in the mood for conversation. He didn't seem to understand what was going on. Lady Melamori hopped off the table gracefully. The poor fool didn't even react to his sudden liberation from her embrace. She grabbed him roughly by the wheat-colored locks that sprouted from the top of his head, and dragged the mountain of meat into Melifaro's office with no visible effort. Melifaro followed after them, shaking his head in amazement.

As soon as I sat down at the table, I began to whine. With the exhausted manner of a hero of all world wars in succession, I demanded that we put in our order at the *Glutton* without waiting for the rest of our colleagues to return. To be honest, I suspect that events would have shaped up that way even without my insistence. Juffin himself was in a hurry to get his kamra.

"I think we should add a few bottles of good wine to our order. I feel a tad tired today," said Lonli-Lokli. "I don't think anyone would object."

Indeed, no one had any objections. The devil take it, we had something to celebrate! Just a few hours ago we had unmasked and disarmed a Phetan, one of the most formidable forces of evil in this World. Not to mention our joint munchkin-extermination mission, and our happy introduction to Juba Chebobargo, the person with the magical hands.

When the trays arrived from the *Glutton*, Lonli-Lokli produced the familiar cup with the hole in the bottom from under the folds of his looxi. But he slyly managed to surprise me a second time. Uncorking a bottle of *Shining*, Sir Shurf took his time pouring its entire contents into his cup. Of course, the size of the cup would not seem to accommodate such greed. It turned out, however, that nothing would spill over the brim of the cup, either. The quivering aromatic column of greenish-yellow wine froze above the vessel. Lonli-Lokli sipped from the top of this liquid iceberg.

I felt the urge to cross all my fingers, just to be on the safe side; but then thought better of it, as this could be interpreted as magic of some forbidden degree.

"Do you feel better, Shurf?" asked Juffin.

"I certainly do. Thank you, sir," said Lonli-Lokli. And, indeed, not a trace of weariness remained on his face.

❀

There was still much that remained unclear to me, so I requested an explanation.

"So it was Juba Chebobargo who made those dolls come alive?"

"Almost. As I understand it, Juba's skills were so great that he made the dolls using only permitted magic—and his amazing hands, of course! It wasn't that the dolls were really alive; but they were very lifelike, and they could perform certain simple tasks. Collecting all the money and valuables they could carry, for example. And he taught them to return to their master. It was an excellent plan, I'll grant him that. If Melifaro hadn't taken on the case, I don't think anyone would have caught on for a few more years; and by then he would have made a fortune. Although today's events probably would have put an end to his scheme, anyway."

"So what happened? What made the dolls go mad like that? Nothing like that has ever happened before, has it?"

"It certainly hasn't! What do you think—who was the kid that jumped out of your neighbors' house and gave the poor lady that overly passionate kiss?"

"One of Juba Chebobargo's dolls!" It finally dawned on me. "Lady Feni bought it, along with the rest of the antique junk that she collected. And the doll went crazy in that lovely little house, just like the protective amulet that attacked me. I can't say I blame them. I'd probably go nuts in that place, too. But what happened to all the other dolls? Was it some kind of epidemic?"

"You can be very perspicacious when you wish to be, Max. That is exactly what it was, an epidemic. The crazed object returned home, and thus made a huge contribution to science. Now it is clear beyond the shadow of a doubt that the properties of magical objects not only change in the presence of a Phetan, but can also share their newly acquired qualities with other magical objects. Today was quite a fruitful day in the area of scientific discovery. And in the area of bodily injury, for that matter."

"And conflicts with one's neighbors," I grumbled.

"I told you not to move there from the very start, if you would care to recall," said Juffin, and kindly poured me some more kamra.

"And I told *you* from the very start that by moving there I was acting in the line of duty. How many souls would he have destroyed if he hadn't come across me?"

"Inhabitants of the Borderlands have a highly developed faculty of intuition; I'm convinced of this now more than ever," said Lonli-Lokli, summing things up.

"And a highly developed lucky streak," said Juffin. He turned to me and said, "You have no idea how lucky you were to receive that royal gift when you did. And I have one more scientific discovery that I can share with you. I hope it's the last one today. I was able to discover the magical properties of the Children of the Crimson Pearl."

"Ah, while we're toiling away, state secrets are being revealed in here," said Lady Melamori, flushed and disheveled, as she appeared in the doorway. She stood at attention, then reported.

"Everything is fine, Sir Juffin! Melifaro will join us in just a moment. He's finishing the interrogation of Juba with Mister, oh what's-his-name, from the police. You know, the one who's fourth on the List. He really is a nice guy. Poor Juba isn't in his right mind. When I started trailing him, I was already terribly angry. I'm even a little ashamed of myself now. He still isn't in very good shape after the run-in with his babies. Still, why is Shixola only fourth on the List? I think he deserves to be second, at the very least."

"If I am not mistaken, Lieutenant Shixola's intellect manifests itself in the following: he is smitten with you, my lady, and does nothing to hide it."

"Nothing of the sort!" Melamori retorted. "We only talked about work."

"As far as I'm aware, that's all that's necessary. There, there; I'm just joking! Go on my girl, what were you saying?"

"Well, it doesn't really matter. I see you have more interesting news here. Sir Juffin, you look truly elated. Come now, don't keep it a secret!"

"I wasn't planning on it. You were the one who interrupted me. Couldn't you have just listened quietly from behind the door? So, gentlemen, in answer to Max's question about Phetans: these creatures are capable of concealing the recollections that people have of them in the dimmest recesses of people's consciousness. The poor victims are unable to remember their terrifying nightmares. They blame their sickly state on other factors. So they stay home and rest, and in their slumber they again fall victim to the hungry beast. In observing your dream today, I had the opportunity to see the Child of the Crimson Pearl in action with my own eyes. It wasn't even necessary to keep it at the head of your bed. It was enough for you hold it in your hands just once. It turns out that the pearls help their owners recall events under any circumstances. That's it! Finish chewing that morsel, Melamori, and tell us what went on over there."

Melamori, heedless of this wise piece of advice, began speaking with her mouth full. Dining etiquette was obviously not held in very high regard among the Echo aristocracy—though I must admit that this sight only made her more attractive to me.

"I told you; everything's fine. I started tracking Juba Chebobargo. Not that it was really necessary—his home address is certainly no secret—but I was really furious. It was all for the best, though. By the time we arrested him, the criminal was as tame as a kitten. Well, we set off for the Street of Little Generals, Melifaro and I and the handsome Sir Shixola. When we arrived, Chebobargo appeared to be in quite a pickle. He was sitting on the floor in the parlor, with those little beasts swarming over him from head to toe. They were trying to decide what to do with him. From what we could make out, some of the dolls considered him to be a sort of parental figure, and the other camp dubbed him a tyrant. When we arrived, they were in a heated discussion. Oh, gentlemen, they weren't actually *saying* anything at all. They just ground their teeth rhythmically, like a cross between normal and Silent Speech. When we killed a few of the dolls from the doorway, total chaos broke out. They were running every which way, and Chebobargo, too. I don't know whether he was running from them or from us! I guess the poor fellow didn't really know what was going on at that point. So I went after him, and Melifaro and Shixola stayed behind to kill the little critters. You know the rest. Oh, one more thing. The police found almost all the stolen valuables in Juba Chebobargo's bathroom—and mine too, of course. They were on top because I was the last person to be robbed. What about that important business that you fellows had to take care of? What have you been up to? Tell me!" And Melamori gave Lonli-Lokli a pleading look. She'd certainly picked a loquacious bard!

"Sir Juffin will tell you himself, I am sure."

Yes, Sir Shurf was far from being the greatest gossip in the Unified Kingdom.

"I'll tell you when everyone else gets here. Don't be angry dear, I just can't stand repeating the same thing over and over."

"Fine! But I may drop dead of curiosity right here in your arms, I warn you!"

❧

Before half an hour had passed, Melifaro arrived. In contrast to everyone else, he had already managed to change his clothes. He was wearing a lettuce-green skaba and red and blue checked looxi. Maybe he kept a whole closet full of garments at work, I mused.

Soon Sir Kofa poked his head into Juffin's office. He said he was just passing by and decided to drop in to find out how things were, because there were amazing rumors making the rounds in the city. For instance, it was said that Juba Chebobargo was the leader of a gang of midgets. And Mister Venerable Head had apparently killed Tolakan Enn, former Heir to the Throne, with his bare hands, because of some debt at cards from way back. And he knocked off the wife of the victim while he was at it. He then falsified the report, to the effect that the Enns were involved in forbidden black magic and were penpals with two dozen Rebel Magicians.

"Nice rumor," Juffin said with a grin. "There's a moral to be learned from it. People should remember it's best to pay their gambling debts on time!"

But the real joke of the day was sir Boboota Box, who, despite his serious injuries, had already written up an official report in which he said that the "city police were following up on a lead that could result in solving the mystery of the recent robberies that had been taking place in Echo." Luckily for Boboota, his more intelligent subordinates were in no great hurry to send the letter and prudently saved their boss from embarrassment.

Juffin spent the rest of the evening telling everyone about our adventures. I almost fell asleep in my chair, lulled by the warmth, my own full stomach, and the opportunity to hear the story of my own adventures recounted so thrillingly, even though the story was horrifying.

"Sir Max, I am sending you home," Juffin announced. "All the mysteries have been solved, and all the pastries have been eaten. What you really need now is to sleep for twenty-four hours without a single nightmare."

"I have no objections to that," I said with a smile, "but I have one last question. Sir Melifaro, do you have any cats at your estate?"

"Of course. Why do you ask?"

"I promised myself that when this ordeal was over, I would get myself a kitten. But since two missions have come to a close at the same time, I'll need two kittens."

"I could give you a dozen if you ask; but tell me what do plan to do with them? Do you eat them?"

"We Border Dwellers eat anything!" I announced. Then, taking pity on my nonplussed colleagues, I said, "I'm going to stroke them, and they are going to purr. Those, I believe, are the ideal relations between humans and cats."

❈

Home, sweet home. My nightmares were over, and I was exhausted by the ordeal I had been through. I lay down in bed and stretched so exquisitely that I almost cried with joy. I slept, not like a baby, but rather like a bear in its den. And I only came to on the evening of the following day. I was hungry. Unlike a member of genus *ursus*, I lacked a layer of fat to sustain me.

An hour later, there was a knock at my door. It was the young courier from the Ministry of Perfect Public Order.

"A package from Sir Melifaro for Sir Max," the boy reported, and handed me an enormous basket. I could hardly lift it. Closing the door after the courier, I removed the ornate blanket that covered the basket. Two dark fuzzy creatures with bright blue eyes were peering out at me. I took them out of the basket. Each of them weighed more than a grown cat in my homeland! I studied them carefully. The black one was a boy, and the coffee-colored one was a girl. The kittens seemed possessed by an utter calm that bordered on extravagant laziness. Naturally, plump as they were! I was so thrilled with my acquisition that I sent a call to Melifaro.

Thanks, buddy! The beasts are awesome! Totally awesome!

Sinning Magicians, Max. You speak so oddly when you use Silent Speech, who would have known . . . They're just cats, no big deal. Bon appétit!

What else was I expecting to hear? I named the boy Armstrong and the girl Ella. The idea came to me when they reminded me in their low-pitched mews that animals must be fed. My pets definitely knew how to croon. And in the old days, before I was Sir Max of Echo, I used to like listening to a bit of old jazz.

CHAPTER THREE

CELL NO. 5-OW-NOX

T HERE'S A SIGN I ALWAYS WATCH FOR: BEFORE EVERY MAJOR CASE, everything goes quiet in the House by the Bridge. If I find myself dozing for several nights in a row in my armchair, my feet up on the desk, it means that some hullabaloo or other will soon be in full swing.

And, in point of fact, I don't mind. Serving in the Secret Investigative Force isn't yet just a routine for me. And if everything continues the way it's going now, it's unlikely that it ever will be.

When urgent matters crop up (and there are more of them than there are agents), my personal time-frame stops coinciding with the pace of the hands on the clock. Sometimes I seem to live through a few years in just one day; but at the end of the day I'm not any older.

I like this. I'm hungry for life. Even those several hundred years that are almost guaranteed to every inhabitant of this World seem like a very short allotment of infinity to me. I admit, hand on heart, that I just want to live forever—preferably without becoming too decrepit, though being old doesn't really frighten me. If you take one look at Juffin or at Sir Kofa, you understand that solid old age is rather an advantage than a burden.

That morning Sir Kofa Yox showed up exactly ten seconds earlier than Juffin. During that time he managed to sit down in a chair, wipe the workaday mask off his face (low forehead; long, fleshy nose; high cheekbones; sensitive lips; double chin), and stretch sweetly, with a bit of creaking here and there.

As though agreeing with his colleague, Sir Juffin gave a leisurely yawn in the doorway. He planted himself in his chair, and yawned again—a protracted one, mingled with a little squeal. These things are highly contagious: I too started to yawn, although I hadn't slept too poorly on the job that night. In fact, I felt completely rested. Finding a night job was all it took to help a night owl like me switch to the ordinary schedule of most of humanity.

I could have gone home if I wanted to. I even should have. But I had already decided beforehand to drink a mug of kamra in the company of my senior colleagues, because I know how they work: as soon as I leave, they start talking about The-Most-Interesting-Things-In-The-World. No more missing out on that! These days you had to drag me off duty by force.

"Judging by what a rotten sleep I had last night, we could arrest the entire population of Echo for abuse of forbidden magic," Juffin spluttered angrily, gulping down half the mug of kamra at one go. "Only where could we lock them all up? There aren't that many free cells in Xolomi."

"That bad?" Kofa asked, frowning skeptically.

"Worse than bad. Every time I started to doze off, another misuse of magic signal would sound, and I'd just about jump through the roof. I was cursed to be born with such sensitive ears. What's been going on, Kofa, do you have any idea? The Let's Make Potions Festival, featuring members of all the Ancient Orders?" The boss drank down the rest of his kamra with an indignant slurp, then proposed with obvious relish, "Is it possible that I have slept through a government revolt?"

From the depths of his chair, Sir Kofa observed Juffin's fuming with paternal benevolence. He waited until he was quiet then permitted himself to launch into an explanation.

"I feel for you, Juffin, but it wasn't really that entertaining. In fact, it was rather sad."

"It sure must have been. Well, don't keep me on tenterhooks! What happened?"

"What's there to say that you don't know already? Old Sir Fraxra is in very bad shape. The wisemen are absolutely powerless to help— after all the fellow's already over 1,000 years old. Not every magician lives that long and Fraxra was just a young novice of some bedraggled Order. They booted him out of there pretty quickly, too, and found him a position at Court. That's where the matter ended."

"Yes, I know all that. Did the old man really decide to try to prolong his existence? There's something suspicious about it. He's a sensible man, and he's well aware of his own limits."

"He is, indeed, a very sensible man. Sensible enough to understand that there are things you have to part with in due course in the World before leaving it. The household staff and servants adore him. Including the cook."

Juffin's face brightened.

"Ah, yes. Sir Shutta Vax, the youngest son of the legendary Vagatta Vax, Head Chef of the Court of Gurig VII. The one who retired after the Code of Krember was introduced."

"And right he was to do so, too. Old Cuisine is Old Cuisine, after all. A kitchen wizard like Vagatta Vax—what would he do without magic of the 20th or 30th degree? Boss around the kitchen boys? I think not."

"But Shutta learned a thing or two from his daddy, from what I understand," Juffin mused.

"But of course. You know that Shutta Vax would go through hell and high water for his old master. And to break the law a little for the dying Sir Fraxra with a speciality of the family house is the least he could do. In short, last night a Chakkatta Pie was born. And the nocturnal merrymakers kept their noses to the wind without knowing why themselves."

"I forgive him for my troubled sleep," said Juffin. "The young fellow, of course, found you and asked you to put in a good word for his blasted noggin?"

"Shutta Vax did, in fact, find me and warn me that he was going to break the law," said Sir Kofa. "His loyalty to the King, of course, is hereditary, not a matter of conviction. The fellow decided to save us the extra trouble. He said that if we considered it necessary to send him to Xolomi, he was ready for it. He requested only that we wait until morning, so he could feed the old man—then off to the executioner's block he'd go."

"That wily old fox knows that Juffin will never lay a hand on a kitchen magician. Well, I only hope that Sir Fraxra dies happy. I wish I could be in his shoes!"

"Shutta really is counting on your kindness. And as a sign of his gratitude, he decided to share responsibility with you," said Sir Kofa. He drew a box out from the folds of his looxi and handed it to Juffin.

Juffin accepted the box as though it were a priceless treasure. I swear I have never seen such a reverent expression on his face! He lifted the lid and carefully folded down the sides of the box to reveal an enormous piece of pie. It looked like a neat triangle of the purest amber, gleaming from the inside with a warm light. Juffin's hands trembled, honest to Magicians! With a sigh, he took a knife and sliced off a thin piece.

"Take it, Max. You can't imagine how lucky you are!"

"You can't imagine what an honor this is," Kofa said with a smile. "If Juffin gave his life for you, I could understand it. But to share a piece of Chakkatta Pie! What's gotten into you, Juffin?"

"I don't know. He's just lucky," Juffin said. "I'm not sharing anything with you, Kofa. I'm sure that you already had your share."

"That's right. So don't let your conscience bother you."

"And I'm sure that slice was even bigger than this one."

"Your eyes are bigger than my stomach! My slice was almost half as big as yours."

I fingered the piece of pie as though enchanted. What kind of pie could this be? I carefully bit off a corner of the shining baked wonder.

There are no words to describe, in any human language, what happened in my mouth that wondrous morning. And if you think that you have already experienced all the pleasures that could possibly tantalize your taste buds . . . well, then, you are living in blissful ignorance. I will seal my lips, because the taste of Chakkatta Pie is simply beyond words.

When the tasting orgy was over, we fell silent for a time.

"Are you sure the ban can't be lifted, at least for cooks?" I asked plaintively, shaken by the injustice of the ways of the World. If this is one of the dishes of Old Cuisine, I simply can't imagine what the rest of it was like. My senior colleagues sadly cast down their eyes. Their faces wore the expressions of people whose dearest possessions have been irretrievably lost.

"Unfortunately, Max, it is thought that the world can come to ruin even through this," Juffin said somberly. "Moreover, we weren't the ones who wrote the Code of Krember."

"The one who wrote it had probably been on a strict diet for about a hundred years, and hated humanity to boot," I grumbled. "Is it really possible that His Majesty and Grand Magician Nuflin can't allow themselves a piece of Chakkatta Pie for breakfast? I don't believe it."

"You do have excellent intuition. Regarding the King, I have my own doubts, while in the city there is talk of a secret kitchen, hidden in the basements of Jafax, the Main Residence of the Order of the Seven-Leaf Clover," Sir Kofa remarked with studied indifference.

"Perhaps I shouldn't have joined the Secret Investigative Force at all," I said, gazing at Juffin reproachfully. "Put in a good word for me at your Seven-Leaf Clover, will you? Maybe they'll take me on as a janitor."

Juffin nodded absently, chugged down the rest of his kamra, then turned a dazzling smile on us.

"Life goes on," he announced. "Therefore, tell me, my dear friend: a pie is a pie is a pie, but did anything else happen here?"

"Everything, one might say, that falls under General Booota's jurisdiction," Kofa said. "Trifles. Simply too many to count for one night. That's why you couldn't sleep. For example, the idiot smugglers tried to hide their contraband from Customs by applying black magic of the fifteenth degree. Can you believe it?"

"Yes," Juffin said drily, nodding his head. "Exceptionally dull-witted. You might as well steal an old skaba, and then blow up the whole Right Bank so no one will find out."

"Then there was a counterfeit job. Black magic of only the sixth degree. And there was an awkward amateur attempt to mix a sleeping potion. Piffle . . . Oh, here's something of a more serious order. Belar Grau, former apprentice of the Order of the Secret Grass, has become a pickpocket. A real professional, by the way! They just about caught him last night . . . see for yourself."

He handed Juffin several self-inscribing tablets. These are an extraordinarily convenient little invention, let me tell you. Just think a thought or two, and it up and writes them down. It must be said that some people think less than grammatically—but there it is. That's one thing you can't change.

Juffin studied the tablets with respectful concentration.

"What I'd like to know is what Booota Box does all day during working hours. And what part of his body does he use for thinking, when it becomes absolutely unavoidable. I doubt it's his behind—it's so big that it would be capable of coming to some weighty conclusions eventually. Okay, then. We'll let him deal with the bungling sorcerers and smugglers. The counterfeiter and pickpocket we'll keep for later."

Sir Kofa nodded gravely.

"With your permission, I'd like to take my leave. I want to drink some kamra in the *Pink Buriwok* on my way home. They don't know how to make it worth a darn, but the biggest tongue-waggers in Echo gather there early in the morning on their way from the market. I don't think . . . although . . ."

Sir Kofa fell silent and almost mechanically passed his hand over his face, which underwent a sudden change. Rubbing his nose, which was growing before our very eyes, he went off to squander the remains of the treasury.

"Juffin," I began in confusion. "Tell me, why don't you give Boboota Box all the cases at once? He's a jerk, of course; but a criminal at large— that's not right, is it? Or have I misunderstood something again?"

"Have you misunderstood something? You've understood absolutely nothing! A petty criminal at large is a mild inconvenience, but a Boboota running around the House by the Bridge is a disaster! And I do have to try to get along with him. To my way of thinking, that means 'taking charge of the situation.' And 'taking charge of the situation' means that Sir Boboota Box will be forever in our debt. It's the only state of mind that allows for constructive dialog. At the same time, we always need to have something up our sleeves that Boboota doesn't know. What if we suddenly have to give him a present; or, on the contrary, to give him a scare? The gratitude of Boboota Box is as loud as the gases he lets out at his leisure—and as fleeting as their odor."

"How complicated it all is!" I exclaimed ruefully.

"Complicated? It's very simple, boy. And, by the way, what's a 'jerk'?"

"A jerk is—Sir Boboota Box. But you, sir, are a true Jesuit!"

"You can cuss a mouthful when you're in the mood," Juffin said admiringly.

🌀

"Excuse me," said the stranger formerly known as Sir Kofa, peeping into the study. "That blasted pie made me completely forget about the most important thing. All night rumors have been circulating through the city that Burada Isofs died in Xolomi. I checked up on it—it's true. He was in cell No. 5-Ow-Nox. How do you like them apples, Juffin!"

"I'm just wondering," the boss muttered, "how do nighttime revelers find out things like that? All the more since it happened in Xolomi."

"You said yourself that Echo is full of two-bit clairvoyants," I reminded him.

"So I did. Thanks, Kofa! You've made me happy. How many people have expired in that cell over the last few years, Kurush?"

The sleepy Buriwok raised his head reluctantly, but starting recounting information about the 225th day of the 115th year.

"Dosot Fer died on the 114th day of the 112th year in cell No. 5-Ow-Nox in the Royal Prison of Xolomi. Tolosot Liv died on the 209th day of the 113th year in the same place. Balok Sanr died on the 173rd day of the 114th year. Tsivet Maron died on the 236th day of the 114th year. Axam Ann died on the 78th day of the 115th year. Sovats Lovod died on the 184th day of the 115th year. Burada Isofs died in the same cell on the 224th day of the 115th year, if I have understood Sir Kofa correctly. Somebody give me some peanuts," Kurush concluded, on an unexpectedly informal note.

"Certainly, my dear fellow!" Juffin reached into the desk drawer for the peanuts, which were far more abundant than secret documents.

"You can be on your way, Kofa. Good work, for remembering to report that to me. Think about what our next step should be."

Our incomparable Master Eavesdropper-Gobbler, as Melifaro had christened him, nodded, and disappeared into the darkness of the corridor. The door closed silently behind him. I shivered under the penetrating gaze of Sir Juffin Hully.

"Well, Max, what do you think? Will you take the case?"

"How do I get a handle on something like this?"

"You look for the only handle we have. You set out for Xolomi, and you sit in the cell yourself. If you throw yourself into the fray, you'll find out what's going on there. And circumstances will instruct you about how to proceed."

"Me? In Xolomi?!"

"Where else, my dear friend. That's where they're dying. You're leaving tomorrow. Oh, don't look so alarmed! All things considered, it doesn't look like it will take too long for events to unfold. And I'm certain no one can manage this case better than you can."

"Manage how? By staying in prison?"

"That, too," Sir Juffin said with an acid smile. "What's wrong with you, Max? Where's your sense of humor?"

"Somewhere out there. I'll go look for it," I said, with a dismissive wave of the hand, as if to show that things weren't really that bad.

"Listen carefully, Max. Sooner or later it would have happened anyway."

"What, you mean that sooner or later they'd clap me in Xolomi prison?"

"Enough already about the prison! I'm serious now. Sooner or later you're going to have to start acting on your own. So it's better that it happened now. It's not a matter of earth-shattering importance for the World. And it's not the most difficult case, it appears. I can jump to your aid at any moment, though I'm sure that won't be necessary. I'm at your disposal, Max: day, night, tomorrow morning, and in between. Think, make a plan. Everything you need will be made available to you. And this evening, instead of reporting to duty, come to see me. The last supper for the future prisoner. Your every gastronomical wish will be fulfilled."

"Thank you, Juffin."

"You're very welcome!"

"But now maybe you'll explain to me—"

"No explanations, don't even ask! Treating you to dinner—I'm always ready to grant that wish."

At that we parted.

※

In the evening I set out for the Left Bank, armed with the hope that someone would finally tell me what the devil I was supposed to do in Xolomi. But what do you think—would that monster change his mind? Not on your life! You came here to eat, he'll say. Well, make me happy, Max, and move your jaws. All this talk about work, work, work—that's what I'm fed up with!

According to Kimpa, dinner had been personally prepared by his Master, the Venerable Head.

As it turned out, Sir Juffin Hully was an excellent cook. But I hungered for something completely different. I wanted instructions.

"Take it easy, Sir Max, relax. Tomorrow is tomorrow. Besides, I'm absolutely sure that once you get there, some silly thing will pop into your head, and it will turn out to be the only real solution to the problem. Take a bite of this, I dare you . . ."

Chuff, Juffin's little dog and my best friend, began to whimper sympathetically under the table. *Max worried. Bad*, the dog's compassionate Silent Speech reached me. *Only you love me and understand me*, I answered.

And I whined out loud, "Juffin, instead of compliments from you I would have preferred a piece of paper with the steps I should take carefully detailed and numbered, and with every action I should perform printed in bold block letters."

"You'd still get confused. Eat up, Max! It's the pinnacle of my accomplishments. For forty years already I've been dreaming of retiring and opening a restaurant. It would even outdo *The Glutton*."

"I don't doubt it. Only the King won't let you retire."

"That, of course, is only a matter of time."

"Does it ever occur to you that people might be afraid of eating at a restaurant like that? And what rumors will start up about the food you serve there? They'll say you slice up carcasses of rebel magicians and add them to all the dishes; that you siphon the blood of innocent children into the soup!"

"Good golly, boy, that's the best kind of advertisement! But innocent children—that's a new one. I'll have to start up a rumor about it."

I didn't expect to get anything more concrete out of him. There was one idea that dawned on me that night just before I left, though.

"I've decided to take Lonli-Lokli with me," I announced, shocked at my own genius. "That's possible, I hope?"

"Actually, the cell is just meant for one. Will you sleep locked in his embrace? Then again, with your notions of comfort—"

"No, you don't understand. I'm planning on shrinking him and hiding him in my fist. Sir Shurf taught me that himself a few days ago. He says I'm quite good at it. True, I haven't had the opportunity to use it on living people, yet," I added uncertainly. Suddenly my confidence dried up like a puddle in the desert.

"Objects or people, it works just the same," Juffin said. "It's a fine idea, Max. I told you that no one could handle this case better than you."

"That remains to be seen. Will Lonli-Lokli agree, do you think?"

"In the first place, Shurf will be flattered by your confidence in him. He takes you far more seriously than you might imagine. And, second, his opinion is beside the point. An order is an order. You'd better get used to it, by the way. You are second in command, and giving orders isn't a choice, but a duty."

"Sinning Magicians! If there's one thing I can't stand, it's giving orders," I said with a grimace.

"Is that so? And who frightened the junior clerks out of their wits with his menacing growls in our half of the House by the Bridge? And who nearly drove Boboota into a conniption fit? Don't sell yourself short, Sir Max. You'll make an excellent tyrant—one of those who kills with pleasure during palace coups."

"The first few times I had the opportunity to give orders, I must admit I enjoyed it," I said sheepishly. "Then I realized that it just wasn't for me. Even when I send the errand boy for kamra I feel that I cease to be that sweet, kind Max I've known all these years. So I feel like it's someone else who gives orders. And I can't say I like that someone else."

"How fastidious we are," Juffin said with a sniff. "Fine. Don't worry. I'll send for Shurf myself and explain everything to him. Any other requests?"

"None for now. I just know that I'll feel much safer in the company of Lonli-Lokli. Juffin, have I ever told you that I'm a rather cowardly fellow? Keep it in mind."

"If you can believe it, I'll feel safer myself," Juffin admitted. "Have I ever told you that I'm a sly old fox, but careful beyond measure? Learn the art of description, Max. I said almost the same thing you did—but how much more flattering to my pride!"

※

I left the hospitable home of my boss in a tumultuous state of mind. I told myself that if Juffin were foolish enough to entrust the operation to me, I wasn't going to answer for the consequences. But a newly awakened A-student syndrome prompted me to do everything to the max (as it were), or to die of shame. Where was it, this A-student syndrome, when I had been going to school, I'd like to know?

However much I grumbled, I knew all too well that when it was over I'd be happy to see the smile on Sir Juffin Hully's face, and to hear the proud exclamation to his protégé (an exclamation, which could buoy up someone who had just fallen off a mountain). "You see Max? I told you everything would work out! And you didn't believe me." I just had to reconcile myself to the thought that I would undertake any exploit to earn the indulgent smile of my mentor. That's how far things had come!

It was a cold night, one of the coldest that winter. In my homeland, the thermometer would probably have read around 32°F. The climate in Echo is more than moderate. There are neither hard frosts, nor heat waves—which, to be sure, is fine with me. The romance of a snowy winter never did capture my imagination. I can't stand going to work in the dusky morning twilight, shuffling along a dirty white sidewalk, feet completely benumbed in soaking boots, and contemplating how much a pair of new ones would cost. And in the heat of summer, I'm ready to sell my soul for a breath of fresh, cool air. So the mild climate of Echo suited me down to my toes. Well, at least something makes me happy, praise be the Magicians.

I was driving home, trying to think not about tomorrow, but about something else—namely, whether I would get the chance to see Lady Melamori in the morning. By that time, my interest in Lady Melamori had begun to assume dangerous proportions. The worst thing was that for the life of me I couldn't figure her out. Since the evening we had met the first time, she had looked at me with undisguised adoration—sometimes even with slight fear. But excessive admiration, as far as I've been able to judge, rarely gives rise to true intimacy. So I didn't know myself whether I should still have hope, or simply get a grip on myself before it was too late. Whether it was already too late—of this I wasn't sure.

Then several days ago she had thoroughly disarmed me by saying, "Come to my place this evening, Sir Max. You don't know where I live yet? It's very easy to find. I live next to the Quarter of Trysts. Amusing, isn't it?"

My head started spinning. I took a deep breath, scrubbed myself in the baths for about two hours, and donned the best looxi from my modest collection. I almost started powdering my nose, since here in Echo men are not ashamed to use makeup—at least on special occasions. But my conservative upbringing restrained me from taking that last fateful step.

I ordered Kurush to guard the office—that bird really beats all!

When I got to Melamori's house, though, I found the Minor Secret Investigative Force assembled nearly in its entirety. At first I couldn't get over my disappointment:

"My lady, you could have warned me that this would be business as usual. Do we not see enough of each other during working hours?"

When I'm upset I always grow tactless. Luckily, I didn't offend anyone.

"On the upside, I don't have Booboota here, Sir Max," the hostess boasted proudly. "What's more, he's not in any of the neighboring houses, either! Amazing, isn't it?"

"Ah, but that's a shame, my lady! Who am I to converse with? I was planning on talking with a competent expert about everything that floats in the swamps and outhouses. Let me just drop in on Lady Melamori, I thought. I'm sure General Booboota is already there."

I tried to make light of the situation. My colleagues were clearly amused by this. At last I cheered up, too—but there was no glimmer of a romance that would eventually burst into flame that night. The iconoclastic Lady Melamori flirted with Sir Melifaro and Sir Kofa, but to me she only threw tender glances from a distance of a dozen steps, no fewer.

I realized I was becoming despondent, and I tried to distract my thoughts from her. But how could I distract myself right there in her presence! The vagueness of our relationship tore me apart. If she had just told me where to go, everything would at least have become clear. No means no. The interested parties hang themselves in the outhouse; life goes on. But every time we met, she stuck to me like a leech, like a five-year old girl to a three-foot tall Mickey Mouse. She stood up on her tiptoes, batted her eyelashes in rapture, and all but called over all her girlfriends to take a look. My heart, obviously, melted from her attentions. And I sank in deeper and deeper . . .

Fie on you, devil! I awoke from these sad meditations when I noticed all at once that I had been sitting for a long time in my own dining room, chewing my food mechanically. My stomach groaned, letting me know that I had already gone overboard. Sinning Magicians, how much had I stuffed in? And why!

The bells were ringing in the city. Morning was breaking. Time for certain gentlemen Secret Investigators to extricate themselves from their armchairs and head for Xolomi prison to while away the hours in a cell where prisoners had a habit of dying.

I still didn't want to go to Xolomi—but not because prisoners kept dying in that cell. After all, that was their problem. I was embarrassed to admit it, but it was the very prospect of being locked up in jail that worried me. Until then, it had never entered my head that I might end up in prison. Especially here, in Echo! It was in the interests of my profession, of course—but, still. Frankly, my knees started shaking when I thought about myself in prisoner's garb, standing before the bars of a window.

By the way, are there any barred windows in Xolomi at all? Actually, why would you need bars, when the jailers have magic of every description and degree at their disposal?

Juffin had been very vague about the term that Lonli-Lokli and I were supposed to be serving. Come back once you've completed the mission—or something to that effect. What did that mean? If we don't complete the blasted thing we'll stay there forever? What a future!

It's one thing for me to be there, but why should poor Lonli-Lokli have to suffer? On the other hand, if they refuse to let us out, we'll tear the whole island of Xolomi to pieces! The very second that Sir Shurf starts missing his neglected wife, we'll start right in.

I had met Lonli-Lokli's wife at the party at Melamori's. Marvelous woman! Brilliant, beautiful, and very amusing. Her good nature probably determined her choice of her significant other. There is nothing more amusing than seeing the two of them together. She is diminutive and plump, and hardly reaches the belt of the spindly Sir Shurf. Moreover, with his lady at his side, Lonli-Lokli, always the butt of many jokes, is incapable of taking offense. She learned to pronounce his name only after many years of conjugal life.

They appeared to me to be very much still in love with each other. When Sir Shurf looked at his wife, his impenetrable gaze became very human. Well, it was a good thing that Lonli-Lokli had a happy family life. The personal welfare of a professional killer promotes social tranquility and equilibrium. After reaching that conclusion, I cheered up a bit.

I could have stayed in that armchair forever. Everyone wants to postpone unpleasant fuss and bother until tomorrow. But it was already tomorrow. It was time to archive the cozy, festive "yesterday" and forget about it. The short, warm "today" was still in the soft armchair, right under my backside. It couldn't last forever.

I stood up and started getting ready. Armstrong and Ella, my erstwhile kittens who by this time were no spring chickens, let me know, in no uncertain terms, that it was time for their breakfast. I was generous, even profligate, before my departure.

"From now on it will be our errand boy Urf who feeds you," I told the beasts, filling up their bowls to the brim. "They say he's a good person and grew up on a farm, where he also fed fat furry creatures like you. And I'll be back soon. I'm just going to jail for a while, and then I'll return." I laughed, aware of the flatness of my own joke.

Armstrong and Ella looked at me with their thoughtful blue eyes, as impenetrable and deep as Sir Juffin Hully's.

※

The morning was just as cold as the night had been. I walked to the House by the Bridge, appreciating every step along the way. The thought that I could expire prematurely like my predecessors at Xolomi honed all my senses and perceptions. Although . . . maybe it was just a chain of improbable coincidences? Could be!

But you can't fool the heart. My heart, at least. And slowly, but surely, it seemed to fill up with lead. What would happen when I showed up at Xolomi? I was getting more and more unnerved by the minute. Even the thought that the terrifying Lonli-Lokli would be hiding in my fist, that I was keeping him in reserve so that I could thumb my nose at danger, gave me only the slightest comfort. I still had to manage to let him out at the right moment, if need be.

Sir Shurf Lonli-Lokli was waiting for me in the Hall of Common Labor—unruffled, dependable, as always. He was noting down something in his "work diary" so as not to waste time. Looking at him, I livened up a bit.

"Are you ready to become my victim, Sir Shurf?"

"Victim? Sir Max, you clearly overestimate the significance of the impending event," he objected phlegmatically. "Believe me, I have no cause for alarm—and you even less."

"Well, thanks for the reassurance."

And I made a motion with my left hand, undetectable to the prying eyes of others. Lonli-Lokli disappeared. In theory, I knew that he hadn't disappeared, but was to be found between the thumb and the index finger of my hand. But this useful knowledge somehow didn't fit into my head.

"Dandy, Mr. Nightmare!" Melifaro beamed, emerging from his

office. "Tell me, might you not be persuaded to keep him there for the next two hundred years or so?"

"Lady Lonli-Lokli would object, and I wouldn't want to grieve her," I replied, smiling. "And why are you here so early?"

"Juffin woke me up. Sent me a message that he wouldn't be here before midday. He ordered me to see you off. He wants me dead! Usually he's here at the crack of dawn, but today . . . Well, there you are."

"He's hiding from me," I informed him proudly.

"From you? You're making progress! To my knowledge (and I do know something about the history of the Unified Kingdom), Juffin Hully hasn't hidden from anyone for the past one hundred years. Well, in the Epoch of Orders there was a case—and it wasn't the only one. Then again, everyone ran from each other during the Epoch of Orders. How did you scare him?" asked Melifaro and sat down in front of me.

"Give me some kamra and I'll tell you," I said, crossing my feet and placing them carefully on the table. It's frightening to think of the number of dumb movies that inspired me to assume this pose. "You're here to see me off, so you must see to it that I leave here happy. Thus, you must bribe me with every possible means at your disposal."

"Well, that's the limit! Bribing a jailbird!" Melifaro grumbled. "Fine. Take advantage of my generosity." He sauntered into the office and brought out a jug of kamra and two mugs of completely improbable dimensions.

"So why is our 'Sir Venerable Head' running away from you?"

"I ask too many questions. Actually, that's why he decided to stick me in Xolomi."

"Oh, is that all? Questions! And here I was thinking that yesterday you tried to get him drunk on Elixir of Horse Dung, the national drink of your Barren Lands."

"That actually did happen," I admitted. "But Juffin said that his Diurnal Backside usually does the dirty work. Thanks for reminding me—I'll have to treat you to some!"

"No thanks!" Melifaro screwed up his face in anxious trepidation, and he shot into his office like a bullet. Several times he peeped out timidly; then the joke grew stale, and he returned.

I killed another half-hour in this pleasant manner. Lady Melamori, for whose sake I was dragging it out, didn't appear.

Finally, I got behind the wheel of the amobiler and set off for Xolomi to turn myself in.

❀

"I see you as though in a waking dream!" The senior commander of Xolomi covered his eyes respectfully, in the ritual of a first meeting. "I'm happy to speak my name: Sir Marunarx Antarop."

I introduced myself, and they led me off to be served breakfast.

"You're so skinny, Sir Max! They really work you hard in the Secret Investigative Force. I know all about it! You need to eat more!" Sir Marunarx exclaimed, refilling my plate over and over again. "Never mind. You'll fill out here with us, I promise you that!"

The sumptuous breakfast was suspiciously reminiscent of a formal banquet. The commander fussed over me like a doting uncle. I thought I was going to prison, but it looked like I had ended up in a resort. And so, it turned out, I had.

"Whew, I've already filled out! By about ten pounds," I said an hour later. "Thank you, Sir Marunarx. I should go to the cell now, I suppose. That's why I came, after all."

"I'm so sorry, Sir Max! I'm afraid it will be uncomfortable for you there! But Sir Hully requested that I put you not in the guest quarter, but in a prison cell. What do you think—could it have been a joke?"

"You never know with him," I laughed. "No, Sir Marunarx, I'm really supposed to go to the cell. No one has died in your guest quarters, I hope?"

"I understand," the old man said with a sigh. "Well, let's go then. By the way, Sir Max, you know that when you're in the cell you can't use Silent Speech? I can't change that for you, I'm afraid. The prison is built that way. You know yourself, Xolomi is a magical place. It's not for us, the employees, to decide what is permitted here and what isn't."

"Yes, that's what I've been told."

"So if you need to get in touch with Sir Hully or anyone else, tell the guards that you wish to take a walk, and they'll bring you to me, at any time of day or night. Here you can do anything your heart desires. My people have already been informed about you, of course."

"Excellent!" I nodded. "And now, arrest me, please!"

❀

Cell No. 5-Ow-Nox seemed to be quite a cozy little place. And, by the way, in my homeland you'd have to plunk down several suitcases of greenbacks for a pad like this! But for a native of Echo, it would probably be difficult to reconcile oneself to such cramped quarters—only three "small" (by local standards, miniscule; by ours, enormous) rooms, all on one floor. And also a bathroom with a toilet one floor below, as is the custom here. In the bathroom there were only three tubs, the same number I had at home. Now I began to understand why my landlord had been unable to find a tenant for so long. When I got home, I'd have him put in a fourth tub. I can't live like I'm in prison!

But praise be the Magicians I had still not completely adapted to local customs, so the modest prison cell seemed to me to be the height of luxury. A half-hour later I realized I had already gotten used to being there.

Actually, I get used to things very quickly. If I move my belongings to a new home in the morning, by evening I feel I have lived there my whole life. It even occurred to me that in a few days I'd grow so used to Xolomi that I'd "remember" why they had thrown me in prison. And then I'd repent, and try to reform with all my might!

❀

And so I sat in my cell and gazed at the ceiling. The marvelous Lonli-Lokli lived some sort of ineffable life between my thumb and the index finger of my left hand. I was terribly curious—what was he feeling about all of this? In any case, the fellow had taken his "work diary" with him. How he could comfortably pass the time away with that notebook is as much a mystery to me as it is to you.

Finally, I decided it was time to go to sleep. I'd have to rest, since the most interesting things would happen at night, I assumed, if they were to happen at all.

I was still afraid that nothing untoward would happen. I wondered how much time I would have to spend in Xolomi before I realized that seven deaths in the space of three years was very sad and awkward, if not idiotic—but finally, that it was just a coincidence after all. Would I be here a year? Two? More? Well, never mind. The gentlemen Secret Investigators would be able to survive for about twelve days without us, after which they'd be the ones raising hue and cry to get us released themselves. Sir Juffin would no doubt be the first to decide that our business trip had dragged on too long.

I slept remarkably well. When I woke up, it was already dark. I received a prisoner's meal, which tasted curiously like the recent festive breakfast. Why do Juffin and I always eat at the *Glutton Bunba*? The food is great there, of course, but prison fare seemed to be more refined. We'd have to introduce the tradition of carousing at Xolomi: purely out of professional considerations, of course. Or perhaps we could spend Days of Freedom from Care on the premises—it's quiet, cozy, and there's nobody to bother you.

Night was coming on. So as not to waste precious time, I tried to do what I truly know how to do well (and it wasn't much): to chat with the objects around me, and to see that part of the past that they "remembered."

It was hopeless. All the prison flotsam and jetsam that surrounded me answered my appeals with surging waves of fear. We had seen that before!—in Makluk's bedchamber, where the little balsam box had sent out the same currents of terror. There was no doubt about it. I had stumbled upon a real story, not a chain of awkward coincidences.

Just then a guard appeared to "convoy" me to a business meeting. One of my guards, by the name of Xaned Janira, had been dying to meet me since morning, but the good commander had tried to preserve my peace and quiet, and ordered him to wait until I woke up.

Mr. Janira bears the title of Master Comforter of Sufferers. As I came to understand it, he was a sort of psychotherapist. He visits the prisoners regularly, asks them how they slept, what they are anxious or worried about, and what messages they want to send home. In Echo, prisoners are treated very humanely. It is thought that if a person has landed in Xolomi, he has no farther to fall, and to subject a prisoner to further discomfort and inconvenience is senseless and cruel. The psychological and emotional comfort of a prisoner is a matter of great concern, and this is, of course, only proper.

"I thought you'd be interested, Sir Max, in some information I possess," Xaned Janira said, after the ritual greeting was over.

He turned out to be an exceedingly youthful fellow, with a round face and a melodic voice, and narrow green eyes that settled on me with a penetrating gaze.

"Strange things have been happening here recently," he said. "I suppose this is the reason for your stay. It seemed only right that before investigations get underway you should hear me out. I've been waiting all day for you to call me, but I finally could wait no longer. At the risk of being importunate, I decided to take the initiative."

"I ate too much for breakfast, Sir Janira! So much that I just couldn't think straight," I said, trying to excuse my behavior. "I should have turned to you as soon as I crossed the threshold, but I didn't sleep very well last night, and I just collapsed in my cell right after breakfast. Forgive me. Thank you for inviting me to talk with you."

From the expression on Xaned Janira's face, I understood that at that moment he was prepared to go through hell and high water for me.

I don't know what it was in me that won him over—the respectful "sir," a form of address not warranted by the station of junior psychotherapist, or my willingness to admit my mistakes. Somehow or other, though, I had traversed the path to his heart without much trouble.

"Not at all, Sir Max! You had every right to rest before getting down to work. I just wanted to explain to you the reasons for my own persistence—I thought I might be able to assist you. Maybe my information will prove useless, but . . . well, just listen to what I have to say, and then you decide. Two days ago the prisoners from cells 5-Soya-Ra, 5-Tot-Xun, and 5-Sha-Pui, which are adjacent to cell 5-Ow-Nox, complained to me about bad dreams. Strangely enough, the content of all their dreams was very similar."

"I can only sympathize with them, poor fellows! And what did they dream?"

"All three of them dreamed about a 'small, transparent man,' as they described it. He came out of the wall, and they all experienced inconceivable horror. From then on their versions of the dreams diverged. Malesh Patu claims that the transparent man wanted to poke his eyes out, and Sir Alarak Vass complained that he 'was groping for his heart.' The third case is rather amusing," Janira related with downcast eyes. "The prisoner insists that he tried to plug up his backside. His biggest fear is that his next dream will see the attempt succeed."

"Goodness! I wouldn't want to be in his place."

It sounded to me as though the prisoners' nightmares had been an eccentric combination of real dangers and individual phobias. This transparent fellow had most likely done something wicked to all of them, but each of them had a personal interpretation of the events. That made sense. What didn't make sense was where this creature who haunted all their dreams had come from in the first place. Sorcery was not supposed to be possible in Xolomi; that's why it had become a prison for those who had a penchant for forbidden magic.

"How is their overall health?" I asked. "Have you shown them to the wiseman?"

"Yes, of course. We cannot just ignore complaints like that, all the more since the trouble began simultaneously with three prisoners. These gentlemen hadn't been acquainted before, and here in Xolomi, you understand, they couldn't organize any kind of conspiracy. And why should they? It turns out that the health of all three of them is hardly anything to brag about, but the organs that the transparent 'dream man' allegedly targeted are in perfect condition."

I noted with pleasure that my theory about the influence of personal phobias on the interpretation of nightmares wasn't so far from the mark. Not bad for a dilettante like myself.

"What could be wrong with them, then?"

"All three of them are gradually losing the Spark," Janira said in a portentous whisper. Then he went quiet, waiting for the significance of what he had just said to sink in.

I let out a low whistle. To lose the Spark means to suddenly lose the life force, becoming so weak that death comes like sleep after a hard day, when you cannot resist it and don't even want to. According to my competent colleagues, this mysterious condition is the most dangerous thing that can befall a person born in this World.

"What's strange is that these unfortunates are getting weaker only gradually, whereas a person usually loses the Spark suddenly, without any alarming symptoms," said Janira. "In spite of that, our wisemen are absolutely sure of the diagnosis. They say that they can still save them, but medicines don't seem to be helping."

"Well, why don't you try this: move the poor souls to other cells—the farther from cell 5-Ow-Nox the better—and let their cells remain empty until I can discover the cause of this misfortune. You can manage that, I hope?"

"Yes, certainly," said the Comforter of Sufferers, nodding. Then he added apprehensively, "Are you certain it will help?"

"Almost certain. But that's always how it is. I can never be completely sure of anything. In any case, give it a try. And do it right now. We may still be able to save them. I don't know what they did before that landed them in Xolomi, but not a single person deserves such a terrible punishment as sleep filled with nightmares. I'm speaking as a longtime expert in this field."

"Do you know how to prevent nightmares, Sir Max?"

"I do," I said, and grinned. "My own, anyway."

❧

I went back to my cell. It looks like I'll have my fill of bad dreams here, I mumbled to myself.

I had hardly returned to my senses after the nightmares from the house next door had paid a call, when I was treated to another round in Xolomi, where prisoners are tormented by bad dreams. A plugged up backside, for instance . . .

Nevertheless, I had slept excellently during the day myself. Perhaps it was *because* it had really been daytime? The heavy cell door closed behind me and . . . disappeared. Here in Xolomi every door exists only for the person in the corridor. From the vantage point of the prisoner, it isn't there at all. Amazing!

Now I was burning with impatience. Would the "transparent man" appear tonight—and what would he do if I didn't fall asleep? I was absolutely sure that I wouldn't. I had slept too soundly and well during the day. What would you have done?

I began waiting for events to unfold, which, in their turn, they didn't exactly hasten to do. The night brought no answers to my questions. On the other hand, it was generous with strange experiences and sensations.

I felt neither fear nor anxiety, but I constantly sensed I was being scrutinized by somebody's gaze. And it was so intense it tickled. The tickling irritated me like a caterpillar that had crawled under the covers. I grumbled and scratched and ran to take a bath three times—but it was no use.

At dawn, everything stopped, and I tumbled into sleep. During the night, however, I had a bright idea—though putting it into practice could wait until dinner. (Putting things off until later is a hobby of mine. From morning to evening all I do is put things off.)

I woke up from the rumble of the cell door. My food was brought in to me. Tasting the cheese soup, I started seriously contemplating what kind of crime against the state I should commit. Being held captive for twenty years in these conditions—not a single Royal Honor could compete with "punishment" like this!

When I had finished my soup, I asked to go for a "walk" to Mr. Commander's office. The time had come to consult Juffin. That night I had realized that the part of the story of Cell No. 5-Ow-Nox I knew about only went back to the first of the seven deaths. Since then three years had passed. What had happened there before? Who had been kept in the cell? That was what I meant to find out. In Echo you have to be on top of things like that. I wouldn't have been at all surprised to find out that a few thousand years ago, some shady Grand Magician or other had been held here, and that today's misfortunes were a logical consequence of that.

I didn't doubt that Sir Juffin knew every detail of the history of this little place. But in sending me to Xolomi he kept as quiet as a fish— either out of perversity, or because he was just waiting for me to ask the right questions. (In the interests of professional training, of course!)

But look at me! Instead of pedantically collecting information, I wasted time and energy on gathering personal amorous experience. It's my own fault! I concluded, and settled myself more comfortably in the commander's chair. After beating myself up like this for a while, I sent a call to Juffin.

Now tell me how it all started, I demanded. *What happened here before the 114th day of the 112th year? One of your mutinous Grand Magicians was held in the cell, I'm guessing?*

Very good, Max! Juffin was ecstatic about my knack for putting two and two together.

I have no idea why you're praising me, I grumbled. *Well, yes, I asked the question that I should have started with only today, and not a year later. For an idiot like me, that's probably an achievement.*

I have any number of acquaintances who would have needed not one, but two hundred years, if they needed a day. You're angry at me; but you're even angrier at yourself. But I meant it when I said "very good."

I don't recognize you, Juffin. Such compliments! You must miss me or something.

I had already forgiven him, of course. I was as happy as a pig in a puddle. Praising me is definitely the right strategy. Someone who praises me in good conscience can twist me around any number of little fingers.

❄

In any case, I received an exhaustive answer to my question, and a half hour later I was home. In Cell No. 5-Ow-Nox, that is. I sat sprawled out in a soft arrestee's chair. I was trying to digest the information I had received. Naturally, you couldn't get around the requisite crazy Magician—that was as clear as day. Maxlilgl Annox, Grand Magician of the Order of the Sepulchral Dog, and one of the fiercest opponents of the reform, served a prison term in Xolomi during the height of the Troubled Times. According to Juffin, the combined efforts of a dozen of the best practitioners of the Order of the Seven-Leaf Clover were needed to imprison his person, remarkable in all respects. At the same time, even the Grand Magicians of other Orders, who had long ago lost any capacity for fear, trembled before him.

He wasn't such a madman, though, this head of the Order of the Sepulchral Dog. Of course, he had traveled a strange and winding road. But if you believed the historical chronicles, which I devoured by the dozens in my spare time, you'd discover that few of the Grand Magicians were guilty of banality and lack of imagination in their chosen paths.

And so, Mister Annox was deeply preoccupied with the problem of life after death. Not only there, where I was born, but here in the World, as well, no one really knows the answer to the question of what awaits us after death. There are myriad hypotheses—murky, frightening, and seductive—but not a single one of them has much value for someone who isn't inclined to take a stranger's word on faith alone.

Of course, the interest in immortality wasn't solely theoretical for the prisoner of Cell No. 5-Ow-Nox. Those Magicians of yore, one must realize, were serious fellows and didn't waste their precious time.

As far as I could understand, Sir Annox expended unimaginable effort trying to continue ordinary earthly existence, even after death, in the human body so dear to his heart. In simple terms, he wanted to be resurrected. I didn't doubt that this old geezer had discovered a sneaky way of returning to the land of the living. But then he died. In this very Cell No. 5-Ow-Nox.

The victors never meant to kill him. It seems they very reluctantly killed their enemies, supposing that every death was an irreversible event. And the Order of the Seven-Leaf Clover maintains the belief that an irreversible event should occur as seldom as possible. This so that the World can become stronger—or something like that . . . I hadn't yet had time to figure out all the fine points of the local eschatology.

Nevertheless, the Grand Magician Maxlilgl Annox had died. It wasn't a suicide in the ordinary sense of the word; I think this death was some sort of "laboratory experiment" essential to his research.

The fact that the walls of Xolomi were the most impenetrable barrier for magic of any degree did not infuse me with optimism. On the contrary, it forced me to think that the posthumous existence of Sir Annox was limited to the walls of his cell. It was evident that proximity to the dead Magician didn't have a beneficial effect on his latter-day cellmates. Being condemned to life in this cell was a kind of death sentence. That was no good, I decided. Unjust. In this sense, prisoners are far more vulnerable than ordinary citizens. They can't change their place of domicile, even when they feel it is urgent to do so. I wouldn't want to be in their place . . . but, in fact, I already was.

I whiled away the night reading the next volume of Manga Melifaro's *Encyclopedia,* which I was able to find, to my delight, in the prison library. Nothing supernatural happened, except that I again felt someone's attentive eyes prickling me. They were even more ticklish this night than they had been the night before. Several times I heard a quiet, dry coughing, which seemed more like an auditory hallucination than the real thing.

Toward morning I got another strange sensation—I felt as if my body hardened like the shell of a nut. So much so that the tickling, to which I was already accustomed, felt not like something touching my skin, but like a slight trembling of the air around me. This wasn't very pleasant, but I felt that the invisible being who monitored my every move all night long was even less pleased. His displeasure translated itself in part to me. Soon I would start berating myself for not letting the possessor of the powerful gaze tickle me to his heart's content. What spiritual callousness and disrespect for a stranger's desires, I would say to myself in reproach!

I couldn't explain these events with any originality. Maybe I'm just imagining it? Or maybe Juffin put a protective spell on me, without my knowing it? He very well could have. And what if the true explanation was that I was a creature from another World—almost like a space alien?

I was so tired from all these conjectures that I went to sleep before dawn. I wonder how poor Lonli-Lokli is spending his time, I thought when I was dozing off. He's probably bored. And hungry. What a jam he's in!

※

But I had no opportunity to be bored. I had no opportunity to sleep, either. I woke up at noon from the familiar tickling sensation. I was amazed. Was this creature, whoever he might be, really able to operate during the day? On the other hand, why not? All of the most terrible things I had witnessed during my sojourn in Echo had happened in broad daylight. It's possible that assuming nightmares lie in wait for us only at night is the most foolish of superstitions, born in that long-distant past when our forebears finally lost the ability to see in the dark.

I washed myself, drank a mug of kamra, and began to go over things in my mind. My predecessors in the cell had died only at night. A coincidence? Or was the reason much simpler—they died at night because they slept at night, like all normal people? And because of me the local ghouls had had to change their schedule? Questions, questions, and no answers.

But what unnerved me most of all was my own equanimity. For some reason, I was still not afraid of anything. Not of what had already happened, not of what, theoretically, could happen still. Somehow I had become certain that nothing bad would ever happen to me. Not here, nor in any other place. Never. Bravery verging on lunacy. Until recently I had never suffered from such a syndrome. Maybe the secret of my courage was the trick up my sleeve—or at the end of my fingertips: the well-concealed Sir Lonli-Lokli. But maybe the person whose identity I was interested in discovering derived some advantage from dealing with a myopic daredevil? And he was boosting my mood, unbeknown to me?

For whatever reason, I didn't fall asleep again that day. Until twilight, I kept pouring myself mugs of kamra, and I read my beloved *Encyclopedia*, which made me smarter with every line.

Then I came to understand that events were unfolding precisely in the tradition of fairy tales. The first and second nights I was just teased mildly. Predictably, the real horror was postponed until the "fateful" third night.

When dusk set in, I was overcome by a heavy somnolence. This was more than strange, since I usually experience an excess of liveliness and energy at that time, regardless of how I spent the day.

Now, though, I had to stave off sleep, and I didn't manage very well. I tried to spook myself by summoning up the lurid horrors that lay in wait for me on the far side of my closed eyelids. No use. Even thinking about the unprecedented shame that would cover me if I failed didn't work. Melifaro's stinging remarks, Juffin's consoling gestures, and (the apotheosis) Lady Melamori's contemptuously pursed lips. Even that didn't help. A blissful drowsiness enveloped me like a downy pillow, the weapon of choice of a gentle strangler. I was just one wink away from the land of nod.

A bottle of Elixir of Kaxar saved me from slumber. It was pure luck that I had decided to bring it with me. I had to drink quite a bit. But I'm not complaining—Elixir of Kaxar is not only a powerful tonic, but darned tasty, too.

Afterward, Juffin explained that drinking the elixir galvanized the force into action. Apparently, the mysterious being decided that if I was using magic only of the eighth degree for self-defense, I wasn't a force to contend with. My seeming helplessness forced it to take the most thoughtless course of action in all its strange career.

I didn't want to argue with Juffin; all the same, it seemed to me that this malevolent chap, fairly unhinged by the loneliness of his transparent existence, just couldn't wait anymore. It wasn't a matter of logic at all. The dead Magician wanted to take my life. He was compelled to try—the sooner, the better. Most likely, my "Spark," or whatever it is, was just the amount or intensity he needed. He had been moving toward his goal for so long already! Drop by drop he had absorbed the strength of those who had ended up in that cell. The time came when Maxlilgl Annox was strong enough to take the first life of another—a life he needed to redeem his own, partly spent, life. Then he was able to claim another, and another . . .

The last portion made the ghost of the Grand Magician so powerful that he was able to invade the dreams of the inhabitants of the neighboring cells, who were soundly protected by impenetrable walls (for magic of the living, but not for him—the dead). He wanted just one thing: to take as many lives as he needed so that he could resurrect himself once and for all. He was already on the threshold of completing this experiment that lasted a lifetime, with a death thrown into the bargain. He needed only a final gulp of the mysterious and precious substance that goes by the name of the Spark. And for the third night in a row, his tantalizing "gulp" had been almost within his grasp—but wouldn't fall asleep. Naturally, the old geezer tried to go for broke. I would no doubt have done the same if I had been in his shoes.

What's more, no matter what Sir Juffin Hully said, my opponent was very close to getting what he wanted. Much too close for comfort!

※

When the silhouette of the intruder materialized like a shadow in the corner of my prison boudoir, I froze in horror. Of course, I had enough information at my disposal to prepare myself for this eventuality. But I wasn't ready. I was completely unnerved.

To be absolutely honest, I was terrified. And I didn't know how to bring myself to my senses, even though the appearance of the intruder was more funny than fearsome. The ghost of the Grand Magician was exceedingly small in stature. This was the result of his disproportionate physique—an enormous head; a powerful, muscular torso; and stumpy little legs with feet as small as a child's.

A comical figure, to be sure; but the brown, wrinkled face of the intruder made an entirely different impression. He had huge blue eyes, a high forehead, and the finely chiseled nose and nostrils of a predator. His long hair, and a beard of the same length, branched out in a multitude of tiny braids—most likely, an ancient fashion. Well, it's hard to keep up with the trends from a prison cell. Especially for a ghost, I thought. This observation was very much in my style, and it suggested that things weren't really so bad.

Having mastered my fear, though, I realized that something worse was happening. I was paralyzed. I couldn't budge. I stood there gazing dully at the reluctant recluse—I was lucky I didn't fall flat on my face. Do something, you moron! shouted the clever little fellow inside me. Unfortunately, he didn't have much influence over the rest of me. Do something already! This is *for real!* Move it!

Nothing helped.

I knew exactly what I needed to do: free Lonli-Lokli with a few energetic shakes of my hand. But even this rudimentary action was too much for me—this fatal thumbing my nose, so to speak, at the night visitor. I was helpless in this situation. It was no longer up to me. I realized that I was goner.

"Your name is Perset. You are a piece of life. I've been looking for you," the ghost whispered. "I have come to you down a long road—one end was prison, the other the grave. And only the wind cried 'Oooooooh!'; but still I came."

He came, you understand. I'd rather he not speak at all, this unsung symbolist poet. A person who burdened his interlocutor with such trite and highfalutin turns of phrase upon first meeting was absurd. I decided to refuse the burden. Besides, I had written better dialogs when I was eighteen. I didn't know how, but I was determined to get the better of him.

At that moment, something utterly bizarre began happening to me. I felt that I was starting to "harden" again. It seemed to me that I had turned into a small, hard apple—one of those that only a seven-year-old boy can munch on (since boys that age are known to chew on everything that comes their way).

Then I had a completely mad thought—I began thinking that there was no way a grownup man like my opponent was going to munch on the hard, bitter apple that I had somehow become. This delirious notion seemed to me to be so self-evident that there was no way around it. And this restored my belief in my own powers. To be honest, I had completely forgotten about my human nature and about the human problems that beset me. We sour green apples live our own inscrutable, carefree lives . . .

My guest began to grimace. He wore the expression of a person who has been wandering around for the last twenty-four hours with a mouthful of vinegar and unripe persimmon. The ancient fellow grew quite upset—and at that very moment the little green apple became a person again. And the person acquired the ability to act. He gave his left hand a good shake—a single deft motion was all it took. In the middle of the prison cell stood Sir Lonli-Lokli.

"You brought Thumbkins!" Maxlilgl cried with indignation.

It was as if we had agreed on the rules of battle beforehand, and I had breached the hypothetical contract.

"You're not Perset!" the ghost added vehemently. Evidently, he was still hoping that I would feel ashamed of my behavior and stuff Sir Shurf back in the closet. I think Sir Annox had become considerably softer over the past years of associating only with defenseless, frightened inmates.

"Don't 'Perset' me!" I growled.

The ghost's confusion was palpable. Sir Shurf needed time to peel off his protective gloves, covered with runes. While the dead Magician and I were squaring off, Lonli-Lokli managed to carry out the necessary preparations. The brilliant light from his death-dealing hands illuminated the cell walls, and life seemed all of a sudden to be a devilishly simple and precious matter. A story with an untold number of happy endings—take your pick.

I didn't even suspect that my chances for staying alive were still approaching zero.

It was my own fault, of course. I had never had to deal with retired Grand Magicians. I foolishly assumed that there was no hurry in killing him. My vanity demanded that I deliver this mistake of nature to the House by the Bridge and drop it screaming and kicking at Sir Juffin's feet. How I was going to capture a ghost I had no idea. But then again, I had had a miserable, third-rate education. I didn't have classes in the foundations of metaphysics, either in high school — which I got through on a wing and prayer—or in college, from which I was unceremoniously expelled. I shared my half-baked thoughts on the matter with my colleague—but Sir Shurf is the most disciplined creature in the universe. As he saw it, I was the leader of the operation. Consequently, my orders had to be summarily carried out. Even the most half-baked ones.

Lonli-Lokli's paralyzing right hand did not achieve the desired effect. Instead of freezing submissively to the spot, the ghost began to increase in size, threatening to assume gigantic proportions. At the same time, he became increasingly transparent. It all happened so quickly that within the fraction of a second his indistinct head was hovering somewhere up near the ceiling.

"Stupid Thumbkins!" Maxlilgl Annox screeched. "He knows not how to kill! Begone, Thumbkins!"

And without paying any more heed to Lonli-Lokli, the thick mist, which by now had almost lost its human form, lunged at me. It managed to touch me—a cold, damp, sticky pudding—that's what it felt like. The touch left a bitter aftertaste in my mouth, for some reason, and the cold pain that shot through my body was such that I still can't imagine how I survived it.

I didn't even lose consciousness. Instead, I screamed at the top of my lungs:

"Liquidate him!"

Sinning Magicians! Where was my head?

As though from a great distance, I watched Lonli-Lokli join his remarkable hands together and cross his forefingers. This promising gesture had no visible consequences, though. Another tormenting second passed. I didn't understand a thing. Why didn't Shurf kill him? The human pudding was already thickening around me.

And then another improbable thing happened. It was like the icing on the cake of this bewitched night. The shining fingers of Lonli-Lokli drew the outline of a wondrous curve in the darkness, and a waterfall came crashing down on us. Tons of cold water swallowed up the transparent silhouette. I still didn't understand what was happening, but I turned my face to the refreshing streams of water. A good wash was surprisingly welcome right then.

Our opponent, however, turned out to have a very tenacious vitality. Of course, the water wasn't able to do serious harm to him, although it did engender another metamorphosis. After his bath, the ghost began shrinking at an alarming rate. As huge and transparent as he had just been, he now became tiny and dense.

My insights into astronomy are catastrophically limited. I don't even know what super-dense heavenly bodies are called. That they are "dwarves" I know for certain. But whether they're "white," or "black" I have no clue. Our dwarf was, in any case, white, a miniscule homunculus, shining with the same blinding whiteness as Lonli-Lokli's hands reaching out for him. In spite of his miniature stature, he looked very threatening.

"You were mistaken, Sir Max," my imposing partner remarked evenly. "Water can't harm him."

"I, mistaken?! Wherever did you get the idea that water would do the trick?!"

"But you yourself told me to liquify him!"

"Sinning Magicians, Shurf! *Liquidate*, not liquify! It means to kill! And the sooner the bet—"

I broke off in mid-sentence. Suddenly I couldn't go on. I wasn't up to talking anymore. The tiny creature glittered in the air, very close to my face. It was muttering something. The bastard's putting a spell on me, I thought indifferently. I didn't have the strength to resist him . . .

🌀

. . . I was blinded by the bright light of the sun. I was standing beneath the spreading branches of a tree, and an unkempt girl, milky-white, as short in stature as Sir Maxlilgl Annox, was offering me an apricot. "Accept the gift of a fairy, Perset!" Why, I don't know myself, but I took it and bit into it. The fruit was worm-ridden. A pale little caterpillar slipped into my wide-open mouth and dove into the tender depths of my gullet. I felt its sharp jaws pierce the sensitive membranes. Poison began coursing through my body, filling me with weak nausea. I should probably have died of pain and disgust, but a blinding hatred filled me, and I began to shout. I shouted so violently and fiercely that it set a rushing wind in motion. Leaves, scorched dry, began falling from the tree, and the milk-white girl, her face distorted from horror, slithered through the withered grass, hissing like a viper. Finally, I spit out the poisonous caterpillar at the feet of Lonli-Lokli, who wasn't in that garden at all; and then the glaring light began to subside.

🌀

What I really admire in our Master Who Snuffs Out Unnecessary Lives is his unflappability. He won't be caught out! While I was wandering through the sunny fields of my nightmare, the guy did what had to be done. He finally put his death-dealing left hand into action— something he should have done straight off. In such cases, everything goes off without a hitch. Whether you're a human being, or a ghost, or a Magician-knows-what, death will be easy and instantaneous.

Then this remarkable fellow pulled on his protective gloves, and with the dexterity of a professional nurse poured the remains of the Elixir of Kaxar into my mouth.

"It's very helpful in cases like this, Max, so drink up. I regret that I didn't understand your order properly. I concluded that you were talking about a new method of destruction by water. It cost me considerable effort to get him wet. Here in Xolomi, even I have a hard time working wonders—although Sir Juffin, naturally, gave me special training."

From the Elixir of Kaxar I not only came to, I also cheered up—a clear sign of an overdose.

"A method of destruction by water—Sinning Magicians! How could that be expected to work? Why water? You should have just pissed on him! That would have killed him, I'm sure! Loki, have you never tried pissing on a ghost?"

"Sir Max," my savior protested in an injured tone, "my name is not Loki, but Lonli-Lokli. Until now you have always managed to pronounce it correctly. I would hope that the ability will return to you in the near future."

The poor chap had decided, apparently, that I was as big a dunderhead as Melifaro.

"That was no slip of the tongue, Sir Shurf. I was simply reminded of a menacing god whose name resembles yours. Please don't take offense, my friend."

"I've never heard of a god by the name of Loki," he admitted in surprise. "Do your fellow tribespeople worship him?"

"Some of them, anyway," I didn't so much as raise an eyebrow. "We of the Barren Lands have a multitude of divinities, you know. Everyone believes whatever he wants to. Every second nomad is a high priest. And some chaps, myself included, don't believe in anything in particular, but take a lively interest in everything."

"It isn't secret knowledge, is it?" Lonli-Lokli inquired. "You could enlighten me about these matters?"

"Yes, I can," I nodded resolutely. "For you—I'd do anything."

For the next hour and a half, over the cold remains of the excellent prison kamra, I waxed eloquent on the subject of Scandinavian mythology, passing it off as legend of the Barren Lands.

I must give Sir Shurf his due—the Scandinavian epic was very much to his liking. He especially liked Odin, the chief of the gods and dead heroes, who brought the honey of poetry to earth. The Master Who Snuffs Out Unnecessary Lives viewed poetry with profound reverence, if not outright trepidation.

Inspired either by the unexpectedness of our shared literary passions or by overindulgence in Elixir of Kaxar, I patted my imposing colleague on the back. I had forgotten that in the Unified Kingdom this gesture is only allowed to close friends. Luckily for me, Sir Shurf didn't object to this official acknowledgment of our newly established friendly footing. Indeed, he seemed very flattered.

Then it occurred to me that I had no idea what obligations my status as close friend of Sir Lonli-Lokli would entail. Here in Echo there must be myriad peculiar rites and customs surrounding true friendship. I decided I'd have to consult Juffin about it. Let him teach me how to be a friend here. And I'd write it down in my notebook and try to check every move I made against it. I just hoped that in the next hour and a half I wouldn't offend him; that would be just like me.

Finally we finished our divinity tutorial and began sending signals to the world outside the cell. We were immediately released and led to the commander's office. They fed us an excellent breakfast and plied us with fresh, hot kamra. It was wonderful. When I began to feel quite chipper again, I hastened to relieve my curiosity.

"Tell me, Shurf. How did you pass the time when you were small? I'm not asking about your childhood, of course. I mean when you were hidden from prying eyes in my tightly clenched fist."

"Time?" Lonli-Lokli asked with a shrug. "Time, Sir Max, passed as it always does. During these few hours I even managed to work up an appetite."

"What? Few hours!"

"Do you mean to say that I miscalculated?"

"We've spent three days and nights here!" I exclaimed.

"A curious effect," Lonli-Lokli concluded impassively. "But it's for the better. Three days and nights is too long an interval to go without sandwiches. One might call it a lucky thing that my temporal perception was distorted."

I would have liked to delve into many more details about his existence in the palm of my hand, but Sir Shurf said that in matters like this you have to take it as it comes—you can't learn about it secondhand. Then he generously offered to give me the experience firsthand—but I decided I'd had enough excitement for one day, and tactfully changed the subject.

✹

After breakfast, we took our leave of the hospitable Sir Marunarx. It was time to head back to the House by the Bridge. I felt superb—though my body felt a bit weightless under the effects of the outsize portion of Elixir of Kaxar. I was tempted to fill my pockets with rocks to prevent inopportune levitation.

"I really don't think you should sit behind the levers, Max," Lonli-Lokli announced, getting into the amobiler. "You are the best driver I know, but even in former times, when it was possible to buy Elixir of Kaxar in any store, driving the amobiler in such a condition was strictly prohibited."

I had to reconcile myself to it.

"Nevertheless, you Borderland dwellers are marvelous creatures," said Lonli-Lonkli, driving onto the wooden planks of the ferry that traveled between the island of Xolomi and the Old City. "I must admit that I can't quite put my finger on what it is that distinguishes you, but you are not at all like other strangers. Unfortunately, I am a poor theoretician." With these words, the fellow buried his nose in his famous "work diary"—to register his fresh impressions, I could only suppose.

"What do you mean by that, Shurf?" I asked with unfeigned interest.

"Don't take offense, Sir Max. It's just that some are of the opinion that Elixir of Kaxar, like ordinary cheering beverages, acts as a depressant on the psychological state of so-called barbarians—please forgive the crudeness of the term. Some wisemen even claim that Elixir of Kaxar endangers the mental balance of your countrymen. It is thought that only natives of Uguland can cope with the effects of magic drinks. But you don't seem to suffer any harm from it. On the contrary, this beverage has a much milder effect on you than it does on many representatives of 'Civilized Peoples.' That is what I meant to say. Again, forgive me for my tactlessness."

"Have you forgotten, Sir Shurf? You are now my friend, and you can say anything you wish."

Needless to say, I heaved a sigh of relief. When Lonli-Lokli started talking about my idiosyncrasies, I almost thought I had given away my true origins, and that all Juffin's labor had been dust in the wind. But no—he was just amazed that I didn't dance naked on the table after a few gulps of Elixir. Well, next time I'd have to make him happy.

✳

Sir Juffin Hully himself was quite happy when he saw us, alive and triumphant, and all in one piece.

"I doubt that the problem of life after death is still relevant for the Grand Magician Maxlilgl Annox," I quipped from the doorway.

"If we had killed him when he was alive, anything could have happened. But we killed him after he had already died. Sinning Magicans, what am I saying! Stop me!"

"In any case, I'm sure his research is finished once and for all," Juffin assured me.

"One hopes so. I didn't much like your Grand Magician. By the way, I wanted to deliver him to you alive—well, as alive as it was possible to consider him to be. But it just didn't work out."

"Magicians be with you, my boy! You might not have come back alive yourselves!"

"That's what I assumed," Lonli-Lokli observed. "But an order is an order."

Juffin shook his head reproachfully. I couldn't figure out which of us he was more dissatisfied with.

"I was an idiot. I'll mend my ways," I repented. I collapsed in a chair, and right away realized I was falling asleep. Just as my eyes were closing, I muttered, "Don't forget to tell him about the water, Shurf. That was something else!"

※

I was still feeling the beneficial effects of Elixir of Kaxar, and so I awoke only an hour later. I felt as light as a feather, and surprisingly chipper. My colleagues were drinking kamra that they had ordered in the *Glutton*, and were conversing quietly.

"Aha, he's up and about," said Juffin.

He stared at me with suspicious enthusiasm, as though I were a holiday pudding that may just have reached the proper consistency. It wouldn't have surprised me if his mouth were watering.

It didn't. But he did launch into a medical examination, though this didn't really resemble an ordinary medical procedure.

Juffin asked me to stand by the wall, and for some time I felt his motionless, light eyes drilling into me—not a very pleasant sensation, I'll have you know. For the first time since I had made his acquaintance I felt uncomfortable under his gaze. Then he told me to turn my face to the wall, which I did with relief. For a time, the boss studied my backside and its environs. Not satisfied with a visual examination, he began patting me on the back. This massage, in contrast to the "I spy" game, was enjoyable. Then his relentless hands—the sizzling hot right one and the ice-cold left one—were on my head, and I felt wretched. It was as if I had died and nothing was left of me. Nothing at all. And then I began shouting—not from pain, but to prove to the whole world that it wasn't true. I shout, therefore I am. A stupid phrase, but it worked.

"Easy, Max," Juffin said, his voice full of sympathy and concern, helping me into the nearest armchair. "Unpleasant, I know; but it's over now."

Almost immediately I felt better physically, but I couldn't vouch for my emotional equilibrium.

"What was that all about?"

"Nothing, really. The ordinary dialog between the body of a healer and the body of a patient. Not everyone likes it. You, for example, didn't. But you have to grow accustomed to these things, and you haven't yet. Are you ready for some news?"

"Depends," I answered cautiously. "Is it good? Bad? Or what?"

"Or what. Depends on your sense of humor."

"Well, that's never been too much of a problem for me."

"We'll put it to the test now. You see, Max, your . . . how can I put it most accurately . . . your physiology has undergone a change."

"What kind? Have I become a woman? Or do I just never have to go to the bathroom again? What do you mean, Juffin?"

"No, everything is fine below the belt," Juffin said with a chuckle. "As for the bathroom and other little joys of life—there's no need to worry."

"Well, that's something."

"Nothing really terrible has happened. But you do have to know, all the same. You've become poisonous."

"Poisonous? Me?" Juffin's revelation sounded simply absurd. "Do you mean to tell me that if someone eats me he'll die? Alert the local cannibals, on the double! They may become victims of their own appetites," I laughed like it was the last laugh of my life.

"No, eating you is no problem. Neither is touching. Someone could even use your silverware or a towel after you with no dire consequences," said Juffin. "There's just one danger. If you become angry or scared, your saliva will become poisonous. The most deadly kind of poison, I might add. It kills instantaneously if it so much as touches the skin—of a person, at least. And you will spit this venom at your offender come what may. Let me assure you that self-discipline and training is of no use here. No amount of willpower will change the situation. It's not a matter of choice. You'll spit even if you decide not to. The only thing you can do if you wish to avoid the instantaneous destruction of your offender is to spit off to the side somewhere. So look to your character, boy. Don't let trifles annoy you, or you'll spit the whole of Echo into oblivion."

"It's not all that bad," I observed uncertainly. "I'm not malicious. If something like this happened to Boboota, humanity really would be in grave danger. Of course, it would be nice to try, at least once. If you don't watch out, I'll leave to become Sir Shurf's assistant."

"Well, that wouldn't hurt," Lonli-Lokli remarked, maintaining his placid, unruffled demeanor. "You know yourself, Max, that I sometimes have more work than I can handle."

"And what about my personal life, Juffin?" I sighed. "No girl will want to kiss such a monster! Maybe we should keep the news a secret?"

"Explain to the girls that kissing you is completely harmless. As long as you're not angry, at least," Juffin shrugged. "As for keeping it secret—I wasn't intending to call a press conference about it, but you know that—"

". . . that Echo is full of two-bit clairvoyants," I finished his thought.

"Precisely."

"But why did this happen to me, anyway?"

"It's your fate, boy. When you're mixed up in magic at high levels, it affects you differently from how it would affect . . . let's just say 'normal people.'" Juffin then glanced over at Lonli-Lokli meaningfully.

Sir Shurf is as trustworthy and reliable as a cliff inside a safe inside a Swiss bank, but it was perhaps not worth announcing to him that I was a refugee from another World. Besides, everything was already as clear as day to me.

"You never know beforehand what or how something will affect you," Juffin added. "Remember what happened when we were at my neighbor's house?"

"But I was only very briefly a vampire," I objected plaintively. "After a few hours everything was back to normal."

"Right. Because my spell was the kind that is only short-term.

But the ghost wanted to kill you. That's why the spell he put on you worked like a charm, so to speak—a very permanent one. What can be more permanent than death?"

"Well, you've consoled me. Thanks a million!"

"Deal with it, Max. Don't think this incident is the last one in your life. Everything is for the best! At Makluk's house you became a bit wiser. Now you have a useful weapon at your disposal. Who knows what's next?"

"That's what I'm afraid of."

For a few seconds I sincerely tried to feel sorry for myself. Then I shook my head and burst out laughing.

"Maybe I just need to see a wiseman. I'll come to him and say, 'Doctor, I have poisonous saliva. What should I do?' And he'll say, 'No problem. A strict diet, a walk before bedtime, and an aspirin for the night. In five hundred years, you'll be right as rain!'"

"Aspirin? What's that?" Lonli-Lokli asked.

"Oh, it truly is a magic potion. It's made from horse dung, and it helps everything!"

"Well, I'll be! And our scholars write that in the Borderlands sorcery is very backward. It does seem to be the case that reason often falls victim to prejudice."

Sir Juffin clutched at his head.

"Stop, gentlemen! I can't laugh anymore. My face will become permanently contorted. A last piece of advice, Max. I suggest you consider yourself to be very lucky. You have plenty of useless and inoffensive habits. It's about time you acquired some dangerous ones. Your new acquisition might come in very handy in our profession. And if some hysterical lady refuses to kiss you, just spit in her direction and all will be well. Got it?"

"Got it."

"Excellent." With that, he threw open the door, took a sizable package from the hands of a courier, and tossed it on my lap. "Now try this on."

I opened the package, and out fell a black looxi embroidered in gold, a black skaba, a turban in the same style, and a pair of marvelous boots. On the boots were stylized heads of toothy dragon-like creatures; the black boot-tops were strewn with tiny golden bells. Of course, I would never wear anything like that in my homeland—but here in Echo, I was stylin'!

"Is this a gift, Juffin?"

"Something like that. But please do try it on."

"Thanks!" I started pulling on the boots.

"You're very welcome. Do you like these?"

"I'll say!" I plunked the black turban on my head. It was decorated with the same tiny gold bells.

"And the looxi?

"Just a second."

I wrapped myself up in the black and gold garment and looked at myself in the mirror. It turned out that the gold patterned embroidery formed glittering circles on my chest and back, like targets.

"It's great! Fit for a king."

"Well, as a matter of fact it is for a king. I'm glad you like it, Sir Max. Now you have to wear it."

"Gladly. But why do I have to? And it's a pity to wear such finery on a daily basis."

"You'll get as many outfits as you need. You still haven't understood the main thing. These are your work clothes, so to speak. Your uniform. You'll have to wear it all the time from now on."

"Fine, but I still don't understand. You yourself said that in contrast to the police, members of the Secret Investigative Force don't wear uniforms. What is this, some kind of innovation?"

"Not exactly. This uniform is just for you. You, Sir Max, have become Death. Death in the service of the King. And for such occasions, one must wear the Mantle of Death."

"And when people see me passing by, they'll run from me like the plague. Is that it?"

"It's not all that bad. When they see you, they'll tremble blissfully and think with nostalgia about the good old Epoch of Orders, when people in garments like this were much more common. Your social stature is so high that . . . to put it bluntly, you are a Very Important Person of the highest rank. You'll see what I mean."

"Ah, a 'big boss,' eh? Well, I can deal with that. But why don't you wear a uniform like this, Shurf? You of all people should be wearing one."

"At one time I really did wear the Mantle of Death," Lonli-Lokli confirmed with a nod. "But times change. The time for white garments has come for me now."

"Oh, and I thought your clothes were just a matter of personal taste. And what do your white clothes mean?"

Lonli-Lokli didn't reply. He clearly didn't want to discuss the subject.

※

"The times when Shurf was Death have passed," Juffin announced solemnly. "Now he has become Truth. At least, that's how his position is listed in the Secret Registry of Practicing Royal Magicians. To put it more simply, our Sir Lonli-Lokli isn't capable of anger, fear, or taking offense—in contrast to you, for example. He can bring death, it's true, but only when it's absolutely necessary, not because he wants to himself. Not even when he is ordered to do it. If, let's say, I order Sir Shurf to pulverize an innocent person, he will, in the line of duty, try to carry out my orders, but his hand will refuse to obey its master. So it turns out that our highly disciplined Sir Shurf, for the most part, answers to no one. That is why he is greater than death. He is Truth because he is, in the last instance, as impassive as the heavens. Whew! I'm getting carried away. All that is, of course, a shameless mixtures of naïve philosophy and bad poetry. But you understand the gist of it."

"I'm glad I don't have to wear orange or raspberry," I said. "Still, I'm not crazy about this idea."

"You don't have to be crazy about it. Come to terms with it, and try to get some satisfaction out of it, at least. Case closed. You won't be working tonight, at least, so let's go to the *Glutton*. I'm starving, and so are you. Any questions?"

"Yes," I muttered. "Who's paying?"

※

By the end of the evening, all the Secret Investigators were sitting around the table. There was nothing unusual in this, of course. Juffin had probably sent out a silent call and told everyone to join our little feast, though it was nice to think that there was some mysterious connection between my colleagues and me, and that walking around the city, everyone inevitably gravitated toward the place where the others had gathered. We attract each other by some principle of collective magnetism: that's how I imagined it.

When she took her leave, Lady Melamori, who hadn't taken her eyes off me the whole evening, invited Melifaro and me to visit her at dawn to drink a mug of kamra. According to her strategic plan, we would arrive together and neutralize each other. I wondered whether she was making fun of us or—worse—whether she, herself, didn't understand what she wanted.

"Spit at her, man!" Melifaro hissed. "Spit at her, I dare you. She deserves it!"

"No kidding," I murmured. "But my spit is a matter of state. To use it for my own purposes is abuse of office. And I'm just out of Xolomi."

I did finally make it home that night, and was greeted by Armstrong and Ella, looking sleek, well-fed, and well-groomed, as promised. I decided that from now on I would use the services of the courier, who had been charged with looking after my little beasts. Unlike me, the fellow was made for this kind of work.

All night I stuffed my furry friends with delicacies from the *Glutton* and was rewarded by their grateful purring. I at last grew weary of this pastime; but they wouldn't leave me in peace.

I was awakened by a knock at the door. Only a civil servant of a fairly low rank would dare knock so boldly. Sleepy, grumpy, and befuddled, I crawled over to open the door. Armstrong marched beside me on my right, and Ella spun around in circles on my left, meowing indignantly. It must have been a sight to behold.

At the door stood an extremely proper-looking gentleman whose elegant, gold-rimmed glasses and graying temples cast an aura of intelligence over his pedigreed face.

"Please accept my apologies, Sir Max," he said, bowing. "Allow me to introduce myself, Kovista Giller, Master Verifier of Sad News. I know that it isn't entirely proper to appear at your door at this time of night, but His Majesty King Gurig VIII insisted on it."

My innate sense of hospitality and the servile tone of the visitor conspired to make me invite him in. Moreover, there was nearly a full jug of kamra from the *Glutton* and a pretty assortment of tidbits, as well. I just had to find some clean mugs. In a large house that's not so easy.

"What happened?" I inquired when the objects of my search were found. "What is this 'sad news' you wish to verify? Did someone finally rat on me? We'll have to celebrate that."

"I'll explain everything to you, Sir Max, but please don't be alarmed. Nothing untoward has happened, I assure you."

"Judging from what you've just told me, you already know about my new position," I remarked acidly. "To be honest, I wasn't about to get alarmed. Whatever may have happened, the death penalty is not held in high repute here, and I just returned from Xolomi. I had a lovely stay there, I hasten to add . . ."

"Generally speaking, my main occupation is to verify the legitimacy of denunciations that make their way to the Royal Court. That really is true," my guest admitted, somewhat abashed. "But I beg you, Sir Max, do not think that the King gave any credence to General Boboota Box's memo. I'm here about another matter altogether."

"Well, well, well! Our conversation has taken a much more interesting turn! Do me a favor, sir, and tell me what kind of memo that might have been. I haven't been at the Ministry for three days. I was carrying out an investigation on the orders of the Venerable Head. What, according to General Box, was I up to?"

"I'm embarrassed even to mention such trifling matters to you, Sir Max. General Box found out that in your absence one of the junior staff members of the Ministry of Perfect Public Order visited your home and—"

"And fed my animals," I nodded. "It's the truth. He groomed them, too. What else are junior staff for?"

"I agree with you one hundred per cent, Sir Max. I'll let you in on a secret: General Box always forgets that the Secret Investigative Force and his Police Force are very different organizations, that what is acceptable in his half of the House by the Bridge is not necessarily so in yours. Boboota Box has not seldom delivered denunciations about the behavior of the Venerable Head himself, not to mention your other colleagues."

"And what exactly does Boboota object to?"

Kovista Giller broke into a shy smile.

"Well, he objects to everything. For instance, that Sir Kofa Yox doesn't show up at work when he should be on duty, because he rarely leaves the tavern."

"Well, yes," I agreed. "That truly is bad form! He should just stay in his office, occasionally making a trip to the john to hear Boboota's underlings rake him over the coals in secret. Instead, he haunts all the dives in town."

My visitor nodded in satisfaction.

"The King even collects letters of denunciation about your department. He sticks them in a special album and illustrates them personally. He says he's going to give the album to Sir Juffin Hully when the pages run out. That's why His Majesty read General Box's letter carefully before adding it to the others. The King was curious: why do you keep beasts at home, and what kind of pleasure do you derive from this?"

"See for yourself," I smiled tenderly. "Look how beautiful my Armstrong and Ella are. And so smart!"

The instigators of social discord heard their names and clambered into my lap. I groaned under their bulk, which was nothing to joke about. The long, carefully groomed fur flowed down almost to the floor. Blue eyes peered out from fuzzy cheeks, and their plumelike tails tickled my nose. I had reason to be proud of them!

"If you only knew how sweet it is to sleep to the sound of their purring," I murmured dreamily. "That, if you will permit me, is pure delight."

"Where did you get them, Sir Max?" my guest asked.

To this very day I don't know what made me tell a fib. I think I felt the cats would be hurt if I admitted to a complete stranger the secret of their plebeian origins.

"These cats are the direct descendants of wild cats of the Barren Lands and a mysterious, wild black beast that inhabits the land where the sun sets."

I tried my best to imitate the speech of an exultant savage until I could no longer restrain myself. I burst out laughing, then said in a normal tone of voice:

"At least that's what it said in the note I found in the basket when the little critters were delivered to me by a merchant. They were a present from an old friend."

"To think of it!" the Royal Messenger exclaimed. "His Majesty guessed correctly! He told me right off, 'I'm sure that this Sir Max has cats that are as unusual as he is. Go over and find out—I'm dying with curiosity!' Now I see with my own eyes, Sir Max, that your cats don't resemble in the least the cats that live on our farms."

"If His Majesty considers Armstrong and Ella to be such marvels, I will be the first to agree with him," I declared, pressing the heavy mounds of fur closer to me. "They are nothing if not extraordinary."

The local farmers simply don't have the time or the strength to groom the resplendent fur of their animals, I thought to myself. My cats, it was true, looked nothing like the scraggly, matted specimens that lurked about the peasants' gardens in search of extra scraps of food.

The Master Verifier of Sad News apologized profusely for taking up my valuable time, and sent out a call to Rulx Castle, the main Royal Residence. Evidently, such a serious matter requires lengthy deliberation—the fellow remained silent for nearly an hour.

Finally, Kovista Giller again turned his attention to me. I was already dozing off in my armchair.

"Sir Max," he began in a respectful whisper. "The King would like some cats just like these. Oh, I don't mean to suggest that His Majesty intends to take your own beasts from you. But you do have a girl and a boy, and it stands to reason that that will eventually result in offspring. Might we have the honor of receiving a cat from the litter?"

This was a sensible solution to an impending problem. Kittens were in the bargain sooner or later, there was no getting around it. I had been planning on sending the Armstrong-and-Ella descendents to the same place their parents hailed from—Melifaro's estate. But the Royal Palace was more convenient. And it was closer to home.

"Of course! When the little ones arrive, I'll be happy to send the King the pair of them with the chubbiest paws!" I promised solemnly.

Kovista Giller showered me with thanks, apologies, and compliments, and then disappeared out the door. I went off to bed.

I didn't have a chance to sleep in the next morning, though. A few hours later my new acquaintance sent me another call. It seemed all the courtiers had to have Armstrong and Ella's future offspring, too. Kovista Giller insisted that we meet again.

That evening I held in my hand a note with the names of all the eager recipients of this "rare" (and with Royal stamp of approval!) breed. It was a list of ninety names. And I suspected this was only the beginning.

Poor Ella, even a very long lifetime was too short to produce that many litters. But all these men of the world hungered to appear on the glorified waiting list, if nothing else.

Naturally, Juffin found out about my dealings with the Royal Court in no time, and summoned me for a meeting. I set out for the House by the Bridge anticipating the amusement to come.

"What are you doing to my World, Max? What kinds of transformations are you unleashing?" demanded the Venerable Head of the Minor Secret Investigative Force with mock severity. "And, be so good as to tell me: why only cats? You should have inspired them to take horses into their homes and to ride from the living room to the bedroom! Why were you so grudging?"

"I can still try, if you wish," I replied, giving the matter some thought. "The size of the apartments in the capital would certainly allow it."

"I don't doubt that you'd succeed! The Royal Courtiers are so eager for novelties . . . but wait a few years, why don't you? At my age, it's hard to get used to newfangled notions."

"I'll wait. But never mind the horses. Let's just stick to cats."

"Really? Well, thank you for that, at least. Sinning Magicians, sometimes I really start believing myself that you grew up in the Borderlands. You don't even take offense anymore!"

"Just watch how I can take offense! Just see me spit!" I grimaced madly.

"I might otherwise be struck with terror, but my position won't allow it," Juffin said, grinning. "It is widely believed that I fear nothing and no one. I can't just up and fly in the face of the honored traditions of the Secret Investigative Force."

"By the way, apropos of traditions," I said, recalling recent events. "What are so-called close friends expected to do for one another? I'm not joking, I really need to know."

"What are you talking about, Max? Who are you calling your 'close friends'? Give me some background."

"Well, last night I overindulged in Elixir of Kaxar and patted Sir Shurf on the back. He seemed perfectly happy with this, so everything's fine. There must be some friendship traditions I have to uphold so as not to offend him, though. Am I guessing right?"

"No, I don't recall anything of that nature," Juffin said, furrowing his brow. "I don't think anyone is required to do anything in particular. You don't have to address him as 'sir' anymore, although you seem to have stopped doing that already anyway. Sinning Magicians! What am I trying to explain? Friendship is friendship! By the way, if you recall, I once did the same to you."

"Yes, but—"

I grew confused and fell silent. It's awkward to admit to a person that you consider him to be the Great Exception to all possible rules. It's too close to crude flattery.

But Juffin understood already anyway.

"You mean to say that I'm just one of the guys, but Lonli-Lokli is a true gentleman? Yes, that's one way of looking at it, but you're in luck, Max! There are no particular rituals for such a situation. Well, except for the fact that now when you visit Shurf, you have the right to take a bath at his house and spend the night. And he has the same right—though I question whether he would take advantage of it. All right, Sir Max, a few Days of Freedom from Care are no less than you deserve, so I won't detain you any longer."

"That sounds like you're showing me the door," I said with a smile. "I even feel a bit hurt. Not show up on duty for two days? I'll die of boredom!"

"I'm glad you like your job. Now you've got to get some rest, though. And no adventures! I'm saying that to you as a healer. Understand?"

In the corridor of the Ministry I ran into General Boboota Box. He bared his teeth in the semblance of a smile, his face crimson. The poor chap seemed to be on the verge of fainting. When he saw my Mantle of Death, the illustrious General Boboota understood that he had acquired a very dangerous enemy. I could only sympathize.

Joking aside, passing by the *Sated Skeleton* I heard two middle-aged ladies in heated argument. If I'm not mistaken, they were playing Krak, the local version of poker. And, inevitably, they were both cheating. They made so much noise that they couldn't hear the melodious tinkle of the bells on my boots. "May Sir Max spit on you!" one of them screamed at the other.

Unbelievable! I plunked myself down on the mosaic sidewalk and let my head fall into my hands. I sat like that for ten minutes or more. I kept repeating, like a mantra, Juffin's advice: "Get used to it, and try to enjoy it."

Then I got up and walked home. What else could I do?

CHAPTER FOUR

THE STRANGER

AS SOON AS SOMEONE DECIDES THAT HE HAS MADE HIS PEACE WITH himself and the world around him, his best friends, as though on cue, will start doing everything in their power to relieve him of the illusion. This has been tested on a live human being. On me, to be exact.

I returned to the House by the Bridge after several days of blissful lethargy, clouded only by the installment of a fourth bathing pool in my house. I walked down the corridor, wrapped in my splendid Mantle of Death, anticipating a pleasant meeting with colleagues. And, to tell the truth, they didn't let me down.

At the door leading into our side of the building, Melifaro rushed up to me. The fact that in his haste the guy stomped on my foot and elbowed me in the side was a trifle. He then tried to turn this petty incident into a kind of vaudeville act.

Melifaro bounded away from me like a tennis ball. His face froze in an expression of utter horror. He collapsed onto all fours and began beating his head against the threshold. To top it off, he let out a scream so shrill it made my ears ring.

"Spare me, O Sir Max the Terrible, who spews death from out of his fire-breathing maw! Do not snuff out my existence with your burning spittle, which flows abundantly over the heads of your sworn enemies! I am unworthy of such a magnificent demise."

Terrified policemen came running up when they heard Melifaro's shrieks. It appeared they sincerely thought that someone was being murdered. They stared at my grimacing colleague. At me they only glanced surreptitiously, as though trying to size up the situation— was he going to spit or not? From our side of the Ministry, only Lonli-Lokli poked his stony physiognomy out of the doorway. Taking it all in at a glance, Sir Shurf sighed and slammed the door shut. In the meantime, the curious policemen still lingered.

Enjoying the all-round attention, Melifaro jumped up suddenly and sidled up close to me.

"Am I forgiven?" he asked innocently. "Or did I overdo it?"

"You overdid it." I tried to stay calm, since I really was becoming a bit overwrought. "In such cases, it's considered only proper to repent for no less than an hour. Moreover, it should be done in the most public place in town. Get thee hence to the Victory of Gurig VII Square, my poor friend, and fulfill your duty. Then you will be absolved of all guilt."

At that, I retreated, slamming the door so hard the handle was left hanging limply by one screw. After that I really did start to calm down.

What's wrong, Max? Melifaro sent me a call posthaste. *Are you actually offended? I just wanted to amuse you.*

Content yourself with the thought that you amused a whole crowd of cops and your own sweet self, I replied.

Where did your sense of humor go, Max? Well, never mind. If you're still in a huff, I'll stand you a drink. Come along to the Glutton *and I'll treat you to something stronger than your own nerves. Over and out.*

He really was sucking up, tossing out my favorite expression. This only made me angrier.

"What if I actually do kill him, Shurf?" I asked.

Lonli-Lokli proceeded to regale me with legal advice, as thougt I really did intend to get even with my friend.

"Lifetime imprisonment in Xolomi, since you are both in government service. That will be an aggravating factor. Or there may be no consequences whatsoever, if you can prove that he committed a particularly heinous crime. All in all, such a situation is very undesirable. You ought not take offense at Melifaro. You know him, Max. It's unfortunate that he was spoiled by his mother and older brothers, since his father, Manga Melifaro, was always busy—"

"Gadding about the World writing his famous *Encyclopedia,* I know. World travelers shouldn't start families. Their passion for adventure gets passed down to their offspring. Well, never mind. I'll just go to the *Glutton* and give him a shiner. He's waiting for me, after all. Did you see the expressions on those terrified policemen, Shurf?"

"Naturally."

"Make sure that none of them gets into the *Silver Leaflet* for the next thousand years. There wasn't an intelligent face among them. And they really believed that I might kill him, the idiots. It's obvious they learned their stuff from General Boboota."

After venting my spleen on innocent people I felt a deep sense of satisfaction and went to make peace with Melifaro in the *Glutton*. There was plenty of time. Already bored at home, I had shown up for work much earlier than necessary.

Melifaro did everything he could to improve my mood—which he had done so much to spoil. When the time came to go on my night shift, I was no longer a menace to society.

※

Sir Juffin Hully sat in his armchair, his nose between the pages of a book. This idyll attested to the peace and tranquility that had already returned to Echo.

"Greetings, traitor," he mumbled. "So, you're sitting in the *Glutton* with Melifaro instead of relieving an old man on duty."

"First of all, I came a half hour early. Second, Melifaro was atoning for his sins."

"I know all that. And third?"

"And third, I'm ready to do it all again in your company."

"What, exactly?"

"Go to the *Glutton*."

"You won't burst at the seams, Sir Max?"

"No way."

"I'm too lazy to go anywhere. Let's have them bring something over here. Sit down. I'm going to gossip."

"For you, Sir, I'm prepared even for that."

"Ha! He's prepared. You're the main character of this story. Do you know what Lady Melamori has been up to? I just found out today. When did you last see her?"

"Two days ago. Melifaro and I went to visit her. If you're talking about that, Juffin, you can rest assured—everything was all above-board and proper. Too much so for my taste."

"I see. I could have predicted the outcome of that visit without the help of clairvoyants—even twelve years before your birth. That's not what I'm asking. Did you see her after that?"

"No. True, Melamori sent me a call several times. She inquired about my health and asked about my mood. Very sweet of her. I was touched."

"By the way, how have you been feeling all this time?"

"You mean after my incarceration in the death cell? I haven't spat any poison, at least, if that's what you want to know."

"What I want to know is something I'll figure out for myself. Give me more details."

"There's nothing in particular to tell. Right afterward I felt I was in tip-top shape. My mood was good. Even too good. I felt cheerful, without any grounds for it, as though someone were tickling me. I wanted to laugh apropos of nothing. So I wandered around the house giggling like an idiot—children would say 'I was feeling punchy.'"

"And that's all?"

"Well, yes. Isn't that enough?"

"Because of you, Sir Max, I have to be surprised so often it's almost indecent," said Juffin.

I couldn't quite tell whether he was praising me or mocking me.

"So what happened? Tell me now—I'm on pins and needles!"

"Well, sit for a while without the pins and needles, and I'll chew my food," Sir Juffin snapped, biting off nearly half of the *Glutton Pie*, specialty of the house, which had just arrived.

He was really as eager to talk as I was to hear, and he began talking with his mouth full.

"The First and Last Lady of the Secret Investigative Force, Melamori, decided to test whether you were indeed worthy of her adoration."

"I know one good way to test it," I murmured. "If she doubts whether I am at her service any time of day or night, let her try me. You can tell her that."

"Oh, Max, come on. Lady Melamori is a very serious woman. She has her methods. That's why our cruel huntress has decided to shadow you."

"What! Has she lost her mind?"

"No, I wouldn't put it that way. She's always been like that."

"Are you sure that she's on my trail? I feel absolutely fine."

"Exactly. You feel wonderful. How did you put it—you feel 'punchy'?"

I didn't know what to think anymore. Lady Melamori on my trail! Unbelievable. But what usually happens to people in such cases? Deep depression at the very least. That's the job of the Master of Pursuit—that's why she's hired. But I'm a rare bird. The queen of my heart is hot on my trail, and I feel nothing at all. Just a bit giddy. I'm a callous, insensitive pig. A monster. I hate myself.

There was another reason for my distress.

"And I thought she was asking because she was really worried. That she thought I was sick, since I wasn't at work. And that she couldn't wait until I turned up at the House by the Bridge again. But it was just her idea of an experiment. How humiliating."

"Don't worry," said Juffin. "The old gal was interrogating you with the best of intentions—according to her own lights. If you had betrayed any sign of suffering, she would immediately have stopped. And she would have been completely happy. You see, for Melamori, her dangerous gift is a question of honor and fate. It's the only thing she really has. Don't worry. All our boys have had to undergo the same torments. Even I did—at the very start of my career, the lady decided to find out what kind of fish or fowl it was ordering her around."

"I can only imagine the blow she got."

"No, it wasn't so bad. For her benefit I demonstrated my 'Primary Shield'—though I could really have lost my temper. I have to hand it to her—the girl came to her senses in under an hour. She's a fine damsel, that Melamori."

"What is this 'Primary Shield'?" I asked. "Is it something you can teach me?"

"The 'Primary Shield' is a poetic name for my own kind of Secret Weapon, Max. 'Primary' means it's the least dangerous for my opponent. What can I teach you? You've got stronger shields than any person in this World. Stronger than I dared hope. And you'll gradually learn to use them, but only through experience. Don't sell yourself short. You just lack the terminology."

"What a formidable character that Lady Melamori has turned out to be," I sighed, pouring myself a comforting portion of kamra.

"Such potent gifts at her disposal, yet she behaves like a little child."

"Are you angry with her, Max? Don't be. It's not worth it. The poor thing is already moping around as it is."

"No, I'm not mad. Just bemoaning my broken heart."

"I warned you from the start that choosing her as a sweetheart wasn't a very wise move. Does it never occur to you to listen to your elders, Sir Max?"

I sighed and cut myself a second slice of the Glutton Pie. I'm a callous human being. No broken heart can spoil my appetite—it's been proven time and again.

"You don't have anything to add regarding this incident except the sad story of your broken heart?" Juffin asked when we had polished off the pie.

"I don't know. Actually, I should be asking you. How can it be that I don't feel anything? Strange things are afoot. It seems that if I commit some crime, I can just calmly flee the scene. I'm a dangerous guy."

"Yes, much more dangerous than many," Juffin observed with a satisfied air. He looked like an artist whose hands had just put the finishing touches on a masterpiece.

"It's all so strange. When I lived at home, I didn't notice any miraculous inclinations in myself at all. I was as ordinary as the next person. I had peculiar dreams, but that was a personal matter. Maybe others dream the same way, but they just don't talk about it? But as soon as I end up here, some novelty or other surfaces every day. Maybe you should just cut me in half to find out what's inside!"

"Excellent idea, Sir Max. But you aren't as invulnerable as all that. You've got your limits. Remember what happened to you in the *Old Thorn*?"

"The place that funny lanky fellow runs? What's his name—Chemparkaroke." I smiled, feeling a bit sheepish.

What happened there wasn't an achievement I wanted to recall. Juffin had taken me to the *Old Thorn* when I was still waiting for my appointment to the service. He decided that I just had to try the Soup of Repose, a dish favored by all citizens of the Unified Kingdom.

As far as I understood it, this soup had a light narcotic effect, so harmless and pleasant that the whole family was accustomed to partaking of it, even the littlest tykes.

For that reason I plunged into the psychedelic adventure with no trepidation at all, although my whole life I had felt a cowardly antipathy toward drugs and drug users. My smattering of experience in this area was acquired, of course, in the last years of high school, and was so unsuccessful that rather than developing a habit, I developed a phobia.

I really fell face-first into the Soup of Repose. All my foreignness, which I simply forget about from time to time, came to the surface as soon as I had finished slurping up the first serving. Juffin suddenly found himself in the company of a blithering idiot, giggling over his empty bowl in a fit of hilarity. For me it wasn't the most pleasant experience, either. In an instant I had become a hallucinating nutcase with compromised coordination. The respectable habitués of the *Old Thorn*, I imagine, were shocked by my behavior.

After this incident followed twenty-four hours of agony, as though I had stopped taking drugs after twenty years of rampant indulgence—and that despite the qualified medical help of Sir Juffin Hully. But even his healing arts were in vain. I had to endure it.

After I recovered, I vowed to make an enormous detour—of at least twelve blocks—around the *Old Thorn*.

Juffin approved of my decision and solemnly vowed not to indulge in Soup of Repose in my presence.

"Just don't tell anyone that I can come undone merely by eating that soup. Someone might pour some into my kamra just to see the effect it has on me."

"What are you saying, Max! That's an attempt to poison a high-ranking government official—exactly the sort of crime that falls under our jurisdiction. Anyway, I think I'll go home. And you try to be kind to Lady Melamori tomorrow. Our Lady is quite beside herself. After this little drama I think she'll have to refrain from working for a few days. In our line of work, self-confidence is as necessary as the air we breathe, and every setback can mean the loss of one's gift."

"You don't have to ask, Juffin. I'll be nice to her. And not because . . . but because . . . well, never mind. Just don't worry about a thing. If I had known what was happening, I could have complained to her about being in a bad mood right off—I wouldn't have minded. And everything would have turned out fine."

"Don't grieve, Max. Just think about how many wonderful things there are in the World! That's an assignment. See you tomorrow."

And Sir Juffin hurried out, to where the faithful Kimpa was already waiting for him in the amobiler.

✸

The chief was absolutely right. The World is full of wonderful things. It was best to acknowledge the wisdom of what Sir Juffin Hully said. It was best to relax, stop sniveling, and start a new life—with a visit to the Quarter of Trysts.

This, by the way, is what the majority of lonely ladies and gentlemen do in Echo. And there is no shortage of them. Marriage in the Unified Kingdom is something people embark upon in their mature years—and not everyone decides to get married even then. It isn't customary here to consider a family to be an unmitigated boon, and a lonely old age synonymous with failure in life. No one tries to claim the contrary either, though. Public opinion is simply silent on the matter, allowing everyone to arrange one's affairs as one sees fit.

I had quite recently received a detailed briefing about the Quarter of Trysts from Melifaro, who fairly took me to task for being so ill-informed. You may be a barbarian, he said, but that doesn't excuse you from knowing something so basic.

This aspect of local custom was completely unexpected for me. Despite my almost panicky desire to embark on some sort of "private life" I wasn't sure I was ready to visit the Quarter of Trysts.

Let me explain. When you are returning home from a party in the company of a girl you don't know very well, and you both realize where things are headed—well, it doesn't always look like the Great Amorous Adventure that you dreamed of in childhood, but the scenario is simple and predictable. Everything happens by mutual consent. Two grown people make a more or less conscious decision. For one night, or longer—the ensuing sexual experiences of a new combinations of bodies will show.

In Echo, however, chance encounters are another matter altogether.

Visitors to the Quarter of Trysts fall into two categories: the Seekers and the Waiters. Every person decides for herself or himself which category to join that day. On one side of the Quarter one finds houses of male Seekers and female Waiters; on the other side are female Seekers and male Waiters. There are no signboards. Everyone knows where to go and why.

Upon entering the appropriate house, every Seeker must take part in a curious kind of lottery and pull a token out of a vase. By the way, there are also blank tokens. They signify that on that particular day fate is preventing you from having an amorous encounter with anyone whatsoever. In that event there is nothing to do but turn around and go home. Theoretically, the unlucky person may proceed to the neighboring house and repeat the process, but this is considered to be a sign of blatant disregard for one's own fate, and there are not many who would want to challenge it.

Once the Seeker gets a token he goes into the living room, where the Waiters are to be found, and starts counting each person in turn—one, two, three, etc.—until he reaches the number that appears on the token. That Waiter is, so to speak, waiting for him or her.

I hasten to add that there is no one there to supervise the activities, so there is nothing to prevent cheating. But Melifaro himself said he couldn't understand how such an idea could even enter anyone's head. He couldn't imagine anything more outrageous. Upon witnessing his reaction I concluded that no one in the Quarter of Trysts engages in such fraud. Here it is taken for granted that Lady Fortune is quick to take offense, and it's best not to play pranks on her.

The newly fledged lovers then leave the Quarter of Trysts, set out for home or a hotel, and try to extract as much pleasure as possible from this arrangement of fate. In the morning, they must part forever. That's a mandatory condition.

As far as I understand it, no one is there to enforce this unwritten contract down to the last point and to punish violations. Nonetheless, the rule is considered sacrosanct, and my suggestion that it would be easy to cheat fate met with a grimace of disgust, as though I had undertaken to expound on the charms of necrozoophilia and had warmly urged Melifaro to accompany me to the nearest pet cemetery. "Please, no more jokes of that kind," he advised me grimly. "Especially around people you don't know. And not around people you do know, either."

So I never was able to understand the real reason for my friend's offended sensibilities. I dismissed his prejudices and soon came up with my own high-minded explanation: the mutual agreement of the lovers, that separation for all time was inevitable, was not the worst means of lending an aura of romance to "intimate relations with a chance partner." (I think this is how such phenomena are described in cold officialese.)

After recalling the above information, I realized sadly that it was still too early for me to make my way over to the Quarter of Trysts. My knees would shake, my tongue would twist into knots, my armpits would become small inverted lakes—and afterward in bed I would hardly show my most flattering side. The manner of acquaintance was too abrupt and unconventional. And what if "my fate" delivered me into the arms of an ancient, toothless giantess with elephantine legs? How, I asked myself, would I survive till morning? No. Better to place my bets on a more conservative approach to courtship, since it isn't prohibited by local tradition.

After reaching this decision, I looked around in search of a way to kill time. The only possible conversation partner, our buriwok Kurush, was dozing, head tucked away under one wing. I reached for a book that Sir Juffin Hully had left lying on his armchair. The title was *The Philosophy of Time*; the author, one Sir Sobox Xes. Sinning Magicians! What people won't read.

All in all, I had a rather distressing night. Thumb-twiddling boredom, fruitless deliberations about the Quarter of Trysts, and philosophical literature can plunge one into a funk much faster than the magical shenanigans of our incomparable Master of Pursuit.

❀

The morning brought with it some favorable changes. Sir Kofa Yox amused me with a few risque jokes. Juffin decided to stay home until lunchtime, but he sent me a good-morning call. At the same time he asked me to wait for Melifaro, so that the Secret Investigative wouldn't be without someone in charge. I didn't object, since I wasn't planning to leave anyway until I saw Melamori. She most likely felt guilty, and I'd be a fool not to use such a chain of coincidences to my advantage.

The lady finally made an appearance. She slunk around the Hall of Common Labor, unsure of whether to approach me. The door to the office was open a crack, so I had the opportunity to overhear a series of bitter sighs, too loud to be spontaneous.

After enjoying the concert, I sent a call to the *Glutton* and ordered kamra for two and a lot of cookies. The order arrived in a matter of minutes. When the courier opened the door, Melamori flitted to the far corner of the hall, fearful of remaining in my field of vision. She seemed to be listening to the clatter of dishes with bated breath.

When the messenger had left, I asked loudly through my wide-open door:

"If I have a tray with two jugs of kamra and two mugs delivered to my room, do you think it's because I suffer from a split personality? I need help—there are no two ways about it."

"Is that for me, Max?" came the plaintive squeak.

"It's for my late great-grandmother, but as she's in no condition to join us—well, I'm not angry, and the kamra's getting cold."

Melamori appeared at the door. Two expressions struggled for mastery on her face: a guilty one, and a satisfied one.

"Did Juffin tattle on me? He might have saved himself the trouble, since I'm so ashamed as it is," she muttered.

"There's no need to feel ashamed, Melamori. I'm just made a bit differently, that's all. Don't worry your head over it. My wise Mamma said that if I ate a lot of horse dung every morning, I would grow up strong and handsome, and no one would be able to shadow me. As you can see, she was right."

My heart ordered me to be magnanimous, but it would be wrong not to admit that I hoped for a little reward. After all, her admiration (albeit treacherous) was a rather pleasant sensation; far better, it seemed to me, than polite indifference. Polite indifference, which I had experienced more than once, was something I didn't even want to contemplate.

As a result of my carefully planned operation, I seemed at last to have charmed the First Lady of the Secret Investigative Force. Sipping her kamra, she exuded ingenuous cheer. Our fingers touched accidentally a few times over the cookie platter, and she didn't cringe from my touch by any means. Suddenly emboldened, I suggested that we stroll through Echo in the evening. The lady admitted honestly that she was afraid, but she promised to be brave—not today or tomorrow, but very soon. No later than a few days from now. We just had to fix the date for accomplishing this feat. It was a serious victory. I hadn't counted on it.

I went home ecstatic. For two hours or so I tossed and turned, unwilling to forfeit my happy excitement to the oblivion of sleep. Finally I dozed off, lulled by the purring of Armstrong and Ella curled up at my feet. I wasn't able to sleep for long, though.

❈

At midday I was awoken by a terrible noise. My head still fuzzy with sleep, I decided that a public execution (not customary in Echo) was underway beneath my window, or that there was an itinerant circus in progress (which does happen here from time to time). Insofar as it was impossible to regain slumber in the midst of that hubbub, I went to see what was going on. When I opened the door, I suddenly felt that I had either lost my mind, or that I wasn't really awake yet.

On the street in front of my house, an orchestra made up of a dozen musicians had taken up its position. The musicians were trying desperately to coax some mournful melody out of their instruments. The magnificent Lonli-Lokli stood in front of them, wailing at the top of his lungs a sad song about a little house in the steppe at the top of his lungs.

This can't be happening, because—because it just can't be happening, I thought, dumbstruck. Hardly waiting until the end of the serenade, I rushed over to my colleague to find out what was happening.

"What is this, Shurf? Why aren't you on duty? Good golly, what's this all about?"

Sir Lonli-Lokli coughed, unfazed.

"Is something wrong Max? Did I pick the wrong song?"

"The song is wonderful, but . . . let's go into the living room, Shurf. They'll bring us some kamra from the *Sated Skeleton*, and you'll explain everything to me. All right?" I was ready to cry from bewilderment and vexation.

Dismissing the musicians with an expansive gesture, my "official friend" followed me into the house. Beside myself with relief, I collapsed onto an armchair and sent a call to the *Sated Skeleton*. Not the worst pub in Echo, it was, moreover, the closest to home.

"I'm not on duty, since they offered me a Day of Freedom from Care and Chores," Lonli-Lokli began calmly. "And so I decided to use this opportunity to carry out my duty to you."

"What duty?"

"The duty of friendship!" Now it was his turn to be surprised. "Have I done something wrong? But I consulted the handbook . . ."

"What is this handbook, and where did you get it?"

"You see, Sir Max, after you and I became friends, I started thinking that the customs of the places you spent your youth might differ from ours. I didn't want to offend you accidentally, out of ignorance. So I turned to Sir Melifaro, since his father is the preeminent specialist on the subject of the customs of peoples that inhabit the World."

"Aha! Sir Melifaro!" I exclaimed, beginning to understand.

"Yes, insofar as the books yielded no information about this aspect of the lives of your countrymen. The only reliable source for this information is Sir Manga Melifaro. Considering that we are both acquainted with his son—"

"Yes, we *are* acquainted. And Melifaro told you that you must regale me with romantic folk ballads?"

I didn't know whether to laugh or to be angry. Someone knocked on the door. The delivery boy from the *Sated Skeleton* had arrived just on time.

"Sir Melifaro told me about this particular custom of the Barren Lands, and about a few others, as well. He said that at the full moon, you and I had to exchange blankets, and on the Last Day of the Year—"

"Yes? And what, in his opinion, must we do then?"

"Visit each other and clean the bathing pools with our own hands. As well as other hygienic spots, including the toilets. Was he mistaken about that, Max?"

I tried to master my emotions. I realized that I needed to spare Lonli-Lokli's feelings. It would be unpleasant for him to find out that he had become the victim of a practical joke.

"Of course not, Shurf. That's all basically true. Only, you don't have to do any of this anymore. I'm an ordinary, civilized person who ended up living in a strange place for a time. Much stranger to me than you can even imagine. But I've never held fast to the barbaric customs of my homeland. So, for one thing, friendship means the same thing there that it means here—straightforward, good relations between two people who are sympathetic to each other and wish each other the best. Exchanging blankets or mutual toilet-cleaning isn't necessary. Agreed?"

"But of course, Max. I hope I haven't offended you in any way. I simply wished to show my respect for the customs of your forebears and to please you."

"You have pleased me with your considerate attentions and companionship, in any case. I assure you."

After feeding and reassuring my guest, I ushered him out the door and was left alone with my own fully justified indignation. The first thing I did was to send a call to Melifaro.

You're forgetting that I can fly into a terrible rage, pal! I growled fiercely (insofar as it's possible to growl fiercely using Silent Speech).

What's wrong? he asked innocently.

What's wrong! Lonli-Lokli was just here with a whole orchestra!

Are you upset? Melifaro asked in a sympathetic tone. *My father said that was the custom where you come from. You didn't like it? Does our Lonli-Lokli have a bad voice? I'd always heard his voice was most pleasant.*

Well, that beats all!

I still didn't know whether to laugh or to get angry. So I decided to take refuge in dreamland.

And it was the right thing to do. As it turned out, it was my last chance to get some sleep. That evening I went off to work—and ended up being detained for several days, embroiled in one of the most desperate of classic criminal cases.

❀

The nightmare began suddenly, and coincided precisely with my arrival at the House by the Bridge. A block away from the Ministry, I heard a familiar bellowing:

"Buffalo tits! If those bony-butts can't find their own crap in an outhouse full of it, they can eat it until the hole is empty! Give the case to those Secret Investigative Crapsuckers? Those Generals of Steppe Outhouses who can't extricate themselves from their own crap without a horde of bare-butt barbarians?"

I was amused. The old geezer was waxing so eloquent that he didn't hear the warning bells on my boots.

You just wait, my fine fellow! I'll fix you, I thought with irrepressible glee, as I neared the Secret Entrance to the Ministry of the Perfect Public Order.

Right, "Secret" . . . as if! The door was wide open, and at the threshold stood General Boboota Box, no longer red, but purple with malevolent rage.

"Now those bare-butt denizens of barren outhouses will be wiping the foam from my crap!"

At this point, Boboota noticed me, and he shut up so fast it seemed that the World had stopped.

I looked wonderful, in my own humble opinion, my Mantle of Death unfurled and my face bright with fury. I summoned all my meager acting abilities so that my malice appeared convincing. The nervous tic—which, according to my directorial method, was supposed to strike Boboota with fear that my venomous spit was headed his way—was particularly effective. I don't know how believable I really was, but it worked on Boboota. Fear hath a hundred eyes.

There are many grounds for reproach of the Dashing Swordsman Boboota Box, though cowardice is usually not one of them. But there is an immutable law of human nature: all people are mortally afraid of the unknown. My newly acquired gift, which had caused so much speculation in the city, belonged to the realm of the unknown. So you could understand the poor guy.

General Boboota gulped frantically. Captain Shixola, his hapless audience, looked at me almost with hope. I advanced toward them steadily. I wanted to push the joke to its bitter conclusion, to spit at him just to see what would happen. Theoretically, my spit didn't threaten the life of the Chief of Police, since I was neither angry nor afraid. But I stopped myself just in time. I decided that it might put too great a strain on the poor fellow, and I would be left to clean up the mess afterward. So I traded malice for mildness, and smiled good-naturedly.

"Good evening, Sir Box! Good evening, Captain!" My politeness dealt the final blow to Boboota, though it seemed to disappoint his subordinate. I left them to their perplexity and sailed off to Sir Juffin Hully's office, which was considered a safe haven for me, his right-hand man.

Juffin was there, and in high spirits.

"Have you heard, Max? We've just been assigned a very unusual murder case. It's really not our department, but Boboota's boys can't cope with it. He's aware of that himself. That's why the poor fellow just isn't himself today. You probably heard his harangue out there. Well, let's go look into this murder."

We went out into the corridor. There we were joined by Lady Melamori, gloomy as I'd never seen her before. Strange, for I had cheered her up considerably that very morning. Or was it the murder that had gotten her upset? Doubtful. For me a human death was an event—for Melamori it must have already been routine.

"Why is it so quiet?" Juffin wondered aloud, listening to the whispering behind the wall that separated our rooms from those of the City Police. "I thought Boboota was going to keep up his ranting until dawn. Could it be that he has lost his voice? I don't believe it. It would be too good to be true."

"Well, I was just passing by, and I pretended to be angry," I announced modestly.

Juffin stared at me in amazement.

"Sinning Magicians! I'll arrange it so that your salary is bigger than my own. You're worth it!"

Melamori didn't even smile. It was as if the brave General Boboota had never even been her favorite butt of jokes. Rather, she looked as though she were about to cry. I put my hand on her shoulder and was about to make some lighthearted, offhand remark, but I didn't get a chance. When I touched her I understood everything. I can't imagine how the secret mechanisms were set in motion, but now I knew exactly what Melamori was feeling as well as she knew it herself. Our Master of Pursuit was temporarily out of order. The unsuccessful attempt to trail me had upset the delicate balance of her dangerous gift.

She needed time to put things to rights again.

It's like the flu, which, thankfully, is unknown to the people of Echo. Whether or not you want to admit it, getting better takes time. And now Melamori was going to the scene of a crime as though to her own funeral, for she already sensed what the outcome would be—failure, and a new blow to her self-confidence. But she was going anyway, because she was not used to backing down, even before insurmountable obstacles.

And however foolish, I would most likely have done the same. I was starting to like the damsel more and more.

I sent Juffin a call.

Melamori can't work today. She won't be able to do her stuff. And she knows it. Why did you call her here? To teach her a lesson?

Juffin stared at me intently, then at Melamori, and suddenly smiled his blinding smile:

"Go home, on the double! March, my lady!"

"Why on earth should I?"

"You know why. Your gift belongs not to you alone, but to the Secret Investigative Force of the Unified Kingdom. And if there is something that endangers your gift, you must take measures to protect it. That's also a talent, like all the rest of it. And no shifting your problems onto the shoulders of a tired old boss, who will inevitably forget about them. Is that clear?"

"Thank you," Melamori murmured. It was painful even to look at her.

"You're welcome," Juffin snorted. "Go home, Melamori. Better yet, drop by to see your Uncle Kima. He's a great Master. He'll patch you up in no time. In a few days you'll be right as rain. The sooner the better."

"How will you find the murderer?" she asked uncertainly.

"Sir Max, this lady is insulting us," the chief said with a grin. "She considers our intellectual faculties to be on the wane. She thinks that we're good-for-nothing nincompoops who can only cling to the skirt-tails of the Master of Pursuit, hot on the trail of the criminal. Shall we get offended, or kill her on the spot?"

"Oh, please, I didn't mean it that way," said Melamori, and a timid smile spread across her face. "I'll get better. I'll bring you something from Uncle Kima. And please forgive me, won't you?"

"I will forgive you, of course," Juffin assented. "But Sir Max, here—they say he's terrible when he's angry. General Boboota completely lost his bearings!"

"I'll make it up to Sir Max somehow," Melamori assured him.

Understandably, I was beside myself with joy.

The darling of my demise graciously retreated and disappeared around the corner, toward the parking lot for official amobilers.

Her parting smile was the last pleasant moment of the day. The rest of it was too lousy for words.

※

A woman had been killed a few steps away from our favorite pub, the *Glutton Bunba*. Young, beautiful, though not quite to my taste. A rich brunette with large eyes, generous lips, and broad hips. In Echo, this kind of female beauty is particularly prized. But this woman had had her throat slit—a second horrific grin that reached from ear to ear.

If Juffin is to be believed, this is not how people are killed in Echo, neither women nor men. No one. As a matter of fact, murder of any description is exceedingly rare (unless, of course, one of the banned Orders of Magic is involved—then anything can happen). But this didn't smell like magic, whether forbidden or permitted. No magic at all.

"To be honest, the thing that surprises me most about this whole mess is the location of the crime," I said when Juffin and I returned to the office. "It's common knowledge that the *Glutton Bunba* is your favorite haunt, Juffin. Not even a crazy paranoiac would get up to no good within a dozen blocks of the place."

"Well, whoever it was sure did," the chief said with a sniff.

"Maybe it's a newcomer?"

"Most likely. In Echo, even in the Troubled Times, damsels weren't treated like that. How inconvenient! We need Melamori now more than ever. She'd solve it in an hour. But here we sit, dwelling on every little piece of nonsense."

While we sat, a second murder occurred, this time not far from the Street of Bubbles. The same bloody "smile," but this time the Mona Lisa was a bit older (three hundred years of age). She was the local wisewoman, old Xrida, whom everyone on the street consulted for toothaches or all manner of bad luck. She was still youthful, energetic, and, in contrast to many of her colleagues, a very sweet lady. The residents of all the neighboring quarters had loved her, and the *Echo Hustle and Bustle* published letters of gratitude several times a year from people she had healed.

I should add that neither of these murders was carried out with the goal of robbery, since no valuables belonging to the victims had been touched. As for money, the women probably didn't have any with them. Here in Echo, it is thought that touching coins cools off love. For this reason, no woman will ever take money into her hands, and only the boldest consider gloves to be sufficient protection. Men, too, prefer to take precautions; but ladies are especially superstitious in this regard.

By the way, this is why the inhabitants of the Unified Kingdom gradually introduced the custom of using various kinds of bonds and IOUs. Several days at the end of the year are set aside for clearing these debts. I myself prefer to pay with cash, and have occasionally gotten into awkward situations because of this. You hand your money to the bartender, and he glares at you because, you see, he's left his gloves in the kitchen and now he has to run hither and thither all on account of you.

Thus, in the space of an hour, we had two corpses on our hands. And very few fresh ideas. The night was generous: we received five more "smiles" that were the spitting image of each other, while the victims differed significantly in age, appearance, and social standing. They even lived in distant regions of the city. The criminal seemed to be mixing work with pleasure—grisly murders *cum* nocturnal excursion: "Echo by Night."

Close to morning we had a breathing spell. The murders seemed to have ceased. Most likely the protagonist was exhausted and had decided to take a nap. Juffin turned the matter over to Melifaro and Lonli-Lokli for the time being. Sir Kofa Yox went to gather information about the murders in the pubs, and our Venerable Head ordered me to stay right by his side. So far I had been of no use to him whatsoever. Maybe I provided him with inspiration—his muse, so to speak? In that case, I was a pretty lame muse; Juffin hadn't been visited by a single interesting notion the entire night.

❧

The seventh murder was bequeathed to us at noon, with the same "signature" and no return address.

Strictly speaking, this was what we knew: the killer was probably a man (the tracks he had left in the dust had all but disappeared, but the size was impressive); he was in all likelihood a newcomer (quite unconventional behavior); he possessed a knife of extraordinary size by local standards; he was indifferent to the property of his victims; and he seemed to have no connection with the rebellious Orders, since he didn't even practice traditional magic in his own gruesome kitchen.

Moreover, he wasn't insane, since madness in this World leaves behind a weak but distinct stench. Sir Juffin Hully detected no trace of it at any of the crime scenes.

"Max, you seem to be present at a historic moment," Juffin said, putting aside his pipe, which he had been turning around and around in his hands for the last five hours. "This time I am absolutely baffled. We have seen seven corpses in the past twenty-four hours, a slew of clues that don't add up to anything, and no magic to speak of, whether outlawed or permitted. It's time to give the case back to Boboota's department and try to live down our shame."

"But you yourself know that—" I began cautiously.

"I know. But it doesn't smell like there is any kind of sorcery afoot here. And using True Magic for such bestial murders? Highly unlikely. I can't even imagine it. Unless he's mad—but it didn't reek of any kind of madness."

"You know best," I sighed. "Let's go eat, Juffin. These walls need a rest from us."

Even the *Glutton* was gloomy. Madame Zizinda looked like she had been crying. The food exceeded all expectations, as usual, but we weren't in any mood to appreciate its merits. Juffin ordered a glass of

Jubatic Juice, sniffed it critically, and pushed it away.

This was perhaps the most incoherent, senseless night I had experienced in all the time I had been here. Hm. *In all the time I had been here.* It hadn't been too long, to be honest. It wasn't at all hard to imagine that in addition to tourists from neighboring cities, inhabitants of other worlds had made their way to Echo, just as I had done. Sinning Magicians!

"Juffin," I whispered. "What if it's a countryman of mine?"

My boss raised his eyebrows and nodded slowly.

"Let's go to the Ministry. A conversation like this isn't for strangers' ears. Tell Madame Zizinda to send kamra and something harder to my office. Only not this stuff," he added, looking at the liquid distastefully.

In the office the chief stared at me with his penetrating gaze.

"Why?"

"Because it explains everything. No magic, right? In any case, no obvious magic. That's number one. Number two, if I'm here, why might there not be other guests like me? A door, no matter how well locked, always remains a door while a house is still standing. And Juffin, you yourself say that it's not customary to kill like that in Echo. Where I was born, back there, treating ladies that way is quite popular among madmen. Some madmen. We call them 'maniacs.' That's my third, and most important, argument. It's all too familiar. I've seen similar things on television."

"Where did you see it?"

"It doesn't matter," I mumbled. I tried to think of a quick and comprehensible way of describing television to a person who had never seen it. "Let's just say that it gives you the ability to stay home and watch what's going on in other places. Not everything, of course, but the main things. Things that are surprising or important. And then there are movies. With the help of a special apparatus. No magic. Although who knows what the gauge on your Magic Meter would show?"

"Exactly. Oh, you should have brought that television along with you—what a fascinating little gadget!"

"But what do you think about the murderer?" I asked, trying to steer my chief back to the problem at hand. "Do you think he might be a native of my country?"

"Well, it's an elegant and logical hypothesis—just something you'd come up with. We'll have to try it out. I'll go see Maba Kalox, and you'll come with me. Maba knows your story, so don't try to impress him with the legend of your origins."

"Sir!" I exclaimed, indignant. "It's not my legend, it's yours. A prime example of the genre of fictional falsification. 'Sir Max is from the Borderlands of the County Vook and the Barren Lands—an uncouth barbarian, but one heck of a sleuth!'"

"It's mine alright," Juffin sighed. "At least I'm good for something. Let's go."

At this point, I must elaborate on how I ended up in Echo, since, strange as it may seem, it is directly connected with how these events further unfolded.

For the first twenty-nine years of his muddled existence, Max, the Max I was then, nocturnal dispatcher at a newspaper, average in every possible sense of the word, had grown used to attributing special significance to his dreams. Events in dreams seemed even more real to me than everyday reality. It even went so far that when matters in my dreams weren't going very well, nothing could comfort me when I was awake. Moreover, even on the best of days, when reality was absolutely agreeable to me, I didn't quite see the difference between the dream world and the waking world. I dragged all my problems around with me, there and back—as well as joys and satisfactions, when there were any, of course.

Among the myriad dreams I saw (for it was like watching myself starring in a strange movie) there were several that stood out for their frequency. A city in the mountains, where the only kind of municipal transportation was a cable car; a shady English park, divided into two parts by a babbling brook; a series of empty beaches on a gloomy seacoast. And another city, whose mosaic sidewalks enchanted me at first sight. In this city I even had a favorite café, though I could never remember the name of it after I woke up.

Later, when I found myself in the real *Glutton Bunba*, I recognized it immediately. I even discovered my favorite table between the counter and window onto the courtyard. I felt immediately at home in this place—the smattering of customers who stood along the lengthy counter all seemed strangely familiar to me, and their exotic mode of dress didn't daunt me in the least. I might add that they, too, looked upon my trousers without any particular curiosity. Echo is, after all, the capital city of a large country. It is also one of the largest seaports in the World. It's hard to shock the local residents, least of all with exotic attire.

In time, one of the regulars began greeting me. I greeted him back. Even a cat, as everyone knows, appreciates a kind word—no less so when it's asleep and dreaming.

Gradually, this person established the habit of sitting down at my table just to chat. And Sir Juffin Hully can do this as no one else can—just give him the chance, and he'll talk your ear off. Things went on like this for a fairly long time. Sometimes when I woke up I would relate to my friends some of the marvelous stories I had heard from my new acquaintance. They all told me to write them down, but I never got around to it. I somehow felt that certain things shouldn't be entrusted to paper. Well, laziness was a factor, too; why hide it?

Our curious friendship began suddenly—and, for me, completely unexpectedly. One day my conversation partner broke off his story in mid-sentence, and with the mock seriousness of a conspirator, glanced around furtively, then said in a mysterious whisper: "But you're sleeping, Max. This is all just a dream."

I was thoroughly shaken, and my body jerked so that I fell off the chair and woke up safely on my floor at home.

For the next seven years I dreamed about everything under the sun except the mosaic paving tiles of the wondrous city. I was sad not to be visited by those dreams, and in my waking life things got worse and worse. I lost interest in my old friends, broke off with my girl-friends, and changed jobs more frequently than underwear. I threw all my books away, since they could no longer comfort me, and when I drank too much I invariably got into fist fights, as though I wished to smash to bits the reality I could not abide.

In time, however, I calmed down. I adopted the whole package of life-affirming values: friends, girlfriends, a tolerable job, decent living quarters, a large library attesting to the affluence of its owner, rather than to his literary tastes. In bars I began ordering coffee instead of spirits. I showered in the morning, shaved no less than every other day, took my underwear to the laundry, and kept my wits about me, resorting to withering glances and biting comments instead of using my fists.

Instead of justified pride, however, I still experienced that dull longing and boredom that drove me out of my mind in my youth. I felt like a walking corpse that had risen from the grave, and had for some reason settled down to a quiet, unobtrusive existence among people who were only half-alive, just as he was.

But I got lucky—and how!

One day, early in the morning, as soon as I had fallen asleep after work, I saw in a dream the long counter of the bar, my favorite table, and my old acquaintance waiting for me at the neighboring table. I remembered right away how our last conversation had ended. I knew I was having a dream. But this time I didn't fall off my chair. I didn't wake up. I wasn't even afraid. I guess as I had grown older I had learned, from necessity, to keep my wits about me.

"What's happening?" I inquired. "And *how* is it happening?"

"I don't know," my old friend answered. "I don't think anyone knows how things like this happen. But they do happen. My hobby is examining that fact, when I'm up to it."

"You don't know?" I asked, flabbergasted. For some reason I assumed this person was bound to know the answer to my every question.

"That's not what matters just now," he interrupted me. "But tell me—do you like it here?"

"Do I? It's my favorite dream! When I stopped dreaming it I thought I'd lose my mind."

"I understand. And do you like it there, where you live?"

I shrugged. Around that time problems had been piling up at home. No major difficulties—they were all in the past by then—but dull, trivial, everyday problems. I was the proud owner of a mediocre, uneventful life, and delusions of grandeur about what I actually deserved.

"You are a nocturnal creature," my conversation partner observed. "And not without eccentricities, am I right? Where you live, it's a problem when you can't sleep at night, I suppose."

"A problem! You're not kidding!"

Before I knew it, I was unburdening my heart to this sympathetic old man. And when all is said and done, why be ashamed of it? It was only a dream, as I had been frankly informed seven years before.

He listened to me rather indifferently; but he didn't laugh at me, either, for which I am grateful to this day.

"Well then," he began, after I had gone quiet. "That's all quite sad, but I have an excellent proposal for you: an interesting, well-paid job here in this city, which you have already come to love. Moreover, you'll work only at night—just like you've always wanted."

I didn't have to think twice. It still hadn't sunk in that a decision I made there, in my dream, could have any real consequences. But I wanted him to fill me in on the details, purely out of curiosity.

"Okay, let's say you've already won me over. But why do you need me? Do you mean to say that there are no other night owls in this entire city?"

"Of course there are plenty of those," he said with a grin. "By the way, my name is Juffin. Sir Juffin Hully, at your service. Don't trouble yourself, I already know your name is Max. And your last name is immaterial to me. You'd be surprised, but I know quite a bit about you already. In particular, I know that you have a certain rare talent that is relevant to the organization I head. It's just that it hasn't revealed itself to you yet."

"What kind of talent might that be? Not a criminal streak, by any chance?" I snickered foolishly.

"You see, you've guessed it already! Fine work!"

"Are you serious? What are you, some sort of a Mafia boss?"

"I don't know what a Mafia is, but I can assure you, what I am is much worse."

"A Mafia boss is the head of a criminal organization," I explained. "A big-shot bandit. And what are you?"

"I, on the contrary, am head of the Minor Secret Investigative Force of the city of Echo. Another version of a 'big-shot bandit,' you might say, but in the service of the law. By the way, my department concerns itself only with magic crimes."

"Tragic crimes?" I asked incredulously, fearing I hadn't heard correctly.

"No. You heard right. Magic crimes. There's no need to wince. I'm not playing a joke on you. I'm quite serious. But never mind about that for now. If we are able to work together, you'll get answers to all your questions, and even answers to questions you didn't know you had."

"Well, I guess you could say we're already working together."

"Really? Well, that's good. I thought it might be hard to persuade you. I even thought of making a speech."

"Why don't you tell me what my job will be, since we're working together?"

"Nocturnal Representative of the Head of the Minor Secret Investigative Force. You see the Force is usually getting some shuteye at night. So you, Max, will be the Nocturnal Head."

"Not a bad career for a migrant worker."

"You're right about that. Tell me, if I really were this 'Mafia' boss, would you nevertheless have agreed to work with me?"

"Oh yes," I replied honestly. "I don't know the ins and outs of life here. So for me there's no real difference between those who commit crimes and those who catch the criminals."

"Good for you, friend; you didn't lie. Keep going in that spirit. The truth isn't such a weighty thing that it ought to be concealed."

This Sir Juffin, with the profile of a bird of prey and the cold eyes of a predator, had a surprisingly gentle smile. I realized I hadn't been that charmed for a long time—either awake or asleep. I truly did want to stay here, with this extraordinary person. What he did, and what role he wanted me to play, didn't really matter at all. This may be why I decided to take our conversation as seriously as I would have if I had been awake. I wanted to believe him; I hadn't desired anything so deeply for a long time.

"Now we just have to sort out the technical details," said Sir Juffin Hully and sighed.

"What do you mean?"

"I mean, Max, that you still have to get here."

"Am I not here? Oh. Well, yes . . ."

"That's just it. Do you think it's the real you here now? You're an ordinary ghost. Well, almost ordinary. People don't shriek and dash aside when they see you, but someone with a trained eye will see through you instantly. And you'll have problems with your body, which is now lolling around under a blanket. If you die, it's curtains for you. No, you must be present here with all your engine parts and accessories, which are who-knows-where at the moment."

"The engine—yes, that's a problem," I said, crestfallen.

"Right you are. But listen carefully. You have to do something well-nigh impossible when you wake up. First, you must remember our conversation. I hope that won't pose a problem for you. And if it does—well then, we'll have to start all over again. Second, you must remember that all this is extremely serious. You have to convince yourself that some dreams can continue while you're awake. And if it doesn't work, you must persuade yourself to verify it. Out of curiosity, or out of boredom, as you wish."

"No problem. I have enough of both in my life."

"Wait before you speak! People are made in such a way that if something inexplicable happens to them, they write it off to an over-heated imagination. You have only a few hours here to convince yourself of my existence. There I'm powerless to help you. All I can do is hope for success."

"Have a little faith in me," I protested, a bit hurt. "I'm no dim-witted fool."

"Neither dimwitted, nor a fool. But the capacity to believe in miracles isn't the strongest trump card in your deck. I've had the pleasure of studying you for many years now, Max."

"How?"

"Not 'how' but 'why'. That's just the way it happened. I saw you here by chance many years ago. I realized you weren't a local. Then I thought that you weren't old enough to be hanging around in bars. Only then did it occur to me that you weren't *real*. You know: a phantom, a ghost, a pale shadow of a distant dreamer. Around here such things do happen, but I didn't sense any of our magic in you. That's why no one caught on to you. Except me, of course."

"And you—"

"I noticed you because I'm well-versed in these things. And you know what? I took one look at you, and I knew: this guy would be an ideal nocturnal replacement for me one day. And he'd be a pretty good one even now!"

I was stunned. It had been a long time since I had received any compliments, and such pleasantly unexpected ones were a first for me. Now I understand that Juffin was praising me in advance, as it were, so that I could more easily believe in his existence. No matter how loudly my common sense shouted that it was just another stupid dream, to accept the fact that the charming Sir Juffin's overweening flattery was also only a stupid dream—well, that just wasn't my style.

"When you're convinced that it's worth a try—if, of course, it comes to that—do the following . . ." Here, Juffin fell silent, rubbed his forehead, closed his eyes, and then commanded, "Give me your hand!"

I extended my hand, which he then grabbed hold of painfully. Then he began muttering quietly, hurriedly, almost incoherently, as though trying to keep up with some invisible understudy.

"Late at night, go to . . . yes, that place called Green Street. Remember. Don't stand still, just keep walking. Well, for an hour, two hours—however long you need to. You'll see a carriage—you call them 'streetcars.' An empty streetcar. It will approach you then stop. Get in and sit down. The streetcar will start moving. Do whatever you wish, but don't take the coachman's seat. It's better not to risk it, you never know with these things. Don't get nervous, and don't worry. It could take a long time, so be sure to bring some sandwiches or other provisions. You should be prepared to spend a few days on the road. I don't think the trip will take terribly long, but anything can happen. And, most important, don't tell anyone anything. They won't believe you, and other people's doubts always interfere with real magic."

Finally, he let go of my hand, opened his eyes, and smiled.

"Remember that last bit of advice well—it will come in handy in the future. Is everything clear?"

"Yes," I said, rubbing my sore extremity.

"Will you do this, Max?"

"Sure I will. But streetcars don't run on Green Street."

"Maybe not . . ." Juffin said indifferently. "What, did you plan to travel between worlds on an ordinary streetcar? By the way, what's a streetcar?"

❀

When I woke up, I didn't have to make any extra effort to remember my dream. I remembered it down to the most minute detail. Trying to figure out where I was at that very moment proved to be more difficult, but I managed.

It was three in the afternoon. I made myself some coffee. Then I sat in an armchair with my cup, and with the first, best cigarette of the day, intent on mulling over everything. By the last gulp, I decided there was nothing more to think about. Even if it was an ordinary dream, what did I have to lose? Taking a walk to Green Street wasn't much trouble. I like to walk, and I didn't have anything to do at night. But if the dream was prophetic . . . then it was the chance of a lifetime!

There was nothing to keep me here. My life stretched before me like a meaningless, empty expanse.

There wasn't even anyone I needed to call to say goodbye to.

Well, there were, of course, people to call. A good fifty names in my telephone book, which I had acquired only a month ago. But there was no one I wanted to talk to, much less see. Maybe I was just depressed. In that case, long live depression! That hypothetical malady made it very easy for me to make the most important decision in my life. It surprises me to this day.

I was possessed by a strangely pleasant lightheadedness. I was moved neither to try to put my effects in order, nor to share my plans with trusted friends. I spent the evening not in tormented deliberation, but over endless cups of tea in front of the TV. Even the last episode of *Twin Peaks* didn't seem to me to be a bad omen. I just thought that if I had been Agent Cooper I would probably have continued wandering around the Black Wigwam—anything was better than returning to reality and messing up the lives of others, along with one's own.

Rather, I behaved as though the most intriguing event of the evening would be the ritual of taking out the trash. Packing my backpack with only a thermos of coffee and a three-day supply of sandwiches, I felt like a first-class idiot, but I thought that even being a first-class idiot would be a welcome change. In recent years I had been a paragon of sensible behavior, and the results were not impressive.

I left home at one o'clock in the morning, and it took me about twenty minutes to Green Street. I had to hang around there for quite a while. One of the last things I recall in that world was the sight of the enormous numbers on the electric clock hanging above the telephone company building: 2:22. I don't know why, but symmetry like that has always struck me as an auspicious sign.

The loud rumble of the approaching streetcar shattered the stillness of the night, interrupting my contemplation of multiple twos. I wasn't exactly afraid, but my head started spinning, my eyes saw double, and I just couldn't get my mind around how the streetcar tracks had suddenly appeared in the middle of the narrow cobblestone street. I was able to make out a sign that indicated I was at the stop for streetcars following route 432. For some time, the number struck me as even stranger than the very existence of the streetcar. In our city there had never been more than thirty routes, at most. I chuckled nervously. The sound of my own laughter seemed so terrifying to me that I immediately stopped. Then the streetcar appeared from around the corner.

I wanted very much to peer at the driver's cabin. (People have a habit of doing on occasion what they know they shouldn't.) When I did, I saw a broad, carnivorous-looking face sporting a sparse growth of whiskers. His tiny eyes, drowning in abundant flesh, burned with unearthly ecstasy. It was hard to determine what frightened me most about his appearance. Let's just say that at that moment I understood what a soul wandering through Bardo must feel when it first comes across the procession of Divine Furies. Ordinary epithets ("fear," "horror," "shock") cannot begin to describe what I felt.

The streetcar slowed as it approached the stop. Then I realized that this was the end: if I got in, it was the end of me, and if I turned tail and ran, all the more so!

I glanced again at the driver's seat. Now it was empty, to my relief. A streetcar without a driver, on a street where streetcars don't run, along route 432, from nowhere to nowhere—that was alarming, but bearable. This form of distorted reality was more to my liking.

The streetcar came to a halt. It was a completely unidentifiable old model with crude letters scrawled on the side that read "Sex Pistols" and "Michael is an ass."

I'll always be grateful to this Michael. He saved my life, or my reason, or both. Contemplating the animal nature of the person immortalized on the side of the streetcar reassured me, and I entered the empty semidarkness of the compartment. I sat down by a window and arranged my backpack on the next seat. The door closed. It closed very gently. There was nothing in the least bit frightening about it. We started moving. Even our speed seemed just right.

The nighttime landscape outside the window was in no way unusual—half-familiar urban streets illumined by the pale globes of streetlights, now and then cheerful yellow patches of windows, the weak neon shimmer of store signs. I felt happy and calm, as though I were on my way to my grandmother's house in the country, where I hadn't been since I was fourteen. My grandmother died, the house was sold, and I had never again been as free and happy as I was then. I looked at my reflection in the glass: cheerful, eager, youthful. What a nice guy I can be.

On one of the seats I discovered some sort of magazine, and I reached for it happily. The magazine was a news digest, a genre I am especially fond of. Some people like things that are a bit hotter, but at that stage in my life I liked to numb my brain with digests—an ecologically clean drug. It made time pass the way I like it to: imperceptibly.

This probably all seems very absurd—jumping without a backward glance into an old jalopy of a streetcar, reaching for an out-of-date magazine, and devouring the day before yesterday's news over fresh sandwiches. But that's just how I am: when I don't understand what's going on, I try to find some activity that will distract me. In everyday life I often behave like a lunatic, but as soon as things start getting strange, I become a psychologically balanced bore. It's no doubt my unique version of the instinct of self-preservation.

When my attention wandered away from the magazine, I noticed that it was getting light outside. Suddenly I felt like there was a taut string inside me, quivering and ready to snap. Two cheery suns were clambering up into the heavens above the horizon—each one above its own horizon, that is. Two sunrises in one—or one sunrise twice? To the left and to the right, so that neither eye would feel left out.

Come what may, I had to gather my wits about me. So as not to panic, I turned away from both windows, screwed up my face, relaxed, yawned, and tried to get more comfortable on the hard seat. Surprisingly, it worked—the seat seemed to become roomier and softer. I laid my head down on the sandwich-stuffed backpack and fell asleep.

I slept soundly. No nightmares haunted me. Apparently, the demons in charge of my dreams were taking a smoke break. Good for them.

All in all, the streetcar-microcosm was kindly disposed toward me. When I woke up, I realized I was lying not on a hard seat, but on a short, soft leather divan. It was possible to fit my whole body on it if I pulled my knees way up near my chin. In addition, a scratchy plaid throw, almost as comforting as the one I had left at home, had appeared out of nowhere.

"How sweet you are to me," I mumbled, and fell into an even deeper sleep.

When I woke up again, the streetcar compartment looked like a dormitory for gnomes. All the seats had turned into short, leather divans, which suited me to a tee. After all, it would be a crime not to take advantage of such creature comforts in the face of the complete unknown. I slept a lot, munched on my provisions, and discovered new magazines now and then, sometimes in the most improbable places—one of them turned up tucked under my armpit; another was stuck in the ticket puncher like a monstrous, interstellar transfer pass.

As for surrealistic landscapes like the double dawn, there were no further surprises. A permanent darkness settled outside the windows of the streetcar, making it easier to preserve my emotional equilibrium.

According to my approximate calculations, this idyll continued for three or four days. Who knows, though, how much time really passed in this extraordinary streetcar? To this day, the most inexplicable phenomenon of that experience remains the fact that I never once felt the call of nature or noticed the absence of a bathroom. This, to put it mildly, contradicts what I know of human capabilities. The whole time I waited with trepidation for the familiar distress signals from my plumbing system, all the while trying to come up with a somewhat hygienic solution to the awkward problem I anticipated —but it turned out to be unnecessary.

My final "awakening" was strikingly different from the previous ones, beginning with the fact that I found myself wrapped not in the scratchy throw, but in a fur blanket. And I could finally stretch out my long-suffering legs. Looking around, I discovered that I was lying not in a bed and not on a divan, but on a very soft floor in a huge, half-dark, and nearly empty room. At the far end of this room, someone was breathing heavily, menacingly, as it seemed to me. I opened my eyes wide, then turned over awkwardly and got up on my hands and knees. The breathing ceased, but a few seconds later something softly nudged my heels. To this day, I don't know how I kept myself from screaming out.

Instead, still crouched on the floor, I pivoted around and found myself nose-to-nose with another one, very soft and moist. Then something licked my cheek. Indescribable relief nearly robbed me of my senses. Before me was an absolutely charming creature—a shaggy puppy with the face of a little bulldog. Later, I found out that Chuff wasn't a puppy at all, but a seasoned canine. His compact size and exuberance had misled me.

Soon, a small figure draped in capacious garments flowing down to the floor materialized in the twilight of the room. Peering closely

at him, I realized that it was not my dream companion. It was someone else. Could I have come to the wrong address?

"Mister Venerable Head is expected later this evening. If you
please, sir, inform me of your wishes," requested the stranger, a fragile, wizened old man with radiant eyes and a pensive, thin-lipped
mouth. This was Kimpa, Sir Juffin Hully's butler. Juffin himself did
indeed arrive later that night.

Only then did it sink in that the unimaginable journey from one
world to another had really taken place.

That is how I ended up in Echo—which I have never had cause
to regret, even on days as hopeless as this one seemed to be.

⁂

While I was lost in reminiscences, the amobiler, manned by Sir
Juffin Hully, was winding in and out among the luxuriant gardens of
the Left Bank. Finally, we turned into a narrow driveway that seemed
to be paved exclusively with semiprecious stones. At first I didn't see the
house amid the thick undergrowth. Sir Maba Kalox is probably a
philosopher, and his philosophy requires that he become one with
nature. That's why he lives in a garden without any architectural super-
fluities, I thought cheerfully, just before we nearly ran smack into the
wall of his house, all but invisible under the opaque curtain of vines.

"This is what you call camouflage!" I exclaimed admiringly.

"You can't imagine how right you are, Max. Now do you see
why I sat behind the levers of this blasted buggy? During my lifetime
I have paid several hundred visits to Maba, and I have always been
forced to find my way to his lair by guesswork. It's impossible to
memorize the way here. Every time you just have to arm yourself
with the hope that you'll get lucky. Maba Kalox is an unsurpassed
master of discretion!"

"Is he hiding from someone?"

"No, not at all. People just have a hard time discovering his
whereabouts. It happens of its own accord, with no help from him.
One of the side effects of studying True Magic."

"And why is your house so easy to find?"

"In the first place, we all have our eccentricities. And, second, I'm
by no means as old as he is."

"Do you mean to say—"

"I don't mean to say anything. But I have to, since you asked. The

Order of the Clock of Time Backwards has existed . . . let me see . . . yes, around 3,000 years. And I have yet to hear that there has been a succession of Grand Magicians."

"Wow!"

I had nothing more to add.

Sir Juffin turned behind the well-concealed building. There we came upon a decrepit plywood door, more fitting for a toolshed than a Grand Magician's villa. The door opened with a creak, and we found ourselves standing in the middle of a large, rather chilly hall.

Maba Kalox, the Grand Magician of the Order of Time Backwards, was known for having peacefully disbanded his Order several years before the onset of the Troubled Times, after which he managed nearly to disappear from sight without ever leaving Echo. This living legend was waiting for us in the sitting room.

The "living legend" was quite ordinary looking. He was a shortish, stocky fellow of indeterminate age with an animated expression. His merry, round eyes were the true embellishments of his face. If he could have been said to resemble any of my companions, it would have had to be Kurush, our wise buriwok.

"Haven't set eyes on you in ages, Juffin!"

Sir Maba Kalox said this with such unfeigned enthusiasm that it seemed Sir Juffin's presence filled him with cosmic joy.

"I'm happy to see you," he said to me, making a low exaggerated bow. "You could have brought your marvel around sooner, Juffin. May I touch him?"

"Go ahead. As far as I know he doesn't bite. He doesn't kick. It's even safe to drop him on the floor."

"On the floor! That's a good one."

Maba Kalox really did probe me with his index finger, then immediately drew back as if he were afraid of getting burned. He winked at me conspiratorially, as if to say, "You and I know this charade is just for Juffin's sake—so bear with me. Let's humor the old geezer." Sir Maba didn't use Silent Speech, but somehow I knew just what the wink meant. I liked his approach, in spite of the fact that he had called me "marvel" and pinched me like fresh dough.

"Sit down, friends," Sir Maba Kalox said, gesturing broadly toward the table. "I'll rustle up some of your best black poison."

By "black poison" he meant kamra, of course.

"It will probably be some potion of boiled herbs again," Juffin commented peevishly. He could grow savage when someone took aim at one of his little weaknesses.

"Well, at least it's not any of that liquid tar of yours. Whoever decided that was fit for drinking at all? No matter how often those misery-mongers muttered spells over it. Don't pout, Juffin. Just try this. It really is something special."

Sir Maba Kalox was absolutely right. The steaming, ruby-hued beverage that appeared on the table had a flavor somewhat reminiscent of Elixir of Kaxar, of which I was particularly fond, infused with some kind of celestial flower.

"Well, at long last I get offered something decent in this house," Juffin said gruffly, beginning to come around.

"I haven't seen you this tired since the Code was adopted," our host said, standing up and stretching creakily. "Why worry so much about these murders, Juffin? When the World might really have collapsed you were much calmer about it—and for good reason."

"First, if I can't solve a case within an hour, it makes me very irritable, you know that. Second, Max has gotten an idea into his head that I don't like one bit. At the same time, it would explain everything. If we left the door open between Worlds—well, Maba, you realize it's nothing to joke about."

"The door between Worlds is never really closed, Juffin. It's time you realized that. In any case, I'm at your service, on the condition that you both drink another cup of my concoction. I'm extremely vain, you know."

"And I was worried that you had left all your human weaknesses far behind," Juffin said, grinning. Then he turned to me, "Sir Max, don't sit there looking so stiff and awkward. This may be the only house in Echo where you have no cause to feel shy."

"I'm not feeling shy. I just always need a little time to—"

"Sniff things out?" Maba Kalox asked. His eyes were the kindest X-rays I had ever been subjected to.

"Something like that. It usually lasts just a short time, and then I realize that I'm already used to things. But sometimes—"

"Sometimes you understand that you'll never get used to it. You don't have to, but you try to swallow it anyway," Maba said, finishing the end of my thought. "Well, I'd say that's a very sensible approach to things. Sniff it out, Marvel. As for me, I've already sniffed you out."

I nodded and reached for the second cup.

"You can check out whether Max is right or not, can't you?" asked Juffin, drumming his fingers on the tabletop nervously.

"Of course. But why check it out? You already know he's right, Juffin. You're just tired. And not only because of this. But it was your choice—wasting your life on trivial nonsense."

"Somebody has to do it," Juffin grumbled.

"And not just anyone, but you in particular. So it's all well and good. You want me to look into the matter, do you?"

"Of course I do. If a fellow from another World is roaming around Echo, I have to know at the very least whether he ended up here just by chance, or—"

"Why don't you call a spade a spade, Juffin? What you really want to know is how many other uninvited guests are likely to fall into your warm embrace."

"Well, you've got my number. Of course that's what I want to know. That's my job."

"Fine. If you want a refill, the jug's on the table. I hope you won't be bored. I'll be back shortly."

With this, Sir Maba, much to my astonishment, crawled under the table. I stared at Juffin, dumbfounded.

"Look under the table and you'll understand."

I looked. There was nothing there. What else did I expect?

"The door between Worlds can be anywhere, Max," Juffin said softly. "Even under the table. What difference does it make? But whoever wants to find it has to hide from the eyes of others. Maba needs only seconds. I'd need a minute or two. How long did you have to wait for that curious contraption that delivered you to my bedroom?"

"About an hour."

"Not bad for a beginner. It's just a matter of practice, son. Pour me some more of that potion. I think I've found just what the wiseman ordered for a weary man."

"I'd like to get the recipe for this out of him," I murmured dreamily.

"The recipe? It doesn't exist. I know how Maba makes his concoctions—he just throws in everything that comes to hand."

"Sinning Magicians, Juffin! That's beyond me."

"Me, too, for the time being. And I've been around on this earth a bit longer than you have, if you care to remember. I haven't wasted my time, either. The problem is that everything happens gradually, Max."

"My problem is that everything happens too suddenly."

"In that case, you're lucky. Try to get used to it."

Somewhere in the far corner of the sitting room a door slammed. Sir Maba Kalox came back to the table, as cheerful and animated as ever.

"Thank you, Juffin. It was a pleasure to examine the Door you opened, and to see the curious place that lies beyond it. I must say, it was grand!"

"I'm glad you liked it. But the more Max tells me about the place, the less I like it."

"I'm not saying it appeals to me. It was simply very interesting. It's been a long time since I've seen anything like it. Are you glad you stole away from there, Max?"

"I can't imagine my life working out any other way. When I first arrived here I felt like I had landed in clover! I felt that someone was rubbing the part of my brain that makes me purr."

Sir Maba Kalox nodded, settled himself more comfortably in his armchair, and thoughtfully drew out a plate with small rolls from under the table. He tasted them, nodded his approval, and placed his souvenir on the table.

"They're edible, and very tasty. But, I won't stall, I'll tell you everything that happened while I was there. In the first place, Max, you were right. One of your countrymen really is at large in Echo. By the way, Juffin, it's the first time I've come across someone of his age and sex who has such a highly developed faculty of intuition."

"Same here," my boss said.

I blushed with pleasure.

"I congratulate you both. Eat up, don't be afraid. I don't know where they came from, but nevertheless . . ."

"Poisoner," Juffin mumbled, stuffing a roll into his mouth. "Chow down, Max. If we die, we're going out together."

The rolls were excellent. The flavor seemed familiar to me, though I couldn't quite place it.

"I don't know how you managed," Sir Maba Kalox continued. "But you, my boys, came up with the craziest mode of transportation between Worlds I've ever seen."

"What do you mean 'we'? Juffin thought it up. I just obediently followed instructions," I protested. I certainly didn't want to be burdened by someone else's laurels. I didn't even know where to put my own.

"Judge for yourself, Max," Juffin replied. "How could I have invented that 'streetcar' when to this day I don't know what it is? Someday it will get through to you that we did it together. But for now, you'll just have to take my word for it."

"Just resign yourself to not knowing what you're doing for the next few hundred years," Maba Kalox added. "It's only frightening at first. After that it gets interesting. Now then, let's get back to my impressions. I found myself in the dark and lonely street where the Door between Worlds opened for you, Max. There was some lunatic wandering around who was obsessed with murder. Nothing so unusual in that, and anyway, I love madmen. However primitive they may be, they always have access to marvels. As for this fellow, it was obvious to me right away that he was tripping over the marvelous with both feet. Some kind of eccentric buggy, clearly man-made, drove up and stopped right in front of him. I've never seen anything more ungainly in my life. A means of transportation should be able to drive anywhere, and not be confined to a little path! All the more since no path is infinite."

"That 'little path' is called 'tracks,'" I interposed, just to set the record straight.

"Thank you, Max. That, of course, changes everything. When I realized how this strange buggy was made and what it was for, I split my sides laughing. But for the madman, the arrival of the streetcar was also a surprise. You see, he was aware that on that street there was no little path like the one I have already mentioned. Yes, yes, Max, I remember. 'Tracks.' Consequently, the poor fellow was sure that this contraption couldn't be there at all. Sinning Magicians, how little it takes for some people to lose their minds!"

"Tell me, Maba," Juffin said, frowning. "How great is the probability that other people will come across this streetcar?"

"The chances are almost nil. The appearance of this anomaly of nature is in some way connected with the phases of the moon there, as well as the positions of the other planets. The necessary conditions of alignment are fairly rare. Also, it's a deserted street. And, more important, this passage between worlds was created especially for him"—a nod in my direction—"so normal people not only cannot use the thing, they don't even see it. Only an experienced person or a lunatic, whose own personality has disintegrated due to the onset of madness, is able to pass through the Door to Beyond. You may rest assured, Juffin, such auspicious conditions occur very seldom, unless we're talking about a few of their Magicians who manage to pass through. But that's possible at any time, under any circumstances."

"All the more since there are no Magicians there," I added.

"I wouldn't be so sure of that," said Sir Maba Kalox. "Are you personally acquainted with all the inhabitants of your world?"

"Of course not, but—"

"Just what I thought. Just because you haven't met any of them doesn't mean they don't exist. Be optimistic, we Magicians are everywhere."

"So you're saying there won't be any invasion from those parts," Juffin said, visibly relieved.

"Of course not. Oh, and one more interesting detail. This 'streetcar' had a coachman. I wish I had had more time to study this strange creature. I'll pursue the matter at my leisure, to be sure."

"A zealous-looking fat fellow with a thin mustache," I said slowly, my lips growing numb with horror at the memory. "As monstrous a mug as earth can produce—was that him?"

"Yes indeed it was. Who else? The first being you ever created, Max. You might be a little bit more charitable. I've never seen the likes of him."

"Who is this coachman you're talking about?" Juffin demanded. "You never mentioned him to me, Max!"

"I thought you knew everything already, without me. Besides, I tried to forget about him as soon as I could. I almost died when I saw him! Praise be the Magicians, he disappeared almost immediately!"

"Oh, right—you no doubt thought he was a good buddy of mine. Well, I'll be. I should have questioned you about your journey. My pragmatism foiled me—I thought that since you had arrived in one piece that was all that mattered. Maba, what kind of creature is he?"

"I can't say. I don't know yet myself. There's only one thing I can tell you: I've never seen anything like him before. If I find time to study him, I'll certainly inform you of the results of my research. But you are so severe toward your own creation, Max!

The lunatic, for example, liked this coachman very much. He decided to talk to him and to find out how the streetcar had found its way to a street where it didn't belong. And at a certain moment he thought that the coachman might become his best friend. You could say they were made for each other, each obsessed in his own way. In short, the streetcar stopped, the fellow got in, greeted the coachman, and off they went. I can't tell you all the details of their journey together, since I was too lazy to investigate any further. But after some time, the lunatic ended up in Echo, in the back courtyard of the *Glutton Bunba*. He was hungry, frightened, and he had finally 'flipped his lid.'"

"He flipped what?" asked Juffin asked.

"His lid. I'm just using his own term. Nuances are very significant in such matters. Max, can you translate?"

"Well," I began. "It means to 'lose your mind' all at once, but at the same to sink deeper and deeper into it, step by step. That's how I would explain it."

"Well said," Sir Maba exclaimed, sounding pleased. "And what happened next you know better than I do, as the Door between Worlds closed and I lost interest in your companion."

"Listen, Maba, couldn't we—" Juffin proposed, before Maba cut him off.

"No, we couldn't!"

"Fine. Goodbye then. Don't forget to let me know about the mysterious mustachioed creature when you figure him out."

"And you come back in a dozen or so days, or even before, but not with such a despondent countenance. You come, too, Max. With Juffin or by yourself. If you can find me, of course. But I can't help you there. Well, gentlemen, you have given me great pleasure, dropping in like this and dumping your personal problems on me. That's a true art. Farewell."

And Sir Maba overturned the table we were sitting at with a violent shove. The table crashed to the floor, shards of dishes went flying in all directions. I ducked instinctively, the chair flipped over, and in the wink of an eye I had landed on the most reliable of all points of rest, after executing a somersault à la Sir Melifaro.

A moment later I realized I was sitting not on Maba's floor, but in the luxuriant grass beside a garden path. I glanced around, stunned. Next to me sat Juffin, roaring with laughter.

"Maba adores surprising novices. After meeting him for the first time I found myself at the bottom of a lake, crawling on all fours looking for some stairs, since I had completely forgotten I knew how to swim. In fact, the very notion that there existed such a useful skill as swimming never entered my head! It was several hours before I reached shore, and several years, if I remember correctly, before I understood how I had ended up there. But by then I couldn't be angry at Maba, even if I tried very hard. Believe me, Sir Max, he was very humane in his treatment of you."

"You call that humane? All the same, I liked Sir Maba very much."

"I'm glad you did. Let's go. You can sit at the levers—finding the way back is a piece of cake."

❅

"What were you and Maba discussing just before we left, Juffin?" I asked when I had come to my senses after our unorthodox parting from the Grand Magician. "I'm pretty quick on the uptake, but that was too fast even for me. 'Couldn't we—' 'No, we couldn't.' Forgive me for being importunate, but I'm terribly curious."

Sir Juffin Hully waved his hand vaguely. "It's no mystery. I meant to ask whether we might be able to find your countryman more quickly using you . . . well, as a model. Maybe there is some scent from your world so subtle that I can't detect it. Or something of that nature, which might speed the case up a bit."

"So?"

"You heard him—it's impossible."

"You mean my homeland has no smell? That's disappointing."

"It may very well smell, but you, Sir Max, are no reliable model."

"I'm hurt," I admitted in dismay.

"You needn't be. Studying True Magic has already changed you too much. You yourself may not notice these changes, but you can take my word for it. If we use you as a model, we might just as likely find me—or Maba Kalox himself."

"That's also relevant," I remarked. "You yourself said that seeking him out to pay a visit was no easy matter."

"Yes, but I'd prefer to find this 'lunatic' for a start—and only then undertake a more intellectual pursuit. Sleeping, for instance. Ah, here we are already."

"And his clothes, Juffin?" I asked, getting out of the amobiler. "I'm willing to bet they are no more fitting for a walk around Echo than the trousers I showed up in."

"Oh, but this is the capital of the Unified Kingdom. There are dozens of visitor here at any given time. It's no secret to the local residents that half the World wears trousers, including those very citizens of the free city of Gazhin, not to mention the inhabitants of the Borderlands so dear to your heart. Trousers will surprise no one here. The time when locals were ready to gawk at every foreign costume is long since past. Now they don't even turn their heads. How are things, Melifaro?" Juffin asked our colleague, whom we found stretching his legs in the main foyer of the House by the Bridge, nonchalantly studying the artwork that adorned the walls.

"Not bad, that is to say, no more corpses," Melifaro reported briskly. "The fellow has wound down, I suppose. He really should take better care of his health. Sir Juffin, are you ready to save my skin from this poison-spewing monster? Not long ago he threatened to do me in!"

I stared at Melifaro in bewilderment.

"When was that?"

I had already clean forgotten about Lonli-Lokli's serenade yesterday, after which the 'diurnal backside' of the Venerable Head really had run the risk of my wrath. Vanity of vanities, to be sure.

"You won't be offended, Melifaro, if I do you in later? In light of recent events, murder seems like a terribly trivial and humdrum affair. I don't want to be just a pale imitation of an unsung genius."

"Give me a break! The victims are ladies, and I'm a man at the height of my powers."

"Death has no gender preferences."

"Spoken like a true philosopher," Juffin remarked approvingly. "Come with me, Melifaro. We need a quick-witted ne'er-do-well like yourself who isn't completely befuddled by these goings-on. I've already sent a call to Sir Kofa. He promised to join us in half an hour."

"Right. He just has to consume half a pie and listen to another new joke," Melifaro quipped, nodding vigorously. "You can't hold it against him, though; it's his job."

When he got to the office, Juffin collapsed in a chair and smiled broadly.

"We've done all we could, Melifaro. Now it's your move. It's clear beyond the shadow of a doubt: the killer is Max's countryman. What do you suggest?"

"Clothes are out," Melifaro observed coolly. "Time was when a person in pants was considered a novelty."

"I told you," Juffin said, turning to me.

"Likewise his accent. Well, we have a few leads to work with, but it'll take some time," Melifaro said, slipping his fingers under his turban.

"Think, Max. What else is there that would distinguish your compatriot from, er, normal people? No hard feelings, of course. Is there anything that might draw attention, something impossible to conceal in a motley crowd?"

"I have to concentrate," I replied. "And the best place to do it is sitting on the porcelain throne. Maybe there a brilliant idea will dawn on me. Excuse me, gentlemen. I'll return in a moment."

I left for the shortest vacation of all—a rest stop to which every person in any imaginable world has an inalienable right.

Passing down the corridor, I heard one of my favorite "arias" again, and I decided to sneak over to catch another performance.

"Bull's tits! What kind of crap does she want from you, Foofloss? She can go over there, where they wallow in it!" General Boboota Box looked around warily and glimpsed my friendly face just as I rounded the corner.

". . . insofar as those good people will undoubtedly be interested in everything she has to say," Sir Boboota finished in a hollow voice without taking his eyes off my face.

In response, Captain Foofloss, his relative and deputy, eyes popping out of his head, carried out the curious and entertaining breathing exercise know as spluttering.

"I was just giving orders that a material witness in the case Hully has been investigating since yesterday evening be sent to you," Boboota reported respectfully. He can actually express himself decently when he wishes! I marveled.

"Excellent," I drawled. "You have acted fully in accordance with the law, Sir Box."

I could have sworn he sighed with relief.

I returned to find a cheerful hubbub in Juffin's office. A spry, red-haired lady in an expensive bright-red looxi was holding a mug of kamra in her hand and beaming coquettishly at Melifaro's chiseled Hollywood features. I had thought that the heyday of the frivolous flirt had passed, but the lady herself clearly knew otherwise.

"And here's Sir Max," Juffin announced solemnly, for some reason finding it necessary to state the obvious. "Please begin, Lady Chadsy."

The lady turned to me. Upon seeing my garment, her face fell. Then she broke into the falsest of false smiles and turned away from me again hastily, all of which I found quite distressing. I took my place without any fanfare, arming myself with a full mug of kamra.

"Thank you, sir. You can't imagine the brutes I had to deal with at the City Police department. They didn't know how to offer a lady a sip of kamra, much less a comfortable chair. I was forced to sit on a rickety stool!"

"Oh, I can imagine," said Juffin. Sincere sympathy was written all over his face. "But I am under the impression that it was an even more serious matter that brought you here."

"Yes, indeed, Sir Hully. Already this morning I had a premonition. I knew I ought not to go shopping. And I didn't, because I trust my premonitions. But then my friend, Lady Hadley, sent me a call. She was very anxious to see me, and I couldn't refuse her. We agreed to meet in the *Pink Buriwok*. I decided not to call for an amobiler, but to go on foot, since I live on the Street of High Walls, so—"

"Yes, the *Pink Buriwok* is just a stone's throw away," Melifaro nodded. Lady Chadsy looked at him with unfeigned interest, and not a trace of maternal tenderness.

"Exactly, sir. I'm surprised at how quickly you understand me. Perhaps you also live nearby?"

"No, but I'm planning on moving there soon," Melifaro informed her in a confidential tone. "Please go on, my lady."

The lady blushed with pleasure. I could hardly keep from laughing aloud, though it would have been quite awkward if I had lost my composure. The lady would no doubt have refused to give a deposition until they had me strung up and quartered—all the more since my Mantle of Death reduced any hypothetical manly charms to zero.

"I left home despite the premonition. And it hadn't misled me. I had not gone a block when some horrible barbarian came around the corner wearing a disgusting, dirty looxi with sleeves, and dreadful-looking trousers. And the boor was swaying back and forth! I had never seen such a drunk man—well, with the exception of my cousin James, whom I once found in a similar condition. But that was well before the Code Epoch, so Cousin James can be forgiven. But this drunken scoundrel started waving a knife around at me. He even slashed my new skaba, which I bought only yesterday at Dirolan's! You can imagine how much it cost. I can't stand men like that, so I gave him a punch in the nose before I really got frightened. He hissed some strange words at me. 'Who-are, who-are!' At first I thought he had the impudence to ask me who I was. But then he hissed 'Old-who-are!' and ran away, so I think it must be some primitive barbarian curse. I went home to change and sent a call to Hadley so she wouldn't be angry that I was late, and I explained the reason I had been delayed. Hadley said that it might be the murderer they wrote about in the *Echo Hustle and Bustle*, and that truly frightened me. And she advised me to come to you—well, not to you personally, Sir Hully, but to the House by the Bridge. Then I hailed an amobiler and hurried over here. That's all there is to tell. Do you think it might be the same killer? But he was such a weakling! I can't understand why those poor women couldn't wrestle him down. Just one punch was all it took."

"Thank you, Lady Chadsy," Juffin announced ceremoniously. "I think your courage has saved not only your own, but many other lives, as well. And now, you may go home. I regret that our meeting was so short, but it is our duty to find the culprit who insulted you as soon as we are able."

"You will find him, gentlemen. Of that I am certain!"

The lady made her exit, swaying her hips gracefully, and now and then casting sultry glances at us over her shoulder. Melifaro, the lucky man, received such a passionate parting smile that he nearly crashed to the floor under the weight of it. When Lady Chadsy had finally disappeared from sight, the poor guy rolled his eyes heavenward.

"Sinning Magicians, what did I do to deserve such punishment?"

"Well, if worse comes to worst, you're guaranteed a position as a salesman at Dirolan's," Juffin said with a grin. "Max, have you remembered how you differ from 'normal people,' to use the terminology of this poor man?"

I shrugged, and drank the rest of the cold kamra. I differed from "normal people" in many ways, especially just now. I would have to try to discern how all my former compatriots differed from my present ones, but the amusing episode with Boboota and the heart-wrenching confession of Lady Chadsy distracted me from my thoughts on the matter.

"Here I am!" Sir Kofa Yox beamed at us with the complacent smile of a man with a full stomach. "I'm sorry I'm late. I was detained by a very amusing incident. I was just going into the *Old Thorn* when your call came, Juffin."

I leaped up and knocked over my chair. The mug, blessedly empty, clattered to the floor.

"What an idiot I am!" I cried. "How could I have forgotten! The Soup of Repose! Remember what happened to me, Juffin? Of course he was swaying back and forth on his feet! He sure must have been! Of course, it was my countryman. The guy tried the soup! No more murders for him!"

"Well, that's that," Juffin sighed in relief. "Our troubles are over. Though we have nothing to be proud of. We're just lucky. Theoretically, the killer could have wandered around Echo forever, eating something else."

"What happened when you ate the soup?" Melifaro asked, perplexed. "I don't quite get the connection, gentlemen."

"Max can't eat Soup of Repose," Juffin explained. "But don't even think about joking about it, son. It affects him like poison. He was knocked out flat for three days after eating a bowlful, and I was powerless to help."

"Poor guy," Melifaro said sympathetically. "That's why you're so overwrought all the time. As though Lonli-Lokli were sitting on your backside. You're really missing out, mate."

"I hope it's the worst loss I experience," I said indifferently. "I can get along fine without the soup."

"Everything makes sense to me now," Sir Kofa announced suddenly. "You can send Lonli-Lokli to the *Old Thorn*. The killer's there. He's the reason I was late."

"I'll go myself." Melifaro jumped up and made it to the doorway in a single bound. "You can't just kill a miracle of nature like that! Moreover, the Master Who Snuffs Out Unnecessary Smiles is busy with my paperwork. It would be a sin to deprive him of the pleasure."

"We'll go together," said Juffin and stood up. "I'm curious, too, not to mention Max, who simply must exchange greetings with his compatriot. And Sir Kofa has full right to his portion of the laurels."

Frankly speaking, I wasn't especially eager to accompany them. I would have to encounter a person who had traveled the same road I had, through the Door between Worlds, to use Juffin's terminology. If it were up to me, I would have postponed the meeting. But no one thought to ask me.

They put me behind the levers of the amobiler—we had some distance to go, and time was short. Along the way, Sir Kofa recounted his experiences.

"Just after midday, a strange fellow entered the *Thorn*. As everyone knows, Mr. Chemparkaroke adores oddities. The stranger, the better—that's his motto. Chemparkaroke is still just as curious as the day he arrived in Echo for the first time from the island of Murimax. Anyway, the visitor made his entrance by shouting out something from the doorway: 'All women are . . .' something or other. A hole in the heavens above, I can't remember for the life of me."

"Whores," I prompted. "He probably said 'all women are whores.'"

"That's it, Sir Max! You're not a medium, by any chance?"

"No, it's just that maniacs like this guy usually get fixated on one idea or phrase, and they keep repeating it over and over. He said the same thing to the red-headed lady. He called her an 'old whore.'"

"What does it mean?" Melifaro wanted to know.

"Nothing, really. Something like 'bad woman.' Or, let's say, 'very bad, depraved woman.'"

When he heard my translation, Melifaro colored deeply. But I thought it necessary to continue my lecture.

"Guys like that always bear grudges against women—against all of them without exception, or just against blondes, or plump ones, or tall ones. It all depends."

"Let's not get sidetracked, here," Juffin grumbled. "Let Kofa have his say."

"Chemparkaroke was in ecstasy over this incomprehensible word. So he agreed with his guest out of politeness. The guy asked whether Chemparkaroke had anything to relieve his suffering. The innkeeper concluded that the visitor wanted to taste some of his legendary soup. He poured him some of the most potent stuff. At first the visitor didn't want to eat it, but Chemparkaroke swore on his mother's grave that it was the best cure for suffering. So the fellow tasted it. He liked it. Did he ever like it! Chemparkaroke claims that he had never witnessed such unequivocal enthusiasm about his home-made soup. When the visitor had finished, he fled. Chemparkaroke realized that the fellow had no money and didn't know that the King picked up all tabs for the hungry in Echo. Visitors are often unaware of this, and so end up getting into scrapes. Chemparkaroke was used to it. He was happy with the new acquisition for his 'oddball collection' and returned to his innkeeping tasks.

"An hour later, his newfound friend came back. Chempar-karoke noticed that he was shuffling his feet uncertainly in the doorway, and shouted to him to come in, since he wasn't obliged to pay for anything if he didn't have the money. Then he served him some more soup. The fellow kept muttering about 'relieving his suf-fering.' By the time I dropped in to the *Old Thorn*, curiosity-seekers were already gathering. Chemparkaroke was doing a brisk busi-ness, so his generosity was rewarded tenfold. And people got what they were looking for. Something extraordinary was happening to the visitor. After the second bowl of soup, he began to babble, and after the third, he broke into the most enigmatic dance I've ever seen. It was probably some kind of folk dance. Then he dozed off, and I thought he was there for the long haul, since he was in no condition to leave. Chemparkaroke promised to keep an eye on him, because by then it had occurred to me that this strange bird could well be one of your clients. I even started to wonder—is he really a human being? But what didn't occur to me was to recall Chemparkaroke's story about how you, Juffin, dragged this poor boy into the *Thorn* one day."

The "poor boy," of course, was me. Juffin sighed penitently, remembering his recent blunder.

At the threshold the *Old Thorn* I winced. It was no doubt a great place, but my digestive system refused to agree with that opinion, and a feeling of nausea hit me the moment I entered. The *Thorn* was so packed that it looked as though the entire citizenry of Echo had received a Day of Freedom from Care at the same time. When our rather intimidating posse entered the tavern, the patrons slowly began to disperse. The red-haired Chemparkaroke assumed a know-ing expression and began wiping off the already spotless dishes.

My countryman was asleep on a broad wooden bench. Luckily, he didn't seem to be one of my childhood friends. That would have been too much. As for his age, he could have been my father—or perhaps the pressure of being a maniac had aged him before his time. This guy looked ghastly—a dirty raincoat, wrinkled trousers, week-old stubble, dark circles under his eyes . . . poor thing. Moreover, he had clearly overindulged in Soup of Repose. His ragged breathing was not a sign of physical well-being. If he had died right then and there, it wouldn't have surprise me. It looked like that's where things were heading.

Juffin sniffed fastidiously.

"We've spent a whole day looking for this . . . this natural phenomenon? Ugh, how unattractive! Take him, Max, and get him out of here. Chemparkaroke, do you have anything to add to Sir Yox's story?"

The good-natured redhead shook his head:

"What's there to add, Sir Venerable Head? An ugly affair. At first he was so funny. Then he started to snore, to moan, to chase an invisible person around the tavern. The customers were amused. People love a clown, even a sick one. But then he fell on the bench and went to sleep. Only I think that soon he'll be chatting with the Dark Magicians. I often get a hunch about things like that. If you give him something to drink, his legs will start twitching, and it'll be all over."

"Thanks for the good news, old boy. I'm all for it," Sir Juffin muttered. "Good work, Chemparkaroke."

The innkeeper was flattered, but he clearly didn't understand why he was being praised. Juffin looked at him wearily.

"Take him, Max. What are you waiting for? He's not going to dance anymore, that's for sure."

I sighed and did the usual prestidigitation with my left hand. The half-dead maniac fit comfortably between my thumb and my forefinger. Chemparkaroke's jaw dropped. He had arrived in Echo during the height of the Code Epoch and was unaccustomed even to small wonders. I frowned in distaste, and we left. I even had to drive the amobiler holding this fistful of iniquity.

※

In the Hall of Common Labor I was able to rid myself of this unpleasant burden, depositing my countryman right on the rug.

Then I went to wash my hands. I'm a typical neurotic, so things like this can easily knock me off course. And I really didn't like this maniac. It was probably because we had too much in common. At the same time, his appearance was extraordinarily repellant to me. I steeled myself and plunged back into the fray.

"Should I bring him back to his senses?" Sir Juffin Hully pondered aloud, staring at our quarry with unconcealed disgust. "It would be a lot of fuss and bother, but I'd like to know."

It seemed I could imagine what my boss wanted to know. Blessed are the ignorant!

"Don't worry about it, Sir Max," Juffin said jovially.

Usually he begins to understand what I'm feeling before I even notice a change of mood in myself. But today he seemed to lag behind a bit with his consolations.

"This is no test of your nerves. It's a form of pleasure, because we have a chance to find out something we didn't know before. Keep your chin up, son!"

"I'm not so sure that this arcane knowledge is going to improve my appetite," I murmured.

Sir Kofa and Melifaro looked at us with incomprehension.

"It's nothing," Juffin told them. "Just a little family quarrel. I'll deal with this handsome devil."

"I'm afraid it's already too late to help him," I replied. "Remember, I was almost done in by one bowl of it. This lucky man polished off three."

"I wasn't planning to help him. But perhaps he wants to make a confession." Juffin crouched down beside the malefactor and began massaging his ears. Then he reached for his throat. The rhythmic motion soothed and lulled me, if no one else.

Better turn away, Max. The silent advice of Juffin resounded in my head. *You really don't have to play any part in this.*

I averted my gaze reluctantly. And just in time. Sir Juffin Hully executed a feat that I never would have expected from such a staid, respectable, middle-aged gentleman.

With a piercing yelp, he leapt on the stomach of the hapless maniac, after which he rolled head over heels out of the way.

"It's been some time since I had to amuse myself that way," Juffin remarked, getting up to his feet. "Well, now he'll talk."

And my countryman did begin to stir.

"Kela!" he called out. "Is that you, Kela? I knew you'd find me! Way to go, mate!"

As though in a dream I moved closer to this unsightly creature.

"What's your name?" I asked.

Dumb, of course. Why could I possibly have wanted to know his name? But it was the first thing that came into my head.

"I don't know. No one calls me by my name anymore. Is there any more of that soup left? It really does help with the pain."

"Well, I wouldn't say so." I stuck to my guns on that point. "Besides, you could die from eating it."

"No matter. I already did, but they woke me up again. Who woke me up?"

"I did," Sir Juffin Hullly answered. "Don't bother to thank me."

"Can someone explain to me where I am?" the unhappy specimen asked. "A person has a right to know where he died."

"You're too far away from home for the name of this city to mean anything to you," I replied.

"All the same, I want to know."

"You're in Echo."

"Is that in Japan? But none of you looks like Japs around here. You're fooling me, right? Everyone here laughs . . . It took so long to get here. I don't remember why. And those whores, they didn't want to tell me where I was, either. They were probably glad that I got stuck here! Never mind. In the place I sent them, they won't think it's funny anymore."

I noted with astonishment that no amount of violent upheaval could inspire this single-minded man to doubt the rightness of his own actions. A lunatic, Sir Maba had called him, and he was right. He was possessed.

"Kela promised me that they'd help me die here," the tormented soul suddenly informed us. "Are you the ones who will help me?"

"Who is this Kela?" I asked.

"A streetcar driver. I don't know who he is. He promised me that everything would be over soon. So I felt calmer. He was going to kill me, but then he changed his mind. He said that other people would do it. Kela's my friend. I used to have another friend, when I was a kid. I killed his dog because she was in heat. It was disgusting. Kela's also my friend. The best one of all. I don't know—" He made an effort to raise himself up, and stared at me with something like horror, or maybe with love. "Oh, a familiar face. I've seen you somewhere before, friend. Only without that cape. In a dream . . . I saw . . . yes."

He started to grow weaker. Then he closed his eyes and was silent.

"Where could he have seen me?" I asked in surprise.

"What do you mean 'where'? In the Great Battle of Horse Dung, when you were the brave commander of a mighty horde of five men!" Melifaro prompted.

"Shut up," Sir Kofa muttered. "Can't you see? Something is happening here that neither you nor I can understand, or even hope to."

"It's not all that bad, Kofa. Hope is the last thing to die," Juffin piped up gaily, and turned to me. "He said 'in a dream'! Where else? Whether you like it or not, there is some very strong bond between you two, Max. And a very dangerous one. This is a special problem. In short, you're going to have to kill him."

"Me?!"

I was beyond dumbfounded. I couldn't believe my ears. The world felt like it was collapsing around me.

"Why do I have to kill him, Juffin? The death penalty was abolished long ago—you said so yourself. And he won't hold out for very long as it is."

"That's not the point. It's about you. This stranger used your Door. I can't explain it all right now; it isn't the time or place. You must understand one thing: if the man dies his own death, he'll open another Door for you. It'll be there waiting for you. It could be anywhere. No one knows how things will transpire, and you have too little experience to figure it out on your own just yet. And behind this new Door will be Death, because now his path leads only there. And by killing him with your own hands, you will destroy this unnecessary and fatal connection you share, which you had no part in choosing. And mark my words, there's no time to lose. He's dying. So . . ."

"I understand, Juffin," I nodded. "I don't know why, but I understand everything. You're absolutely right."

The world around me shuddered and melted away, subsiding into a million tiny flames. Everything became shiny and dull at once. It was, as I saw—no, sensed, felt—a kind of short corridor that stretched between me and this dying madman. And I very much doubted that we were two distinct people. We were Siamese twins, freakish sideshow monsters, connected not by a tissue of skin, but by something else, concealed from the gaze of the crowd in some other dimension.

Perhaps I hadn't been aware of this from the start, but when I rushed off to wash my hands, as if that would help, I already knew.

I had managed to hide this terrible knowledge from myself, until Juffin uttered out loud what I had been too afraid to think.

I dropped down on my knees next to my abhorrent double, and took the splendid Profiline butcher's knife from the inner pocket of his coat. And I planted the knife in his solar plexus, without shrinking back and without even flinching.

I've never been a strong man, rather the opposite. But this act completely changed my notions of what I was capable of. The knife went into his body like it was butter—though it doesn't really happen that way.

"You got me, friend . . ."

In the last words of the dying man I heard more reason than I had heard during all the other events of that absurd, sickening day.

And then I went to wash my hands again. It was the only way I knew to reward myself for my courage.

🌀

When I returned to the place of execution, junior officials were already bustling about with buckets and mops.

"Thank you for removing the body so quickly," I said, taking my seat. "You'll think it's funny, but I've never killed anyone before. I've never even gone hunting. Juba Chebobargo's doll doesn't count, I suppose. It's a loss of innocence in a way, so please be kind."

"No one removed him, son," Kofa said in a quiet voice. "He simply disappeared, as soon as you left. The blood on the carpet stayed, though. They're already cleaning up the mess."

"How's it going, Sir Max?" Juffin shoved a mug of hot kamra over to me.

"You already know. Fine, I guess. It's strange, though. The World hasn't completely come back to me, if I may express it that way."

"I know. But that will soon pass. You did everything just fine. I didn't expect you to manage as well as you did."

"I'm wearing the Mantle of Death, after all," I laughed. Laughter is the best way I know to return you to your senses.

"Sir Juffin, I need a drink," Melifaro announced. "I thought I was used to everything in this job at the Refuge for the Mad. Now I understand that I desperately need a drink. Right this second."

"I've already sent a call to the *Glutton*. Do you think you can hold out another two minutes?"

"I'm not so sure. First those pagan rites of yours, then the disappearance of the primary material evidence. And you have no intention of explaining anything, I suppose?"

"No, I don't. I'd be glad to, but . . . we had to do it that way, old chap. Take my word for it."

"Really? Or maybe it was just a new form of entertainment, and I'm lagging behind? Sir Kofa, you, at least, might try to calm my nerves."

"I need a drink, too," Kofa Yox said, smiling good-naturedly. "Then I'm at your service."

"This is no Secret Investigative Force. It's some kind of orphanage," I snorted. "So I kill a guy. Just one, mind you. He disappears afterward. It's really no big deal! Besides, I think I need a drink, too. I'll join you."

"My team has taken to drink," Juffin moaned. "Lonli-Lokli is my last hope—where is he, by the way?"

"Did you call, sir?" Lonli-Lokli appeared suddenly at the door. "Have you still not found our killer?"

Turning around to look at him, the four of us burst out laughing. At first it resembled mass hysteria, but in a few seconds we really did begin to find it funny. Shurf stepped into the office, sat down in a chair, and regarded us with warm interest, waiting until we had regained our composure. Then he asked:

"So, what about the murderer?"

"Everything has been taken care of, since Max killed him and the corpse disappeared," Melifaro informed him, laughing heartily again.

I didn't have the strength to join in his merriment. Luckily, the messenger with a tray from the *Glutton Bunba* was already at the door. Excellent timing!

I had never in my life thought I would be capable of drinking a whole mug of anything at one go, much less Jubatic Juice. Evidently, however, the body knows its own needs. If necessary, it will perform miracles.

"Sir Juffin," Lonli-Lokli urged calmly. "Perhaps you will tell me."

"Melifaro is absolutely right, Sir Shurf. That's just about how it all happened, save a few spicy details."

"Max, why did you do it on your own? And in such a primitive manner?" objected the professional in Lonli-Lokli, somewhat scandalized by the shoddy job of a dilettante.

"I'm bloodthirsty, Shurf," I admitted eagerly. "Sometimes I just can't help myself."

This time it was Juffin Hully who laughed loudest of all. I think it was just relief for he realized I was finally myself again.

"But that's very bad, Max!" Lonli-Lokli exclaimed in alarm. "With your abilities you need to learn to exercise self-control. If you don't mind, I'll demonstrate some simple breathing exercises that will aid in the development of your self-control and peace of mind."

For the sake of my "official friend" I tried to be more serious.

"Thank you, Shurf. I'd love to see them. But to be honest, I was just joking. Later I'll explain everything that happened. Everything I can, anyway. I'm afraid it isn't much."

"If this has anything to do with a mystery, I'd prefer to remain in the dark, since a mystery made public is an insult to Truth."

"Do you understand?" Sir Kofa asked Melifaro. "That's an answer to all your questions at once."

"I couldn't give a flying buttress," Melifaro announced dreamily. "I've had my drink and all is well. You can go to the Magicians with your terrible mysteries. Even without them, life is wonderful. Oh, by the way, since Sir Shurf is here with us—do you still think that I was making fun of you both, O Bloodthirsty Monster? Sir Max, I'm talking to you!"

"Of course," I said indifferently. "But I didn't give a flying buttress, as you expressed it, either."

"Then you absolutely must meet my father, who will give you evidence of my innocence. Sir Juffin, can you possibly do without us both at the same time? At least for one day?"

"What would I need you for? Get out of my sight this instant, if you wish," Juffin said. "But just one day, mind you! Agreed? Sir Kofa, Sir Shurf, get used to the idea that tomorrow the two of you alone will answer for the safety and security of the Unified Kingdom. And tonight—only Kurush. Right, my friend?" Juffin stroked the bird's fluffy little cap of feathers tenderly. "As for me, I intend to sleep for a whole day and night. Lady Melamori is probably already sipping expensive wine under the watchful supervision of her uncle. These two are planning an outing to the country to terrorize cats. We're a pretty pack of Secret Investigators, bulwark against threats to our society's well-being. It can't be denied."

"Well, how about it, Max?" Melifaro said, turning to me. "We'll leave tonight, and get there in a few hours. If you're at the levers of the amobiler, we'll get there in one. Fresh country air, heaps of good food, and my Pa. It will be something, believe me. And Mama's a treat, too."

"Heaps of food, Papa, and Mama," I repeated in rapture. "That sounds perfect. And a fast drive sounds even better. You're a genius, Melifaro! I'm forever in your debt. Thank you, Juffin. You're both lifesavers."

I wasn't exaggerating. A change of scenery was exactly what I needed just now. I hadn't dared dream I would be lucky enough to get it.

"Well, shall we go?"

Melifaro was already dancing in the doorway in anticipation. He didn't like sitting in one spot for very long, especially after a plan of action had been laid down.

"Yes, yes. Juffin, tell me, am I required to wear these rags of baleful splendor wherever I go?"

I meant, of course, the Mantle of Death. Not the most appropriate attire for a jaunt to the country.

"No. You only have to wear it within the city limits," Juffin said acerbically. "But I thought you liked your little uniform."

"I do like it. I'm just afraid the chickens out there will stop laying eggs from fright. Did I say something wrong?"

"Oh my gosh, another mystery!" Melifaro exclaimed wringing his hands. "Max, a hole in the heavens above, what on earth are 'chickens'? Only turkeys lay eggs. Take it from a country boy!"

❀

While Melifaro looked over my apartment in bewilderment, trying to understand whether it was asceticism or stinginess that had inspired me to settle down there, I cuddled with Armstrong and Ella, delighting in their throaty purrs and murmuring whatever banal endearments came into my head.

Then I went up to the bedroom and rummaged around in the closet until I found some duds that more or less corresponded to my foggy notions of the requirements country living. I went back down to the living room with a half-empty weekend bag in tow.

"I'm ready. I'm afraid you've gotten a sad impression of my way of life. I can't do anything to change it. I love tenement living!"

"What do you mean? It's great here!" Melifaro cried, brushing off my remark. "No frivolous extras. A real den for a lone hero. Truly, Max, it's very romantic."

"Shall we have a drink for the road? I'm the most inhospitable host in the whole darn town. Actually, I don't have anything to offer you, unless we decide to go out to the *Sated Skeleton*."

"I took all we needed from the Ministry. Drink, kamra, and everything else I could grab. Let's go, Max, or I'm going to collapse. You, no doubt, are even more exhausted."

"I'm nowhere near collapse. You forget I'm the 'nocturnal backside.' My shift is just beginning. Off we go!"

"You know, Max, there is an aura of evil about you," Melifaro remarked, getting into the amobiler. "Your nocturnal habits, your fast driving, your gloomy expression, the black looxi, you don't eat soup, like normal people do . . . Not to mention your absurd habit of killing crown criminals. It's too much for one person. It's no wonder Melamori is afraid of you."

"Afraid of me!"

"Of course, didn't you know? When I saw how she looked at you, I thought, 'That's it, pal. You can go scratch your backside. You've got a serious competitor!' Then I realized that my stakes hadn't fallen so low. The lady fears you like a nightmare."

"That's ridiculous. Why should she be afraid of me? Melamori isn't one of those prissy city girls who are ready to pee in their pants whenever I go out to the store for some useless crap."

"That's just it. She's no priss. She understands people better than anyone. That's her job. Ask her yourself. How should I know? Anyway, I think I'll doze off while we're driving."

"Then we'll be on the road for a very long time. Because the only road I'd be able to find without your advice leads directly to the Barren Lands."

Of course I was lying shamelessly, since I didn't even know that road.

"And I thought you knew everything, like Juffin."

"Everything except addresses, birthdays, and other such nonsense."

"Too bad. Besides those things, there's usually nothing to know about people. Well, all right. I'll be the navigator. You're not going to tell me anything about what happened today, either, Max? Mystery of mysteries, but I'm dying of curiosity!"

"He was my illegitimate brother," I answered in a malicious whisper. "And since we both claim the inheritance of our Papa—two old nags and a heap of their manure—I just took advantage of the privileges of office and finished off my rival."

"Very funny. So it really is a terrible secret?"

"If it were up to me, it might not necessarily remain a secret. But terrible it certainly was. So terrible that it's not even funny. Actually, if I hadn't killed him, he would have died anyway. It was something like losing the Spark, only even more unpleasant."

"How exciting!" Melifaro had an unending supply of good humor. "Fine. Never mind. You can keep your secret to yourself. By the way, there's a left turn here. Wow, you'd make a great race car driver, mate!"

"What should I know about the customs you keep at home?" I asked, changing the subject. "When Juffin dragged me over to old Makluk's to pay a visit, I nearly had a heart attack: bearers, palanquins, packs of servants everywhere, dressing for dinner. I shouldn't expect anything like that, should I?"

"Take a good look at me, Max. How could I be the son of people who observe formalities? Mama believes that every guest has one sacred obligation: to remain full at all times. My father adheres to only one rule: no stupid rules, end of story. Do you know that it's because of this I don't have a name?"

"Really? I couldn't understand why everyone always called you by your last name. I wanted to ask, but I thought maybe the problem was that you had some completely bizarre first name."

"And you spared my vanity? You shouldn't have. I don't suffer from that, and I wish others didn't, either. I just don't have a name. When I was born my father had already left on his famous journey. Mama sent him a call every day asking what to name me, and every day he had a new idea. Each day she would ask again, just to make sure—always with the same result. When I turned three, my mother finally got tired of this shilly-shallying, and she asked the question point blank. Well, magnificent Sir Manga was very busy at the time, and his answer was: 'Why does he need a first name at all with a last name like ours?' My mama has her own notions of marital harmony. She said, 'Well, may everything be as you wish, dear. You'll be the one to protest later on.' So she didn't argue with him, all the more since it wasn't a matter of her name, but of mine! And that's how I've gone through life, though it's the only thing I have to complain about—that's for sure."

"That's great. I have the opposite situation. I was lucky with my name; but that's the only thing I'm grateful to my parents for."

"That's right—you have just one name, too." Melifaro nodded sympathetically. "You're happy with it?"

"Actually, no. But you saw my living quarters. I don't like anything superfluous."

"You're right there, too. Now you have to turn left. Slow down a bit. The road gets bad here."

"Slow down? Never!" I cried out proudly, as we flew over the bumps and potholes, and the landscape whizzed by.

"Here we are," Melifaro said with relief when we had come to a high wall hung with fragrant, trailing greenery. "But are we still alive? No, Max, there's something monstrous about you! And I've invited this monster to my own home. But what can I do? I won't call for Juffin to come to the rescue. He's even worse. Let's go, Mr. Bad Dream."

The inhabitants of the enormous estate were already asleep, so we went out to the kitchen, where we silently devoured everything we could get our hands on. Then Melifaro showed me to a small, cozy room.

"When I was a child, and I was sick, or just sad, I would always sleep here. It's the best place in the house, believe me. Make yourself comfortable. This room does wonders for people who've had a hard day like you have. First, you'll fall asleep right away, no matter what your ordinary habits are. And then—well, you'll see for yourself. My runaway grandfather, Filo Melifaro, built this part of the house himself. And he was not the least significant person in the Order of the Secret Grass."

"Really? Juffin gave me a turban from their Grand Magician as a gift."

"That's really something! You're a lucky man. Try not to lose it—it's a powerful thing. I'm off. If I don't go to sleep right now, I'll expire, that's for sure."

�֍

And I was alone. A pleasant weariness lay on my chest like a pillow of soft ivy. It was wonderful. I undressed, got down on all fours, and fastidiously examined the local "dream station." I discovered the blanket and wriggled down into the warm darkness underneath. I felt calm and happy. I didn't much feel like sleeping, but lying on my back and silently contemplating the ceiling—what could be better!

The dark beams above enchaned me. They seemed to undulate ever so slightly, like waves of a tranquil sea, and eventually their rhythmic motion lulled me to sleep. In my dreams I saw all the places I loved—the city in the mountains, the English park, empty beaches. I didn't dream about Echo anymore, though. There was nothing surprising about that—Echo had become part of another life, and I roamed its streets awake now.

This time it was very easy for me to pass from one dream to another. I changed dreams at will. When I was bored by walking in the park, I stepped over to the beach. Sad and lonely among the sandy dunes, I suddenly found myself in the cabin of the cable car. Several times I thought I heard the quiet laughter of Maba Kalox nearby, but I couldn't find him anywhere. Even this seemed like a remarkable incident to me, however.

I woke up before noon, feeling absolutely free and happy. Events of the recent past seemed to me to be part of a good adventure film, the future didn't scare me, and the present suited me to a tee. After I had washed, I wrapped myself in a skaba and looxi of fiery bright colors, which I had picked out yesterday for the vibrant contrast they made with my malevolently glowering uniform, and sent a call to Melifaro.

You're already up? You've got to be kidding! And I'm still so tired I can't move! Well, go downstairs and drink some kamra with my esteemed father. Or by yourself, if he's already gone. I'll join you in an hour and a half.

I went down to the living room, where my eyes were met by a remarkable spectacle. A fellow of enormous proportions, his eyes downcast, stood by the table, wheedling and moaning.

"But Father, why?"

"Because it will be better that way," answered his elder in the voice of someone losing his patience. It belonged to a shortish, elegant man whose red hair was woven into a luxuriant braid. I swear to the World, the braid extended all the way to the floor! Sizing up the situation, I realized that this must be Sir Manga Melifaro, the author of the *Encyclopedia* I so ardently admired.

"A good morning to you, gentlemen."

I was beaming with pleasure as I entered the living room. This was strange, since I am usually shy around new people, and I can't stand introductions.

"Good morning, Sir Max Baxba, greet our guest."

"Good morning, Sir Max," the sad giant repeated obediently.

"Well, all right. Go to your trader, boy. Only remember—we need six horses. Six, not twelve! As far as I'm concerned we don't need them at all, but since you have your heart set on it. But not a dozen! Is that clear?"

"Yes, Father! Goodbye, Sir Max. You've brought me luck!" And the giant, already cheerful, bounded out of the room.

"My eldest, Sir Max," Sir Manga said with evident disbelief. "A child of 'youthful passions,' as they say. I can't fathom how I produced something like that!"

"You are truly a man of passion, Sir Manga," I smiled, and poured myself some kamra. It was as good as the kamra from the *Glutton*, hands down.

"I can't believe it myself. Besides Baxba and Melifaro, which would be more than enough to break a father's heart, I have another, middle son—Sir Anchifa Melifaro. I'm embarrassed to admit that he's a pirate. And one of the most cutthroat, if I'm to believe the dockside rumors. Although he's quite as homely and diminutive as I am myself."

"That's good for a sailor," I said. "It's best to travel light, and insofar as it's hard to leave one's own body at home, it should be as compact as possible."

"You no doubt bonded with my youngest," Sir Manga grinned. "You've both got the gift of gab."

"Moreover, he just has a last name, and I only have a first name. Together we make up one whole person."

"True, that. Were you really born on the border of the County Vook and the Barren Lands? I don't recall meeting any young fellows like you there."

"Me either," I had to shrug indifferently. "Maybe I'm just one of a kind."

"It looks that way. Sir Max, I'm afraid I owe you an apology."

"Sinning Magicians, why?"

"While Melifaro's still sleeping I can let you in on a secret. Recently he asked me about some customs of your countrymen. Now I understand why he needed to know."

"Close friendship rituals?"

"Exactly. Did Melifaro already engage in some strange antics?"

"No, but someone else did."

"A hole in the heavens above, Sir Max! You see, I'm quite vain. And when there's something I don't know . . . In short, I couldn't shame myself in front of my youngest son. I had to think up a story about singing some idiotic songs outside at midnight."

"That fellow sang them at midday. Besides, I work the night shift, so I couldn't be present for a midnight serenade. But I came to an agreement with him. He promised to limit himself to the music that sounds in his irreproachable heart."

"Praise be the Magicians! Because I got carried away and told him that—"

"That on the Last Day of the Year we had to clean each other's toilets? That certainly came as a surprise to me."

"Oh no, Max. I could never have said anything of the sort! I know a thing or two about the Barren Lands. There are no toilets to speak of, much less to found a friendship on!"

"Hm, so that was a collaborative invention. Melifaro swore on the veracity of your story."

"Don't give me away, Max! It could be very awkward," Sir Manga begged, laughing heartily.

"Throw you to the lions to be torn apart limb from limb? Never!" I swore. "But only on the condition that you let me taste some of that dish over there."

I helped myself to the tiny crumbling pastries in culinary ecstasy.

After breakfast I left the house without waiting for Melifaro to wake up, and wandered about the countryside until I got hungry. I rolled around lazily in the grass, sniffed the flowers, and filled my pockets full of little colored stones. I stared at the clouds in wonder. In short, it was one of the pleasantest days of my entire life.

In the evening I met Melifaro's mother, whose monumental stature gave away the secret of the giant Baxba's origins. At the same time she was so beautiful that it took my breath away. Not a human being, but a sculpture; moreover, a vibrant, life-affirming one.

I was surprised at myself. I fell asleep just after midnight like a good boy! And I had a serious motive. That night the little room treated me to another round of magical dreams. And I was worn out after a long day of prancing through the fields and meadows.

Morning began with a race with the wind in the amobiler. I had to deliver Melifaro, who had overslept, to the House by the Bridge in record time. He received no pleasure from the race, as he was in dreamland, blissfully unaware in the back seat. I had a hard time persuading the Diurnal Representative of the Venerable Head not to carry on his engaging pastime in his own office after we finally arrived. Upon my success, I went home to enjoy the advantages of my nocturnal schedule: I crawled under the covers again, back in the company of Armstrong and Ella.

※

At sunset I reported to the House by the Bridge and was pleasantly surprised. Lady Melamori had already returned, cheerful and ready for new feats of derring-do and renown.

"Well, you're a sight to behold!" I said from the doorway. "You owe me a walk, my Lady, remember?"

"I remember. Shall we go now? Sir Juffin will let you go."

"Sure I'll let you go," the gloomy voice of the boss resounded through the door to his office, slightly ajar. "I'll be here till late, anyway."

"Has something happened?"

"Has something happened? The annual report to the Royal Court happened. In a dozen days this blasted year ends, remember? But in a disaster of this magnitude, you can't assist me, unfortunately. So enjoy life—but only till midnight."

I whistled ecstatically—there were still five hours left until midnight, by my calculations. Somehow, things had recently taken a sharp turn for the better. It even made me a bit wary.

※

"I have just one condition, Sir Max," Melamori announced as we were about to leave. "No amobilers. I've heard frightening tales about your driving."

"All right," I agreed. "We'll go on foot, along crowded, well-lighted streets. When the full moon rises and I start turning into a werewolf, you can call for help. By the way, you can follow the example of Melifaro and drop the 'Sir' when you address me. Why stand on ceremony with werewolves?"

Melamori smiled, somewhat taken aback.

"Oh, I can't simply call you 'Max.' I wasn't raised that way."

"But I can call you Melamori. Practice for ten minutes or so—and I'll just be rude for the time being, all right?"

"Of course, Sir Max. You probably think I'm silly, but—actually, your suggestion about a crowded place is just what I had in mind. For the time being."

"'For the time being.' That sounds promising. Onward, my lady!"

We walked very chastely and modestly through the center of Echo. Only I kept having the feeling that something was missing. Then I realized: Melamori didn't have a bag or a purse that I could offer to carry, to display my chivalry. Nonetheless, at the very end of our sojourn we enjoyed the local version of ice cream in a small artificial garden on the Victory of Gurig VII Square. Thus, the illusion of childhood revisited was complete. I felt I had grown younger by about twenty years, and Lady Melamori, all things considered, by ninety. Our babbling conversation was playful and innocent, until I felt it was proper to touch upon a matter that greatly interested me.

"Melamori, I've wanted to ask you for a long time—"

"Don't, Max! I think I know what you want to ask, dear Sir, uh, yes—"

"Really? I'll bet a crown that you can't guess what it is."

"Can't guess!" she cried, her voice growing shrill.

I had found the perfect ruse. She was as reluctant to let a wager slip as a habitué at the horse races.

"You wanted to ask why I was afraid of you," she blurted out. "Hand over the crown!" She blushed with pleasure at this absurd, small victory.

"Take it, my lady," I plunked down a gold coin on the table where we were sitting. "Shall I wrap it into something, or are you superstitious?"

"Please do. I'm not superstitious, but . . . you never know."

"Excellent! But I'll bet ten crowns that you don't know yourself why you're afraid."

"Don't know? I'm not so crazy as to be afraid of who-knows-what nonsense. It's just that you, Sir Max, are—I don't know what you are! And the unknown is the only thing I'm afraid of. You lose, Sir Max. Money on the table! I'll treat you to something a bit more pricy. Would you like some King's Sweat?"

"How about some King's Piss! Whatever is it?"

"The most expensive liqueur available. Over the counter, that is."

"Fine. We'll order some of your 'Sweat.'"

"Not mine, the King's! Anyway, it looks like you have managed to loosen my tongue after all, Sir Secret Investigator."

"Frankly, I don't understand. I'm a fairly ordinary person. Well, not without a few quirks that may be explained by my origins. Sir Manga Melifaro could deliver a whole lecture on the subject."

"I don't give a flying buttress about his lectures. Let him read them to Lookfi, he adores any sort of ethnographic nonsense. Try some of the liqueur, Max. It's truly out of this world, despite the dubious name. But it's time for us to go. Sir Juffin is bored without you, Sir Max . . . uh, just plain Max."

The liqueur really was superb, though I'm not very fond of liqueur in general.

Naturally, I accompanied the damsel home. This is probably the custom in all Worlds, even when the lady is the incomparable Master of Pursuit. Along the way we were silent, until Melamori decided to dot and cross the leftover i's and t's.

"There's nothing amiss, Max. It's just that I have some doubts that I can't completely dispel—not that I attach much credence to them, either. Of course, you're no evil spirit. And you're not a Mutinous Magician, recently returned to Echo. That's obvious. But you still don't strike me as being a normal person; even one with eccentricities. I really can't figure you out. I like you very much, if you wish to know. But I sense some sort of threat emanating from you. Not just a vague, general kind of threat, but one that concerns me, personally. Though it's hard to say for sure. Sir Juffin could probably help me, but he doesn't want to. You know how he is. So I have to sort it all out myself. And I will, a hole in the heavens above you!"

"Go ahead and sort it out," I said. "And when you've sorted it out, share the information with me. Because I for one am not aware of this hypothetical 'threat.' Do you promise?"

"I promise. But this is the only thing I can really promise. Good night, Max."

With that Melamori disappeared behind the massive, ancient doors leading to her living quarters. And I went to the House by the Bridge, unsure about how to interpret the results of our evening together. On the one hand, they seemed more than promising. On the other . . . Well, time would tell. In any case, I would have to remind Lonli-Lokli to teach me some of those breathing exercises. I sensed that I would need some superhuman self-discipline in the near future.

※

A few days later, when it had started to seem that the incident involving my countryman had receded into the past, a call from Sir Juffin Hully got me out of bed somewhat earlier than I would have wished.

Wake up, Sir Max! the voice of my boss boomed through my sleepy brain. *There are things in the World that are much more interesting than the dull slumber you've been plunged in for six hours straight. A visit to Maba Kalox, for instance. I'm coming to pick you up in an hour and a half.*

I leaped out of bed as though on fire. Ella meowed indignantly at the disruption. Armstrong didn't even twitch an ear.

I bathed, dressed, and downed a mug of kamra in record time—a quarter of an hour. That still left time for me to sit down in a chair and properly wake up.

"Maba says he's ready to answer a few questions. We're in luck, Max. The old man doesn't keep his promises very often!" Juffin seemed quite pleased. "Have you already begun your training with Sir Shurf? You might need to exercise some self-control."

"I've just started, but it will be enough for me just to see Sir Maba. His face is the most effective tranquilizer I know."

"You're right about that, lad. Although this is, of course, an illusion. In fact, I don't know a more dangerous creature; or a more peaceable one," Juffin mused, leaving me completely confounded.

It didn't take as long for us to find Sir Maba Kalox's house as it had the first time. The living room was empty, but the master of the house came out to greet us in a few minutes.

In his hands, Sir Maba held an enormous tray that he was examining curiously.

"I wanted to surprise you with something tasty, but this seems to be quite inedible." He hurled away the tray, and I shrank back, anticipating a thundering crash. But the tray disappeared before it reached the floor.

"I know you don't like repetition, Maba, but we would be thrilled to be offered some of that red potion you treated us to last time," Juffin suggested hopefully.

"Well, by all means—if you are such dullards that you spurn new sensations." Sir Maba crawled under the table and drew out a pitcher and three small, delicate cups. They looked familiar.

"You haven't caught on yet, Max? Maba has compassionately stuck his nose into your own past," Juffin said laughing.

"Of course! Sinning Magicians, these are the cups from Mom's best tea set! I'll tell you a secret, Sir Maba: I hated it! And the rolls you served us last time—they sold them in the greasy spoon across the street from the editorial office where I used to work! Gosh, I'm slow."

"Probably just not very observant. Besides, you weren't expecting evidence of things from your world. A person usually sees only what he is expecting to see beforehand. Remember that for the future!" With these words he pulled a pie out from under the table.

"My grandmother's!" I exclaimed with absolute certainty. "My grandmother's apple pie! Sir Juffin, now you'll understand that my homeland isn't all that bad!"

"No, Max," Sir Maba said, surprising me yet again. "Not your grandmother's, but her friend's. The one who gave your grandmother the recipe. I thought the original would be better than the imitation. Now then, as you have already understood, boys, I solved the riddle. Congratulations, Max. You have created a Tipfinger! Which is quite extraordinary for a novice in our profession. For that matter, is quite extraordinary any way you look at it."

"What have I created? What's a Tipfinger? How could I have created something when I have no clue what it is?"

"That's how it usually works," Juffin observed. "I don't think the creator of the universe had any clue what a 'universe' was, either."

"I hate giving lectures, but for the sake of such a promising student, I am willing to abandon my scruples," Sir Maba said with a sigh. "Everything boils down to this—that in the World there are many ineffable creatures. Among them are Tipfingers. It isn't that they are so terribly hostile to human beings; but we are too different to arrive at a mutual understanding. Tipfingers come out of nowhere and feed on our fears, anxieties, and forebodings. Occasionally they take on the appearance of a particular person and visit his acquaintances, scaring them with the most uncharacteristic capers, or simply with a look. I can tell you whose appearance you unwittingly gave to the Tipfinger you created. You saw his face only once, on the street, when you were a small child. The face scared you and you began to howl. Then you forgot it, until it came time to open the Door between Worlds. You were well-prepared for this event—you lost no time or energy on unnecessary doubts.

I think you both simply chose an opportune moment, Juffin. My congratulations—that took real skill. In fact, Max, you not only opened the Door, you also planted this uncanny creature there, so you would have something to fear. You thought that the unknown had to be terrifying. And insofar as Juffin had not prepared any nightmares for you, you rectified his oversight yourself—unconsciously, of course. I could explain things in more detail, but you wouldn't understand beans about it, no offense. But you, Juffin, I'll dream you up tonight without fail and show you everything. It's very exciting! By the way, Max, until now no one knew exactly where Tipfingers came from. With your help we cracked another mysterious nut. They are the offspring of someone's inclination to fear of the unknown."

I really understood almost nothing of these explanations, though a thing or two did actually sink in.

"But that ghost, the one that lived in Xolomi, that's what he called Lonli-Lokli! He said to me, 'You brought the Tipfinger here, fellow!' Could our Shurf also really be—"

Sir Maba burst out laughing.

"Ah, Maxlilgl Annox! Don't give it another thought. That was his favorite curse. He called nearly all adepts of other Orders 'Tipfingers.' And your Lonli-Lokli, back in the day, as far as I know, was . . . where did he seek the Power, Juffin?"

"In the Order of the Holey Cup."

"That's right, the Mad Fisherman. He made some heavy-duty mischief in his day."

"Sir Lonli-Lokli? Heavy-duty mischief?" I was flabbergasted.

"Why are you so surprised, Max? People change. Take a look at yourself. Where is the pathetic little chap who trembled at the approaching footsteps of his boss?" Sir Maba said with a grin.

"This is true."

"By the way, I saw how you put the old man out of his misery. The waterfall was priceless! That was the best show I've seen since the beginning of this dreary Code Epoch."

"You saw that?" I was becoming accustomed to this nature of surprise.

"Of course! It's my hobby—keeping track of the fates of my former colleagues. That's why I couldn't pass up such a performance. But don't you entertain any illusions about the future, young man. I never intervene. I only observe. That's why Juffin Hully exists—to intervene.

For the time being we have some differences of opinion on life."

"Which has never prevented you from accepting fees for your, let us say, 'consultations,'" Juffin interposed drily.

"Of course not. I love money. It's so pretty. Actually, as for your personal Tipfinger, Max—you'll have to kill it sooner or later. It's not good to litter the Universe with any old thing. Besides, a Tipfinger in the Door between Worlds is an unprecedented outrage. There you have my consultation; and just try to accuse me of taking money from the King's coffers without deserving it!"

"Oh, that's a good one. Suddenly he's the guardian of the State Treasury!"

"How does one kill a Tipfinger?" I asked.

"When you kill it, you'll know it. Don't worry, Max. Theoretically, the matter can wait for a few hundred years. But sooner or later, you just won't have any other choice. Life is very wise. By that time, you'll certainly know what to do."

"Well, if you say so, then I will," I said. "You have confused me once and for all."

"That's how every good story must end, Max. When a person stops understanding something, he's on the right track," Juffin assured me. "We won't take any more of your valuable time, Maba. All the more since we've already eaten everything up. Don't forget: you promised to dream me up tonight."

"I won't forget. Farewell."

I was expecting some kind of escapade or outburst, but nothing of the sort happened. Sir Maba Kalox left the living room by the same door he had entered, and we went out into the front hall.

"Have I been promoted?" I asked. "Have I been accepted into the ranks? Somehow there don't seem to be any more surprises in store."

"Are you sure, Max?" Juffin said, smiling, as he threw open the door into the garden.

"Of course, I—" I stepped over the threshold and froze. Instead of the garden we found ourselves in our own office.

"Well, what do you think of that?" Sir Juffin Hully winked at me. "Never let down your guard when you're dealing with Maba Kalox."

I sat down in my chair and started to practice those very breathing exercises that the unflappable Sir Lonli-Lokli had taught me. I had only the faintest hope that they would help.

CHAPTER FIVE

KING BANJEE

I N MY HOMELAND, WE CELEBRATE THE NEW YEAR. HERE IN ECHO, AT the end of winter, they see the old year out. At home we say, "Happy New Year!" Here they say, "Another Year Has Passed."

About a dozen days before the year ends, the citizens of Echo begin to recall that life is short, and they try to do everything they didn't get around to in the past 288 days: fulfill the promises they have to others or themselves, to pay off their debts, receive what they are owed, and even willingly plunge into all kinds of unpleasantness so as not to sully the bright vista of life that awaits them (so they think) just on the other side of the "terrible year" now coming to an end. Practicality taken to an absurd extreme. In a word, the Last Day of the Year is no celebration, but a ridiculous excuse to begin—and just as suddenly to cease—mind-boggling activity.

This frenzy passed me by completely. Sir Juffin Hully was drawing up the annual report. After rushing around tearing his hair out for two days, he transferred this task onto the iron shoulders of Lonli-Lokli. The only thing I had to do was pay the debt I had run up at the *Sated Skeleton,* which took exactly fifteen minutes. In other establishments I always paid right away in cash, not so much out of contempt for local superstition, but rather in the hope that "touching metal" really would cool off love. In my case, however, it was ineffectual.

Troubles, it seemed, were not on the horizon for me. The bad habit of making promises didn't apply to me, either. The only thing left to do was to pick up the rest of my annual salary from Dondi

Melixis, the Treasurer of the Ministry of Perfect Public Order, who, it must be said, parted with the treasury funds with such a display of relief that it seemed they were burning a hole in his hands.

After wrapping up my affairs, I was forced to contemplate the haggard faces of my colleagues. They glanced enviously at my healthy pink glow, that of a lay-about who got more than enough sleep. Sir Melifaro was the most assiduous of all during these trying days. His exuberance disappeared, and he even seemed to get thinner.

"It's not just a matter of work and other troubles. I have too many relatives, too many friends, I'm too goodhearted to refuse them anything, and there are too few Days of Freedom from Care for me to be able fulfill my promises! Only orphaned ascetics like you, friend, are happy and free," Melifaro said bitterly.

It was after midnight, about four days before the End of the Year. I had arrived, as usual, for night duty. Melifaro, working practically since dawn, had just finished putting in order the next of a pile of self-inscribing tablets, wherein records of 300-year-old interrogations, and letters from one Lady Assi, peacefully coexisted. (Melifaro swore on the health of his own mama and all departed Magicians that he had no clue who she was.) He dragged himself to my office to drink some kamra in more comfortable surroundings. About eighteen distant relatives from all corners of the Unified Kingdom, who had long ago been invited to visit, had descended on Melifaro's house. I knew I had to save the poor guy.

"Send them a call and tell them . . . Well, for example, that someone is planning to assassinate Grand Magician Moni Mak, and no one but you can prevent this dastardly deed. Make something up. Then go to my place and get some sleep. True, I have merely four bathing pools as well as two cats, but when it comes to the lesser of two evils—"

Melifaro wouldn't let me finish.

"O Lord of the Endless Plain! My savior! From this day onward I am forever in your debt. Max, you're a genius. Now I know the value of true male bonding."

The pale shadow of Melifaro began again to resemble that natural disaster to which I was accustomed. He even bounced slightly in his chair—a far cry from his normally unmitigated exuberance, but it was better than nothing.

"Nonsense," I said, making light of Melifaro's praise. "You can hit the sack as soon as you get there, and sleep as long as you like. I'll stand in for you in the morning until you show up for work."

"You'll stand in for me? No offense, Max, but I'm irreplaceable. Although . . . maybe. Why not? Yes, of course! Oh, thank you!"

"I'm doing it for myself. I'm a person of habit. When I see you in this state, I feel like the World's caving in. My offer is valid until your relatives pack up and leave for their respective homes."

"The day after tomorrow. They're leaving for the estate to torment my papa and mama. But that's no longer my problem. Gosh, Max! I'm going to cry."

"Cry in the morning when you want to take a bath. Don't forget, I have only four bathing pools: just one more than a prison cell has."

"Shall I let you in on a secret, Max? I have nine washtubs, but I usually finish after the second. I'm a terrible slob. Well, I'm off. To sleep, a hole in the heavens above, to sleep!"

I stayed alone with the slumbering Kurush, somewhat abashed by my own magnanimity.

※

An hour later I had left the bird all alone and was hurrying to the outskirts of the Old City, to a tavern with the gothic name of *Grave of Kukonin*. Sir Kofa Yox had sent a call for help.

The matter was more funny than serious. It struck me as some kind of "pre-holiday fireworks." The unpleasant moment of paying the bill had arrived for a certain Mr. Ploss, one of the regular patrons of the *Grave*. A bill for the whole previous year, no less! He had no money on his person. Mr. Ploss would have had to wait only until the next day to get his salary for work and to discharge his debts.

If he had just explained this to the innkeeper of the *Grave*, everything would have been fine. People in Echo are peaceable and compassionate. But the chap had downed a few too many. I suspect that he just felt awkward asking for an extension in the presence of a dozen of his acquaintances. Mr. Ploss took the risk of casting a spell that required magic of the 21st degree. That's a serious overdose of the stuff. He made the innkeeper "remember" that he had already paid off his debt the day before. The misled innkeeper even began apologizing for his mistake, saying it was a result of the confusion of that time of year. The scoundrel humbly accepted the apology.

Mr. Ploss could have gotten away with his little prank in the pre-holiday madness if Sir Kofa Yox hadn't blown into the *Grave of Kukonin* like an ill wind. Our Master Eavesdropper has the unique talent of appearing just in that place where his presence might spoil the lives of basically good people to the maximum degree. The magic-meter on Sir Kofa's miniature snuff box reported to him that some-one was dabbling in Forbidden Magic. Discovering the fledgling sor-cerer was just a matter of technique.

When Mr. Ploss realized that his naïve practical joke and the twenty crowns he saved were worth a decade in Xolomi, he figured he had noth-ing to lose, knocked back another glass of Jubatic Juice, and decided to do battle rather than surrender. To this day, I don't understand whether it was courage or imbecility that drove him to this reckless act.

Locking himself in the bathroom, Ploss began to heckle the other patrons, claiming that his esoteric skills would suffice to turn every-one there into swine, which he could sell to the neighboring tavern for good money.

The other visitors, just in case, quickly fled from the establish-ment, and the innkeeper, in tears, began begging Kofa not to destroy his family, moreover right before the End of the Year. Then, at the request of numerous members of the public, Sir Kofa Yox summoned me. Our Master Eavesdropper could make short shrift of a dozen amateur Magicians like Ploss, but not with a gaggle of kitchen-boys sobbing in terror.

Wrapping myself tighter in the black and gold Mantle of Death, and twisting my face into a terrifying grimace, I burst into the tavern. The bells on my boots tinkled like a Christmas carol. My mouth kept twist-ing into a crooked smile. Unruly locks of hair stuck out every which way from under my turban. I didn't resemble Death in the Service of the King so much as the victim of a pre-holiday tussle. But the innkeeper of the *Grave* sighed in relief. His workers gazed at me like intellectually backward adolescents ogling Arnold Schwarzenegger. Now that's what reputation can do for you!

Stopping on the staircase that led to the bathroom, I sent a silent call to the hapless criminal. *Sir Max here, pal. You'd best come out now, before I get real mad. Don't play any games with me; the food in Xolomi is first-rate!*

That worked. To my indescribable astonishment, Mr. Ploss aban-doned his lavatory hideout then and there. He was so frightened that Sir Kofa and I had to bring him to his senses again. I even turned my pockets out for him, standing him a glass of Jubatic Juice. Actually, he had afforded me great pleasure. I think the owner of the *Grave of*

Kukonin cherishes the coin he got from me to this day, certain that it is the most potent of protective amulets.

Finally, the officials from Xolomi arrived, summoned by Kofa Yox. We handed over our quarry, who by this time was in a hopelessly gloomy state of mind. It was the first time I had been present at the ceremony of taking someone into custody and it proved to be quite a show!

One of the officials, the Master of Accomplishment, raised a small, but weighty staff over the head of the arrestee. I was afraid that he was going to brain the poor fellow: bam! and that would be that. But that wasn't what happened. What I witnessed was magic, not crude corporeal reprisal. The staff burst into scarlet flames above the head of the suspect, and a fiery number 21 hung in the air momentarily. This was precisely the degree of magic Mr. Ploss had used, according to Sir Kofa's evidence.

Then an unwieldy tome of the Code of Krember in a snow-white binding was produced. On this "bible" of the Unified Kingdom, Kofa, myself, the innkeeper, and three kitchen-boys solemnly swore that we had truly witnessed the aforementioned silent fireworks. In fact, one witness is enough, but when there are more, servants of the Chancellery of Rapid Justice note down all of them. An abundance of names attests to their professional dedication. Your everyday bureaucratic tricks, in other words.

After these legal procedures, they led the poor, half-crazed fellow away. I was pleased to see Sir Kofa again, and I would gladly have prolonged the happy reunion, but . . .

"At the End of the Year there's so much to do, Max. You understand," our Master Eat-Drink-and-Be-Merry Eavesdropper replied to my innocent suggestion that we go together to the House by the Bridge to share some gossip over a jug of kamra. "But something is telling me, 'Drop by the *Tipsy Bottle*, Kofa!' So I am forced to decline your invitation."

"Of course. Go, Sir Kofa, do what you must. Thank you for remembering Mr. Bad Dream. Was I ridiculous? My grand entrance, I mean."

"Ridiculous? It was terrifying! Just like the good old days. I almost teared up with emotion."

I went back to the Ministry.

An hour later Sir Kofa sent me a call, *Max, I was right! Magic of the seventh degree. A lady tried to pass off a one-crown coin for a whole dozen. She was also trying to pay off her debt for the year, blast it! I'm going to the* Hunchback Itullo *to enjoy myself. My heart tells me it's going to be hopping there tonight, too.*

I was taken aback.

That's the most exclusive establishment in Echo! It's frequented only by highly respectable gourmets who don't know what to do with all their money. Do you think they've started getting stingy?

The End of the Year is the End of the Year, Max. In any case, be on your guard. Over and out.

All the Secret Investigators had latched on to that expression, making Silent Speech feel like communicating via walkie-talkie.

Sir Kofa no longer needed my help, not because the Echo-dwellers had suddenly become more sensible, but because they simply didn't put up such a fuss when they were being arrested. It allowed them to hope that they could get away with only a fine and a warning.

Juffin arrived at the House by the Bridge just before daybreak, and only for a moment. He didn't even drink any kamra—an event hardly less significant than the end of the world. He took numerous parcels out of the drawer of the desk, told me confidentially that he was determined to lose his mind, and dashed off with a speed that Melifaro couldn't fathom even in his wildest dreams.

Then Lady Melamori appeared in the doorway and began complaining about life.

"Sir Max. Just Max, I mean. You can't imagine!" (The poor thing still stumbled over my name.) "You can't imagine how awful it is to have a big family!"

"I can imagine it very well," I sighed. "As we speak, another unhappy victim of family ties is snoozing over at my house, while his three million relatives think he's saving the Unified Kingdom."

"You mean Melifaro? Lucky man! I have it worse. My relatives are influential enough to free me from duty if duty interferes with family gatherings. So there's no one who can save me. I'm glad the End of the Year doesn't come every dozen days!"

"Have a mug of kamra," I suggested. "Sit down with me for half an hour. It won't be the most exciting adventure in your life, but you'll be able to relax. Maybe you'll even be inspired to comb your hair."

Melamori stared at her reflection in the convex side of the glass mug.

"Oh, how embarrassing! You're right, Max. A half hour of ordinary life wouldn't hurt right now." She took off the small lilac turban she was wearing and began arranging her wild tresses. "Well, never mind. In three days it will all be over."

"I suggest celebrating your return to ordinary existence with the most exhausting of strolls." I had decided that a little pressure wouldn't hurt. "Crowded places, brightly lighted streets, and no monkey business."

"Not necessarily," Melamori said with an unexpected smile. "I mean, crowded places aren't absolutely necessary. Who, I wonder, could protect me from Sir Max, the Terror of all of Echo? Boboota's boys? Anyway, it's bad form to promise something at the End of the Year. So I make no promises. When the year ends, though—"

"I get it. Next year I'll try to make as many promises to as many different people as possible so I won't feel I've just escaped from a Refuge for the Mad. I'll be just like everyone else."

"Thanks for the kamra, Max. I've got to run. My parents have finagled Days of Freedom for me—alas, not Freedom from Care, but from ordinary human existence. If they discover that I've come here only to wish you good morning rather than fulfilling the duties of a son—"

"You mean daughter."

"No, I made no mistake. I meant what I said: a son. My father, Korva Blimm, desperately wanted a boy. He is sure to this day that I was born a girl purely out of stubbornness. Someday I'm going to run away to your Wild Lands, I swear by the World."

Melamori, gloomy again, gave a dispirited wave and left the office and the House by the Bridge.

I yawned, more out of a feeling of helplessness than from want of sleep. The World was clearly at sixes and sevens.

Even the indestructible Sir Lonli-Lokli was destined to drink of the bitter cup at the end of the year. Even if the report Juffin had dumped on him appealed to his lower bureaucratic instincts, the guy still had worries piled up over the year waiting on his doorstep back home. And everyone needs to sleep, even Lonli-Lokli.

So he wasn't looking his best. It was the first time his impassive face had looked completely human to me. It seemed to suggest that the fellow was sick of everything.

After he had downed my kamra as well as his own, Sir Shurf boldly embarked on the last part of the report.

I wasn't the only normal person in this pre-holiday bedlam,

though. The life of our Master Curator of Knowledge, Sir Lookfi Pence, didn't seem to have suffered any change. Before it was even noon he dropped by for a chat. Well, if the chap has time for this, it must mean everything is as it should be, I surmised.

"It seems that you, too, are burdened neither by promises, nor by reports, nor by relatives," I said, looking at the cheerful boyish countenance of Sir Lookfi with pleasure and relief.

"What makes you say that?" he asked in surprise.

"Because you're the only other person whose face doesn't bear witness to the exhausting send-off of the passing year."

"What, is the year ending already?"

"In three days."

"Goodness gracious! I completely forgot! I'll have to ask Varisha if there's anything I must do. Thank you for the reminder, Sir Max."

Lookfi bounded headlong out of the office, upsetting a cup and overturning a chair. The remains of the kamra settled into the green pile of the carpet in the shape of a mournful question mark. I had no choice but to call the messenger. Someone had to clean up this mess!

After midday I began to nod off and secretly to curse the sleepy-head Melifaro. I adore the opportunity to save a human life, of course; but charity begins at home. And that was just where I wanted to be.

Melifaro showed up before I had fully exhausted my supply of curses. He looked so healthy and robust that I felt like a saint. This was even more pleasant than scaring the population of Echo with my Mantle of Death.

"All hail, Sir Max, the one and only bestower of sweet dreams!" Melifaro exclaimed from the doorway.

He could have continued this panegyric until kingdom come, but I wasn't in the mood to listen.

"I'm going home to bestow sweet dreams on myself. If someone tries to wake me up, I'll start to spit, so beware," I threatened, and called for a Ministry amobiler. Just then the ten-minute walk home didn't seem like the best way of getting there. I so desperately wanted to sleep that I began undressing in the amobiler. But who would be surprised by that at the End of the Year?

❀

The following two days passed in a similar fashion. The general tension continued to mount. But on the morning of the Last Day of the Year, I suddenly realized that everything was over.

Sir Juffin Hully arrived at the expected time, sat down in a chair, and was lost in contemplation for a time.

"You still haven't learned how to make kamra, Max?" he asked out of the blue.

"I don't think I have the knack for it. Do you remember my first attempts? The results were so disastrous I decided not to repeat the experiment."

"Fine. Now I'll teach you how to do it. Otherwise my conscience will bother me. Luring a person to a strange, unknown World, and then turning him loose without teaching him the most basic of skills . . ."

I was so surprised that I took the risk of agreeing to try. And we began casting spells over a miniscule brazier that he fished out of the bottomless drawer of his desk. Our joint creation was not bad at all, although it could never have competed with the "piece de resistance" of the *Glutton*. After this success I had to repeat it on my own.

"A hole in the heavens above you, Max," Juffin grumbled, as he tasted my creation. "You're never going to learn. It's hopeless."

"I'm a newfangled newcomer," I announced proudly. "A barbarian, a savage, and an ignoramus. You should pity me, instruct me, and not criticize me. Besides, if you had warned me that you needed a fellow who could make kamra, I would immediately have admitted that you had come to the wrong address."

"Ignorance is no sin," said Juffin. "But I don't understand. Why can't you learn this one thing? You do much more difficult things with the greatest of ease."

"Talent," I insisted. "You need talent for everything. In this area of expertise, I happen to be all thumbs. It's lucky for you, Juffin, that you never tried one of my omelets. Not to mention the rest of my culinary quirks. Sandwiches are the acme of my abilities."

"Really? That's terrible. Fine, let's go to the *Glutton*. And if someone comes when we're not here, Kurush will take care of him. Right, my dear?" Juffin said fondly, stroking the buriwok's soft feathers.

Kurush looked very pleased.

❧

Naturally, when we got to the *Glutton*, we couldn't settle for just two mugs of kamra. We had a lengthy, hearty breakfast, and I was finally convinced that the pre-holiday nightmare had been left behind.

"Don't even think of hightailing it home yet, Max! The Royal Showering of Gifts is scheduled for noon. If I'm not mistaken, you're also on the list for receiving some unadulterated nonsense or other."

"And Sir Kumbra Kurmak couldn't be persuaded to part with my souvenir an hour earlier?"

"What a sly one you are! No, you'll just have to be patient. Kumbra won't show up before noon, anyway."

"Maybe it could be a reward for saving Melifaro's life two days in a row. The only thing I'm dreaming about is going to bed."

"You'll have to wait a while. Don't pout, Max. I picked out an excellent present for you. It far outshines a present from the King."

Juffin handed me a ceramic vessel with delicate cracks on it that witnessed to a venerable old age.

"This is—!"

"Sh-h-h. Yes, it's the real thing!" The smile on the face of my boss revealed that this could be nothing other than Elixir of Kaxar, the sweet offspring of Forbidden Magic, the only potion capable of restoring my composure in any situation. Just in time!

"You're hushing me up like someone is about to rat on us as we speak. I'd like to know who—is Sir Kofa somewhere around here?"

"It's always the same," grumbled a bald, sharp-nosed old man who had just seated himself at the next table.

Yes, it was none other than Sir Kofa Yox, in the flesh—though skillfully disguised, as usual, in the interests of the profession.

"And I was just about to arrest you, gentlemen. Well, never mind. I'll insist on a bribe, though, Max. In contrast to you, I haven't slept a wink for four nights straight. Well, hardly at all, anyway. A hole in the heavens above this Last Day of the Year!"

I began to open the bottle eagerly.

"You're really letting yourselves go, boys," Juffin smirked. "Magic of the eighth degree in a public place and abusing professional privileges, that's what it is."

"Oh, give us a break, Juffin! Well, do you want Max and me to turn ourselves in? We'll turn you in, too, while we're at it. I'd like to see what you would do if we tried."

It had been a long time since I'd seen Sir Kofa so happy. He had grown younger by . . . oh, I've never been much good with numbers of that magnitude.

At midday we reported to the Chancellory of Minor and Major Inducements, where those who were eager for awards had already gathered. Never in my life have I seen so many cops in one place at the same time, I thought, and could hardly stop from laughing.

Luckily, ever since the irony of fate had wrapped me in the Mantle of Death, I could afford to overstep the protocol of almost any official ceremony. In the House by the Bridge I was granted almost everything my heart desired. Who cared about the trembling subordinates of General Boboota Box, and their boss, grunting and groaning under the weight of his own significance?

Actually, today Boboota was somewhat subdued. I recalled that it had been a while since I'd heard his refined soliloquies, redolent with a thorough knowledge of the techniques of defecation. Most likely the pre-holiday commotion had put a damper even on the brave General of the Police.

Finally, the corpulent and amiable Sir Kumbra handed me the generic Royal Trinket Box and I went home. For one thing, I had had only the smallest nip of the reviving tonic: these things must be saved for the appropriate occasion. And for another thing, the cats were waiting for me. The poor things were somewhat overwhelmed by their recent close confinement with Sir Melifaro. They, too, deserved some rewards and comfort.

"Max!" Juffin's voice reached me just as I was on my way out. I turned around.

"Something else?"

"Yes. You still have an unfulfilled promise hanging over you. You should take care of it before the New Year."

"What promise is that?" I had no idea what he was talking about.

"The last time you were at my house you promised Chuff you would visit him soon."

"Is that an invitation?"

"It's a reminder. If my company hasn't become irksome to you, just know that I'll be home by sunset, and not a minute later. I don't think anyone has to sit at the Ministry tonight. Kurush can manage without you until midnight, in any case, especially since there will probably be nothing to manage."

"Thank you. Of course I'll come. I'll eat everything that's put on the table. And then I'll go rummage around in the closets."

"I don't doubt it. All right, go get some shuteye."

꒰꒱

Armstrong and Ella greeted me with petulant meowing. As a consequence of Melifaro's deep sleep, they had received their breakfast several hours later than usual over the past few days, and they didn't intend to welcome the innovation.

"That's all over, my little furries," I reassured them, filling their bowls. "Everything's back to normal now."

Curiosity proved to be stronger than weariness. Before I fell asleep, I opened the Royal Trinket Box to see what was inside. Not a hundred days had passed since I had tried to open just such a box. Now I did it almost mechanically. Hmm, yes. Magic of the fourth degree we had already mastered, and much else, besides, a hole in the heavens above!

This time I had received a surprisingly beautiful little medallion made of white steel, which is prized far more highly than gold in this World that lacks precious metals. On the medallion was the likeness of a fat, peculiar-looking, but very appealing little creature. Peering closely at it, I gleaned that the unknown artist had tried to depict Armstrong (or Ella, his nearly identical other half).

꒰꒱

Three hours of sleep was more than enough. Even a tiny drop of Elixir of Kaxar can do wonders, it seems. In my joy, I straightened up the house, cleaned up after the cats, and even shaved. Then I sat in the living room, filling my pipe with the local tobacco, the taste of which I had never been able to get used to. But the ritual of fiddling with the pipe is itself one of the true pleasures of domestic leisure.

At sundown, I carefully packed myself into the amobiler and set out for the other side of the Xuron, to the quiet and respectable Left Bank. I drove through completely empty streets. Restaurant proprietors were peacefully nodding off in the doorways of their establishments, not really hoping to take in any profits that night. Birds wandered about on the mosaic pavements. The residents of Echo were resting from the cares of the year gone by. There was no trace of noisy celebration, only the deep, unbroken slumber for which the capital had so desperately longed.

꒰꒱

Juffin opened the door for me himself. Kimpa, his butler, had gone to sleep right after he had laid the table. Our eagerness to stay up and talk had no doubt struck him as the height of eccentricity.

The first thing I did was embrace Chuff, who was practically swooning in ecstasy. The little dog licked my nose carefully, and then started in on my ear. I prefer other modes of washing, but I vowed to enjoy this one.

"I've come bearing no gifts," I apologized, sitting down in a comfortable chair. "You know how thrifty I am. But I think I can find something for you, little fellow."

I unwrapped a small parcel. Inside were Chuff's (and my own) favorite cookies from the *Hunchback Itullo*, delicious beyond description, and just as pricey. Sir Juffin Hully claims that making this delicacy without resorting to forbidden degrees of magic is nearly impossible. Be that as it may, the chef there is above suspicion. They inspect him every dozen days, and no trace of mischief is ever found.

That's what true culinary talent is—the lack of which, in yours truly, we were bemoaning only that morning.

Max is good. Chuff is fluent in Silent Speech. Better than I am.

"Did you squander your whole life's savings on those cookies?" Juffin asked.

"Only half of it. The other half I squandered, as you put it, on this." And with the dramatic flourish of a seasoned conjuror, I gave my left hand a shake, and a small, pot-bellied bottle of dark glass appeared on the table.

"You're lying about the cost. These things can't be bought or sold," said Juffin in rapture. "Is it possible that Melamori is sharing again? I thought that she had broken your heart; but it seems to have been a well-laid plan. You're a genius, Max! You discovered the only foolproof way of filching wine from the cellars of the Seven-Leaf Clover. Very practical! I'm impressed."

"Do you think that she would filch something from her uncle to give to me, as if to a bosom buddy? No way. We just had a bet, and I won hands down."

"You were betting?"

"Well, yes. She loves taking a gamble. But you must be aware of this."

"I never attached any significance to it. What was the bet?"

"I told her I could talk to General Booboota for fifteen minutes without him using the words *butt*, *crap*, and *gaseous expulsions*, as it were. She didn't believe it was possible. Then I went to Boboota and began discussing the latest news. As you can imagine, he listened, snorted, and nodded his head. In the privacy of his own thoughts he probably cursed me a thousand times. I simply took advantage of the situation. Melamori hadn't been around for a few days and wasn't aware that relations between me and Boboota had taken a new turn."

"I heard about it, though. Some say he's developed a nervous tic. Whenever Boboota begins to express the fruits of his contemplation out loud, he keeps glancing around furtively to see if you're anywhere nearby. Gosh, Max, I never expected you could make me so happy!"

"There might have been an easier way—just hire some werewolf."

"Life has proven that you are far more terrifying. So you won the bet?"

"There's the evidence," I said, nodding at the bottle. "*Dark Essence*, one of the best varieties, according to Melamori. She said that it was a fair exchange."

"The girl is absolutely right, on both counts. You surprise me, Max. Wines like this are meant to be drunk in solitude, behind locked doors in a distant room, so that an evil wind doesn't blow your best friends over on an inopportune visit."

"And I'm sucking up to you. I gather that in your cellar you keep not only the skinned hides of magicians, but also a couple cases of Elixir of Kaxar."

"Why should I store it away? I can make that stuff myself! It's not forbidden to disregard the Code in the interests of the Crown. Grand Magician Nuflin Moni Mak thinks the same."

"All the more. I share those views completely. It's too bad I'll never learn how to make it myself."

"No, you probably won't. You can't even learn to make kamra, poor boy," Sir Juffin Hully seemed to feel truly sorry for me.

"I have to have at least one fault," I consoled my long-suffering teacher, and pushed the bottle of *Dark Essence* toward him.

※

By the time I got back to the office, I felt more like a human food vendor cart than a human being. I needed to stretch my legs and wiggle my toes.

Despite Sir Juffin Hully's optimistic prognosis of a quiet night ahead of me, a matter awaited that wasn't exactly business as usual.

In the Chair of Despond in the Hall of Common Labor, a charming, middle-aged lady, wearing an expensive looxi that she had pulled on right over her everyday skaba, was wailing and keening. The damsel was in that stage of shock when incoherent mumbling is over, but the gift of speech has yet to return. For that reason I didn't dispute the citizens' right of our guest to quiet moaning, but obeyed some latent instinct and handed her the mug of kamra I had tried to make myself earlier. I decided that such liquid muck would restore her emotional equilibrium no worse than smelling salts—which, by the way, are prohibited here as magic of the third degree.

She gulped the stuff down mechanically and finally grew quiet. Even her sobs ceased. It was surprising that she was still alive at all.

Kurush was the only one capable of giving a full account of what had happened to the unfortunate visitor before she came to her senses. He was the sole witness of her surprise visit. I turned to him expectantly, and the buriwok conveyed the following information without a moment's hesitation:

"My husband turned into a piece of meat, my husband turned into a piece of meat, my husband turned into a piece of meat."

I looked at Kurush mournfully, then at the damsel, then at Kurush again, then—at the ceiling, which got in the way of the sky. Why, O Dark Magicians? I'm not such a bad person. You might even say I'm a very good person. So spare me, please!

The paltry "please" changed nothing. The madness progressed. Kurush kept up his refrain about a husband and meat. I knew that now he wouldn't be quiet until he had scrupulously reported every word that had been spoken in my absence. Hearing her own monologue from the mouth of the talking bird, the lady made a reverse turn on the path toward tranquility and was soon back on the verge of hysteria. I forced another gulp of the black muck on her, and it helped. The poor woman raised her beautiful, forlorn eyes to me and whispered:

"It's horrible, but in the bed there really is a huge piece of meat, and Karry is nowhere to be found."

The buriwok finally fell silent. He seemed to be quite upset, too. I stroked his feathers gently.

"Good boy. What a smart fellow you are! Everything's all right now. You were brilliant, Kurush. If I had known what was going on here, I wouldn't have stayed away so long."

Kurush puffed up in satisfaction. Sir Juffin Hully knew how to raise the most spoiled buriwok in the entire Unified Kingdom, though also the most kindhearted.

"People usually don't come to the House by the Bridge on the Last Day of the Year," he said. "So it's not your fault, Max. It's amazing you came back at all."

I turned to the woman again.

"What is your name, my lady?"

She smiled through her tears. (Excellent, Max. You're a real playboy, Mantle of Death notwithstanding.)

"Tanita Kovareka. My husband is Karry—I mean Karwen—Kovareka. We have a little inn here in the Old City, the *Tipsy Bottle*. Maybe you know it? But now Karry—" and she burst into quiet sobbing again.

"I think we ought to go to your house right away," I said firmly. "You can explain everything along the way. If there's anything you wish to explain, of course. You won't object if we go on foot? As far as I know, it's about ten minutes from here at the most."

"Of course," she said. "I could use some fresh air."

Before leaving, I stroked Kurush again. Indulge him and indulge him some more—that's the treatment both Juffin's and my own heart insisted on.

❄

The night's warm velvety haze seemed to gather us into its comforting arms. Soon, Lady Tanita had almost calmed down. A person simply cannot suffer longer than she can suffer. When strength is exhausted, our attention turns to other things, whether we wish it to or not; and that is a great boon.

"Everyone's always afraid of you, Sir Max, but I feel so peaceful in your presence." Lady Tanita's even embarrassed me with her compliments. "People gossip and say that Sir Venerable Head found you in the other world. Is that true?" she asked suddenly.

"Almost in the other world," I confessed, trying to squirm out of this one. "On the border of the County Vook and the Barren Lands."

"Too bad," my companion sighed. "If it had been true, you would have been able to tell me how Karry was doing."

Mr. Kovareka was a lucky man, I thought. Even if he were really dead, he had been wrapped in love and concern when he was alive, that much was certain.

"Don't jump to conclusions yet, Lady Tanita," I said, trying to console her. "Maybe nothing irreparable has happened."

"It has!" she whispered. "It was not just an ordinary piece of meat, Sir Max. It was a piece of meat in the shape of a human being. And it was wearing Karry's pajamas!"

Lady Tanita began sobbing again, but no tears fell from her eyes. She continued to talk, the only way she knew to relieve her pain.

"We were tired and went to bed very early. There were no customers. There are no customers anywhere tonight. Then I suddenly woke up. You know, Sir Max, I always wake up when Karry is in pain, or even when he's thirsty. We've lived together a long time, now—I suppose that's why. We married very young. Our parents objected, but they just didn't understand. So I woke up absolutely certain that something was amiss with Karry. Then I saw that horrible piece of meat wearing his pajamas. There was even something resembling a face. Here we are, Sir Max. I don't want to go up to the bedroom, though."

"I'll go upstairs alone. And you know what I suggest? If I were you, I'd find the company of my friends, or a relative, just in case worse comes to worst. Get them out of bed and tell them your sorrows. They'll give you all kinds of potions, and finally you'll grow tired of simple consolations and fall sound asleep. It may seem unbearable, but . . . it's a way to keep from losing your mind. I'll send you a call when I need to question you, but it will most likely not be before morning."

"I'll go over to Shattraya's. She's Karry's youngest sister. Lady Shattraya Kovareka is her full name. She's a good girl, and I'll have to comfort *her*. And that's better than . . . You're a very kind person, Sir Max. Only a person who truly knows what pain is could give me such advice. Thank you."

"Shall I accompany you?" I called into the darkness.

"Shattraya lives just on the next street over!" The faint voice of Lady Tanita melted away in the dull orange mist of the streetlights.

❀

I went into the house through the relatively small living room. Of course, a large part of the house was occupied by the *Tipsy Bottle,* a cozy little restaurant whose atmosphere was completely incongruous with its silly name. I had been there once during the fall, I seemed to remember. I recalled that I had even chatted with the proprietor, a short, stocky man with an exceptionally thick crop of chestnut hair. At that time I wasn't yet wearing the Mantle of Death, and I wasn't constantly being bombarded with polite, strained smiles and terrified looks.

I went upstairs. If only Lady Tanita had known that, without her, I was as scared as a child whose parents risk leaving him alone for the first time to go to the movies! But there was nothing I could do about it.

I threw open the door to the bedroom with a heavy heart. My nose was greeted by a smell of tasty food so unexpected that I froze in my tracks. Then I groped around for the light switch. A warm orange light filled the room. Here in Echo, special glowing mushrooms are often used for lighting streets and interiors. They multiply eagerly in special vessels like lampshades. The trick is that the mushrooms begin to shine when something irritates them. The light switch sets brushes in motion that gently but insistently tickle the mushrooms caps. They react instantaneously.

The orange hue of the angry mushrooms doesn't appeal to everyone. Many esthetes prefer candles, or spheres with glowing blue gas. Sir Juffin Hully is partial to the latter. I got used to blue light when I lived with him, and I acquired the same kind of spheres for my own living quarters. But now the orange illumination also seemed sweet to me; the people who lived here thought so, too, apparently.

Thus, the mushrooms worked themselves into a temper, and I was able to glance around.

Something was lying in the middle of the fluffy carpet among the scattered blankets. That something was indeed dressed in garb resembling pajamas—a roomy skaba made of soft fabric. I had never taught myself to use this unappealing garment. To romp around in a skaba and looxi, that was one thing. But to sleep in a shapeless parachute of a thing that looked like your grandmother's nightgown—excuse me! That was asking too much. And in a good bed, one must sleep in one's birthday suit—a time-tested rule.

The mysterious "something" clearly belonged to the opposing camp, since it was wearing pajamas. Its resemblance to a human being seemed to stop there, however. In front of me was a real piece of meat, well-cooked and appetizing. It gave off a dizzying, tantalizing, and vaguely familiar aroma.

I inched closer. This was very trying on the nerves. I almost got sick, despite the wonderful aroma. The meat really did have the wretched face of a human being. The remains of its features were encircled by a halo of chestnut curls that even I recognized as belonging to Karwen, though I had only once laid eyes on him. Lady Tanita was right. There were no grounds for hoping otherwise.

"Sinning Magicians," I exclaimed aloud. "Now what am I supposed to do!"

※

I went down to the living room, entered the dark restaurant, and poured myself a full glass of the contents of the first bottle I grabbed. I couldn't make out the name of the drink in the darkness, but the taste wasn't too bad. Then I stuffed my pipe with tobacco. The taste of the local tobacco didn't matter at all—under the circumstances, it was better than nothing.

I sat alone at the bar in the light cast by the dim orange nimbus of the streetlight, sipping the anonymous drink, and smoked. This simple ritual was enough to restore some semblance of order to my thoughts. I realized there was no need to bother Melifaro, and especially not Sir Juffin. Let them catch up on their sleep. I'm not such a moron that I can't handle these routine matters. It's my job, after all.

Having resolved my moral deliberations, I went back to the bedroom. The tantalizing smell again seemed familiar to me. Where could I have smelled it before? Not in the *Glutton Bunba*, that's for sure. The smell in the *Glutton* is unique: sharper and spicier. Certainly not in the *Sated Skeleton*, which delivered my breakfast every morning. And not . . . it remained just out of reach. It didn't smell like my grandmother's kitchen. Although . . . I finally went completely astray, as so often happens when you try to fish out a single kernel in the rice pudding of your memories.

Abandoning this olfactory wild-goose chase, I dug into my pockets for the dagger. The gauge mounted on the handle showed evidence of magic of the second degree. This was not only officially permitted, but also absolutely logical, since I was in the presence of the remains of a restaurant proprietor. And who is more adept at practicing permissible Black Magic than a chef? This modest degree of conjuration, in my humble opinion, was nowhere near potent enough to transform a human being into something like what I saw before me. Fine, we'd deal with that question later. Now I had to remove the body to the House by the Bridge, I reasoned, because that was the proper procedure. Further, I couldn't bear thinking of that abomination in the marital bower. Sooner or later the sweet Lady Tanita would return. What an incompetent figure I'd cut if she had to see that gruesome piece of meat again!

It wasn't that I felt sorry for this woman, nor could what I experienced have been called pity. It was just that everything that had happened to her seemed to be happening to me, as well. Lady Tanita's sorrows washed over me like the sound of a television blaring in the next room. It wasn't inside me, but I couldn't escape it. In short, I experienced in the flesh the literal meaning of "empathy."

There is nothing simpler than carrying out the impossible. You just have to imagine what you must do, and turn your mind off completely. When you come to your senses, everything is already behind you.

I swear by the World that when I was wrapping the piece of meat in the blanket, I felt not a shred of emotion. I didn't feel anything later, either, when I was enacting my favorite trick, as a result of which the disgusting mummy fit between the thumb and forefinger of my left hand. And while I was walking through the empty city to the House by the Bridge, my feelings were dormant, as though some part of myself, tender and vulnerable, had been put into cold storage until better times.

When I reached the Ministry, I wondered where I should unload my burden. Perhaps in the small, dark chamber, thoroughly insulated from the rest of the world, where material evidence was stored? Or in one of the chilly, spacious basement rooms that served as the morgue and were nearly always empty? I was so perplexed about this dilemma that I decided to consult Kurush.

"If you're sure that this was once a person, it can only be a corpse," said the wise bird.

I felt relieved. Here was some degree of certainty, in any case.

Only after the aromatic corpse was on the stone floor did I allow myself to become a bundle of nerves again.

I went to wash my hands. I washed them for a full half hour, scraping away at the skin with my fingernails.

After this ritual purification on my upper extremities, I felt better and went back to the office.

"An auspicious End of the Year, eh?" I said, winking at Kurush. "A visit from a beautiful damsel and a mountain of food."

"Are you serious, Max?" asked the buriwok cautiously. "I don't think you can eat that. In fact, people are constantly eating all kinds of junk they shouldn't."

"Of course I'm joking," I said, petting the bird's soft feathers.

"Do you know whether there's any good kamra left over around here, Kurush? The kind I didn't make, that is?"

"In Melifaro's office there's most likely a whole jug of it," the buriwok replied. "I saw them bring it in, and I know the master of the office left a few minutes later. They also had pastries with them, so who knows."

"Great."

I catapulted headlong into the office of my "daylight half." On the table I found a jug of kamra and several pastries. The fellow had been so eager to return to his home, now emptied of relatives, that he didn't bother to finish the treats, though at his habitual rate of consumption they should have been gone in seconds flat, so Kurush and I were in luck. We were unlikely to reach the ever-hospitable Madame Zizinda with a call. Any other time or season, sure, but not the Last Night of the Year.

※

Toward morning, I managed not only to drink all the kamra and help Kurush clean the sticky cream off his beak, I did more: I drew up a plan of action. I was ready to accept the challenge, in the spirit of Melamori and her gambling fever. It was the first time in my professional life that I had been on a case from the word go. With all my heart I wanted to see it through to the end, and to do everything properly. Naturally, there could be no thought of dealing with it all on my own. That wasn't necessary. But I felt that when Juffin arrived, I simply had to greet him, not only with the news of the sordid case, but also with an aim to solving it.

Juffin, it seemed, had sensed something was up, arriving much earlier than he was expected.

"Couldn't sleep," the chief announced gloomily, sitting down in his chair. "Everything all right with you, Max?"

"With me, yes. But as for a certain sweet lady—no, I wouldn't say so. This wondrous night has left a widow in its wake."

Then I reported to Juffin what had happened, down to the last detail.

"Hm, is that why I jumped out of bed this morning like I had been stung? What I want to know is whether Zizinda has opened her lair already, or whether she's still in the land of nod. Never mind, she won't refuse to stir her stumps for such an old customer. Now I'll just take a glance at your 'piece of meat,' and it's off to breakfast. Let's go, Sir Max."

After a visit to the morgue, we went out to the *Glutton.* Just where was the logic in our actions, I wondered. Madame Zizinda greeted us at the door. Evidently, her intuition was in fine working order, too.

"Juffin, I've had some time to think," I mumbled, turning red and staring at my plate. "Actually, I have a plan."

"What's wrong with you, Max?" the chief raised his eyebrows in surprise. "Where is your ever-ready supply of self-confidence?"

"Well, you see, when I was mulling it over I felt so smart and clever; but now . . . Of course, you'll have your own plan of action. And mine is no match for it, I'm sure."

"Nonsense," said Juffin and patted me on the back. "So what if I have? And what makes you think I have one at all? Come on, then. Out with it."

"This is what I think. It's all very strange, of course. I don't know whether this is unprecedented—maybe during the Epoch of Orders . . . In short, I would submit a request to the Main Archive. Let Lookfi question all the buriwoks. If there was a precedent, it could help us. Then we have to find out more about Mr. Karwen Kovareka. Maybe he got mixed up with some Mutinous Magicians, stumbled on a secret of the Order, for instance? We have to find out. I think for Kofa, finding out is just a matter of one, two, three. And Melamori probably has to visit the bedroom to discover whether anyone else was there who shouldn't have been. I don't think so myself, but just to make sure I can talk to Lady Tanita. She seems to like me. I gave her some advice about how not to lose her mind, and we made friends. Now, Melifaro, I think, should lead the parade. He knows how to ignite everyone's interest, and he can manage Boboota's boys, as well. That's about it."

"Wonderful!" exclaimed Juffin. "This means I can even retire tomorrow if I want to. You're really a fine fellow, and I mean that with all my heart. Eat up!"

I tucked into my food, already growing cold, with relish.

"We'll put your plan into action," Juffin said in a decisive tone. "You seem to have all the bases covered. I have only one comment to make."

"What is that?" I said, my mouth full of food, and happy that there was just one comment.

"You must remember how you recognized the smell," he said earnestly.

"Oh, Juffin. I've already broken my head—my nose—over that one. It's no use."

"I know one thing for sure: it's not from your world. You can trust me on this one. It's a very strange scent, but it is indigenous to this World. There's not the slightest doubt about it. So start walking around town. Visit one by one all the taverns you've been in before. And sniff them out. Who knows?"

"Okay, but what's to say that when I find the place they'll be serving the same thing?"

"You're lucky, Max. That's your only guarantee. The main thing is not to come down with the sniffles—this is absolutely the wrong time. Let's go to the Ministry. You'll be in command, and I can enjoy myself."

"Are you making fun of me?"

"Why should I want to do that? Your plan deserves the highest praise. So implement it."

"Juffin, it's much easier for me to do things myself than to explain to a bunch of people what I think they should be doing."

"I know. I'm the same way. But life doesn't always live up to our expectations. You have to get used to that."

❋

We returned to the House by the Bridge. Then Juffin went home to have a few dreams, since, as he said, his faith in me was absolute. He had finally convinced me of that. I also understood that I had to crack this case before sunset or die. Or at least burn up from shame, and become a silver residue of ash somewhere in a dark corner of the Ministry for Perfect Public Order. And it has plenty of dark corners.

I heaved a sigh, gathered my wits, and got down to work. I sent a call to Melifaro, to Sir Kofa, and to Melamori. I told them to report to work. All three of them were shaken down to the soles of their feet. I wasn't so fluent in Silent Speech, though, that I could offer my colleagues the opportunity to say everything they thought about me and my idiotic appeal at daybreak on the First Day of the Year. "Over and out!" I barked, and signed off, realizing further cause for why Juffin had been so willing to give me a chance to prove my mettle.

There was no point in bothering Lookfi. The buriwoks from the

Main Archive don't open their beaks before noon. They have their own daily rhythm of existence. It's only our Kurush who is a saint.

❀

Melamori was the first to arrive. It seemed I had given her a reasonable pretext for escaping the parental embrace a few hours earlier than planned. In any case, she wasn't angry.

"You look fabulous!" It was impossible for me not to gush. "Have you had enough sleep?" I gallantly filled her cup with kamra.

"Has something happened, or did you just miss me?" Melamori asked with a grin.

"Of course I missed you, but that's no reason to wake you up at dawn. I'm not such an ogre as they claim I am. Well, I wouldn't think twice about devouring a few dozen old men and babies. But not allowing a lady to sleep her fill?"

"Well, whatever has happened?"

"A corpse happened. And a strange one it was. You can come to admire it—and to enjoy the aroma at the same time. I'm not kidding: take a deep whiff. Then come back here. There will be another cup of kamra waiting for you, and an assignment."

Melamori obediently carried out my orders and went down to the morgue.

She came back with a troubled expression on her lovely face.

"Smell familiar?" I asked.

"Yes! But I have no idea why."

"Same here. Well, don't worry. If you can't remember, you can't remember. Here's your kamra. Drink up, and forward, march to the *Tipsy Bottle*."

"What am I to do there? Drink myself into oblivion while the sun rises?"

"Precisely, and in between your eighth and ninth glasses of Jubatic Juice, don't forget about going up to the master bedroom. Find out whether anyone besides the legal owners of the place was there last night. Except for me, of course."

"So was that Karwen in the morgue? I'm slightly acquainted with his wife. Gosh! What a present on the Last Day of the Year!"

"The first day of the year, Melamori! Be optimistic. There's a saying in my homeland: 'The way you celebrate the New Year is the way you'll live it.' Can you imagine?"

"Do you believe that, Max?" Melamori looked at me in almost superstitious horror. "And nothing can be done to change it?"

"In my homeland, no. But in Echo, the silly signs and superstitions of the Barren Lands are not in force. So off you go to the *Tipsy Bottle*!"

"I'm going, I'm going. Just between you and me, you're a worse tyrant than Juffin!"

"I hope I am. Speaking of tyranny, it seems I'll have to hit all the diners and snack bars in town trying to track down that scent again. And since you recognized it, too, I order you to accompany me."

"You're ordering me to hit all the diners and snack bars in town with you, Sir Max? I mean, just plain Max?" said Lady Melamori with a laugh.

"Of course," I said. "I'm abusing the privileges of office in the best of interests. I've dreamed of this my whole life, and here I am in the driver's seat. Now you won't be able to wriggle out of it."

"I wouldn't think of trying," said Melamori, and gazed at me, so clearly delighted that I suddenly turned red as a tomato. Then she left to carry out the task I had so tyrannically assigned.

※

Sir Kofa Yox arrived exactly two seconds before Melifaro, and both of them were burning with curiosity about whether my poor head was still in working order. They were alarmed when I related the events to them. This was the first serious crime that had taken place in Echo on the Last Night of the Year since the beginning of the Code Epoch. This was what Sir Kofa Yox claimed; and that was saying something.

By the time they arrived, I was already very tired. So I laid out the plan of action for them, and when I issued my orders, I was so cool and matter-of-fact it seemed I had been issuing them my whole life.

"I don't think poor Karwen could have been involved in any dark matters," said Sir Kofa, plucking the hem of his looxi thoughtfully. "But you're right, my boy. We need to investigate his recent activities. People are capable of things that are so out of keeping with their characters, you can hardly credit it."

"Especially at the End of the Year," I said with a grin.

"Precisely. I'll return at sundown, and if I uncover anything unusual I'll send you a call."

Kofa passed his hand in front of his face, changing his features without missing a beat. He turned his purple looxi inside out, so the modest brown lining was facing outward. Our Master Eavesdropper was ready to embark on a hard day's work.

"And what is your command for me, O Terrible Child of the Night?" Melifaro had already jumped up from his chair, ready for action.

"Take a whirl through the Ministry. Stop in at the morgue and admire my catch. If you're in the mood you can have breakfast. Wait for Melamori. Find out what she's dug up. Actually, I'm sure that no one but the master and mistress had been in the bedroom. Ask around on Boboota's side of the Ministry. Maybe one of the police-men knows something. Even the devil has a sense of humor."

"And who is this 'devil' who likes a good joke?"

"Well, something between a vampire and a Mutinous Magician."

"Ah, something like yourself."

"I saved your life! I hid you from your hordes of relatives under my own blankets," I said reproachfully. "And instead of falling at my feet or inviting me to dinner, all I get is—"

"I'm a swine," Melifaro admitted, sounding aggrieved. "I'm inviting you. Today. No matter how much work there is, we still have to fill our bellies."

"It's nice to hear such pearls of wisdom. Mind you, it's the *Hunchback Itullo* or nothing."

"I wouldn't settle for less. Do I have your permission to depart, Sir Great Commander?"

"Permission granted. Hey, wake me up in about two hours, all right? I have a date with a beautiful lady."

"Maybe I could stand in for you?" Melifaro said enthusiastically.

"Dream on. You're not quite the man inconsolable widows are searching for. Moreover, you'll be meeting the magnificent Sir Lookfi at that time. Have you forgotten? Anyway, let me get some sleep!"

"Right here?"

"Yes. If I go home, wild horses wouldn't be able to drag me out from under the blanket."

"True. It's virtually impossible to get out from under your blanket," Melifaro said with the confident air of an expert. "Did you cast a spell over it? And what if Juffin comes here and wants to get some work done?"

"It won't bother me," I said, rearranging the chairs into the piti-ful likeness of a bed.

"It's beginning to dawn on me," Melifaro mused. "You've done away with our unfortunate chief, and now—"

"If you don't let me get some sleep, I'll do away with you," I mumbled, already feeling the sweet tug of slumber. "I've changed my mind. Wake me up in two and a half hours, not two. In fact, make it three. And tell Urf to feed my cats. I just promised them yesterday that life was getting back to normal."

"All right, go to sleep. I'll take care of everything. Otherwise you might start spitting," said Melifaro, and he disappeared out the door.

It seemed I had closed my eyes for no more than a minute. When I opened them again, Melifaro was there, looking down at me.

"Well, what now?" I said.

"What do you mean 'what now'? You asked me to wake you up. Come on, upsy-daisy, Mr. Bad Dream. It's time for me to go to the Main Archive. Besides, I've got some news for you."

"A hole in the heavens above this World!" With a groan I tore my head away from the spot where normal people usually have a pillow. "It's already been three hours? How unfair!"

"Three and a half," said Melifaro, handing me a mug of hot kamra. "Juffin hides the Elixir of Kaxar in the lower left drawer of the desk. He made the bottle invisible, but you'll find it if you fish around for it."

"I know how to find it without your prompting," I growled. I tore into Juffin's desk drawer with the express goal of appropriating his personal property. A few seconds later, I was chomping at the bit to move a mountain or two.

"Now I can at least stand being around you," Melifaro said approvingly. "Have you known about this hiding place a long time?"

"Since my first day on the job. After the scandalous adventure of the Soup of Repose, our chief realized that Elixir of Kaxar provided me with my only chance to wallow in vice. So, what's the news?"

"First, our department: Melamori couldn't find any traces of intruders or strangers. Except yours, of course. As you predicted. Master Mouthful-Earful hasn't reported back yet. On the other hand, the City Police have a piece of news that makes everything else pale by comparison. Boboota has disappeared."

"What?!" I spluttered, spewing kamra everywhere. "Are you serious?"

"Never been more so. He left for his meal right after the Royal

Showering of Gifts. Since then, no one has seen him. His subordinates figured that the General had gone home, and were too happy to entertain any doubts. His servants at home thought Boboota was on duty. I think they were quite happy with the situation, as well. This morning, his wife finally decided to send a call to her beloved Boboota."

"And?"

"Very strange, Max. He's alive—Lady Box is sure of that. He's alive, but he doesn't respond to any calls, as though he is sleeping very soundly."

"And Melamori? Has she been looking for him?"

"She's still looking."

"How's that? I thought she worked fast."

"That's just it. In the Chancellery of Encouragement there's not a trace of Boboota."

"That's impossible. Yesterday at noon he was stomping around over there."

"That's right, stomping around. Life, you know, is a complicated matter. It's only in your homeland where everything is simple and straightforward: either there is horse dung, or there isn't."

I made a frightening grimace. Quick as lightning Melifaro hid under the desk, where he continued his story in the trembling voice of a scared little boy.

"Not in the Chancellory, not on the stairway, not by the entrance. There isn't a trace of Boboota anywhere! Rather, the traces are everywhere, but they're very old. Twelve days at least. They don't count. Mr. Vampire, you're not mad anymore, are you?"

Instead of answering, I laughed like a maniac, not so much at Melifaro's antics as at the news. And what news!

"The entire City Police Force is looking for Boboota." Melifaro went on. "If they don't find him by sunset, they'll hand over the official case to us."

"Does Juffin know?"

"He certainly does."

"Is he happy?"

"You bet he is. He'll arrive here at sundown to start the investigation. Maybe he had a hand in the disappearance himself?"

"I wouldn't be at all surprised," I smiled. "Are you planning to stay under the desk until he gets here? What about the Main Archive?"

"You promise you won't spit?"

"I might. The only thing that will save you is sheltering under the wing of a buriwok."

"Fair enough." Melifaro dashed out from under the desk, finished his kamra in a gulp, and disappeared into the corridor, waving goodbye.

Then I was alone. I sent a call to Tanita.

I'll come in a quarter of an hour, Sir Max, she replied. *You know, the advice you gave me—well, everything was just as you said. I didn't lose my mind. I even slept for a few hours. Thank you.*

I ordered the junior staff to straighten up the office, and then sent a call to the *Glutton*. If I had to turn poor Lady Tanita inside out for information, let her at least eat something. It was unlikely that anyone but me would be able to persuade her to take some breakfast. I wasn't even certain I'd be able to, but I'd have to try.

Lady Tanita Kovareka arrived within fifteen minutes, as promised. She had managed to change her clothes, and she looked the picture of elegance. Here in Echo, they don't have the custom of dressing in mourning. It is thought that each person's pain is a private matter, and broadcasting your loss to passersby on the street is uncouth.

"Good day, Sir Max," she greeted me, not without a trace of sarcasm. She had the courage to acknowledge the bitter irony of the traditional form of greeting. Lady Tanita rose even higher in my estimation.

"You know why I called you. I have to find out what your husband had been doing, especially in the recent past. I know it's painful to talk about, but—"

"I completely understand, Sir Max. Things like that don't just happen out of the blue. Of course you have to find out who . . . But I'm afraid I won't be of any help here."

"I know what you're trying to say. There was none of *that*. It always seems that nothing was amiss until a misfortune befalls someone. Then it becomes clear that a few completely insignificant actions were the first steps along the path to calamity."

I had devoured enough detective novels in my time to be able to resort to this commonplace. I just hoped that the authors of the books knew a bit about life.

"All right, Sir Max. I can still only tell you one thing, though. Our life was passing just as usual—"

"Right, Lady Tanita. But you understand—I'm an outsider. I don't know how your life usually passes. So explain it in a bit more detail."

"Of course. Every day Karry got up before daybreak and went to the market. We have plenty of servants, but he preferred to select all the meat and produce himself. Karry is—was—a very good cook. For him this was not just a way of making a living, but something more—an art—a matter of honor and love, you might say. When I woke up, he was almost always at the helm in the kitchen. We opened two hours before midday, sometimes earlier, if there were customers who requested it. Beginning in the morning, one of the servants was on duty at the bar, so Karry and I had time to do other things if we wished, or even rest a while. Toward evening Karry went into the kitchen to prepare one or two specialties of the house. Our employees took care of the rest. I stood behind the bar, but sometimes Karry let me go out for a walk. He adored serving the visitors and hearing their compliments. He usually went to bed before midnight, as he was used to getting up early. I stayed on at the restaurant. Not alone, of course—there were servants with me, as well. Right after midnight, I would retire upstairs. We have a young fellow by the name of Kumaroxi who is always happy to work nights, on the condition that we let him sleep during the day."

"I understand. I'm the same way. Tell me, Lady Tanita, what did Mr. Kovareka do in his spare time? You have to take a break sometimes, even from your favorite work."

"Karry wouldn't have agreed with you. The only kind of leisure that he wanted was to stand behind the bar shooting the breeze with the customers. You may not believe me, but the only reason he ever went to other people's taverns was to sniff out their secrets. And he was very good at it! Karry had never learned to cook; never studied to be a chef, I mean. In his younger days he served as a coachman at the Chancellory of Pleasure. You see, I inherited the *Tipsy Bottle* from my grandmother. In the beginning we had to rely completely on the servants. We didn't even know how to brew kamra! For the first few years Karry hung about in the kitchen with the cooks, helping peel the vegetables. Then one day he threw a salad together. Just an ordinary salad; but people claimed they hadn't tasted anything like it since the beginning of the Code Epoch! It turned out that he had just watched our cook prepare it and then come up with a few innovations to the recipe. That's how it all began."

"Did your husband go hunting often?" I asked. Lady Tanita stared at me, baffled. "I mean, hunting for other people's culinary secrets."

"Fairly often. Well, once every dozen days, and sometimes more frequently. He even learned to disguise his appearance, since chefs don't like sharing their secrets with their colleagues."

"You see, Lady Tanita? You said you lived a quiet life, yet all the while Mr. Kovareka was in disguise, delving into the culinary mysteries of his colleagues in disguise. You have to agree that not every Tom, Dick, and Harry behaves like that. Oh, please forgive my bad manners! I'm so used to expressing myself like—"

"Don't worry, Sir Max. Even if you began talking like a gravedigger it wouldn't change anything. It's even better that way. When you smile, I forget Karry is gone."

"Lady Tanita," I said earnestly. "Remember, there are other Worlds besides this one. That's something I can vouch for, at least. So he is somewhere, your Karwen; only this somewhere is far away. When my grandmother died—and she was the only one in the family I truly loved—I told myself she had just gone away. I also told myself, of course, that we couldn't see each other, and that was bad—but all the same, she was somewhere. And life went on there, as it did here. Believe me, if anyone knows something about death, it's me." Here I twisted the black hem of my Mantle of Death significantly.

Who would have thought my childishly naïve belief was exactly what this unhappy woman needed? She smiled thoughtfully.

"You're probably right, Sir Max. For some reason I feel that you're always right. I would like to know what kind of other World it is, and if Karry is happy there. Actually, being in another world is better than being nowhere at all. And then, maybe when my time comes, I can find him there. What do you think?"

"I don't know," I admitted. "But I very much hope so. There is always someone we all want to find beyond the Threshold."

"You really are a good person, Sir Max."

"Just don't spread it around town, or I won't be able to do my job. It's better for everyone—as long as the criminals are afraid of my garb, there's no need to resort to more dangerous weapons."

Suddenly, the memory of the terrified Ploss brought an involuntary smile to my lips. It turned out to be very apropos. I finally knew what to ask her.

"Lady Tanita, think hard. Did your husband have any special plans for the Last Day of the Year? Maybe he made some sort of resolution that he shared with you? For instance, sniffing out another culinary secret, or inventing a new recipe? And maybe he even carried out his resolution."

I couldn't abandon my favorite hypothesis about the involvement of a mysterious Mutinous Magician. I was used to seeing the fraught legacy of the past behind every significant incident. A fellow is capable of consulting even such dangerous advisors in the interests of a consuming passion.

"Karry never let me in on the details of his culinary affairs. He loved surprises. You know, Sir Max, Karry felt that he himself was almost like a Grand Magician. That's what he was, when he entered a kitchen. But come to think of it, you may be right. Recently he had been going off somewhere every day, for two or three hours at a time. In his hideous platinum blond wig. And, he bustled about in the kitchen when no one was there. That last evening, he looked so pleased! Yes, Sir Max, you're absolutely right. I'm sure that Karry had found out someone's secret, may it be cursed."

"And do you know whose secret Mr. Kovareka might have wanted to find out?" I asked without much hope.

"No, Sir Max. I really don't. The only thing I can tell you for sure is that Karry had no interest in anything but the very best. Are you familiar with the fare at the *Sated Skeleton*?"

"And how! I live in that quarter. I can admit this to you, Lady Tanita. When I found out that the chef dabbled slightly in magic of the second degree, I knew I could get a good breakfast there."

"Precisely. Karry wasn't interested in that degree of magic. It didn't meet his expectations of fine cuisine."

"Hm. The circle of suspects has just narrowed considerably. You're certainly making my job much easier. What establishments met with his approval?"

"Let me think. He didn't like praising competition, but the *Glutton Bunba* and the *Hunchback Itullo*, it goes without saying. They're the cream of the crop. The *Greasy Turkey*, *Fatman at the Bend* . . . Yes, and of all the *Skeletons* he was fondest of the *Dancing Skeleton*. You know, the chef there once worked under the legendary

Vagatta Vax. Actually, Karry has always considered the best chefs to be those in the service of wealthy families. They have enough leisure time to devote themselves to the culinary arts, rather than 'feeding any old junk to a bunch of tipsy hicks,' as he put it. He dreamed of meeting Shutta Vax, son of the famous Vagatta Vax. But it was impossible. The family has its own social circle, very exclusive. Maybe Karry was able to insinuate himself into someone's private kitchen? I doubt it, though. That would be too unlikely."

"Thank you, Lady Tanita. This is more than enough for the time being. Don't be angry if I send you a call again. My foolish brain might come up with a question at any hour of the day or night, so be prepared for the worst."

"If only that were the worst of it," Lady Tanita smiled. "Sir Max, I have no one else to ask for advice. Perhaps you could tell me what I should do now? So as 'not to lose my mind,' as you put it yesterday."

"What should you do? I don't know. I only know what I would do in your place."

"What? What would you do?"

"I would leave everything behind. I'd begin a new life. I mean, I'd try to change everything completely, right away—a new house, even a new city; but a new house at the very least. I'd get a new job, if I had even the slightest chance of getting one. I'd start dressing differently, I'd change my hair. I'd make a bunch of new friends. Things like that. I'd try to work till I was dead-tired, so that sleep would seek me, and not the other way around. And in a dozen days I'd take a look in the mirror and see some unfamiliar person, someone who had never experienced the woes I had gone through. Strange advice, don't you think?"

Lady Tanita stared at me in disbelief.

"It is very strange advice, but I'll try it, Sir Max! It's better than returning home, where there's no Karry, anyway. What you're saying is so simple—but it would never have occurred to me! Are you giving me advice based on your own experience?"

"Yes. Twice I've taken that step. The first time it wasn't very successful. But it wasn't a complete disaster, either, and I didn't go mad. The second time, though, I managed very well. You might even say I was wildly successful."

"Was that when you moved to the capital from the borders of the Barren Lands?"

"Just so. But I was lucky! If Sir Juffin hadn't—"

"It was *our* luck!" Lady Tanita said. "If the Mantle of Death conceals such a fine person as you are, it means the World won't collapse any time soon. Today I will move to the New City, to the very center of town. And I'll open a new tavern. There is fierce competition there! And I'll hire new people. By the time we're able to stand on our own feet or go under, I think I'll have had time to get used to the idea that Karry has just gone away."

"Give it all you've got, my lady!" I said in all sincerity.

And I thought to myself that I hoped I had the courage to follow my own advice, if at some point the curious heavens chose to test the mettle of my foolish heart.

Lady Tanita took her leave, and I set out for the Main Archive. Sir Lookfi Pence wandered pensively among the preening buriwoks, absently knocking over chairs as he passed. Melifaro sat in state on the desk, dangling his legs, lost in thought.

"Well, anything to report?" I asked from the doorway.

"Nothing. Not a thing," Melifaro said, enunciating each syllable. "For all intents and purposes, it looks like not a single crazy Magician has ever before attempted this simple way of preparing a quick and delicious holiday meal. Speaking of a meal, I'm ready to fulfill my side of the bargain right now, with you, Mr. Bad Dream. With you or without you, I'm going out to eat. Otherwise you'll have one more corpse on your hands."

"Will you accompany us, Sir Lookfi?" I asked.

"I can't, Sir Max," the Master Curator of Knowledge said apologetically. "I must stay here until sundown. And my wife is the proprietress of a restaurant, you know. A very good one. When we had just gotten to know one another, I promised Varisha—that's her name—that I would never go to another establishment for as long as I lived. Except the *Glutton*, of course, but that's in the line of duty. Working for Sir Juffin Hully, it's impossible to avoid going to the *Glutton*. She understands that. I wanted to please her, and now I have no choice but to keep my word."

"And what is the name of her establishment? I'd like to try it sometime."

"Of course, Sir Max. It's the *Fatman at the Bend*. It's in the New City. Have you heard of it?"

I certainly had! The thought that the adored spouse of Sir Lookfi Pence was one of the prime suspects raised my mood considerably, and my appetite, too.

꙰

The *Hunchback Itullo*, the most expensive restaurant in Echo, is located at some distance from our Ministry, which explained why I had only been to the *Hunchback* twice. The first time I wandered in purely by chance, when I was studying Echo and its environs. The prices astounded me. They were extremely high, even by comparison with my beloved *Glutton*—not the cheapest place in town. This only whetted my curiosity. I simply had to find out what you could get with money like that.

But it was the interior of the place that surprised me most of all. I had never seen anything like it in Echo. There was no bar, nor were there small tables scattered about. Instead, there was a spacious hall and many small doors. A middle-aged lady with raven hair and a gloomy expression opened one of them for me. Behind the door was a small, cozy booth with a round table, in the center of which was a fountain. Tongues of rainbow-colored flames from myriad candles dispelled the soft darkness. Yes, the ambience was very impressive! And the food was no less so, though I came away feeling I lacked the education and background to appreciate the nuances of this sophisticated cuisine.

The second time I went there was quite recently, to buy the tiny packet of gourmet cookies for Chuff. From the looks of it, Melifaro wasn't exactly a regular here, either.

"I feel like a complete dolt," he admitted, sitting down at the little table. "A completely rich dolt who does nothing except torment his belly with delicacies."

"That's why I was so eager to come here," I remarked.

"To feel like a rich dolt?"

"No, so that you could learn your own worth!"

"You've overindulged in your Elixir, Mr. Bad Dream. I feed him, and he mocks me! Mysterious Soul, Child of the Barren Plains—what will become of you?"

The door opened. The proprietor of the establishment had favored us with a visit. It was the legendary Hunchback Itullo himself, famous for preparing all three hundred dishes on the menu single-handed. For that reason, the customers of this elegant restaurant were required to have the patience of a saint. It was sometimes two hours before your meal was served.

"Please don't close the door," I requested as Mr. Itullo entered. "It's stuffy in here."

"I told you you went overboard with the Elixir," Melifaro muttered with a knowing wink. "Shortness of breath is the first sign of poisoning."

"Oh, you'd be singing a different tune if you had to go around smothered under this blanket," I cried, nodding with repugnance at my splendid Mantle.

"Mr. Itullo, one of the secrets of the universe has been revealed before my very eyes. Now we know it for a fact: Death sweats! Sometimes, anyway."

Melifaro mimicked an expression of inspired ecstasy, and waved his arms around under the proprietor's nose. Alas, our host was not the most good-natured fellow in Echo. He smiled grimly, and placed a weighty tome on the table. It looked like a first edition of the ancient Gutenberg Bible. This was the menu.

I gave Melifaro free rein, since he was paying. If he wanted to waste half an hour of his life trying to understand the difference between Cold Sleep and Heavenly Body, who was I to deprive him of his intellectual enjoyment?

"Good gentlemen, if you prefer a crystal clarity of taste, I would advise you to turn your attention to this page," Mr. Itullo announced with a flourish.

"And what would you recommend for a person who is accustomed to partaking of horse jerky?" Melifaro asked snidely.

"I have just the thing. This is a marvelous stew, which I prepare from the heart of a winded racehorse according to an ancient recipe. A very expensive pleasure, since one must pay for the whole horse. You do know, gentlemen, how much a thoroughbred costs, as well as the cost of the jockey's labor? Not to mention the seasoning."

"How about it, Sir Max?" Melifaro asked solicitously. "I'll grudge you nothing, you know."

"No," I mumbled. "I'm more interested in the 'crystal clarity of taste,' if it comes right down to it. And it's beastly to torment animals like that."

"Some Child of the Steppes," snorted the amateur anthropologist.

Disappointed, Melifaro poked his nose in the menu again. The hunchback muttered anxiously as my friend turned the pages in rapture; I listened out of the corner of my ear as their exchange dragged on. I held my burning face up to the cool draft that escaped into the booth from the hall. And suddenly . . .

Sir Juffin Hully was absolutely right about my luck. I was devilishly lucky. A weak aroma, that same wonderful smell of delicious food that was so out of place in the morgue of the Ministry of Perfect Public Order, now tickled my nostrils again.

"That's what I want," I said triumphantly and pointed in the direction of the open door.

"What might that be, sir?" the host asked in alarm.

"Whatever that smell is. And that's what you want, too, right?" I stared meaningfully at Melifaro, whose nose was already turning toward the door in wonder.

In just a fraction of a second, his dark eyes glittered with absolute comprehension.

"Yes, Mr. Itullo. We've made our decision. That smell is simply incomparable. What is that dish? Well, spit it out!"

"I'm afraid that's impossible, gentlemen," the hunchback said, shaking his head vigorously. "And it's not on the menu, so don't bother looking for it."

"Why isn't it?" Melifaro asked, leaping out of his chair.

"The fact is that it's a very expensive dish."

"Excellent!" I exclaimed. "That's just what we had in mind— something a bit more pricey. Isn't that right, my poor friend?"

"Yes, my insatiable foe!" Melifaro didn't even bat an eyelid.

"Nevertheless, gentlemen, it can't be done." Our host was unyielding. "It takes more than two dozen days to prepare such a dish. I have several old customers who order it in advance. I am willing to accommodate you, but your order will only be ready in . . . I don't quite know how many days, since some of the ingredients are supplied by merchants all the way from Arvarox. I can put you on the waiting list and let you know when it will be ready. But I can't promise anything."

"Fine," I said, with a dismissive wave. "In that case bring me something with a 'crystal clarity of taste.' We'll discover your skills by beginning at the beginning. But please, no horse's hearts. Apart from that, we are placing ourselves in your hands."

"I'd recommend that you consider numbers 37 and 89, gentlemen." The hunchback clearly felt that a weight had been lifted off his shoulders. "The wait will be less than an hour. These are true culinary masterpieces! What would you like to drink in anticipation of the meal?"

"Kamra!" I almost shouted.

"Kamra? *Before* the meal? But your taste buds, your palate—"

"Yes, we'll need a jug of water, too, to rinse the palate before the most significant culinary event of our lives. And don't shut the door, please. It's hot in here!"

When we were at last alone, Melifaro launched right in.

"That smell is the one in our morgue, a hole in the heavens above your long nose, Max! Am I right?"

"I'll take that as a compliment. My whole life I've wanted a larger nose. One like Juffin's, at the very least."

"You have terrible taste. Your nose is the very height of fashion."

"Well, at least it's good for something. Send a call to Kofa. Unfortunately, I grow tired too fast using Silent Speech. Let's hear what our Mouthful-Earful thinks about all this."

"Does it really tire you?" Melifaro asked in surprise.

"Try to imagine. Have you ever tried learning a foreign language?"

"I'll say. My papa was always forcing us to memorize the mumbo-jumbo of some idiots who didn't have the sense to learn normal human speech."

"Well, then you know how it is for me."

"I understand. Only it's so funny to hear you try."

"Come on, call Kofa, Mr. Ninth Volume of the *Encyclopedia* of Manga Melifaro. Or I may burst from curiosity."

"All right, I'm sending the call," Melifaro's face assumed an intelligent expression to let me know that he had made contact with our Master Eavesdropper.

In a few minutes, two jugs were served to us, one containing kamra and one with water. Melifaro's face melted into a more human expression again. As a matter of fact, the poor fellow was laboring under an overload of information and all the implications thereof. By the time the gloomy lady who was serving us had departed, Melifaro looked as though he was on the verge of fainting.

"Your nose is really something!" he blurted out. "Sir Kofa is almost certain that he knows the dish in question: King Banjee Pâté. The most outlandish rumors have been circulating about it for a long time now. Even in the Epoch of Orders not every chef had it in his power to make a dish like that. The problem is that rustling up King Banjee requires magic of no less than the tenth or eleventh degree. But Itullo is the most law-abiding citizen in Echo. He's never been caught so much as dabbling in the second degree since the Code was written! So there you have it. According to Kofa, the whole King Banjee business is shrouded in mystery. It isn't anywhere on the menu. Sir Kofa himself tried ordering the infamous pâté several times, but he got some vague promise that they would 'put him on the list.' Sound familiar? Among the citizens of Echo, there are several people who, in their own words, have tasted the delights of this pâté. Sir Kofa has overheard talk of this unique experience of the taste buds. Another curious fact—the lucky ones were not terribly rich. They were average citizens, the kind who would come to the *Hunchback* a few times a year if they could afford it, but not more. And Itullo suggested to us that it was so expensive, a whole month's salary wouldn't buy a portion of the grub."

"He doesn't want to get mixed up with us, that's for sure," I said nodding.

"With the Secret Investigative Force? Stands to reason. There's something fishy about this pâté."

"Was that all the news?"

"No, there's more. Do you know where Boboota ate yesterday?"

"Gosh, it wasn't here, was it?"

"It most certainly was. And it wasn't the first time. It turns out that General Boboota developed a passion for luxury a dozen days ago. And recently he's been eating exclusively at the *Hunchback*."

"I don't think his salary is less than ours; but every day, that's a bit excessive!"

A curious and thrifty little fellow with an inordinate interest in Boboota's pocketbook suddenly took over in me.

"Oh, it's much less, Max. A general of the Police Force makes half as much as an ordinary Secret Investigator. Didn't you know?"

"Well, that proves my point. I don't like the sound of this, Melifaro. Not one bit. From what I know of fellows like Boboota, they don't like throwing their money around on the sly. They want everyone to see them. And here . . . these idiotic private booths! Like some underworld den. It's convenient for a fellow like me. I can lose my appetite when I'm surrounded by the unpleasant faces of total strangers. But that can't be a problem for Boboota. Why would he eat in such an expensive place, if not to let everyone see him indulging his taste buds in solitary contemplation?"

"What's a 'den,' Max?" Melifaro asked. "You're a fount of new words today."

I scratched my head. How do I explain what a den is? And why were the characters of my favorite books, with Sherlock Holmes leading the procession, always hanging around in 'dens'? Oh, right, to smoke opium! And how did those visits sometimes end up? Right! Poor Boboota. But would someone mind telling me how opium would have found its way into Echo? And of what possible use it would be for people who can absolutely openly and legally, in the company of their families at home, partake of their Soup of Repose and boggle their minds to their heart's content?

"Kofa didn't happen to say which booth Boboota had eaten in, did he?"

"Just a second, I'll ask."

Melifaro again seemed to turn to stone, this time only briefly.

"Great," he said in a moment. "People always take notice when it's such a renowned person. Several times Boboota was seen coming out of the far booth—the one on the right, if you're standing at the entrance."

"Excellent!" I said. "That's just where I wanted to go. How about you, Melifaro?"

"Absolutely! Shall we go now, or after we eat?"

"However we can, without being noticed."

"Why?" Melifaro asked in surprise. "Do you think anyone would dare try to stop us?"

"No. But all the same, I don't want anyone to see us. We Borderlanders are so shy and inscrutable."

"Yes, especially when you've had a drop too much of Elixir of Kaxar. Well, if you don't want anyone to notice us, so be it. How do you suggest we pull it off?"

"For a start, we tactfully send a call to that booth, to find out whether anyone is there. If there is, we'll just have to wait while they split their sides laughing. If not, we'll have to hurry before someone comes. Shall we?"

"I'm only doing it for your sake. Yes, there's one fellow in there. A very sleepy one! He didn't notice a thing. He didn't even twitch."

"Well, we're in luck. That means we'll have time to eat."

"I hope so. I was already starving when we were in the Archive, if you'll remember. Then what will we do?"

"Nothing much. We'll wait till that gloomy damsel returns to the kitchen. Then we'll just slip into the booth and find out how it smells."

"Smells? Do you think—"

"I don't think anything. We'll just have to wait and see. But I smell a rat."

"A rat? What's a rat, Max? Is it some delicacy from the Barren Lands and you recognize he smell?"

I was already weary of idiomatic misunderstandings, so I didn't say anything.

The gloomy old lady, who entered bearing two trays in her muscular hands, distracted us from the talk of rats that so confounded my colleague. Then we attacked the food with gusto. 'Crystal clarity of taste' was a very apt description. Even I was able to appreciate it.

"Try to exercise a bit of restraint," I suggested to Melifaro. "Don't eat everything at once. Leave a bit on your plate."

"Why should I? Oh, I understand. You mean we might have to hang around here a while. Don't worry. The sleepyhead's on his way out, I'm keeping track of him."

"Ah! Well, don't hold back, then. Dig in. I grant you permission."

"Thank you," Melifaro mumbled, his mouth full of food. When we both had nearly cleaned our plates, he said, "I think we can venture out now . . . no, wait a second. He's still standing in the hall." He paused. "Perfect. I needed to finish chewing that last morsel. Come on, Max. The moment has arrived. The old shrew isn't anywhere in sight."

❧

We slipped out, and in a matter of seconds we were inside the booth, which the magnificent General Boboota had lately graced with his world-renowned presence.

"Sinning Magicians! That smell!" Melifaro whispered in alarm. "The smell was coming from here. The sleepyhead was feasting on

King Banjee, or whatever the dish is called. They've already cleared away the dishes, but it smells just like the kitchen!"

"Not 'like' the kitchen. It's coming from the kitchen."

"No, Max. The kitchen is to the left of the entrance. Didn't you see where the hunchback went with our order?"

"That means there are two kitchens," I murmured. "Think about it. The smell is very powerful just here. And it's the only smell around. Why don't you tell me something else, Sir Ninth Volume—can your limitless wisdom lead us to find a door that a blockhead like me would have to look for until tomorrow morning?"

"A secret door? Good thinking, Max. Let me look."

Melifaro closed his eyes. He shuffled around the room uncertainly. I froze, expecting the loud crash of overturned furniture.

It didn't come. He carefully skirted a chair standing in his path, then continued to inch forward. By the far wall, he stopped, and got down on all fours. Then he went on with his search.

"Here it is!" Melifaro looked up at me, beaming. "Come here, Max. I've got something to show you."

I shuddered. His half-closed eyelids shone with pale green phosphorescence in the murky semidarkness.

"Look!"

"Well? It's just a regular floor. Ah, I see. It's warm!" I discovered that one spot on the floor was almost hot to the touch.

"Warm!" Melifaro huffed. "Well, you could have found the blasted door yourself, then!"

"It would have taken me hours to find it, crawling around on my hands and knees. Your way is much better."

I couldn't admit that I still had no clue about my own abilities in this area.

"Do you want me to open it for you, too?" Melifaro inquired spitefully.

"It's in your own best interests. Didn't Juffin ever tell you how I once tried to open a box containing the Royal Gift?"

"He told us. He gathered us all together and said, 'People! If you want to stay alive, don't allow Sir Max to open cans of preserves in your presence!' We were terribly frightened, and there was much wailing and gnashing of teeth."

"'Preserves'? Is that what you said, 'preserves'?"

For some reason it struck me as very funny that there were also preserves in Echo. Well, where would I have seen them? I almost always ate in restaurants, or was invited to someone's home as a guest.

"Are you hungry again already?" Melifaro asked in surprise, moving the floorboards aside with a careless gesture.

We stared into the darkness, from which a cloud of delicious odors wafted toward us.

"Let's go," I said. "Though we'll look like a pair of fools if it turns out just to be a side entrance to the main kitchen."

"Right, disguised like the secret passage into the garden of the Order of the Seven-Leaf Clover? Not likely, Max."

We descended a narrow ladder. Melifaro replaced the false floor behind us, and we found ourselves in utter darkness.

"You don't have a problem finding your way in the dark, I hope?" I asked.

"Do you?"

"I think I do. I don't know. In any case, I can't see a thing."

"Fine, I'll guide you. Some Child of the Night you are."

Hand in hand we groped our way toward the divine aroma that grew stronger with every step. Gradually I discovered that I instinctively knew where to turn so as not to bump my forehead against a wall, and where to raise my foot a bit higher to step over an invisible, but hard impediment in our path.

"Are you joking at my expense?" Melifaro asked, trying to withdraw his paw from mine. "You sure don't miss any opportunity to make me look like an idiot."

"My whole life I've dreamed of holding hands with you, and now I've found a pretext. Don't be so touchy. I'm absolutely serious. I don't know whether I can find my way around in the dark or not. I never know anything for sure about myself beforehand.

"You are a lucky fellow, after all. What an interesting life you have. Here we are. We still need some light, though. You are a smoker, I recall."

"To the degree that I can tolerate the rubbish that passes for tobacco around here. I do have matches, though, don't worry."

"I'm afraid that won't be enough light. You'll have to smoke your pipe. It's the only light-bearing apparatus we have that gives off a steady glow."

"Are you trying to hasten my demise? Well, so be it."

I quickly filled my pipe. The idea was brilliant. I had only to draw on the pipe, and the dim reddish glow dispelled the darkness around us. We we were standing on the threshold of a small storeroom, stuffed to the brim with huge, oddly shaped cupboards. Strange furniture. I had seen things like this a number of times at home, but never here in Echo, where the spare, elegant objects that functioned as domestic furnishings looked more like works of art.

Since the capacity of my lungs was limited, we were once more plunged in darkness.

"What was that?" Melifaro tugged on the sleeve of my Mantle of Death. "Puff on that pipe one more time, please."

"If you want to boss me around, you'd better learn to smoke," I growled.

"When I was eighteen I swiped my older brother's pipe, smoked nearly all the contents of the snuffbox, and got terribly sick. Please, Max. Give us some light! What are these things?"

I went right up to the nearest 'cupboard' and took a mighty draw on the pipe.

Holy cow! It wasn't a cupboard at all, but a cage! And a person was trapped inside it. He seemed to be sleeping. In any case, the fellow didn't react when we appeared right in front of him, and the clouds of tobacco smoke that enveloped him didn't faze him, either.

"He's neither alive nor dead," Melifaro observed after a brief silence. "Try sending him a call, Max! Very curious sensation. It's like talking to a sausage."

I immediately regretted it. The 'curious sensation' turned out to be one of the most uncanny and horrible experiences of my life. I suddenly felt as though I myself was a large, living sausage that had somehow preserved the very human characteristic of being able to contemplate his essence and his fate. I was a sausage that dreams of the moment he will be eaten. I couldn't extricate myself from the sticky spiderweb of nightmarish sensations. A slap in the face, fairly powerful, made me drop my pipe, then sent me reeling to the opposite wall where, I banged my knee against the corner of yet another cage.

"What's wrong, Max?" Melifaro asked in a trembling voice. "What is happening to you? Who taught you to do that? What is it?"

"I don't know," I murmured, fumbling around for my pipe, which had gone out. Now a good draw on the pipe was just what I needed. Sausages don't smoke, I knew that for certain. The foul taste of the substance that they mistakenly consider to be tobacco here in Echo convinced me I was a human being, and a moment later, I even remembered who I was.

"You know, friend, I sometimes surprise myself," I admitted. "I'm afraid of myself. I'm a danger to my own existence—that's what I think."

"Maybe you're just some former Grand Magician? And Juffin gave you a good whack, so you lost your memory?"

"I hope not. Speaking of good whacks, thanks for slapping me around there. You seem to have saved my life. You ever tried that with the deceased? Maybe it would work on them, too."

"Nonsense, Max. I wanted to slap you around a long time ago, and now there was a reason. But really, what happened to you?"

"I sent him a call, and I probably tried too hard. Some hundredth degree of your blasted magic, instead of the second. It's always that way with me. My whole life I've always put too much salt on my omelets, too. That's the sort of thing that happens to me."

"Hey, look over there, Max! There's another curious spectacle."

I turned around to look. That cage contained a person, too. I puffed on my pipe so we could see it better. Sinning Magicians! It was a piece of meat that still hadn't lost the outline of its human form. A piece of aromatic meat dressed in a skaba and a looxi!

My nerves were ready to snap. We seemed to have unraveled this cursed affair, and much more quickly than we had anticipated. But I still felt no sense of relief.

"Do you see what I see, Melifaro? He *cooks* them! He cooks them, somehow, the swine! Send a call to our boys. We need Lonli-Lokli here. The sooner the better."

"Yes," whispered Melifaro. "And I really need the bathroom. I feel sick. We just ate what he cooked."

"Go ahead and hurl," I replied with a forced calm. "Don't be ashamed. But I don't think they fed us human flesh. I have a feeling the hunchback has only one Speciality of the House."

"Lonli-Lokli will be here soon," Melifaro reported. "I requested that he bring a few boys from the Police Force. What is this filth we've dug up, Max? Let's go look at the rest."

"Are you sure you want to? Go without me, then. I don't want to barf after a good meal. I wasn't raised that way. My mother thought that after visiting a good restaurant you shouldn't even do number two for a week."

"Still joking, Mr. Bad Dream? How would you have known about expensive restaurants living in the Borderlands? It can't get worse than it already is. But what if there are live people in the other cages?"

"Maybe there are. Go take a look. I've seen enough."

I turned away from the loathsome House Special and puffed on my pipe with genuine pleasure. Honestly, it wasn't so bad after all, this local tobacco.

"Max, I was wrong!" Melifaro's voice sounded improbably loud. "It just got worse! Come here and shed some light. Come on, puff on it one more time. You can close your eyes if you don't want to look."

I looked, of course. I had always known that my curiosity would be my undoing. A piece of meat in a looxi—that's disgusting enough. But when above the belt there's meat, and below, a pair of legs . . . Nevertheless, I didn't get sick. My stomach is quite a reliable piece of equipment. No matter what kind of filth crosses its path in life, it continues to function. All of a sudden, though, standing upright became too much for me, and I sank to the ground with a dull thud, like an overloaded shopping bag.

Only then did I realize we were no longer alone.

※

The rest was like a dream. A second that seemed to last a whole lifetime—that's what they usually say. "A whole lifetime" is an exaggeration; but that a few hours fit into the span of this second is something I'll stake my life on.

In the doorway, I saw a darkness thicker than that which surrounded it and a short, stooped silhouette. The chef was hurrying to restore order to his kitchen. He was enraged, and wasn't thinking about the consequences. One split second was enough for me to become this person, then to stop being him, and to realize—he's a madman.

Itullo the hunchback was armed with a hatchet and a silk noose, which they use here to kill turkeys before plucking and roasting them. The hunchback had come to kill us, filthy rotten little boys who were making mischief with his frying pans. From the very start he didn't stand a chance; but madmen don't bother their heads with such trifles.

I turned around and looked again at the monstrous creations of this kitchen wizard. There are many ways to meet one's death, but people shouldn't have to die like that. Not that way.

I wanted to fly into a rage. I wanted to desperately, but it didn't happen. I remained utterly calm. It was almost a matter of indifference to me. The breathing exercises that Lonli-Lokli had taught me turned the nervous Max into an extremely steady and composed beast. That meant there would be no show. As long as I was calm and good, spitting was useless. It would flop.

The hunchback did try his best to enrage me, poor thing! He charged at me, flourishing his implements of destruction, the tools of his trade. I think the certainty of this "culinary genius" that he could really kill me and Melifaro with his paltry weapons was the last straw for me. Truly, what was there to be angry about? I grew downright cheerful.

Since I hadn't managed to lose my temper, I decided at least to scare Itullo a little, and to amuse Melifaro, who was looking terribly serious just then.

I winked conspiratorially in the darkness and spat juicily at the distorted face of our hospitable host. Then I drew back my right hand for a good blow to the throat of our attacker with the back of my palm— it was already clear that there would be no getting around a fight.

What does a snake feel when it sinks its teeth into the flesh of a stranger that disturbs its repose? At that moment, I knew: it feels nothing in particular. Nothing, really, at all.

What was bound to happen sooner or later happened just then. The monstrous gift of Grand Magician Maxlilgl Annox finally manifested itself in the full glory of its power. Contrary to Juffin's prognosis, it happened when I was neither angry nor afraid. Itullo the Hunchback fell dead, conquered by my spittle, the deadly power of which now left no room for doubt.

"Oh, boy," Melifaro stared at me in unfeigned rapture. "You're reviving the best traditions of the Epoch of Orders. Without you the World would be a terribly dull place."

"Did I kill him?" I asked in disbelief, still needing confirmation.

"Do you have any doubts about it? Do you think you just told him 'Begone, creep!'?"

Melifaro, praise be the Magicians, doesn't have the weakest nerves in the World. His smile stretched from ear to ear.

"You know what? I'm happy," I said frankly. "I've never in my life seen anything so lowdown and loathsome in my life. Feeding people such filth, and at such outrageous prices! That mad chef has spoiled my appetite for a long time to come, and he has been fairly punished for his services. By the way, Melifaro," I remarked, "I did spare your wallet. You never paid for the meal, did you?"

"A good way to save money, I can't deny it. Not to mention that this Grand Magician of the Order of the Giant Sausage was planning to cut you into little pieces and serve you up in a gravy made from my blood I'm sure."

"I'm still wondering, though." My senses were rapidly returning to me. "That fellow, Karry; Mr. Karwen Kovareka. He was transformed into meat at home in his bed, instead of in some cage . . ."

"Leave it to me, Sir Max. Your job is to kill far-from-innocent people. I'll deal with everything else. Believe me, in about two hours I'll be able to answer all your questions. I'll send a call to Lonli-Lokli and let him know he can just take it easy, maybe go out for a quiet meal. You've put the poor fellow out of a job. What I really need now are a dozen of Boboota's smartest men."

"No problem, friend. You just need to arrange it with their boss," I muttered. "Did it never occur to you, genius?"

"You think—"

"I don't think anything. Thinking is your job. My job is killing far-from-innocent people. General Boboota ate here, then disappeared without a trace. Take my matches and go look for him. If he's already well done, we'll put him aside for Juffin. Who knows, maybe Sir Venerable Head wants to eat him for dinner."

"Ugh! That's revolting. Hand over the matches."

A few minutes later, Melifaro's jubilant voice echoed through the room.

"Juffin's going to fire us, Mr. Bad Dream! Boboota's here, but he seems to be all right. He doesn't even look like a sausage—he's just sleeping."

"He's been here since yesterday. Evidently, turning into pâté is a fairly lengthy process. Oh, if it hadn't been for my darned good luck, poor Juffin would have been so happy! It looks like it just wasn't meant to be."

"What's going on here? Are you here, Sir Melifaro?" It was the voice of Lieutenant Shixola, a policeman, and our good friend.

"Over here. Keep it down, boys. Your boss, it seems, is taking a nap."

"What?! Our boss?"

Shixola quickened his pace, and tripped over the corpse of the mad chef at a rapid clip. I managed to catch him at the very moment his thoroughbred nose was an inch from the floor. His colleague, following close behind, miraculously avoided the same fate, and several more policemen reached for their weapons in alarm. Melifaro guffawed.

"Good day, Sir Max," Shixola mumbled, freeing himself from my embrace. "Lucky for me you have excellent reflexes. What did I trip over?"

"Over the body of a state criminal—a poisoner, a cannibal, and the abductor of General Boboota. Mr. Itullo tried so hard to make your life easier and more pleasant! Truly, gentlemen, Sir Melifaro and I are terribly sorry. We are to blame. Here is your boss, healthy and all in one piece."

"Not 'we'—just you, Max!" Melifaro hurried to rid himself of the undeserved laurels. "I just came here for dinner. So, gentlemen, if you have come to punch the living daylights out of the one who rescued your boss, Sir Max is your man. I ask you to observe the proper protocol!"

The policemen looked at Melifaro as though he were a slow-witted sick child. It seemed to them that saying such things about a person wearing the Mantle of Death, in his presence, no less, was not courage, but suicide. I made a horrible grimace and showed Melifaro my fist. One shouldn't let down one's defenses in front of strangers, all the same. Otherwise, how could you keep them quaking in fear?

"I won't disturb your work, gentlemen," I said, bowing to Melifaro. "Carry on."

"And you?" Melifaro asked indignantly.

"What more is there for me to do here? I'll go cheer up Juffin. By the time you get there, he will already have had time to kill me for the good news. Then, you'll see, you'll be relieved. I'm saving your skin, friend. It's nothing to me—I'm immortal."

The poor policemen listened to me, mouths agape.

As I was going out the door, Melifaro's voice reached me. "Were you serious about that immortality business, Max?" I sighed and resorted to Silent Speech, which I had been avoiding all day, *Who knows who I am? I told you.*

I set out for the House by the Bridge. I really couldn't wait to repent before my boss. And I hadn't seen Melamori since the morning.

※

Since I was driving the amobiler, I was in Sir Juffin Hully's office, in less than ten minutes.

"I never expected you to be so prompt, Max. Finding Boboota a dozen seconds after sunset! That's a record even for our office—cracking a case less than a minute after it was officially opened. We have something to celebrate. Let's go to the *Glutton*. And you can stop peering around in hopes of seeing Lady Melamori. She has been home for two hours already, by my estimation. I let her off, poor thing: first her relatives, then that foolish call from you at sunrise. What brought that on? A surge of tender emotion? Come on, let's go."

"Did Melifaro manage to report *everything* to you while I was on my way here?" I was a bit hurt. "And here I thought my tongue would drop off before I finished telling my tale."

"What do I need with someone's report? I'm always with you, in a manner of speaking. And not because I so desperately want to be."

"Always!?" I was flabbergasted. "That's news to me!"

"Oh, Max. Don't exaggerate. I would go off my rocker if I had to keep an eye on you all the time. But when I'm worried, it's easier just to look in on how things are going than to keep fretting about you. Take it easy."

"Well, as long as you don't peek when I'm in the bathroom . . . I guess I won't fret about it. But were you really worried?" I asked uncertainly, and accidentally bumped my forehead against the doorframe.

"Do you think yours is the only heart that sends out distress signals?"

Juffin finally took pity on me and casually placed an icy palm on my sore forehead, which relieving the pain instantly.

"Let's go! If you stare at the door another minute, it may disappear altogether. Don't get vindictive, now: you made two major blunders, which only someone as lucky as you could have gotten away with."

"Blunders?" I echoed, mortified. "But I thought this was when you'd start praising me."

We entered the *Glutton*.

"I am praising you. In our profession, being lucky is much more important than being thorough or quick on the uptake. Luck isn't something you can learn. Don't pout, son. You don't need me to tell you about all your genius and the consequences thereof. What will you order?"

"Nothing!" I exclaimed in disgust. "After a spectacle like that . . . Well, maybe I'll have some pastries. Anything, as long as it's not meat."

"Are you that impressionable? Well, it's up to you. How about a drink?

"No. That is . . . If only . . ."

"Good golly! That potion's going to be the death of you! Fine. Take it—but just a drop, mind you."

Juffin held out the invisible bottle of Elixir of Kaxar.

"Oh, you brought it along!"

I broke into a grateful smile and took a sip. That was all I needed.

"Tell me about my blunders, Juffin. Now I'm ready even for a public thrashing."

"To begin with, Max, you forgot to ask Sir Kofa to go to the morgue to sniff out and identify the smell. He would immediately have told you what it was. And you might have been able to get along without your uncanny good luck. What made you decide to eat at the *Hunchback*, of all places? Can you explain that to me?"

"I can. My preternatural intuition," I said, and burst out laughing. I couldn't help myself. "Not really. It was my preternatural pettiness. Melifaro owed me a good meal in exchange for the use of my favorite blanket. I value my blanket very highly, so we had to go to the most expensive restaurant."

"Hm. Life hasn't seemed this entertaining in a long time! All right, then. You got the point about Kofa?"

"Got it," I said. "Sheer stupidity on my part. At least I did send all the others down there."

"A sound decision. Never mind, it happens to everyone."

"What else?" I asked dully. "What else did I do wrong?"

"You and Melifaro didn't sense the danger. Do you know the

hunchback had every intention of poisoning you? From the very first, he was sure you had come to look for Boboota, and because madmen have their own logic, I myself didn't anticipae it until it was too late. Or maybe it's just hard to see through a madman. In short, after you had sniffed the King Banjee, Itullo was determined to treat you to a good dose of poison."

"What happened?" I asked.

"Nothing, obviously. I was all ready to intervene, but the hunchback just forgot to do it! As soon as he entered the kitchen, the decision evaporated from his sorry head. So you were spared, and I was very surprised. I haven't been so surprised in, well, about five hundred years! That a poisoner forgets to add the poison—well, that flies in the face of the basic laws of the universe."

"You said yourself I was lucky," I said with a shrug. I finally decided to ask a question that had been bothering me for a long time. "Did you say about five hundred years? How old—"

"How old am I? Not as old as I might seem. Just seven hundred, and then some. Compared to Maba Kalox I'm just a spring chicken."

"Seven hundred? You've got to be kidding!" I shook my head in admiration. "Will you teach me?"

"This, coming from the fellow who frightened poor Melifaro with his talk about immortality? Better keep quiet . . ."

At that moment, a flaming red comet seemed to burst into the *Glutton*, collapsing in the chair next to me. Melifaro's speed astonished me—this force of nature had even managed to change his clothes!

"Everything's fine, Sir Juffin. I can imagine how upset you were, but at least a few dozen days without Boboota are guaranteed. He has been taken to Abilat Paras. This great healer claims that bringing Boboota around will be difficult—and Boboota was lucky. The others can already be buried: the changes were irreversible. How crafty that hunchback must have been to lure them into his clutches!"

"Have a drink, you poor fellow! I won't offer you food, if even Sir Max turns up his nose at it."

"Well, perhaps a little something sweet," Melifaro drawled. "Only, please—no meat!"

"How fastidious my reps are! Who would have thought," Juffin said grinning. "Eat your pastries then. I'll get down to something more serious."

The chief solemnly lifted the lid off the pot filled to the brim with Madame Zizinda's renowned hot pâté. Melifaro and I exchanged queasy glances, before launching right into the platter of sweet confections—just to take our minds off the days' horrors, of course.

"All right, let's hear it, son," Juffin demanded with his mouth full. "Max here is bursting with curiosity; and, I must admit, it's not all that clear to me, either. How do you think he lured them there?"

"Rumors about that blasted pâté had been doing the rounds in Echo for a long time. Lots of people went to Itullo's to partake of the secrets of old cuisine. The fellow really had learned to make the dishes without resorting to Forbidden Magic. I found his papers, and the police questioned the servants already, so I can explain everything with some certainty. This is how it worked. The hunchback made a list of gourmets. He collected information about them, and then invited them, preferably those who both lived alone and were prosperous, to his establishment. There he fed them his foul delicacy. As soon as they tried it, some people—not all, only the weakest and most vulnerable—were instantly hooked. They felt they couldn't live without it. When a customer like that came to Itullo in the middle of the night, fell on his knees, and offered his whole fortune in exchange for a serving of the pâté, the chef knew that he had caught another one in his snares. He started making them pay in earnest; and they had to pay a high price to be led down the garden path to the graveyard. The poor fellows sank into debt and would even begin selling their property to buy the cursed dish. One of them sold two houses, at least; I know that for a fact. Within a few dozen days, the hunchback succeeded in reducing the poor gluttons to rags. By then they were ready to be lured to the next step. One fine day, the customer would just fall asleep over his plate. To be more exact, he would fall unconscious. It didn't take much effort for the hunchback to put him into a cage in the cellar. Then the last stage of feeding began. The denizens of the cellar were fed another mixture of ingredients: the vile invention of the great chef, resembling the pâté itself in taste and aroma, but much more radical. Another few days, and a heaping portion of King Banjee was ready to be served to a new batch of unfortunate gourmets. What will they do now, poor things?"

"Go to the wisewomen," Juffin said. "Better late than never. So the pâté itself reduced them to a state of stupor, then knocked them out completely. After which they were fed some other junk that turned them into pâté themselves. Extraordinary! What a brilliantly devised vicious circle! And he did all this without resorting to Forbidden Magic? Now that's talent, a hole in the heavens above him! What a waste."

"Poor Karwen!" I blurted out. "Hunting for culinary secrets turned out to be a dangerous pastime. He no doubt found his way into Itullo's covert kitchen and swiped the first pot he came to that smelled like King Banjee. He took it home, studied it, tasted it, of course—then perhaps got carried away and ate it all at one sitting. What terrible luck!"

"Ah, the hapless proprietor of the *Tipsy Bottle*," Juffin sighed. "This is not an auspicious start to the New Year, boys. Echo has lost two of its finest cooks. We'll have to do something about it."

"Still, there's something not quite right here," I objected. "If the hunchback chose his candidates so scrupulously, how did General Boboota get caught up in this mess? He can't be considered a lonely man by any stretch of the imagination. After all, he's the Head of Public Order. Did the hunchback go completely mad?"

"He certainly did go completely mad!" said Melifaro. "But there was more to it than that. There was a curious misunderstanding. One day Boboota took his wife to Itullo's. It was a festive family outing, everything was very sweet, until the General saw Sir Balegar Lebda, one of his former colleagues, in one of the booths. He was a lonely old retired General of the Royal Guard. The same one, by the way, whose appearance just about did me in today."

"The one who had become pâté above the belt?"

"That's the one. That night they had served the unlucky fellow his final helping. The door opened, Boboota saw his old comrade, ran to embrace him, and helped himself to a morsel from his plate, as a sign of their friendship. The next day he appeared before the hunchback demanding more. The hunchback tried to send him to the wisewomen; he realized the risk he was running. But Boboota raised a ruckus."

"I can imagine," Juffin said with a grin.

"In short, the hunchback was afraid that Boboota would bring the entire City Police Force to his door, and he chose the lesser of two evils. By the way, I saw the accounts. Boboota's culinary pleasures were almost free of charge, in contrast to what the others laid out, of course. That's the whole story, Max."

"Not quite all," Juffin corrected. "The most interesting task is still ahead of us. Now we have to save the reputation of Boboota Box, brave General of the City Police Force. We'll have to give him your laurels, boys."

"Why?" I protested, nearly choking. "You longed to send him into retirement, and this is the perfect pretext!"

"Max, you'd better stay away from politics. Just leave it to your daytime half. No, on second thought, better not. I see the same baffled look on his face. I might have expected you to understand, Sir Melifaro."

"Do you mean to say—" Melifaro's dark eyes lit up a flash of understanding.

"Well, yes. Topple Boboota and make the City Police Force the laughing stock of everyone in Echo? And how will they work then, those brave boys? And who will do their job? The seven of us? No, thank you very much. Moreover, every cloud has a silver lining. We'll report to the King how the brave General Boboota went right into the thick of it to expose the criminal. But we'll keep the truer version on hand for future use. So Boboota will be as good as gold. Although, even without that the poor thing is so scared of Max he's developed a nervous tic."

"And I was sure you'd kill us for finding him so soon," I sighed in disappointment. "What a schemer you are."

"Scheming is the most exciting thing in the world, Max. Magic alone isn't enough to provide first-class entertainment. Ah, Sir Shurf is here! Where's my office, anyway: in the House by the Bridge, or here in the *Glutton*?"

"Good evening, gentlemen," Shurf Lonli-Lokli bowed with perfect aplomb and sat down next to Juffin. "I'm not disturbing you?"

"Did you miss us, Lonki-Lomki?" Melifaro inquired acidly. "Did Mr. Bad Dream steal your job again?"

"My name is Lonli-Lokli," said the Master Who Snuffs Out Unnecessary Lives in an even tone. "And our colleague is called Sir Max. You have a terrible memory for names, Melifaro. There are many exercises for improving the memory, you know."

Sir Shurf grabbed the last cream puff and popped it into his mouth. I was stunned. Could Lonli-Lokli have learned how to joke? No, I must have imagined it. There were no exercises for developing a sense of humor—not in this World, nor in any other.

"Did you actually use your Gift, Max?" asked Lonli-Lokli. "I was certain that at this stage in our studies it wouldn't be easy for you to lose your spiritual equilibrium. I probably underestimated the fieriness of your temperament."

"No, on the contrary. My temperament is just fine. Something strange happened, though. I wanted to tell you, Juffin, so I stored it away in my memory. I didn't get angry, and I didn't get scared, during all that commotion, although I understood that under the circumstances that was exactly what was required of me. But the hunchback was so pathetic, with his absurd hatchet and his turkey-strangler, that I decided to play around. I thought that after all the rumors about my poisonous spittle he might be afraid of regular spit, too. It's good that I hadn't tried any games like that before."

"Are you serious, Max?" Juffin stared at me with the most fearsome of his icy gazes. After a moment he sighed wearily. "Of course you're serious. Well, it turns out you're not the only one who can make blunders. On the other hand, it's not a bad thing that questions of life and death don't just depend on your unreliable emotions. You're always dangerous! Always. It's good that you know that now. We'll just have to take life as it comes. You haven't changed your minds about the pâté, fellows?"

Melifaro and I shook our heads vigorously.

"What affectation! Do you think I buy into your delicate spiritual sensibilities? Perhaps you're even planning to request a vacation?"

"I wouldn't think of it," I protested, "especially if you'll allow me to return what you have in your pocket to its proper place."

"No way! The amount you downed already is enough until the day after tomorrow." Juffin was trying very hard to be a gruff boss. "All right, here's what we'll do. You're in luck, Melifaro, you can go home. And Shurf, it wouldn't do you any harm to relax for a while. This End of the Year has wound everyone up—everyone except Sir Max. So let him report to duty. That clear, hero?"

Juffin looked at me so meaningfully that I knew there was something else in store.

"Right then, I'm off!"

Just as I was standing up to leave, I remembered something and grinned cunningly. "You still owe me dinner, Melifaro! As far as I remember, you didn't have to pay a farthing in the *Hunchback*."

"There's only one thing on your mind!" Melifaro exclaimed. "As soon as you get up from one table, you're making a beeline for the next. Don't you care about anything in the World besides food?"

"Besides food? Of course I do! I'm also fond of bathrooms. Like my best friend, General Boboota Box. He's taught me a lot."

"But that's very unfortunate, Max," Lonli-Lokli said mournfully. "There are so many wonderful things in the World. Don't you like to read?"

"I was only joking, Shurf," I said, and left with a dignified air to the accompaniment of the friendly guffaws of Juffin and Melifaro. Only Lonli-Lokli had the presence of mind to wish me goodnight.

✿

Juffin's call reached me when I was already in the office.

I didn't let you go home because I wanted you to try to fall asleep in my chair. You must try it, at least by around sunrise. I'm not joking! Other than that, do as you wish. Over and out.

I was puzzled. In any case I didn't feel like sleeping. "Do as you wish." That sounded tempting. I thought a bit, then sent a call to Melamori. I was glad to learn that she was in good spirits.

I'm very sorry. We closed the case already, so my morning order about the eateries has become invalid.

I know, Max. But maybe the hunchback had accomplices? They could be making King Banjee in my favorite café on the Victory of Gurig VII Square. Sir Kofa went home to sleep before I did. So if you're ordering me to—

Of course I'm ordering you. The Unified Kingdom will simply perish if we don't carry out an inspection. And I can't go there alone. I'm terribly scared of the dark. I'm waiting for you. Over and out.

I even tossed my head in delight—how beautifully everything was turning out!

She arrived in half an hour, gazing at me in joyous anticipation, as only she could.

"Only no dark, deserted streets," Melamori whispered with a smile. "But who will take your place on duty?"

"Kurush, of course. Who else?"

The buriwok opened one eye just a crack, then puffed up its feathers again.

We went for a walk along the well-lighted streets. And where else was there to walk, may I ask? In Echo, praise be the Magicians, there are no dark alleyways or backstreets.

🌀

"I'm probably a terrible bore, Max," said Melamori. "I promised you that I would try to figure out why I was afraid of you. But I haven't been able to. And that's probably very bad, because—well, because . . ." her voice trailed away and she stared gloomily at her glass.

"What is there to understand?" I grinned. "I'm just a very scary fellow. Don't worry. Everyone's afraid of me. And don't make a tragedy out of it. In fact, you don't have to try to figure anything out. In matters like this, people should just consult their hearts."

"But I have two hearts!" Melamori retorted. "One that is brave, and another that is wise. And they want completely different things!"

"Well, then you'll just have to draw up a schedule. Let one of them lead the way today, and tomorrow it will be the other one's turn. That's a solution."

"Why are you in such a hurry, Max? Life is so long. It's good not to know everything there is to know, and everything that is to come. When everything has already happened . . . something wonderful disappears . . . I don't have the words to explain this."

"We've had different upbringings, Melamori. I prefer things to be more definite. Somewhat, anyway."

"Take me home, Max," Melamori said suddenly. "I've overestimated my own abilities—in all respects. Please don't be angry."

"Oh, I'm not angry," I said. "Maybe we can just do this more often? Walking together, I mean. While your two hearts are trying to sort things out between them, I would have a bit more happiness."

"Certainly, Max," Melamori said, "as long as it doesn't annoy you. The walks, I mean. They're not exactly what people expect when they have feelings for someone. I just happen to be a stubborn exception to the rule."

"When I was young, living very far away from here," I intoned like a thousand-year old man, "I had some difficult times. Let's just say I had only one pie, but I wanted to have ten. But I never threw away that single pie just because I wanted more. I've always been a sensible fellow, Melamori."

"I understand, Max," said Melamori, and smiled. "I would never have believed that you had to get by on just a single pie."

"I still do, as you see, in a certain sense. Let's go, you look like you're about to drop off to sleep."

"I feel like I'm already dreaming," Melamori murmured. Then I took her home.

When we arrived I was rewarded with a playful, smacking kiss on the cheek. Don't let yourself be seduced by that, I thought to myself. That innocent kiss doesn't mean anything But my head was spinning with joy. My breathing exercises were powerless to combat it.

I took a roundabout way back to the office. It was easier to think while I was walking than it would be sitting in the chair, and I certainly had things to think about. About Melamori's two hearts, for instance. If it were any other girl, the confession about the two quarreling hearts would have struck me as a silly, high-flown metaphor. But what did I actually know about the physiology of the inhabitants of Echo? Very little, when it came right down to it.

Returning to the House by the Bridge, I sent a call to Lady Tanita. My modest experience in matters like this told me that she would hardly be sleeping soundly, even at this late hour.

Good night, Lady Tanita. I wanted you to know that at around sundown I killed the man who caused Karwen's death.

I decided not to explain to the widow that her husband's horrific death had come about, in fact, by chance. It was unlikely to comfort her in any way.

Thank you, Sir Max, she answered. *Revenge is better than nothing. You know, I took your advice. I've already moved so I can start a new life. And that's better than nothing, too.*

When you open a new tavern, send me a call. I'll definitely come by and save you from any possible chance of bankruptcy. Good night, Lady Tanita.

I don't think you'll care much for what my new cook prepares, but you must come anyway. Good night, Sir Max. And thank you again—for the advice, and for avenging me.

When the invisible connection with Lady Tanita was broken, I was again alone, except for the sweetly sleeping Kurush. Soon, sleep stole over me, as well, and recalling Sir Juffin's order, I dozed dutifully in his chair.

I was extremely uncomfortable. My back ached, my legs went numb. I woke up every five minutes, then slipped immediately into slumber again. "Don't fidget, don't get distracted," the voice of Maba Kalox, the most mysterious creature in this improbable World, repeated to me in my dream. I couldn't really see his face, though. Toward morning, I also dreamed about Juffin, but I didn't have the strength to understand, much less remember, the contents of these importunate visions.

※

"You look terrible, Max."

The cheerful voice of Juffin restored me to life. It was morning. I felt quite sick.

"Were you playing tricks on me me?" I asked wearily. "What were you and Sir Maba up to?"

"Do you remember?" Juffin asked. "Do you remember what you dreamed?"

"Not really. Only that you were there, and it was exhausting, I hasten to add. Well, and Sir Maba's voice—he told me 'not to fidget.' What was it about, Juffin?"

"Never mind. You'll go home, sleep a bit, and you'll be as good as new. Before you go, though, try making some kamra again."

"Juffin, are you taking revenge on me for Boboota?" I asked. "What a beast you are, after all."

The chief looked at me with genuine compassion.

"Why, is it that bad? Please, Max, try it. I beg you. Honestly, I'm not teasing you. Or if I am, just the very slightest bit."

I went downstairs and had a good wash. I did feel better, though my body still ached all over. Returning to the office, I clattered the dishes around humorlessly. Sir Juffin Hully behaved like a director on premier night. He was terribly nervous, but he tried hard to conceal it. I hurried to get the culinary experiment over with.

"Here," I said. "Who are you planning to torture? What's that you say—the hunchback's waitress wouldn't talk? Let her drink that, the old shrew."

To my surprise, Juffin not only sniffed the contents of the pot, he even tasted it himself. When he tasted it a second time, my jaw dropped as far as it could without falling off altogether.

"Don't you want to try it, Max?"

"Come off it," I said, sighing. "That's all I need."

"As you wish." Sir Juffin filled his mug to the brim. "It's not quite as good as the kamra in the *Glutton*; but still, I like it."

"What are you talking about? Why are you drinking that stuff? Are you getting stingy? I can put it on my tab in the *Glutton*—I'm rich and generous. Don't do it, sir!"

"Don't you get it, Max? Try it yourself—stop fooling around!"

I tried it. The kamra wasn't as good as the *Glutton*'s; but it was better than the kamra in the *Sated Skeleton* in my neighborhood.

"Did you teach me how to make kamra in my sleep?" The truth was starting to dawn on me.

"Not me—Maba! It wasn't within my powers. In time I may be able to teach you to move between Worlds—but not how to cook. It wasn't even easy for Maba."

"But why? Do you need a new chef?"

"Far from it, son. There's no power in the World that will make a good chef out of you. To be honest, Maba and I just wanted to find out what we were worth. We weren't sure we could do it. But now we know that no one else can match us. And it may come in handy for you. Go home to bed, poor fellow. Tonight you can enjoy life. Come back tomorrow exactly one hour before sunset. We have an important call to pay."

"To Sir Maba?" I asked, brightening.

"Dream on! Life can't be one unbroken chain of pleasures. We're going to Jafax."

"To the Main Residence of the Order of the Seven-Leaf Clover!"

"Right you are. We're going to reshape history."

"What do you mean by that, Juffin?"

"I'll tell you later. Go get some rest. Good morning, Max."

When I got home, I snuggled down under the blanket on my bed and buried my nose in Armstrong's soft flank. Ella purred loudly in my ear.

"Happy New Year, little furries," I said to the cats. They yawned indifferently. I also yawned, and then blanked out.

CHAPTER SIX

VICTIMS OF CIRCUMSTANCE

WHEN I WOKE IT WAS NEARLY DARK IN THE BEDROOM. THIS WAS a record—it had been a long time had passed since I had slept till sundown.

Are you sleeping? Well, I'll be, mate! Melifaro's call resounded in my sleep-muddled brain. *Good for me. I just earned a crown.*

What for? I asked, uncomprehending.

Nothing much—it's just that I made a bet with Melamori. She claimed you'd wake up before sundown, and I bet on later. I was ready to lose, but you've done me a good turn!

So now you owe me not one, but two meals, I said. *Your debt to me is growing by leaps and bounds. Over and out.*

I yawned and dragged myself downstairs, my head buzzing like I had a hangover. Ella and Armstrong were slumbering by their bowls in the middle of the front room. Urf, the farmer's son, a junior official at the Ministry of Perfect Public Order, had most likely come in while I was sleeping. The cats looked full and contented, and their fur had been carefully groomed—not by me, of course. In childhood I sometimes frightened my parents by sleepwalking down the corridor, but I would hardly have known how to carry out such a delicate hairdressing operation with my eyes shut.

When most of the sticky cobwebs of sleep had fallen away, I began feeling like a person again. The delivery boy from the *Sated Skeleton* whined plaintively at the door. Just as I was about to answer it, I realized I hadn't managed to get dressed yet, so I quickly wrapped myself

in Armstrong's colorful mat. It was a far cry from the Mantle of
Death, but I wasn't prepared to open the door completely naked. One
look at the boy informed me that a cat's mat wasn't the most appropriate domestic attire either; but by then it was too late. My poor,
beleaguered reputation!

I closed the door behind the disconcerted youth, returned the
mat to its customary place, and happily sat down to breakfast. After
the first mug of kamra, my head grew less fuzzy. It occurred to me
that Lady Melamori could have found dozens of other pretexts for
a bet with Melifaro. She probably wasn't against taking a stroll with
me, but she was embarrassed to take the initiative. The argument
about the hour I awoke was an excellent way not only of getting
information about my habits, but of tactfully reminding me of her
existence. So I immediately got in touch with this incomprehensible
creature.

Good day, my lady!

*Not day—evening, Sir Sleepyhead. I lost a whole crown because
of you!*

*I'm guilty. I repent. But I had a terrible night. I dreamed about
Juffin. Can you imagine? You should pity me, not scold me. And I
need to be aired out, as well, like an old winter looxi.*

*I'll fetch you in half an hour. Sir Juffin informed me in strictest
confidence that you would be free tonight, so I have great plans.*

First I nearly died of happiness. Then I went to get dressed. If
Lady Melamori caught me wrapped in Armstrong's mat, my chances
would plummet, no doubt. Or . . . would they?

When the Master of Pursuit appeared on my doorstep, looking a
bit dazed by her own boldness, I was already in fine fettle and prepared for anything. "Anything" in this case meant walking thousands
of miles, if need be, along Echo's mosaic sidewalks, in the company
of Lady Melamori. According to her, long walks in one another's
company are just what a man and a woman who are not indifferent
to each other need. It was possible that I had been hasty with my conclusions about "each other"; but Melamori's tender look confirmed
my most daring conjectures.

This time we traipsed all the way to the New City (about an hour
and a half from my house, by the way). Melamori managed to tell me

heaps of new gossip, but I only listened out of the corner of my ear. I was too happy to be all ears.

"There's a remarkable place around here," she said, slackening her pace. "An old mansion with a garden. In the evening they sell some vile drink here, that's why it's so deserted."

"I know of many deserted places with vile drinks. My house, for instance," I laughed. "It wasn't as far to seek."

"This is a special place. It used to be the Country Residence of the Order of the Secret Grass. Back then, Echo was much smaller than it is now, you know. I'm sure you'll like it. Here it is."

We passed through the gateway, the appearance of which was none too promising esthetically. The first impression was deceiving. A narrow dark flight of stairs leading to a neglected garden, illuminated by the bluish light of tiny glass globes filled with some incandescent gas. Here there were none of your ordinary small tables—only low benches nestled among the evergreen Kaxxa bushes, which resembled the juniper of my homeland. The air was wonderfully cold and transparent. It didn't slow the blood, but just chilled the skin, like menthol. My head spun. It seemed to me then that I was amazingly young, and the world around me was full of mystery. If you think about it, that was the honest truth, and just what I should have been feeling.

I broke into a smile.

"You're right, this is a marvelous place!"

"Yes. But don't even think of ordering kamra. It's disgusting here. Better get something stronger—a drink like that can't be spoiled under even the most adverse circumstances."

"Stronger? Don't forget, it's still morning for me."

"Oh yes. Of course . . . well, all the worse for you, Sir Max. I'm going to indulge, with your permission—it's already long since evening for me."

"Indulge to your heart's content. I hope they can find water from some sort of sacred spring around here. That's what I need right now."

They didn't serve water there, alas, so I was forced to content myself with a glass of some kind of sour fruit compote. Melamori and I made quite a couple—she, a delicate creature gulping down the most potent Jubatic Juice, and me, the hefty fellow in the Mantle of Death, sipping bland fruit compote.

"If you want to talk, this is where to do it," Melamori blurted out, already blushing from the effects of her drink.

Then she went quiet, as though frightened at the sound of her own voice. Just as I was about to nudge her back to life, she started up again unexpectedly.

"As for my fears, Max—I've dug up a few things. So tell me, what color are your eyes?"

"They're . . . brown, I think," I stammered.

I was stunned. Sinning Magicians! What was happening to my memory? How could I forget the color of my own eyes?

"Um-hmm. You see, you don't even know yourself. Take a look," said Melamori and held up a small mirror she pulled out of the folds of her looxi.

A pair of gray eyes, round with surprise, stared back at me.

"What's gotten into me? I completely forgot! Amazing!"

"You forgot? It's no wonder you forgot. Yesterday they really were brown. In the evening, that is. And in the morning they were green, like a descendant of a Draxx. When I went to Headquarters three days before the End of the Year, they were blue. I even fancied they looked just like Uncle Kima's."

"It's very sweet of you to pay attention to such trifles, Melamori. But it's news to me. It's even hard to believe. Are you sure you're not confused yourself?"

"Do you want to bet?" Melamori said, grinning. "Look in the mirror an hour from now. They change constantly!"

"I'm not going to bet with you," I mumbled, handing back the mirror. "You'll have me penniless. But for the life of me, I don't understand why that should fill you with fear. So my eyes change color. You call that a miracle? Your whole family is from the Seven-Leaf Clover. You can't seem to get used to it."

"That's just it. I know a lot, but I've never heard of anything of the kind. Yesterday evening, when I finally realized I wasn't just imagining it, I even asked Uncle Kima. I didn't mention your name; I said I had noticed it in one of the messengers. Kima also told me I was imagining it, that such things just don't happen. I didn't want to insist, but today I asked Sir Juffin. You know what he said?"

"Let me guess. 'The world is full of wonders, girl.' Or, 'Don't fill your head full of nonsense, Melamori.' Am I right?"

"Almost," Melamori said with a sigh. "He let out a big guffaw and answered that this wasn't your only achievement. And he added that this city was full of ordinary lads, without any eccentricities, and that's why they weren't working in the Force."

"That's very nice of him," I said and smiled. "I'll have to thank him next time I see him."

"Joking aside, Sir Max, are you absolutely sure you're human?"

"I don't know," I said with a laugh. "It's not something I've ever really thought about!"

"Sir Juffin answered me the same way. And he laughed just like you. But what am I supposed to do? Leave the Force so that I don't have to see you? Or drink too much before every meeting with you just to pluck up my courage? Answer me, Sir Max!"

I probably should have thought up some comforting drivel for her. It was in my own best interests. But I liked Melamori so much I couldn't lie, and I didn't want to try to wriggle out of the situation.

"I really don't know!" I insisted. "I was always sure that you'd have to look far and wide to find a more normal person than myself, however strange that may sound. But don't try to pull the wool over my eyes, Melamori! You're not such a coward, as far as I can judge."

"No, I'm no coward, but . . . I grew up among special and unusual people, Max. My father was appointed to the throne during the Troubled Times, in the event of the deaths of both Gurigs. My aunt and uncle are from the Order of the Seven-Leaf Clover, and my mother's side of the family is descended from an ancient royal dynasty. You can imagine what it was like for me when I was growing up. And I'm used to being 'special' myself. The 'most important,' even. I grew up thinking I knew everything, understood everything, and could make anyone do my bidding. Well, nearly everyone. I've had to reconcile myself to the idea that Sir Juffin Hully is beyond my comprehension, insofar as I know the history of the Troubled Times not from books, but from witnesses. He'll tell you, too, if he hasn't already. But I want to love a person who—"

"Who will do your bidding?" I asked, suddenly realizing what she was trying to say.

"Yes, most likely. Moreover, that's how I was raised. If I don't understand something, it frightens me. This is what the Order of the Seven-Leaf Clover stands for, if you'd like to know—circumspection and comprehension, precisely in that order! So since I know quite a bit, and can explain things to myself somehow, I'm usually no coward. But as soon as I look at you, Max, I just fall apart!"

"Then there's only one way out for you," I said with a wink. "Get to know me better. Throw caution to the winds and find out who I am. You'll discover that I'm a terrible bore, and then everything will be fine. Hurry up, though. By the next full moon I'll completely lose my human form."

I couldn't help feeling amused. I've had all kinds of problems with girls, but never this kind. It was usually other things they disapproved of. I had believed quite optimistically that putting Lady Melamori's inchoate fears to rest would be a piece of cake. She'd get a closer look at me and realize that fear was the last thing she should feel around me. I'm not very convincing as some "beast flying on the wings of darkness."

The evening ended with us indecorously sharing another bottle of the Order's exclusive wine in Melamori's living room. True, we weren't alone. There were also eight (imagine!) of Melamori's girlfriends keeping us company. The young ladies were all very pretty, and they chattered so incessantly it made me dizzy.

Melamori seriously overindulged in strong beverages, so when I was taking my leave I received a passionate kiss from her. Almost genuine. I was so taken aback that I decided just to be happy with what I had—come what may!

All the rest of the night I wandered through Echo, frightening the solitary passersby with my Mantle of Death. My mind was on fire with wild premonitions. Some atavistic instinct demanded immediate and desperate action. But my good upbringing prevailed, and in the end I did not scale the wall and crawl through Lady Melamori's bedroom window.

I couldn't fall asleep, either, even by midday. After tossing and turning under the covers for a few hours, I dispensed with my daily schedule and set out for the House by the Bridge, arriving much earlier than I was expected.

"You couldn't sleep, Sir Max?"

I very rarely had the occasion to see my boss in a bad mood, but I couldn't remember ever having seen him as happy as he was today.

"What's going on?" I asked. "Did Boboota Box die after all?"

"Don't be silly, Max. He's all right. He's going to invite you and Melifaro over to visit him as soon as he can get out of bed. So prepare yourself! It's hard to be General Boboota Box's rescuer. I suspect the gratitude of this wonderful man will be much more tormenting than his rage. Be that as it may . . . Do you remember Chakatta Pie?"

"And how! Did you really manage to get another piece?"

"Look at things from a broader perspective! Even Chakatta Pie will be available to any Tom, Dick, and Harry in town. And us, too!"

"What do you mean by that?" I prodded cautiously. "Do you plan to rewrite the Code of Krember?"

"I always knew you had exceptional intuition. You guessed it! Not rewrite it completely, but . . . we'll just make a small amendment. One neat and proper little change. Everything's ready to go; we just need the official sanction of Grand Magician Nuflin. That's why we're going to see him. And when I say 'we,' I mean both you and me. Actually, three of us are going. Kofa is invited, too."

"Juffin," I stammered, almost losing the power of speech altogether. "Why would you need me there? I'm flattered, naturally. But are you sure that I'm someone you want tagging along with you to the Residence of the Seven-Leaf Clover? What about the color of my eyes? You don't think they'll clap you in Xolomi for consorting with an otherworldling? Lady Melamori would probably approve of such a harsh measure."

"Oh, she unburdened herself to you already? Silly girl. Well, unlike her, Nuflin is a serious chap. He's lived an exceedingly long life. He understands True Magic and all the rest. At the dawn of the Troubled Times his emissaries fell at my feet. By the way, it was because he was *well-informed*. Without people like me and Sir Maba, the Order of the Watery Crow—"

"The 'Watery Crow'?" I asked, and burst out laughing.

"Go ahead and laugh. It doesn't matter now. But a century and a half ago it wasn't funny at all. He had a real Power behind him, and not some paltry bag of tricks. It was through their kind offices that the World was on the verge of going to wrack and ruin and succumbing to the Dark Magicians. The others just helped in whatever ways they could."

"Still, it's funny. So in fact the victory of the King and the Seven-Leaf Clover in the Battle for the Code was your doing?"

"Partly. I'll tell you about it someday when we have time—when you're ready to understand even half of what I say. Don't be offended. Your ability to understand depends on your personal experience, and not on your mental powers. So, getting back to your question. I'm taking you and Sir Kofa with me for the simple reason that Nuflin requested me to. He's the master of the house, he decides these things."

"He wants to see a savage from the back of beyond?"

"He wants to take a look at my successor, if you really must know."

I nearly fell out of my chair, but started to do Lonli-Lokli's breathing exercises instead. I think they saved my life.

"Don't worry," Juffin grinned. "What does it matter to you what will happen in three hundred years? As far as I know, you never hoped to live that long. So just take it as information about my posthumous life. Agreed?"

"Agreed," I sighed. "All the same, don't joke like that anymore, all right?"

"Who says I'm joking? Well, enough of your wailing and moaning. You knew from the very start why I was bringing you here. The fact that you concealed this from yourself is another matter altogether. Why don't you brew up some kamra; you don't want to lose your touch."

"Oh, that's more like it," I said, getting down to business. "Now I'll make a fool of myself, you'll demote me to janitor, and everything will be fine."

"No need for false modesty," Juffin said, tasting my concoction. "Today it's even better than last time."

❀

Exactly one hour before sundown, Sir Kofa Yox appeared, this time in his own guise, and enveloped in a splendid dark purple looxi. Never before had I seen such a rich hue. It almost seemed to glow from within.

"Only Sir Kofa has the privilege of dressing like that," Juffin informed me. "After all, he's been keeping the peace in this blasted town for two hundred years. Back then, the position of Head of City Police inspired far more respect than the title of Grand Magician. And it wasn't just by chance—it was thanks to Sir Kofa that the philistines of Echo went almost unscathed in the Troubled Times. I could kill him for it: I'm sick of them, these philistines!"

"Mea culpa," Sir Kofa muttered, his eyes downcast. "What could I do? I'd taken an oath."

"But how did it come about that General Boboota occupied your post?" I asked. "Intrigue?"

Juffin and Kofa exchanged glances and exploded in laughter.

I blinked dully, uncomprehending.

"Boy, you still don't understand where you're working," Sir Kofa said, after he had regained his composure. "Let me explain—it was a promotion. And what a promotion it was! What you don't seem to realize is that Sir Juffin is second-in-command in the country."

"After the King?"

"No, after Magician Nuflin, of course. And you and I and His Majesty Gurig VIII are trailing behind somewhere among the first twelve."

"Well, I'll be!" I said, shaking my head in vexation.

"Don't worry, Max, that's just the unofficial version of the ladder of hierarchy. It doesn't change anything. Let's go."

And off we went to Jafax.

⁂

The Transparent Gates of Jafax Castle, the Residence of the Order of the Seven-Leaf Clover, the Single and Most Beneficent, open only twice a day: at sunrise and sunset. Early in the morning they are opened for representatives of the Royal Court and other important people. And at dusk, shady characters like us make our way inside. People think that the Minor Secret Investigative Force is the most sinister organization in the Unified Kingdom, though an initiate knows this is absurd.

The Grand Magician of the Order of the Seven-Leaf Clover, Nuflin Moni Mak, was waiting for us in a dark, spacious hall. It was nearly impossible to make out his face in the thick gloom. Suddenly I realized he hadn't had a face for a long time already. To be more precise, the old man had forgotten what his own face looked like, and therefore no one else was able to descry its features. I also understood that the Grand Magician himself had seen fit to convey this silent information to me.

"You can't imagine what a great joy it is that I've been able to stay alive until your visit, gentlemen! And what do you know, stay alive I did, until this very day!"

Magician Nuflin's voice witnessed to a venerable old age, but its jangling chords concealed such incredible power that I shrank from him. He sounded slightly mocking and thoroughly amiable. He seemed to feel no need to intimidate his guests—like anyone who truly knows his own power.

"Have you been under Juffin's tutelage for a long time already?" Nuflin Moni Mak asked, staring at me in frank curiosity. "How do you like it, this apprenticeship? They say you're doing quite well. No need to be shy around Old Man Nuflin, Max. You should either be terrified of me, or not fear me at all. The first alternative seems rather pointless—we're not enemies. You don't have to answer, just sit down and listen to what the wise old folks say. You can tell your grandchildren about it. But then again, you can't possibly have any grandchildren at your age!"

I took the Grand Magician's advice and sat down on a comfortable, low divan. My older colleagues followed suit.

"Juffin, you are fond of a good meal," Nuflin remarked affably. "It's a wonder you waited so long with this amendment. My boys are simply thrilled about it. They say the opposition will be forced to shut up for two hundred years or more. Some theoreticians they are! Kofa, you're a wise man. Tell me honestly, have you ever seen this 'opposition'? I don't believe in it, myself. It's a childish fancy. My boys think that without enemies Old Nuflin will get bored with life. Tell me, Kofa, have I got things all wrong?"

"You're quite right," the Master Eavesdropper affirmed. "If there is an opposition, it's not in Echo. And if someone's grumbling about something in some Landalanda—"

"Ooooh, we're scared, aren't we?" Nuflin interjected. "We don't even know where to hide. Well, that's enough of that. Juffin, tell me how your little plan is going to work, and let's be done with it. By the way, your boy here hasn't had a wink of sleep in more than twenty-four hours. Are you aware of that? You shouldn't drive your people so hard. You always were such a mean fellow."

"He's driving himself, without any outside help," the boss said with a grin. "As for the reforms, for every chef an Earring of Oxalla, the same as your novices have. And let them experiment in the kitchen with Forbidden Magic, whether black or white. Only up to the twentieth degree, of course. More than that is out of the question."

"Oh, Juffin. Why would they need more? That's all an honest person needs to make a great meal."

"Yes. And at the same time we can be sure that they will never resolve to ask for more. Whatever else it may be, it's an extra safety measure."

"Why didn't you say something sooner, Juffin? Were you waiting until I came up with the idea myself? They cook very well for me already. Who would have thought! Now everyone will be able to get a tasty meal, just like in the good old days! They'll put up statues of us in front of every tavern! And young Gurig, too, so his nose won't be out of joint."

I followed the conversation with rapt attention, and while much of it was over my head, I was able to figure out that the Code of Krember would no longer prevent culinary masterpieces from seeing the light of day. This rather alarmed me. If I had been a terrible glutton until now, what would become of me under the new dispensation? What if I expanded to Booboota's dimensions? Lady Melamori would fear me even more than she did already.

At a certain moment, I began to sense that there was another witness to our conversation—an invisible one. I even detected a familiar condescending chuckle. Was it possible that Maba Kalox's curiosity extended to such pedestrian affairs? In any case, I knew only one person who was fond of being invisibly present at important events.

Magician Nuflin interrupted my musings.

"What do you think about all this, young man? Do you also like to eat well?"

"I do. True, you'll never make a chef out of me. So my views on the subject completely coincide with those of Maba Kalox—it doesn't matter where the food comes from, as long as it goes down well. Am I making myself clear?" I asked in a servile tone, fixing my gaze on a spot on the ceiling, from which Sir Maba seemed to be observing us.

Frankly speaking, this was a joke meant especially for Sir Juffin Hully. I thought my boss would pick up on the allusion, and that the others wouldn't notice it at all. Instead, all three of them began staring at me like amateur botanists examining a rare carnivorous plant—in horror mixed with ecstasy.

"Oh, Juffin," the Grand Magician exclaimed, breaking the silence. "What a nose your boy has! To sniff out the old rascal Maba—who would have thought? Where did you find him?"

"About where we buried Loiso Pondoxo in his time. A place even more remote, though."

"What can I say Juffin—he's worth his weight in gold!"

I instinctively sensed that the Grand Magician was staring at me again. I won't say I was entirely happy about this, but I tolerated it patiently. Nuflin watched me intently for a time, and then began to speak again.

"Young man, ask that sly old fox Juffin when the last time was that old Nuflin was taken by surprise. Well, you don't even have to ask him. If I don't remember, he won't remember either. But if someone asks you, you can tell him that old Nuflin was very surprised on the evening of the third day of the year 116 of the Code Epoch. And that would be the truth, because I was surprised today! What can I do for you, my boy? It's better to say thank you right away for something like this, and not regret it later."

I was completely stunned by what had just happened, but I decided that I shouldn't explain or excuse myself. If Grand Magician Nuflin Moni Mak thought I was a genius—well, so be it! I was embarrassed, though Juffin looked pleased. And I did have a request.

"If you really want to make me happy, it's all in your power," I said, making an effort to be deferential, although this didn't really seem necessary.

"Oy vey, Max, I already know that everything is in my power without you telling me so," the old man said with a grin. "Just give it to me straight."

"Please allow me to wear my regular clothes. Not when I'm on duty, of course, but in my free time." I fiddled demonstratively with the hem of my black and gold Mantle of Death. "It's crucial that I wear it at work, and it is truly very beautiful. But sometimes I just want to go unnoticed, to have a rest from people's stares. All the more since it turns out that I don't have to be angry or frightened to be poisonous. Experience has shown that this ability is always present in me. You needn't be afraid of upsetting me, though. I'm very even-tempered when I keep myself in check."

"Who would have suspected—such a good boy, and so lethal!" Nuflin exclaimed gaily.

"Thank Magician Maxlilgl Annox for that," Juffin said, smiling. "Do you remember him?"

"How could I forget? Such a small fellow, and so serious. So he's the one who presented you with that gift, Max? How wise of him—to do something of benefit to someone in the end. So, Juffin, does he speak the truth? Does he really have such a poisonous mouth? And is it possible to work with him even when he's being kind?"

"Max isn't wise enough to begin lying to you. Perhaps in about three hundred years . . ."

"Oy, Praise to the Heavens, I refuse to live that long! Here's what I would say to you, Max. When you're not working, dress however you please. And keep in mind that you'll be in my debt for this favor! It's not every day that old Nuflin changes established tradition."

"I can't tell you how grateful I am to you!"

I was elated. I had been granted freedom—the priceless freedom of being a person no one notices. I would be able to chat with pretty tavernkeepers, share my tobacco with nice old men, make friends with stray dogs. What else do you need to be happy?

"When you get older, you'll understand that it's not all these other silly people who need the Mantle of Death, but you yourself," the Grand Magician said meaningfully. "Think about wise old Nuflin then! The Mantle of Death, like the Mantle of the Grand Magician, is a good way of saying no to the World. Other people have their own lives, and you have yours, independent of anyone else. Just don't protest, saying you don't want to say no to this World! Come to me again in about five hundred years, and let me hear what kind of tune you'll be singing then."

It seemed the old man had blithely forgotten his own recent promise not to live another three hundred years. Or did he believe he could still receive visitors after his demise? But who in the World knows what he'll be able to do after death?

"I won't take up any more of your valuable time, Nuflin," Sir Juffin said, standing up. "I remember how trying you find visitors, even such worthy visitors as ourselves."

"Now don't sell yourself short, Juffin. For all I know, you just want to go get something to eat . . . and rake my old bones over the coals! You think I'll try to stop you? Or invite you to dine with me? Well, then, you don't know me very well yet! Take yourselves off to your *Glutton*. And you, get a good night's sleep, boy. You'll be needing it."

Sinning Magicians, what did he mean by that?

❀

We left Jafax via an underground passage that connected the castle to the House by the Bridge. I learned that this was a very important part of the ritual: one must enter the Residence of the Order of the Seven-Leaf Clover in plain view, but leave this sacred place in secret, through one's own previously arranged exit. The services of a guide are not offered to guests, and they won't even consider unlocking the gates for them.

"And who is this Loiso Pondoxo you buried who-knows-where?" I asked when we had crossed the threshold.

"Ah, Loiso, Grand Magician of that same Order of the Watery Crow—the name of which was such a source of amusement to you. Listen, go get some sleep, hero," Juffin said with a wink. "Some Nocturnal Representative you are! You're practically asleep on your feet. All the same, Sir Kofa and I will be working all night."

"Working on such a sacred task is no chore," Sir Kofa announced, nodding solemnly. "My congratulations, Juffin! It was so easy for you to push through those changes in the Code. You know how to wrap the old man around your little finger."

"It's a good thing I was the one to do it. Imagine what would happen to the World if someone else were able to do the same!"

"Horrors! Do as Juffin says, Max. Go to bed. You aren't up to making any sense, anyway."

I didn't object. Making sense was a fairly remote prospect just now.

I was terribly drowsy on the way home. All the same I sent Melamori a call.

How are things, my lady?

Not much to report. While you were waltzing around Jafax, I had to entertain Melifaro. And the girls, of course. They all took to each other immediately. Poor fellow, his head's probably still spinning after so much heavy-duty flirting. He's used to taking on the ladies one by one. But here—what a range of possibilities!

And how did they like me?

I don't know. I can't remember. I really overindulged in the liqueur and the hard stuff yesterday. Sweet dreams, Max. I'm falling asleep.

Will I see you tomorrow?

Sure! Over and out.

Melamori had also picked up my inane little expression. It was pleasant, as though she had a keepsake of mine in her pocket that she took out to show her friends from time to time.

As soon as I fell asleep, my life—interesting though it already was—became even more interesting. I dreamed that an invisible guest had just made himself at home in my bedroom.

"Greetings, clairvoyant!" I recognized the voice of Maba Kalox instantly. "You were very clever to discover me back there. But in future, don't show off, all right? Everyone already knows how smart you are, and I like to stay incognito."

"I'm sorry, Sir Maba!"

I was already asleep, but I was still aware enough to understand just what he was saying.

"It wasn't such a terrible *faux pas*. Those three would have sensed my presence even without your help. From now on, though, remember—if you want to talk to me, well, that's what Silent Speech is for. Announcing to everyone that 'Sir Maba is here!' isn't the thing to do. Agreed?"

"Agreed," I mumbled. I was ashamed of myself.

"Good. Now, since I just blew in on a wild wind, I'm going to give you a present."

"What kind of present?"

"What do you mean 'what kind'? A good one! Keep an eye on your pillow from now on. Make sure no one tries to move it from its proper place."

"Why?"

"Because the pillow of such a great hero can be an excellent plug in the Chink between Worlds. Am I making myself clear?"

"No," I admitted.

"Oh, Max. How does poor Juffin manage to teach you anything? I can't imagine! Fine. Remember how I fetched all those silly treats for you from under the table?"

"Oh yes," I said, smiling broadly in my sleep. "Do you mean to tell me that I can do that, too, now?"

"Well, let's just say that you can't do it like *that* yet, but if you set your mind to it, you may be able to rustle up a few of those funny smoking sticks from distant Worlds that you so crave. Try it when you wake up. And nail your pillow to the floor so it won't get lost, is my advice to you!"

"What do I have to do?"

"Stick your hand under the pillow. Then everything will happen on its own. Only you must exercise patience, my boy. It takes a long time at first. You'll see what I mean."

"Well, Sir Maba, if I can get hold of just one regular cigarette, I'll be forever in your debt!"

"That's just fine. Your funny habit is the best guarantee that you'll practice hard. Practice is what you need now."

"Uh—will I dream you again?" I asked eagerly. "Maybe there's something else I can learn from you."

"Of course there is. Even without my help. I can't promise I'll visit you often. You're young, and I'm so old. It's not much fun for me to teach you. Let Juffin run around after you! All the more since you want to dream other things now. And it's completely within your power."

"What do you mean?"

But it was too late. Sir Maba Kalox had already disappeared. In his place, Melamori appeared at the window. I was glad, but somehow not surprised.

"Good dream, my lady!" I called out gaily. "How glad I am to see you!"

"Is this really a dream?" asked Melamori. "Are you sure?"

"Yes. And it's my dream, not yours. I'm dreaming you."

Melamori smiled and started melting away. Her fragile silhouette became completely transparent. I wanted to stop her, but suddenly I realized I couldn't budge. I weighed a ton—no, who was I kidding? I weighed far more . . .

"Yes, I'm already almost home," Melamori squeaked in surprise, and disappeared completely.

※

I woke up. It was early morning. Armstrong and Ella were breathing contentedly somewhere down by my heels. The kitties! They could accidentally nudge the pillow—the plug, that is—and other Worlds would come gushing into my poor bedroom! I fretted, only half awake.

I rushed over to the small cupboard at the far side of the room to find a needle and some thread. My stashing habits are sometimes truly remarkable. I got into bed again and sewed the corners of the pillow firmly to the thick sleeping-rug. I took a deep breath. Now everything was all right. I could sleep some more.

My head dropped onto the rug, next to the tightly secured pillow, and I blanked out. This time, no dreams came to me; none that I was aware of, anyway.

I finally woke up again around noon. The sun, enchantingly impertinent as happens only in early spring, peeped from behind the curtain. I stared at the firmly attached pillow in wonder—what kind of nonsense was this? Then I remembered.

Guess what I did next. I stuck my hand into the alleged Chink between Worlds and waited expectantly. I didn't experience anything out of the ordinary. It must have looked absurd—a person on all fours, naked, one hand under the pillow, while on his face a look of tense anticipation of something miraculous. Thank goodness the windows were covered with shutters!

In about fifteen minutes, I began to think that Sir Maba Kalox had played a trick on me. A tiny trick, to be sure, but it was a fine way of taking revenge on me for recently blowing his cover. He had warned me it would be a lengthy process, however. So hope was still keeping itself warm in one of the dark corners of my heart—presumably the left ventricle.

Another ten minutes or so passed. My legs grew numb, my poor elbow screamed for mercy. Hope entered its final stages: the death throes. Then I realized that my right hand was no longer lying on the soft nap of the rug under the warm pillow. It was—horrors, it wasn't anywhere at all! All the same, I was able to wiggle my fingers. To do this, though, I needed to make an effort of the will, rather than a physical effort of the muscles.

I was so afraid that I forgot about everything else in the world. My benumbed legs, my convulsively cramped shoulders—who cared?

Where was my poor paw, was what I wanted to know. Forget the blasted cigarettes! I'd smoke the stinking pipe tobacco. Just give me back my beloved hand!

Though I could do with a cigarette at a moment like this . . .

Suddenly I lurched backwards, so unexpectedly that I lost my balance and fell over on my side. Luckily, I didn't have far to fall when I was already on all fours. I burst out in nervous laughter. My hand was with me again. More than that, between my middle finger and my forefinger I found a half-smoked, burning cigarette. There was a red lipstick stain on the filter. Aha! I had robbed some dame! The blue number 555 below the filter . . . Sinning Magicians, what's the difference! I took a puff, and swooned. Deprivation had turned me into a terrible skinflint; seconds later I carefully put out the cigarette and went to wash. Then I warmed up the remains of yesterday's kamra, sat in an armchair, and tenderly smoked the crumpled stub. What a glorious start to the day! It was as though I had dropped into the middle of a fairy tale.

Need I say that I didn't emerge from the bedroom until sundown? I swear that even the desire to see Melamori couldn't dislodge me until it was time for me to report to the House by the Bridge.

The first attempt, as it turned out, was the most successful. The next few times I had to wait even longer. Now, at last, I knew why I had to suffer. By the time I left for work, I had four cigarettes— three that someone had already smoked, and one whole one. After wrapping up my loot and carefully hiding it in the pocket of the Mantle of Death, I set out for the Ministry of Perfect Public Order. With all the excitement of these otherworldly experiments, I had even forgotten to eat.

After yesterday's historic occasion, I must admit I expected a huge crowd of chefs at the visitors' entrance, all of them longing for permission to apply magic of the heretofore-forbidden 20th degree in their kitchens, and to wear the Earring of Oxalla to top it off.

Nothing of the sort. There were no visitors, either outside or in the corridor, or even in the Hall of Common Labor, where a temporary reception space had been set up. Melifaro was sitting in state on the table with the bored expression of the well-rested.

Sir Juffin Hully came out of the office to meet me.

"Unbelievable, Max. You're on time today, and not three hours early. What's gotten into you?"

"Don't you know? I saw Sir Maba in my dream."

"Really? And was this vision too wonderful to wake up from?"

"You really don't know? He taught me how to forage for cigarettes. Underneath my pillow!"

"How thoughtful of him. I never would have expected it. And did it work? It did, of course—it's written in big letters across your happy forehead. Strange, Maba never was a very good teacher. He's too impatient to bother with neophytes. We're talking nonsense over here, Melifaro. Don't give it a second thought," said Juffin, finally noticing that the eyes of his Diurnal Representative were popping out in surprise. "It means you're going to have to work that much harder, poor boy. It seems that from now on Max is going to be spending all his time fishing around under his pillow."

"Well, that beats sitting in an office all day," said Melifaro.

I was feeling magnanimous, like every truly happy person.

"I'm not yet a lost cause. But tell me, where are all the chefs? What happened this morning?"

"Not a thing," said Melifaro and yawned. "Chemparkaroke, the innkeeper of the *Old Thorn,* dropped in. It was really something. He claims that he can prepare his house special, the *Soup of Repose,* without any magic whatsoever, as long as the seasoning herbs are potent. But the Earring of Oxalla, he said, was a beautiful thing, and the customers would like it. He's quite a character. He insisted on looking into a mirror while the earring was being affixed, so he could see the whole process. I thought I'd have some fun, and called in the junior staff. The boys crowded around Chemparkaroke, each of them holding a mirror so that he might see his reflection from many different angles at once. I put the earring in, wailing some terrible incantations at the top of my lungs, half of them made up right on the spot. The fellow was ecstatic! He pirouetted in front of the mirror for half an hour, at the same time inviting all the policemen to his establishment. Finally he turned to me, told me he liked the earring, and left. Now there's a full house at the *Old Thorn,* no doubt."

"Do you mean to say that Chemparkaroke was the only one who came by for an earring? And he didn't need magic at all, if he is to be believed? What is this, Juffin?" I asked my boss in consternation. "It was such an achievement—persuading Grand Magician Nuflin, and so forth. And now the idiots . . ."

"That's precisely the point. They're not idiots at all. They're just sensible, cautious gentlemen. Do you think they would come running on the very first day? The Earring of Oxalla is no trifling matter. Do you know what will happen to the person who decides to indulge in magic of even the 21st degree if he's wearing that little doodad? There aren't many who could withstand the shock of pain that is inevitable in that case. Our amazing culinary wizards are living people, and they're not quite ready to be hemmed in that way. Everyone thinks that if he breaks the prohibition only once he can hide from us, if he's lucky. And it isn't even the end of the world if he ends up in Xolomi. Almost half of the most important people in the Unified Kingdom have done time in Xolomi. But about the Earring of Oxalla there can be only one opinion—either you have it or you don't."

"Why not take it off?" I didn't understand a thing. The day before I was so sleepy that I hadn't managed to pin Juffin down and ask what the Earring of Oxalla really was.

"Oh, Max! Give me a break, Marvel of the Steppes!"

Melifaro held out for my inspection a fairly large ring of some kind of dark metal, clearly different from ordinary jewelry. It was solid, without any break in the hoop, nor was there any clasp. I took the thing in my hand. It felt heavy and warm.

"Affixing it to someone's ear is quite easy, but it can only be done by a competent person. Me, for instance. This metal, as you see, can't penetrate human flesh without the accompaniment of specific charms," Melifaro explained. "And to remove it . . . In the Order of the Seven-Leaf Clover there are several fellows who specialize in such procedures. To go to Jafax, however, and say, 'Hey, guys, take this hardware out of my ear! I'm itching to make some magic!'—well, it's not the wisest move. Am I right, Boss?"

"Absolutely," said Juffin and yawned. "You are so very right that my presence here is becoming superfluous. I'm going home to sleep, fellows. I'm as tired as a mad murderer."

"Wait, so it was all for nothing?" I asked. "Your diplomatic stunt, I mean. The cooks aren't going to flock to you in record numbers?"

"Don't be silly. Everything will fall into place. Today the whole city will throng to Chemparkaroke's. Tomorrow a few of his bolder fellow-chefs will report to us. In the evening all his customers will be lined up at his door. The day after tomorrow another ten cooks will show up. In a week we'll be fending them off. Everything in its own good time, you see."

"Yes, I see," I said. "I guess I'll be able to hold out for a few days."

"What a glutton," Sir Juffin exclaimed in admiration. Melifaro rose.

"I suppose I'll stop in at the *Thorn*. I'm very curious—was Chemparkaroke telling the truth when he said he wanted the Earring just for esthetic purposes, or did he have other motives? What kind of soup will he cook up now? Poor Mr. Bad Dream, you'll never know, will you?"

"Big loss. Run along, you pathetic opium-eater, you."

"What's that? Your tongue really runs away with you sometimes. I take it that must be something very improper."

"Why improper? In the Borderlands that's what we call nomads who hanker after fresh horse dung—so much so that it can be habit-forming. They also claim that it 'brings them repose.'"

"You're just envious," Melifaro said, putting an end to the matter. "Well, Magicians be with you, I'm off to enjoy myself."

"Who isn't going to enjoy himself?" I murmured as my colleagues departed.

When I was finally alone, I went to the office I shared with Juffin. I poured myself some kamra and took out a little stump of a cigarette. Life was already wonderful without the *Soup of Repose.*"

That night I didn't go anywhere, since Lady Melamori, it turned out, hadn't slept well the night before and was too tired to go for a walk. But I did get a promise in return: "Tomorrow your poor feet will be cursing you, Max!" In lieu of something better, that promise was quite satisfactory.

Juffin's prognosis was correct. The next day, Madam Zizinda came to the House by the Bridge with her cook, and toward evening, yet another plump, red-haired beauty with violet eyes arrived, with two terrified cooks in tow. Since I had come to work fairly early, I was lucky enough to witness the spectacle. Only when Lookfi ran downstairs, red in the face and getting tangled in the hem of his looxi, did I realize this was the famous Lady Varisha, adored young wife of the Master Curator of Knowledge, and proprietress of a restaurant renowned throughout Echo: *The Fatman at the Bend.*

Sir Lonli-Lokli made a long speech about "how happy we were," and so forth. Our Master Who Snuffs Out of Unnecessary Lives was simply indispensable in such situations. Melifaro stared at the guests in frank admiration, nudging Lookfi with his elbow occasionally, and bellowing with approval: "Good show, fellow! Good show!"

At last, flattered by our attentions, Lady Varisha left, gripping her treasure tightly. Poor Lookfi's legs were buckling under him from the emotional strain. The cooks, whose ears were already adorned with the cunning embellishments, followed their mistress gloomily.

Then Melamori and I went out for a walk, leaving only Kurush behind in the Chancellory. The buriwok didn't object—I promised to buy him a pastry.

This time there were no fraught conversations about my "non-human origins." Alas, neither were there any passionate kisses when we parted. But I wasn't bitter or sad. If this wonderful lady needed time to make room in her heart for me—so be it. I could allow myself the luxury of being patient. Nowadays, besides our waking meetings, I had my dreams, too.

I had only to close my eyes, and she appeared at the bedroom window. In contrast to her original, the Melamori of my dreams wasn't the least bit afraid of me. She came very near, smiled, and whispered sweet nothings in my ear. She couldn't touch me, though; it was as though an invisible glass partition sprang up between us every time. Nor could I take any action—it was so hard to move in this dream. I could begin to stir, but my mobility stopped there. Then she would disappear. I would wake up and toss and turn for a long time in bed, trying to pick up the pieces of my dream so I'd be able to hold it in my memory.

The days passed very quickly. At home I spent hours fumbling with my pillow. The process was still long and tiresome, but I didn't mind. I was glad that at least something succeeded. How and why were questions I avoided asking myself. I couldn't come up with anything sensible, so it was better if things just unfolded as they wished.

In the evenings I hit the streets with Melamori, and at night, on my shift, I twiddled my thumbs and chatted with Kurush. Then, a few hours before dawn, I went home to see another Melamori, the Melamori of my dreams.

Juffin seemed to guess that there were some strange things happening to me. In any case, he had nothing against my absences from duty. Whenever I saw him, I noted the flash of unfeigned curiosity in his eyes. A chemist leaning over his beaker—that's what our Venerable Head looked like at those moments. Evidently, to him I resembled some sort of rare virus. I suppose I should have been pleased.

The culinary wizards really did start pouring into the House by the Bridge. After Mr. Goppa Tallaboona graced us with his presence (he was the proprietor of all the *Skeletons*: *Sated, Tipsy, Fat, Happy,* etc.), it was clear that Juffin's brilliant idea had conquered the folk.

Goppa didn't really need the Earring of Oxalla at all. Not only did he not know how to cook, but he ate his food cold and raw. Mr. Tallaboona brought two dozen of his head chefs to us. And while Melifaro performed the appropriate ritual on them, he gave his colleagues from the Secret Investigative Force an edifying lecture on the dangers of gluttony. The sly old fox knew no one would pay the least bit of attention.

It had been ten days since our historic visit to Jafax, when I received a call from Sir Kofa Yox an hour before sunset. I was just about to fish out a sixth cigarette butt from the Chink between Worlds. Getting more than five cigarettes before leaving for work was a rare achievement, but I kept right on trying.

Take your regular clothes with you today, Max. You'll need them, Kofa advised.

Has something happened? I asked in alarm.

No, but something will, believe me. Wait for me after midnight, boy. Over and out.

I was so intrigued that I even forgot to be glad about the sixth cigarette, which I found in my hand.

At the House by the Bridge, the usual chaos reigned. An angry, already thinner Melifaro was fighting off hordes of cooks who were lusting after the Earring of Oxalla.

"I work until sundown, gentlemen. Sun-DOWN. You know what that is? It's when the sun goes beddy-bye. Do you know what the sun is? It's that shiny round object that crawls through the heavens! I think I'm making myself clear. Come back tomorrow!"

The cooks shuffled disconsolately around the Hall of Common Labor, hoping Melifaro might just be blowing off a little steam before getting down to work again.

"Indeed, why don't you come back tomorrow, gentlemen?" I suggested amicably. "Or if you're so determined, I guess I could try my hand at it. Any volunteers?"

The cooks began to depart, eyeing my black and gold Mantle of Death suspiciously. A moment later, Melifaro and I found ourselves alone.

"Thanks, Mr. Bad Dream!" Melifaro smiled wearily. "I never realized there were so many cooks in Echo. Today alone I obliged a hundred fifty of them. It is magic, after all. And I'm not made of steel, as this monster Juffin seems to think I am. I'm going home to bed. Tomorrow it's sure be more of the same!"

I went into the office. Sir Juffin Hully had already left, most likely to some tavern to sow the sweet fruits of his government labor.

"Max!" Melamori peeked through the half-opened door. "Are you here, yet?"

"No," I said, with a shake of my head. "You're hallucinating."

"Oh, that's what I thought," said Melamori and perched on the arm of my chair. This was a sudden change of events!

"Will you treat me to some kamra, Sir Max? Let's sit here and talk a bit. I don't feel like walking today. You know, I just can't sleep these days. I wanted to ask you . . ."

"Ask away."

At that moment, the delivery boy from the *Glutton Bunba* interrupted us. Melamori poured herself some kamra and leaned her face over the mug to catch the soothing steam. I understood this meant we would begin to talk in another ten minutes or so. I was already familiar with all her little habits. After thinking a bit, I reached for a cigarette. To heck with conspiracy and discretion—if worse comes to worst, I'll tell her the cigarettes were sent to me from my long-lost homeland.

But Melamori wasn't concerned about my cigarettes.

"I dream about you every night," she announced gloomily. "And I just wanted to know, are you doing this on purpose?"

I shook my head. I had a clean conscience. I really didn't have anything to do with it. And I actually had no idea how to pull something off like that off "on purpose."

"I dream of you, too. What's so surprising about that? I think about you, and then I dream of you. That's all. That's the way it always is."

"I'm talking about something else. Are you sure you don't do even a bit of magic?"

I burst out laughing.

"I wouldn't even know how to do any magic like that, Melamori!

Ask Juffin. He has to make such an effort to teach me the simplest things."

This was something of an exaggeration. I learned easily and quickly. It just seemed to me that it wouldn't hurt to lay it on a bit thick. Let the lady think I was a dullard, and sleep soundly.

"Fine. I probably think about you, Max—but these dreams truly frighten me. I just wanted to say that if you do making magic, you don't need to. You don't have to force me into anything. I want to myself, but . . . just wait a while. Nothing like this has ever happened to me before. I have to get used to it."

"Certainly! Everything will be just as you say, my Fierce Lady. I can wait. I can learn to stand on my head, or dye my hair red. I'm a very agreeable guy."

"Dye your hair red! Red!? Oh, you're joking!" Melamori laughed out loud, sounding relieved. "How did that idea ever enter your head? Can you imagine what you'd look like?"

"I'll look magnificent!" I announced proudly. "You won't believe your eyes."

When I was alone again, I shook my head in amazement. My long-suffering, longed-for office romance was slowly but surely approaching the finish line. And the dreams—well, we had "stepped all over each other's hearts," as they say here in Echo. That's why we each had the same dreams.

It never occurred to me that I should take Melamori's questions more seriously. I should have realized that we were both having the very same dream, but I didn't want to. Sometimes I'm surprisingly thickheaded; especially if it's more convenient for me.

❀

"Are you bored, boy?" Sir Kofa Yox appeared so suddenly that I jumped up. "Get dressed. Let's go."

"Where?"

"What do you mean 'where'? To the place they make miracles. We're going to work on your education. Change your clothes."

"But who's going to stay here?" I had already taken off the black and gold Mantle of Death, underneath which, Praise be the Magicians, I was wearing a completely neutral, dark-green skaba. I started changing my other clothes. Boots with bells on them and dragons' heads would have blown my cover.

"Kurush. He's the one who's been holding down the fort while Lady Melamori dragged you around to hideaways only fit for ruining your digestion."

"Max never stays in one place," the buriwok complained. "He comes and goes. People are so flighty and fickle."

"You speak the truth, clever fellow," said Kofa. "But you don't mind, do you?"

"I don't mind, as long as you bring me some pastry," the conniving bird replied.

"I'm bringing you at least a dozen, you smart thing," I promised, wrapping myself in a modest swamp-colored looxi. I adore looking unobtrusive!

"I'm ready, Sir Kofa!"

"Ready? No, you're not. You don't want anyone to recognize you, do you? Do you think you have the most ordinary physiognomy in Echo? Come here."

Sir Kofa scrutinized me for a minute. Then he sighed and began to massage my face gently. It was pleasantly ticklish. At the end, he gave my nose a tug.

"I think that'll do. Come look in the mirror."

I went into the hall and stared at myself in the mirror. I saw an unprepossessing character gazing back at me—beady eyes, a long nose, with a protruding lower lip and a powerful, receding forehead. My good old pal Max was nowhere to be seen.

"Sir Kofa, can you put me back the way I used to be?" I asked nervously. "To tell you the truth, I don't much like this sort of guy."

"A lot you know! Like him or not, the important thing is that no one will recognize you or pay much attention to you. Faces like that are a dime a dozen. Haven't you ever noticed?"

"Regrettably, no. I'm very slow about certain things. I'm not against it for the time being—just don't forget to give me back my old face!"

"It will come back of its own accord, no later than tomorrow morning. Tricks like this don't work for very long. All right, now we can go."

Kofa then altered his own features with a swift movement of the hand. Now he and I looked like a wise daddy and his not-so-bright sonny boy. Our new faces clearly belonged to the same general category, but Kofa's looked older and slightly more intelligent.

"Where are we going, anyway?" I asked. I was bursting with curiosity.

"A hole in the heavens above you! Haven't you guessed? We're going tavern-crawling. A new era has begun: the Epoch of Good Food. I don't want your poor training in this area to condemn you to a dreary existence in this wonderful new World. I'm actually a very good person—has it never occurred to you?"

"Do you mean to say that I skipped out on work to go on a pub crawl? Sir Kofa, that's incredible!" I said, starting to laugh.

"I see nothing funny about it. I assure you, Juffin considers our outing to be a very serious matter, even if the House by the Bridge were to go to hell in a Dark Magician's handbasket in your absence. Besides, I'm doing my job. And you're assisting me."

"By the way, Kofa, do you know what Melifaro calls you?"

"Of course I do. What do you expect from the Master Eavesdropper-Gobbler? I see nothing wrong with it. Who are you to laugh, Mr. Bad Dream?"

Much to my surprise, we went right past our favorite *Glutton Bunba*.

"You come here almost every day with Juffin, anyway. He's so conservative," Kofa said dismissively. "He's convinced that the *Glutton* is as good as it gets. The cuisine in the *Glutton* is good, I admit. But every day the same thing—that's too dull!"

First we went to the *Merry Little Skeletons*. The numerous *Skeletons* scattered about Echo reminded me of the McDonald's of my homeland. I smiled.

"What is it?" Kofa asked, taking a seat in the far corner of the room.

"Oh, nothing. I was just thinking that there are too many 'skeletons' in Echo."

"Do you know the story behind them? Of course, you don't. Juffin has never had a clue about which stories are the most interesting ones. So listen up. The proprietor of all the *Skeletons* is Goppa Tallaboona. You've seen him—he brought all his cooks over to the Ministry. The fellow comes from a wealthy family, the Tallaboona clan, descendants of gourmands. Back in the day, they were very influential people. These gentlemen so loved to eat, and to eat well, that sometime after the beginning of the Code Epoch they fell into despair. They gathered together and ordered their cooks to prepare food as they had done in the 'old days'—that is, not neglecting to use Forbidden Magic. And they ate fit to burst. Those were happier times, back then; Juffin and I had our hands full already with other matters. When we were able to find a half-hour to look in on the Tallaboonas, there was no one to arrest: only dead bodies. Some of them weren't able to eat so much, so they lost the spark. They got food poisoning. Nice story, isn't it? Goppa received a huge inheritance, including the houses of his relatives, and in them he opened his taverns. It's funny, since Goppa had always practiced asceticism in his youth. He constantly quarreled with his elders, and felt nothing but contempt for the family traditions. He didn't take part in their final feast, of course. They say that to this day Goppa eats only sandwiches, and I believe it. The fellow has a very original sense of humor. Look over there."

Sir Kofa pointed to a brightly lighted niche at the opposite end of the room. There was a small table with two small skeletons sitting in state.

"They're real, Max. The real skeletons of Goppa's late relatives. You'll find them in every one of his establishments, if you recall. And the name of each tavern accurately describes the character of the deceased. The master and mistress of this house were a married couple—both of them small in stature and truly merry people. Good people. They were friends of mine. Now they're going to serve us something special, so save your strength, Max. The chefs here are still the same ones. The Tallaboonas have always been able to afford the very best. The solemn moment has arrived—they're bringing out the *Big Puff*!"

When I looked at the head chef wheeling his cart in the direction of our table, I was nonplussed. The fellow's cart was laden with something that looked like Chinese dumplings, except that each dumpling was about three feet in width.

"Sir Kofa, I do love to eat, of course," I whispered. "But I'm afraid you have overestimated my abilities."

"Don't be silly, boy. It's going to be all right. Be quiet now, and watch."

When he stopped at our table, the cook bowed in a dignified manner and placed two relatively small plates in front of us. I had no time to wonder how the small plates could accommodate the *Big Puffs* before the cook grasped the uppermost dumpling carefully between two small shovels. Then he began to blow on it. He blew as gently and patiently as a grandmother blowing on a spoonful of oatmeal, begging her beloved grandchild to outdo himself and take just one more bite.

Unlike a grandmother's spoonful of porridge, though, the "dumpling" began shrinking rapidly. When the *Big Puffs* had become the size of a statistically average pastry, the cook quickly transferred it to Kofa's plate, and he began to eat.

"Start right in, boy!" my culinary "Virgil" informed me with his mouth full. "Its best to eat it straight away."

I considered it wise to heed his advice, so as soon as the pastry landed on my plate, I got down to business.

Inside the *Big Puffs* I discovered an ample, but light meat filling and a whole ocean of aromatic juices. It was divine!

The cook kept tossing more and more Puffs onto our plates, but we didn't give up. Finally, the cart was empty and we were alone.

"Remember, Max, you should only order the *Big Puffs* here. It's not the same in other taverns. Believe me, I've tried it."

Kofa rolled his eyes to the heavens in delight.

"Once upon a time, it was the most ordinary dish imaginable. Over the last hundred years or so the cooks of the capital have forgotten the finer points of their profession. Never mind, they'll make up for lost time and pick up their tricks again now. Time heals all. Let's go, boy."

And off we went.

※

"I've never failed to give the *Skeleton* cuisine its due," Sir Kofa Yox said. "Of course, with legitimate magic alone they could never outdo Madame Zizinda or the Hunchback Itullo, may the Dark Magicians protect him. They're Old School—without a good spell they don't know how to butter a piece of bread. Aye, what's true is true. Now their time has come again, though."

"By the way, how could Goppa have been allowed to keep the cooks? Why didn't you throw them in Xolomi?" I asked.

"In Xolomi? For what?"

"Well, you said yourself that they prepared food like in the 'Good Old Days.' They must have used plenty of spells, I imagine."

"Ah, that . . . You see, Max, the cooks were just carrying out orders. They didn't even have to try to defend themselves. Their superiors presented them with a paper that stated that they took all the responsibility. If any of the Tallaboonas had survived, they're the ones we would have 'thrown in Xolomi,' as you put it."

"Where I come from, everyone would have to bear the blame: the ones who gave the orders, as well as the ones who carried them out."

"That's absurd! How can you punish a person if he's not acting on his own volition? What a system you have there in the Barren Lands."

Kofa stared at me so attentively that I realized: he doesn't believe Juffin's legend about my origins. He doesn't believe it, but he's keeping mum. So I did, too.

Our next stop was the *Happy Skeleton*. Sir Kofa nodded toward another niche at the opposite end of the hall, just like the one we saw earlier. It was occupied by a solitary smiling skeleton.

"Here we're going to eat 'Hathor' turkey," Sir Kofa announced.

"What's it called?" I wanted to make sure I had heard correctly.

"'Hathor.' It's a completely baffling sort of animal god from another World. I can't figure it out. I don't know whether anyone can. One thing for sure—it has the head of a bull."

"A cow," I corrected him. "'Hathor' is female, so her head is that of a cow, not a bull."

"Where did you study, boy?" Sir Kofa asked in astonishment. "The things you know!"

"Well, I certainly didn't learn it in school," I admitted. "I just read everything I that came my way. A good way of fighting insomnia."

"Everything that came your way! Do you go out of your way, by any chance, to dip into the forbidden library of the Seven-Leaf Clover? Come on, you'll never get me to believe that!"

I thought that informing Sir Kofa that the goddess Hathor was one of the many zoomorphic figures in the Egyptian pantheon probably wouldn't be such a good idea. What if it was some kind of sacred mystery?

This time two hefty kitchen boys plunked down a huge platter on our table. On the platter was a horned bull's head. A "braised" turkey's carcass hovered between the horns. At first I thought it must be resting on a skewer, but then I realized that the delicacy really was floating weightless in the air.

"Don't even think of putting the turkey on a plate," Sir Kofa whispered. "It has to stay right where it is. Slice the meat with a knife using a fork to hold it steady . . . And don't touch it with your hands. You'll ruin the taste!"

I obeyed for that would truly have been a sin.

✺

After the fourth tavern, I began to beg for mercy. I felt there was a good chance I would share the sad fate of the Tallaboona family.

"What a weak stomach you have, boy! I never would have expected it. There's one more excellent establishment I want to show you. They have delicious desserts, and very small portions. Honest!"

"All right," I grumbled. "But this is the last one. For today, anyway."

The tavern was called the *Irrashi Coat of Arms Inn*.

"Who's Irrashi?" I asked without thinking.

"Come off it, lad! You know who Hathor is, but forget the name of the neighboring country?"

"I just ate so much I can't think straight anymore."

I felt ashamed. Even though the eight-volume *Encyclopedia* by Manga Melifaro had long ago found its way from the bookshelf to my bedside table, the geography of the World was still not one of my strong points.

Sir Kofa Yox shook his head disdainfully, and we entered.

"Xokota!" a friendly bartender called to us in greeting.

"Xokota!" Sir Kofa answered solemnly.

"What did you just say?"

"Ah, that's one of the the nice customs of this place. The proprietors are all locals, from Echo. But the cuisine is Irrashi, and they try to speak to the customers in broken Irrashi, to the best of their abilities. It's funny—Irrashi is one of the few countries where they don't speak in normal human language. Our homegrown snobs consider their babbling to be the height of refinement."

"Right. And you just greeted each other, as I understand it."

"Of course. Look over there, Max. You see that fellow in the gray looxi? He's dressed very strangely, don't you think?"

"Strangely? Why do you say that, Kofa?"

I looked over at the modestly clad, middle-aged stranger who was hunched over his mug at the bar.

"You didn't notice? And the belt?"

"I can't see any belt from where I'm sitting. Move over! Ah! Sinning Magicians, that's beautiful!"

The stranger was wearing an elegant, broad belt under his looxi—a remarkable thing that glistened like bright mother-of-pearl.

"That's what I was talking about. Hm, it really is quite strange. The fellow is dressed modestly in the extreme. He couldn't be dressed worse, in fact. His skaba is downright tattered, did you see?"

"What a nit-picker you are, Kofa!"

"That's my job. Oh, here's our dessert."

The portions were indeed quite small. We were each served a piece of weirdly oscillating pie. It didn't resemble jelly—the pie seemed to move of its own accord, not as a result of its internal consistency. And the spoons they gave us! They were gigantic. I couldn't imagine how we were supposed to eat our dessert with them. They would never fit into a human mouth.

"Excuse me, my fine friend," I said to the young waiter. "This is not a spoon; it's a travesty, a mockery of a spoon at best. Couldn't you find some other kind of utensil for us?"

"Xvarra tonikai! Okir blad tuu."

After this utterance, the fellow disappeared. I looked quizzically at my dinner companion.

"What was he saying, Kofa?"

"Magicians only know. I'm no Irrashi interpreter. First he apologized, then . . . I think he said he'd go look for something. But you're selling yourself short, Max. These amusing ladles are one of the charms of the *Coat of Arms*. Such a refined dessert— and such enormous spoons! You won't see anything like it anywhere else in Echo."

"I can do without the 'charms.' There's no way I'm going to eat with that shovel! I'd rather eat with my fingers. Oh, where is my Mantle of Death when I need it? If I were wearing it, the proprietor of this place would have pulled out the family silver passed down from his great-grandmother. Sir Kofa, my old face hasn't returned yet, has it? I'm about to start raising a ruckus."

I was having fun. So was Sir Kofa, judging by the look on his face.

"Is it hard being an ordinary mortal? Nuflin was right when he warned you. Oh, well, go ahead, kick up a fuss. And I'll eat. I like these spoons."

But I didn't have to make a scene. The fresh-faced waiter was already hurrying over, waving a small spoon above his head victoriously. It was just what I imagined an ideal dessert-eating instrument to be.

"Shoopra Kon!" the fellow said, bowing obsequiously, and handed me the wonderful utensil. Then he turned to Sir Kofa and mumbled: "Xvarra tonikai! Prett."

"Never mind," Sir Kofa mumbled back. "Get along now, you poor fellow." Then he turned to me. "Well, you've really done it now, boy. You don't even need the Mantle of Death. People are afraid of you without it. Instinct, most likely. For Sir Max they find a spoon; but not for me, it seems. Incredible . . ."

I felt very satisfied with my petty victory. And the dessert lived up to my highest expectations.

"Don't look now, Max!" Sir Kofa nudged me. "There's another one. I don't understand: is this some kind of new fashion?"

"Another what? I don't—" I was brought up short.

I only had to glance toward the entrance, and everything was clear to me. A handsome young man in a splendid yellow looxi froze on the threshold. Underneath his elegant overcoat was a tattered skaba and a magnificent mother-of-pearl belt, the same kind that the fellow at the bar was wearing.

"It can't be a coincidence," Kofa said with a sniff. "It's the first time in my life I've ever seen anything like that—and, suddenly, along comes his twin! Look, they've spotted each other! Well, well, well . . ."

The belted ones did a double-take, staring intently at one another. The face of the youthful newcomer in yellow registered surprise, fear, and, it seemed, even sympathy.

He opened his mouth, made a step as if he was going up to the bar, then turned on his heels and left. The first fellow was getting ready to rise, but he waved over the proprietor, instead. The tavern-keeper placed another mug in front of him, and the fellow began studying its contents again with great intensity.

"How do you like them apples, Max?"

"It is strange," I replied uncertainly. "Oh, he's leaving! Shall we follow him?"

"Hold your horses, hero! We don't need to follow him."

"Why not, Kofa?"

"Because . . . how can I explain it? It's just not done. Secret investigators don't go rushing around Echo, chasing down every suspicious Tom, Dick, or Harry that comes along. Preventing crime is not our job. But if something happens and they ask us politely to look into it—well, that's another story. In short, we're not going anywhere."

"Well, you know best."

I must admit, I was disappointed.

"That's the way it is, boy," Sir Kofa said with a wink. "Don't be sad. All your chases and crime-hunting are still ahead of you. For the time being, you should just enjoy life."

"Enjoy life? You're making fun of me, Kofa. After tonight I'll never be able to look at food again."

"You're in for a surprise. Now I'm going to reveal to you the oldest secret of Old Cuisine."

"No!" I grimaced and shook my head. "With all due respect, Kofa, I refuse."

"Never indulge in hasty decisions. You don't know what's in store for you yet. Don't worry, Max. I'm not going to feed you, but cure you of your culinary overindulgence. Honest."

"In that case—onward!" I exclaimed happily. "If I've ever needed a cure like that, now's the time."

And with that we left the *Irrashi Coat of Arms*.

"If you ever overeat like this again, you must go to the *Empty Bowl*," Sir Kofa informed me. "Remember this address, friend: 36 Street of Reconciliation. I have a feeling you'll be coming here often."

The *Empty Bowl* was full of people, but they worked fast there! In just a few minutes a cook with a small cart came up to us. He rattled the bottles and vials with the concentration of an experienced pharmacist. I looked at the cart. Sinning Magicians! I almost threw up. The fellow drew out of a jar what looked like a huge piece of soft, greenish bacon grease and placed it on a tiny brazier. A minute later he poured the turbid, runny fat into a tall colored glass. He then plopped the second piece of fat onto the brazier. I shuddered, swallowed back some of my own saliva, and turned away. Sir Kofa took the glass calmly and emptied it down, without so much as wincing.

"It's not as bad as it looks, boy. Drink up. I'm not joking—I want to help you. Some hero you are! Well, sniff it, at least."

I sniffed it obediently. The smell was not in the least nauseating. On the contrary, a pleasant menthol scent tickled my nostrils. I sighed and gulped down the terrible looking stuff. It wasn't so bad. Not bad at all, in fact. It was like drinking a glass of mint liqueur, diluted with water.

"Well, how did you like it?" Sir Kofa asked in concern. "You certainly are impressionable. I would never have expected it. Fine, let's go. For your information, it's called *River Rat Bone Marrow*. A strange name, of course. Remember it, though—it'll come in handy."

When we were outside again, Sir Kofa studied me attentively.

"Are you sure you're not hungry, Max? We can stop into a few more places . . ."

"Magicians be with you, Kofa! I don't even want to think about it!"

"Well, suit yourself. Now then, run along to the Ministry. It will be morning soon, anyway. Don't forget to take Kurush the snacks you promised him. He's earned them."

"Of course. Thanks for the experience. It's a night I won't soon forget."

"That's the spirit. Good night, Max."

❁

On the way to the Ministry, I carried out my promise, stopping by the *Glutton* to pick up a dozen pastries. Kurush wouldn't be able to eat all that—but it's no sin to skip out on work and then try to make up for it later.

The delicious aroma of freshly baked pastry made me think it wouldn't be a bad idea to have a little bite to eat myself. Sinning Magicians, was I crazy? How could I eat after a night like that?

Kurush was delighted, and he started right in on them. I changed into the Mantle of Death and went to look at myself in the mirror. What a bizarre sight! My own features could already be made out under the unattractive false face. I had two distinct faces, one showing through the other. I shuddered and went downstairs to wash up. On the way back I glanced in the mirror again. Finally! There was my trusty old mug looking back at me. I wanted to cry with relief. I was, after all, quite a guy. It's a matter of taste, of course, but it was a face that agreed with me.

I went back to the office. Kurush had just finished the fourth pastry, but his enthusiasm was flagging. I looked at the bird enviously, and—well, I ended up eating five whole pastries myself! I really had worked up an appetite already. That *River Rat Bone Marrow* was a devil of a concoction. Wonder of wonders, I felt I hadn't eaten in days.

❁

At home I dreamed of Melamori again. The invisible wall dividing us disappeared all at once, and she sat down next to me. She was amused by my immobility. Not only was she amused, but it made her very brave. I was showered with kisses, such real ones that it almost made me start thinking that . . . But my poor brain didn't want to think at all, and then she disappeared. And I woke up.

Melamori always disappeared from my dreams at about the same time, just after dawn—the time people wake up to go to work. But I tried not to pay attention to this coincidence. Once I get hold of something, I'll hold onto it for dear life, even if it's only a dream, and in my case, especially if it is a dream.

❀

Not long before noon I dozed off again to the deep, guttural purrs of my cats. Almost immediately, I got a call from Sir Kofa.

Enough lounging around, Max. Something very interesting is happening here, so—

Time to eat again? I asked, horrified.

No, time to work. Remember those clowns with the belts?

And how I do! Oh, Kofa, do I have an hour, at least? To wash.

What a squeaky clean rascal you are! Fine, go hose yourself down. But we'll be expecting you in an hour.

I jumped out of bed. Armstrong was so deep in sleep he didn't twitch an ear. Ella woke up with a diminutive feline roar and rushed down to her bowl. After feeding the cats and bathing, it turned out that I had no time to replenish my tobacco supply with my pillow prestidigitation. It's a good thing I hoard things like a squirrel: I had hidden away several cigarette stubs for a rainy day. Like today.

❀

The Hall of Common Labor was swarming with chefs again. I gave Melifaro a sympathetic nod, and continued through to our office. An unrecognizable Sir Kofa Yox (curly haired, ruddy faced, large eyes) was whispering to Juffin. When he saw me he fell silent.

"Secrets?" I inquired. "Dreadful ones? Or not very?"

"Somewhere in between," Juffin said. "How's your stomach, hero? Are the city toilets running over after your busy night?"

"Are you trying to compensate for the absence of General Boboota?

That's not your forte, Juffin. Moreover, Boboota's irreplaceable."

"Well, just take a little walk to the morgue and back. It's bound to be an instructive excursion. We'll just finish up our secret-swapping session while you're gone—and don't let your nose get out of joint. In fact, these are secrets of Grand Magician Nuflin. Not very exciting."

I dutifully set out for the morgue, which was located on the premises of the Echo City Police. Sinning Magicians, I sure hadn't expect everything be this simple! There lay the fellow we had seen yesterday in the elegant yellow looxi. Only now his belt was gone. Was it murder with the intent to rob? Not the most popular kind of crime in Echo. I twirled my magic dagger in my fingers. The gauge didn't budge. No Forbidden Magic around here. But if Juffin wanted me to see it, there must have been some foul magic involved. What kind, though? For one thing, there was no blood nor any trace of violence. Had he been poisoned? No. If this were just about "murder with the intent to rob," Juffin wouldn't have been summoned in the first place

I looked at the dead man one more time. There was something about him . . . something very obvious that still eluded my grasp.

I went back to the office without having figured it out. Pre-occupied with heavy thoughts, I bumped right into Shixola, the former lieutenant of the City Police. After the remarkable rescue of Boboota, Shixola had been promoted to captain, which (unlike most of his colleagues) he richly deserved.

The fellow reeled, but stood his ground.

"Did you come to admire our discovery, sir?" asked the unfortunate victim of my absentmindedness, rubbing his bruised chin.

"Yes. There's something not quite right about your discovery," I said and looked at Shixola thoughtfully.

"I agree. There must be. First Sir Kofa came by, then Sir Venerable Head himself graced us with his presence, and now you arrive. This ragamuffin is really running you ragged."

"Ragamuffin . . . ?"

The expensive yellow looxi and the fancy boots of the dead man seemed very much at odds with that description. Then it dawned on me. Underneath this expensive looxi the man was wearing the old, tattered skaba I had glimpsed yesterday. It looked as though the fellow hadn't changed it for years. This glaring contrast seemed significant.

"Yes, a ragamuffin, of course!" I shouted enthusiastically, and rushed off, leaving Captain Shixola bewildered and alone.

❧

"Well, what do you say?"

Juffin smiled broadly, as though getting the chance to look at the corpse had been a birthday present, perhaps the best I had ever received.

"Nothing much to say. The fellow's not dressed too well. I'll be honest with you, it took a while for me to realize it. It looks like he hadn't changed his clothes in years. By the way, who took his belt away from him? The killer, or you?"

"Whoever did, it wasn't us, unfortunately."

"How did he die? I didn't see any wounds. Was he poisoned?"

"Possibly. It's not clear. You have something to add?"

"No, nothing."

"Nothing at all?"

"Well, my heart lurched unpleasantly. That happened yesterday, already, when Kofa and I saw him in the *Irrashi Inn*. There was nothing more concrete than that."

"I'm not interested in anything 'concrete.' What really intrigues me are the messages your darn-fool heart sends out. If you had a few hearts to spare, I'd pass them out to our boys instead of those good-for-nothing gauges. Every time something halfway interesting happens, they stick at zero and refuse to budge. It's ridiculous! Imagine, Kofa and I didn't sense that anything at all was amiss. Your new friend sure did, though."

"Who's my new friend? Shixola?"

"What a short memory you have," said the chief and grinned. "Grand Magician Nuflin Moni Mak was kind enough to send me a call an hour ago. He says it's urgent that we get to the bottom of this case. He has a terrible foreboding, and no clues whatsoever. Are you related to him, by any chance?"

"You should know," I said, heaving a sigh. "You're the one and only expert on my genealogy. Give me some kamra, Juffin. First I don't get enough sleep, then I have to gaze on a corpse . . . life just all-round sucks."

"What, the trick with the pillow didn't work?" Juffin laughed out loud. "Well, win some, lose some. And make your own kamra. Why did I waste my time teaching you? And don't grind your teeth like that, Sir Max. Kofa hasn't tasted your culinary invention yet. Please."

"You can't fight the magic word," I muttered, mollified. "What a despot you are, Sir Juffin."

"Could be worse."

I carried out the motions mechanically, but the results were the best ever! Even Sir Kofa didn't turn up his nose at it.

A feeling of justified pride dispelled the forebodings that had taken hold of me since my visit to the morgue. I pulled a parcel of cigarette stubs out of the folds of my Mantle of Death. My senior colleagues frowned in distaste, but I couldn't have cared less. If people are doomed to smoke some reeking muck that they mistakenly consider to be pipe tobacco, one can only pity them.

"In what country do they make those belts?" I asked. "You must know, Kofa."

"Good question, Max. At this point, I don't have the answer. That is, as far as I've been able to tell, they aren't made anywhere. But that's clearly insufficient information. Actually, I was just about to go to the Customs. Since we've decided to take the bull by the horns, we can't get by without Nulli Karif. That's his job, to be in the know about all our dear foreign visitors. That's why I woke you up, so you'd keep me company."

"Did you like it?"

"What, your company? How could I not have liked it? It was a barrel of fun. Especially your heroic struggle over the spoon!" Kofa burst into peals of laughter.

"Well, I have had about all I can take, Sir Kofa," I exclaimed. "I'm abandoning you for General Boboota. You're cruel, and he's kind and good. We're going to go to the can together, sit in stalls side by side, and tap on the walls."

"Why tap on the walls?" My colleagues were now beside themselves with mirth.

"So we can understand each other without words," I explained. "It's a spiritual bond you two could never even dream of."

"Let's get going, genius," Sir Kofa said. "I can't promise you spiritual bonds, but I guarantee you won't be bored."

꧁

The Head of Customs of the Unified Kingdom, Sir Nulli Karif, was a remarkable character in all respects. Small, garrulous, and, I assumed, very young. Round glasses in thin frames completed the image of this delightful personage.

"Well, whom do we have here! Sir Kofa! And you must be Sir Max. Splendid! Has something happened? You don't have to answer that. I understand. Otherwise you wouldn't have dragged yourselves over here from the other side of town. How's Melifaro? What's the news about his older brother? Is that pirate going to descend on Echo any time soon? They say Melifaro fastened the Earring of Oxalla on Chemparkaroke with such a powerful spell that no one will ever be able to remove it, even someone in the Seven-Leaf Clover. So much has happened around here! Do you remember Kaffa Xani, Sir Kofa? Well, he's not with us anymore. He rented a ship and set sail for Magicians know where. Splendid! Attaboy! Way to go! Have you killed a lot of people, Sir Max? I don't doubt you have. Is that true about Chemparkaroke? Has something indeed happened, Kofa, or did you just drop by to shoot the breeze?"

The monologue of the Head of Customs threatened to go on indefinitely, but Sir Kofa thought of a way to dam up the torrent of words, if only temporarily.

"Are you going to make us wait out here forever, or will you invite us into your office?"

"Oh, it's not much of an office, really. Look here, Kofa. It's a pantry, a storage room, not an office. This is where half the confiscated goods end up, since storing the junk elsewhere is too dangerous. And the fellows from Jafax can't be bothered with nonsense like that. It's a vicious circle. Soon I'll have to start receiving guests right at the docks. Well, I'll just set my chair down there and . . . oh, did you know our Kaffa Xani had become a captain? I suspect he'll join the pirates and end up on the gallows in some Tasher jungle or remote Shishin Caliphate. But that's how it goes. What sense is there in being a sailor if you don't ship contraband? It's foolish, that's what it is. I don't understand people like that. All the same, Sir Kofa, it's splendid that you dropped by for a visit—though I don't believe for a minute that's the only reason you came to see me. I'm right on target, aren't I?"

"Of course you are, Nulli. But perhaps you'll offer us some kamra and keep quiet for three minutes? I'd never think of requesting five, I realize that's out of the question. Well, are you finished?"

"But of course! They'll bring us kamra directly. What kind do you prefer, Max? Local or Irrashi? Or maybe you're a fan of Arvarox kamra? Though I think they already drank that up. The boys in this outfit do nothing but drink kamra—and from such enormous mugs." He spread his small arms out wide to illustrate this phenomenon. I was duly impressed.

"If you aren't exaggerating, Sir Nulli, the poor fellows must be hard at work," I said. "It's even hard to fathom the existence of a mug that big."

"Certainly, Sir Max. We're not playing the fool here. Those lads have to sweat," said the remarkable fellow, without missing a beat. "I must say, though, the pay here is quite good. That same Kaffa Xani worked all of three years for us, and he's already managed to hire a ship. Didn't I tell you? Now he'll sneak in contraband, and I'll have to catch him. Magnificent! Ah, here's the kamra."

Sir Nulli sniffed the contents of the jug and launched into another flood of words.

"That's Irrashi. It's actually rubbish; but then, it's imported. Where else can you get anything like that? Help yourselves, gentlemen. Though I'd prefer to just pour it out, I'm so sick of it. Well, if it isn't old Tyoovin!" Nulli gestured toward the corner of his office, filled to the brim with all manner of bales and bundles, where a blurry white spot was just visible. "Sir Max, you haven't yet met our Tyoovin. Let me introduce you to my predecessor, Sir Tyoovin Salivava, who was killed in the fifty-second year of the Code Epoch when he attempted a raid on the most famous smuggler of the Epoch of Orders. A great man, when all is said and done. I don't remember his real name. They called him the 'White Bird,' and sometimes 'Slippery Sun.' Smugglers have always been a romantic bunch. But the fellow didn't survive the brawl. Old man Tyoovin was a sight to behold. If he hadn't had so much to drink that night, White Bird would never have caught him. Marvelous, don't you think?"

"So, you mean he's a ghost?" I interjected, staring incredulously, staring at the distant blur.

"Of course he's a ghost. What else could he be? The old man's not in very good shape today. By that I mean that Tyoovin usually appears with a completely human outline. I guess he's feeling shy. Actually, Mr. Salivava was so drunk when they killed him that his ghost is never fully aware of what's going on. But he's a fine fellow. He's a big help to me. It's enough for him to materialize in front of some dapper, jaunty captain and bark, 'Worthless nincompoops!', and the chap starts spilling all his secrets at once, without any effort on our part. I can just go to sleep, which is usually exactly what I do. He's quite something, that Tyoovin. He does love his work. Yes, indeed. But Sir Kofa, what on earth is wrong? I can see in your eyes that this isn't just a social visit."

"Nulli, I'll give you another ten seconds. If, by then, you don't shut up of your own accord, Max and I will tie you up, gag you, and then get down to business. Is that clear?"

"What do you mean, Sir Kofa? When have I ever refused to get down to business with you? I guessed right. You do have something to talk over with me. Excellent! I'm all ears, gentlemen. But first tell me: this concerns Melifaro and Chemparkaroke, am I right?"

"Sinning Magicians!" Sir Kofa rolled his eyes heavenward. "Of course not! You should know better than that. Why are you so wrought up over Chemparkaroke? Now, Nulli, put on your infamous thinking cap. This has nothing to do with smuggling, so—"

"Well, then, I'm not the one you should be talking to," Sir Nulli Karif prattled on merrily. "I know who you need to see."

"First hear me out!" Sir Kofa roared.

This had the desired effect. The fellow went quiet, adjusted his round spectacles, and focused his attention on Sir Kofa, who heaved a sigh of relief and continued.

"I know that you notice any little thing that smacks of the unusual. I want you to try to remember whether you've seen anyone lately whose belt kindled your imagination in any way. Wait a minute, though. Don't even think about giving me the run-down on every belt you've ever seen in your life! I'm interested in a certain wide belt made from some unknown substance that looks a bit like mother-of-pearl, only much more vivid. Okay, you can open your mouth now. You've been very patient. It was good of you, Nulli."

"I have seen it!" Sir Nulli Karif proclaimed victoriously. "I saw one, and not so very long ago. Now I have to remember where, and on whom. You know how many people there are hanging about here, Sir Kofa. That stands to reason—it's a port. Why should it exist at all, if people are going to go around it, instead of passing through? Right? Well, it happened this year. Less than a dozen days ago, to be exact. What else? Um, yes, well, I saw the belt and said to Doo Idoonoo, 'I'd arrest those pirates in the wink of an eye, if you and I were counted among the more fashion-conscious blokes in town!' Not singular, but plural—*pirates*—so there were two of them in those belts. Maybe more. And it just so happened that Doo Idoonoo and I were there together, and then he didn't show up at work for half a dozen days. He was sick. He's quite a sickly chap . . . or he's a malingerer. I don't know to this day. My head is filled with Magicians-know-what kind of nonsense, but Doo Idoonoo will remember what he was doing before he fell ill. He's a real hypochondriac. When he comes down with something, he starts to recall every person he's come into contact with, and tries to make his wife believe they cast the evil eye on him. I'll send him a call and ask him, and you help yourselves to some kamra, gentlemen. If it runs out, they'll bring more. You can't imagine how much of that junk we have here."

Sir Nulli Karif went quiet, then grew tense. I realized he was engaging in Silent Speech.

A half hour later it was clear to me that Silent Speech had not made our host any less loquacious. Sir Kofa grimaced and coughed loudly. Nulli nodded, shrugged apologetically, and went back into a trance. A few minutes later he got up from his desk and left the office. I glanced at Kofa in bewilderment.

"He's trying to be discreet, Max," he explained. "There's a rumor going around that I can eavesdrop on other people's Silent Speech."

"Only a rumor?" I asked.

"Well, actually, I can, but it's too taxing. And it's bad for my health. You know, son, there are some things that are better left alone. All the more since it's easier to read the thoughts of my interlocutors once they've finished their conversations. So I had no intention of . . . But there's no way of convincing anyone of that, so he might as well hide."

"I beg your pardon, gentlemen," said Nulli Karif. His face expressed more satisfaction than compunction. "Speaking frankly, I also felt the call of nature. Have you seen our new facilities? The boys have decorated it with all the smuggled talismans that held no interest for Jafax. Quite an educational spectacle! I found the answer to your question, Sir Kofa, so don't fret."

"Well, spit it out, Nulli. We'll talk about your privy some other time."

"That's too bad, Sir Kofa. You'll never see anything like it again. Well, it's up to you, of course. It's all fresh in my memory now. It was a ship owner from Tasher and his captain. They dropped anchor in the port on the morning of the fifth day of this year. They had a magnificent washtub of a vessel, better than many of our own. You can see for yourselves, it's still moored there. It's called the *Old Maid*. Funny, isn't it? That's what seamen sometimes call their perfectly innocent ships—it's enough to make you split your sides! Now let me tell you the name of the ship owner . . ." Nulli rummaged around in the desk, found a stack of registry records and buried his nose in them. "Aha! His name is Agon. That's all. Tasherians have such short names. Yes, Doo Idoonoo reminded me that their cargo did contain belts like that. We were joking that we would have liked to have been able to pin something on them, and confiscate the belts for ourselves. It was only White Magic of the fourth degree, though, nothing forbidden. We had to let them through."

Sir Kofa took the records and began studying them.

"Very curious," he said after some time. "It looks like they had nothing to sell but those belts. Some tourists!"

"They said they were planning to buy goods in Echo. That's their right," said Nulli Karif.

"Hmm, quite interesting indeed. Buying here, and selling back home in Tasher, where the prices are much lower. What a wise merchant this Agon is, how well he carries on his trade! A commercial operation like that makes sense only when you're stealing goods from the capital, not buying them. Now that's an idea. Is there anyone on the vessel, Nulli?"

"Naturally. The captain and some of the crew. They're either saving on the cost of a hotel or standing guard over their old tub. She's worth it, a floating bathtub like that, didn't I tell you? But there's nothing there that would interest you, Sir Kofa. I've gone over everything with a fine-tooth comb."

"Now we'll find out what kind of 'floating bathtub' this is, and whether there really is anything of interest in it. Thank you for the kamra, Nulli, but let me give you some advice. Go back to the local brand. I suspect that foreign muck is just what's making your assistant sick. It burns, and gives you a stomach ache. And keep your ears open—if you hear anything else about those belts, send me a call right away, day or night. I'm taking all the papers on the *Old Maid*—

let me sign for them." Kofa slapped his hand on a fat little tablet Nulli had produced from under his turban. "There we go. Good day, Nulli. Let's go, Max."

I bade farewell to the friendly customs officer, and we went to the port to look over the *Old Maid* and meet her captain.

❄

The contours of the elegant sailing vessel were a vision to behold, The captain was equally impressive. A handsome, stately man with a long braid and a beard that fell below his belt met us at the mooring. A severe black suit put the finishing touches on his appearance: baggy trousers and a loose-fitting tunic down to his knees. The belt, if he was indeed wearing one, was concealed beneath this garment.

"Captain Giatta, at your service, gentlemen," he intoned drily.

The captain spoke with an amusing drawl. Praise be the Magicians he's not from Irrashi. We'd have a hard time finding an interpreter, I thought to myself.

"The Secret Investigative Force of Echo. Allow us to board your ship, Mr. Giatta," Sir Kofa Yox replied no less drily.

"This vessel is the personal property of Mr. Agon, and I'm not authorized to take strangers on board."

"Anywhere in Unified Kingdom the Secret Investigative Force is fully authorized to turn inside out not only your 'personal property,' but also your personal backside, if we think we might find something interesting there." In Sir Kofa's voice I detected notes I hadn't heard before—mellifluous and ominous at the same time.

"There's only one thing I can tell you, gentlemen. I was ordered not to let anyone onto the ship. I have only one option: to die carrying out my duty. I'm very sorry."

Captain Giatta did not in the least resemble a dull-witted fanatic. He also had no likeness to a dyed-in-the-wool criminal, though who knows what a dyed-in-the-wool criminal is supposed to look like. The captain had sad, tired eyes, and he pronounced the word "die" almost dreamily.

Sir Kofa sent me a call, *Be on your guard, Max. I wouldn't want to kill him, but . . . you can see for yourself that this fellow is a bit shady.*

Then Kofa turned to the captain again.

"Well, I understand that an order's an order. In that case you'll just have to take a ride with us in the amobiler. I hope your boss has no objections to that?"

"No," Captain Giatta said uncertainly, but with evident relief. "There was no mention of that. So I won't refuse."

"Excellent. Command your subordinates to guard the ship, and you'll have a clear conscience."

The captain went to give the orders, and I looked at Sir Kofa in some confusion.

"Is this normal behavior for Tasherians, Kofa?"

"Of course not. The chap is bewitched, it's as clear as day. But there's an aura of White Magic of only the fourth degree emanating from him, and that's perfectly legal. Juffin will figure him out, you'll see. That will be interesting for you, too."

"And the ship?"

"Never mind the ship. I've already sent a call to the House by the Bridge. Lonli-Lokli and a dozen policemen will be here in half an hour. They're the best team for a first-rate search. Here comes our brave captain now. We're lucky, all the same, that he decided to come with us," Kofa whispered as our new companion returned.

"I'm at your service, gentlemen," Captain Giatta said with dignified bow.

The captain stared out the window in rapture the whole way. He seemed completely unfazed that he was under arrest and was being transported to the House by the Bridge; rather, he was thoroughly enjoying the sightseeing excursion. I shared his enthusiasm: Echo really is a dazzlingly city. I should have grown used to it, but I was still awestruck by its beauty.

Meanwhile, big changes were underway at the House by the Bridge. The Hall of Common Labor was deserted. The cooks had been abandoned to the whims of fate for the time being. Neither Melamori nor Melifaro were anywhere to be seen. They were probably running around chasing after the tantalizing loose ends of secrets, which are abundant in every respectably good-sized mystery. Sir Juffin Hully greeted us practically licking his chops and staring at Captain Giatta like a hungry cat eyeing a bowl of cream.

At first the interrogation seemed improbably dull to me. In his questioning, Juffin zeroed in on some details concerning the technicalities of the ship's rigging, the commercial practices of the captain's boss, and the biographies of all the crew members. Mr. Giatta calmly answered some of the questions, and resolutely refused to answer others—questions that seemed completely innocuous to me. Sir Juffin greeted this obstinacy with perfect serenity.

"So you say that your assistant, what's his name—ah, yes, Mr. Xakka. He used to be employed on vessels of the Unified Kingdom? That's very interesting, Captain," Juffin said. "Very interesting, indeed."

Suddenly the handsome captain rolled his eyes and collapsed on the floor like a sack of potatoes. Juffin wiped the sweat off his brow wearily.

"He's a tough one. Real tough. And scared to death. I was hardly able to pacify him," said Juffin. He sighed and continued as though he were delivering a lecture. "You must be very careful with a bewitched man, Max. I could put a strong spell on the captain, but we don't yet know what exactly they've done to him. You know, the combination of spells sometimes leads to unpredictable results. When I was a young and foolish deputy sheriff in the city of Kettari, I came across a bewitched lady once in the line of duty. She was behaving like she was possessed, and I had to practice some sorcery just to save my own skin. This happened far from Echo. The magic in the provinces is far more primitive than we're used to here. No one expected any surprises. But then my suspect screeched and exploded into pieces. I was absolutely stunned, and my boss, the old sheriff of Kettari, had to devote many days and nights to returning me to my senses."

Juffin smiled dreamily, as though it were the most pleasant memory of his entire youth.

"So what have you done to him? Was it hypnosis?"

"I have no idea what you mean by 'hypnosis.' I just pacified him. Very effectively. Our captain has never been so tranquil, Magicians' honor! Now we can take that ghastly tunic off him."

As was to be expected, Captain Giatta's black garment concealed a valuable belt, an exact replica of the one we had seen yesterday.

"This is a serious matter, of course," Juffin smiled. "Kofa, Max, look closely at his unkempt clothes. Can you draw any conclusions, Max?"

"Well, it's not easy to keep up your appearance on a long journey," I surmised.

"Nonsense. The captain's trousers and tunic are perfectly neat and tidy. No other ideas?"

"He just hasn't taken his shirt off in a long time," Sir Kofa said, taking pity on me. "That's because—"

"Because he's wearing the belt over the shirt!" It suddenly dawned on me. "It's impossible to remove the belt, right? So that other guy in the morgue, he wasn't a ragamuffin. He just couldn't remove his belt and was forced to wear his old skaba for days and days."

"Now you're talking!" Juffin exclaimed. "By the way, about that fellow in the morgue—he hadn't taken off his skaba for much longer than just several days. Perhaps a few years. That was plain to see. But the *Old Maid* sailed into Echo only eight days ago. You've got to get to the bottom of this, Kofa. Get in touch with Nulli Karif and ask him to dig around in the archives. You can occupy Melifaro's office for the time being. I sent him to find out who the victim was. I have a feeling that it won't be easy. Max and I will work on the poor captain. You can't assist us there, anyway."

"Juffin, what do I need with your mysteries? I have enough of my own to solve," Sir Kofa said with a sly grin, and shut the door behind him.

"You sent him away, because—" I ventured cautiously.

"Yes, yes. Don't ask foolish questions. Practicing True Magic in the presence of strangers—well, Sir Maba Kalox might be able to permit himself such luxuries, but I can't. Nor can you. And without True Magic we'll end up killing our brave captain. That would be unjust, for one thing. And for another, he can tell us a thing or two. For the time being, just watch me, Max; we never know how something will pan out when you're involved. If you sense that you can help me in some way—be my guest. If not, don't try to show off."

Juffin sighed, rolled up his sleeves, and began tapping lightly and rhythmically with his fingertips—not on the mother-of-pearl belt, but in the air. His fingers stopped just fractions of an inch away from the belt. His movements were mesmerizing, and I seemed to doze off in spite of the obvious importance of what was transpiring.

I slept and I dreamed that I was Captain Giatta. I felt rotten, since I knew what was going to happen. This queer old fellow, the Honorable Head of something or other, wanted to help me. But I knew only too well that all he had to do was touch the Belt (in my own mind it had now become a belt with a capital B)—all he had to do was to touch it with the aim of taking it away, and I would die. And my death would be worse than death. It would be an infinitely long and tormenting demise.

"Juffin!" I cried, hardly able to get my tongue around the word, so drowsy was I. "Don't do it! We'll end up killing him, no matter how you go about it. It's something I know."

"You're not the one who knows it, Max." Juffin countered calmly. "It's Captain Giatta who knows. But he only knows what they told him. Consequently, it might not be true. Take it easy. Don't allow your empathy to distract you. That can be dangerous."

And Juffin's hands finally touched the belt.

※

A dark wave of pain enveloped my head. It wasn't simply pain, it was death. What imbecile said that death is a soothing balm? Death is nauseating helplessness and infinite physical pain, gnawing the body into tiny pieces with the voracious teeth of oblivion. In any case, that's what the death of Captain Giatta was like.

But I'm not Captain Giatta, thought someone next to me. No, not "someone," of course. That was me doing the thinking, me, Max, a living being, not one of the rough, sinewy scraps of the body of the unfortunate Tasherian captain. Realizing this bare fact held out the promise of salvation.

The alien sensations subsided, and my own returned to me slowly and solemnly, like lazy dancers to Ravel's *Bolero*. To see, to breathe, to feel the hard seat of the chair with my own backside—it was wonderful! My clothes were wet through, but even that seemed like something miraculous. I thought of the ridiculous local saying "The dead don't sweat," and smiled.

Juffin got up from his crouching position and looked at me in amazement. The cursed mother-of-pearl belt flopped onto the carpet.

"Everything all right, Max?"

"I'm checking. And the captain? Is he dead?"

"No. You saved him, boy."

"Saved him? Me? Sinning Magicians, how could I have done that?"

"You took on half of his pain for your own. A strong person is quite capable of surviving half of it. I've never seen anything so strange—the belt itself was *pretending*, Max. It was putting on an act, like a regular cunning human being. And when I had ascertained that it was already harmless—well, you now know it all."

I nodded, exhausted. My head was spinning, and it wasn't so much that the world seemed to be receding from me as that it was trembling like jello. Juffin's voice seemed to reach me from someplace very far away.

"Come on. Take a gulp of your favorite potion."

Juffin poured some Elixir of Kaxar into my mouth. That meant I would be in tiptop shape in no time. Soon the world did stopped quivering, although I still didn't experience my usual buoyancy.

"You both underwent the same thing, but it will no doubt be some time before the captain begins to function normally again," Juffin observed. "Never mind, we'll turn him over to Sir Abilat now. You'll see, by morning he will have recovered. I think everything will be much easier when our brave captain begins to talk. By the way, Max, now you can imagine what the effects are when some daredevil begins casting spells while wearing the Earring of Oxalla. Do you remember asking why they were afraid? Well, there's no better answer to your own question than personal experience. Well done, Max!"

"I didn't do anything. I'm a victim of circumstance," I sighed. "I had no choice about whether I wanted to save the poor bloke or not. Now if I had really done all of that of my own free will—"

"That's just fruitless sophistry," Juffin declared dismissively, with a wave of his hand. "If you did it, you did it. That's what matters. You don't really have to know exactly what you're doing or why. You did it because you could. And that's why I say you've done well. Am I making myself clear?"

"Clear enough. Give me some more Elixir, or you'll be seeing the corpse of the great hero by dinnertime. You can add it to your stew of dried Magicians."

"Take it, but don't get carried away," Juffin handed me the bottle. "Listen, you probably haven't heard the news yet. Now you can buy this potion in any store, since magic of the eighth degree is all you need to brew it. It didn't occur to me to tell you before."

"Now I'll never die," I said with a blissful smile. "No one's going to wipe me off the face of the earth. Finally, my life has a meaning! I'll drink a bottle of Elixir a day, and reach enlightenment."

"That sounds like our good old Max," Juffin announced happily. "Just a moment ago there was some pale, washed-out shadow in our midst . . . Still, I think you ought to rest. Go home, try to sleep, or at least just lounge around for a while. We'll manage until morning."

"Go away at the most interesting moment? Do you take me for a fool?"

"There won't be any more surprises tonight, Max. Kofa and I will sniff out what we can, and we'll wait till Captain Giatta wakes up. I've already dismissed Melamori for the day, and Lonli-Lokli is heading for home right after the investigation at the port. I'll let Melifaro go, too, as soon as he tells me the name of our deceased friend. You, Max, would be getting at least a dozen Days of Freedom from Care if it weren't for this blasted case. So, homeward, march! That's an order. Can you stand up?"

"After three slugs of Elixir? I could do a jig!" I said.

I stood up—then collapsed in a heap on the floor. My legs knew what they were supposed to do, but they refused to obey.

"I suspected as much," Juffin sighed. "Well, let me give you a hand."

"Strange, I felt fine until I tried to stand up," I said, leaning on his shoulder. "Now I feel more like a bag of potatoes than a human being."

"Never mind, it will pass," the boss said, trying to console me. "By morning you'll be as right as rain. Be here by noon, all right?"

"Of course! I can be here even earlier."

"That's not necessary. I'm no good as a nurse. I hate looking after invalids."

Juffin stuffed me in the back seat of the official amobiler, relieved to get me off his hands. And home I went.

❀

I was able to get out of the amobiler on my own devices and made it to my living room without too much effort. Things weren't going badly, all things considered. After a while, I sent a call to the *Sated Skeleton*. I had just managed to hobble to the bathroom when the delivery boy arrived, so I had to turn around and go back. My rate of progress was nothing to brag about.

I stripped off my clothes, still damp with sweat, splashed around in the water, and then had something to eat. An hour later I felt much better. My exhaustion gradually turned into a pleasant fatigue, so I crawled into bed. I fell asleep before midnight. Some night owl I was!

My sweet dream visited me afresh. Melamori appeared at the window, paused, then started to approach. I tried to move, but as always in these marvelous dreams, I could only just raise myself off my pillow. Melamori came still closer, and sat down beside me. I lifted my hand and tried to embrace my vision. The vision didn't protest.

I still don't know whether it was the unpleasant recent events that were to blame, or whether the hefty portion of Elixir of Kaxar had given me unprecedented strength. This time, though, my heavy, unwieldy body, and she who was the cause of my grief, both obeyed me. When the vision of Melamori was finally under my blanket, I mentally congratulated myself on my victory.

Then something happened that couldn't be explained by any stretch of the imagination. I got scratched. I actually got scratched; and the culprit was the sharp edge of a medallion adorning the lovely chest of my wondrous vision. For a moment, I stared bewildered at the tiny droplet of blood on my palm. Then I woke up. At that very instant, I received a monstrous jab in the belly.

"That was . . . that was worse than swinish, Max!" Melamori shrieked—a flesh and blood Melamori, who was drawing her elegant little foot up for the next attack.

The lady was aiming for the place that should never be targeted under any circumstances. Without even thinking, I grabbed hold of her bare foot, and yanked with all my might. Melamori collapsed onto the floor, curled up into a ball, and rolled into the far corner of the bedroom.

"You did cast a spell after all!" she hissed. "I asked you not to, but you had to bare your fangs and do it anyway! You're worse than the ancient Magicians! At least they didn't lie when they performed their malicious tricks!"

"I didn't lie to you!" I said with the equanimity of absolute shock. "Don't you see I'm just as surprised as you are? I didn't really do anything unusual. I just dreamed about you, and I felt glad that I did. I don't see that there's any reason for a brawl. You should be glad that miracles—"

"I don't need any of your filthy miracles!" Melamori snapped.

I was astonished at how much venom could fit into such a small lady.

"No sniveling vampire would dare force me to do such a thing! It's disgusting! To go to sleep in your own home and wake up in someone else's bed. In the bed of some creature who doesn't even deserve to be called human. It's outrageous! You make me sick, Max!

Do you know what I'm going to do now? I'm going to the Quarter of Trysts. At least there I'll be able to meet a real live man and forget about this nightmare. I'd kill you if I could! You're lucky that I can only kill humans!"

Slowly, my blood began to boil. When someone dumps so much rubbish on you all at once, no amount of breathing exercises promoted by Lonli-Lokli will do any good.

"Fury! Shrew!" I bellowed. "Coward! Go find some weakling whose head you can turn with your pathetic wiles! You need a man you can kill at the drop of a hat! 'Get on his trail' and it's all up with him! I'm telling you, there was no spell! It was a wonder—a mi-ra-cle!"

"You dare say that to me, after all you've done?" Melamori asked, her voice tight with rage.

"I've done? I didn't do anything. I just went to bed, closed my eyes, and dreamed about you. That's the extent of my 'magic.' If you don't believe me—fine! Suit yourself."

I remembered how happy my dream had made me, and the consciousness of loss gave me a hollow feeling in the pit of my stomach. A new wave of rage swept over me. A dense ball of bitter saliva collected in my mouth. Lady Melamori was lucky that I was able to control myself. I spat on the floor, then stared dully at a hole in the carpet that gave off a cloud of reeking steam. When I got a grip on myself, I turned around. Melamori had shrunk into the corner, trembling. I felt sad and ashamed. At that moment life struck me as some monumental joke.

"I'm sorry, Melamori. I said some very foolish things. And you did, too, believe me. Take my amobiler and go home. We'll talk later."

"We have nothing to talk about," Melamori said, creeping out of her hiding place and inching toward the door. "Even if you're not a liar, all the worse! That means you can't help it! Never mind—I'll find a way. No one will ever force me to do anything! You hear me?"

She slammed the door so violently that one of my small fragile cabinets crashed to the floor. I clutched at my hair and shook my head—everything had gotten completely out of hand! It seemed my romance was smashed to smithereens. Yes, Max, that's exactly what had happened.

❀

I got out of bed and went downstairs. Dirty, rotten vampires like me have the bad habit of pouring gallons of kamra into themselves after forcing themselves upon sweet ladies. Besides that, we smoke our revolting, stinky cigarettes from another World, and this creates an illusion of emotional equilibrium in us. True, it doesn't last very long. I was so tense and on edge that my lethargy evaporated like magic. Adrenalin is a powerful thing.

The fact is, I don't have a drop of patience. If something goes wrong in my life, I'm not able to wait for an auspicious moment to remedy the situation. I'd rather spoil everything once and for all, as long as it's today, than subject myself to anguished expectation and breathing exercises with an eye toward the future. Of course, it's stupid, but there are things that are stronger than I am. Waiting and hoping is a path that may lead to sudden madness, but running amuck through town like a complete idiot—that's sometimes just the ticket! Almost any action I take gives me the illusion that I'm stronger than unmerciful circumstances. I have to do something. This is my form of reasoning: a protective reflex, the uncouth, visceral reaction of a body in trouble. In short, what I truly hate is sitting in one place and suffering.

I went back to the bedroom and started getting dressed. I thought—I was absolutely certain—that I was going to go to work. I'd go help Juffin. What kind of work would he have me do, though? In any case, with a sip of Elixir of Kaxar in the morning I'd feel as good as new.

Only when I had gone outside did I realize that I was dressed not in the Mantle of Death, but in the swamp-colored looxi I had been wearing during my recent gluttonous outing with Sir Kofa. I shrugged. I didn't have the strength to go back and change. The house awakened painful memories, too fresh for me to want to run up against them again. But going to work in these clothes wasn't exactly appropriate, either.

I'll take a walk through town, calm down a bit, do some thinking, and then we'll see, I decided, turning into the first alleyway I came to.

My legs carried me along wherever they wished. I tried not to interfere. My memory, and the urge to get my bearings in my surroundings, were suspended for the time being. My thoughts also seemed to have taken a short vacation, and this was wonderful. I must admit, I hadn't counted on this kind of relief.

My headlong flight through the night was interrupted by the rind of some exotic fruit. I slipped, plopping down on the sidewalk in the most inelegant manner. It was good I wasn't wearing the Mantle of Death—this clumsy footwork could easily have soiled my sinister reputation. The unexpectedness of my fall from grace also jolted my memory, letting loose a stream of curses from my far-off homeland, long slumbering in the recesses of my memory. Two men who were coming out of a tavern stared at me in unfeigned delight. I went quiet, and realized I should pick myself up off the mosaic sidewalk. Praise be the Magicians, at least it was dry.

I got up and looked at the signboard over the establishment from which the two men had just emerged from. The name of the tavern struck me as more than fateful: *The Vampire's Dinner*. I smiled bitterly and went inside. What I found was fully in keeping with my expectations, and filled me with a sense of foreboding. In the semidarkness stood the solitary silhouette of the barkeeper. His hair was disheveled and his eyelids glowed phosphorescent. From his ear, naturally, dangled the Earring of Oxalla. I began to feel more cheerful. This is where I should have brought Melamori for our discussion today. I think the proprietor of this establishment would certainly have been on my side.

I sat down at the table farthest from the door. The surface was daubed with red paint. These were supposed to represent spots of blood. I considered for a moment, then ordered something from the Old Cuisine. I was lucky that unhappiness always improved my appetite.

I was served a harmless-looking piece of pie with no outward signs of the vampire esthetic. When I made a tiny incision, the pie literally blew up like a piece of popcorn that explodes over a sizzling hot fire. On my plate there was now an airy cloud of a substance so delicious I had to order another one as soon as the first portion was gone. By the way, this culinary confection was called *Breath of Evil*.

When I had fallen into a blissful stupor, I ordered some kamra and began to fill my pipe. On top of all the other misfortunes, my meager supply of cigarette butts had dried up. That's how it always was with me: if it rains, it pours.

I smoked, and stared at my fellow patrons with the lively interest of an imbecile. One of them was about to leave. His hairdo was just like that of Captain Giatta, whose life I had inadvertently saved: a braid down to his belt and an ample beard. Was this fellow perhaps from the *Old Maid*? Some ship's cook adding to his stockpile of trade secrets? I scrutinized the stranger more carefully. He was just fishing around for his wallet in the mysterious depths of his flowing robe. Sinning Magicians! The dull gleam of mother-of-pearl: a belt. More precisely, *the* Belt! Another bewitched sailor. I'd have to do something.

Of course, I could simply have arrested the fellow. It was my duty to do so. But I understood very well the remarkable behavior of Captain Giatta. A bewitched man was quite capable of believing that he had to face death rather than surrender. So I decided just to follow him. My clothes, Praise be the Magicians, were completely unobtrusive. Why not do a little spying? A much better diversion than moaning over my broken heart. I tossed a crown down on the blood-spattered table. This was, of course, too much to pay for a few pieces of pie in a dive like this, but I felt very sympathetic toward the proprietor of the *Vampire's Dinner*. The disheveled slyboots caught the gleam of shiny metal and his eyes lit up. I put a finger to my lips and slipped out the door. My bearded friend was just disappearing around the corner. I quickened my pace.

I didn't recall having been in this part of Echo before, or perhaps it was just that at night it was hard to recognize. Anyway, I wasn't in the mood for sightseeing. I didn't take my eyes off the back of the stranger. Where was he taking me? I already envisioned how I would discover the hideout of a whole band of belted long-beards, and Juffin and I would swoop in and save them from their benighted existence. Actually, I wasn't too eager to repeat my recent flirtation with someone else's death. Never mind, we'd get out of it somehow.

Sinning Magicians, who would have thought! The bearded object of my undivided attention had led me not just anywhere, but into the very heart of the Quarter of Trysts. Bewitched or not, it seemed he still suffered from loneliness and wanted to try his luck. I smiled bitterly. Lady Melamori was kicking up her heels somewhere nearby, if she hadn't reconsidered her vow to come here seeking oblivion from my repellent embrace. I couldn't just let this smart fellow slip away, getting his happiness for a night! And jumping into bed with the happy couple was out of the question.

But life was wiser than I was. I didn't have to find a way out of a ridiculous situation. The stranger stopped short and turned to me.

"You're too late, mate," he said in the same distinctive Tasherian drawl that Captain Giatta spoke with. "Do you know how many people there are all around us? If you take another step I'll shout for help."

Then it dawned on me. He thought I was trying to rob him. Of course, what else would a wealthy stranger think if he had been pursued by a suspicious character in a nondescript looxi for the last half hour?

"I'm no robber," I said, with my most charming smile. "I'm much worse. There's no stopping me. You came at it from the wrong end. I'm from the Secret Investigative Force of the Unified Kingdom. Are you in the mood for a walk to the House by the Bridge?"

I winked at the bearded chap. The stupid circumstances of my conversation with the suspect in the middle of the Quarter of Trysts suddenly filled me with a senseless buoyancy. I swiveled my hips suggestively and pursed my lips in a Cupid's bow.

"Tonight, I am your fate. What's your name, handsome?"

"Handsome" gasped for air. My unbridled approach seemed to have disarmed him. But the Tasherian's voice remained firm.

"I can't go with you, sir. I very much regret it, but I am forced to stand my ground."

And the bearded one drew an enormous butcher knife from under his looxi—the kind of knife that is probably considered to be an ordinary dagger in distant Tashera.

"No one loves me," I concluded. "Fine, let's fight it out. All the more since I know your weak point, my friend. I'm not going to slice you up into pieces. I'll just undo your wonderful belt and see what happens. Well, have you changed your mind? Give me your little toy."

Recent events had made me absurdly reckless. I was even surprised at myself. I seemed to have decided I had nothing to lose. My opponent seemed to think likewise.

"It's all the same to me," the stranger said gloomily, grasping his instrument more deftly. "We'll have to fight. I'm very sorry, sir."

With a sudden movement of the hand, a silver bolt of lightning pierced my stomach. Rather, it should have pierced me—only I suddenly had no stomach for it to pierce.

To tell the truth, to this day I don't understand what happened. I was behaving like a second-rate hero of a B movie, so I should have died right there, on the mosaic sidewalk of the Quarter of Trysts. Why didn't it happen? It's hard to say. I think that some of Juffin Hully's lessons must have gotten through to me, though I'm still not sure he taught me anything of the sort.

The knife fell on the mosaic, and I tried to figure out what was happening. I wasn't there. I just wasn't. That's all. I had disappeared somehow, gone "nowhere" and ceased to be "something"—for the space of a second. Then I appeared again. Just in time to step on the knife with my foot, as well as on the hand of the stunned would-be killer.

"Hi!" I said. "Now we're going to undress. Or we'll just go straight to the House by the Bridge. As you wish, darling. Take your pick. Today is your day."

The bearded fellow jerked with such force that I almost flew head over heels, along with my tasteless jokes. It finally dawned on me that my chances for winning this contest of wills were very slim. The Mantle of Death and lots of good food had made a very benign fellow out of Max. An uneasy feeling of doom had crept up behind me and was about to leap out and put an end to my existence. I didn't like it a bit.

I knew very well that I wouldn't spit at the bearded chap. It would be cruel to kill him, not to mention foolish. Who knew what kinds of secrets the angry old salt was keeping inside him? On the other hand, how could I fight a strapping fellow like that? I had never been any good with my fists. Making a big noise, yes, but standing my ground in a fight to the death was not my cup of tea. Whatever Sir Juffin Hully said about the possible dire consequences of mixing two curses, I had to take the risk and do a bit of sorcery.

Praise be the Magicians, at least I knew how to do *something*. With a practiced gesture, I hid the long-beard between the thumb and the forefinger of my left hand.

Exhausted, I sat down on the pavement and hung my head between my knees. I should take this souvenir to Juffin, I thought gloomily. I'll go presently. Let me just sit here a minute, then on to the House by the Bridge, blast it!

I felt stunned. It seemed as if an enormous heavy stone had settled on me, and I couldn't move.

Then I felt a gentle hand come to rest on my shoulder.

"Has something happened, sir? We heard some noise. Perhaps you need some help?" asked an elegant, bright-haired lady in a richly adorned looxi.

Her broad-shouldered companion sat on his haunches and stared searchingly into my face. What could I tell them, these fine, upstanding young people?

After all, just recently I had been Sir Max, the most lighthearted, frivolous civil servant on either side of the Xuron.

"It's all right, kind people," I said with a smile. "I came here with a friend, and that idiot refused point blank to visit the Trysting House. He cried half the night about how lonely he was, but as soon as we were here he got cold feet. I'm ashamed to say that he was afraid. He punched me and then ran off."

"Your friend must be crazy," the lady said, shaking her head in disapproval. "How can someone fear his own destiny?"

"It turns out that it's possible," I said, staring at my left hand, where, inconceivably, the arrestee was being held. "So I'm all right. Thank you kindly. Good night to you."

"We certainly will have a good night," the lady said, smiling.

Her companion finally stopped studying my face and took the woman by the hand.

"Magicians be with your mad friend. Drop in yourself and meet your destiny. Morning is a long way away," she grinned archly, waving goodbye.

Left alone, I looked pensively at the Trysting House. Had this fair-haired stranger bewitched me? I didn't know why, but I suddenly wished very much to go inside. After all, I still hadn't been with a woman in this World. Except in my dreams—but that didn't quite count.

⚙

As though from a distance, I observed a tall young man in a modest garment, who stood up from the pavement and reached for the doorknob. That young man seemed to be me. In any case, I discovered that I was already on the threshold of that establishment. When someone asked me to pay two crowns, I dug nervously in the pocket of my looxi. The building was located on that side of the street where the Seekers were men, and the Seeker paid a double entrance fee.

I paid the money, but had no idea what to do next. Melifaro's explanations had evaporated from my memory. What the heck was I thinking, coming here with an arrestee in custody! I felt slightly panicky. I realized that in my other hand I was grasping a tiny, smooth ceramic tag with the number 19 stamped on it. How and when I had managed to come by it was a mystery.

I stared thoughtfully at a huge glass receptacle that was sitting on the floor by the entrance. It was full of tags of the same kind. I had probably taken it from there. What now? I wondered in horror. I started to tremble. I no longer remembered that I had come here to meet an unknown woman, to meet my own destiny. I had only one goal: not committing another blunder. I had already screwed up enough for one night!

"What are you waiting for, sir?" the affable host asked in surprise. "Your number is 19. Go meet your destiny, my friend."

"Yes, of course. Thank you for reminding me why I came here. People are so absent-minded; and I'm a person, after all."

I finally remembered what I was supposed to do. I slowly entered the rooms where the Waiters, lonely women both beautiful and plain, were biding their time. An absurd thought flickered through my brain: I was no doubt the first cop who had ever sought a lover with an arrestee in his fist!

One, two, three . . . I couldn't even make out any faces. They all swam together in a blurry mass, and I walked through it with a foolish grin on my face. Six, seven . . . too bad, I have another number, sweetheart. Ten, eleven . . . May I get past, please? Eighteen, nineteen . . . You're the one I'm looking for, my lady.

※

"Are you doing this on purpose? Are you casting spells again?" asked a familiar voice. "You shouldn't be doing this, Max. Well, anyway, that's that. You can't fool fate, can you?"

I finally managed to focus my eyes. The pale splotch of a face slowly acquired a sweet, familiar outline. Lady Melamori looked at me guardedly. It seemed she couldn't decide what to do—whether to throw herself at me in a warm embrace, or run for her life.

"That's it!" I said. "This really is the limit!"

Then I sat down on the floor and began to laugh. I couldn't have cared less about propriety and all the rest. My good sense simply refused to take part in this implausible adventure.

My little tantrum seemed to convince Melamori better than any rational argument could that there was no plot against her, and never had been. Ever.

"Let's get out of here, Sir Max!" she begged, sitting on her haunches next to me. She carefully stroked my poor, crazy head, and whispered, "You're scaring the visitors. Let's go. You can laugh all you want when we're outside. Come on, get up."

I leaned obediently on the strong, small hand. Sinning Magicians, this delicate lady lifted me up without any effort at all!

Outside, the fresh breeze seemed to put everything in its proper place, and I no longer felt like laughing.

"Strange things have been happening lately, Melamori," I said. Then I was silent. What else was there to say?

"Max," she cried. "I'm so ashamed. When I was in your bedroom—well, now I understand that I did something very foolish, but I was so frightened! I completely lost my head!"

"I can imagine," I said. "You fall asleep in your own house, and you wake up the devil knows where."

"What's 'the devil'?" Melamori asked.

It wasn't the first time I had had to explain my way out of such idiomatic scrapes. Now I didn't even try.

"It doesn't matter. But you know, I really don't know what I did. I still have no idea how it happened."

"I believe you," Melamori said, nodding. "Now I realize you didn't know your own powers, but . . . it's too late."

"Why?"

"Because it has already happened. Only we're going to your place, not mine. I live too close. Let this last walk be a long one."

"The last walk? Are you out of your mind, Melamori? Do you think I'll bite your head off in a burst of passion?"

I tried to be upbeat, so that I could raise my spirits.

"Of course you're not going to bite my head off. It wouldn't fit in your mouth," Melamori replied with a weak smile. "But that's not the point. Don't you realize where we just met, Max?"

"In the Quarter of Trysts. You'll never believe how I got there. Think what you wish, but I ended up there in pursuit of a fellow in a mother-of-pearl belt. You remember all that business with the belts, don't you?"

Melamori nodded, and I went on.

"We had a little scuffle on the street, and then I arrested him. He's still here." I pointed to my left fist.

"Do you mean to say—" Melamori burst out laughing.

Now it was her turn to sit down on the sidewalk. I sat next to her, my arm around her shoulders as she howled with laughter.

"And I thought that you— Oh, it's too much! You're the most extraordinary fellow in the World, Sir Max! I adore you! What a shame!"

At long last, we got up to go.

"Have you never been to the Quarter of Trysts?" Melamori asked suddenly.

"No. In the Barren Lands everything is much simpler. Or much more complicated, depending on how you look at it. So, no. This is the first time."

"And you don't know—" Melamori's voice broke into a whisper. "You don't know that people who meet in the Quarter of Trysts are supposed to spend the night and then part forever?"

"In our case that's absolutely impossible," I said, and smiled, although my heart was slowly sinking down to my toes. "We aren't both going to quit our jobs, I suppose."

Melamori shook her head.

"That's not necessary. We can see each other as often as we like, Max, only we will be strangers. I mean—well, you know what I mean. It's the tradition. You can't do anything about it. It's my own fault. I went there to get back at someone. I don't know who, or why . . . I shouldn't have gone there, and you shouldn't have either. Although, who knows whose fault it is? People don't really have any choice in the matter."

"But—"

I was completely bewildered. My mind was such a mess I should have just shut up.

"Let's not talk about this, all right Max? Tomorrow is still a long way away, and . . . they say destiny is wiser than we are."

"We won't if you don't want to. But I think all this sounds like primitive malarky. We can decide for ourselves what to do. Why do we need all those silly traditions? If you wish, we can just walk around today as though nothing happened. No one will tell anyone anything, and then—"

"I don't want to, and it's impossible," Melamori sighed, smiling, and covered my mouth gently with her ice-cold hand. "I'm telling you, enough about that, all right?"

We continued on our way in silence. The Street of Old Coins was quite close already. Another few minutes, and we entered my dark living room. Ella and Armstrong began meowing pitifully. Day or night, in female company or all alone, as soon as I walk in the door they demand food! I was distracted for a moment by the feline distress signals. Melamori examined the cats with astonishment.

"So those are the parents of the future Royal Cats? Where did you get them, Max?"

"What do you mean? They were sent from Melifaro's estate, didn't you know?"

"Why does the whole Court consider them to be an unknown breed, then?"

"Magicians only know. I just started taking care of them. It seems never to have occurred to them that cats need to be groomed. Melamori, are you sure everything's all right? More than anything on earth I hate coercion."

"I already told you. Nothing depends on us, Max. It's out of our hands. What's happened has happened. The only thing we can do now is waste even more time than we have already."

"All right. I won't argue with you. For now," I said, and put my arms around her. "I'm not going to waste any more time, either."

"Just try not to let your arrestee escape. The one thing I'm not planning on doing tonight is chasing him all over the house."

Melamori smiled a sad, ironic smile. I tried to imagine our pursuit, and laughed so hard I almost fell down the stairs, taking Melamori with me. Melamori struggled with her imagination for a second and then started giggling, too. Perhaps we weren't behaving too romantically, but that was just what we needed. Laughter spices up the passions much better than the languid seriousness of lovers clinging to one another in melodramas. And I hate melodramas.

❀

Of course, the thing that kept nagging at me was that crazy talk about "the last time," which Melamori had started and ended so abruptly on our way to my place. They say that the anticipation of parting heightens pleasure. I'm not too sure about that. I think that night might have been perfect if it hadn't been for the thought that morning would soon arrive, and I would have to wage a hopeless struggle against the prejudices and superstitions of my newly acquired treasure. These thoughts did not enhance my desperate attempts to be happy.

"How strange," Melamori said. "I was so afraid of you, Max. But now I find that it's all so peaceful and easy to be with you. So peaceful and easy . . . As though it was all I had ever needed my whole life. How stupid it all is."

"What are you calling stupid?" I smiled. "I hope you aren't refer-ring to what just happened."

"Well," said Melamori, laughing. "That wouldn't be the right word for it. It's not exactly an intellectual activity."

Now we were both laughing. Suddenly, Melamori broke out in a wail I wouldn't have been able to imagine possible. I was so upset that it took me a whole minute to think of a way to calm her down. Some "thinker" I am!

The dawn that I had been dreading the whole night nevertheless crept up in the heavens at the appointed hour. Melamori dozed on my embroidered pillow, smiling in her sleep.

At that moment, I became absolutely certain of what I must do. The plan of action, a very simple but effective one, was as clear as the morning sky. I simply wouldn't let her go. I'd let her sleep, and when she woke up I would sit beside her. I'd throw my arms around her. She would start to squeal and try to break free, and would spew all kinds of nonsense about traditions, and I would silently hear her out and wait as long as necessary for her to be quiet. Then I'd say to her, "Sweetheart, while you were asleep I came to an understanding with destiny. It won't object if we stay together a little bit longer." And if Lady Melamori still protested, I just wouldn't listen.

I finally started feeling a bit better, and I even felt sleepy, but I couldn't afford to take any chances. I took a hearty swig of Elixir of Kaxar. My drowsiness evaporated, muttering an apology. There remained one problem to take care of: I really wanted to use the toi-let. I didn't want to leave my outpost, but my upbringing wouldn't allow me to wet the bed.

A half hour later I realized that there were a few things a person couldn't postpone indefinitely, and I looked attentively at Melamori. She was sleeping, there could be no doubt about it. I left the room on tiptoe, and shot downstairs like a speeding bullet. The trip didn't take too much time. When I got back up to the living room, my heart suddenly cried out, wrenched with pain: "That's the end of that, boy!"

Completely dejected, I slumped down on the step and heard the outside door slam followed by the clacking of my own amobiler. I realized it was all over. This was truly the end.

I wanted to send a call to Melamori, but I knew it wouldn't help. Nothing would. The destiny that I had reached an understanding with thumbed its nose at me.

After I had somehow mastered my emotions, I bathed, got dressed, and went to work. After all, the bearded arrestee, who might have been considered quite an effective love potion, was still balled up in my fist. The fact that this bizarre talisman hadn't brought me luck was another matter altogether.

※

The amobiler wasn't in front of the door, of course. I wondered whether stealing the personal property of a lover from the Quarter of Trysts was also a hallowed tradition.

I had to go to the House by the Bridge on foot. Every stone on the pavement screamed out my loss. "A few hours ago you were passing us together," the ancient, one-story houses on the Street of Old Coins reproached me heartlessly. I felt absolutely forlorn. Then I did the only thing that promised to bring me any relief: I sent a call to Sir Juffin Hully. *I'm on my way, Juffin. I'm bringing a present. In the meantime, how are things?*

They almost did you in last night, didn't they? the chief inquired.

Yes. Last night, and then again this morning—in a manner of speaking. Not more than fifteen minutes ago. But that's beside the point right now. Talk to me, Juffin. Just tell me how the case of the belts is going, all right?

Silent Speech, as always, required my full concentration, so I couldn't think about anything else when I was using it. And that was just what I needed.

Of course. When have I ever refused to save time? Listen carefully. First, Melifaro was able to identify the victim yesterday. He was a young man named Apatti Xlen. Ah yes, this name doesn't say anything to you. It was a celebrated case, Max. It happened about two years ago, in the Moni Mak family home. Yes, Max, it was Sir Ikas Moni Mak, grand nephew of Magician Nuflin himself. He had received a visit from some old friends of his wife, the Xlens, who had settled on their estate in Uruland during the Troubled Times. When it was time for young Apatti to decide what to do with his insignificant life, they sent him to the capital, where the boy lived for half a year in the home of Moni Mak. I think he was going to school. Then he disappeared, taking with him the White Seven-Leaf Clover. We know for certain that not long before this Apatti had bought an elegant, gleaming belt in one of the harbor shops. Sir Ikas remembered this object, so there can be no doubt—

"Good day, Sir Max. You walk almost as quickly as you drive."

Silent Speech broke off, and live conversation started up, for I was already in the office I shared with Juffin.

"Or I drive as slowly as I walk. But there's something I don't understand. What did he swipe from the magician's grandnephew? I asked, trying to put up a good front, as though nothing at all had happened to me. Juffin should hardly have had to pay for my fatal inability to lead an office romance to a "happily ever after."

The boss shook his head and thrust a mug of kamra into my hand. His eyes expressed ordinary human compassion. Or was I just imagining it?

"He stole the White Seven-Leaf Clover, Max. That's just a pretty bauble—only a copy of the Shining Seven-Leaf Clover, the amulet of the Order of the Seven-Leaf Clover. Already during the Epoch of Orders there were rumors about the extraordinary power of this object, but I'll tell you a terrible state secret: all these rumors were complete hogwash. The only thing the Shining Seven-Leaf Clover is capable of is bringing personal happiness to Sir Nuflin . . ."

"That's no small thing!"

"Yes, but on the other hand it's not all that much. And the White Seven-Leaf Clover can't even do that. It's just a pretty, useless gew-gaw. But the boy snatched it and disappeared for two years. We checked up on it: the *Old Maid* was anchored in our harbor at that time, so I personally haven't a single doubt that poor Apatti spent a long vacation in Tashera, and has now come home, only to be killed. Do you know how he died?"

"He decided to foreswear all ornamentation? Took off the belt?"

"You guessed it. Almost. The fellow didn't do anything so foolish of his own accord. He was robbed. And because the robber was interested in the belt, he removed it right then and there. You can imagine what happened to Apatti. A terrible death."

I shuddered.

"But why are you so sure that it was a robber? Maybe the fellow decided to challenge the ban on removing it. Maybe he decided to do just what he felt like doing?"

"And experience all the charming consequences firsthand? Don't you think that hypothesis is a bit too daring? Besides, they already found the robber. Dead. He was being fitted for some new clothes and he took off the belt, poor chap. The police took him to the morgue yesterday evening, soon after you left. Now the two of them are lying there side by side, a vision to behold."

"I see," I replied. "And what about our captain?"

"He's sleeping sweetly after a heart-to-heart talk. Here's what he told us: Agon the merchant hired him four years ago for a trading voyage. He gave him the belt as a 'token of friendship.' The captain immediately put it on and fell right into the trap. They showed him the power of the belt. Not the full extent of its power—but enough, as a warning. Then Mr. Agon explained to the poor blighter that his job was to carry out orders unquestioningly. If he did, everything would be fine. The captain didn't have to do anything very unusual. He just sailed the *Old Maid* from Tashera to Echo and back. And he protected it from curious eyes. Giatta recruited his crew himself, although before the last journey Agon brought a new cook on board. He didn't consult Giatta about the decision—he just showed the old cook the door. The main thing was that the new cook wasn't wearing a belt. All the while, Giatta is sure that Mr. Agon was afraid of his own protégé. Do you smell an intrigue, Max? I think that's our protagonist. Never mind, we'll get around to him eventually. By the way, when the cook arrived in Echo he disappeared, so food was brought to the crew from a nearby inn. Actually, he didn't really help us out all that much, the great Captain Giatta, belts notwithstanding. Agon understood that you can't trust captives or slaves. By the way, the captain intends to devote the rest of his long life to kissing your feet. He believes you saved his skin and his soul, and he's absolutely right." Juffin paused. "So, what kind of 'present' have you brought for me?"

"Another happy belt-owner. He was about to slash me to pieces.

But everything turned out all right in the end, as you see. I still don't know how I managed. I witnessed a knife pierced my insides, after which I disappeared, and then suddenly I was there again—completely unharmed."

"I know," Juffin grinned. "You managed that trick very well. All the rest was pretty awful, though. You behaved like a child, Sir Max. Aren't you ashamed?"

"Nah. I'm a fool, of course—but I always suspected it. I didn't need any more proof."

I recalled how I had frightened the stranger with my bawdy antics, and smiled involuntarily.

"Melifaro would have been amused, don't you think?"

"I do think so," Juffin said laughing. "But the way you followed him—that was a very poor performance. The fellow spotted you within a few seconds and made a beeline for the nearest populated area. I'm afraid it won't be any easier to teach you the art of shadowing than it was to make a decent cook out of you. Turning you into a ghost was less difficult."

"Juffin," I asked cautiously. "Were you watching me the *whole* time?"

"As though I have nothing better to do! I only came near when I smelled trouble. I wanted to help you, but you wriggled out of it somehow on your own. Do you remember how you did it?"

"Are you joking? I had no idea what was going on!"

"Naturally. That's the misfortune of talented people, Max. You act first, and then you try to understand how it got you into trouble. We ordinary folks are much more reliable. All right then, let's examine your discovery."

"Shall I let him out?" I asked, getting ready.

"Wait, don't make any rash decisions. First, tell me, what does he look like, this unsuccessful butcher of live meat? I was watching you, not him."

I began describing the appearance of my companion from the Quarter of Trysts, but as I babbled away, bitter memories clutched at my heart again. I fell silent and stared dully at the floor.

"Excellent, Max!" Juffin held himself aloof from my worldly sorrow. "Do you know who you've captured? It's the owner of the *Old Maid* himself—Mr. Agon in the flesh. Your famous luck is better than any amulet."

"Great," I said morosely. "You can tear me to pieces and dole me out to the poor and suffering. I won't object. So what should I do with him now? Keep him as a memento of a wonderful night?"

"That's not such a bad idea. I suspect that Mr. Agon is closer than anyone to solving the unpleasant mystery of these foolish belts. Among the other bans placed on him by the owner of the belt is no doubt the prohibition against having anything to do with the authorities. Once he's in the House by the Bridge, he's bound to die. We simply won't be able to save him."

"And if I do what I did yesterday?" I suggested. "I'll share the pain with him, and he's sure to survive!"

"Would you really agree to that? I wouldn't advise it."

I shrugged.

"What else can we do? Besides, I've never felt as bold as I do today. *Carpe diem*!"

"That's all I need," the boss muttered. "To bury you while saving this worthy son of the distant south. No, today we'll be wiser. We'll go to Jafax. The women of the Seven-Leaf Clover will think of something. All the more since we're making efforts for their boss."

"For Magician Nuflin? Wait, Juffin—are there really women in the Seven-Leaf Clover?"

"Whatever made you think that there weren't?" Juffin asked. "There are more women than men. That was the case in all the other Orders, as well. Didn't you know?"

"How could I have known? I've never seen any of them. And all the Grand Magicians I've heard about are men."

"Yes, I suppose so. But, you see, women are inclined to secrecy. When they enter the Order, they break their ties with the world so effectively that it's almost impossible to have any contact with them. There are quite powerful personages among them, but no one has been able to persuade them to accept an important office. They claim that it would 'distract them from the most important things.' In a way, they're right. You'll see for yourself when we get there."

"But what does Magician Nuflin have to do with this?" I asked as I settled behind the levers of the amobiler. "You said we were doing this for him."

"Where is your renowned intuition, Max? You can figure it out. The young man who became a captive of the mysterious belt stole the copy of the Shining Seven-Leaf Clover, which is only good for a souvenir. Now people are appearing in Echo again with similar belts. What do you think they might want?"

"Magician Nuflin's real amulet?"

"Congratulations, you hit the nail on the head!"

"I wonder how they intend to pilfer that little trinket from Jafax?"

"It's very simple. If they managed to put the same kind of belt on Nuflin, he'd give them anything they wanted."

"How could they foist something like that on the Grand Magician himself? That's impossible, Juffin."

"Well, it would probably be hard to get it on Nuflin himself. But that's not really necessary. There are many people in the Order of the Seven-Leaf Clover, and there are secret passageways connecting Jafax with Echo—like our House by the Bridge, for instance. It would be enough to fasten a belt like that on one of our messengers for him to dive into hell and bring out a bunch of Dark Magicians, not to mention the Shining Seven-Leaf Clover. If he's lucky, of course. But people sometimes are! In short, lad, someone who had the wits to forge those belts would be fully capable of clinching a deal like that. I know I could."

"You, Juffin?"

"Among the Mutinous Magicians were young men who were much more sharp-witted than I was. What they weren't smart enough to do was to take a critical view of foolish superstitions."

"So you think there is some Mutinous Magician behind all of this?"

"Of course. Who else do you think would need the blasted amulet? Unless it were a jeweler—but there are many more valuable things in the World. We're here, Max, don't you see?"

"Oh, yes. I didn't even notice. It's neither dawn nor dusk, though. How will we pass into Jafax?"

"Through the Secret Door. It's the only way of reaching the women of the Seven-Leaf Clover."

Juffin climbed out of the amobiler and I followed behind him. The boss walked along a high dark wall, then stopped and slapped his palm hard against a slightly protruding greenish stone.

"Follow me, boy. Better close your eyes—it will steady your nerves."

Without looking back at me, the boss began walking directly into the rock.

There was no time to think. I closed my eyes obediently and plunged after him. My muscles tensed instinctively, bracing in anticipation of a blow. But none was forthcoming. A moment later, Sir Juffin intercepted me, my body still poised to ward off obstacles in a fierce struggle.

"Where did you think you were going, Max?" he asked gaily. "We're here. Open your eyes now if you don't believe me."

I looked around. We were standing in the middle of the thick undergrowth of an ancient overgrown garden.

"Good day, Juffin. How's the earth treating you, you old fox?"

A vibrant voice resonated from behind my back. I shuddered and turned around. The voice was coming from someone who resembled the fairytale ideal of a grandmother: a shortish, plump lady with silver hair and a benevolent smile, and cheeks graced charming dimples.

"What a fine boy, Juffin!" she said, looking me up and down with undisguised admiration. "Are you Sir Max, dear? Welcome!"

The old lady embraced me with unexpected affection. I felt I had returned home after a long absence.

"This is Lady Sotofa Xanemer, Max," the chief said. "She's the most frightening creature in the Universe, so be on your guard."

"No more frightening than you are, Juffin," Lady Sotofa laughed. "Let's go, gentlemen. You and Nuflin have some problems on your hands, Juffin. That's for sure. And you must come with me and have something to eat, my dear," she added for my benefit.

"What a good idea," Juffin said drily.

"No matter what, you're always ready to eat," she remarked to Juffin. "I know you. But I love you all the same. Where have you been lately? You stopped visiting me. Maybe you think you bore me? Well, listen here, you old coot. You are tiresome, but my heart goes its own way, and it's always glad to see you. And one must listen to one's heart."

Lady Sotofa scurried ahead, showing us the way and looking back now and then with a comical expression to illustrate her running commentary. Her little hands gestured wildly, her looxi fluttered in the breeze, and her dimples became ever more pronounced. I simply couldn't credit her with great magical powers, however hard I tried.

Finally we arrived at a cozy garden pavilion that seemed to serve as Lady Sotofa's office. There we were greeted by another sweet lady, somewhat younger than Lady Sotofa. With age she promised to become an exact replica of her elder associate. She already had the soft plumpness and the charming dimples.

"Oh, Sotofa! You're always entertaining men! Don't you want to take a rest?"

Her laughter rang out like tinkling bells.

"Of course I entertain them, Reniva. Don't you remember? We agreed that I'd bring the menfolk around, but you would feed them. Now scoot! Off to the kitchen with you! The silly youngsters that pass as our chefs will never be able to cook as well as you can."

"Are you suggesting that the food should be tasty?" Lady Reniva asked, arching her brows. "I thought men didn't care what they ate as long as it filled their bellies. Fine, I'll feed your swains, but you'll have to reckon with them in the meantime."

She disappeared behind a partition, and the three of us were alone.

"Well, Sir Max, were you frightened?" Lady Sotofa giggled. "Did you think that this daft Juffin had brought you here to see some crazy old biddies? You don't have to reply. I can see in your eyes that that's what you thought. Well, give me your fist. Come on, come on—don't be timid."

I stared at Juffin in confusion. He looked at me sternly, and nodded. I extended my sweaty left hand to Sotofa, the one in which Mr. Agon, the no-good Tasherian merchant, had been languishing for the last dozen hours. The merry old lady stroked my fingers cautiously, lingered a moment, frowned, and then broke into a smile again, displaying her enchanting dimples.

"Easy as pie, Juffin! I'm surprised you didn't manage to do it."

"You know I could have," the Venerable Head of the Secret Investigative Force muttered. "It's just that everything comes to you so naturally."

Lady Sotofa shook her head reproachfully and applied a sudden sharp pressure at the base of my palm. I yelped in surprise and pain, and opened my fingers. The unfortunate merchant tumbled onto the carpet, and Lady Sotofa triumphantly displayed the marvelous mother-of-pearl belt, which, by some miracle, she was left holding.

"There you are, Juffin! Are you starting to regret that nature has rewarded you with this old crone you're still so proud of?"

"Don't exaggerate, my lady," he murmured. "I still have a few tricks up my sleeve you haven't yet learned."

"What do I need those for? Your tricks don't put bread on the table." She turned to me, "How did you like that, my dear?"

I nodded in astonishment and stared at my recent captive.

"Is he alive, Lady Sotofa?"

She waved her hand with a flippant air.

"Why wouldn't he be? I could revive him right now, but it makes more sense to do it just before you leave. I don't intend to feed this blockhead, and if we eat while he looks on—well, it wouldn't be very polite, would it?"

After dinner, which affected me like a dose of horse tranquilizers, Lady Sotofa leaned over the immobile body of the merchant Agon.

"How long can you just loll around like that, you no-count?" she roared in an alien, shrieking voice. The unfortunate chap began to stir.

"I'll let you in on a little secret, Juffin," said Sotofa, beaming. "It's possible to return any person to life if you shout in his ear the same thing he was used to waking up to in childhood. As you see, the mother of this gentleman couldn't control her emotions. Just like my own mother, in fact. Do you remember my mamma, Juffin, may she rest in peace? I think she was what turned us into such good sorcerers: we had to save our skins somehow. Well, collect this dolt, boys, and clear out! You have work to do, and so do we. Life's not just for pleasure."

We loaded the gradually reviving merchant whose life we had just saved into the amobiler. I was so taken aback by what I had seen that I didn't even ask any questions.

"Well, what do you think of her?"

I had never known Juffin's voice to sound so tender.

"Oh . . . I can't even imagine what all the others are like."

"You can take it from me that the others are no match for her. Sotofa is the cream of the crop. Even Grand Magician Nuflin is scared of her. Has this shaken your faith in me, Sir Max?"

"Not at all, but she's really something."

"Sotofa hails from the same place I do. Did you catch that?" Juffin smiled. "She's my closest friend from those parts, although we see each other rarely, and mostly on official matters. About five hundred years or so ago we had a very stormy romance. The people of Kettari were tickled to death when, after the latest in a long chain of quarrels, I arrested her in the 'name of the law' and escorted her to the House on the Road. That's what the local Ministry of Perfect Public Order is called. Five hundred years ago, can you believe it? Then Sotofa got it into her head that she had to enter some Order, and she tripped off to the capital. I was devastated by her little escapade. But life proved the girl right—there was a place in the Order for her."

I stared at Juffin.

"Are you telling me this for a particular reason?"

"Naturally—you need to know why she treats me with such a lack of decorum," the chief said, winking at me. "Otherwise you might start thinking that any woman older than three hundred can wrap me around her little finger."

❀

At the House by the Bridge Melifaro dashed out to meet us.

"Juffin," he said in a mournful whisper. "I don't understand what's going on. Melamori has locked herself in my office, and she won't let me in. I think she's crying."

"Well, let her have a good cry," the boss advised him. "Why shouldn't a good person cry when times are bad? Everything will be all right, just don't try to comfort her. She'll kill you on the spot, and I won't be able to jump in and set things right. I'll be too busy. Find Lonli-Lokli. Let him drop whatever he's doing and wait for us here. And don't you go anywhere, either. Tell Melamori that in half an hour we'll be working to beat the band. She can join us if she wishes. Let's go, Max."

Without giving me time to reconsider, Juffin gripped the unfortunate merchant Agon under his arms and dragged him into his office. I shuffled after them.

"Now then, Max," the chief addressed me in a clipped, energetic tone, seating our captive in an armchair. "I hate interfering in other people's affairs, but sometimes one must. This is one of those times. Don't even think of pursuing this affair of the heart—it will only make matters worse. Lady Melamori is feeling as miserable as you are, if not more so. But she is under no illusions about what happened this morning. She knows something that you don't know. For example, she knows what happens to people who fly in the face of tradition and try to fool fate. It's not customary to speak of such things aloud, since it's common knowledge—common for everyone but you and other newcomers, that is."

"What is it, then? What does everyone know?" I wailed.

"You see, one of the lovers who ignores the ban on subsequent trysts will surely die. Which of them it will be cannot be predicted. But I'd be willing to bet that it won't be you, since . . . well, never mind. Take my word for it: you're luckier than Melamori. That's just the way it is."

"It's the first I've heard of it," I muttered. "And, excuse me, but I don't believe it. It's like some cheap mystery romance."

"For some time now your whole life has been some cheap mystery romance, as you put it. Why would I lie to you? You and I, Praise be the Magicians, didn't find each other in the Quarter of Trysts."

"That's true," I said with a crooked smile. "But I don't like any of this one bit. I thought the lady was just shy and superstitious. I had hoped I might persuade her eventually."

"You might be able to if you try. But I wouldn't advise it. 'Not my girlfriend' is much more pleasant to the ear than 'dead girlfriend,' don't you think? A solid friendship has its advantages over a flaming passion, which you will come to realize sooner or later. Okay? So case closed. Back to work."

I looked at Juffin, stupefied. He shrugged, as though giving me to understand that the laws of nature didn't depend on him.

"I trust you won't try to strangle me if I give this pathetic specimen a few drops of your precious elixir?" he asked casually.

"No, not if you give me some, too. I'm as tired as can be."

"Certainly, you sponger. Why haven't you bought yourself a bottle yet? I told you—"

"I'm economizing. Is that more than you can fathom?"

Sir Juffin Hully laughed out loud. He seemed relieved that I was behaving like my old self again. And truly, knowing that my grief was shared half and half was enough to return me to life. Something similar had happened yesterday with Captain Giatta. I came to understand that I wasn't a "spurned lover" from a mawkish novel, but simply a person compelled to accept his fate. It was painful, but much more tolerable.

米

After he had swallowed some Elixir of Kaxar, our captive began to understand what was what. When the merchant finally grasped the fact that he was no longer wearing the belt, he tried to kiss our feet, which didn't flatter us in the least.

"We'd rather you spilled the beans, on the double!" Juffin grumbled. "Who fastened that silly belly-embellishment on you in the first place?"

"His name is Xropper Moa. He's from your part of the world, sir."

"Say no more." Juffin turned to me. "The one and only Grand Magician of the Order of the Barking Fish. The Order was a lightweight outfit, but the fellow always had an uncommonly vivid imagination."

Juffin scrutinized the merchant again. The merchant shuddered under his gaze. I can understand why: Juffin's range of meaningful stares includes some that are absolutely terrifying.

"What did he want from you, Agon?"

"He wanted to steal something, some 'Great Talisman.' I myself am not sure what it is. My task was a petty one—to palm the belt off on certain people. Then Xropper sent them a call or met them personally, and told them what was required of them."

"Excellent. On whom did you foist the belt during the present journey?"

"No one. This time Xropper came with me himself. He seemed to have realized that without his participation it wasn't going to work. I did everything he told me to do, but . . . my single greatest success was the boy Apatti. He procured only a useless copy, though. After this fiasco Xropper fumed for a whole year, and then thought for another one. Finally we set out for Echo again, and he promised that it was our last voyage. After that he would set me free."

"And you would conveniently be able to carry on your business, isn't that right?" Juffin asked, narrowing his eyes. "Those belted lads make very good thieves, don't they? They do everything you tell them to, and they never give away their boss. You liked that—admit it, Agon! How much wealth from the capital were you able to cart off to sunny Tashera?"

"I didn't—"

"Hold your tongue, Agon! I've studied all the unsolved cases of apartment burglary that plague the conscience of our municipal police. The dates of these memorable events correspond fairly exactly to the dates when your *Old Maid* was anchored in our docks. Shall I go on?"

The bearded fellow stared at the floor in embarrassment. Sir Juffin smirked.

"I see that won't be necessary. Now then, you tell me where your friend Xropper is. And if I can find him with your assistance, consider yourself lucky. You'll pay your captain; I'll send you away from the Unified Kingdom with no right of return—end of story! Your exploits don't fall under my jurisdiction, after all. But if I don't find him—well, I'll just buckle this marvelous little trinket on you again, this amazing belt fashioned by Magician Xropper Moa himself. Are you feeling lucky, merchant?"

"I don't know where Xropper is!" Mr. Agon stammered in panic. "He didn't tell me anything!"

"Commendable precautions," Juffin agreed affably. "It would be strange if he reported to you. But you still have one more chance. Imagine that I would be satisfied if you told me where he was yesterday. I ask for no more than that."

"Yesterday . . . Yesterday, we met at the *Golden Rams* after dinner, but I don't know—"

"It's good that it was after dinner and not for it," Juffin said, screwing up his face with disdain. "A vulgarly expensive dive with terrible food. Just the ticket for a rogue like Xropper! Fine, Sir Max. Pack up our guest. We'll take him with us. He might come in handy."

I stared at the chief in perplexity until it dawned on me what he wanted.

"Sure!"

With one deft movement, the merchant occupied his usual place between the thumb and the forefinger of my left hand. It began to seem that Mr. Agon and I would be together forever.

※

Melifaro peeked into the office.

"Everyone's assembled, Juffin. You shouldn't work so hard, Mr. Bad Dream. You don't look yourself at all!"

"I'm longing for fresh horse manure," I informed him gloomily. "They call it nostalgia."

"Ah, well, why didn't you say so? I thought you had just grown tired of killing people. It's no surprise—Lonli-Lokli himself gets tired of it sometimes."

"Any job grows wearisome," I said didactically.

I left the Hall of Common Labor like I was jumping headfirst off a skyscraper: fast, determined, and with no regard for the consequences.

"Let's go, boys," Juffin's voice rang out cheerily behind me. "Destination: the *Golden Rams*. Lady Melamori, remember: yours is the first move."

"With pleasure," Melamori nodded. She tried not to look at me, which was probably wise. "Attagirl! Way to go!" Sir Nulli Karif would no doubt have said.

"It's a formidable adversary: Magician Xropper Moa. Heard of him?"

"Ah, from the Order of the Barking Fish? Formidable my foot!" Melamori twitched her shoulders haughtily.

"Certain Orders of Magic that had no pretensions to supremacy had very dangerous secrets," said Sir Lonli-Lokli, shaking his head in disapproval. "You should keep this in mind, Lady Melamori, in the interests of your own safety. And the interests of the case, naturally."

"Do you understand? Don't put on airs," Juffin said. "Let's be off. Sir Max, get behind the levers. Your folly will serve us well now. Every minute counts. This is your one chance to bury the Minor Secret Investigative Force nearly in its entirety. What Kofa and Lookfi will do without us I find hard to imagine."

"What do you mean? Sir Kofa will keep on eating, and Lookfi never notices anything anyway," Melifaro snorted. "And no one will shed a tear over our mangled bodies."

"I think a catastrophe like that would be a serious loss for the Unified Kingdom," Lonli-Lokli said in an imposing voice.

Melifaro snickered with quiet mirth, but refrained from his usual guffaw.

"No time to bemoan your fate; here we arrive at our destination," I said with a grin. "Some heroes you are! Jump out. Forward, march, Lady Melamori! Show all those Magicians from the *Grunting*

Kitty-Cat what a pound of Booboota's crap is worth in a bad harvest year!"

My outburst surprised even me. Juffin and Melifaro exchanged glances and exploded in laughter. Even the glum Melamori smiled. Sir Shurf Lonli-Lokli looked at us like we were all unruly but beloved children, and got out of the amobiler.

Then the Master of Pursuit took off her elegant boots, entered the tavern, and circled through the large hall.

"He's been here! Magicians are always easier to track down, Sir Juffin," she shouted. "Here is his trail. He's somewhere nearby, I swear by your nose!"

"Swear by your own, girl. I need mine."

Sir Juffin Hully looked like a fisherman who had caught a twenty-pound trout.

Melamori left the tavern, then set off by herself, hot on the trail. We piled back into the amobiler to await her summons. After half an hour, I felt Juffin's hand on my shoulder. He said:

"The Street of Forgotten Poets, Max. You know where it is?"

"It's the first I've heard of it. Is there a street with such name?"

"No time to wonder—just press on the levers and let's get going. Drive toward Jafax, it's in that direction. It's a small alleyway. I'll show you where to turn."

The Street of Forgotten Poets lived up to its name. It was so deserted that tufts of pale white grass grew between the intricate designs of the paving stones.

There was only one house on this street—but what a house! It was a veritable castle, surrounded by a high wall that still bore the indistinct traces of ancient inscriptions. Beside the gate, tapping her bare little foot impatiently, stood Melamori. She displayed a reckless, nervous joy that I found somewhat unsettling.

"He's here," the Master of Pursuit said through clenched teeth. "When he sensed me near, the little stinker first grew sad, and then started losing the remaining scraps of his pathetic mind. It's too bad you made me wait for you, Juffin! I could have already been through with him. Well, I'm off. Follow me!"

"Not so fast!" Juffin barked. "Lonli-Lokli will go in first. That's his job. It would be far better for you just to stay behind in the amobiler. Where is your praiseworthy caution, lady?"

"What do you mean, stay behind in the amobiler?" Melamori erupted in fury. "I'm the one who tracked him down. I should go in first."

She spoke with a vituperative intensity I had never before witnessed in her. Even during our heated row the night before, the gleam in her eyes hadn't filled me with such alarm.

What's all the rush about, my dear? I wondered to myself. Then I understood.

"That's not Melamori talking! Or, rather, it's Melamori, but she doesn't know what she's saying. He's 'caught' her, too, Juffin! Melamori sniffed out Xropper, but he . . . well, he caught hold of his end of the trail she was following, when he realized what was going on. I don't know how else to put it. The fellow thinks that he's only being followed by one person, and he's in a hurry to do battle. It's a wonder she even waited for us at all."

Sir Juffin squeezed my shoulder hard.

"That's exactly right, only I— very well. Is that clear, Melamori? Are you going to let the Magician of some paltry third-rate Order make your decisions for you? Now get yourself over here, on the double!"

Melamori stared at us in astonishment and shook her head.

"I can't, sir . . . I really can't. And I'm sure we have to go into that house before he gets away. Vampires under your blankets, though, you're right! These aren't really my thoughts. And I didn't want to wait for you. If you had come just a minute later . . ."

Meanwhile, Lonli-Lokli had managed to get out of the amobiler and pick up Melamori, lifting her high in the air without any visible effort.

"There we go! Do you feel better now, lady?" he asked, seating the bewildered Melamori on his shoulders. "Why don't we study the aforementioned phenomenon a bit later, gentlemen?" suggested this remarkable individual in his most imperturbable manner.

We exchanged glances.

"Indeed, why not?" Juffin asked, and Melifaro and I peeled our backsides from the seat of the amobiler in seconds flat. The chief was right behind us.

"Well, do you agree to wait for us in the amobiler, girl?"

"Right now I'll agree to anything." Melamori clutched at Lonli-

Lokli's neck like a monkey. "I'm terrified of heights! But maybe you'd let me go in with you, after all? I'll stay in the back, honest! I don't want to have to sit in the amobiler."

"All right, I suppose you may come. Only put your shoes on. You won't have to do any more tracking for the time being, and you're bound to cut yourself on a shard of glass," Juffin said. "Do you know whose house this is? This is where old Sir Gartom Xattel Min lives. About a hundred years ago, terrible stories went the rounds about the disorderliness of his home, until everyone finally grew bored with the topic. Sir Shurf, let the lady down. Then grab Max and get a move on! The three of us will follow you."

Sir Shurf looked me up and down, and then picked me up with the gallantry of a professional stevedore.

"Shurf, I can walk!" I shouted. "Juffin didn't mean it like that."

"Is that true, Sir Juffin?" Lonli-Lokli asked politely.

"What? Oh, Sinning Magicians! You're driving me out of my wits, boys! Of course I only meant for you to go in together. What kind of an outfit is this? Secret Investigative Force, terror of the universe, my foot! It's a circus, that's what it is!"

Lonli-Lokli and I finally entered the yard, and then the dark, dank-smelling hall of the enormous deserted building.

"How are we going to find this fellow, Shurf?" I asked in panic. "This house is as big as a town!"

"Yes, the house is rather sizable," Lonli-Lokli agreed. "Don't worry, Max. At this distance, even I'm able to pick up his scent. I have quite a bit of experience in this area: before Lady Melamori joined our force, we had to get along without a Master of Pursuit. It's a very rare talent, and finding the right person for the job is difficult. Our previous Master of Pursuit, Sir Totoxatta Shlomm, met his end in a situation very much like this one. Only his adversary was much more formidable—he had acquired a glove like my own."

I gave a low whistle.

"Sir Totoxatta was an unimpeachable Master of Pursuit, though not one distinguished by his caution. You know Max, it's still very painful for me. We began working in the Secret Investigative Force on the same day, and we became fast friends—go left and sidestep this shard of glass, no boot could withstand a specimen like that—

that's why I warned Lady Melamori that all the Orders, even those that are not too powerful, have their dangerous little secrets. She was in serious danger. Get back! Quick!"

Lonli-Lokli's white looxi flitted through the darkness like an eccentric ghost. His shining right hand, which brought not death, but petrifaction, illuminated a frightened elderly face for one split second. Then everything went dark again.

I inched closer and found myself staring at a wrinkled, swarthy old man in a tattered looxi. His body lay immobile on the floor in an unnatural pose. His hands were raised above his head, and his legs were bent at the knee. It could have been the pose of a toppled statue, but not of a living being, conscious or otherwise.

"Is this the Grand Magician?"

Lonli-Lokli shook his head.

"No, Max. This is the master of the house, Sir Gartom Xattel Min. See, he's wearing the same kind of belt as the others. That was very shrewd of Xropper to have a complete stranger lie in ambush. When a Master of Pursuit is close to her prey, she has no awareness of anything else: that's how they are. That's why he wanted Lady Melamori to enter alone. I consider that to be justified only when tracking down simple civilians, but even then it's undesirable to my mind."

"But what could this old man have done to her?" I asked, confused. "Surely he's no great warrior."

"Never judge too hastily, my friend. Once a person has learned to shoot from the Slingshot of Babum, he never loses the skill. And a shot to the head is capable of killing anyone, even the Master of Pursuit. Do you see what he has in his hands?"

My head was spinning. Melamori could have died by some primitive slingshot in the junky recesses of a dank old corridor—this was too much! Never mind my ill-used broken heart. Let her do what she wishes. Let her even get married, like countless other old girlfriends of mine; but let her stay alive! I don't really know whether a good friendship has advantages over a flaming passion, as Juffin claims it does, but it has a decided advantage over death!

"Let's hurry and get out of here, Shurf," I said hoarsely. "We'll get rid of this Xropper character, and then scram."

Lonli-Lokli had no objections, and we went on our way, wandering through littered corridors and steep staircases until we found ourselves in a basement room.

"Stay behind me, Max," Lonli-Lokli said in a tone that brooked no argument. "Today hasn't been the most uneventful day, and there may be more excitement in store. He's somewhere nearby, so . . ."

The lustrous white shimmer of Lonli-Lokli's death-dealing hands began cutting intricate designs in the darkness.

"What are you doing, Shurf?"

"It's better to force your victim out than to seek him yourself. Do you really think that killing is my only accomplishment, Max? My profession requires a much wider spectrum of skills." He paused and squinted into the darkness. "See? There he is. This spell is foolproof—with people, that is. *Yowzer shazam, bim bam!*"

His final exclamation was accompanied by a bright explosion, and I realized that Sir Xropper Moa, the Grand Magician of the Order of the Barking Fish, had left the world of the living. At that moment, his name assumed an honorable place on the list of the latest accomplishments of the Secret Investigative Force.

"There you have it," Lonli-Lokli said, pulling on his gloves. "Finishing a case is always easier than starting it. Have you ever thought about that, Max?"

"No, but I promise I will."

"As always, Sir Shurf has been equal to the task!" Juffin's voice rang out from behind us. "I apologize, but we were detained, boys. I used the opportunity to lecture Lady Melamori over the body of the slovenly old codger."

"I told you we would miss the most interesting part," Melamori protested in an injured tone. She was still shrouded in darkness. "Everyone's already been killed. How disappointing!"

"The most interesting part, you say?" Juffin's eyebrows shot up. "Gentlemen, do you know what's in this basement?"

"Of course we do," Melifaro's face appeared in the doorway. "Somewhere here is the secret entrance to Jafax. The eldest son of Sir Gartom Xattel Min is one of the most prominent junior Magicians of the Order of the Seven-Leaf Clover, hallowed be its name, and greetings to your Uncle Kima, Melamori. Is that what you meant, Sir?"

"It's impossible to surprise any of you," Juffin said, pursing his lips in mock displeasure. "My congratulations, boys. Today Grand Magician Nuflin will be able to sleep peacefully, which doesn't happen every day. It's too bad, of course, that you had to kill Xropper, Sir Shurf."

"But you know yourself, Sir Juffin, that this is the lot of every

Mutinous Magician who has made three attempts at murder, whatever the outcome."

"Don't take it amiss, Sir Shurf. Your actions were perfectly correct. I just wanted to know what this madman intended to do with the Shining Seven-Leaf Clover. As far as I know, this object is of no benefit to anyone else in the World but Magician Nuflin. Perhaps I'm wrong?"

The tremor of uncertainty in Sir Juffin Hully's voice lent a certain charm to the end of the case. Besides, there was still trouble in store for us.

We returned to the House by the Bridge and put old Xattel Min in a a detention cell for those awaiting trial. It was decided not to revive this poor apology for a marksman while he was still wearing the belt. Why borrow trouble?

"Go home to rest, boys," Juffin ordered. "Everyone but . . . How about you, Max? Are you ready to roll?"

"I'll say!" I admitted readily.

I was even afraid to think of going home. Armstrong and Ella were waiting for me; but so were sweet memories that were better kept at bay.

I looked at Melamori, who was intent on studying the floor under her own feet. The prospect of going home to rest clearly did not fill her with enthusiasm, either. She was as unhappy as I was, proof that I wasn't alone in having found at last what I had sought for so long. Sooner or later she would have to try to make her life bearable—and the sooner the better. So I did the first thing that occurred to me: I sent a call to Melifaro.

If you don't walk her home, friend, you're a miserable louse!

Melifaro nearly fell off his chair in astonishment, then looked at me quizzically.

Do what you're told!

What's gotten into you, Mr. Bad Dream? I always thought you dwellers of the endless plains were as jealous as—

But I'm a crazy dweller of the endless plains, so . . . hold your tongue, Ninth Volume of the Encyclopedia! Over and out!

I saved face by running off and closing myself in the office that Juffin and I shared. Since I really am "as jealous as . . . ," I do wonder "what," or "whom"?

Sir Juffin Hully joined me after a few minutes.

"Are you sure you can hold out one more night, Max? I can probably do without your help. Only you'll have to release your bosom buddy. Can you get along without him?"

"Bosom buddy? Oh, Sinning Magicians, Juffin! I completely forgot!"

Now this was amusing: I had grown so used to carrying around Agon the miniscule merchant that I had ceased paying any attention to him at all. "Do you need him now?"

"Not really. You can wait a while if you're not in any hurry. Lady Sotofa promised to arrive in a few hours. I need Agon to send a call to his captives, all those belted fools. They'll come to the House by the Bridge and Lady Sotofa will undress them. That's nothing to her, as you know."

"In that case, I'm not going anywhere. Lady Sotofa is a queen among women! Don't you think so?"

Sir Juffin sniffed.

"That she may very well be. Well now, Sir Max. We'll have some dinner, and you can set your companion free a bit later. You aren't very anxious to go home, am I right?"

"You know I don't want to," I said.

"Excellent. That means that I won't be the only one who's dead tired at daybreak. But you know what? Your favorite Elixir of Kaxar can help you for another two or three days. Four if you're lucky." Juffin looked at me closely. "Has it ever occurred to you that it would be easier and much more practical to pack up and move, rather than shuffling around Headquarters with your eyes glued shut?"

"No, it didn't. I'm an idiot, aren't I?"

"Yes, now and then," Juffin said smiling. "So do you want to stay in the Old City or move to the New? Then you'd have the chance to demonstrate your chief talent every day—driving the amobiler into the ground."

"If you need to change things, you should do it all at once. I'll move to the New City! Somewhere there a sweet lady has opened a tavern. At one point I had the sense to give her the same advice I just heard from you. Funny, isn't it, how much harder it is to take advice yourself than to give it to other people? By the way, you're slandering me. I've never driven the amobiler so hard it broke down."

"Not yet, anyway. Here, take the key, and remember this address:

18 Street of Yellow Stones. I tried to find something awful, so you'd think it was cozy."

"I have a feeling there won't be fewer than ten bathing pools."

"Only eight. Of course, there are sometimes fewer, even in the most elegant houses in the New City; but you see, I have principles I find hard to ignore."

"For certain things you should just say thank you immediately, so that you won't be kicking yourself later, as Grand Magician Nuflin said." I had just realized the magnitude of what my boss had done for me. "Juffin, you're saving me! Do you want me to kiss the hem of your looxi? I see you don't . . . But when did you have time to arrange all of this?"

"What do you think Silent Speech is for? And the junior officials of the Ministry of Perfect Public Order? Better to eat now than spoil your appetite worrying about trifles. One of the messengers can move your menagerie and other household effects. How about good old Urf? He's already used to helping you with your household affairs."

"You're so wise, and I'm a dolt. You know, I'll probably keep the house on the Street of Old Coins. I have a pillow fastened somewhere there, a plug in the Chink between Worlds."

Juffin began to laugh. That's not the right word for it, though. He let out a guffaw that came from the bottom of his soul, infectious and long. I stared at him blankly. Whence this merriment?

"What a bunch of baloney, Max! Maba was just joking with you. He loves practical jokes. You didn't have to fasten that pillow to anything. You can take it with you wherever you wish, and continue your activities with the same amount of success. The secret isn't under the pillow. It's not even inside the pillow . . . Oh, Max, you're so funny, you really are!"

"So he was pulling my leg?" I felt a bit embarrassed. Still, I somewhat liked Sir Maba's joke.

"It's all right, Juffin. Let there be one more deserted house on the Street of Old Coins. Who knows, maybe I'll want to return there someday."

"Time will tell. Now then, release your captive."

❧

Agon the Merchant, completely discombobulated by his metamorphosis, immediately sent a call to all his comrades in misfortune, after which he went into the detention cell.

I rested my head on the table, exhausted. After all, we were all comrades in misfortune: the fashionable dandies in their gleaming belts, the chefs of the capital sporting the Earring of Oxalla, Melamori and I, and other visitors to the Quarter of Trysts, and the countless dwellers of all Worlds, bound hand and foot by spells, obligations, and destiny.

"It's not so bad, dear," Lady Sotofa's voice jerked me out of my dark whirlpool of homegrown philosophy into the bright world, where fresh kamra and a bracing nightshift awaited me.

I smiled. "As soon as I meet a good person, I find out that her favorite hobby is reading my mind."

"Why would I need to do that, Max?" The old lady sniffed. "It's just that you looked wise and mournful, like all boys when they're thinking about their silly problems. Well, where are your poor devils hiding?"

"You arrived nearly an hour before you promised," Juffin exclaimed. "So don't be too hard on us. You'll have to wait."

"Oh, what luxury! I can't remember the last time I had a whole hour to do nothing."

"Don't count on having a whole hour. They could start arriving any minute now. What did I tell you? Here comes the first one."

The first one, by the way, was the same fellow that Kofa and I noticed in the *Irrashi Inn* at the very beginning of this story. Such coincidences do happen.

❈

Lady Sotofa's hands worked wonders. Her lips weren't still for a second. She managed to sympathize with every patient, and to joke with us at their expense simultaneously. The recent hostages of the belts, now free, informed her where they could be found in the upcoming dozen days. Kurush grumbled at the large amount of tedious work, but managed to process all the information. With a memory like his, he couldn't forget anything if he tried.

"They haven't run afoul of the law, have they?" I wanted to know.

"No, of course not," Juffin assured me. "How can you condemn someone who had no choice? The only candidate for unpleasant repercussions is your friend Agon, since he took some of the illegal actions on his own initiative. But let him set sail for his sunny Tashera. I don't ever want to see his backside again. Ah, yes, Sotofa! We have one more handsome specimen for you. You'll like him, I promise. Let's go."

Soon Xattel Min, the old Slingshot King, appeared in the doorway of the office, his eyes blinking in confusion. Seeing him now didn't awaken any negative emotions in me. In a few minutes, the old man was dismissed, after being provided with a long list of qualified repairmen and housecleaners, though there wasn't much hope he would make use of it.

I greeted the dawn in my new house. Ella and Armstrong pattered about through all six rooms, meowing in delight. Sir Juffin Hully had strange notions about a "modest dwelling." After a perfunctory glance around the house, I collapsed on the new bed and fell fast asleep. This time I didn't dream about Melamori. As before, I had no hand in it. That part of my life had simply receded forever into the past, it seemed.

At sundown, I was awakened by a call from Sir Kofa.

I'm waiting for you at the Golden Rams, *Max. Do you know how to get here?*

But Juffin said the food there was terrible! I objected sleepily.

Of course he'd say that. Juffin's the biggest snob in Echo. He's like all provincials who've lived here a hundred years. I promise you'll like it. Besides, your debtor is with me.

Oh, Kofa, let me wake up first. What debtor?

Captain Giatta. You saved more than just his life, and the fellow is determined to repay the kindness. To tell you the truth, Max, I don't envy you. The captain has an extremely serious expression on his face, and his intentions are every bit as serious. He's ready to wait three hundred years, if he has to, to return the favor you've done for him. In other words, the sooner you come, the more food you'll get. Over and out.

CHAPTER SEVEN

JOURNEY TO KETTARI

"**G**OOD DAY, MR. BAD DREAM," MELIFARO'S SMILE SEEMED TO spill beyond the edges of his face.

"Bad night, Mr. Daydream."

For a fraction of a second, he stared at me in perplexity, then nodded with relief.

"OK, I get it. That's a good one, I must say. Did you think it up yourself?"

"No, Lonli-Lokli did."

"Ha!"

We were sitting in the *Glutton Bunba*. My colleague was dining after a hard day of work, and I was having breakfast before a no less hard night of work. Most likely I would sit in my own office, inhaling the dizzying smells of spring invading the office through open windows, and do the breathing exercises Lonli-Lokli had recently taught me. Our humorless Sir Shurf really was the preeminent expert in this department.

The onset of spring is not the best season for mending broken hearts, which is why recently I hadn't been the happiest of men. If Melifaro had known me longer than half a year, he would immediately have recognized the biting tone of my ordinarily inoffensive jokes. Good golly, could that be true? Not even half a year had passed since I turned up in Echo. I shook my head in disbelief.

"What's wrong?" Melifaro asked.

"I just thought about how long I've been hanging out here in Echo. Not that long at all."

"Yet you've already destroyed so many lives," Melifaro said by way of praise, "and I'm sure you're not going to stop there."

"True that," I said. "You just wait and see."

"Juffin asked me to tell you not to worry about chewing too carefully," Melifaro said with a hearty laugh. His voice expressed a tinge of envy.

"He must want to try out a new enema on me, but his hopes are all in vain. My stomach can digest pieces that haven't been chewed at all," I said. But my heart skipped a beat. If Sir Juffin was planning to burden me with some insoluble problem—gosh, that was just what I needed!

"He's getting ready to reveal a secret to you. Huge letters reading 'Caution! Dangerous Information Enclosed' are printed across his forehead. I suspect you'll have to gnaw the remains of several dozen Mutinous Magicians to wrest the great secret of a Universal Laxative from their criminal hands. Alas, I fear that my whole life I am destined to remain an ignorant witness of your malevolent intrigues."

"I'm leaving, then. Malevolent intrigues just sound too tempting."

"You're not even going to finish your meal? You'll starve to death while you're on duty, and I'll be dancing a jig on a little heap of ashes that remains of you."

"I'm not going to finish the meal, nor am I paying for it," I replied, wrapping myself in my warm Mantle of Death. "I'm so fearsome that it doesn't matter what I do."

With that, I strode boldly to the door. Our repartee could go on forever, and I was spurred on by a tantalizing mixture of curiosity and hope.

§

When I arrived Sir Juffin Hully was just sniffing the contents of a jug of kamra. Then he nodded in satisfaction and filled his mug.

"For the sake of experiment I compromised my principles. This kamra is not from the *Glutton*, Max. I ordered it from the *Fatman at the Bend*. I thought I'd just see how the little wife of our Lookfi earns her bread and butter. It's not bad, not bad at all. Have you ever been there?"

I shook my head.

"That's very bad of you. I'd go so far as to say it's unpatriotic. Since the proprietress of the *Fatman* is the wife of our colleague, we have an obligation. But do sit down, Max. You could have finished your meal back there. That's very unlike you, choosing work over food."

"You aren't the only one who's surprised," I said. "You seem to know everything about me that there is to know, Juffin, even what

I've left behind on my plate. It boggles the mind."

"Not everything. Just the most important things. I need to have a serious talk with you, Max. Very serious, indeed. I want to burden you with a problem."

"Finally!" I said ecstatically, and reached into my pocket for the little parcel with cigarette butts that I still managed to salvage from the Chink between Worlds. In other words, from under my own pillow.

The teaching method of Sir Maba Kalox breaks down like this: many little treats, and no whip. All carrots, no stick. It works like a charm, every time. Tormented by the disgusting taste of the local tobacco, I spent days filching cigarettes from the inaccessible reaches of my own homeland, not bothering to struggle to understand how I was able to pull it off.

"I've been saving this problem for you from the start," Juffin began. "Only it seemed to me that we'd need to wait several years, to give you time to get used to our World. But it turns out that you're already used to it. There's nothing to wait for."

"I was just thinking about that myself," I said, nodding. "It just occurred to me that Melifaro and I have known each other only half a year. And you brought him home only a few dozen days after I—"

"You can say that again," Juffin said. "I myself can hardly believe the speed of your progress, even though I knew what a clever fellow I was dealing with. I should have been prepared. In any case, I'm certain you'll manage with this, and now is just the right time. A short journey to the end of the world—that's just what you need, wouldn't you say?"

"Juffin, don't hedge! You've whetted my curiosity to such a degree already that my head is spinning."

"I'm not hedging. I'm just waiting for you to make yourself comfortable, light up a smoking stick, and perk up your ears. It's a long story, Max, and very convoluted."

"A hole in the heavens above you, sir! I adore long, convoluted stories."

And Juffin began.

"There's something going on in my home city of Kettari, Max."

I gaped at him. I had anticipated any beginning to the story except this one, that's for sure! Juffin smiled an understanding smile.

"Your knowledge of the geography of the Unified Kingdom is still rather superficial."

"Please don't spare my self-confidence, sir. I never take it with me when I leave home. I know nothing about your geography. It's a fact."

Juffin nodded and began unfolding a map. I stared at it, enchanted. Local cartography is its own branch of art. My chief tapped the neatly clipped nail of his narrow finger on a small, bright dot nestled in the west among finely delineated mountain peaks.

"That's Kettari, Max. And Echo is here. See it?" His finger came to rest on the miniature depiction of a town in the lower part of the map. "Not too far, but not so very near, either. Do you know what this brightly colored circle means?"

I shook my head.

"It means that the main occupation of the city's inhabitants is arts and crafts of various kinds. From time immemorial Kettari has been known for its carpets. Even when I was a boy they were inimitable, though there used to be many more fantastic things in the World than there are now. No one makes such fine rugs anywhere else. Naturally, the Capital is eager to do trade with Kettari: they like luxury here."

"That enormous carpet the color of dark amber lying in your drawing room is from there. Am I right?"

"Right you are. How did you guess?"

"Because . . . because on the edges there is an embroidered inscription 'Kettari Honey.'" I burst out laughing. Juffin did, too, of course.

"A vampire in your mouth, son! Are you going to listen or not?"

"Yes, yes." I poured myself some more kamra and assumed an expression of intense concentration.

"Several dozen years ago in Echo it became customary to travel to Kettari in large caravans. It was quite convenient, so no one was surprised by the new practice. Even early on, I noticed that a native of Kettari always accompanied every caravan. I figured that if my countrymen wanted to earn a little money, what right did I have to prevent them? Of course, at first not everyone who wanted to go shopping was willing to go in a large group and pay for the services of a guide. There were a few curious incidents: for example, some of the blockheads from the Capital couldn't find the road to Kettari. They returned home distraught and spread around some nonsense about Kettari being destroyed. That was no surprise, since idiots abound everywhere, and a person will invent all kinds of justifications for his stupidity. But all these stories convinced our merchants that a small fee for the Master Caravan Leaders, as my countrymen like to call themselves, is the lesser of evils. No one wants to lose time, to suffer setbacks, and to become a laughing stock, do they?"

"You say that grownup people with all their wits about them couldn't find the road to your Kettari?" I asked, amazed. "Are the roads in the Unified Kingdom really so bad?"

"Good question, Max. A lot of people were amazed about this. How was it possible to get lost? The County Shimara is not the most outlying province, and Kettari is hardly what you might call the sticks. The caravan leaders claimed that most of the towns around Kettari were destroyed during the Troubled Times. Since life in these population centers depended solely on the needs of provincial Residences of the Orders around which they were built, there was no sense in reviving them.

"They mentioned that the roads had been destroyed, as well. That already seemed a bit strange. I never heard of anyone destroying roads, even during the Troubled Times. Why should it have happened now? There was a curious incident involving one of the Magicians of the Order of the Secret Grass—a close relative of our own Melifaro, by the way. When he was leaving the Capital, he anticipated that he would be pursued, and he caused the road along which they were traveling to veer up skyward. It must have been a strange spectacle— you're traveling along a road and suddenly you realize you're moving up into the clouds! I even proposed to Magician Nuflin that he leave everything that way; but in those days he wasn't very compliant. They brought the road back to earth almost immediately; and that happened not in County Shimara, but right here outside of Echo. So I was very skeptical about the stories of ruined roads.

"Then I started thinking: if the local inhabitants are saying it, they must know what they're talking about. And what difference does it make to me anyway? In short, the guides all believed it, and they believe it to this day. And why not? Our merchants return from Kettari loaded down with carpets. They also complain about the terrible condition of the roads. Kettarian carpets, by the way, become finer all the time, and the travelers are all unanimous in praising the beauties and riches of my native city. I don't remember Kettari being a flourishing cultural center, although everything changes, and it's a good thing when it's for the better."

"And you, Juffin, how long has it been since you were there?"

"A very long time. I seriously doubt whether I'll ever go back. I have neither family nor friends in Kettari anymore, so I have neither ties of tenderness, nor obligation to this dot on the map, and I am not at all sentimental. In this I resemble you, by the way. But that's not really why I don't want to go there. I feel there's some sort of inner ban on my returning there. I know that not only do I not need to go to Kettari—I shouldn't. And my experiences witness to the fact that an inner ban is the only authentic kind. Are you familiar with that feeling, Max?"

I fiddled with the cigarette butt pensively.

"I think I know what you mean. A genuine inner ban is a thing of great power. Only I often can't distinguish it from the other inner stuff: self-defeating, paranoid thoughts, superstitions, habits of mind."

"Don't fret about that. Emotional clarity is something that comes with time. Now then, back to the matter at hand. A few years ago, a bizarre chain of events began to unfold. In this very office, two fugitives from the law showed up. One of them kept shouting maniacally that they wanted to turn themselves in to Mr. Venerable Head personally. The other didn't say a word, just stared at the same spot the entire time. They had been sent to the City Police Department for some trifling offense and had been able to escape the guards, which doesn't surprise me in the least. Considering the chaos that reigns in Boboota's office, I'd say it was predictable, if not inevitable.

"One of the fugitives, someone by the name of Motti Fara, turned out to be a countryman of mine. Like me, he hadn't been in Kettari for quite some time—since the beginning of the Code Epoch, at least. When he got into trouble, he decided that his native city wasn't the worst place to hide from the police of the Capital. So the two of them set off for Kettari. And got lost."

"And that seemed too unlikely to you, right?" I asked, and added knowingly, "Maybe your countryman just had something wrong with his head? That happens sometimes, you know."

"My countryman did not strike me as an idiot," Juffin said drily. "In my humble opinion, Mr. Fara had quite enough intelligence to make it back to his hometown. But nothing came of it. After that failure, the fugitives returned to the Capital. Instead of hiding, they went straight to the House by the Bridge, which in itself is quite improbable, and started begging for a meeting with me. My curiosity did not allow me to ignore their request—people don't often commit such foolhardy acts."

"Oh, yes they do," I murmured. "Even worse ones."

"You're right, for the most part," Juffin smiled. "But for us, natives of Kettari, pragmatism is in the blood. Pay attention now; the best is yet to come. Don't let your mind wander."

"I'm sorry, Juffin. I don't seem to be very cheerful, today."

"That's an understatement, if I've ever heard one. You've been so lacking in spirits lately that it's nauseating just to look at you!" the chief said with a sigh.

Then he got up from his chair, came up to me, and tugged at my ear. It made me feel so awkward that I began to laugh nervously. When I stopped laughing, I realized with amazement that my mood really had noticeably improved. Even my broken heart felt like it had been reassembled.

"You deserve a break," Juffin said. I felt his heavy hand on my shoulder. "It's my little gift to you. To be honest, everything that is happening to you, you'll have to come to terms with yourself, without anyone else's help. But one can stray from any rule—if not too long, or too far. All the more since I need all your attention right now, not pathetic little shreds of it. Right-o?"

I nodded silently, delighting in the absence of the familiar gnawing pain in my chest, the trusty companion of every loss I ever experienced. Juffin went back to his chair and continued his story.

"My countryman seemed to be mortally afraid. He swore that Kettari had disappeared. Or, rather, that it lay in ruins. His companion was in a twilight state of consciousness, and the stench of madness hung about him like the smell of sweat on a farmer. The poor thing should have been sent to a Refuge for the Mad, not to prison. He couldn't even say his own name, but mumbled incoherently. However, Motti Fara seemed to be a very sensible gentleman, however. He announced that the two years in Nunda Prison that he had been sentenced to were nothing compared to the disappearance of our native city. Then this true patriot of Kettari did this," (here, Juffin tapped the tip of his nose with the index finger of his right hand) "and asked that, as one countryman to another, I not extend his sentence for running away.

"That's our favorite Kettarian gesture, Max. It means that two good people can always come to an understanding. I was so moved I was ready to let him off altogether. Unfortunately, Booboota's boys already knew that the sly fellow had found his way under my wing. Now that's something I understand: old fashioned patriotism!"

I couldn't suppress a smile, so loaded with irony was the chief's remark.

"To continue, Max. A few days later, another caravan arrived, loaded with carpets from Kettari. Here were a few dozen reliable witnesses from the flourishing town. I could take comfort in the knowledge that my fugitives had simply gotten lost, after all. Yet a nagging voice inside me kept insisting that it wasn't all as straightforward as that; and if I lose sleep over a problem for more than one night, it's a sure sign that something smells fishy. When all is well in the World, I sleep soundly. That's just the way I'm made. You're the same way, if I'm not mistaken."

"Me, sir? Why my rest depends on more down-to-earth matters. If I don't forget to go to the bathroom before I go to bed, I sleep like the dead. If I forget, I toss and turn, and I'm tormented by gloomy premonitions about the imminent demise of the Universe. My constitution is very primitively designed, didn't you know?"

Juffin grinned and poured me some kamra.

"To add to my own suspicions, my countryman wrote me letters nearly every day. I can still see that seal of the Nunda Royal Prison of Hard Labor in my mind's eye. I even had to create a special box for his correspondence so it wouldn't get mixed up with the other papers. The content of the letters was not distinguished by its variety. Here, take a look at one of them. It is paper, of course. Prisoners aren't allowed to use self-inscribing tablets. But you're used to paper, aren't you?"

Juffin opened a small box, extracted a little square of thick paper from it, and handed it to me. With a voyeuristic thrill, I started reading the crabbed handwriting of this missive meant for someone else:

> Sir Venerable Head, I'm afraid that all the same you didn't believe me. But Kettari true enough is no more. There is just an empty place, a pile of ancient ruins. I could not have gotten lost. I know every stone for miles around. I remember the seven Vaxari trees by the city gates. They're still there. But the gates are gone! There's just a bunch of stones that still bear the remains of the carving of old Kvavi Ulon. And behind them, just dusty rubble.

I handed the letter back to Juffin, who turned it over in his hands a few times and then placed it in the box again.

"Then he died, this unlucky fellow. It was more than a year ago now. Here's his last letter. It's different from the others. Another law of nature: the farther you go, the more interesting things become. Take a look, Max."

I took the next folded paper square from him, and stumbling over fragments of the small, unfamiliar handwriting, began to read:

> Sir Venerable Head, I have once again decided to take pen in hand and take up your time. I hope they are passing my letters along to you. Last

night I couldn't sleep. I kept thinking about the ruins that greeted me from behind the tops of those trees. And I remembered how Zaxo and I wandered around in those ruins for a long time. Probably that was when he lost his senses. As for me I just lost my memory. You see up until now I was sure that we had just left right away, and I couldn't understand why Zaxo lost his mind. He isn't from Kettari, so if someone was going to go off his head, it should have been me!

But last night I remembered that we went into the destroyed city, and I even found the ruins of my old home. But Zaxo said that I shouldn't worry—there is the square, he said, and there are the tall houses, and there are people walking around everywhere. But I couldn't see anything. My friend ran in that direction, and I was looking for him for a long time. And sometimes I could hear people's voices, somewhere far away, so I couldn't make out what they were saying. Only once I heard very clearly that they were talking about the old sheriff, Sir Mackie Ainti, and I was very surprised. He disappeared about 400 years ago, before my parents were even born, and someone said that he was on his way and that he would take care of everything.

Then I found Zaxo. He was sitting on a rock, crying, and he couldn't answer any of my questions. I took him away from there, and we set out for Echo again. Sir Venerable Head, don't think I just made all of this up on the spot. I really only remembered these details last night, and I doubt very much I remembered everything that happened to me there. I beg you, please try to find out what happened to Kettari. I love that city, and I left my younger sister behind there. I would like to find her when I leave Nunda, and that will happen very soon.

Here the letter broke off.

"How did he die?" I asked.

"Good question! Everything happened more than suddenly. They took him out for a walk, when the weather was fine and dry. Out of the blue there was a bolt of lightning. The poor fellow was reduced to a pile of ashes, while the guard came away only with singed eyebrows. Then came a peal of thunder and a downpour. Rain fell for two dozen days without ceasing. The first floor of the prison was flooded, and almost a dozen inmates were able to escape in the chaos. Nunda isn't Xolomi, by a long shot! The incident created quite a furor. You know, Max, from the very start I was inclined to believe my countryman. Just the fact that he had voluntarily turned himself in to the authorities speaks volumes. Imagine how scared a person must be to subject himself to something that stupid. But you know, this letter and his strange death were the last straw. I realized that the fellow had led me to the brink of one of the most mysterious cases I had ever . . . Did you want to ask something, Max?"

"Yes. Besides the adventures and terrors of your unfortunate countryman, was there something else you wanted to tell me?"

"Your intuition works even when it doesn't need to; I was going to tell you anyway. It's nothing earth-shattering, just one little observation. You see, my doubts were sufficient to prompt me to take a good long look at the carpets they were bringing from Kettari. I'd stake my life on it that they smell faintly of True Magic, although they were made without resorting to it. Nevertheless, you know, it is strange. Until now I've been able to sense its presence in a person when he was up to his knees in mystery, even if he didn't suspect it himself. As it was in your case, Max. But things, inanimate objects? I had never encountered anything like that before."

"But what about Sir Maba Kalox's house? It's so shrouded in mystery it's hard to find it. A house is an inanimate object, isn't it? Or have I got it wrong again?"

"No, you're absolutely right. And you've proven yet again that I've hit upon the best solution to a small but compelling problem."

"And what might that be?" I asked him, even though my heart, thudding desperately inside my ribcage, already knew the answer. Juffin nodded.

"I see you already understand, Max. Yes, you're going to Kettari. You'll join a caravan and take a look at what's going on there. If it all comes to naught, you can at least bring back a carpet; you need to make your new apartment a bit more homey. In any case, since it's better for me not to show my face there, why not send you? All things considered, it amounts to the same thing."

"'The same thing,' that's a good one! Of course, I'm ready to go anytime, but it doesn't make much sense for me to go there."

"What makes you so sure? Mysteries love novices, especially fine ones like you. Aging wisemen like me should sit at home thinking deep thoughts. In short, I decided long ago that this case is just made for you. I never dreamed that you'd be so willing, though. Oh, and by the way, I don't think it will be too dangerous."

"I've heard that one before! When you sent me to Xolomi to deal with the stumpy-legged ghost, you were also sure that I would manage with no trouble at all."

"What do you mean? You managed beautifully, just as I predicted."

"I just about spoiled everything! Twice running."

"'Just about' doesn't count, Max. You acted quickly, and almost all your decisions were sound. Don't you think that for a person who has lived in the World just a hundred days or so that's nearly impossible?"

"Melifaro once came up with a theory about my origins," I recalled. "He suggested that I was a Mutinous Magician who lost his memory after you whacked me upside the head, as it were. Are you sure nothing like that happened, sir?"

Juffin was delighted with this hypothesis. I let him have a good laugh, then went on.

"You know I don't object to danger, especially now. But please explain to me, in the name of all Magicians, why are you so sure that this trip won't be dangerous? Are your feelings about it propitious?"

"Yes, that too. But there's more to it. I've already spoken about Kettari to Maba Kalox. He is no doubt aware of what is happening, but he's beating about the bush. Maba has his own ideas about things, as you know. He assured me that whatever was happening in Kettari didn't threaten the World, and could in fact be considered a 'joyous event.' Then again, Maba has his own notions about such things. By the way, he is thrilled that you're going there. I wish I knew why. Come what may, I must learn all the details of this story. My curiosity has always taken precedence over my sense of duty, and in the case of Kettari, both these factors come into play. But the most important consideration is that I've found an excellent pretext for making your already-difficult life a little harder. What do you say, Max?"

"I can't tell you how happy you're making me. But what about the 'old sheriff of Kettari'—that Sir Mackie Ainti the 'voices' were talking about? You yourself used to be the sheriff of Kettari. Did you change your name or something, Juffin?"

"Me? In the name of Magicians, of course not! I succeeded him as sheriff. In the beginning old Mackie was my boss. And much more than just a boss. If they ask you in three hundred years 'Who was Juffin Hully?' and you're in the mood to talk, you'll probably say the same things about me that I would tell you about Sir Mackie. He didn't drag me out of another world, though. That's the difference between you and me."

I stared at Juffin. So this Sir Mackie Ainti taught my boss all the inscrutable things that go by the name of Invisible or True Magic? I wondered. The boss nodded. The question that was on the tip of my tongue was no secret to him. This instant mutual comprehension sent a thrill up and down my spine.

"I might add that the old man really did disappear about four hundred years ago. That is to say, he didn't disappear, but just up and left Kettari, saying goodbye to me in these words: 'It's time for you to have a bit of fun, Juffin—only don't even think about sending me a call. For your own sake.' Mackie was never distinguished by garrulousness; not like yours truly. So thank the Dark Magicians, Max—you didn't end up with the worst mentor in the World."

"I already do thank them, on a daily basis. They're probably sick of hearing from me by now," I said, smiling. "So when do I leave, Juffin?"

"Caravans to Kettari form once every two dozen days. The next one leaves about four days from now, if I'm not mistaken. I hope everything will be ready for your departure by then."

"Everything?" I asked in surprise. "What is there to get ready? Or haven't you finished yet?"

"I've hardly begun. First, you're not to go alone. Don't even think of arguing that point. It's not just some idiosyncrasy of mine. It's a rule."

"I wouldn't think of arguing. Who's going with me?"

"I'd like to hear your suggestions first."

"I'm a creature of habit. If I'm going to set out for who knows where and who knows why, I want Lonli-Lokli by my side. I've tried it once, and I like it. But who will strike the fear of the Magicians into the bad guys of the Capital if both of us high-tail it out of Echo at the same time?"

"Don't worry, Max," Juffin grinned. "You've never seen me in action. I've become lazy with both of you around, but even I can come out of hibernation if need be. And it's time to shake some of the fat off Sir Kofa."

"You can say that again. I must admit, it never occurred to me that you might want to come out of hibernation. So you don't object to Lonli-Lokli as my traveling companion?"

"Object? Those were my thoughts exactly. Only curiosity prevailed. I wanted to find out whether you'd guess where my sympathies lay, or whether you'd slip up this time and land in a puddle. Congratulations!"

"I assume that Shurf and I will have to disguise ourselves. The whole city recognizes us at a glance. I'm sure no one wants to go to Kettari in the company of two professional killers from the Secret Investigative Force." I glanced at Juffin. "Did I land in a puddle?"

"Not yet. Keep going, Max."

"It won't be a problem for me," I said confidently. "But how will Shurf pull it off? He's so conspicuous. I guess Sir Kofa is our only hope."

"Plop!"

I looked at the chief, stunned, then burst out laughing.

"Oh, you mean I fell in the puddle after all?"

"You sure did." Juffin was beaming. "How modest you are, Sir Max. If there is to be a problem with anyone, it's going to be with you. You don't seem to be very observant. Praise be the Magicians, Shurf has an extremely inconspicuous appearance. The city is full of fellows just like him! Change the color of his hair, dress him in something bright and colorful instead of his white looxi, take off his gloves—and even you won't recognize him. And there are plenty of tall people in the World."

"All the better. But why should I have problems disguising myself? Do I have an unusual face or something?"

"To tell the truth, your face really is unusual. Have you ever seen anyone in Echo who could be mistaken for your brother?"

I was somewhat abashed. In fact, I had never paid any attention to such matters.

"You're a rare bird in these parts. But that's not the problem. Sir Kofa can transform your face into anything that strikes his fancy. The problem is your accent, Max."

"Do I really—" I blushed.

"Yes, you do. You're the only one who doesn't notice it. And half the city already knows that only the 'fearsome Sir Max, wrapped in his Mantle of Death' speaks in such an abrupt and choppy manner. They'll see through your disguise, however you might dress up. I won't even mention your Silent Speech—sometimes it's downright difficult to understand you."

"But what will I do? Feign muteness?"

"Mute people use Silent Speech better than anyone. It's the only way they can communicate. But don't despair, Sir Max. We'll turn you into an elegant damsel."

"A damsel? Elegant? Me?!" My astonishment knew no bounds.

"Why are you so surprised? Sir Kofa will do some work on your face and voice, pick out a wig for you . . . It's all quite simple."

"I'll become the laughing stock of the House by the Bridge this season!" I wailed. "Juffin, just what kind of damsel would I make?"

"A tall, skinny, and fairly broad-shouldered one. Perhaps not the type that appeals most to men, but that's Lonli-Lokli's problem. He'll just have to travel with an ugly wife."

"A wife! Surely you're joking!" I was on the verge of tears.

"What's gotten into you, Max?" the chief asked. "Of course you will pass yourselves off as a married couple. Married couples are the most frequent travelers to Kettari. They mix the pleasant with the practical; the purchase of carpets with shared relaxation and rest. If a woman with an accent like yours joins the caravan, everyone just assumes she's from your part of the World. Why shouldn't an upright citizen marry a lady from the Barren Lands? In Echo we love the exotic. You won't inspire any doubts, and everything will work out just fine. And don't look at me like I'm an executioner. Why are you so alarmed?"

I couldn't explain why myself. Most likely, some slumbering prejudices had been awakened in me. If a man dressed up in women's clothes, it meant he had some issues. Although the clothes themselves wouldn't really pose a problem, I considered. In Echo the attire of men and women is so similar, the differences so minimal, that I still couldn't distinguish a woman's looxi from a man's at that point.

"I don't know what to say. I just feel rather awkward."

"I see nothing in the least awkward about it. Good night, Sir Kofa."

I turned around to look. There in the doorway was Sir Kofa Yox, our Master Eavesdropper, and the unsurpassed master of masquerade. He was carrying a sizable parcel.

"This sweet lad does not want to become a girl at all," Juffin told him in a thin voice. "What do you think, Kofa, shall we overpower him, just the two of us, or call for assistance?"

Sir Kofa bestowed a patronizing smile on us both and hoisted his burden onto the table.

"Are you going to do it right now?" I asked plaintively. "Maybe you'll let me go out for a little walk first?"

I was always assaulted by thoughts like this in the dentist's chair. I wanted to dash off and come back "tomorrow"—that is to say, never.

"You've had your little walk," said Juffin. "Listen, Max, it's just ordinary dressing up. Like a carnival! Haven't you ever been to a carnival?"

"Yes," I grumbled. "I was six years old, and I dressed up like a rabbit."

My colleagues hooted with laughter.

"A rabbit? At a carnival? In the Barren Lands!" Sir Kofa moaned. "Boy, do you ever think before you speak?"

I couldn't help laughing myself.

"All right, come off it, Kofa. I really don't have much experience of carnivals, so . . ."

"That's better," said Juffin. "Say, maybe you thought that we were going to turn you into a real woman? And that you'd have to fulfill your marital duties?"

"It wouldn't have surprised me."

"Don't worry, son. For one thing, although making a woman out of a man and vice-versa is possible, Kofa and I aren't powerful enough wizards to accomplish it. Sir Maba probably could, though. Well, no; even that's unlikely. Why would he want to? I wouldn't be surprised if Lady Sotofa could manage it. I'll have to ask her."

"And another thing; Sir Lonli-Lokli would never cheat on his wife with such a skinny, broad-shouldered alien. Praise be the Magicians, Shurf's got sense when it comes to women."

"What nonsense you're talking, Juffin! Why 'skinny' and 'broad-shouldered'? We're going to end up with a very pretty girl, you'll see," Sir Kofa objected with the air of expert whose pride had been hurt.

He was already unpacking his parcel. I looked with horror as he pulled out some reddish curls—my future wig, no doubt! Juffin saw the expression on my face and burst out laughing again.

"We decided to do this early so you'd have time to get used to it," Sir Kofa said compassionately. "I've dressed up as a woman many times. Oh, yes, you remember our first meeting at the Glutton! You see, women have a different bearing and posture, different gestures. They respond to things differently. Four days isn't much, but you're a quick learner. If anything, you'll just pass for a damsel with a few eccentricities. And don't worry, all the changes in your appearance are only temporary. By the way, Juffin, how long will he have to be in Kettari? I need to know."

"Let me think. The journey there takes three days. In Kettari the caravan usually stops for six or seven days. Maybe that won't be enough. It will be necessary to stay and wait for the next caravan—that's two more dozen days. And then there's the return trip. Yes, Kofa, I think the spell will have to last for four dozen days. Better to have some extra than not enough."

"Four dozen days?" I moaned. "And what if we get back sooner? What will I do looking like that?"

"You will work, Max! What does it matter what kind of face is hiding under the Mantle of Death?" said Juffin with a shrug. "Just wait, you'll end up liking it."

"Oh, I'm sure I will. I can just imagine how Melifaro's going to enjoy this. He'll laugh like he's never laughed before."

"Why are you so sure that anyone will laugh at you?" Juffin

asked. "Is that another pleasant custom from your native land?"

I nodded. "Do you mean to say that in Echo things like that aren't considered funny?"

"Sir Kofa just reminded you that he often dresses up like a woman. Have you ever heard anyone joke about it? Even Melifaro?"

"No."

I was forced to admit that nothing of the sort had ever happened in my presence. Only the very unobservant weren't amused now and then by Sir Kofa's appetite, but they viewed his dressing up as something he did in the line of duty. Work is, simply, work. I had again been caught out, measuring other people's looxis by my own yardstick.

"All right, take your clothes off," Kofa commanded. "There are likely to be some problems with your figure, so let's start with the most difficult thing. The face won't need more than a minute."

"Undress all the way?" I asked in confusion.

"Of course all the way," Juffin said. "Haven't you ever gone to the wiseman?"

"Almost never, praise be the Magicians! I'm afraid of them."

"What is there to be afraid of?" Sir Kofa asked in surprise. "Wisemen help us get to know our own bodies. That's why their manner is so kind and mild. It's an absolute pleasure to deal with them!"

"Oh, you don't know our wisemen. They'll cut you into tiny pieces, and then figure that it's easier to bury you than put you back together."

"A hole in the heavens above you, Sir Max—what kind of place is it, your homeland?" Juffin shook his head in wonder as he had done so many times before. "All right, do as you're told. And you, Kofa, lock the door, or an ill wind might blow someone else our way."

"The World will see the severe working methods of the Secret Investigative Force and shudder," I said under my breath, unwrapping my looxi.

❧

I stood immobile in the center of the room for almost an hour, while Kofa diligently massaged the air around my body. He didn't touch me; but the sensation was pleasant all the same.

"That should do it, Max. Think about how you want to be addressed, by the way. You'll need a good woman's name."

I looked myself over warily. Everything was just as it was supposed to be—unchanged. My hips were no broader, my bust hadn't blossomed.

"It's not a real woman's body," Sir Kofa said, smiling. "It's simply an illusion—but an excellent one! Get dressed and you'll see what I mean. No, you can't wear that!"

Confused, I laid my skaba back on the arm of the chair.

"Take a look at what I brought, over there on the table. They're all the latest style. The fashion victims of the Capital will be green with envy."

I dug around in the pile of multihued rags, pulled out a dark green skaba, and quickly put it on.

"Wow!"

It was the only thing I could say. The delicate fabric outlined the tender curves of some unfamiliar female body. Juffin looked at Kofa in delight.

"It's perfect! Far better than I could have imagined. Well, keep going—such a sweet lady, with such an unbecoming stubble. It's painful to look at. You could shave once in a while, Sir Max!"

"I did shave. Yesterday." I rubbed my chin. "You call that stubble?"

"Never mind, Max. You won't have to worry about that anymore," Sir Kofa said, lathering some black muck on my bewildered face. "There we go! This stuff lasts even longer than you'll need it to."

"That's the best news since the culinary amendments to the Code. Do I rinse it off now or should I wait a while?"

"Why should you wait? There's nothing to rinse," Kofa said in surprise as he fitted a light red wig on my head. The long curls instantly started to tickle my shoulders.

"No, it disappeared along with the stubble. I'm a sorcerer, after all, not a barber! And don't even think of trying to remove the wig. It'll hurt. Now it's your own hair—for a while. Sit down in the chair, lady. I'm almost done."

I had to endure a five-minute facial massage, which was rather unpleasant this time. My nose had an especially hard time of it. I was sure the poor thing would turn red and puffy after such treatment. Tears sprang to my eyes, but I suffered through it bravely.

"Done," Sir Kofa Yox said, and gave a weary sigh. "Juffin, do we have anything to drink? I haven't sweated like that in a long time."

"It's brilliant, Kofa!" Sir Juffin exclaimed, staring at me. "Who would have thought? Even if this lovely lady goes to the middle of the Victory of King Gurig VII Square and starts shouting at the top of her lungs that her name is Max, they'll just have a good laugh, and there the matter will end. I'll have someone bring us all something to drink. And not only drink: it's a sin not to celebrate on such an occasion! Put on your looxi, Sir Max. Come admire the work of an old pro. You'll like it, I promise!"

I wrapped myself in a patterned looxi the color of river sand with a feeling of trepidation. Who would be looking back at me from the large mirror in the corridor?

"Not like that, lady," Kofa warned me. "Women never pin up the hem of their looxi. They just drape it over their shoulder. And they're quite right to do so—it's simple and elegant that way. All right now, let's see you walk."

I strolled through the office obediently.

"Hm. We'll have to do something about your gait. It spoils everything," Kofa said. "Fine, go admire yourself. Get used to it, and then we'll teach you how to walk."

"What about the turban?"

"That isn't absolutely necessary. Girls with such abundant hair prefer not to cover their heads, especially if they've come from afar. And you've come from afar, lady, judging by your accent. Come on, step up to the mirror. How shall we name our girl, Juffin?"

"Let him choose," said Juffin. "This poor fellow will have to decide something on his own, at least. What do you say, lady?"

"Marilyn Monroe!" I bellowed, and burst out laughing.

"What's so funny?" Juffin asked. "It's a pretty name. Sounds foreign, but that's good. Wait a minute—is it some kind of rude curse?"

"Well, almost," I said, deciding not to go into detail on the matter.

I made my way down the corridor, my heart in my throat. I approached the mirror, gathered all my courage, and stared at the revealing surface, darkened by time. There, gazing at me with unfeigned curiosity, was a tall, nicely dressed lady, very much to my taste.

I peered into her pleasant face, hoping to discover even the slightest resemblance to myself. Not even a hint of the old Max remained. I walked back and forth, not taking my eyes off the mirror. Yes, the lady was a bit angular. What's true is true! It started to seem funny to me; my head began to spin. When the elegant lady in the mirror broke into a loud guffaw, I felt like I might just lose my mind. I returned to the office. My senior colleagues were already setting the table.

"It's a shame to give such a beauty to Lonli-Lokli," I objected. "He won't be able to appreciate her, anyway. You're a genius, Kofa. I love her! I mean, me."

"Oh, yes, I completely forgot about the voice," sir Kofa said. "Drink this down, Lady Marilyn."

He handed me a small vial with some suspicious-looking blue liquid. I sniffed it daintily, took a deep breath, and drank it down. Not too bad—something akin to dry sherry, only not very hot.

"And you have nothing else to offer—"

I broke off suddenly. Now my voice had become someone else's, too—not a squeak as I had feared, rather a fairly low, husky voice—but definitely a woman's.

"Take it, boy," Sir Kofa said, and held out a mug of Jubatic Juice to me. "You really do need a drink."

After a few gulps of the tasty drink with its kick-boxing strength, I perked up. I think the source of my good mood lay in the dark depths of this unprecedented madness. My good friend Sir Max, the Nocturnal Representative of Juffin Hully, had been transformed into some red-haired girl entirely too quickly.

"You'll have to work on your mannerisms, lady," said Juffin. "You still look more like the village idiot than the wife of a prosperous member of society."

"Mannerisms? Now wait one second!"

I jumped up and sashayed around the room provocatively. Then I pursed my lips for a kiss.

"How do you like me, gentlemen?"

Sir Kofa looked crestfallen. He didn't say a word.

"How awful, Max!" Juffin blurted out. "Is that really customary in your homeland?"

I went back to my chair.

"Not really. Not always, anyway." I became more composed. "That's how dissolute women behave; and only on occasion."

"All the same, it's hideous! I think you owe me more than a good meal for pulling you out of there in time."

"What do you mean, 'in time'? If only you had been about ten years earlier."

"I'm not sure that would have been wise. Someday I'll explain why. You must be worn out, Kofa," Sir Juffin said compassionately to our Master Eavesdropper.

The latter just chewed his pie with a melancholy air.

"Praise be the Magicians, one doesn't have to perform tricks like that every day. And now I have to try teaching this lady some manners."

"Don't bother, Kofa. We'll manage. The situation is almost hopeless, but I have another idea."

"You're right, Juffin. I do think you're going to need a good miracle."

"Excellent. You and Kurush just nod off for a while, and Max and I will go for a walk. Come on, Max . . . Uh, I beg your pardon. Lady Marilyn."

"I am not nodding off. I'm memorizing what you're saying," the wise bird piped up. "I always knew people were strange creatures, but what I've seen today beats all."

"That's for sure," Juffin snorted, smoothing down the buriwok's soft feathers as we left the office.

"Where are we going?" I asked, getting into the amobiler.

"Can't you guess? I know only one old lady capable of making a real lady out of this crazy dame."

"Are we going to Jafax?" I asked. "To Lady Sotofa?"

"Yes. I've already sent her a call. She's also from Kettari, after all, so it's a matter of concern to her, as well. Sotofa was surprisingly quick to agree to help us. Actually, it's not her style, but she seems to have a soft spot for you."

"And that is completely mutual."

"Then let's go, Lady Marilyn."

※

Lady Sotofa met us at the door of a small garden pavilion that served as her study.

"Oh, what a pretty girl! Too bad she's not the real thing. If she was, I'd bring her here to live!" she said smiling, and hugged me.

I was, as usual, a bit flustered. I felt that no one had ever been so unabashedly delighted about a visit from me as this formidable wise-woman with the mannerisms of a doting grandmother.

"Sit down, Juffin! Remember the kamra they used to make five hundred years ago in Kettari, in the *Country Home* on the Square of Joy? Well, I managed to make it even worse. Try it. You'll approve! And for you, my girl-boy, I have something very special."

Lady Sotofa produced a miniature jug from under her looxi. Its appearance witnessed to origins deep in the ancient forest.

"It's delicious and very good for you, in some cases."

"You haven't found some Heavenly Half, have you, Sotofa?"

Juffin shook his head in amazement. "I haven't laid eyes on it in at least three hundred years!"

"What use is it to you, Juffin?" Lady Sotofa retorted, her laughter ringing out. "It's all the better you haven't. And if you haven't seen it, no one else has, either. Things like this should be secreted away in the dark. But do sit down, Max. No, not at the table. Over here in the armchair. It's more comfortable. Here you are!" She held out a glass with some thick, dark-red liquid. She thought a bit, then nodded. "Yes, one's enough. It's better not to go overboard with such things."

I took the small glass obediently and sipped it. It really was delicious, almost as good as Elixir of Kaxar.

"Look at that, he's drinking it," Juffin said gruffly. "With me he would have asked a thousand questions to make sure it wasn't poison."

"Good boy. I'd ask a thousand questions myself before accepting a potion from your hands, Juffin, you sly old fox," Lady Sotofa said gaily.

Sir Juffin Hully looked quite satisfied.

"And now, you can just relax," Lady Sotofa said. "I can explain to you the properties of what I just gave you to drink. I don't mind. You know, back in the good old days, they gave Heavenly Half to the mad."

"Thank you, Lady Sotofa," I mumbled gloomily. "That's a comfort."

"Hear me out, silly." The good nature of the fearsome sorceress was inexhaustible. "They gave this potion to the mad, and the poor things immediately regained their senses. That's why it's called Heavenly Half —it was thought that the drug would help the mad find the half of their souls that was groping about in the dark. This continued until one wise person discovered that these unhappy creatures hadn't really become healthy and whole, but only seemed so. In fact, their tormented souls remained who-knows-where. Do you understand?"

I shook my head sadly.

"Never mind. Such are your years. It will come with time. Now you'll sleep a bit, and when you wake up, you'll be the same old silly Sir Max. But you'll behave like a true lady. You'll stay just as you are, but people will think they are in the presence of a completely different person. To be honest, it's not a very good potion, boy, for if people want to seem different from how they really are, they must make an effort themselves. And wonder-working concoctions dissipate the spirit. But just this once, for a good cause, it won't hurt, I suppose. I don't think you'll find it necessary to study to be a real woman. You're very good at it already!"

"Thank you, Lady Sotofa. You're the only one in the World who loves and compliments me . . ." I murmured, dozing off.

"Hush, and go to sleep. Don't try to fight slumber, or everything will come to naught! You see, wondrous things prefer to happen when a person sleeps. That's the way things are arranged."

Lady Sotofa covered me with a fur blanket and turned to my chief.

"Have we really found some time to talk at long last? You don't have to rush off anywhere?"

Through a haze of sleep, I noticed that Juffin tapped the end of his nose twice with the forefinger of his right hand, the famous Kettarian gesture. Well, well . . .

When I woke up, it was already light. The beaming Lady Sotofa sat by my side and peered at my face with interest.

"Goodness, Max, you've been asleep for so long." Her smile grew even wider. "Where did you learn that?"

"It's an innate talent," I replied in a strange, velvety voice.

I didn't experience any emotional reaction, which couldn't help but make me happy. I realized that Lady Sotofa and I were now alone. Had the chief really abandoned me in Jafax? He would do that.

"Where's Juffin?"

"Home or on duty, I don't know. I didn't try to find out. Do you know how long you've slept? Juffin and I like to wag our tongues, of course, but in the time you've been asleep, we could have discussed all the causes of the origin of the Universe, which isn't terribly entertaining."

"How long was I asleep?"

"More than twenty-four hours, Max. That did surprise me."

"Wow! Juffin's going to tear my head off!"

"Of course, he could do much worse, that awful Juffin. But I don't think anyone intends to tear anything off you in the near future. Take it from an old soothsayer."

"All the same, I've got to run," I said anxiously. "I have to leave tomorrow . . . or the day after tomorrow. I don't know."

"Of course you must leave, boy," Lady Sotofa said, nodding. "But first you have to bathe, and if there's time, I'll whip you up some kamra. I hate fussing around with the brazier, but I'll make an effort for your sake."

I smiled.

"You spoil me, Lady Sotofa."

"Of course I do. Someone has to. The bathroom is downstairs, just where it should be. Nothing newfangled or out-of-the-ordinary around here, boy."

"And I thought it might be in some other World altogether!" I shouted on my way downstairs.

"One doesn't exclude the other," Lady Sotofa called after me.

In the bathroom, I immediately started scrutinizing myself in the mirror. Yes, Lady Marilyn Monroe was no longer angular, thanks to Lady Sotofa and her Heavenly Half! I couldn't take any credit, that was certain.

The illusion was so convincing that I undressed almost with a feeling of panic. Under the skaba, however, I discovered my own body. I sighed with relief and began to wash.

I ran back upstairs in leaps and bounds, from a surfeit of energy. Sleeping for more than twenty-four hours in a chair, and feeling so good afterwards—that is magic of a higher order!

※

The plump, gray-haired old woman, undoubtedly one of the most powerful beings in this World, was waiting for me at the table.

"Here's the kamra, and here are some cookies. That's all there is. But you don't like having a real breakfast."

I nodded.

"You know that, too!"

"It's no mystery to me. You're too young to have secrets from me, boy."

"You frighten me. To know everything about me—that's scary."

"There's nothing in the least scary about it, Max. On the contrary, it's all very sweet. Even your dark past in some, please excuse me, insane place."

"I completely agree with you that it is insane. Perhaps you might mend my broken heart, Lady Sotofa? That sadist Juffin claims that I have to learn to deal with all these misfortunes on my own. But I'm not managing too well."

"Good gracious, me. What kinds of misfortunes can you possibly have? All your sorrows are like summer snow: now it's here, now it's gone, as though it never was. Just don't bury your nose in the past all the time or keep dreaming of the future. Today you're in masquerade. You should enjoy it!"

They were only words, but I felt as relieved as I had when Juffin had tweaked my ear.

Yes, what kinds of sorrows can you have, friend? I said to myself. You ran away from a place where you felt miserable, and ended up in the best of all Worlds, surrounded on all sides by marvelous people who do nothing but try to share their wisdom with you and treat you to delicious delicacies the rest of the time. And you just whine and complain, you ungrateful swine!

"Lady Sotofa, you are truly the best of women," I said.

"Of course I am. And a great beauty, besides, if you'd care to know."

"I can imagine," I said. "I'd like to peek into the past, to get a glimpse of you in your merry youth!"

"To see how that crazy Juffin chased after me, brandishing a warrant for my arrest after I refused to leave the city with him? Well, fine, since now we can have a 'girl to girl' chat, I can boast a bit. Watch out, though! Make sure you don't fall in love—you'll fare worse with me than you did with Kima's niece."

And before I had a chance to register what she had just said, she jumped up and began swinging her arms in circles with astonishing speed. I couldn't make anything out—only her hands flickering and flashing before my eyes.

"Well, what do you think?"

By then I had already been fairly showered with wonders, and had begun to think I would never again react with my former passion and fervor. But now, standing before me, I saw a petite young beauty. Rooted to the spot, I inhaled spasmodically. Exhaling proved to be problematic, however. The fantastic Lady Sotofa patted me on the back absently.

"Oh, come on. It wasn't that scary."

Somehow managing to breathe out, I closed my mouth and stared at this vision. She was the one who had the famous figure of Marilyn Monroe—whose name I had so carelessly appropriated. Lady Sotofa, however, was a dark brunette with almond-shaped green eyes tilting slightly upward toward her temples, and snow-white skin.

❀

"Please go back to the way you were!" I was nearly overcome with the turmoil of my emotions. "But why don't you—"

"Why don't I always look like this? Of what use is it? So one of the young Magicians of the Order of the Seven-Leaf Clover might dream about pinching my behind at night? That holds no interest for me anymore, and I would just feel sorry for them, the silly men."

Lady Sotofa again carried out her strange aerobic exercises, only this time her arms gyrated in the opposite direction.

"I think it's really time you got back to the House by the Bridge."

The smiling, plump old lady placed her warm and heavy palm on my shoulder. I nodded. I didn't feel like talking. I had received a small miracle, and a fragile little piece of the odd wisdom of the women of the Seven-Leaf Clover into the bargain.

"Don't be sad, Lady Marilyn. You're pretty, too!" Lady Sotofa's joyful laughter followed me. "Promise me that you will try to enjoy your adventure. Agreed?"

"I promise!"

And Lady Marilyn Monroe set off for work. Along the way, I stopped in at the first jeweler's I came to and bought several expensive rings. Let's make ourselves happy, sister! I had begun to make friends with my new persona.

※

I entered the House by the Bridge through the Secret Door, as was my habit. Only afterwards did I realize that could seriously blow my cover. Luckily, no one noticed my blunder. In fact, there was no one to be seen, either outside or in the corridor.

Juffin's call reached me when I was already in our half of the Ministry.

It's good you woke up, Max. Better late than never. I'll be there in no time—I want to see what's become of you. Melamori and I are on the trail of a very attractive poisoner. Nothing too serious, but I don't like to let her go alone on excursions like this.

You're absolutely right, I concurred.

I was happy for Melamori: on the job, and out of danger. That's how it should be.

I don't need you to tell me I'm right, son! Sir Juffin Hully snapped back at me. *Over and out already!*

A genuine idyll reigned in our office. Melifaro was sitting in state on the desk, his legs crossed, still as a statue. So that's what he's like when nobody's there to see him, I thought.

When he noticed me—or rather the fetching Lady Marilyn—he started up, flitted from his pedestal, and stared at my new face with such undisguised admiration that I realized right away: here it is, Marilyn's and my finest hour!

A crazy notion took hold of me.

Lady Sotofa had urged me to "enjoy the adventure," and one must obey one's elders.

"What seems to be the problem, my lady?" Melifaro inquired with tender sympathy.

Without a moment's hesitation, Marilyn and I vowed: come what may, just don't laugh and spoil everything.

"Nothing, praise be the Magicians," I smiled shyly. "Father asked me to visit this place and convey his gratitude to Sir Max and one other gentleman. I think his papa wrote some important book. Oh yes, of course: Sir Mefiliaro!"

"Melifaro," the Diurnal Representative of the Venerable Head corrected me gallantly. "That would be me, my lady. But tell me, who is your father, and why did he wish to thank us?"

"I'm afraid you aren't very friendly toward my father. Nevertheless, he owes you his life. My name is Lady Marilyn Box."

"You're General Boboota's daughter?!" Melifaro was flabbergasted. "Sinning Magicians, why haven't I seen you here before?"

"I just recently arrived here in the Capital. Just after I was born, during the Troubled Times, Father sent me to relatives in the County Vook. My mother wasn't his wife, you see, but my father always took care of me. After my mother died, he persuaded Lady Box to adopt me officially. Papa has a difficult character, I know, but he's a very good person."

"And very brave!" Melifaro praised him enthusiastically. "Your father is a real hero of the War for the Code. So don't pay any attention to stupid rumors, Lady Marilyn. I for one respect your daddy very much."

Inside, I was howling with glee, Sir Melifaro respects General Boboota very much. How was the poor guy going to look me in the eye after this?

"Yes, my papa is like that. Crude, but sincere" Marilyn said. "Unfortunately, he's still very ill."

That was no fabrication. The adventure with the *King Banjee* pâté had put the scandalously famous General of the City Police out of commission for a long time. I went on:

"But father doesn't want you to think he's ungrateful, so he asked me to come here and find Sir Max. And you, of course."

I fished out one of my newly purchased rings and gave it to Melifaro.

"This is for you, Sir Mefilaro, as a token of friendship and gratitude."

Melifaro admired the ring, and immediately tried to put it on. Oh, of course; my hands must be daintier than they used to be. My poor friend could only wear the ring on his left pinkie, and that with difficulty.

"Tell me, do you think I could see Sir Max?" Lady Marilyn asked dreamily.

Melifaro grew fidgety. It was truly a sight to behold! He came right up to me, put his hand on my shoulder, leaned close to my face, and informed me in a conspiratorial tone:

"You know, Sir Max isn't here now. I'm not sure whether he'll be coming back any time soon. And, really, it's for the best. I wouldn't advise you to meet him."

Things were getting more and more interesting.

Could I really compete with his Hollywood looks, I wondered, brightening when I realized he was actually worried.

"But why, sir?" Lady Marilyn and I tried to appear very naïve. We opened our mouth childishly and batted our lashes.

"It would be very dangerous," Melifaro confided. "Our Sir Max is a terrifying creature. You know they even made him wear the Mantle of Death. Can you imagine?"

"But Father said—" I began timidly.

"Your father is very sick, my lady. Moreover, he's under the sway of his gratitude. I'm sure if it weren't for the circumstances, he would never have allowed you to meet this terrible person. You know, Sir Max does nothing but kill people day in and day out. And not just criminals. The poor fellow can't control himself. Just two days ago he spat poison at a lady as sweet as you! He was under the impression she was speaking to him disrespectfully."

"Why didn't they lock him up in Xolomi?" I asked, trying with all my might not to laugh.

"Oh, you wouldn't believe it, lady. It's all due to the intrigues of Sir Juffin Hully, our Venerable Head. Sir Max is his favorite, and the chief always protects him. If you only knew how many corpses of innocent people they have burned in this very office! I'm a brave man, I like to take risks—that's the only reason I haven't resigned from duty. My colleagues, every one of them, are asking for voluntary retirement."

Melifaro was on a roll. He told one fib after another, and couldn't stop. I covered my face with my hands and tried to laugh soundlessly. For better or worse, I succeeded.

"What's wrong, miss? Did I scare you?"

I nodded silently. Saying something out loud was more than I could manage. Another word and I would explode with laughter.

"Oh, but this is the Secret Investigative Force, the most fearsome outfit in the Unified Kingdom. Worse things can happen here, you know. Compared with Sir Juffin Hully, Sir Max is a puppy."

Aha! I thought. It's not enough that I'm a "cold-blooded killer"; now I'm a "puppy," too. Oh, you'll pay dearly for this, Sir Melifaro. You'll pay for this with your life. To lie so brazenly to a poor country girl!

"I'm the only normal person in this office," said Melifaro, putting his arm around me. "Why are you so upset? This is Echo, Capital of the Unified Kingdom. You must get used to it. But life in the Capital has its pleasant sides. And if I've upset you, I am obliged to rectify my mistake. Let me show you Echo by evening. I'll treat you to a dinner you're unlikely to get anywhere else. How about it?"

What a ladies' man, I thought with contempt. Gosh, do women fall for such cheap tricks? Or does he think he'll get away with it just because the girl is from County Vook?

I shook my head.

"I can't, sir. We barely know each other."

"But that's what I'm suggesting, that we get to know each other better."

Melifaro smiled disarmingly. "Honestly, miss, you'll have a good time. I promise."

Lady Marilyn and I smiled timidly. "Well, if you promise to behave—"

"Of course! I'll call on you just after sundown," said Melifaro, and glanced cautiously at the door.

Indeed, the arrival of potential rivals at this moment would have been undesirable. According to Melifaro's way of thinking, the beautiful Lady Marilyn would now make haste away from the House by the Bridge to avoid meeting Sir Max, Mr. Bad Dream the baby-eater, to be out of harm's way.

I slowly got up from the visitor's chair and headed for the desk.

"I'd rather just wait here, Sir Fulumaro."

I began rummaging silently through the desk drawer, until I produced an invisible bottle with some remains of Elixir of Kaxar.

"What are you doing, miss?" There was distinct note of panic in Melifaro's voice.

I was probably taking a risk. This peace-loving fellow was as dangerous as anyone in our charming company. If he had taken me for some Mutinous Magician newly returned to Echo, the matter might have ended in a skirmish. But praise be the Magicians, the lovely red-haired Lady Marilyn was above suspicion.

I opened the bottle and took a tiny swallow. There was no need to do this—even without the Elixir I was able to turn the world upside down now. But Lady Marilyn and I wanted a little nip of something.

"What do you think you're doing, Ms. Box?!" It was pitiful to look at Melifaro. "That's Sir Juffin Hully's desk. You can't dig around in there!"

"I can," I replied calmly. "We inhabitants of County Vook love snooping around in other people's desks. Sometimes you can even find a bit of fresh horse dung. So, put that in your pipe and smoke it, Melifaro."

Melifaro's face fell. I seemed to have gone slightly overboard. I didn't even want revenge anymore.

"Oh, come on, old friend," I said softly. "Haven't you ever been to a carnival?"

Melifaro, who was made of pretty stern stuff, took what was coming to him. He laughed nervously. I thought back on the conversation we had just had—and then it was no holds barred.

※

Sir Juffin Hully found us sitting on the floor locked in an embrace, tears of laughter streaming down our faces. We wheezed weakly, since we were already hoarse from laughing so hard.

"Max you were such a romantic boy," the chief remarked acidly. "You were even too shy to go to the Quarter of Trysts. And what do I see here? All it took was for you to acquire a bust and to spend twenty-four hours in the company of Lady Sotofa—and you fall into the arms of a complete stranger."

"Sir Juffin," Melifaro moaned. "If you leave him like he is, I swear I'm going to marry him!"

"I won't marry you, sir. You deceived me," I said coquettishly. "Oh, Juffin, you should have heard him."

Melifaro and I started howling with laughter again.

"What exactly has been going on here?" asked Juffin.

"Nothing I wouldn't tell my mama," I said. Now Sir Juffin joined in our laughter.

Fifteen minutes later, Melifaro and I had come to our senses and even found it possible to relate to Juffin the circumstances of our "acquaintance" with one another.

I had to hand it to Melifaro—he didn't hesitate to recount his own idiocy in the most lurid colors.

"Well, Lady Marilyn, you've made some progress," the chief said. "And who was so shocked by the prospect of turning into a woman two days ago?"

"I didn't realize I'd be such a beauty. By the way, someone invited me out to dinner. You haven't reconsidered, sir?" I said, winking at Melifaro.

"With a beauty like you, I'd go to the end of the world! Where will we go after dinner—your place or mine?"

"My place, naturally. My papa happens to be home. General Boboota, if you recall. He'll tell you all about his military exploits. Sir Juffin, am I free this evening, or do we have a new lady colleague? Does the Mantle of Death look becoming on me, boys?" My new persona behaved much more frivolously than the old one.

"I don't think a walk through the city would hurt you, Lady Marilyn. And you, Sir Melifaro, don't lose your head over this flirt. The day after tomorrow she abandons you and sets off on her honeymoon with Sir Lonli-Lokli."

Melifaro whistled under his breath, beginning to get the picture.

"So this is serious, gentlemen? And I thought—"

"That Max and I had lost our minds from boredom? Take your new girlfriend for a walk. And make sure she answers to her own name and doesn't go into the men's room by mistake."

"I can assure you, everything's in order in that department, judging from her recent performance," Melifaro said. "What kind of life is this, Sir Juffin? As soon as you meet a nice girl, she turns out to be Mr. Bad Dream. And to top it off, she's going to marry Lonli-Lokli! Do you think I'm made of stone?"

"You? You're made of iron, beyond the shadow of a doubt!" the chief consoled him. "Max—er, Lady Marilyn, I mean, Sir Shurf and I will be expecting you tomorrow at sundown. You probably won't be going home again, so try to arrange all your affairs and pack. And don't worry about your furry beasts. Our junior employees will soon be climbing all over each other, vying to be the ones to look after them."

I grew a bit sad thinking of my poor kitties. What a ne'er-do-well they had for a master.

"I think Ella's expecting kittens soon," I said. "Future royal felines. Though she's so fat already that you'd never know."

"Oh, Max, if only I had your problems," Juffin said. "Sir Melifaro, grab your heartthrob and be off. I have a meeting to attend with Mr. Poisoner."

❊

"You know, Lady Marilyn, with such a sweet little face and Mr. Bad Dream's amusing tricks, you'd make an ideal wife," Melifaro said, seating me in the amobiler.

"I'll say," I replied, and then decided to ask about something I never would have dared mention in my original state. "And what about Lady Melamori?"

"Lady Melamori mumbles your name in her sleep, if you must know. And she devotes the rest of her time to deep, long-winded monologues about the advantages of living alone. What happened between the two of you, I'd like to know? Perhaps Lady Marilyn likes to gossip?"

"Perhaps she does. Only nothing happened between us except fate. We met in the Quarter of Trysts, to my misfortune."

"Oh, that happens," Melifaro sighed sympathetically. Then he grinned from ear to ear. "On the other hand, if you become a real girl, my mother will get a chance to marry me off at last! And remember—I've never said anything like that to a girl before."

"Thanks. But I'm not ready for family life just yet. Let's go. You still owe me dinner."

❊

Three hours later, a full, happy, and slightly tipsy Lady Marilyn stopped her amobiler by the doors of Lady Melamori's house. Her woman's heart told me I should, so I didn't try to argue. Not deliberating too long about my actions, I sent a call to Melamori.

It's me, Max. Peek out for a second, I'm standing at the entrance.

I can't, Max. Melamori returned the call. *Do you know what you're doing? We can't see each other for the time being. Until . . . until it feels right.*

If I dragged myself here in the middle of the night, it's probably not so that things between us would become even worse. Just take a look outside—then you can decide whether to let me in or not. I swear by Sir Juffin's favorite pajamas that you won't regret it. No one but me will ever surprise you like this again. I'm waiting.

Healthy curiosity proved stronger than her apprehension. In a minute, the tip of Melamori's nose was poking out the door.

"Who are you?" she asked sharply. "And where is Sir Max? Is this some kind of joke?"

"Of course it's a joke," I smiled. "And a very good one, too, don't you think?"

"You . . . What do you mean by that?"

"Try to get on my trail. All your doubts will disappear with the wave of a hand. Well, what are you waiting for?"

Melamori jumped out of her slippers quick as a flash, and in another flash she was standing at my back. A few seconds of constrained silence, and then a sharp intake of air.

"Oh, Sir Max, what's happened?" she asked, her lips turning pale. "Did someone cast a spell on you?"

"Yep. It's only for a while, though. I have to marry Lonli-Lokli right away. Shhhh! It's a deep, dark secret. Maybe you'll let me come in after all?"

"I think it will be all right," Melamori said, smiling. "Will you please explain to me what's happening?"

"Of course I will. Two girls have to have a heart-to-heart chat about something. You know, I thought it would be hard for us to become friends, since . . . Well, you understand exactly what I mean. But being girls—it's just right for a start. By the way, I'm Marilyn. I think it will be easier for you that way."

"Oh yes, much easier."

We went into the living room. Melamori suddenly began laughing in relief.

"Sit down, Lady Marilyn. It's wonderful you've come! I wanted very much to see you."

"Female intuition," I grinned slyly. "It's a formidable power. By the way, it tells me that you have some kind of souvenir from Uncle Kima around somewhere. What better time than now to let the drink flow freely? I'm leaving the day after tomorrow."

"Forever?" her voice expressed genuine anguish.

"Forever? Don't get your hopes up. For a few dozen days in all."

"Where?"

"To Kettari. Our chief succumbed to an attack of nostalgia and ordered us to dig up some cobblestones from the streets of his youth. Open your cache, sweetheart. When I have too much to drink, it will loosen my tongue and I'll tell all. Honest I will."

"Would you like to drink Gulp of Fate, Marilyn?" Melamori asked. I shuddered from the unexpectedness of it.

"Gulp of Fate? Hmm, it seems we've already tried that before."

"I wonder where you could have tried that wine, Marilyn," Melamori parried, as calm as ever. "It's very rare."

"It certainly is rare," I laughed, feeling with surprise how the last heavy stone dropped from my heart. "Of course I'd like a drink. Who am I to refuse Gulp of Fate?"

"Wonderful."

The ancient wine turned out to be dark, almost black, in color. Some hardly visible blue sparks played at the bottom of the glass.

"It's a good sign, Marilyn," Melamori said, tapping the edge of the glass with her finger. "Kima told me that these little flames appear only if the wine is being drunk by people who . . . how can I explain it. People between whom everything is *right*. Understand? Not 'good,' and not 'bad,' but *right*."

"I think I do understand. Only I have another way of saying it: *for real*. Am I expressing myself properly?"

"If there's one thing you and Max really know how to do, Marilyn, it's express yourself 'properly.' Taste good?"

"You bet!"

"Then tell me your story. I can take an oath of silence if you wish."

"I need no oath from you, Melamori. Just watch and listen. Lady Marilyn and I are real storytellers."

And I narrated in great detail the story of the strange costume ball, with me starring as the beauty queen. Melifaro the lover was the hero of the finale.

"My goodness! I've never laughed so hard in my life!" Melamori said, wiping away tears. "Poor Melifaro. He has no luck with girls.

You should have given him a chance, Marilyn. Where will you find another boy like him?"

"Maybe you're right. I'll take your advice into consideration. Look, it's already getting light! Will you have time to get some sleep?"

"Oh, I'll just be late for work. No big deal. I'll tell Sir Juffin that I was giving you lessons in feminine wiles."

"Yes, those will come in handy, considering who my future life companion is supposed to be." I struggled to get up from the low divan. "I'm going to go get some sleep, Melamori. It's time you did, too. Better too little than none at all."

"It doesn't matter how much, but how you sleep . . . And today I'll sleep like the dead. Thank you, Marilyn. Please tell Sir Max that it was an excellent idea."

"I'll tell him," I yawned and waved to her. "Good morning, Melamori."

I'd like to note that Marilyn also slept like the dead, which hadn't been the case for a long time with my good old friend Max. This girl had a first-rate heart of stone, much more reliable than mine.

❧

At sundown I reported to the House by the Bridge. I had a suit-case with me that accommodated a large bottle of Elixir of Kaxar, masses of clothes (Lady Marilyn enjoyed shopping), and my enchanted pillow—"Stopgap in the Chink between Worlds," in the words of my greatest benefactor, Sir Maba Kalox. Whatever might happen, setting out for the unknown without my one and only miracle-method for getting a normal cigarette just wasn't my style.

Sir Juffin Hully was chatting animatedly with some middle-aged, suntanned blond fellow in a light-blue and white looxi. He had the appearance of a sports coach: muscular arms, ruddy complexion, and a stern, unsmiling expression. Unwilling to interrupt their conversation, I sent my chief a call.

Are you busy, Juffin? Should I wait in the lobby?

"What do you mean, Lady Marilyn?" Juffin flashed a welcoming smile. "Did you think I had a visitor, Max? And who said we'd have a problem with Sir Shurf's appearance? My compliments to both of you, boys. You make a perfect couple."

"You look ravishing, Marilyn!" the unrecognizable Lonli-Lokli observed politely, rising to greet me, and (Oh, sinning Magicians!) considerately helping me to my seat.

"I must ask your forgiveness, Max, but from here on out I'll be addressing you with various terms of endearment, since it's customary between husband and wife."

"There's no need to ask my forgiveness. You can address me any way you like at any time, Shurf!"

"Now my name is Sir Glamma Eralga, dear Marilyn. Of course, you must simply call me Glamma."

"Maybe we can just call each other by our regular names for the time being? It's so disconcerting otherwise."

"No, Sir Shurf is absolutely right. The sooner you get used to your new names the better. Later you'll have bigger worries," Juffin said.

What kinds of worries was he referring to, I would have liked to know?

I stared at Lonli-Lokli curiously. It was the first time I had seen him without his death-dealing gloves, which I tended to think of as his real hands. I knew, of course, that they weren't. But the heart, which is stronger than reason, was certain that the shining hands were the real thing.

"Gosh, what's wrong with your hands, Shurf? I mean, Glamma."

"Nothing. If you are referring to my gloves, I have them with me, in the trunk. You don't suppose, do you, dear Marilyn, that all citizens have gloves like that?"

"Of course I don't, but I've never seen you without them, Shurf —er, dear!"

"Maybe this Shurf you speak of is still wearing them; your dearest Glamma, as you can see, is not."

"Oh, of course. I'm sorry, sweetheart," I said laughing. "And what's with your fingernails?"

"These are the first letters of the words of an ancient spell. Without them, the gloves would be lethal for me, too. I'm afraid I'll have to wear these." Lonli-Lokli showed me some elegant gloves made from the thinnest blue leather. "On the road they won't attract attention, but when I dine, I anticipate they might arouse suspicion."

"It doesn't matter in the least. Any person can have eccentricities. Let people think that you're squeamish, that you're just afraid of germs."

"Greetings, sugar pie," said Melifaro, bursting into the office. "Well, have you considered the possibility of remaining a girl and accepting my proposal? My mama would be ecstatic," he said, leaning on the armrest of my chair. "Our Loki-Lonki is much improved in appearance—but I'm still better-looking!"

"Sir Melifaro, stop soliciting my wife," said the transformed Lonli-Lokli. "And please be so good as to learn my name, at least by the time I return. You've known me for years."

"You got that?" I asked bitingly. "I'm no damsel in distress."

It was Juffin who got the biggest kick out of our absurd and spirited repartee, which was just as it should be. He's the boss, after all.

❄

"Juffin, I hope you won't object?" asked Sir Kofa Yox, the incomparable Master Eavesdropper *cum* Personal Cosmetologist, entering the office and clutching a sizable parcel to his chest. "You still have time to explain to these unfortunate boys what kind of hellish place they're going to. You have the whole night ahead of you, and I have something extremely yummy to help pass the time."

"When did I ever object to parties, Kofa?" Juffin rejoined. "But why did you bring all this with you? We could have just called for a courier to deliver it."

"No way! I won't entrust a matter like this to just anyone. Shutta Vax, one of the virtuoso cooks in the ancient style, has retired from the profession and cooks only for himself now. But when I asked him for seven Chakkatta Pies, he couldn't refuse. We're lucky—it appears that he's the only one left who has the slightest idea how to make them."

"Do you mean that, Kofa?" Juffin looked truly alarmed.

"It's no joking matter. Ladies first, so get over here before I reconsider."

Melamori didn't wait for him to repeat the invitation.

"Good evening, Marilyn," she greeted me, placing her hand affectionately on my shoulder. "It's too bad you're leaving tomorrow."

"But if we weren't leaving, there wouldn't be any Chakkatta Pies," I said. "It's the law of natural compensation."

"We've forgotten about poor Sir Lookfi," Melamori said. "We should call him."

"I did, but he must first say goodbye to about a hundred buri-woks. Now bring on the pie, Kofa. I can't wait."

The dull thud of an overturning chair announced the arrival of the Master Keeper of Knowledge.

"Good evening. It's so kind of you to remember to call me. Sir Kofa, you're a good sort to arrange this celebration for all of us. And good evening, Sir Max. I haven't seen you in a long time. What have you done to your hair? Is that the style these days?"

Melifaro nearly fell off the arm of the chair, Melamori and I exchanged bewildered glances, and Sir Kofa was crackling with annoyance. Sinning Magicians! What happened to my disguise? Could people really still recognize me as Max?

"Don't worry, Max," Juffin came to my rescue just in time. "And you, Kofa—you should be ashamed for being surprised. You know our Sir Lookfi sees things as they are, and not as they seem. How else could he tell all his buriwoks apart?"

"Sir Lookfi is a truly insightful person. I've always said that," Kurush interjected. Juffin nodded, agreeing with the wise bird.

"Still, it's disappointing. I considered this girl to be such a masterpiece," muttered Sir Kofa Yox. "I thought I could fool even Lookfi."

"Juffin, are there any other 'truly insightful' people among the collectors of Kettarian carpets?" I asked with a sudden rush of anxiety.

"No. I personally know of only one other natural phenomenon like Lookfi—the sheriff of the Island of Murimak, the most imposing personage on that entire scrap of dry land. I think his main duty is to count the hairs on the fur of the local species of Royal Polecats. So take it easy," Juffin turned back to Lookfi. "Have you had time to notice by now that our Max has temporarily become a lady?"

"Ah, yes. Now I see. Your hair is longer," Sir Lookfi Pence said with relief. "It's good that this isn't the new fashion. I don't look good in hairstyles like that—and they're so much trouble."

The improvised party was a brilliant success. If I had known that they would give Lonli-Lokli and me such a sendoff, I would have gone on a journey every day. Finally, just the three of us remained behind.

※

Sir Juffin Hully devoted a large part of the night to telling me and Lonli-Lokli the fabricated story of our conjugal life, for it was very likely we would meet curious travelers who wished to chat over dinner. I must admit, I only listened with half an ear, since I'd be with Lonli-Lokli, sturdy and reliable as a cupboard. He wouldn't forget a word of the boring biography of Sir Glamma Eralga and Lady Marilyn Monroe.

"That's all well and good, Juffin," I said, staring thoughtfully at the steadily brightening dawn sky. "But I must admit, I still don't understand why we're going to Kettari."

"Precisely for that reason: to understand why you need to go to Kettari once you've arrived. I can tell you honestly, Max—when I sent you to confront the ghost of Xolomi, I really was a bit greedy, that is, I kept a few things to myself until you asked me the question I was patiently awaiting. But this time it's different. You really do know everything I know myself. So I'm sending you to Kettari to find answers to questions that are still a complete mystery to me. If you want my advice, when you get there, you should lie low for a few days. Don't do anything. Walk around the city with Shurf, buy some carpets. Maybe the secret will find you, you have that lucky streak. But if nothing happens—well then, try leaving the city without the caravan or any other company, and then just return. Take your time, though, it seems to me that it would not be very wise to hurry. Right now I'm not sure of anything, though. All right, boys, it's time. The caravan to Kettari leaves in one hour. You can each take a swallow."

Juffin handed me his famous invisible bottle of Elixir of Kaxar, almost empty due to my efforts. I gladly took a gulp of the tasty drink, capable of relieving not only morning somnolence, but almost any other serious complaint.

"Have some, dear. There's a bit left," I offered the bottle to Lonli-Lokli.

My "significant other" declined politely, saying, "Thank you, Marilyn. But I don't drink."

"As you wish. We have a whole day of travel ahead of us."

"There are special breathing exercises that dispel exhaustion far more effectively than your drink," Lonli-Lokli said loftily.

"Will you teach them to me?" I asked.

"I'll teach you, but only after you master the exercises I've already shown you."

"But I already—"

"You just think you 'already.' Forty years from now you'll under-stand what I mean."

"Oh! As the Great Magician Nuflin likes to say, 'I'm just glad I won't live to see the day.' Fine, let's be off, honey."

"Yes. Get a move on," Juffin nodded. "You'll have plenty of time to talk. The road is long. And don't forget to bring me a souvenir from my homeland."

❊

Sir Lonli-Lokli eased in confidently behind the levers of the amobiler.

"Maybe we should change places?" I suggested.

"You want to drive the amobiler right after you've imbibed Elixir of Kaxar? No, you may not do that. I've told you that before. When we're on the road you'll have to relieve me sometimes, Marilyn. But are you sure you can drive like normal people do? If our amobiler keeps overtaking all the others, we'll end up without a Master Caravan Leader. Not to mention shocking our fellow travelers."

"Don't worry," I reassured him. "Unlike our friend Max, Lady Marilyn is a careful damsel. Everything will be fine. I'll step on the throat of any song."

"What's that, some secret spell?" Lonli-Lokli asked quaintly.

"Yep. I could teach you, but it would take forty or fifty years," Lady Marilyn's tongue was as sharp as that of my old friend Sir Max.

Actually, a few seconds later I decided that the joke might lead to unpredictable consequences, and I turned guiltily to my companion.

"Just between us guys, Glamma, it was a joke. It's just a harmless expression."

"That's what I thought. But you're not a guy, Marilyn. I'd advise you to watch your language."

"Yes, my dear. You're absolutely right."

I began to suspect that a journey in the company of Lonli-Lokli would do more to hone my character than the severest pedagogical system of ancient Sparta.

❊

My spirits finally lifted when I caught sight of at least a dozen amobilers accompanied by group of people in elegant traveling attire. When I was a child, I had always loved going to railroad stations to watch trains. It seemed to me they were going somewhere where everything was different from where I was. They were on their way

There, and I envied the passengers as they wearily arranged their baggage in the overhead luggage racks. You could see the enchanting spectacle through the illuminated windows of the train while you stood on the platform. I preferred not to pay too much attention to the trains coming from *There* to the dreary *Here*.

Now I had the same feeling, only much stronger. Not a vague dream about a nonexistent wonder, but a near certainty about it. I even temporarily forgot that Echo was not at all the kind of place I wanted to leave. Comfortably wrapped in the elegant body of Lady Marilyn, I dove into the small human maelstrom, Sir Shurf Lonli-Lokli following close behind.

In a few minutes, Lady Marilyn and her solicitous companion by the name of Glamma had already made the acquaintance of Abora Vala, Master of the Caravan—a short, gray-haired, but not at all old Kettarian, extremely charming despite his sly little eyes. We immediately paid eight crowns, half the cost of his services. The rest of the money was to be paid on the central square of the City of Kettari at the end of the journey. We were assured that the return trip to Echo would be free of charge.

There was another half hour of polite mutual sniffing out and exchanging names among fellow travelers, all of which I immediately forgot in the confusion of the moment. My Lady Marilyn behaved beautifully, not making a single gender blunder and answering consistently to her own name. Finally Mr. Vala called for everyone's attention.

"I think we are all here, ladies and gentlemen. Let us depart. I'll take the lead. I hope you'll approve of the places I choose to stop and rest. I have a great deal of experience in this matter, you may be sure. If you run into trouble of any kind, just send me a call. I don't recommend that you stray from the caravan, but if you get left behind, please don't demand your money back. I hope, of course, that our journey will progress without any untoward events or unpleasant circumstances. Bon voyage, ladies and gentlemen!"

We all dispersed to our amobilers. I must admit I was even glad that Lonli-Lokli hadn't allowed me to take the driver's seat yet. It gave me the chance to admire the mosaic-laden pavement and the low buildings of Echo.

I had grown to love this city so much that the impending departure made me happy—I was already looking forward to the poignant joy of returning.

We passed through the enormous, lush gardens of the outskirts, which finally gave way to fields and woods. I was dizzy with all the new sights. Sir Shurf stared silently at the road in front of him. Even after he had become Sir Glamma Eralga, he was the most dispassionate of mortals. Our journey in one another's company was not the worst pretext for finally satisfying my burning curiosity, I thought.

"Glamma, what do you prefer, the opportunity to keep silent, or the opportunity to talk?" I asked cautiously.

"I always enjoy talking to you, Marilyn, just as I enjoy talking to my friend Sir Max," Lonli-Lokli replied sedately.

Did I detect some warmth of feeling in his voice? Either I was imagining it, or Sir Glamma, the new persona of the Master of Snuffing Out Unnecessary Lives, was a bit wayward (from the point of view of his former self).

"If you don't want to answer my question, just tell me, all right?"

"Of course I'll tell you. What else could I do under the circumstances?"

Lonli-Lokli's iron logic restored my self-confidence.

"Fine. I've made my decision. All the more since the subject concerns not you, Glamma, but my friend Lonli-Lokli."

"I can't help but admire your sense of timing," my companion said approvingly. "All things should be done at the proper time, including asking questions. Ask away. I think I'll be able to satisfy your curiosity."

"I hope so. Once, the name Sir Shurf Lonli-Lokli was mentioned in a conversation with an old Magician, a friend of Juffin's. When he heard the name, he said, 'Ah, the Mad Fishmonger!' Juffin nodded, but a certain Sir Max was very perplexed. Madness was the last thing he would have associated with his friend Shurf."

"We haven't known each other for very long. This explains your surprise. If you're interested in the history of the person I was in my youth, it's no secret whatsoever, in contrast to the history of Sir Max himself."

"Really?" I replied, somewhat confused.

I have to admit, Shurf's last remark (or Glamma's, if you will) sent me into something of a panic. Melamori, Sir Kofa, and now Lonli-Lokli—they all sensed that something wasn't quite right with me. Actually, that's why they are secret investigators, isn't it? Ah well, it's Juffin's fault, after all. Let him explain whatever he wishes, or keep it to himself.

"I don't intend to ask any questions, since I feel the time isn't right yet," Lonli-Lokli said. "You need to learn to control the expressions of your face. Actually, if you don't forget to do the exercises I taught you every day, that skill will develop of its own accord."

"In about forty years?"

"I can't say exactly. Maybe sooner."

"All right, Glamma. Never mind my facial expressions. Let me hear your story, if it's no secret."

"Of course it isn't! Exactly seventeen dozen years ago, a certain youth by the name of Shurf became an apprentice of the Order of the Holey Cup, with which his family was closely connected. So the young man didn't really have much choice in the matter. Actually, for those times it was a more than enviable fate. Not six dozen years had gone by and this young man became the Junior Magician and Master Fishmonger. In other words, he became the watchman over the holey aquariums of the Order. As far as I know, Sir Juffin once told you in fairly great detail about the ways of the Order of the Holey Cup, so I won't repeat it."

"All members of the order ate only fish that lived in holey aquariums and drank from holey vessels, like your famous cup, right?"

"That's a rudimentary, but generally true, characterization. So, for several years the Junior Magician Shurf Lonli-Lokli carried out his duties splendidly."

"Oh, I don't doubt it for a minute."

"Well, you should, since the person we're talking about is completely unknown to you. He was one of the most intemperate, capricious, and emotionally volatile people I've ever met; and believe me, I'm putting it mildly. The path on which members of the Order of the Holey Cup sought their strength did not help them to curb their own vices. You should know that this holds true for many other ancient Orders, as well."

I nodded.

"Yes, Juffin told me about it. I just wish I could get the tiniest glimpse of what really went on during the infamous Epoch of Orders."

"I recommend that you discuss it with Sir Kofa Yox. He's a gifted storyteller, in contrast to me."

"Nonsense, Glamma! You're an excellent raconteur. Please go on."

"I'm terrible when it comes to telling a story. It's just that the subject is interesting to you," Lonli-Lokli said. "I brought up the lack of restraint I had as a young man, because this aspect of his character explains his foolish action." He frowned and fell silent.

"What foolish action would that be?" I urged him on, burning with curiosity.

"He wanted to acquire power at all costs: a great deal of it, and very quickly. So he drank the water from all the aquariums that he was supposed to be looking after."

I couldn't help laughing. I could imagine the fantastic spectacle, as though it were happening right in front of my eyes. Our Shurf drinking the aquariums dry, one after another. Sinning Magicians!

"Pardon me, Glamma, but it strikes me as very funny," I confessed with a guilty air when I had caught my breath.

"Yes, I'm sure it does. The fish that lived in the aquariums perished, naturally, and the reckless young man gained enormous power. Except he couldn't deal with it. That is knowledge one must learn over the course of centuries. It's difficult for me to describe further events in any great detail; my memory is simply unable to retrieve a large part of what this foolish youth did after he left the Residence of his Order. But I can tell you that in the city they called him the Mad Fishmonger—and for a person to be called 'mad' during the Epoch of Orders, he really had to make an effort! I remember none of the residents of the city dared deny me anything I demanded. I was surrounded by terrified women, many servants, a great deal of money, and other things that crude people find entertaining. But I grew weary of all of this very quickly. I became obsessed. In those days, I liked to frighten people. More than that, however, I liked to kill. However, killing ordinary city-dwellers was demeaning. I longed to drink the blood of the Grand Magicians. I would appear at the necessary place, and then disappear. Too many hollow marvels, which I myself couldn't understand, were committed at that time; but the blood of the Grand Magicians lay nevertheless beyond my reach."

"Gosh, Shurf! Can this really be true?"

I realized that our Sir Lonli-Lokli wasn't the cleverest liar in the Unified Kingdom—but all the same I couldn't believe my ears.

"Call me Glamma. You forgot again, Marilyn," the stern tone of my companion put an end to my doubts.

"People change, don't they?" I asked quietly.

"Not all of them. But sometimes it happens. Actually, that's not the whole story."

"That's what I thought."

"I wanted even more power, more than the famous Magicians about whose blood I dreamed back then. One day the Mad Fishmonger arrived at the Residence of the Order of the Icy Hand to seize for himself one of the mightiest of all hands."

"Your gloves!"

"Yes. My left glove, to be exact. The right one I received when I fought with a Junior Magician of this Order. The fellow tried to stop me, so I bit off his right hand."

"You bit it off!"

"Of course. What's so strange about that? It was far less eccentric than most of my other escapades at the time."

"Juffin told me that there was a tremendous amount of powerful magic in the Order of the Icy Hand. Did they really—"

"You see, after I had drunk dry all the twenty dozen aquariums, I received the power meant for the six hundred members of my Order. So it was very difficult to stop me, and when I got the gloves that you are familiar with, I became even more dangerous. But they finally did stop me."

"Who? Was it Juffin?"

"No, Sir Juffin Hully came into my life a bit later. Two dead men stopped the Mad Fishmonger. They were the owners of the hands I took for my own. On one night they came to me in my dream. At that time, I became defenseless when I slept. Not completely, but almost. They wanted to take me away to somewhere between life and death in a place of endless tormented dying. I'm not very adept at describing things, so it would be better if your imagination would tell you what I was threatened with."

"Never mind my imagination," I murmured. "I'm hanging on to your every word. I won't be able to get to sleep."

"Well your words assure me that you're close to understanding the problem I'm trying to describe, Marilyn," said Lonli-Lokli. "I was very lucky that night. I awoke suddenly in great pain, as the old house where I was sleeping began crashing down. One of the stones hit me on the forehead. You may be wondering why the house started falling down; Sir Juffin Hully can tell you the details of his unsuccessful hunt for the Mad Fishmonger. There was no Secret Investigative Force at that time, but Sir Juffin was already entrusted with special missions by the King and the Seven-Leaf Clover. He was terribly renowned—and he deserved it, I suppose. But the Kettarian

Hunter, as Sir Venerable Head was called back then, saved my life purely by chance. I managed to get out of the collapsing house in time, without even realizing what was happening. Meanwhile I was worried about something completely different. It was clear that the next dream would be my last. So I decided to live life to the hilt, mustering all my resources for that purpose, and then to kill myself before suffering the wrath of the dead Magicians. I succeeded in living without sleep for almost two years."

"What?!"

Lonli-Lokli shocked me more with every word he uttered.

"Yes, it was around two years," Sir Shurf insisted. "Just so. Of course, it couldn't go on indefinitely. It is no exaggeration to say that I was already mad with that extra strain, and two years of insomnia turned me into something utterly unspeakable. Sir Juffin Hully followed every move I made, as I later came to understand. He was waiting for the right moment."

"So that he could—"

"No, Marilyn. Not to kill me. You see, that night when he destroyed my house and saved my life, the life he was going to extinguish, it was a serendipitous event. The Kettarian rarely made a fool of himself, and he concluded that fate was showing him the way to me. So instead of capturing the Mad Fishmonger, Sir Juffin decided to save Shurf Lonli-Lokli, who had become entangled in his own marvels."

"It's all so romantic," I said.

"Yes, quite. Of course, Sir Juffin has an unimpeachable sense of timing. He arrived at my side just at the moment when I realized that the period of insomnia was coming to an end—and with it, the end of my life was nigh. I was glad to die. Death seemed to me an appropriate way of avoiding a much worse fate. Then when the famous Kettarian Hunter caught up with me, I experienced an incomparable joy, for I was going to die in battle, and that was much more fun than suicide."

"What did you say? 'More fun'?" I was sure my ears had deceived me.

"Yes, of course. Contrary to the Lonli-Lokli of the present, the Mad Fishmonger loved to joke around and have fun. But Juffin and I never came to blows: instead of trying to kill me, Sir Juffin put me to sleep. I don't suppose it was too hard for him at that point, as I was obsessed with the thought of sleeping. Juffin shoved me into the embrace of the dead men, who were obsessed with revenge. That began a whole eternity of weakness and pain. Oh, you shouldn't grieve for me Marilyn. It happened long ago; and not to me, you may believe. And then the Kettarian pulled me out of the nightmare. He just woke me up, brought me to my senses, and explained that there was only one way out."

"What was the way out, Glamma?"

I didn't know very much about the local miracles, but I had experienced for myself the monstrous power of the nightmares of this World.

"It was all quite simple. Those two were seeking the Mad Fishmonger, so, I had to become someone else. Of course, an ordinary masquerade, like the one you and I performed before beginning this journey, wouldn't have helped. It's not that easy to deceive dead Magicians. Some people, yes; but not them. Sir Juffin transported me to some strange place, gave me a few words of advice, and left me there."

"What kind of 'strange place' was it?" I asked, my heart at a standstill.

"I don't know. Or, rather, I don't remember. It's impossible to preserve in your memory things that happen beyond the boundaries of your comprehension."

"What kind of advice did he give you? Excuse me for pressing the matter, but I want to understand. What kind of advice can you give a person who has been struck by such misfortune?"

"It was nothing, really. He explained what I had to do, and why. He showed me some breathing exercises like the ones I showed you. Don't forget that at the time I possessed enormous strength, enough to perform any wondrous feat. Juffin simply created the ideal conditions for it to manifest itself. I remember that in that strange place I couldn't do anything but these breathing exercises. It was impossible to eat, sleep, and think. Time, as we ordinarily perceive it, didn't exist. My personal eternity fit into a single moment, that's the only way to describe it. I didn't even notice when the Mad Fishmonger died. The young man I had once been died, too. After that, the me you know by the name of Shurf Lonli-Lokli emerged. I have no complaints about my new personality—it doesn't prevent me from concentrating on the things that are really important. And, all in all, it doesn't get in the way."

"It's simply unbelievable. Who would have thought?" I whispered.

"Yes, it is fairly improbable," Sir Shurf agreed phlegmatically. "Then I was able to leave the strange empty place and return to Echo. Sir Juffin Hully found decent work for me. By the end of the Troubled Times a person with hands like mine didn't have to worry about finding something to do. So in the end I did learn to taste the blood of the Grand Magicians; but by then it was a question of duty, not desire. In fact, for my new self it is a matter of complete indifference. I don't think a single murder I've had to commit has had any meaning for me, or for anyone else." He paused. "Excuse me, Marilyn. I'm not a very good philosopher."

I was astounded. My own world, the world I had inhabited so cozily and comfortably, had fallen apart before my very eyes. Infallible Sir Shurf, solid and dependable as a rock, imperturbable and pedantic, completely devoid of a sense of humor and ordinary human weaknesses—where had he gone? And my other colleagues, headed by Sir Juffin Hully, who turned out to have been the staid "Kettarian Hunter"—what did I really know about them? What other surprises were in store for me?

"Now is a good time to do some of those exercises I taught Max, Marilyn," my companion advised me. "You shouldn't get so upset about things that happened long ago, when we weren't even there."

"Words of wisdom!" I exclaimed, and threw myself into Lonli-Lokli's breathing exercises.

※

In about ten minutes I was absolutely calm. The mysteries of an exciting new World were gradually being revealed, and this was a great boon. Nonetheless, I still thank fate that the wonderful revelations of my colleagues didn't come down on me all at once.

"Mr. Abora Vala just sent me a call," Lonli-Lokli said. "The caravan is going to stop for lunch now. You have behaved perfectly this morning, Marilyn. Try to keep it up. By the way, I have long wanted to remark that in doing his breathing exercises, Sir Max breathes just as sharply and unevenly as he speaks. You should do something about it."

"All right, I'll try," I murmured. "Do I really speak so poorly?"

"Yes, of course, but it will pass in time. Let's stop, Marilyn. Get ready to change the subject, all right?"

"Agreed. By the way, our Master Caravan Leader doesn't have bad timing, either. I could eat a horse."

"No, Marilyn: 'I'm hungry as a horse,' or, simply, 'I'm famished.' Mr. Vala has no sense of timing whatsoever. Our caravan leader just stops at the taverns whose proprietors pay him for delivering clients."

I laughed.

"How do you know, Glamma?"

"I looked him in the eye when we met."

"Oh, I see! Still, he stopped just on time. I'm very hungry."

"Here we go, then," said Shurf, and chivalrously helped me out of the amobiler.

✿

The meal was nothing to write home about; for me, anyway. As a budding gourmet and the favorite pupil of Sir Kofa Yox, I wasn't about to jump for joy at your average country cooking. But our traveling companions turned out to be ordinary, dull tavern philistines. I was surprised to realize that the wonderful new World I so adored was not perfect. I suppose the average inhabitants of all Worlds are rather lackluster. I wasn't exactly dizzy with delight at the prospect of socializing with a large number of these good-natured, simple souls. But a journey is a journey, and even such annoyances as bad food and the uninspiring company of fellow travelers had its charms.

After lunch I persuaded Lonli-Lokli to let me drive the amobiler. He didn't want to risk it at first; my common sense didn't exactly fill Sir Shurf with confidence. But Lady Marilyn begged him so!

After an hour of crawling at a snail's pace, I was rewarded.

"I would never have imagined that you could exercise such restraint," Shurf said.

It occurred to me that this was the biggest compliment I had ever been paid before.

"Why are you so surprised, Glamma? If someone tells me 'you mustn't,' I fully intend to heed the advice."

"This isn't merely about things one must or must not do. The amobiler moves at the speed its driver wishes it to, and our wishes are often at odds with necessity."

"Really? Are you serious? Good golly! I had no idea."

"You didn't know?" asked Lonli-Lokli. "I was sure you were

simply fulfilling your childhood dream of high-speed racing when you got behind the levers."

"No! Up till now it just seemed to me that I wasn't as cautious as other drivers, and pushed it to maximum speed."

"Of course, that's what I had in mind when I didn't want to let you behind the levers. Only there's no 'maximum speed.' It's all a matter of the driver's inner speedometer. I underestimated your self-control, however. I believe I owe you an apology."

"You shouldn't apologize, Glamma. That's nonsense. So all this time I've been driving this jalopy, I didn't know how it worked. I'll be a monkey's uncle!"

I sighed, and wiped the drops of perspiration from my forehead. Too much strange, new information for one day.

"The important thing is that you know how to drive it. And you can't be an uncle, even a monkey's. You keep forgetting who you are, my dear."

We rode in silence until deep in the night. Lonli-Lokli, no doubt, had already exhausted his quota of words for the next three years. And I was mortally afraid of asking another questions—I'd had enough amazing revelations for one day, thank you very much.

We spent the night in a large roadside motel. Our guide sat down at the small bar for a game of Krak. Some of the travelers were happy to join him.

"This is how to do business," Lonli-Lokli said. "Two nights on the road to Kettari, and two nights on the return trip. This Master Caravan Leader is a very rich man, I'm willing to bet."

"Do you think he's a cardsharper, too?"

"No, but Kettarians are very good at card games. They have a true talent for it. So fleecing even the luckiest dwellers of the Capital comes naturally to them. I think we need a good sleep. We have a hard day ahead of us."

"Yes, of course," I said uncertainly, knowing I'd hardly be able to go to sleep this early, even after a hard day.

"You know, Lady Marilyn," Lonli-Lokli said, arranging himself under a fluffy blanket. "I don't think it's a good idea for you to leave our room. It won't look very plausible—pretty married women don't usually sit in the bar until dawn after a hard day on the road. People might think things aren't quite right between us."

"It would never have entered my head. No nocturnal ramblings! If tipsy barflies begin making passes at Lady Marilyn, I'll have to spit at them. And that doesn't conform to my notions of propriety and discretion."

"In that case, I beg your pardon. Good night, Marilyn."

My companion dozed off. I crawled under my blanket and let my mind wander. I had quite enough to think about after our instructive conversation. At the same time, I could take advantage of the free time and snatch a few cigarettes from under my wonder-working pillow.

I only managed to fall asleep at dawn, and an hour later Sir Shurf, already impeccably groomed and alert, thrust a tray with kamra and sandwiches under my nose.

"I'm very sorry, but we're leaving in half an hour. I think you ought to use some of your supply of Elixir of Kaxar."

"No, it's better if I sleep in the amobiler," I said, lifting my heavy head from the pillow. "Thanks for your concern, Glamma. Your wife—I mean the real wife of Lonli-Lokli—must be the happiest of women."

"I hope so," said Shurf. "I have a strange fate, Marilyn. Real wife or no, I'm the one who serves her kamra in bed, and not the other way around."

"Sinning Magicians, was that a joke I just heard?"

"It's simply a statement of fact. If you wish to bathe, you'd better hurry."

"Of course I want to!" I swallowed the kamra down in one gulp, I couldn't even look at the food.

※

I settled down in the back seat of the amobiler, leaving my fellow travelers to contemplate the dreary, monotonous plains stretching to the west of Uguland. I fell asleep so soundly that Sir Lonli-Lokli's attempts to make me come out for lunch proved futile. "Just tell them that the lady is suffering from motion sickness," I grumbled sourly, and dove headfirst into the sweetest of sweet dreams.

I awoke not long before sundown. I was as happy, rested, and hungry, all at once, as I had been in a long time.

"I took a few sandwiches from the tavern where we had lunch," Lonli-Lokli said. "I think it was the right thing to do."

"You got that right," I said gratefully. "I hope it's not some inedible stuff again."

"The local cuisine differs from that of the Capital, naturally," said Sir Shurf. "But one shouldn't underestimate the benefit of some variety in life."

"Oh, I'm conservative in these matters," I said with my mouth full. "Maybe it's time for me to take over from you, Glamma? I hope you trust me behind the levers by now."

"Of course I do. You can do as you wish, though I'm not really tired yet."

"One shouldn't underestimate the benefit of some variety in life. End of quote."

"Touché."

My Lady Marilyn made herself comfortable at the levers and daringly lit up a cigarette. I couldn't wait to partake of the fruits of my night's labor.

Lonli-Lokli grew visibly uneasy.

"I don't know where these strange smoking accoutrements come from, but you should hide them from the gaze of strangers. What is all right for Max is not necessarily acceptable for an ordinary citizen, Lady Marilyn."

"I'm a stranger myself, if you care to remember! And it's very unlikely that anyone is observing us now."

"Not now, no, but during the stops."

"I'm not a complete dunce!" I retorted. "Do you really think I'd light up a cigarette in the company of other people, Shurf?"

"It's always better to be forewarned. Besides, you probably haven't considered that it would be better to burn the butts than to throw them away. You really must mind your manners, Marilyn," my companion reprimanded me.

I burst out laughing. Our dialogue was becoming heated. When I had recovered, I carefully burned my cigarette butt. Lonli-Lokli was, after all, the wisest of mortals. And I was a frivolous ninny who knew nothing about the paramount demands of secrecy.

That night we had already reached the County Shimara. Our Master Caravan Leader sat down at the card table again, and we dined on something exotic—too spicy and oily for my tastes—then went to the night's lodgings.

Only then did I realize that the huge residential hall was outside the territory of the Unified Kingdom. Our room was not much larger than an ordinary hotel room in my own world, and the bed was a regular double bed. I looked at Lonli-Lokli in dismay.

"Well, I'll be! It looks like we'll have to sleep in each other's embrace, my darling!"

"That may be rather inconvenient," Sir Shurf said. "Besides, since it has come to this, I can offer you the possibility of using my sleep. When people sleep side by side, it's fairly easy to do so."

"How do you mean?" I asked, puzzled. "I'll have your dreams instead of my own? And anyway, it won't work—Lady Marilyn slept until sundown."

"When one person shares his sleep with another, they fall asleep simultaneously," Shurf explained. "I'll put you to sleep, and then I'll wake you up. But I don't know in advance whose dreams we'll have: yours, mine, or both at the same time. It's up to us to decide. Anyway, I think this solution to the dilemma is a reasonable one. Tomorrow after lunch we'll be in Kettari, and you'll have to be awake and alert the whole day. If I've understood correctly, Sir Juffin wanted us to pay close attention to the road leading into the city."

"That's true," I agreed. "Do you have good dreams, Glamma? After the story about some of Sir Lonli-Lokli's dreams—"

"I would never propose that you share my nightmares. Luckily, I have been free of them for a long time."

"Well, I can't vouch for my dreams," I said, and sighed. "Sometimes I see such terrible things in my dreams that it's enough to make you despair. Do you like taking risks, Glamma?"

"There's no risk involved, since I'm always able to wake up at will. Lie down, Marilyn. We mustn't waste any more valuable time."

I quickly undressed, surprised again that my body had remained the same beneath the illusion of Lady Marilyn, so very plausible and genuine.

It's time to sleep in your pajamas, kid, I thought. You're not going to walk around naked in your friend Shurf's dreamworld, are you? It's wouldn't be polite.

"It's best if our heads are touching," Lonli-Lokli said. "I'm not an expert in these matters by a long shot."

"Okay," I said, and obediently shifted my head. "All the more since putting to sleep such a live-wire as myself . . ." I yawned without finishing my thought, ready to peek into my companion's dreams.

It turned out that the "projectionist" in this small dream-cinema for two was me. My favorite dreams of all visited us that night—the city in the mountains, where the only kind of municipal transport was a cable car; the marvelous English park that was always empty; the line of sandy beaches on the shore of a dark, gloomy sea.

I wandered through these extraordinary dreamscapes, now and then exclaiming, "It's wonderful, isn't it?" "Wonderful!" my partner agreed, an astonishing fellow who didn't look at all like my good friend Sir Shurf Lonli-Lokli, nor like the Mad Fishmonger who once terrorized all of Echo, nor like Sir Glamma Eralga.

I awoke at dawn, happy and full of peaceful well-being.

"Thank you for that wonderful excursion," I said, smiling at Lonli-Lokli, who was already pulling on Glamma's blue skaba.

"I'm the one who should be thanking you, since our dreams belonged to Sir Max. I've never had the opportunity to be in places like that before. Without the slightest doubt, they're marvelous. I never expected anything like that from you, Sir Max."

"The name's Marilyn," I said, and burst out laughing. "Gosh, Shurf, can you really make mistakes?"

"Sometimes one must make mistakes to be understood correctly," Lonli-Lokli remarked cryptically, and went off to bathe.

"All the same, it wouldn't have happened without your help! I don't know how to find those places whenever I feel like it!" I called after him. Then I sent a call to the kitchen; Lonli-Lokli shouldn't have to be the only one to bother with the trays.

❦

A grand, dusky spring morning, a drive through endless green glades, a languorously long lunch of five identically tasteless courses in a remote tavern, the monotonous chatter of the other travelers . . . I don't think I said more than ten words all day. I felt too pleasantly contented to break the tranquility with any sound at all.

"When do we arrive in Kettari?" Lonli-Lonli asked our Master Caravan Leader after we had finished our midday meal.

"It's difficult to say exactly," said Mr. Abora Vala. "I would guess in about two hours. But you see, in this part of the County Shimara, the roads are pretty rough. We might have to take a detour. But we'll cross that bridge when we come to it."

"A very competent answer," I grumbled under my breath, getting behind the levers of the amobiler. "'We'll cross that bridge when we come to it.' That's just dandy. I've never received such exhaustive information in my life. It makes a guy happy to be so well-informed."

"A girl," Lonli-Lokli corrected me. "Are you nervous?"

"Me? Where did you get that idea? Actually, I'm always nervous. It's my normal state. But today I happen to be feeling as calm as I've felt in eons."

"Well, I'm nervous," Shurf admitted unexpectedly.

"Whoa! I didn't think I'd ever be hearing that."

"I didn't think so either."

"We people are strange creatures," I mused. "You never know beforehand what we're going to do."

"Indeed, Marilyn," Sir Shurf said solemnly.

We continued on our way. Lonli-Lokli drove the amobiler, so I had an excellent opportunity to gaze about, savoring the foretaste of mystery.

The road was as predictable as a road can be when you're seeing it for the first time. After an hour and a half I grew bored, and my vigilance tried to go into early retirement. Just then, the caravan turned off the main road onto a narrow path whose usefulness as a thoroughfare looked extremely doubtful.

Several minutes of merciless rattling and rolling and we turned again. The new road was fairly tolerable, looping a bit through the foothills. Then it suddenly soared upward at a dizzying angle.

To the right of the road loomed a cliff, overgrown with dusty bluish grass. On the left yawned the emptiness of an abyss. At that moment I wouldn't have agreed to relieve Lonli-Lokli at the levers of the amobiler for all the wonders of the World I had a mortal fear of heights.

Struggling to reign in my panic, I recalled the breathing exercises and started in on them with a vengeance. Sir Shurf glanced over at me in concern, but didn't speak. In a half hour my torments were over. Now the road was winding between two identically towering cliffs, which seemed to me to offer some guarantee of safety.

"I just sent a call to Mr. Vala. He claims that Kettari is still about two hours away," said Lonli-Lokli.

"He said the same thing after lunch," I grumbled.

458 / MAX FREI

"Well, nothing to get too alarmed about. But it does seem a bit strange, doesn't it?"

"A bit? I'd say it's *very* strange. As far as I understand it, the fellow makes this journey several times a year. This must have given him enough time to get to know the road."

"That's what I would have thought."

"'We'll cross that bridge when we come to it,'" I said with a wry smile. "Maybe that motto is emblazoned on the Kettarian coat-of-arms. Looking at Juffin you'd never think so, but—actually, let me send him a call. There's nothing much to praise, so we might as well grouse to a dyed-in-the-wool Kettarian."

And I sent Sir Juffin Hully a call. To my great surprise, I didn't get the slightest response. It was just like the days when I was a bumbling novice in the World and about as competent in Silent Speech as a lazy first-grader at his multiplication tables. I shook my head vigorously and tried again. After the sixth attempt I finally became alarmed and sent a call to Lonli-Lokli, simply to convince myself that I was capable of doing it at all.

Do you hear me, Shurf? Glamma? Whatever your name is?

"Are you enjoying yourself, Marilyn? It would be better if you—"

"I can't contact Juffin!" I exclaimed out loud. "Can you imagine?"

"No, I certainly can't. I hope this isn't another joke."

"As though I don't have anything better to do than joke around! Try it yourself. It just isn't working for me."

"Fine. Take the levers. I have to sort this out—things like this can't happen for no reason."

✹

A yawning emptiness like an ironic grin now appeared in the terrain to our right. It wasn't terribly close if you tried to look directly at it, but terrifying all the same. I tried to control my fear, and gripped the levers. To admit to Sir Lonli-Lokli that I was afraid of heights—no, better we both plunge to our deaths.

My companion was silent for about ten minutes. I waited patiently. Maybe he's talking to Juffin, I thought. Of course—he must be talking to Juffin. There's a lot to tell him and Lonli-Lokli's always very thorough. Everything is fine. Something is just wrong with me, and there's nothing unusual about that.

"Silence," Lonli-Lokli announced finally. "I've tried contacting Sir

Juffin. And there is no answer from my wife, Sir Kofa Yox, Melifaro, Melamori, and Police Captain Shixola, either. And at the same time, it's no problem for us to communicate with our Master Caravan Leader. By the way, he still claims that Kettari is about two hours away. I think I ought to continue trying to get in touch with someone in Echo. Allow me to remark that this is one of the strangest incidents of my entire life."

"Oh devil's thumbs!" was all I could spit out.

Lonli-Lokli didn't pay the least bit of attention to this exotic curse—a good thing, as the last thing I wanted to do at this point was to try to explain who in the devil the devil was.

A few more anguished minutes, and I had already forgotten about the abyss to the right of the road. Apparently, my fear of heights was something akin to a bad habit, and getting rid of it was a piece of cake. All it took was concentrating on a problem that was much more serious.

"I tried a few more people. Everyone was silent except for Sir Lookfi Pence, who answered immediately," Lonli-Lokli said. He was as calm as though we were talking about the ingredients of a lunch we had already eaten.

"Everything's fine at the House by the Bridge. Something strange seems to be happening just to us. You can talk to Sir Lookfi. I think Juffin is right there beside him by now."

"This game is called 'broken telephone,'" I said.

"What? Which game is that?"

"Oh, never mind. Just take the levers, friend."

We changed places yet again, and I sent a call to Lookfi, not without trepidation. This time everything worked without a hitch.

Good day, Lookfi. Is Sir Juffin with you?

Good day, Sir Max. I can't tell you how glad I am to hear from you. Sir Shurf told me that neither of you was able to send a call to anyone but me. Isn't that a bit strange?

Indeed it is! I couldn't help but smile. *I'm sorry we're causing you such inconvenience, Lookfi, but you'll have to repeat every word I say to Juffin, and then report to us what he says. Can you manage?*

Of course, Sir Max. Don't worry about me. No inconvenience whatsoever. It's very flattering and . . . interesting. Taking part in your conversation with Sir Juffin, I mean.

Excellent, Lookfi, I said, and carefully recounted the few, but very curious, events of the day.

Sir Juffin requests that you describe the route you have been traveling up to this point, after turning off the main road, Lookfi said.

I described in as much detail as possible the narrow, almost impassable lane and the twisting mountain road, the gloomy cliffs overgrown with bluish grass, and the bottomless precipices that opened up now to the right, now to the left of our route. After reflecting a bit, I recalled again the vague answers of the guide to the simplest and most reasonable questions—when, devil take it, would we finally arrive in that blasted little town?

Sir Juffin asked me to relate to you, Sir Max, that he lived for four-hundred some years in Kettari, caught well over several dozen robbers in the surrounding forests, and didn't spend all his free days in the city. So it's no surprise he knows every blade of grass in the entire area. But never in his born days has he seen anything like the landscape you've described, Lookfi said. *And Sir Juffin also says that . . . Oh, Sinning Magicians, but that's impossible!* And Sir Lookfi Pence's voice disappeared from my mind without a trace.

I tried sending him another call, without much hope of success. No response, just as I suspected.

"Now there's no answer from Lookfi, either," I told Lonli-Lokli gloomily. "Sir Juffin managed to catch the story of our absurd post-prandial journey, and announced that in the environs of Kettari there is nothing resembling the terrain we're passing through. Then he asked Lookfi to relay something else. Lookfi heard what the chief wanted to tell us, said that it was 'impossible,' and then the connection went dead. I wish we knew what Juffin wanted to say!"

Lonli-Lokli didn't seem in the least bit perturbed about any of this.

"Let's think about it," I said. "Lady Marilyn is a simple, uneducated country girl. I won't even mention the poor fool Sir Max. We don't know the most elementary things, but I assume that Sir Glamma does know these kinds of things, and Shurf Lonli-Lokli all the more."

"Can you express yourself a bit more clearly? What exactly do you mean?"

"Wow! My whole life I've thought that the only thing I knew how to do was express myself clearly. Fine. I won't boast—I'll just ask you a few basic questions."

"That's a reasonable decision, Marilyn. Ask away. Maybe you'll be able to make some sense of information that seems useless to me."

"All right. First, from what I understand, when you send someone a call using Silent Speech, distance is immaterial. Is that right?"

"That's exactly right. The main thing is to know the person you're trying to communicate with. And reaching him in Arvarox, if need be, poses no problem."

"Excellent. Let's move on. Is there somewhere in the World where Silent Speech doesn't work?"

"In Xolomi, naturally—you know that yourself. I've never heard of anyplace else, though. Of course there are people who simply don't know how to use it, but our situation is somewhat different."

"All right, that all makes perfect sense. Tell me, Shurf, maybe you've heard about a problem like this one? Not necessarily a true story—perhaps a legend, or a myth. A joke, if nothing else."

"In the Order we used to say: 'A good sorcerer can shout even as far as the next World.' That's more likely to be a joke than the truth. You can't send a call to the next World. Luckily, we have ample evidence that all our colleagues are alive."

"But what about us?" I blurted out.

"I'm used to trusting my senses. And my senses tell me I'm absolutely alive."

"Well, gosh! Of course you're alive! And I am, too, I hope, but . . . Oh, the devil with all my secrets! You're the best grave for secrets, your own and others', I imagine. It seems we're in serious trouble. It will be easier for us to figure out just what kind of trouble it is when we're both on the same page, I suppose. What I'm trying to say is that the 'next World' isn't necessarily a place inhabited by the dead. There are many different Worlds, Shurf, and I'm living proof of it. My homeland could also be described as the 'next World.'"

"I know," Lonli-Lokli said serenely.

"You know? A vampire under your blanket! How? Did Juffin brief you about me, or something?"

"It's all much simpler than that. The ruse about the Barren Lands was really a good one, so for a while I didn't doubt its veracity. All I needed was enough time to observe your breathing to grow suspicious, though. Then there were Juffin's mysterious explanations about how our magic works differently on you than on others. Finally, there's the color of your eyes. You are aware that they constantly change color, are you not?"

"I know," I murmured. "Melamori told me."

"I never thought she could be so observant. Well, that's a special case. Don't worry. People don't usually pay attention to such trifles. I wasn't sure myself until I traveled in your dreams last night. You were much more talkative than usual. But we're for now not talking about you. Tell me, where did you want this conversation to go?"

"All right," I mumbled. "Let's just hope that Professor Lonli-Lokli really is the one and only expert on the matter of how creatures from other Worlds breathe. I began this conversation with the aim of informing you that it's highly unlikely I'd be able to send a call to my mom, even if I really wanted to. Am I making myself clear?"

"Absolutely. But it would seem that a journey between Worlds is a highly unusual event. And nothing out of the ordinary has happened to us. So far, it's a journey like any other."

"A journey like any other? For several hours we've been driving through terrain that, according to Sir Juffin Hully, doesn't even exist, and a local inhabitant can't tell us when we're going to arrive at his home town! I can understand your skepticism. It wouldn't have occurred to me, either, if I hadn't traveled between Worlds in a regular old streetcar—which in my homeland is as mundane a means of transportation as the amobiler is here."

"All right then, you seem to know best," Lonli-Lokli said. "Let's drop the subject for now. Sir Glamma will think that he's just driving to the city of Kettari, and Lady Marilyn can maintain otherwise. That seems reasonable to me—to watch the situation as it unfolds from two different vantage points."

"As our respected Master Caravan Leader would say, 'We'll cross that bridge when we come to it.'"

"That's just what I wanted to say," Lonli-Lokli said. "Don't you think we might finally be approaching Kettari?"

"Yes, the road has suddenly become very smooth, though the surroundings still don't look very hospitable. Wait a minute, what's that up ahead? Is it the wall of the city?"

"That's what I was referring to."

"Soon we should be seeing the seven Vaxari trees by the city gates, and the gate itself, which still contains the vestiges of the carving of old Kvava Ulon," I said. "Now that we've finally arrived, I'm as excited as though this were my own hometown and not Juffin's! What am I blathering on about, though? If it were my hometown . . . Oh, never mind."

"Eleven," Lonli-Lokli said.

"Eleven what?"

"Eleven Vaxari trees. You can count them."

I stared at the approaching stand of trees.

"Ha! There really are eleven! And Juffin said there would be seven."

"Who knows how many there used to be," Lonli-Lokli said.

"Do you know anything about botany, Glamma?"

"A bit. Why?"

"Doesn't it look to you as if these trees are all the same height?"

"Yes, it certainly does. But they're very old, because the trunk of the Vaxari becomes knotty like those are only when it reaches the age of five hundred years."

"Exactly! Don't you see? That means that when Juffin was here there should already have been eleven. If now there were fewer trees, that would stand to reason. But more? Oh, and here are the city gates—brand new! No ancient ruins decorated by the long deceased Kvava Ulon. Simple and tasteful. Congratulations, dear. We've made it to Kettari. I can't believe it!"

"Sooner or later it had to happen. Why are you so happy?"

"I don't know," I admitted, looking around in excitement at the curiously elegant little houses.

An abudance of mismatched, crudely arranged flowers decorated the windows. They would have horrified an ikebana artist, but they warmed my heart. Intricate designs of tiny paving stones in every tint of gold and yellow ran every which way along the narrow streets. The air was clean and bitingly cold, despite the hot rays of the sun beating down on us. But I wasn't cold, and I felt as though I had been cleansed from the inside out. My head spun slightly and my ears were ringing.

"What's wrong with you?" Lonli-Lokli asked.

"Lady Marilyn's in love!" I smiled. "She and I are crazy about Kettari already! Just look at that little house . . . and that narrow, three-story one! What kind of vine has curled around it so that the weather-vane doesn't even budge? And the air—you can eat it with a spoon! Can you feel the difference? When we were driving through the mountains the wind wasn't half so transparent and clean. Who could have thought that the World contained such a . . . such a . . . words fail me!"

"Well, I don't like it."

"You don't like it?" I asked. "That's impossible! Glamma, friend, are you ill, or just tired out from the last hundred years? You just need to take it easy. If you can share my dreams every night, if you want. You liked them, didn't you?"

"Yes, they were wonderful. I must say, your offer is very generous. Even too generous."

"Yes, and so what if it is! Oh, Glamma, take out the money—we must pay the rest of the fee. There it is, the bazaar! Where do you suggest we settle for the night? Preferably not too near our sweet fellow travelers. Let them think whatever they want. We've reached our destination, and *après nous, le déluge.*"

"'After us the flood'? You know that expression?"

"Why is it so surprising?" Now I myself was caught off guard.

"That saying was written on the entrance of the Order of the Watery Crow. Didn't you know?"

"What sincere, warmhearted people," I mused. "What I can never manage to get my mind around is the thought of their potency and might, with a name like that."

"Sometimes you really amaze me. What is it you don't like about the name?"

"Perhaps we should settle our accounts with Mr. Abora and take a spin around town," I suggested, unwilling to take the time to explain why the name of the Watery Crow inspired amusement rather than awe. "We're not going to live in a hotel that's full of tourists from the Capital. If you want to get to know a place you have to find yourself real living quarters. And it will be more restful without other people around."

"A very wise decision," Lonli-Lokli agreed. "I imagine the old fox Master Caravan Leader can give us some advice. I'm sure that these kinds of caprices among his tourists provide an extra source of income for him."

"Like heck he's going to earn something else off of me!" I said with a grin. "Let's go, Glamma. I'm in love with this town. Believe me, I'll find a place to stay within an hour that's better and cheaper than something that rogue would dig up for us. I'll bet in his free time Mr. Vala lies to himself just for fun, and it makes him happy not to trust anyone."

"As you wish," Lonli-Lokli said. "Look for a place to stay, then, Marilyn. I won't be any help. I can, however, get the money out of the purse."

"Oh, right. You're wearing gloves. Give him what we owe him, then turn down that alley. It looks like something's gleaming there. I'm hoping it's water. All I need are riverfront lodgings for my happiness to be complete."

Lonli-Lokli slowly got out of the amobiler, then went to pay our guide. When he came back, he looked me over from head to toe. He had eyes that inspired trust, like a good psychiatrist. I lowered my gaze demurely. Sir Shurf got behind the levers again, and we turned down the alley I was so smitten with. A moment later we were driving along the bank of a river. Small, delicate bridges, and an occasional stately, massive one, crisscrossed the dark crease of the narrow, deep river.

"Oh," I sighed. "How can you not love all this, you sourpuss? Look at the bridges! Just look! Gosh, what's the name of this little river? You don't happen to know by any chance, do you?"

"I haven't the faintest idea," Lonli-Lokli said. "We'll have to look at a map."

"Around here is where we have to stay," I said dreamily. "And then we'll go home, and my poor heart will be broken all over again."

"Again?" Lonli-Lokli asked, as though he hadn't heard me correctly. "Excuse me, but Sir Max doesn't create the impression of someone with a broken heart."

I nodded cheerfully.

"It's one of my inconvenient qualities. The worse things are going, the better I look. More than once I tried borrowing money from friends when I looked like I had just won the lottery. My absolutely true stories about living for a week on just bread and water went over like a load of baloney."

"And you really experienced such hard times?"

Spending time with me clearly encouraged the development of Sir Shurf's facial muscles. A look of surprise crept into his usually expressionless countenance.

"Yes, can you imagine? Sometimes I didn't have anything to eat at all. Thank goodness everything changes. Sometimes."

"That explains a lot," Lonli-Lokli said thoughtfully. "That's why it's so easy to be around you, despite your madness."

"What? Well, you sure know how to flatter a guy."

"It's not a compliment, but an observation. Maybe you put another construction on the term."

I sighed. Who said anything about semantics? It was already clear to me that Lonli-Lokli wasn't trying to praise me this time.

"I didn't mean anything by it," Sir Shurf said in a conciliatory manner. "A completely normal person just isn't cut out for our line of work. When I was in the Order they used to say, 'A good sorcerer doesn't fear anyone but a madman.' A bit of an exaggeration, naturally, but I think Sir Juffin Hully operates on this principle when he chooses his colleagues."

"Fine," I said. "I am what I am, and whatever you call me won't change anything. Let's stop here, Glamma. I want to walk along the riverbank and mingle with the locals. Something in my heart tells me they're dying to give shelter to two rich idlers from the Capital. Don't worry, I remember. My name is Marilyn; and I'm planning on having a little chat with some sweet little old ladies."

"Do what you must," said Lonli-Lokli. "After all we shouldn't forget that Sir Max is my boss."

"Oh, come on." I couldn't restrain a nervous chuckle. "All right, I'll be back soon."

I felt a thrill when my feet touched the amber sidewalk. Through the thin soles of my boots I felt the tender warmth of the yellow stone. My body felt light and happy, like I was about to take to the air. Kettari was wonderful, like my favorite dreams, and I now felt more like a sleepwalker than someone wide awake.

I crossed the street with Lady Marilyn's light step, then strolled along, peering at the tiny ancient houses in ecstasy and smiling all the while. "The Old Riverfront," I said, reading the name on a plaque. Well, here's something else I like!

Oh, Juffin! I thought. If I could shout loudly enough for you to hear, I would be sure to say that a remarkable old fellow like you could only be born in such a magical place as this. I'm hardly likely to be able to say this when I see you. So I'm telling you now, just so you know, all right?

I was so absorbed in thinking about what I would want to say to the boss that I almost knocked over a small, frail old woman. Luckily, the dexterity of her tiny frame was hardly in keeping with her years. At the last moment, she swerved aside sharply and grabbed on to the carved handle of a small garden gate.

"What's wrong with you, child? Where did you leave your pretty eyes? In your husband's snuffbox?" she snapped at me angrily.

"I'm awfully sorry," Lady Marilyn said, embarrassed. "I just arrived a half hour ago in this town I've been hearing about since childhood. I never imagined it would be this beautiful! That must be why I've gone a bit out of my head—but it will soon pass, don't you think?"

"Oh? And where have you arrived from, dear?" the old woman asked, clearly moved.

"Echo," I replied with a slight feeling of guile. When you tell someone from a small provincial town that you are from the Capital, you are overcome with a sense of awkwardness, as though you have just snatched a silver spoon from your conversation partner's sideboard.

"But you don't have an accent like someone from the Capital," remarked the observant old lady. "And it's not like ours, either. Where were you born, young miss?"

Lady Marilyn and I began to lie with gusto.

"I was born in County Vook. My parents fled there in the Time of Troubles, and they were quite happy. But I married a man from Echo just a few years ago. My great-grandmother is from Kettari, though, and so . . . In short, when I told my husband, 'Glamma, I want a good Kettarian carpet,' that wasn't really what I was after. What I really wanted was to—"

". . . to visit the land of fairy tales you had heard so much about when you were a child," the old woman said, finishing my thought. "I can see you really like it here."

"I certainly do! By the way, would you mind telling me what the custom is in this city? I'd like to find a place to live for a few dozen days. Not a hotel, but ordinary citizen's lodgings. Is that possible?"

"It is, indeed," the old lady said with enthusiasm. "You can rent one floor, or a whole house. A whole house is quite expensive, though, even for a short stay."

"Oh, goodness!" I exclaimed. "I just wish I could meet someone who would offer me something suitable—and whether expensive or not, we could simply discuss the matter." And I tapped the tip of my nose with the forefinger of my right hand.

"Welcome, young lady!" the old woman said with a merry chuckle. "You certainly deserve a little discount. Just imagine, I'm on my way home from my friend Rarra's house. We were just talking about how we might as well settle down in one house, either mine or hers, since we visit each other every day. The second house could be rented out, so that we could afford a few extras for ourselves. We've been talking over this plan for a dozen years or more, and we can't come to a decision. A few dozen days is just what we need to begin with. It will give both of us enough time to figure out whether we're capable of living under the same roof. My house is nearby. I'd only ask ten crowns for a dozen days."

"Ouch! Prices are steeper here than in the Capital!" I exclaimed.

"All right, eight; but you and your husband will have to help me move some of my indispensable belongings to Rarra's," the old woman said resolutely. "There aren't too many. Since you have an amobiler and a strong man at your disposal, I don't think it will trouble you too much."

The "indispensable belongings" were so numerous that the move had to be carried out in six runs. But the time was well spent. Lady Xaraya, our landlady, managed to show us a place where we could get a good breakfast, and another place for an evening meal. She also warned us (about a hundred times) not to play cards with the locals—very thoughtful of her.

After we paid in advance for two dozen days, Lady Xaraya wished us a good night and disappeared into her friend's house.

"It looks like the little old ladies are planning to get a bit tipsy tonight," I said. "Let's go home, Sir Shurf. Don't be mad, but I'm sick of having to call you Glamma."

"As you wish, but I prefer to be as careful as we can. What difference does it make what you call someone? What's really important is that you not slip up in front of other people."

"What 'other people'? Our companions of the road are slumbering happily in some flea-bag hotel. I assume that they were fleeced out of more money than we were for that opportunity. Aren't you thrilled at what my lucky streak has found this time?"

"Yes, to be sure," Lonli-Lokli admitted. "But I had been expecting something like this all along, so I'm not surprised. I hope my reaction is not cause for disappointment."

"Of course not! It inspires me with the wonderful feeling that everything in the World is in its proper place. Your placidity, Sir Shurf, is the true underpinning of my spiritual equilibrium. So just stay as you are, no matter what. Now let's go home, get washed up, and change our clothes. Then we'll have dinner and take a look around. Juffin, as far as I remember, gave us some astonishing instructions—enjoy life, and wait until a wonder finds us."

"Juffin gave those instructions not to us, but to you. He told me just to guard you from possible trouble."

"My heart is absolutely sure that I can't experience anything remotely like trouble in Kettari! Not a thing!"

"We'll see," Lonli-Lokli said. "Wait! Where are you off to? This is our home. Number 24 the Riverbank. Have you forgotten?"

"Yes, I did forget! As one Sir Lookfi likes to say: 'people are so absentminded.'"

❋

The bathroom was in the basement. Obviously, the inhabitants of all the provinces of the Unified Kingdom had come to a consensus on this matter.

There were no luxuries or extras available to us—just a single bathroom, somewhat larger than we were used to in my homeland, but otherwise nearly identical.

Sir Shurf frowned in displeasure.

"I must say, after a few days on the road I was counting on three or four bathing pools."

I sighed sympathetically.

"I'm sure that you have no less than twelve at home. Well, you'll just have to get used to a life of deprivation and do without."

"I have eighteen of them at home," said Lonli-Lokli with palpable longing in his voice. "And I don't think that's excessive."

"Are there any holey ones among them?"

"Alas, I am not privileged with such," my friend said. "You may bathe, Lady Marilyn. I'll wait in the living room."

When I went back upstairs a half hour later, my friend raised his eyebrows quizzically.

"You didn't have to hurry. I would have waited. Or are you always so quick with bathing?"

"Almost always," I said. "I'm terribly uncouth, don't you think?"

"To each her own," Lonli-Lokli said reassuringly. "But I'll apologize in advance for not being able to clean myself up in record time like you can."

"Nonsense," I said, brushing off his apology. "It so happens that I have a little matter to attend to."

When I was by myself, I reached for my pillow, thrust my hand under it, and waited. Only a few minutes passed before the first cigarette was within my grasp. It had only been smoked halfway to the end. Putting it out completely, I hid it in the small treasure box where I kept my loot. It was a sort of cigar-case with two sections: one for butts, and another for whole cigarettes, which came to me so rarely I was beginning to forget how they tasted. I was loathe to complain, though; they were better than nothing. The few weeks that I tried to get used to the local tobacco were a heroic and bitter memory for me.

About three hours later Shurf finally deigned to come out of the bathroom. By this time, I had already managed to snatch four cigarette stubs, each one longer than the last. It was an uncommonly good harvest. My right hand had rested motionless under the pillow for twenty minutes already, and I didn't intend to interrupt the procedure. Why should I? This fellow knew too much about me as it was. What kinds of secrets could I keep from him?

"May I know what you are doing?" he inquired politely.

"Well, I'm just making magic to the best of my abilities. This is how I come by my smoking sticks. It takes a long time, but it doesn't cost a thing. A habit is very hard to break."

"Is that—are they from your homeland?" Lonli-Lokli asked.

I nodded and tried to concentrate. Sir Shurf examined the butts with skeptical interest.

"Go ahead and try one," I offered. "It's like your tobacco, only much better. You'll like it so much that I'll have to retire just to have the time to rustle up enough for both of us."

"You don't mind? Thank you, you're more than kind." Lonli-Lokli chose a shorter butt and lit up.

"Well, how do you like it?" I asked.

My right hand was still empty, and I had promised myself that I wouldn't light up until I had finished my tedious work.

"The tobacco is rather strong, but it really is much better than what I'm used to," Lonli-Lokli said approvingly. "Now I understand why you wore such a sad expression whenever you smoked your pipe."

"My expression was sad?" I asked, and burst out laughing. "Ah, here it is, the sweet little thing—the wait is over! Out you come!" I quickly extricated my hand from under the pillow and studied my quarry.

Oh, great. That's all I needed: in my hand was a self-rolled joint. The sight and the smell left no room for doubt.

"The devil take it! All my efforts in vain!" I felt cheated.

"What's wrong?" Lonli-Lokli asked. "You don't like that kind?"

"Something like that. But it's worse than that. Most of my countrymen smoke this to relax, but it just gives me a headache. I suppose I am abnormal. Do you want to relax, Sir Shurf? We can trade."

"Interesting," Lonli-Lokli looked bemused. "I never refuse the opportunity for a new experience."

"You want to try?" I beamed. "Then my efforts weren't all in vain after all. And who knows, it may really help you to relax. That's something I wish for you with all my heart, Shurf, since you're not crazy about Kettari."

I offered him the joint and happily smoked the rest of the cigarette myself. I desperately wanted another one immediately upon taking the last drag, but I only had three left, and a whole evening ahead of me. I turned to Lonli-Lokli.

"Well, are you relaxed, old friend? Let's go eat dinner."

Then my jaw dropped so low I could almost hear the thud.

I have no words to describe my astonishment. Sir Shurf Lonli-Lokli was grinning from ear to ear. It just didn't seem possible that it was his own face. I shuddered.

"That's some funny smoking stick. A fine little thing," Lonli-Lokli winked at me, and giggled foolishly. "If you only knew, Max, how funny it is to talk to you looking like red-headed girl."

The giggles grew into outright laughter.

"Is everything all right, Shurf?" I inquired cautiously.

"Why are you staring at me like that, mate? The big bore that I have been for quite a while now just went for a stroll. And you and I are going out to eat, only . . ." He burst out laughing again. "Only just try to close your mouth. Otherwise everything will fall out of it and . . . and there won't be anything to swallow!"

"Sweet," I muttered. "And I thought I'd be able to get a rest from Melifaro for a while. All right, let's go. Only don't forget that my name is Marilyn, and yours—"

"Do you really think that all the people of Kettari are going to eavesdrop on our conversation?" Lonli-Lokli asked. "Drop what-

ever they're doing and crawl around under the windows of some
tavern to hear the names we call each other?" He laughed again.
"Sinning Magicians, Max! It'll be a tight squeeze for all of them!
How many people live in this town?"

"I have no idea."

"Well, however many there are, it's still going to be a tight
squeeze!" Lonli-Lokli brayed like a donkey. "Let's go. I've never been
so hungry in my life! Just don't wiggle your behind, Max, or you'll
have trouble with the male population. Or don't you object to trouble like that?"

"I object to any kind of trouble at all," I retorted angrily.

"Let's go, Marvel!"

"Me, a Marvel? Take a look at yourself!" I said, but Lonli-Lokli
was already groaning helplessly with laughter. Nevertheless, we managed to leave for our outing.

Along the way, Sir Shurf giggled without stopping. Everything
sent him into gales of laughter: the way I walked, the faces of occasional passersby, masterpieces of local architecture. And you could
understand why. By my calculations, he hadn't even smiled in two
hundred years. Here was the opportunity of a lifetime! He was like a
Bedouin who had just found himself in a swimming pool. It was
pleasant to watch him enjoying himself so thoroughly, as long as he
didn't choke from joy. Whether I had done a good deed or committed the most terrible blunder of my life remained to be seen.

"What are we going to eat?" I asked, seating myself at a small
table in the *Country Home*, an old-fashioned tavern that I remembered Lady Sotofa mentioning.

"Whatever we order, we'll end up eating crap again. You can bet
on that!" said Lonli-Lokli, and dissolved in mirth once more.

"In that case, let's take the easy way out." I closed my eyes and
pointed randomly at one of the meals listed on the menu. "Number
eight. I know what I'm getting. How about you?"

"What an excellent way to make a decision!" Shurf frowned and
pointed at something. As one might have predicted, he missed, and
knocked over my glass, which crashed to the floor. Lonli-Lokli guffawed again. I sighed. And this was the fellow who was supposed to
keep me out of trouble?

"Oooh, I'll have to try again!" Lonli-Lokli gasped, his laughter
finally spent. This time I was ready for him, and propped up the

menu in front of him just in time. Sir Shurf's forefinger pierced right
through the menu at about the thirteenth item. The owner of this
dangerous weapon exploded in laughter all over again.

"You must be hungry," I said. "I think a hole in the menu means a
double portion. I hope with all my heart that it's something tolerable."

"Don't ever hope! It will be crappier than crap!" Lonli-Lokli
announced cheerfully. Then he roared at the proprietor who was
timidly making his way to us, "Crap No. Eight, and Double Crap
No. Thirteen. And make it snappy!"

"You've scared the living daylights out of him," I said, watching
the stooped shoulders of the retreating prorietor. "I can only imagine
how—"

"No, you can't! You can't imagine the teeniest tiniest thing! All
the better. Oh-ho! Now it's time to start stuffing our bellies! Look
how he waddles, it's hilarious! By the way, your way of choosing a
meal is really something. Do you see what they're bringing us?"

"Yes, I see it," I said. I was completely at a loss.

They served Lonli-Lokli two minute vase-like glasses, each of
which contained a fragment of some whitish substance that smelled
simultaneously of mildew, honey, and rum. I was presented with a
huge pot, filled to the brim with meat and vegetables.

"Bring me the same, immediately!" Lonli-Lokli demanded.
"Otherwise I'll feel embarrassed in front of the lady. And take back
that Number Thirteen! We smelled it, and that was enough!"

"You may leave one," I interrupted. "I'm very curious about
what kind of junk you ordered."

"Go ahead and try it. Personally, I'm not willing to risk my life
over such a trifle. Goodness, Sir Max—how funny you are!"

The proprietor stared at us in mute bewilderment and disappeared, taking one of the much-maligned little vases with him.

I poked around at the whitish substance with squeamish fascina-
tion, sniffed it again, and cautiously tasted a bit of it.

It tasted like a horrible mixture of lard and smelly cheese, soaked
in some variety of the local spirits.

"Disgusting!" I pronounced with a certain respect. "This is what
we need to take back with us as a present for Juffin. It's the best
medicine for homesickness and nostalgia, which he doesn't suffer
from anyway."

"If we ever see that sly old fox again, that is," Lonli-Lokli said with a smirk. "Actually, you have a lot of experience traveling between Worlds, don't you?"

"Not too much," I replied, a bit shamefaced. "You've changed your tune, it seems. You never liked me talking about my World before."

"It's not my tune I changed—but myself! You're so slow to catch on. Don't you see, that dullard Sir Lonli-Lokli whom you had the misfortune to know couldn't immediately accept the outlandish story of your origins, even it if were the only logical explanation. But I'm not such an idiot as to deny the obvious. I think the unbearable fellow I was unlucky enough to be then will also accept it in time. But it doesn't really matter, does it?"

"Probably not," I sighed. "Ah, here's your meal. Bon appetit, Glamma!"

"What a name!" Shurf chuckled. "Someone really had to think to come up with that one."

He polished off the contents of his pot with unbelievable relish and demanded more. I reached for the kamra, which they made no worse here than in Echo, Lady Sotofa's uncomplimentary remarks notwithstanding.

"You're not such a madman, Sir Max," said Lonli-Lokli, and winked slyly. "I thought I wouldn't be able to let you out of my sight so that you wouldn't get up to mischief in that get-up. But as soon as Uncle Shurf let down his defenses a smidgen, you were already on your guard. You're a little vixen! No matter what happens, you'll always land on your feet. You're made of the sternest stuff."

"I never thought it would come to this, but you know best."

"That was a compliment," Lonli-Lonkli said. "People like you went a long way during the Epoch of Orders, believe me. I don't know where you came from, but . . . Okay, this conversation is getting boring, and I need to grab my good luck by the tail."

"What do you mean by that?"

"Nothing, really. I can't sleep yet, so I'm going out to look for a way to pass the time. When next will I get the chance to neglect my duties with an easy conscience?"

I raised my eyebrows in consternation and quickly assessed the matter at hand. In fact, I had in my arsenal an excellent means of getting out of this sticky situation. One dexterous motion of my left hand, and a miniscule Lonli-Lokli would have the perfect opportunity to come to his senses, resting between my thumb and my forefinger. On the other hand, who am I to deprive this wonderful fellow of his well-earned leisure? After all, he was a grownup man, a few centuries older than me. Let him do as he wished. And the main thing was that it might not be a good idea to let him sleep. If the dead men he had robbed were still looking for the Mad Fishmonger . . . Heck, now was their chance to find him!

"Enjoy yourself, Shurf," I said. "Lady Marilyn and I will go sniff out the situation and see whether there are any wonders to be found around here."

"You are a very clever fellow, Max," Lonli-Lokli stared at me with a new kind of respect and interest. "I just can't describe how clever you are!"

"What, you mean the trick with my left hand might not work?"

I was already used to dealing with people who read my thoughts, so I knew right away what he meant.

"It's not just that it might not work—you can't even begin to think what I might do in return."

"Why not? I have a rich imagination. What I really can't imagine is what I might do myself."

"Bravo!" Lonli-Lokli exclaimed. "That's how you should answer any high-handed crazy Magician." And once more he cackled with glee.

"You know what they say, 'If you lie down with dogs, you'll come up with fleas.' Good night, friend!" I stood up to leave.

"Goodbye, Sir Max. Tell that bore Sir Lonli-Lokli not to be such a show-off. He's a good fellow, but sometimes he goes overboard."

"I couldn't agree with you more. Send me a call if you're headed for trouble."

"Me? Never! But if someone else is headed in that direction . . ."

"Naturally."

I waved to him from the doorway and went on my way.

The first thing I did was return to Lady Xaraya's house, which had turned willy-nilly into the Kettarian branch of the Secret Investigative Force. I settled myself comfortably in the flowery rocker, lit a cigarette, and pondered my reflection in the large, old mirror. Lady Marilyn, it seems our husband has abandoned us. I hope you're satisfied, dear?

In fact, my new persona was wild with happiness. She squealed in an excess of delight and demanded immediately to go for a walk, to breathe the sweet air of freedom. Perhaps somewhere on the streets of nighttime Kettari she might succeed in finding a few adventures?

I thought of the recent transformation of Lonli-Lokli. I didn't know how it would end, but the new image suited him as long as the fellow didn't get into any trouble. On the other hand, a guy like that get into trouble? Come off it!

I decided to banish all thoughts like this from my head. You can't undo what's already been done.

Now Lady Marilyn and I had to resolve one small dilemma. I longed for a walk around Kettari, but was it wise for a pretty girl to gallivant about at night in a strange city?

I have the perfect idea, my little pumpkin! I informed my reflection. Why not dress up like a man? It's pure madness, of course; but what to do?

I ransacked my colleague's bags, found a suitable turban, and even a pin for the looxi. That was all I needed. But now what about Marilyn's illusory curves? Sir Kofa had really outdone himself when he created my new appearance. I could have gotten away with simple falsies! I sighed and grabbed the next cigarette. How do you turn a girl into a boy? I needed the resourceful eye of a designer.

In a few minutes I came up with what initially seemed to be an absurd idea: to conceal my virtual figure in the way a real woman might mask her very real figure. I would bind the illusory bust tightly, pad my sides to hide the difference in size between waist and hips, and stuff a rag in the shoulder area.

Well, it was worth a try. I wasn't sure whether it was really so dangerous for a girl walking alone through nighttime Kettari, but I decided that once I was a fake man I would feel much more sure of myself than I did as a fake woman. But how confusing it all was!

Half an hour later I glanced cautiously in the mirror. To my satisfaction, the effect was much better than I had dared hope. Of course, the youth in the mirror didn't resemble in the least my good friend Max. Nevertheless, the sexual identity of this creature admitted no doubts. The boy was a boy—was a boy! Natural-born.

Just then I remembered Lady Sotofa's story about the potion she had given me to drink. Wondrous Half, or Heavenly Half—something like that. "You'll just stay who you are, but people will think they're dealing with a completely different person." That's what she had said. Did that mean I could now be seen exactly as I wished to be seen? Well, all the better.

Before leaving the house I stuck my hand under the magic pillow. One cigarette was too meager a supply for the long night ahead of me. In a few minutes I was examining in awe a half-empty pack of Camels. Six cigarettes—untouched! I raised my eyes to the heavens in gratitude. "Dear God," I solemnly declared. "First, you do exist! And, second, you're a great guy and my best friend!"

I opened the door and ducked into the bracing menthol breeze of the Kettarian night. My legs carried me to the other bank over a steep, high-backed stone bridge, with faces of dragon-like creatures carved in the railings, and then even further, through quiet, labyrinthine lanes and moon-white splotches of squares. I didn't even try to pretend I had any aim. I was just enjoying the stroll. The wonders would have to find me themselves, in the words of Juffin Hully, I thought.

All night I wandered through Kettari, drunk on mountain air and new sensations. I traveled the length of a dozen streets, drank at least a jug of kamra and other local beverages in tiny, all-night snack bars. I silently opened garden gates and entered dark, empty yards to smoke, staring at the huge, strange greenish moon in the ink-black sky. In someone's little plot of paradise I drank from a fountain; in another I plucked several large, tart berries from a luxuriant spreading bush. It didn't look like the Tree of Knowledge, praise be the Magicians.

The dawn caught up with me on the same bridge where my enchanting journey had begun. I was considering planting a kiss on the funny dragon gazing at me from the railing, but I decided that was going too far—a vulgar act, a false note, the finale of a play in an amateur theater. But here, in Kettari, I wanted to reach perfection. That was why I simply returned home, undressed, and fell asleep right in the living room, curled up in a ball on the short, low divan.

❁

I woke up before noon. I felt as though someone had given me an intravenous of Elixir of Kaxar. Pure ecstasy!

Lonli-Lokli wasn't anywhere to be seen, however. His absence made me a bit nervous. I didn't feel truly alarmed, only a mild discomfiture—a weak mixture of curiosity and compunction about my own role in the matter, more than anything else.

After hesitating a bit, I sent him a call.

Everything all right with you, Shurf?

Yes, I'm just a bit busy, so let's talk later. Don't be upset.

He's busy, he says. I'd just like to know with what, I grumbled to the ceiling. In any case, the matter was settled. It was clear that Shurf was safe and sound—that was all that was required of him.

That most important matter out of the way, I decided to seek out my breakfast. After some consideration, I resolved that Lady Marilyn could go for a walk in Kettari in the light of day. Why should I trouble myself with changing my clothes again? Soon, an elegant damsel was breaking all feminine records in the *Old Table*, a small restaurant where she astonished the proprietor with her preternatural ability to consume huge amounts of food. The appetite I had worked up during my nighttime wanderings was anything but dainty and ladylike.

Having eaten her fill, Lady Marilyn went shopping for a map of Kettari. I might need it in the future; and also, there was no better present I could give myself. Maps and atlases have a hypnotic effect on me, and if I had a different kind of character I could easily have become a collector. But collecting is not my forte. My things seem to spread out through the homes of my friends and disappear forever into dark corners. Even nailing them down wouldn't help.

I purchased a small thick map with a carefully drawn plan of Kettari. I found a seat at a tiny table in a nameless tavern, sampled the kamra, and began examining my acquisition. I managed to locate my house, my beloved bridge with the dragon faces, *Country Home* tavern on Cheerful Square. Yes, that place fully deserved its name, if Lonli-Lokli's antics were any proof.

After gulping down the last drop of kamra, I continued on my way. I was in love with the bridges of Kettari, and I wanted to cross the Meaire—this was the name of the dark little river—two hundred times, no fewer!

This time I crossed to the other bank over a large stone bridge that resembled an intricate underwater fortress. I roamed the city trying to find the places that had caught my fancy the night before. I came to understand yet again that night transforms the world completely; I wasn't able to find a trace of them. This prompted me to do something that seemed quite senseless. I went into a tiny store, bought a fine, almost toy-like pencil, and marked my current route on the new map. I decided that it wouldn't be a bad idea to retrace this path by dark and compare my impressions.

When I had finished, I looked around. The store was chock-full of wonderful bric-a-brac. It looked just like the thrift stores and antique marts of the Old City, where I was used to throwing to the winds, without much effort, the better part of my enormous salary. This store, too, brought out the spendthrift in me, and I dreamily fumbled through my pockets.

Oh, goodness! I suddenly remembered that the money for traveling expenses, our abundant expense account, was in a pouch strapped firmly to the belt of the wayward Lonli-Lokli, still missing in action. Just yesterday it had seemed like such a safe, reliable place for it. In my pockets I had only a bit of change—not more than ten crowns. Any resident of the Capital would consider that to be a veritable fortune, but not I. Almost thirty years of modest, humble making-do hadn't done me any good, and I was now going through an extended period of pathological squandering. I had a physical need to throw money away, and the habit of keeping track of expenses, weighing what I could or could not afford, gave me a headache. Berating myself for being a brainless moron, I looked around helplessly. Well, it was impossible to leave such a marvelous place without a souvenir. All the more since my eyes had alighted on yet another map of Kettari, embroidered on a delicate piece of leather, a true work of art.

"How much is this little trifle?" I casually asked the proprietor, who was watching me intently.

"Just three crowns, miss," he replied saucily.

The price was outrageous. Even in the Capital things made in the Code Epoch were cheaper.

I frowned. "For some reason it seems to me that even one crown would be too much. But one I'd be willing to pay, I suppose. I've done sillier things."

The merchant stared at me mistrustfully. I made the ubiquitous Kettari gesture, tapping the tip of my nose twice. It worked like a charm. This seemed to be the way out of any situation. A few minutes later I was already sitting in another cozy bistro, examining my purchase.

Now, I've never been especially observant, so if it hadn't been for the very common practice of first trying to locate the place you're staying on the map of a strange city, I might never have noticed. Never mind my lodgings—on this map there was no Old Riverfront whatsoever! There was, however, a Cool Riverfront, which was not on the map I had bought a half hour earlier. I put the two maps side by side and peered at them closely. They were similar, very similar, but in addition the name of the riverbank I had already grown to love, there were several other discrepancies. I shook my head in wonder. It looked like the first map I had bought was the right one. I had checked my route against it. Or perhaps both of them were misleading in their own ways?

I drank down the rest of my kamra, grabbed my enigmatic souvenirs, and went outside. I read the street sign carefully: Circle Lane. Then I peered at my little leather map. This time everything corresponded. There was Circle Lane. But the first map told me I should be standing on Seven Grasses Street. Interesting.

It looks like there's a doggone mystery on my trail, I thought. And it doesn't look pretty.

Now I was only interested in bookstores and souvenir stands that sold maps. I amassed maps of Kettari, haggling like a gypsy and wheedling the storekeepers down to less than five times the asking price. Where there's a will there's a way. The only thing I didn't manage was to force the merchants to pay me for taking their wares off their hands.

✿

By sundown, I was tired and hungry, and a quick glace around proved I was standing under a sign that read *Down Home Diner*. The tavern was on the corner of High Street and Fisheye Street, so there were two entrances. The door around the corner from where I stood seemed to be the main entrance. Above that door was picture of an old lady of epic proportions armed with a ladle. The immediate entrance was far more appealing, an ordinary wooden door draped with some local variety of wild grapevine. I pulled it toward me with a decisive tug, but the door wouldn't budge. It looks like I'll have to pass under that cannibal of a cook! I said to myself unhappily. But first, I tried the overgrown door once more, and on my third try I realized that I had to push, rather than pull. This is one of my more embarrassing personal traits—I always have to struggle with new (and sometimes even long-familiar) doors. They say the malady is incurable.

After I had made my peace with the door, I went inside the nearly empty dining hall, chose the farthest table, and plopped down in a comfortable, soft chair.

No sooner had I sat down than a cheerful, plump lady appeared and handed me a weighty menu. I was duly impressed. It's not every restaurant, even in the Capital, that offers such abundant fare.

"A cup of kamra, please," I said. "I think I'll have to study this beautiful book for some time."

"One kamra, coming up!" The tavern-keeper smiled graciously. "Kamra, and something a bit stronger, as well, miss?"

"If I drink something stronger I'll fall asleep in the chair before my meal arrives. I'd like something more vitalizing," I said. The Elixir of Kaxar was resting safely in my travel bag in the house at 24 Old Riverbank St., which I had located on only six of the eleven maps of Kettari. Needless to say, this did not infuse me with optimism.

"I'd highly recommend Elixir of Kaxar," suggested the tavern-keeper, brightening. "Ever since the rules for cooks were relaxed in the Capital, we have been able to stock this marvelous drink. Are you familiar with it?"

"And how!"

I noted to myself that I had probably discovered the "best darn diner in this crazy town," as Sir Juffin Hully would have said. What luck!

The mistress of the tavern left, and I buried my nose in the menu. It didn't take long for me to realize that the names of the dishes contained not a whit of useful information, and were a bunch of abstract lyrical malarky. I waited until the mistress returned with a diminutive glass of Elixir of Kaxar, and explained to her that I needed a hefty portion of something tasty, but not too refined. Yesterday's experience with the lard had made me wary. After a long exchange, the mistress concluded that what I was after was one order of Wind Kisses. I did not object. The mistress said that the dish would take at least a half hour to prepare. I nodded my approval. It's always easy to come to an agreement with me. Then she disappeared into the semidarkness of the kitchen.

I sipped the Elixir of Kaxar. My spirits perked up, and I started to look around. I'd been wanting a cigarette for a long time. I just needed to find out whether it was permitted.

The hall was almost empty. Apart from me there was only one other customer who sat by the window with a view onto a curious fountain with colored streams that didn't simply fall downward, but twisted in intricate spirals. I tried but was unable to make out the face of the stranger. I could only see his back, hunched over a board game. By a leap of the imagination it could have been considered a local variant of chess. The figures were more or less similar, but the board was divided into triangles and painted three different colors.

This fellow seemed to be so engrossed in his intellectual conundrums that not only would it have been possible to smoke a cigarette from another world in his presence, but one could have organized an entire striptease without him noticing. So I lit up without further ado. Lonli-Lokli was totally living it up in this grand city of Kettari—did I deserve any worse?

※

Wind Kisses turned out to be tiny patties made of tender fowl. After I finished, I drank the rest of my divine Elixir and placed my souvenirs on the table. Again I studied all eleven versions of the map of Kettari. Now I had another surprise: High Street, Fisheye Street, and the *Down Home Diner* were there on all eleven maps. This coincidence astonished me even more than the numerous inconsistencies I had found earlier. Not trusting overmuch my own powers of perception, I again pored over the tiny letters on the map. Maybe everything on the map had been just as it should be from the start—only my senses had been confused by the jumble of new impressions. But no, the discrepancies I had found were still there.

I sighed. I would just have to wait patiently for the errant Lonli-Lokli to return so I could dump this problem on his strong shoulders—assuming, of course, I'd be able to find the road home. What if, indeed, Old Riverbank Street wasn't where it was supposed to be?

"Don't fret so, Sir Max. That's all neither here nor there. By the way, you've hardly collected all the variants."

I stared silently at this suddenly chatty gentleman. Did he say "Sir Max" to me? No, I must have misheard. I couldn't possibly have heard correctly! My Lady Marilyn was a perfectly executed illusion, a masterpiece of Sir Kofa Yox's artistry, the pride of both of us.

The chess player smiled slyly under his reddish mustache, stood up, and came toward me. He had a marvelously light gait, and a very unremarkable face that I already couldn't commit to memory—but that gait I'd no doubt still remember in another thousand years!

"The name's Mackie Ainti," he said softly, sitting down in a chair near mine. "Sir Mackie Ainti, the old sheriff of Kettari."

I nodded in silence. My heart was thumping against my ribcage, trying to escape so it could fetch the suitcases and get out of town as soon as possible. The arm of the chair creaked loudly under the convulsive grip of my fingers.

"There's no cause for alarm," Sir Mackie Ainti said, and smiled a slow smile. "You wouldn't believe how long I've waited for this moment, even if I told you myself!"

"A long time?" I asked faintly.

"Yes. Quite a while. I'm awfully glad to see you! You can't imagine just how glad I am!"

"Glad?"

I was completely at a loss. Couldn't wait to see me? How was that possible? He didn't even know me. As far as I knew, Sir Juffin Hully was not exactly corresponding with his first teacher.

"Fine. If you've got it into your head that you just have to be surprised—well, I'll just head back to my board over there. When you're over your shock, send me a call."

"What? No, it's not worth going back and forth. I'll be quick about it," I said. "Naturally, the person who taught Sir Juffin Hully what's what in his time would know everything in the World."

"You got that right. You know, Maba and I had a falling out—"

"Sir Maba Kalox is here?"

"How should I put it . . . At the moment, as we speak, no. And you never can say anything for sure about Maba. Whatever the case may be, he does sometimes pay me a visit. That's how we got to arguing about you, and neither of us guessed. I wasn't at all sure you'd drop in here, and I was getting ready to pay you a visit. But Maba talked me out of it. He reckoned that within a dozen days or so you'd come round to *Down Home Diner*. But we sure didn't expect to see you this soon. Have you any notion how lucky you are, partner?"

"Sir Juffin tells me all the time. I've got a whole slew of arguments to the contrary, but they don't count, I guess?"

"You got that right. You lucky dogs are all like that. It was even a miracle that you were born, did you know that?"

I shook my head in bewilderment. Up to this point I had thought that the story of my conception contained no dramatic plot twists.

"The details are immaterial to you, but you can keep it in mind, anyway. Well, no matter. Looks like you want to smoke?"

I nodded. The problem was that my cigarette box was empty and my magic pillow was at my lodgings.

"Maba left you a present. He asked me to tell you that you're a very quick learner, so it's probably not so much a present as a well-earned reward."

Mackie handed me a whole pack of my favorite cigarettes, with three gold stars on a yellow background.

"Whoa! Looks like I won the jackpot!" I exclaimed. "You were absolutely right, Mackie. I'm the luckiest person in the universe!"

"Almost," he nodded distractedly. "What else can I offer you? I think a good dose of nostalgia would do the trick. Hellika!"

The smiling tavern-keeper hurried over, put a tray with a cup on the table silently, and disappeared as quietly and abruptly as a shadow.

"She is a shadow," Sir Mackie said, seconding my thought. "But a very sweet one. Well, are you happy?"

I looked at the cup. That smell . . . Kamra is, of course, an excellent thing. But nothing beats the smell of . . . *good coffee*!

"I'm going to cry!" I said. "Sir Mackie, I'm in your debt forever."

"Don't bandy words like that around. It's very dangerous, especially in your case. Your words sometimes possess a special power, and some of your wishes do, too. They come true, you know. I think this World is going to see some interesting times ahead, if you don't become old and wise in the very near future. But neither one nor the other is likely to happen any time soon, I reckon."

"Sir Mackie, do you always speak in riddles?"

"Only some of the time. The rest of the time I'm silent as the grave. So just be patient."

"No problem," I nodded, and greedily slurped down another gulp of coffee. "Now I'm going to have a smoke—and you can do whatever you like with me. I'll agree to anything."

"Is that right? By the way, your sense of duty isn't very strong. If Juffin were in your shoes he would already have fired a dozen questions at me, made a few million deductions, and formed a hypothesis. Don't you plan to interrogate me about the mysterious fate of Kettari?"

"I know that you'll only tell me what you consider necessary for me to know. And you'll tell me that without any prompting on my part."

"Bravo!" Sir Mackie said. "I can't help but envy Juffin. It's very easy to deal with you."

"I feel the same way," I agreed. "But I wasn't like this before. Juffin's jokes and lots of good food will turn anyone into an angel."

"Juffin's jokes? That's funny. He used to be the gloomiest fellow in Kettari. I had to work two hundred years to get him to crack a smile. The smile came out crooked, but at least he tried."

I stared at my conversation partner in disbelief.

"Aw, come on! As though I had nothing better to do than sit here and lie to you! So you thought he was born old, wise, cheerful, and with a silver spoon in his mouth to boot? My, oh my, Max. You and I are the lucky ones. There's nobody left to gossip about my youth, and you're growing up so fast there won't be time for your mistakes to stick in anyone's memory. Well then, drink down your strange brew before it gets cold. If you want more, you'll have it. Today's your lucky day. I have to make up for my sins. It's my fault you nearly went off your head about the Kettari maps. I was surprised you even noticed!"

"Well, it was just by chance. I have that habit of first looking for where I live on any map."

"All the same, good for you. But why did you get so agitated about it? Another habit?"

"Indeed. By the way, you promised me a refill."

"Are you always in such a hurry, Max?"

"No. I usually sit on the toilet for a long time."

"Bread has to sit before it rises, too. At least you do something thoughtfully." Mackie hid his smile under his ruddy whiskers.

Suddenly the mistress appeared again out of nowhere, carrying another tray. Then again, a shadow is a shadow.

"Okay," I said, starting in on a second cup of coffee with gusto. "I guess I'll have to play along and ask this question: What's happening in Kettari?"

"You already had the right idea," said Mackie, taking a swig of coffee from my cup before setting it down in disgust. "Are you sure you can drink that stuff? It won't make you sick?"

I shook my head, then asked:

"You're talking about the line I gave Lonli-Lokli, about the 'other world,' and how there are many Other Worlds, aren't you?"

"Of course. I don't object to that explanation. You see, Kettari really doesn't exist anymore. Or, rather, it exists—you can see that for yourself—but it's not where it should be, and it doesn't exist in the ordinary sense of the word."

"And the local inhabitants?" I asked with a sinking heart. "They seemed quite ordinary to me."

"They are. True, they had to die when their time came, but not for long, and . . . just 'for pretend.' You found an excellent little word for it; I'll have to remember it! They think that they live in the Unified Kingdom, just like they did before, and they have no evidence to the contrary. They can always go wherever they like. They can invite their relatives to visit them; only they know it's best to go out to meet them so they won't get lost. It is a small inconvenience that 'the roads around Kettari are in terrible condition since the time of the Great Battle for the Code,' and so forth. So when you leave, you must have a good protective amulet: a guide, a key to the Door between Worlds. I think you like metaphors like that, or am I wrong?"

"Sure I like them!" I said. "So I was right? Kettari is another World altogether, like my homeland?"

"Well, not exactly like your homeland. You were born in a real place—a rather strange one, but real nonetheless. Kettari, in contrast, is the beginning of a new World that will someday become real. The beginning is a wonderful time, a time of marvels, whether we're talking about a whole World or about a single human life. Oh, by the way, you should try going for a walk outside the city gates. I highly recommend it. For you the walk is completely safe. And when else will you have the opportunity to see absolute emptiness?"

"Are you serious?"

"You bet I am! You must go for an outing. Only do it alone, all right?"

"But I'm alone now! I was abandoned."

"It's your own fault. You're lucky your friend is such a beefy fellow. Narcotic substances from one World sometimes have the most unexpected effects on inhabitants of other Worlds. You've experienced that yourself, by the way. Remember what happened to you after just one bowl of that harmless Soup of Repose? And there's no need to fret. Your friend will be fit as a fiddle in no time."

"I'm not a bit worried. But how can you know so much about me, Sir Mackie? I understand that for you it's a trifling matter . . . but why, exactly?"

"What do you mean, 'why'? Vile little word. After all, you happened to appear in Juffin's life, so for me you're a sort of nephew. Excuse me for resorting to such primitive terminology. But they really are like family ties."

I smiled. This made sense to me.

"Well, now. I think that's enough for today," Mackie announced abruptly. "First, walk outside the city, then come back here and we'll continue our family reunion in the evening. Otherwise I may end up telling you more than will fit into your hapless head."

"True, that!"

I didn't know whether to be glad or to regret the sudden end of the conversation. Maybe I really was in need of some time-out.

"Just tell me one thing, please. How should I get home? I mean, which of these maps is right?"

"They all are," Mackie said with a shrug. "The fact is that I couldn't remember exactly how Kettari really was arranged, so there are several floating around out there. The bridges connect the fragments of my reminiscences. You see, I had to create Kettari again from scratch, because the real Kettari was completely destroyed. It's a sad story—and no witnesses remain alive."

"Some Mutinous Magician or other?" I asked knowingly.

"Who else? And not 'someone or other,' but the cream of the crop: Loiso Pondoxo, the Grand Magician of the Order—"

"—of the Watery Crow!" I added triumphantly, unable to conceal a smile.

"I'd like to see you smile if you met up with this fellow. Although, maybe you would be the one who could really keep smiling," Mackie said. "Loiso Pondoxo was so formidable, I still can't imagine how Juffin managed to win that Battle. Perhaps I'm just used to considering him to be young and foolish. Most likely—it's always like that with pupils. I guess it's the same way with children. Well, then, to answer your question, it's all very simple. The *Down Home Diner* is on all the maps, right?"

"Right."

"You bet it is. It was my favorite tavern down through all the peaceful centuries. From here you may reach any destination you have in mind. Just use any of the maps that show the house where you're staying. The bridges themselves will take you where you need to go. Just remember—if you ever get lost, try to find your way back to the *Down Home Diner*. It's your point of reference, your touchstone."

"Great!" I said. "But my heart tells me I'll have to try to find Lonli-Lokli. What if he ended up in the Kettari where there's no Old Riverbank Street?"

"Don't worry. Your friend didn't cross a single bridge. I'll let you in on a little secret—he never even left the *Country Home*."

"You're kidding! And he calls that 'entertainment'? What's he been doing all this time, eating?"

"He'll tell you all about it. Don't worry about him, Max."

"Thank you, Sir Mackie. I'm grateful to you for the coffee, and to Sir Maba for the cigarettes. I never dared hope—"

"We had nothing to do with it," Sir Mackie Ainti said. "It was all your own doing. You always get what you want—sooner or later, somehow or other. Strictly speaking, that's a very dangerous quality. Never mind, though, you'll manage."

"I get everything I want?" I was astonished.

This announcement, in my view, didn't conform to reality at all. Just what "everything" did he mean?

"Yes, that's what I said. But don't forget—sooner or later, somehow or other. That changes things, doesn't it?"

"Yes," I sighed.

Then we both fell silent. I thought over the new formula for my own happiness, and Mackie observed this process with kind curiosity.

"As I understand it, I can come here anytime?" I asked, getting up to go.

"You? You sure can. Good night, Lady Marilyn."

"Good night, Sir Mackie."

I went outside, armed myself with the first map I hit upon, and turned toward my lodgings. I had to gather my thoughts, but the main thing was to make sure my new home still existed.

Everything went off without a hitch. The bridges led me back, just as Mackie had promised they would. And lucky for me, unlike Maba Kalox, he didn't have the distressing habit of playing tricks on novices.

✿

Making myself comfortable in the rocker that I had grown to like, I lit up a cigarette. The meaning of what Sir Mackie had told me was sinking in very slowly. I would have preferred to be a complete blockhead. My head was spinning in circles, my ears were ringing unpleasantly, the world consisted of a million tiny points of throbbing light, and, it seemed, it was about to implode.

Max, I told myself earnestly, get a grip on yourself, all right? Whatever those mighty Creators of the World may have done, it's no reason for you to lose your mind.

This helped, as it had helped me occasionally in the past. I decided to take a bath. Twenty gallons or so of cold water on an overheated head is an ancient, time-tested remedy for all misfortune.

When I went back to the rocker, I lit up again and noticed with pleasure that the living room looked just as it was supposed to—without even the throbbing points of light. There was an ordinary human floor, ceiling, and four walls, all exactly where they were supposed to be.

"Okey-dokey," I said out loud. "Now it's safe to go wherever you wish, honey, whether to the Country Home in search of wayward Lonli-Lokli, or beyond the gates of the city to observe absolute emptiness, or whatever I'm supposed to discover there. I suspect that the first option is more tempting, but Sir Mackie was very insistent in urging the second on me, so—" I shut up then, as there was a clear hint of madness in that soliloquy. I smiled an apologetic smile at Marilyn, staring at me from the large antique mirror, then stood up and left the house with a determined air.

My legs took over and led me in an unknown direction, beyond the uncanny bridges and the narrow dark wrinkle of the Meaire River. To the city gates—where else would my crazy limbs be destined? It looked as though I had no choice but to go along with them.

Forty minutes later I was already walking along the ancient wall of the city. It was so high it seemed the inhabitants of Kettari had tried to block out the sky, and only after many centuries of stubborn effort finally abandoned the hopeless endeavor. I was able to find the gates easily. Too easily for my taste, since my fear was far stronger than my curiosity, and only a strange feeling of helpless doom pushed me to undertake this expedition. I passed quickly beyond the gates as I had once dived headfirst off an enormous cliff.

Instead of a yawning abyss, I was relieved to discover the massive silhouettes of the famous Vaxari trees, blacker than the sky. The greenish disk of the moon kindly agreed to light my path, and I gazed at it in gratitude. I had never thought a distant celestial body would do so much to help out a lowly human creature.

I found myself walking down a wide road. There was no doubt that it was the same road that our caravan had driven along into Kettari just yesterday. I ambled along straight ahead, realizing with pleasure that my mood was steadily improving. My silly, childish fears scattered into the dark lairs of my unconscious like scampering mice. For the time being, at least.

I don't know how long this stroll lasted, but at a certain moment I noticed it was already getting light. I stopped abruptly and stared, flabbergasted, at the sky. It could hardly have been later than midnight when I left home, although . . .

Are you sure your sense of time is in working order? I asked myself. After the instructive conversation with Sir Mackie Ainti and your pathetic attempt not to cave in under that small avalanche of information?

I looked around, and my heart thudded behind my ribcage—but this time from joy rather than fear, though it was most likely a mixture of both. A few yards ahead I saw the end station of a cable car, and up ahead loomed a city in the mountains—the wondrous, seemingly uninhabited city in the mountains I always dreamed about. I was certain that these were the silhouettes of its massive buildings; its fragile, almost toy-like towers; and the white brick house on the edge of the city, atop its roof a weathervane like a parrot that spun even on a windless day.

This fantastic city was already quite near, and I realized I could use the cable car to reach it. It was the only means of municipal transport, as I well remembered. I also remembered that I was never afraid of heights sitting in the flimsy little car. I simply wasn't afraid of anything there at all.

I crawled into the cable car as it slowly floated past, and ten minutes later I was standing on a narrow, crooked little street that I had been familiar with since childhood. Melamori, I thought, here's a place where we could walk after all! How is it possible? A place so marvelous, and I'm all alone. I'm going to explode, it's so wonderful. It's too much for just me alone!

I didn't explode, of course.

I knew this city better than the one where I was born. It seemed to me that now I had really come home. I had finally returned, not in my dreams, but for real, and wide awake.

I don't remember all the details of this mind-boggling stroll. I can only say that I conscientiously walked around the entire city, the name of which I don't know to this day. It was no longer uninhabited. Occasionally passersby would come my way. Their faces seemed vaguely familiar, and many of them greeted me cordially with strange guttural sounds. None of it really surprised me. I just remember that by the time my legs were numb with weariness, I sat down at a table in an outdoor café, and someone served me a tiny cup of Turkish coffee. An inch above the surface floated a puffy cloud of cream. You could either eat it, or spare it and just admire it. I took out a cigarette and snapped my fingers mechanically. A neat greenish flame burned close to my face. The cigarette started to puff smoke, and I took a drag, as though I had always been certain of my ability to summon fire.

Getting used to magic was a trifling matter—as long as it happened with the same regularity as ordinary events.

I continued on my way, crossing the empty English park (this place was from another dream altogether!), and was soon gazing on the eleven Vaxari trees by the city gates. Then I was in Kettari again. The tiny red ball of the sun was just resting on the horizon. I realized I was as tired as though I had been walking for a few days. Sinning Magicians, how long had I been roaming around? But did it even matter? Now I needed to go home. And sleep, sleep, sleep—come hell or high water!

❀

Sir Shurf Lonli-Lokli was waiting for me in the living room, sad and stern.

"I'm glad to see you in one piece," he said. "When I got home, your absence didn't seem strange. After all, we came to this city on business. But by the next day—"

"What? The next day! Gosh, how long was I gone?"

"To answer that question, I'd have to know when you left. I've been waiting for you for four days—but I was gone for a while myself."

"Oh, my!" I groaned. "No time to sleep now. First, I have to figure this all out. Where is my only joy in life? Where is my sweet little bottle of Elixir?"

"In your traveling bag, I guess. I took the liberty of putting it in the closet, since you had managed to leave it right in the middle of the living room floor for all the World to see. For a while I thought maybe you had measured the room and made it the centerpiece for a special reason. Then I realized that wasn't your style, and I cleared it out of the way."

"Sir Shurf, what a nice treat!" I took a hefty gulp of Elixir of Kaxar. My weariness abated for a time. "Good Old Shurf, who's not calling me 'Lady Marilyn' or braying like an insane donkey, but only lives to look after my welfare. I think I must have died and gone to heaven!"

"I don't think it makes sense to call you 'Lady Marilyn' any more, just as it doesn't make sense to stand on ceremony with someone who's been with you through thick and thin, and has even gotten to know—"

"A very sweet and kind version of Shurf Lonli-Lokli," I said with a laugh. "It's for the best. Decorum has its place, but it's only right that it should yield eventually to openhearted familiarity. But why no more 'Lady Marilyn this' and 'Lady Marilyn that'?"

"Take a look in the mirror, Max. It's lucky there aren't many people in Kettari who know your face. I believe we'll have to find our way out of here without the caravan, though. If, of course, we want to keep our mission a secret."

I stared into the mirror in astonishment at a face that looked haggard, bedraggled, and exhausted. Goodness! Not just any face, but my own!

"Yikes!" I blurted out. "All my life I was sure I was anything but plain, but now . . . but how did Lady Marilyn's pretty face get left behind? Actually, who could possibly know but me—and I haven't the foggiest notion. So let's talk about you, Sir Shurf. You probably haven't spent the last few days in the best possible spirits? What I mean is that I should have sent you a call, but I felt sure I was only gone for—"

"I don't know where you were, Max, but I tried to contact you several times."

"And?"

"To no avail, as you might have guessed. But I knew you were alive, because—well, I tracked you down. I'm not as good at it as Lady Melamori, but I do know how, if you'll remember. The trail of a living person is always distinct from that of a dead one, so I wasn't afraid for your life. But duty required me to follow your trail, though from the very beginning I felt I shouldn't meddle in your affairs. Anyway, the trail led me to the city gates, and there I had to turn back home. I felt I couldn't pursue you further than that. It was a very unpleasant sensation. I hope I don't have to experience it again. But at least I realized you weren't in any danger."

"I'm very sorry, Shurf," I said. "You won't believe where I was. My dream, the city in the mountains, the cable car—do you remember?"

Lonli-Lokli nodded.

"You don't have to explain anything, Max. I have a feeling that that secret isn't yours to tell. So it's better to keep quiet, all right?"

"Yes, all right." I stared at him in consternation. Then a light went on in my head. "Did you just have that same unpleasant sensation again that you had by the city gates?"

Lonli-Lokli nodded.

"Holy moley! In that case, I'll zip my lips. In fact, I think I'll go take a little snooze. After the Elixir two or three hours of sleep will be enough. Then you can tell me—no, you'd better tell me now, or I'll die of curiosity. What have you been doing all this time? Not you, I mean, but him—that cheerful chap. How did he entertain himself?"

Lonli-Lokli frowned.

"I'm afraid the news isn't very good, Max. He—that is, me—we played cards. It was so pleasant and exciting! Oh, I was just going to ask you, did you have any money on you when we parted? Because I have nothing left."

"You blew all the money?" I laughed so hard I wanted to collapse to the chair, but missed and fell into a heap on the floor instead. "You lost all the money? How long did you play? A year? Two?"

"Two days and two nights," Lonli-Lokli admitted in embarrassment. "But a round of Krak usually doesn't last more than a dozen minutes, so—"

"I see. As for me, I have three crowns and a bit of change left. Never mind. We'll survive. I have a lot of experience in frugal living. If worse comes to worst, we'll just murder someone. It's a piece of cake! Or become robbers. Do you know how to rob, Shurf? I'm sure you do."

"Yes. It's not a very sophisticated kind of trick," he said somberly. "But I don't think it would be right. We are serving the Crown, in case you've forgotten."

"Oh, yes, of course," I said quickly. My wonder-saturated body had been seeking an outlet for mild hysteria for some time already. "You're delightful, Shurf! A fine fellow. And I'm a dolt. I was ready to rob a jewelry store. Well, we'll live modestly, tighten our belts. Honest poverty has its advantages. I've read heaps of books that claim it does, anyway."

"You're a very magnanimous person, Max," Lonli-Lokli said. "I assumed that you'd be quite displeased with me."

"I'm not a bit magnanimous. It's just that I have loads of more serious problems. And besides, it's my own fault. I shouldn't have given you that joint."

"Your treat afforded me great pleasure," Shurf exclaimed. "A person needs a rest from himself, at least from time to time. As I understand it, that substance is available to you whenever you wish to have it?"

"Alas, no. Remember how surprised I was myself?"

"I understand. But if you ever . . . If I remember correctly, you don't like to resort to this form of release, so . . . well, don't throw that thing away, but hide it for me. Maybe someday, in several dozen years . . ."

"Well, in several dozen years, I figure I'll be able to procure most anything at all!" I announced confidently. "You don't want to have a good time before then?"

"Oh, no, Sir Max! How could I? A person shouldn't neglect the opportunity for relaxation, but it's inadmissible to indulge in it too often."

"I'll take that into account. How wise you are, Sir Shurf. You don't mind if I just lie down here on this divan, do you? I've already grown used to it—I've never been upstairs to the bedroom. I don't have the strength to get used to yet another new bed. Wake me up in two or three hours. I've got so much to do . . . don't I?"

With these words, I closed my eyes and bid farewell to all the Worlds. I had no dreams, only one infinitely long moment of complete repose.

✵

When I awoke, it was nearly dark in the living room. The windows let in a meager, dusky gray twilight. A fat greenish moon had already begun its triumphal ascent above the horizon. I looked around, dazed, to see Lonli-Lokli sitting stock-still in the rocker. He seemed to be practicing his breathing gymnastics.

"W-hat happened, Sir Shurf?" I mumbled in dismay. "I asked you to wake me up! Are you getting absentminded?"

"I did try wake you up," Lonli-Lokli's said. "In three hours, as you requested. I never could have imagined how lustily you can curse. I must admit, I didn't understand more than half the words—but I jotted them down. And I would be much obliged to you if you would explain what they mean."

"You jotted them down! Sinning Magicians, what did I say? I'm even curious myself. Come on, show me the list."

"It's quite dark in the room. We should probably light a lamp. You can't see in the dark, as far as I know."

"I don't need a lamp. I'll figure it out somehow. I'm not yet awake enough to be able to stand bright light."

I took the neat, small piece of paper covered with Lonli-Lokli's large, evenly spaced handwriting, and read the words. Well, I'll be! Some of them were words I hadn't even resorted to in my moments of greatest despair. I felt very ashamed.

"Ouch! Shurf, I'm terribly sorry! I hope you understand that I don't think that way."

"No need to trouble yourself with apologies, Max. I know very well that a person can say anything at all in his sleep. But I'm truly interested in what these words mean."

"All right," I sighed. "First I'll bathe, and then we'll go out somewhere to eat. Honestly, I'll have to drink some courage if you want to hear a real translation and not some pathetic attempt to beat about the bush!"

"That's a reasonable suggestion," Shurf nodded. "I must admit, I'm hungry."

"Oh, and our last pennies are in my pocket! What a scoundrel I am! Well, never mind. We'll get back on our feet again."

✵

A half-hour later we were sitting in the *Old Table*, where I had breakfasted so enjoyably not long ago. As it turned out, the place became even cozier and livelier toward evening. In any case, according to our landlady, "some people spend every waking hour of the rest of their born days in the *Country Home*; and there's nothing better closer to home." As for the *Down Home Diner*, I would drop in there later, and alone. I had to play that game without Shurf—for the time being, anyway.

I began my "morning" with a jug of kamra and a glass of some sort of burning hot infusion. Drinking directly upon waking isn't my style, but we had to celebrate the return of my own dearly beloved countenance. I had also promised to deliver a lecture on uncensored profanity for Sir Shurf Lonli-Lokli, seeker of fresh knowledge. Without a hefty dose of a strong beverage, this just wasn't going to happen.

After I had started to relax, I examined Shurf's handwritten list. He eagerly scooted closer to me.

"Well, this is nothing very exciting. Just a female dog. And this . . . how should I say it, Shurf—a man who is undeserving of respect and who has some serious problems with the plumbing in his backside. It's a word that describes stupid people, although the root is directly connected to the process of reproduction."

"Oh, that's an entire science," Lonli-Lokli said respectfully. "In my opinion it's very hard to understand how it works."

"Really? I never thought so. It's fairly simple. Well, shall we go on?"

"Certainly."

"Very well. Now this expression may be used interchangeably with the straightforward human expression 'go away,' but it makes the one on the receiving end doubt his own ability to procreate. And this is a kind of animal, and at the same time a man who is undeserving of respect, and who has problems with his back passage—"

"And what kinds of problems are they that beset the poor man?"

"It's hard to say," I muttered, frustrated. "Magicians be praised, nothing like that ever happened to me."

In about fifteen minutes we had come to the end of the list. Toward the end I was inclined to blush; but Sir Lonli-Lokli was happy, and that was the main thing.

"I'll probably go home to bed, if you don't have any other plans for tonight," my friend suggested uncertainly.

We had just left the cozy little tavern, and I was feverishly trying to think of a way to make my escape. I had an appointment to keep at the *Down Home Diner* with Sir Mackie Ainti.

"Sure, Shurf," I said, secretly relieved. "I do have plans tonight, but—"

"I understand. It's better this way. Since I came to after trying that strange herb, all I want to do is sleep."

"All the better. Sweet sleep is an excellent thing. By the way, I really hope you weren't terribly shocked by the cursing."

"Why are you so worried, Max?" Lonli-Lokli asked, surprised. "Words are just that—words, and nothing more. Even if you had said them in a conscious state, I would have considered the situation to be more amusing than alarming."

"You've taken a load off my chest! In that case, good night, Sir Shurf. I hope it won't be three or four days before I return. After our meal I have just a little more than two crowns left. Here, you take one. At least we won't starve."

"I also hope I see you in the morning," said Lonli-Lokli. "Thank you, Max. You are demonstrating enviable foresight."

❄

I didn't even have to look at the map. I remembered the way to the *Down Home Diner*, although it was unusual for me not to be disoriented in an unfamiliar town. Soon I had arrived at the intersection of High Street and Fisheye Street. I had already heard the gurgling of the fountain several blocks away.

Sir Mackie was sitting in the same place, hunched over the Kettarian version of chess, as before. He was the only one in the hall.

"Welcome, partner," he said, turning to me. "I have to admit, I didn't think you'd go that far."

"What do you mean?" I was taken aback.

"Stop pulling my leg. All right, all right—I just want to say that you cook up Worlds like nobody's business. I wish I could do it so easily. True, you didn't actually realize what you were doing, and so forfeited the lion's share of pleasure. But that's just a temporary hitch."

I drew in a sharp breath. "Do you mean to say that this city of my dreams wasn't there before? I was the one who—"

"Sit down and take a breather, Max. You seem to have several primitive, but extremely effective ways of making yourself relax. Go ahead. Hellika!"

The smiling tavernkeeper appeared at his table instantly. Rather than sitting down with Sir Mackie, I went over to the place I had been sitting the first time. Mackie stopped his solitary game and came over to join me. Judging by the expression on his face, I had done the right thing.

"Hellika, sweetheart, this boy wants the same thing he had last time. As usual, I don't need a thing, to my great consternation."

She nodded and vanished. I shrugged. Another miracle, big deal!

"Sir Mackie, tell me how—"

"'How!?' Pshaw! That's something I'm not able to tell you. The world is full of inexplicable things. There's just one thing I can say to you: from the very start I expected something like this. That's why I suggested you take a walk outside the city gates. I was right, as you could see. Kettari used to be surrounded by emptiness, and now a marvelous city has sprung up out there—a city very much to my taste. And with a splendid park, too! And stop calling me 'sir,' partner. That just doesn't cut it. Ah, here's your preferred beverage! You've earned it, there's no gainsaying it! Did you ever think that someone would be paying you with a cup of coffee for creating a World?"

"Coffee's not a bad form of currency. I'm fine with it. But what I would like to know is what happened to Lady Marilyn? Can you at least tell me that? Sir Kofa devoted a lot of time and energy to casting that spell. I was supposed to go around with that fetching face and hairdo for at least a few dozen days, if not longer."

"It's a strange story," Sir Mackie said with a wink. "I've never seen the like, I must say. She just really took a fancy to that park."

"What?"

"The park! You heard right. You see, that park of yours—it was no ordinary park. I had to do some serious scoutin' before I could figure that one out. In short, these days there's one pretty ghost wandering around in your favorite park. The ghost doesn't hold any grudges, though. Lady Marilyn still preserves her easy-going nature, so don't worry on that score."

"This is too much!" I said. "All my life I was sure that the creator of something certainly had to be aware of what he was creating."

"And now you know that's not so. Experience isn't the worst way to come by reliable information, what do you say? Drink up that foul-smelling stuff of yours, or it'll get cold."

"The smell of coffee is just something you have to get used to," I said, smiling.

"I'm willing to believe it! Well, I'll have to try it anyway. In that amusing city born of your tenderness and solitude, everyone drinks that stuff, don't they?"

"I don't doubt it. But what do you mean by 'tenderness and solitude'? That's just a manner of speaking, right?"

"It's just a habit of mine to tell it like it is. Someday you'll understand that these were the feelings that governed you when you first saw the vague outline of that place that never existed until you summoned it up. Don't rush it, Max. You'll have plenty of time to get to the bottom of your own escapades. The main thing is that they succeed—and so easily! Too easily I might have said; but no one asked me now, did they? But why should I waste my breath heaping praise on you? And praise really isn't called for, since everyone just does what he can, whether he wants to or not. Did you want to ask me something, Max?"

All my carefully prepared questions had vanished from my head. Never mind, they weren't important. I lit a cigarette, anticipating my enjoyment, and looked at Mackie with avid interest.

"And can you explain to me why you—or, why we, together—are doing all this? I mean why do we need to create new Worlds at all? I suspect that even without our help there are an infinite numbers of them."

"Didn't I tell you I couldn't stand that darn-fool word 'why'? Try using it a little less often. Or, better yet, drop it altogether. At least when you're talking to me. 'Why' isn't the right way of putting the question when you're talking about creating a new World. Everything that's truly interesting and worthwhile exists somewhere beyond the realm of cause and effect."

Mackie tossed his head angrily, and methodically lit his short, oddly shaped pipe. Then he smiled under his mustache and went on, his tone much gentler now.

"Worlds, both inhabited and deserted, are far more numerous than you're able to imagine. But we have to do something, you and I, don't we? And then, who knows, maybe it'll turn out better for us than it has thus far for others. Not a bad reason either, is it? Is that enough for you?"

"To be honest, no."

"Well, ask Juffin sometime. There's one who never objected to the word 'why.' On the contrary, he always loved to explain the reasons behind his own and others' actions. And it's easier for you two to communicate—you're almost the same age."

"The same age!"

"Well, compared to me, anyway. I can't even remember how long I've been knocking about the World. It's like I just got lost here at some point and then decided to stay. Though I'm not at all sure that's really how it was."

I shook my head in disbelief.

"All my life I wanted to live forever. Let others die, I thought, but I'll hold out, somehow. And now you've given me hope."

"Hope is a darn-fool feeling," Sir Mackie said sternly, tossing his head again. "It's best not to hope for anything, that's my advice to you. Well now, let's drop these serious matters. I have something else to discuss with you. From what I hear, your companion doesn't know about any of this?"

"That's something I wanted to ask you. Poor Lonli-Lokli couldn't get beyond the city gates. When he tried it made him feel sick and uncomfortable. I wanted to let him know about my city in the mountains. He saw my dream, too, one time. Why should I have to hide something like that from Shurf? Besides, he's good at keeping secrets."

"I'm not the one you should be asking," Mackie said, smiling. "A newborn World is always very capricious. They have their own idiosyncrasies. Take Juffin, for example. It never wants him to get too close to it. Why might that be? No idea. Though if anyone should know, it's me. Honestly, I don't have a lot to say in the matter. Maybe later, at home, your friend can hear the whole story without even wincing. I think that's how it's likely to unfold. But I do have a request that's more for your friend than for you. Alas, I'm unable to invite him here."

"A request?" I asked, surprised. "You have a request for Lonli-Lokli?"

"Yes. That comes as a surprise to you?"

"Of course it does. I didn't think there was anything you lacked or couldn't take care of yourself."

"Well, to be honest, it's not that I can't take care of it myself, but that I don't want to. I'm lazy, you know. And then, this matter will be quite intriguing for your friend, you'll see. As far as the caprices of newborn Worlds are concerned, what they're always ready to indulge is any kind of culprit or evil spirit. Not long ago, a gentleman showed up in these parts—someone I didn't take a liking to at all. Not that he's all that dangerous for the locals, but it's unpleasant for me to have to be aware of his constant presence."

"Another Mutinous Magician?"

"Worse, Max. A Dead Magician. Believe me, there's no evil spirit more restless than a Grand Magician killed unjustly. And your friend is an expert in such matters, as I understand it."

"You got that right." I smiled. "He'll take care of him in no time."

"Well, I don't know about 'in no time'—I think you're being a bit hasty there. But he'll take care of him, I'm pretty sure. Just tell your companion that Kiba Attsax is on the loose. That'll be enough, you'll see."

"Sure, I'll tell him. Is that all?"

"You can also say it's a big problem, that in Kettari things were just fine till that ornery varmint came around. That claim is very close to the truth, and a person should always be sure he's doing something important. It's more pleasant that way, and things will progress better." He rose from his chair. "Well, I'd say you've had enough of my company for one day. Last time it was a bit too much for you, wasn't it? Did it take long for you to recover?"

"Twenty gallons of cold water on my poor crazy head. The secret cure of Sir Maba of Echo, or Magicians only know where he's from. Seriously, Mackie—I almost went totally bonkers! Maybe you've got a better cure?"

"A long walk. But it's even better to busy yourself with something completely meaningless. Doesn't matter what. Read a book. Play cards with someone. The main thing is not to sit in one place, and not to try to reason it all out. Nothing will come of it, no matter how hard you try. Got it?"

"Got it," I said. "Well, I'll think of something. By the way, you don't happen to know the name of that city? My city in the mountains, I mean?"

"No idea. You should have asked the people who live there. G'night, partner!"

"Good night, Mackie. I'm off to do something meaningless, as you suggest. That's what I do best."

❦

I left the *Down Home Diner* with fairly firm plans for the night ahead. For one thing, I was determined not to lose my mind. And I liked Mackie's idea about taking up cards. I reckoned it would give me a chance not only to pass the time pleasantly, but also to improve Shurf's and my financial situation.

It was a fairly casual proposition, but not a groundless one—I could play a mean game of Krak. Sir Juffin Hully himself had taught me to kill time that way. And he was the luckiest card player in the Unified Kingdom.

Then some hundred-odd years ago, the late Gurig VII issued a special proclamation that prohibited Sir Juffin from playing Krak in public places. The old King was forced to take this measure after the fortunes of several dozen of his courtiers migrated into the pockets of the enterprising Kettarian. Juffin, by the way, didn't object. There was no one left who could keep him company at the card table, and the unprecedented Royal Proclamation flattered him no end.

With me, Juffin played purely for pleasure, of course, since this took place at the time I was still financially dependent on him. Anyway, the first day, after a dozen embarrassing losses, I won two games against Sir Juffin Hully. He couldn't believe his eyes. The next evening, we continued playing. Our luck fluctuated. I still lost more often than my experienced teacher. But, in Juffin's words, even that was highly improbable.

I should note that I myself saw nothing improbable in it. Already as a child, I had concluded that a great deal depends on who teaches you to play a game. It doesn't really have anything to do with pedagogical gifts—you just need to learn from a lucky player. If you do, in addition to getting useful information about the rules of the game, some of your teacher's luck will rub off on you, too.

For this small discovery, I had my unusual lifestyle to thank—rich in nighttime pursuits and friends, lucky and not-so-lucky, who managed to teach me every card game known to man.

So I had the opportunity to compare, and then draw my conclusion. When I proudly announced this conclusion to Juffin, he nodded absently, which could very easily have passed for agreement.

In any case, I had nothing to lose except one crown and a few bits of loose change, the entire paltry fortune that remained to me and Lonli-Lokli. If I lost, it wouldn't be a great disaster. Otherwise I would just end up spending these riches in the first diner I came across, on some junk like the local liqueur—the mere thought of which, frankly speaking, turned my stomach.

I headed resolutely in the direction of Cheerful Square. I had no doubt about what the customers at the Country Home were doing at the spacious bar at the back of the main dining hall. I had a reliable witness—Sir Lonli-Lokli, who had lost his shirt.

There was one hitch in this whole affair. I hate playing with strangers. I'm embarrassed to admit it, but it seems I am really quite shy. But no one could help me there. And anything was better than sitting in the living room, watching poor Max lose his mind. A few trivial problems might make you forget about your one and only true problem. I crossed the brightly lighted dining hall of the Country Home and headed straight for the bar, plunged in semidarkness, where I found the epicenter of Kettarian card-playing society, just as I had predicted.

I sat down on a barstool, and without much deliberation ordered some Jubatic Juice. This was a tried and true beverage. In sufficient quantities, not only would it cure me of shyness, I wouldn't even hesitate to sit, lost in thought, in a glass bathroom in the middle of the city's central square after imbibing enough of it. For a while I wondered, would it be too dramatic to light up a cigarette without leaving my seat in the middle of the hall? Lonli-Lokli was at home asleep, and there was no one to keep an eye on me.

Finally, I decided that the more exotic I looked, the better. The sooner the locals understood I was a simple alien dork, the better were my chances of being invited to join in their sordid doings. A big gulp of Jubatic Juice gave me courage in my reckless, but essentially judicious, decision.

I waved aside all my qualms and lit up. If only poor Sir Kofa, the unsurpassed master of masquerade, could see me now! After all his efforts, here I was sitting in the middle of Kettari with my own inelegant face and unkempt hair, smoking something that doesn't even exist in this World, and planning to drink some courage and fraternize with the locals! But whom did I need to hide from in this nonexistent city, in this heart of a new World—a World, moreover, that I myself was helping to create? It was crazy, but it made sense. So I finished my cigarette with great enjoyment, took a few more swigs from my huge glass, and reached demonstratively for the yellowish-gold, already half-empty, pack.

"Well, you seem to be rather bored, sir," someone behind me observed politely.

"I can't tell you how bored I am. Since the moment I arrived in Kettari I've been dying of it."

I almost laughed out loud at my own awkward fabrication, as I turned to face the person who had addressed me.

Well, what a surprise! It was an old acquaintance of mine, Mr. Abora Vala, our Master Caravan Leader in the flesh. He didn't recognize me, of course. Lady Marilyn, the most beloved of the fictitious wives of that passionate gambler Sir Shurf Lonli-Lokli, was the one who had traveled in his caravan.

The fellow studied my face curiously.

"Have you been suffering from boredom in Kettari for a long time already?" he asked casually.

"Five days or so, why?"

"Oh, no reason. I just know most of the visitors to Kettari by face, and yours is unfamiliar."

"It would be strange if it were familiar to you. I arrived here to visit my aunt five days ago, as I've already said. And she didn't consider it proper to end the dinner celebration for my arrival until half an hour ago. She went to sleep it off; then she'll start preparing another feast for my departure, I'm sure. That's why today is the first day I've ventured outside in the five blasted days since I arrived!"

In my mind I gave myself an A for quick-wittedness, thought a bit, then added a "plus."

"Ah, that explains it," my new-old friend nodded. "I'm acquainted, you see, with the visitors who arrive in Kettari on my caravan. And your aunt, I presume, met you herself?"

"Yes, she sent her sonny boy to some roadside tavern to pick me up. The blockhead is already about two hundred years old, but he's still a mama's boy. Can you beat that?"

"Yes, that's the way it is sometimes," the gray-haired gentleman agreed politely. "It sounds like you're sick and tired of your relatives?"

I nodded mournfully. By that time, I had so warmed up to my role that I began sincerely to hate my hypothetical silly aunt and her hypothetical dimwit of a son, my cousin.

"Would you like some diversion?" he asked innocently. "Excuse me for being so forward, but that's our custom around here. My friends have been enjoying their game for an hour, and I have no partner. We're not playing for high stakes, so you won't be risking your fortune."

You're darn straight I won't, I thought maliciously. A certain cheerful and overzealous fellow already had.

"My name is Ravello," he said.

Oh no it isn't, you debonair player, you—it's Abora Vala, as I recall.

"Don't be shy, sir," this cavalier liar whispered to me. "In Kettari it's the custom to dispense with ceremony in making one another's acquaintance, in particular if the gentlemen have the chance to while away the evening at a game of Krak. What is that you're smoking, if I may ask?"

"This? A friend of mine brought it back with him from somewhere—from Kumon, I believe, the capital of the Kumon Caliphate." I had read this name in Manga Melifaro's *Encyclopedia of the World*, and, to be honest, I wasn't sure whether such a place really existed. I truly hoped he hadn't gotten it wrong.

"The chap is a merchant, or pirate—you never know with these sailors," I added. "You've never seen anything like these smoking sticks before?"

"Never."

This time I had every reason to believe that Mr. "Ravello" was telling the truth.

"And where are you from yourself?" he asked me.

"From the County Vook, the Borderlands. Isn't it obvious from my accent? Well, let's play, then, if you haven't reconsidered. But no high stakes."

"One crown per game?" my tempter suggested.

I whistled. Right—no high stakes.

The speed at which Lonli-Lokli had emptied our money pouch no longer seemed so improbable to me.

"Half a crown," I insisted. "I'm not such a rich man, especially tonight."

He nodded. A half crown for a game is no small potatoes either, I thought.

The only thing left to do now was to place my hopes in Sir Juffin's success. Two losses, and I could begin to undress, or go home—which wasn't really part of my plan.

We finally settled down at a small table by the far corner of the bar. Several pairs of sly Kettarian eyes stared at me from the nearby tables. I shivered. I felt sure they were going to try to bamboozle me. I wasn't sure how, but I knew they would try.

"Be so kind as to tell me your name, sir," "Ravello" probed cautiously. "Perhaps you have your reasons for not introducing yourself, but I have to address you in some way or other."

"My name? Of course, it's no secret." I deliberated a moment. "Sir Marlon Brando, at your service."

It was completely logical. Who else could accompany Marilyn Monroe? A bird of the same feather.

Of course, "Ravello" was no more surprised than Sir Juffin had been upon hearing my choice of names for Marilyn. Such is the fleeting nature of earthly fame. Whoever you might be in one World, in another World you might as well be nobody.

"You can just call me Brando," I said. If this fellow started calling me by my full name, I'd laugh in his face for sure.

※

I won the first two games easily and swiftly, to my great relief. Now at least I had a bit of breathing space—enough for four more hands anyway. And by that time, my poor head, tormented by incomprehensible matters, would be right as rain again. Well, that's what I was hoping.

I lost the third game due to sheer stupidity. Mr. Abora Vala, alias Ravello, was suddenly no longer nervous. He realized I was that very provincial numbskull he had taken me for at first, and that I had just gotten lucky. I took this into account. If I started winning again, I'd have to force myself to lose from time to time. Otherwise my newfound friend would get bored.

Then I won four times in a row. Mr. Ravello began to get agitated and I realized needed to cut short my winning streak for a time. The fellow dealt the cards. I looked at mine and discovered that I wouldn't be able to lose even if I wanted to. My paltry intellectual baggage was incapable of letting me lose with a hand like that. So I won again. It was pitiful to look at my partner. A thief who has just been robbed is a sorry spectacle. I took my cigarettes out of my pocket.

"Care to try one, Ravello? If there's anything good about living in that backward caliphate, it's the fine tobacco."

"Really?" the distracted fellow asked with some hesitation. His furtive eyes stared at me as if trying to detect a local cardsharper behind Marlon Brando's disguise. But my strange accent and the exotic taste of my cigarettes clearly witnessed to other, faraway origins. We started in on the next round. After considerable effort I managed not only to lose, but also demonstrated my indisputable dimwittedness. This worked to my advantage. I decided to raise the stakes.

"I seem to have just gotten richer," I said thoughtfully. "And in an hour I think I'll want to turn in. What do you say we raise the stakes to a crown per game?"

It was amusing to look at Mr. Ravello. The struggle between greed and caution on his expressive face was something to behold. I understood his problem perfectly. On the one hand, I was too lucky by far; on the other, I was a perfect dolt. Moreover, if the stakes were raised in the hour remaining, there would be plenty of time for him to win it all back. Otherwise, who could say? Of course, he agreed. The fellow was both daring and cunning—just ripe for taking the bait.

Then I won six rounds so easily I was surprised myself. My theory about inheriting a sizable chunk of luck from your card-playing mentor proved to be a sound one. Here was the proof, clear as day. Sir Juffin must have a huge surplus of this blasted luck.

"Not having any luck today, Ravello?" someone asked with studied indifference from the nearby table.

Up to now, the other patrons hadn't paid the slightest bit of attention to our game.

He's probably the local champion, some sort of rescue squad. Now he'll have to come to grips with me. In my joy, I ordered another glass of Jubatic Juice. I never thought I'd let myself go like this.

"No luck," my partner admitted mournfully.

"Well, if you're not having any luck, you'd better go home and go to bed," the new gentleman advised. "The moon is out tonight, and you haven't so much as glanced at it."

"You're right about that, Tarra," my victim said with a sigh. "Today the only luck I'm going to see is when my head's on my pillow. But Mr. Brando here isn't tired yet, is he?" He looked at me quizzically.

Not a chance, I said to myself. I guess the idea was that this local ace would step in and save the day. Well, we'll just have to see about that. I'm rather curious to see how it will turn out myself.

"I think I'm just getting the hang of it," I said, assuming the bemused expression of a victor who has won by chance rather than skill. "But if you want to stop the game, I won't insist."

"My friend's name is Tarra. As far as I know, his partner, Mr. Linulan is always expected home by this time. But Tarra is a solitary man. Maybe you'd like to keep him company?" Ravello asked. It seemed I was meant to take the bait; and take the bait I did.

Mr. Tarra closely resembled his predecessor. He even had the same silvery gray hair surrounding a long-nosed face of indeterminate age. Is it just coincidence, or a widespread Kettarian phenotype? I wondered. Maybe it's even simpler than that—they're brothers, and this is a family business. Without engaging in too much idle chit-chat, Mr. Tarra and I got down to work. Suffice it to say, the so-called Mr. Ravello had the temerity not to go anywhere at all, but just to move to the next table. Of course, I pretended not to notice.

I lost the first round without much difficulty. Evidently, my new partner really was an ace. I won the second, though, since my luck seemed to be just revving up.

"Two?" I suggested.

"Two crowns per game?" Tarra drew out the words. "Well, I'll be, Brando. You're a guy who likes to take risks, aren't you? Three!"

"Three it is!" I tried my best to look like a fool you could reason with.

Then I won six games in a row. I realized that Mr. Tarra might also be overcome by a sudden need for sleep, so I quickly lost two in a row. My new partner played well enough that it didn't take much effort to lose to him.

"Six!" he wagered, after his second win. I nodded, and then won almost a dozen games. It happened so fast he didn't know what hit him.

"Good morning, gentlemen, It's already getting light," I said as I stretched and stood up.

"Are you leaving already, Brando?" Tarra asked. It seemed to have just dawned on him that his money was leaving with me. "You could at least give me a chance to win it back."

"I wouldn't advise it," I said. "You'd only lose more. Don't be sad, friend! You'll get lucky someday, too. Kettari's full of tourists, as far as I understand. It's just that your moon is crazy about me!"

"Moon? Well, well, well . . ." my partner drawled in confusion. "Who taught you to play Krak, Brando?"

"My aunt. You're lucky she hasn't left her house in three hundred years. Don't grieve, Tarra. There won't be any more visitors like me in Kettari in your century. You really can play! I hardly had to try at all to let you win now and then."

"To let me win! Are you mocking me?" The fellow seemed to take it as an insult.

"Well, of course I had to lose occasionally," I said in a conciliatory tone. "But it hasn't been such a great blow to your business, has it? So a good morning to you all. I'm going to call it a night."

With that, I left the sweet place, hoping wih all my heart that I wouldn't have to play the hero in a big fistfight.

Nope! Made it out without a scratch.

❀

At home, I carefully counted my winnings.

Eighty-one crowns and some change—a whole handful of it. It was still far less than Shurf had in his pouch before his charming antics got underway, but at least we could live like people again. I looked around. Lonli-Lokli was probably sleeping upstairs, and I decided I could sleep a spell, too. Right here, on the short divan I had already grown so fond of. Too short, to be honest, but I'm a creature of habit. That's for sure. After thinking about it a while, I wrote a note: "Wake me at noon! No matter what," and attached it to the wall above my head. We had things to do today.

This time I was shaken violently out of my sleep. Sir Shurf is nothing if not disciplined. And very thoughtful—he had prepared the bottle of Elixir of Kaxar beforehand, so my morning suffering lasted just a few seconds.

"Thanks, Shurf." I was already able to smile not only at my tormenter, but at the pathologically bright noonday sun.

"I have two pieces of good news. First, we're rich."

"Max, I hope you didn't do anything that—"

"That I wouldn't risk telling the Police General Boboota Box? No, I just decided to find out what you found so fascinating in the local game of chance. I completely agree with you. It was great!"

"You mean to tell me you played cards with the locals? I never thought you'd turn out to be a cardsharper."

"A cardsharper? Give me a break! I'm a very honest fellow. Just luckier than they are."

"How much did you win?"

"Count it," I said proudly. "You can subtract one crown and some change—that's what I started out with. I'm going to bathe."

When I came back to the living room, Lonli-Lokli gazed at me in almost suspicious admiration.

"Your talents truly are inexhaustible," he declared solemnly.

"Oh, no, they're limited, believe me. I don't know how to sing, to fly, or bake Chakkatta Pie. Let's go get some breakfast, Shurf. Good gracious, it's nice not to have to count every penny."

❀

We breakfasted at the *Old Table*, where we had been the day before. The dyed-in-the-wool conservative who told me to leave well enough alone had gained the upper hand in me. The hospitable tavern-mistress recognized us, which was gratifying in itself. But my appetite was roaming around elsewhere and promised to catch me later. On the other hand, Lonli-Lokli ate for two people. This touched me. I felt like a concerned father and sole breadwinner. A strange feeling.

"What about the second?" Shurf asked suddenly, still chewing his food.

"The second what?" I have to admit, I had clean forgotten.

"This morning you said there were two pieces of good news. That we were rich was the first. What was the second? Or is it—"

"A secret? No, Shurf, this news is especially for you. A bit of work for your capable hands, after which we can split this crazy town in good conscience. You see, a certain Sir Kiba Attsax is wandering around Kettari, if I'm not mistaken about his name."

"You're not mistaken."

"Well, it's excellent that his name is familiar to you. As I understand it, things in Kettari are just fine and dandy—but the presence of this gentleman changes the picture somewhat."

"I understand," Lonli-Lokli said somberly. "Everything in Kettari is just hunky-dory. I'm glad you're so certain about that."

"Shurf," I said gently. "Take my word for it. Things are fine in Kettari. Something very strange did happen here—but it's most likely a good thing. I like it, I must say. And Juffin will, too, as far as I can foresee. But this gentleman must be stopped dead. His presence may destroy everything. What, did I spoil your appetite, Shurf?"

"No, it has nothing to do with you. You know that the person whose name you just mentioned died quite a long time ago?"

"I know. That seems to make matters even worse."

"It certainly does. It's always harder to come to grips with a dead Magician than a living one. What else do you know, Max?"

"That's all." I shrugged. "I thought you would know how to find him and all that."

"Finding him won't be hard. I'm curious about what you know about Kiba Attsax."

"Nothing. Only that he's a dead Magician, and he somehow poses a threat to Kettari. Or intends to. I didn't quite understand. Oh yes, of course! He's an 'unjustly killed Grand Magician.' Strange way of putting it, isn't it?"

"Why strange? That's the way it was. When I killed him I didn't know how it was done. Moreover, I didn't realize I was killing him."

"You killed him?" I finally began to understand. "He wasn't by any chance the original owner of your gloves?"

"The left one, to be exact. The owner of the right one is one of the junior Magicians of the Order of the Icy Hand. I would have far less trouble with him."

I was starting to feel very uneasy. "Listen, Shurf, I remember your story very well. But it would never have occurred to me that . . . I suppose it's not absolutely necessary to deal with this fellow. Let him—"

"You don't understand, Max," Lonli-Lokli cut me off gently but firmly. "I'm not afraid of an encounter with him. It's more like I can't believe my luck."

"Your 'luck'? I don't understand a thing, I guess."

"Of course it's a rare opportunity. To meet Kiba Attsax, not in my sleep, when I'm quite vulnerable, but wide awake, when I can do battle with him. I think you can understand how lucky I am."

"Judging by the expression on your face, I wouldn't have thought it," I murmured.

"That's natural. I have to consider the situation that has come about, and try to understand how I should behave. You see, Max, it's not every day that a person is given the chance to relieve himself of such a heavy burden. And I can't allow myself to make any mistakes, so I think I need to begin to act right away."

"We," I said. "I'm a third-rate fighter, Shurf, and not a very good sorcerer. Maybe I'm just good at the card table. Or when I spit poison—that I know how to do. But I'm very curious. Do you think I'd be satisfied with a short synopsis of this Battle of the Titans? No offense, Shurf, but your oratorical style is quite laconic. Besides, I'm lucky here in Kettari. So you can take me with you as your talisman."

"Very well," Lonli-Lokli said with an air of indifference. "Maybe your luck will be far more useful than my skill. Besides, I have to obey you."

"Oh, I forgot!" I burst out laughing. "Instruction number one: act like you don't notice anything."

Lonli-Lokli looked at me in surprise. I took my next-to-last cigarette out of my pocket. Sir Maba Kalox could have been a bit more generous; I deserved a few packs of cigarettes, at least. I don't have time to hang over that blasted pillow all the time. I'm out there creating Worlds, or playing cards. I laughed, and lit up.

"Max, don't you think that's too much?" Lonli-Lokli asked sternly.

"No," I replied. "I'll explain later if you want me to. For the time being, just do my bidding, since I'm the big boss. By the way, instruction number two: banish from you head all this nonsense about doing my bidding. I'd never advise anything very sensible anyway. Eat, Sir Shurf. Nothing's worth a spoiled appetite."

"That pearl of wisdom could have dropped from the lips of the ancients," Lonli-Lokli said placidly.

I looked at him out of the corner of my eye—could he have learned how to joke? No, I was hallucinating. My nerves had always been unreliable.

"Well, let's go look for your friend," I suggested when Shurf's plate was finally emptied. "By the way, how will we do it? Can you pick up his trail?"

"Sometimes you say the oddest things, Max," Lonli-Lokli said. "How, I wonder, can you pick up the trail of a dead man?"

"Me? I never intended to pick up his trail at all. It's not my department. Do I look like Melamori?"

"You're wrong there. You can do it; you just have to try. But it's not the proper topic of discussion now."

"What do you mean 'not the proper topic of discussion'?" I said indignantly. "It wouldn't ever have occurred to me that I

THE STRANGER / 513

could do anything like that. Will you teach me how to pick up a scent, Shurf?"

"Sir Juffin gave no orders. He's not sure of the consequences, and I'm not the one to decide something like this. You can ask him yourself when we get back."

I sighed again. It seemed that in this crazy world everyone was fully briefed about my hidden talents but me.

"Fine, Shurf. What a bunch of conspirators you all are. How are we going to sniff out this dead granddad of a Magician? Do we look for the smell of carrion, or—"

"Don't be foolish," Lonli-Lokli said coldly. "We're going home."

"Home?"

"Of course. I need my gloves."

"Oh, right. See what an idiot I am? Then what?"

"Then it's very simple. Simpler than simple," Lonli-Lokli said. "But you probably don't understand. Now I need the left glove, but not so I can do battle with him. It would never harm its owner; rather the contrary. But it will make finding him very easy."

"Wait," I said, growing alarmed. "How do you intend to fight him without—"

"We'll see," Lonli-Lokli said with a shrug. "I hope you don't believe that I can't do anything without gloves?"

"Of course I don't think that, but . . . Well, it would be better if they were on our side, your 'mitts with a mind of their own,' that's for sure."

"Of course it would be better," said Shurf. "Let's go, Max. I'll need some time to get ready, and I'd very much like to meet up with Kiba before the moon rises."

"Does the moon empower creatures like him?" I asked fearfully, lifting my behind from the seat of the chair in alarm.

"No. It's just that when Kiba Attsax and his assistant came after me in my sleep, the moon was out. I didn't like the spectacle one bit."

"I see," I nodded. "I do see, and that's a fact."

"I'm sure you do. Who could understand things like that, if not you?"

❦

When we got home, Lonli-Lokli headed straight for the bedroom. When he was on the stairs, he turned around unexpectedly.

"Don't come upstairs while I'm there, Max. There are things that can't be done in the company of others—you know that yourself."

"I understand. I also have to get ready for your colossal battle, by the way. I'm going to be very nervous tonight, you know, and that means I'll be smoking a lot of cigarettes. And I'm completely out. So I'm going to do some sorcery. Maybe something you like will come my way, too." I made the last remark to an already closed door.

§

"Oh, boy," I said aloud, seating myself more comfortably next to my favorite pillow, which, through Maba Kalox's kind attentions, had long since ceased to be only a pillow, and had become a plug in the Chink between Worlds. I had already thrust my hand underneath it, ready to wait patiently for my catch. My hand grew numb almost immediately, and I withdrew it in confusion. I had acquired a whole box of chocolates. Sweet, I punned. What was happening to me? I thrust my hand under the pillow again and was surprised at how swiftly it sank into the unknown. A half hour later I was the proud owner of several bags of cookies, a collection of keys, four silver spoons, and a box of expensive Cuban cigars, which I had never learned to smoke since I had never been able to afford them. I stared at the treasures in bewilderment. What the devil was going on? Until now I had only succeeded in getting hold of cigarettes—and I was perfectly content with things that way. Somewhat at a loss, I sent a call to Maba Kalox.

Sir Kalox, can you enlighten me about what's happening? You taught me to catch cigarettes, not all this junk!

I have nothing to do with it, Max! You learn magic completely on your own. You're just diversifying. What's the problem?

That's great, I said plaintively. *But I still can't get used to the local tobacco.*

It's a matter of taste. Personally, I like it. Well, I'll let you in on a secret. Don't get too attached to the pillow. Try it with other objects. The main thing is not to see what your hand is doing—that will only throw things off. You happen to have some free time, I know. So just practice. And don't waste time with trifles anymore. And Sir Kalox disappeared from my mind.

After a time, it occurred to me that I had easily gotten through to Sir Maba, who was in Echo, I presumed. Maybe that meant I could finally contact Juffin?

After the first try, I realized it was futile. Dead silence, as before. I tried once more, just so no one could say I hadn't. Nothing.

Could this mean that Sir Maba was also lurking around Kettari? It's becoming a very fashionable watering hole, I told my reflection aloud. Then I got down to work again, which I won't deny was quite entertaining . . . It turned out that I could get a pizza right from under my favorite divan. After the third pizza, I realized this was the limit of the divan's capabilities. I stuck my hand under the rocker. A bottle of grappa, then a can of Belgian beer. All right, got that figured out. That's where they keep the drinks. But it was high time for a cigarette. I had only one left. Well, live and learn! I stuffed my hand in the pocket of my looxi almost mechanically— and to my astonishment, it grew numb almost immediately. I quickly drew my hand from my pocket. I couldn't believe my eyes! There was a golden-yellow pack. A full pack of my favorite cigarettes, a hole in the heavens above your head! Unopened! But of course, where should you find cigarettes but in your own pocket? I stuck my hand in the same pocket again, and out came the crumpled, empty pack I had counted on finding from the very first. My head felt giddy from my own power, so I had to smoke and calm down a little. And try to get a grip on myself. These miracles were all well and good, but I still had to take charge of the situation somehow.

"What's that, Max?" Lonli-Lokli asked in surprise. I hadn't heard him come downstairs. The protective gloves, covered with runes, adorned his already enormous hands.

"Food from another World," I said with a weary sigh. "It seems today I'm on a roll, though I'm quite baffled myself. You're not hungry, yet? It might do you good. Maybe it's wonder-food?"

"Maybe," Lonli-Lokli drawled, sniffing cautiously at the pizza. "It does seem edible." He tore off a piece, chewed it a while, then shrugged. "You know, I don't really like it."

"I don't like it much, either," I said, feeling a bit guilty. "Let's try the chocolates. Do you want a drink, by any chance? A shot of courage, and all that? Do you have your holey vessel with you?"

To my surprise, Lonli-Lokli nodded enthusiastically and drew from his looxi the bottomless cup.

"In any case, I intended to resort to this, since I need to try every possible means," he explained. "And a drink from another World could only increase my chances of victory."

"So all my efforts weren't in vain!"

It took only a minute to open the bottle, and I poured the grappa into the holey cup.

"May I try, perhaps? I mean, drinking from your crazy vessel?"

Lonli-Lokli stared at me, then emptied his cup in one gulp, and shrugged.

"Well, try it if you wish."

And he handed me the cup. I poured a little grappa into this truly bottomless object and drank it down with gusto. I don't much like the taste of grappa, but since I was privileged to be using Lonli-Lokli's cup I was prepared to brave even this.

"Thank you. What am I supposed to feel now?"

"You? I have no idea!" My friend seemed quite bewildered. "I almost thought that your strange, powerful wine would pour straight through it. You haven't undergone the initiation into the Order. I had some doubts about you—completely silly, unfounded ones—so I let you try it. Tell me, Max, are you aware of your own powers?"

"I didn't even know there might be a problem," I replied. "I thought that it all depended on your magic cup."

"The cup is the most ordinary kind. Just an old cup full of holes," Lonli-Lokli said. "What matters is who drinks from it. You know Max, you're a very strange creature."

"I've always thought so, too. Especially recently," I said. "Well, let's go find your friend. I must say, I've never felt so superb, even after a good dose of Elixir of Kaxar." I stood up and went to the door. At the threshold I turned around, as Lonli-Lokli hadn't budged from his seat. "Do you need to do something else? Did I jump the gun?"

"Max," Sir Shurf asked slowly, "Tell me. Do you always walk without touching the ground, or . . ."

"Only in Kettari. Why do you ask?" I looked under my feet suspiciously. Between the soles of my boots and the floor there really was a small space—almost too small to be seen. "Holy moley! I don't have the strength to be surprised anymore. I don't think it will affect the matter at hand, so let's go before that silly fool of a moon starts scrambling up the sky. You know, I seem to have a strong urge to drink some blood. Is that a normal reaction after using your cup?"

"Absolutely," Lonli-Lokli said, nodding his head. "But try to keep yourself in check, and try not to confuse your real strength with an illusory sense of power."

"I'll try. I must say, I've really never received so much opportune advice before."

"It's just that I know what your present condition feels like. Which means I also know that you can control your behavior if you want to." This weighty compliment committed me to a great deal, whatever miracles might befall.

୫

When we were outside, Lonli-Lokli cautiously took off his left glove, stopped for a few seconds, and then set off toward the bridge with a determined stride.

"Is he nearby?" I asked. My heels, which suddenly tore away from the earth, were buzzing like crazy.

"Not yet. We'll have to walk for about half an hour. That will give us time to discuss a few details of what awaits us. I was going to ask you not to interfere in the fight, and suggest that you generally keep your distance from Kiba Attsax, but—"

"You changed your mind?" I asked. Shurf nodded earnestly.

"Yes, you taught me a good lesson. Underestimating your enemy is an unforgivable blunder. But underestimating your ally is even more dangerous. So go ahead and interfere, if need be."

"That's all well and good," I said, somewhat confused. "But how do you kill dead Magicians? Until now, I knew of only one method—your famous left hand. An excellent thing. But as I understand it, it won't shine for us?"

"No. If it were a matter of any other creature, perhaps. But my glove was at one time Kiba's hand, so it won't offer us any help. I can still do some other tricks, maybe they will be sufficient. Each person has his own best way of killing a Grand Magician, living or dead. You have a chance now to find out what your own best way is," said Lonli-Lokli, and fell silent. I decided not to burden him with conversation.

Meanwhile, we continued along the streets of Kettari. I enjoyed this walk as I had enjoyed no other. Every step sent a pleasant tickling sensation through my entire body, starting as a pleasant itch in the soles of my feet.

"Why am I levitating, Shurf? Has anything like this ever happened to you?"

"Yes. After I drank dry all the aquariums of the Order I didn't touch the earth for several years. It happens from a surcharge of strength and the inability to use it properly. That befell you after a surprisingly small dose, so your case might differ from mine. I must note that Kiba Attsax is now very close by. A bit closer, and I'll have to take off my glove. It's burning my hand."

"Wow!" I said, and immediately shut up. What a thing to say at such a moment!

"Well, Max, I'm taking off the glove," Shurf said quietly. "I have to give it to you now. Together with the protective one, of course. You have no part in the old dispute, so you can hold it without any problem."

"Maybe I should just shrink it and hide it away? That's my favorite trick. Would it be safe?"

"Yes, go ahead. Take it and follow me." Shurf nodded at me, already somewhat aloof.

The dangerous glove obediently settled down between my thumb and the forefinger of my left hand. One thing I had certainly mastered was transporting bulky physical objects in this supremely practical way.

"Whatever you do, try to stay alive," Lonli-Lokli said all of a sudden. "Death is a horrifying prospect if you're dealing with Kiba. I know that for a fact."

"I have a long lifeline," I said, glancing stealthily at my right hand. "Do you?"

"I don't know what you're talking about, save it for later, Max. He's there in that house. Let's go!"

The house Lonli-Lokli pointed to was a small, two-story structure with a signboard that read *Old Refuge* on the façade.

"A rooming house?" I asked in surprise. "A dormitory for dead Magicians, room and board for a modest fee?"

"I think it is some sort of hotel. Do you really consider that to be important?"

"No, it's just funny. A dead man living in a hotel. Where does he get the money, I'd like to know? Or did he have an account in a local bank when he was still alive?"

"Well, he had to be somewhere," Lonli-Lokli murmured glumly.

I threw open the heavy lacquered door for him with a determined gesture.

"After you."

The ancient steps creaked under the weight of his tread.

"Here we are," Lonli-Lokli observed calmly, stopping in front of a completely nondescript white door with the vestiges of a number 6 in faded gold—something only I would notice, with my habit of paying attention to random nonsense.

"Open it, Max. Don't hold back."

"Oh, I forgot—your hands are tied up, in a manner of speaking."

I grinned, and opened the door. Somewhere in one of the numerous magazines I devoured long ago in a previous life, I read that they asked Napoleon what the secret of his victories was. "The main thing is to throw yourself into the fray. After that you can sort out the details," he quipped. Or something to that effect. Quite a fellow, that Napoleon—though he met with a rather unfortunate end.

By the window, with his back turned to us, sat a completely bald, withered old man in a bright looxi. Suddenly, a ball of lightning, white as snow, flew out from under Lonli-Lokli's looxi. It struck the bald man right between the shoulder blades, and he flared up with an unpleasant pale light, like an enormous streetlamp. The ball of lightning didn't seem to hurt the stranger in the least, but he turned around.

※

"Greetings, Fishmonger," said Sir Kiba Attsax, the former Grand Magician of the Order of the Icy Hand.

The most horrifying thing was that Kiba Attsax looked very much like Lonli-Lokli himself. I remembered that Juffin had said our Shurf had an unremarkable appearance—that people who look like him are a dime a dozen. Blockhead that I was, I hadn't believed him!

The many years he had spent in a non-living state had not made him more attractive. The bluish, pock-marked, unnaturally gleaming skin was what really compromised his charm.

The whites of his eyes were dark, almost brown, and the eyes themselves were light blue—a lovely combination, it can't be denied. I even felt a bit calmer when I got a good look at him. How could such a pathetic, dilapidated old creature possibly harm the fearsome Lonli-Lokli?

Oh, how wrong I was!

The dead Magician, it seemed, welcomed the opportunity for a chat. Completely ignoring another ball of lightning, which struck him in the chest this time, he went on with the performance.

"You succeeded very well in hiding from me, Fishmonger. You hid yourself very well indeed! But you weren't smart enough to stay away from a place like this. Did it never occur to you that a newborn World is like a dream? Here your powers don't work. You don't believe me?"

I turned to Lonli-Lokli. I still thought that this dead man would put the fear of the Magicians in us, and then we would make short shrift of him, as the genre required. But the expression on Sir Shurf's face—Sinning Magicians, what's happening to him? I wondered, starting to panic. He was really afraid, and—it looked like he was falling asleep!

The jangling voice of Kiba Attsax jolted me back to reality. "I have no quarrel with you, boy. You may leave. Don't interfere. We have old accounts to settle," he said. The dead Magician waved the stump of his left arm in front of my nose. "He stole my left hand. How do you like that?"

A cold lump of panic shot into my throat. The situation completely knocked me off course. Until that moment I had been sure that I could calmly observe this World full of dangers safely behind the shoulders of the invulnerable Lonli-Lokli. But "even old ladies make mistakes," as they say where I come from. And today we had mistakes galore—enough to share among widows, orphans, and other have-nots, if they wanted them, I thought with crazed glee.

And then I stopped thinking and went into action. It seemed I had been pinned against the wall. For a start, I spat at the dirty mug of the dead Magician. It wasn't that I seriously believed this would help matters, but I couldn't come up with anything more original. To my surprise, the spitting improved the general situation. Of course, it didn't kill my opponent—he was already dead on his feet, so to speak. But I was lucky. It turned out that my spit left proper holes in corpses—just like the ones that adorned my rug at home. The dead Magician seemed very surprised. For the time being, anyway, he was distracted from his cryptic plans for giving Lonli-Lokli his comeuppance.

Behind my back I sensed Shurf coming to life again. He would still need a few moments to recover. I'd just have to buy a little time.

I charged forth, almost up to the alcove where the dead man was sitting. I decided that it wouldn't be such a bad idea to spit right into the dark pupils of his eyes—eyes are so fragile and vulnerable. But I had never been a crack shot, and this time the poison landed on his forehead! Some sniper I'd made.

I laughed nervously, moved closer, and spat again. This time I did myself proud—where his right eye had been, there was now a gaping hole.

Kiba Attsax backed up toward the window in confusion.

"Are you dead?" he asked, with such intense scrutiny that it seemed nothing on earth was more important to him than a candid report on the state of my health. "In this place, the living can't stand up to the dead in an argument, so you must be dead. Why are you on his side?"

"That's my job—to be on his side," I said.

And then I got just what I deserved. I felt Kiba Attsax's right hand on my chest. Idiot! Why did I move so close to him? I berated myself.

Suddenly, I grew cold and calm, and I had no desire to fight with anyone anymore. I just needed to lie down and think a bit. It felt like the most primitive sort of narcosis. That infuriated me, so instead of shaking his hand off, I spat into the dead Magician's face, already seriously disfigured by now.

"Shurf, hide him, quick!" I shouted. "Between your fingers, like I did with your glove. Hurry!"

I dropped to the floor to make sure he wouldn't accidentally shrink me to keep the dead man company.

I just had to hope that Shurf was feeling well enough again to follow my advice, or to think of something better himself. I had run out of ideas.

Then, to my intense relief, I realized that Magician Kiba Attsax was no longer beside me. I turned around. Lonli-Lokli silently showed me his left hand. His thumb and his forefinger were pinched together in a peculiar fashion. It had worked!

We left that inhospitable room and went downstairs. I was shaking all over. Sir Shurf was silent, as before. I think he also needed time to come to his senses after his ordeal. I couldn't even begin to imagine what this had been for him.

❋

Outside there was a cold wind and a soft dusky twilight. We were alive, and we were walking away from the small two-story building.

I turned around almost mechanically, and froze in my tracks.

"Look, Shurf! The house is gone!"

Lonli-Lokli turned around and glanced indifferently, then shrugged.

It's gone all right, said the expression on his face. I realized it didn't really make much difference to me, either. We kept going. Still, I couldn't master my trembling. Even my teeth were chattering.

"Try some of my breathing exercises," Shurf said suddenly. "They seem to have helped me."

I tried. Ten minutes later, when we dropped into a tiny, deserted tavern, I could already hold a cocktail glass in my hand without spilling it or crushing it to pieces.

"Thanks," I said. "They really do help."

"What would they be for, if they didn't help?" Lonli-Lokli asked stolidly.

"What are we going to do with him?" I said, trying to think practically. "Or do you want to keep him as a souvenir?"

"I doubt I'll be needing it," Lonli-Lokli replied. "In any case, I have to say your idea was praiseworthy. So simple, and at the same time it was something even I could do, although my chances of success were slim. You realize you saved much more than my life, Max?"

"Well, I think I can guess. I'm very impressionable. Your story about the dreams of the Mad Fishmonger are still ringing in my ears. Did this fellow do the same thing again? He managed to inform me that meeting him in Kettari wouldn't be such a good idea, that here your chances would be no higher than in your dreams."

"That's how it is, indeed. You know, Max, we'll have to kill him all the same. To kill him once and for all, I mean. Your mysterious friends, the ones who told you about Kiba Attsax—will they help us?"

"I really don't know. We can ask, of course. Let's have something else to drink, Shurf. Your breathing exercises work like a charm, but it's better to take a comprehensive approach to restoring one's health, don't you think?"

"You're probably right," said Lonli-Lokli. "I guess I'd like to drink something myself."

We silently drank some dark, almost black, biting wine. I felt astonishingly good: lightheaded and sad, and no thoughts at all—not one.

I wasn't in the least worried about what we were going to do next. Deep down, I probably already knew, but—

Shurf gave me a quizzical look.

"Let's go," I said. And I stood up resolutely. At that very moment, it became absolutely clear to me where we were going, though I still don't remember how I arrived at the decision. I felt I was being carried along and I couldn't resist. I had no strength to do so.

Lonli-Lokli didn't ask any questions. His trust in me seemed by this time to be unlimited. Maybe that was just as it was supposed to be.

We walked to the city gates. A few days earlier, Shurf hadn't been able to leave the city, but for some reason I didn't doubt for a second that now he could. If need be, I'd just say, "the guy's with me," and everything would be fine.

This wasn't necessary, however. We left Kettari as easily as if we were passing beyond the city gates to admire the famous grove of Vaxari trees or other pastoral beauties. We walked down the road, and still my feet didn't touch the ground. Or maybe they did, I didn't know. I couldn't think about that. An extraordinary sense of my own power filled me like warm water to the very top of my head. It seemed that during this outing I really could do anything I liked; but it never entered my head to take advantage of it. I just wanted Shurf to take a ride with me on my favorite cable car, and then— come what may!

"What's this, Max?" Lonli-Lokli asked in surprise. In front of us was the boarding station for the cable car. In the distance we could see the delicate towers of my city in the mountains, and still further off was the white brick house with a restless parrot-weathervane. I looked at my companion happily.

"Don't you recognize it? You were here not so long ago."

"The city in your dreams?"

"The very one. And in your dreams, too . . . Let's go for a ride."

The little cabin of the cable car was meant for two, so we fit snugly. Sir Shurf stared, enchanted, now to the left, now to the right. His silence was not so much a sign of aloofness as it was the thrill of ecstasy. I felt as if I had just won the Nobel Prize or in any case, that my "outstanding contributions to mankind" were deemed worthy.

The enthusiasms of Sir Lonli-Lokli were not dispensed lightly.

I laughed. It was as if I had been given a certificate that read: "The bearer of this document is immortal, and free to do whatever he wishes, now and forever more."

❋

"Now," I said, when I had stopped laughing. "Throw your dead man into this abyss so that he doesn't prevent us from enjoying the landscape. I think it's is my favorite way of killing dead Magicians. I highly recommend it."

A shadow of doubt flickered in Lonli-Lokli's eyes, but he glanced again at the ghostly landscape that stretched out below us, then nodded and shook his left hand. Kiba Attsax plunged downward. He wasn't the least surprised. Of course, he knew what I was capable of—the dead know everything. Somehow, I felt that Sir Kiba was not at all opposed to such a strange end to his long, tiring existence that confounded common sense. He disappeared; just disappeared, without reaching the earth. Which, to be honest, wasn't underneath *us*, either.

I burst out laughing again, raised my eyes to the sky, and asked, gasping for breath in my merriment, "Did you like it, Maba? Surely you did!"

I liked it, I liked it! Are you happy now? The muffled Silent Speech of Sir Maba Kalox reached me so suddenly I shivered. *Only stop this foolish habit of getting in touch with me aloud in public! Can't you at least try?*

I'll try, I said, shamefaced, this time without opening my mouth.

"Excellent!" said Lonli-Lokli, looking glad and youthful.

Now, however, there was nothing unnatural in his good cheer. He was like the fellow who had walked with me here not long before, when the city in the mountains was still just one of my favorite dreams. Shurf didn't seem to have paid any attention to my yelps into the emptiness.

"Were you sure?" he asked.

"Yes. Don't ask me why. I have no idea! But I was absolutely sure that this was how it would be. Look, Shurf, we're almost there. Yes, take your mitten. I think you can make friends with it again. I shook my left hand and gave Lonli-Lokli back his shining white sharp-nailed glove, which, Magicians be praised, now had only one owner.

❋

The city was glad to see us. There was no doubt about it. The nearly empty streets, occasional friendly passersby, and a warm breeze carried the weak aromas of my favorite memories through the outdoor cafés. There was nothing special about it; but all the same, to me there was no better place in a single other World. Though I would never have considered staying here. I knew it was impossible.

We decided to moor at one of the outdoor cafes. Shurf didn't like coffee, but he did like the frothy clouds of cream sailing on top of it. So we split our portions two ways, which was tasty, and rather funny. I remember that Lonli-Lokli punctured his spoon—he just looked through it at the sun, and the hole appeared of its own accord. He winked at me, and with this handy implement he scooped up the cloud of whipped cream floating on top of the cup. The tall, fantastically slender girl who was busying herself with our orders gave me a smacking kiss on the cheek. That was unexpected, but altogether pleasant. I just shook my head in wonder. We didn't say anything to each other, as I recall. I think we just smiled every now and then; but I'm not at all sure.

After long hours of walking from one end of the city to the other, we finally came across the shady English park. My Lady Marilyn was roaming around there somewhere, if the wise Sir Mackie Ainti was to be believed. And who else was there to believe?

"Oh," I sighed. "I forgot again! I wanted to find out the name of this city. I should have asked someone."

"Nonsense, Max," Lonli-Lokli said dismissively. "The important thing is that it exists, your city. What difference does the name make?"

"Come to think of it, none at all; but I'd still like to know, but, there's no sense wondering about it now."

And then we returned to Kettari, and I went to sleep. I think I was asleep even before I got home.

❁

In the morning, everything was back to normal—maybe it was all too normal, but I didn't object. My legs were planted firmly on the ground, and I wasn't performing any supernatural wonders, except for fishing out a can of Coke from under the rocker. That was hardly a wonder!

It was finally possible to be bored again at breakfast. Lonli-Lokli seemed to be the same reserved and unflappable fellow I was used to, except that there was a trace of almost imperceptible lightness about him, as though all my life I had been acquainted with a slightly ill man who had suddenly recovered.

"I suppose we've done everything we had to do in Kettari?" Shurf asked, reaching for the kamra that we had ordered from the neighboring tavern. I was too lazy to drag myself anywhere early in the morning, even for breakfast.

These were his first words all morning. It seemed the fellow had really decided he'd had enough.

"We'll see. I don't think so, but we'll see. I still have to meet someone. If you like, we can go together to get something to eat at . . . yes, why not? The fare at the *Down Home Diner* is very tasty!"

"Fine," Lonli-Lokli said. "As you wish. But I plan to spiff myself up a bit, so don't wait for me. Go to your meeting, and I'll be along later."

"Fine," I echoed. "As you wish."

Everything seemed to have fallen into place again. I smirked, and Shurf didn't even notice. Life was settling down.

❄

I didn't delay my meeting with Sir Mackie Ainti. Suddenly I was very eager to get back to Echo. Actually, I was sure we could push on already with no regrets or doubts. But I was itching to have one last chat with Mackie. A goodbye chat.

The wooden door of the *Down Home Diner* opened with a quiet creak. I didn't think it had creaked before when I opened it, but maybe I just hadn't noticed?

"Howdy, partner," Mackie smiled hospitably under his reddish mustache. "Did you enjoy your adventures?"

"Did you?" I asked, sitting down in the chair I already considered my own. Indeed, the chair was mine, and only mine. I would wager my life that no one had ever sat there but me. "Did you like my adventures?"

"Me? Very much so. I'm thinking maybe I won't let you go back to Juffin at all. There's plenty of work for you here. Hey, I'm kidding! What got you so scared, Max? Do I look like a kidnapper? You've got a very expressive face. But that's an advantage, if anything. I get a heap of pleasure out of talking to you. And hiding one's feelings—there's no point in that. Might as well not have them at all, and be done with it. I guess you've got some questions?"

I shook my head.

"No. No questions. Your answers only make me feel unwell. Mackie, could I send you a call when I'm ready to ask?"

"I don't know, Max. Try it. Why not? Everything works for you sooner or later. Somehow or other." He winked at me and burst out laughing.

It was the first time I had heard Mackie Ainti laugh. Until then he had just smiled under his mustache. I didn't like his laugh. I didn't know why, but it sent chills up and down my spine.

"You laugh like that sometimes, too. And you also give innocent people a fright," Sir Mackie remarked. "Don't fret, it's all for the best. Well, now, you've got a more important problem. You want to get home, and it would be awkward for you to wait for the caravan. Here, take this." He handed me a little greenish stone, amazingly heavy for a thing of such trifling proportions.

"Is this a guide? A 'Key to the Door between Worlds'? Like the kind all Kettarians have?"

"Better! A man who helped me create my World has the right to a few privileges, and I'm not joking. An ordinary key only works for Kettarians themselves. It won't work for people from another world. Your key is for you alone. If you give it to any of your friends, I won't vouch for the consequences. That clear?"

"Yes. You didn't have to warn me. I'm very possessive."

"Ah, that's good. Don't give it to Juffin, either. Above all, don't give it to Juffin, all right? But he wouldn't take it anyway. I keep forgetting that Juffin is already old and wise. You know, I really am glad that your friend's problems were resolved so easily. He's an extremely nice fellow. And highly entertaining. I'm very sorry that he can't visit me. When are you leaving?"

"I don't know. Soon, I expect. Tomorrow, or maybe even today. We'll see. But why do you say that Shurf can't visit you? I have to confess, I invited him here today. Was that a blunder?"

"No, not at all. It's all right. He's sitting in the next room, since . . . Well, you'll understand soon." Mackie stood up abruptly and made for the door. Then he turned around. "That stone, your 'key.' It only opens one Door between Worlds, Max. Though it works in both directions. Do you catch my drift?"

"You mean I can come back here?"

"Whenever you wish. Come back, and then leave again. I don't think you'll have any time for pleasure trips in the near future, but, who knows what you'll do? Oh, and keep in mind that someone can pass through with you—but not just anyone, so don't take any foolish risks. Make sure you think it through, first. And don't even think of trying to get into the business of being a Caravan Leader. Don't take the bread out of the mouths of my countrymen. Got it?"

I smiled and swiftly tapped my nose with the forefinger of my right hand twice. Sir Mackie smiled, too, under his reddish mustache, then left.

The door creaked loudly, then slammed shut, and I was alone. I hid the green stone in my pocket. How am I going to keep from losing it? I wondered. Would I have to have a ring made from it? I don't like wearing hardware—but maybe it was the only way. I looked out the window. The multihued spray of the fountain was sparkling in the sun. The street was empty. Mackie had most likely already turned the corner, out of sight.

Right, as though he had had time! Stop fooling yourself, Max, I told myself wearily. I got up from the comfortable chair and went into the next room, where Lonli-Lokli was no doubt lolling about, bored as could be.

Shurf had, indeed, already settled down at a table by the window. He was studying the menu, so I stole up to him unnoticed.

"Where did you come from, Max? Have you already found your way to the kitchen?"

"Why would I want to visit the kitchen? I was just sitting in the room next door."

"What room next door? Max, are you sure this tavern has more than one dining room?"

"I just came from there." I turned back toward the door, of which not the slightest trace remained, of course. "Oh, Shurf, more local exotica! Kettarians are very eccentric folk, don't you think? Let's just eat, how about it? A hole in the heavens above this wondrous town, it seems I really am a fervent patriot. I can't wait to get back to our Echo. And we can start our journey this very minute. Does that appeal to you?"

"Of course it does, Max. We can leave without the caravan, if I understand correctly?"

"Precisely. No caravan and no stops, since I'll be sitting behind the levers of the amobiler. You don't object to speed, do you Shurf? We'll set a record and go down in history in one of the simpler and more reliable ways. Listen, you must buy some Kettarian carpets to take home with you. That's why we came, isn't it?"

"Yes. I was intending to. But are you going to be at the levers the whole way back?"

"You can't even imagine how fast we'll get home," I said dreamily. "After you explained the principle of operation of the amobiler . . . You know, I think that until now I drove so slowly because deep down I was sure the old jalopy couldn't move any faster."

"Slowly?" Lonli-Lokli asked incredulously. "Well, I guess in that case we'll be home in no time at all."

When we had finished our meal and gone outside, I turned the corner and headed for the rainbow-hued fountain.

"I always went though that wooden door, Shurf," I told him.

"Of course you did, Max. I don't doubt it. But it's not a real door. Just a stage prop."

"As Sir Lookfi Pence likes to say, 'People are so absent-minded!'" I sighed. "But what am I supposed to do, one might ask? Should I be surprised? No—I'm through with surprises for now."

❦

We spent the rest of the day like real tourists. Shurf did, if fact, set out to buy carpets, and I tagged along to keep him company. As it happened, I couldn't resist the dark and silky nap of one enormous rug. It would match the fur of my cats perfectly. I was most likely the first customer who had ever bought a rug to go with his cats.

We loaded the rugs into the amobiler and went home to pack. Lonli-Lokli only needed about ten seconds to get ready, but I wasn't ready until dark. When and how I had managed to spread my belongings through every room of this spacious house was a mystery to me. Finally, I came across the pile of junk that I had pulled out from under my magic pillow only yesterday. The box of candy was already nearly empty, but there were still some cookies, the collection of keys, four silver spoons, and the box of Cuban cigars. I thought a bit, then stuffed these riches in my traveling bag—you never know when they will come in handy.

When we were already outside, I was struck by an absurd notion, so our departure was delayed by another half hour. I needed to stop by the *Country Home*. This time I didn't want to play cards, though.

❦

When I had settled myself behind the levers of the amobiler, I happily lit up a cigarette, and the vehicle started to move. I drove fairly slowly to the city gates. But when we had passed the eleven Vaxari trees, I drove like a bat out of hell—a hundred miles an hour, at least. I couldn't believe I had managed to get that kind of speed out of the absurd old jalopy. And that was just the beginning!

Shurf sat frozen in the back seat. I couldn't turn around to see the expression on his face, but I could have sworn I heard him breathing rapturously. It was indescribably wonderful. We flew though the darkness along an unknown road. There were no gray cliffs, none of the bottomless precipices we had passed on our way into Kettari. The cable car on the edge of my nameless city, and the city itself, were nowhere to be seen, either—only the darkness and the cold minty air of Kettari. I didn't even notice when the air lost its biting freshness.

"I just contacted Juffin," Lonli-Lokli told me. I raised my eyebrows in surprise

"Good news, Shurf. Tell him . . . tell him your part of the story of what happened in Kettari. I can't afford to get distracted when I'm driving this fast—and slowing down would be too much to ask. Tell Juffin that, all right?"

"Of course. I realize you don't really like using Silent Speech. In any case, by my calculations we'll be in Echo very soon—no later than tomorrow at noon, if you don't get tired."

"Well, what's Elixir of Kaxar for? I know, I know, the driver isn't supposed to indulge. But since I'm the big boss these days, I think I can."

"Yes, Max. You can," said Lonli-Lokli.

Then he was silent for a long time. He and Juffin clearly had a lot to talk about after their long separation. I didn't envy them. If anyone was enjoying life now, it was me. Tomorrow I would talk my fill. Oh, poor Juffin! I'd talk his head off.

After about two hours, Lonli-Lokli touched my shoulder gently. I shuddered in surprise. The dizzying speed at which we were traveling had made me forget about everything else on earth, including my silent passenger.

"Sir Juffin and I have finished our conversation. Besides that, you know, I'm hungry. It would be nice to stop at a roadside diner."

"Dig around in my bag there—you'll find some cookies. They're imported, but edible, I hope. And pass me some. I've also got the munchies."

Lonli-Lokli rummaged around in my bag for a while, then produced a bag of cookies for me, and some for himself, which he munched with gusto.

"Are these from another World, too?"

"Most likely. Oh, Shurf! I have an excellent idea. Wait a minute."

I stopped the amobiler and stuck my hand under the seat. I waited for a minute or two. Ah, there they were! Then I started to laugh.

"What happened, Max?"

"Nothing, it's just that yesterday, when I was trying to get hold of some cigarettes, I kept finding all kinds of edibles. And now, when I'm trying to forage for our dinner—voilà!" I waved a long cardboard carton in front of his face triumphantly. "There are tens packs in here, Shurf! And they're my favorite kind—555! I'm in luck!"

Greetings, Max, Mackie Ainti's call reached me so suddenly I gasped, slumping down in the seat. It wasn't the most pleasant feeling—like getting slammed by a dump truck. Not a real one, of course; but still, what a greeting! It was lucky that I hadn't been driving just at that moment.

I've got to thank you, Mackie went on, sounding somewhat guilty. He probably imagined what I was experiencing just about then.

Maybe I'm too pragmatic, but I somehow thought you'd be glad. Farewell, partner. I'm a man of few words, as you can see.

Thank you. I tried to make my Silent Speech calm and intelligible. *You can't imagine—*

I can. With that, Sir Mackie Ainti disappeared from my mind. I sighed a deep sigh of relief. He was a complicated man. Simply unbearable, for all the tenderness I felt for him.

"Is that a present?" Lonli-Lokli asked. "I think you deserved it, Max. You left the most precious part of yourself in that World."

"Did you hear our conversation?"

"In a way. You know, now that I don't have to waste so much energy fending off Kiba, I can use it for other purposes. Of course, it takes time, but some simple things just happen of their own accord. And you know, it's not hard at all to keep track of what's happening to you. In that sense, you're much more vulnerable than other people. You have an expressive face."

"I am what I am," I said. "I'll try again. Maybe we'll still be able to get some dinner."

A half hour later, after stockpiling several bottles of mineral water and a fistful of tokens for gambling machines, Shurf and I found ourselves the proud owners of a huge cherry pie. After eating a large portion, I started up the amobiler and set off down the road again. The vehicle ate up the miles hungrily. Never had I been such a speed-demon behind the levers as I was on that drive!

"Listen, Shurf," I began. "Did you by any chance ask Juffin what happened the night we tried to get in touch with him? I mean the night we had such a strange conversation with Lookfi, since we couldn't reach anyone else. Why did Lookfi break the connection?"

"I didn't have to ask. Sir Juffin brought it up himself. He thought that you would be eager to find out. You guessed right when you suggested that it was another World. And Sir Lookfi Pence is such a scatterbrain that he didn't even notice my call had come to him from a place where it shouldn't be able to reach him. In this case, his absent-mindedness served a good purpose. Then something happened that you might find amusing. Sir Juffin immediately realized where we had ended up, and wanted to explain it all to you through Lookfi. Lookfi listened calmly to Juffin's conjectures about another World, and began relating it to you. Only then did he grasp the significance of his own words. He realized that the impossible was happening and that's when it ended. Why aren't you laughing, Max?"

"I don't know," I said. "I'm probably just trying to understand, I don't know, something, at least! But you're right. Usually things like that seem funny to me. You changed very much in Kettari, Shurf. Do you know that?"

"That's logical, since . . ." Lonli-Lokli sank into thought.

"Well, of course. First Glamma Eralga's face, then a wife like Lady Marilyn, may she rest in peace, a journey to another World, a joint, and Kiba Attsax for dessert. You poor fellow, Sir Shurf. What a jerk I am, always moaning about my own problems!"

"Well said!" I detected something strange in his voice, so I turned around. Shurf was smiling, ever so slightly. The corners of his mouth were turned up, Magician's honor!

"Not so fast, buddy," I winked. "There's still another dead Magician. What's his name, by the way?"

"Yook Yoggari. But he's far less dangerous. I don't regret these changes, Max. I don't intend to deny who I am. As I've already said, it doesn't prevent me from concentrating on the really important things. It doesn't get in the way of anything, and that's what matters."

"All the same, if this dead fellow starts bothering you, you can count on me," I announced airily. "I'll come to him in his dreams, and make him sing for his supper!"

"Magicians be with you, Max. Dead people don't dream."

"Really? All the better. That means I'm alive, because your little friend suggested that I also . . . well, died . . . in my time, way back when."

"Dead Magicians seldom say anything sensible," Shurf said. "As far as I know, they always dwell in a darkened state of mind."

"Now that makes me prick up my ears," I said grinning. "It's a painfully familiar state."

I sped up so that talking wouldn't be necessary.

⁂

We drove into Echo at dawn. Even Shurf's boldest predictions turned out to be too modest. Noon, had he said? When we arrived in Echo, a fat, pleasant-looking sun had just begun to peek over the horizon, trying to figure out what people had managed to do in the short time it had been away. I waved at the puffy-cheeked luminary and turned into the Lane of Northern Paths. Oh, what a beautiful name! I had never heard it before. I had to slow down considerably, but there was nowhere to hurry to, and Echo in the morning seemed to me to be the most beautiful place in the World. In this World, in any case. In other Worlds there were a few rivals. But now Echo was the best place in the universe, because I was coming home, and my heart loved what it saw, without regretting what it had lost.

"You're going to take a wrong turn," Lonli-Lokli warned. "What's wrong? Don't you know this part of town?"

I shook my head, and Shurf took the task of navigation upon himself. After a good earful of his instructions, I noticed with surprise that we were already on the Street of Copper Pots, approaching the House by the Bridge.

"Are we here?" I was even short of breath from anticipation.

"We're here. I'd like to go home, but I guess my wife will still be asleep. At this hour she won't even be glad to see me, all the more since I don't look like myself these days. You know, she didn't care at all for Sir Glamma Eralga."

"It would be convenient if Sir Kofa happened to be on duty. He could reverse the spell right away."

I parked the amobiler by the Secret Entrance to the Ministry of Perfect Public Order, and was suddenly stupefied. The vehicle began to disintegrate. Lonli-Lokli's reaction was lightning quick. His arms shot upward, then dropped slightly to his sides, and tiny strands of metal and wood remained poised in midair.

"Get out of here, Max!" he roared.

He didn't have to ask twice. I flew out of the amobiler like a bullet. How I managed to grab the carton of cigarettes remains a mystery to me to this day!

I turned around when I was already in the hall. Shurf was pensively removing our traveling bags from under the debris of the amobiler.

"Give me a hand. What are you looking at?" He smiled as naturally as if he had been doing it for the last hundred years.

"You really are a fantastic racer, Max, if I do say so myself. I've never seen anything like it in my life!"

"If there's anything this guy can do, it's travel far and travel fast," a familiar voice sounded from behind me.

I turned around and stared at Sir Juffin Hully in delight.

"You wouldn't believe me, Juffin, if I told you how long I'd been waiting for this meeting," I said in the ingratiating voice of Sir Mackie Ainti, and burst out laughing at the unexpectedness of it.

"Stop it, Mackie!" Juffin exclaimed merrily. "I can't listen to that. Now try to greet me again, Max."

"Juffin, what's going on?" I said in my own voice, and laughed, my head a-spin.

"That's better. Good morning Shurf. This fellow totaled the amobiler, just as I predicted. And it was an official Ministry car, if I'm not mistaken."

"He's a superb racer," Shurf insisted, dragging his valuable carpet out of the rubble. "Max, perhaps you'll help me with this?"

I grabbed the bags nimbly, leaving my friend to deal with the carpets, and Juffin and I went into the office to drink some kamra and shoot the breeze. The prospect was so tempting it made my mouth water.

I got carried away, and talked without a break for four hours.

During that time, Juffin had managed to return Shurf's own nat-ural-born face to him by some surreptitious gesture. ("It's easier to destroy than to create, boys. Why should we wait for Sir Kofa?") I was even slightly shocked at first. I had completely forgotten what Shurf looked like.

"So that's that story," Lonli-Lokli drawled thoughtfully when I finally shut up.

My ears were ringing, whether from exhaustion, or from listening to myself talk. Shurf, in the meantime, had gotten up from the table.

"I'm going home, if you don't have any objections, gentlemen."

"Of course, go on home," Juffin said, nodding. "You could have left long ago. I understand, though. You had a right to hear out the whole story. It's your story, too. I'm very glad Sir Shurf. About the adventure with Kiba Attsax, I mean. You think you may owe Max another serenade now."

Sometimes Juffin's sarcasm went overboard, and this time Shurf and I glanced at each other. I smiled ear to ear, and he with the cor-ners of his mouth, a hole in the heavens above him!

Juffin gazed on this rare spectacle with pleasure, smiling from ear to ear as well. Such an idyll reigned in the office of the Secret Investigative Force that all the rosy tints in the universe would not suffice to describe it.

❋

Then only Juffin and I were left.

"And where's Melifaro's curious nose?" I asked. "Where is every-body else?"

"I ordered them not to disturb us. There will be plenty of time later for hugs and kisses of joy. I don't want anyone else to overhear your report about the events in Kettari. It's top secret, Max. I hope you under-stand that. All my life I've expected something like this from Mackie, but never anything on this scale. I can't even claim that I understand it all now, but that's not unusual. Mackie is the kind of fellow who isn't capa-ble of clarity. Show me all the maps of Kettari again, Max."

"Shall I give them to you, Juffin? I know you aren't sentimental, but in the interests of the case . . ."

"No. Keep them. You may need them. It looks like Mackie is count-ing on several more visits. By the way, did it ever occur to you that you needed to be very careful? It's the most dangerous kind of scrape of all, the one you got mixed up in. Though it's also the most useful."

"I liked it," I exclaimed dreamily. "What do you mean, Juffin? Dangerous how?"

"Because you learn too quickly. And you display your powers so ingenuously. Mackie is very crafty, but he can't always come to your aid when you need him. He loves confronting a person with his fate, and then—just leaving him to it. You know, in every world there are hunters who are looking for people like you. Compared to some of them, the late Kiba Attsax is like a sweet dream. Speaking of dreams, Max. I hope you haven't lost the personal kerchief of the Grand Magician of the Order of the Secret Grass? I strongly recommend that you not go to sleep without it, no matter what. Never. Understood?"

"Yes," I nodded uncertainly. "But what—"

"I don't know," Juffin said sharply. "Maybe nothing at all will happen, you're a lucky one. But I want to be certain that no matter what you dream you'll be able to wake up. That's all. Now we can move on to more pleasant things. Praising you, for instance. You truly exceeded not only your own, but also my expectations."

"I guess so," I said with a shrug. "But it doesn't seem like such a big deal to me. Maybe I'm just tired."

"You must be. You need a good rest—reporting to work every evening, and so forth. Our notions of what constitutes rest are the same, are they not?"

"They are," I said. "We'll start today. I'll just go home for a few hours sleep. Or maybe I won't sleep at all."

"Better take a few slugs of your Elixir and stay here till evening. Tonight you'll stay over at my house. I want to figure out once and for all what exactly happened to you in Kettari. So you'll slumber, and I'll satisfy my curiosity."

"Wonderful," I said. "Sleeping at your house like I used to, just after I arrived in Echo. Yes, it's just like then! I've popped in, fresh from another World. It's a good excuse for me to visit Chuff."

"He'll lick you from head to toe," Juffin said. "I wish I had your worries, boy! Fine, let's quit gabbing for a bit. You should eat something, and I want to take a minute to try puzzling out these blasted maps."

He puzzled not for a minute, but for a good half-hour.

"Now it's clear to me why Mackie won't let me into Kettari," my boss said at last, grinning.

"But Mackie said—"

"Never mind what he said. It seems the old man still thinks I don't catch on too quickly. He's the one who won't let me in, who else? You see, Max, I remember too well what Kettari was really like. And when authentic and reliable memories of sorcerers like Mackie and myself collide, and even contradict each other—well, any World at all, not just a newborn one, runs the risk of flying to pieces."

"So I was led by the nose," I sighed. "And it was Mackie who wouldn't let Shurf follow me, and not some unknown force."

"And a good thing it was he didn't let him. You were very busy just then. You were creating a new World, as I understand. It's very natural, Max. You were led by the nose a bit, but the true purpose was to lead me astray. So don't fret about it. Mackie doesn't always know himself what is true and what isn't, believe me. He's come up with more than a dozen versions of Kettari! It's too bad you couldn't collect all the existing maps of my dear old town."

"Well, what can I say? Juffin, are you in the mood to tell me a little about Sir Mackie Ainti? I just can't figure out what kind of creature he is. He told me he's been alive since time immemorial, and that he rolled into the World from who-knows-where, and somehow I believe him implicitly. Last night he sent me a call, very friendly, thanking me one last time. I hardly survived that short exchange with him! And what happened after I met him for the first time—I've already told you about that."

"Believe it or not, I can't help you there, Max," Juffin smiled. "I spent more than twelve dozen years by his side, but I could never get to the bottom of him. It's most likely my fate, to live in proximity to strange creatures like you and Mackie all the time. You may laugh when I say this, but you and he are like two peas in a pod. But you're young and foolish, while he, in a sense, is perfection. That's the way I remember him. There wasn't a single human weakness in him. To this day, I'm still not sure he ever goes to the bathroom! I swear by the World I never caught him at it!" Juffin said with a hearty laugh. "But I'm sure you'll be better at talking to him in his own language than I was in my time. You and he already see eye to eye. Oh, you're a lucky fellow!"

"Yes, lucky! Only you advise me not to go to sleep without your protective rag, since all the Monsters of the Universe are out hunting. All the same, everything's just hunky-dory!"

"Well, what is it you really want, Max?" the boss asked, knitting his brow. "A tranquil life? A little house with a garden, where you can wait patiently for old age in the company of your dear wife and a horde of grandkids? A royal pension for 'outstanding service'? I can tell you right now that's not going to happen. Never. All the other joys of life are there for the taking, though. Including the Monsters of the Universe, as you call them."

"That's fine with me. Better monsters than hordes of grandkids! You're good at scaring people, Juffin—I'll grant you that."

And I was sent on my way.

There was a free-for-all of everyone else who wished to smother me in hugs, starting with Melifaro, who was the first to tackle me (he had been waiting in line, it seemed, since the evening before), and ending with the shy Sir Lookfi Pence and Sir Kofa Yox, who was too heavy for such strenuous exercises. Even Melamori dispensed with the demure restraint that had characterized our not-very-businesslike dealings lately. It appeared that she wanted us to be friends again. That was no small thing, since friendship was the only thing on the horizon for us. But I had already learned to live with this prospect. And she had, too. In any case, it didn't hurt me anymore. I was glad to see Melamori and all the others. And they were glad to see me with my own face again. I was loved! Darn, it's worth a lot if in some World or other there's a place where you're loved by at least five people. And then there was Lonli-Lokli, who was already at home asleep, and the mighty Lady Sotofa, who was so genuinely pleased with my rare visits. And a few more good fellows who also seemed to have a soft spot in their hearts for me.

"Hey gang, you know what?" I shouted when we had started in on the next jug of kamra from the *Glutton Bunba* (we had polished off so many I had lost count.) "I'm happy."

Why in the World were they roaring with laughter? They couldn't possibly have seen the Droopy Dog cartoons.

※

In the evening, I felt even happier, since I got to spend time with Chuff. He really did lick me from head to toe, but I didn't mind. Then my eyelids started growing heavy. Had they cast a spell on me? But who needs a spell when a person hasn't slept for two days or overindulged in Elixir of Kaxar?

In the middle of the night I woke up, unable to remember where I was. Looking around, I realized I was in my own bed at Sir Juffin's, and that he was sitting over by the wall. His eyes seemed to glitter in the dark—but whose eyes don't play tricks on them when they're fresh from sleep? Anyway, the sight of him sent shivers down my spine.

"Sleep, Max. Don't bother me," my boss said drily. And I dropped off to sleep like a good boy.

❀

In the morning Juffin looked tired, but satisfied.

"Go home, Max. I think I'll sleep a bit. Come to the Ministry after lunch, or even later. It doesn't matter when, just show up. And don't forget about the kerchief if you feel like taking a nap. You're just going to have to get used to it."

"Well, if you say so. What did you find out about me?"

"Loads of things that wouldn't interest you. Now scram, you monster! Let this old geezer get some rest."

At home I was set upon with loud meows by Ella, who was even stouter than when I had left. Armstrong, in his turn, demonstrated brilliant logic: he stared at me pensively, then lazily walked over to his bowl. Well, it made perfect sense.

"Did you miss me?" I asked cheerily. "You don't have to put on an act. I know you didn't. I just cramp your style! I come in here making all kinds of noise; but that's all right, I'll feed you now."

After feeding my beasties, I began unpacking my bags. It's hard to imagine anyone returning from a trip to another World with such useless stuff! The clothes and knick-knacks of Lady Marilyn; the flotsam and jetsam I had accidentally pulled out of the Chink between Worlds, including the box of Cuban cigars. I'll have to take it to the Ministry, I thought. Some aficionado will surely step forward to claim them. The eleven maps of Kettari I would gladly have hung in the living room, but Sir Juffin had warned me that these souvenirs should be safely hidden from prying eyes. So I would have to hide them more carefully.

Finally, I pulled out a small, crumpled parcel. Sinning Magicians, I forgot! My one and only surprise for Sir Juffin, Dish Number 13 from the evening menu of the *Country Home*—that Kettarian delicacy, that reeking bacon grease, that acme of unfathomable vileness, a "remedy for nostalgia," etc. Never mind, I'd give him his treat later in the day. Better late than never.

❀

I left for work just after noon. The black and gold Mantle of Death seemed to me like the best of all possible garments. I must really have been homesick.

Sir Juffin wasn't there yet. But in the Hall of Common Labor, Lonli-Lokli was already sitting in state, dressed all in white, his hands in the embellished protective gloves clasped over his chest.

This vision completely satisfied my esthetic expectations, and I broke into a smile.

"Shall we run down to the *Glutton* and back, Shurf? Or shall we pretend that you're too busy?"

"Too busy I'm not," he replied. "The *Glutton Bunba* is a place I missed even when we were in the *Country Home*."

"Even in the back room of the *Country Home*, where stern, gray-haired men threw themselves into games for small stakes, to kill time? I don't believe it!"

"You're right, Max. Let's go, before I change my mind. Sir Melifaro, I'm leaving."

"Has something already happened in the dark alleys of our capital, gentlemen killers?" Melifaro's quizzical face poked out of the doors of his office. "Whose blood are you planning to drink? Really—has something happened?"

"No," Lonli-Lokli said. "We just think that your backside alone will be more than enough to wipe the dust off the chairs of our side of the Ministry. And Max and I will be doing just about the same thing, but in another place. I deeply regret that your working schedule won't allow you to accompany us to the *Glutton* at this time of day." He turned to me. "Let's hurry, Max, before something does happen. You're too lucky in attracting adventures."

Melifaro's mouth fell open. The airy monologue of the deadpan Lonli-Lokli, the last bastion of seriousness in our small, zany organization, was too much for him.

"Where's our good old Lomki-Lonki? What did you do to him at that resort town, Max? Cast a spell on him? Admit it, you beast you!"

"There's nothing to admit. I just gave him a piece of my mind a few times and swore at him like it was going out of style. Right, Shurf?" I winked at Lonli-Lokli. "I'll have to try the same thing on this fellow here. Who knows what kinds of transformations—"

"Yes, Max, that was some first-rate cussing you did there," Shurf said with an air of nostalgia. "As for Melifaro, I think you might want to give it a try in his presence. Maybe after that he'll finally learn my name. You must do it soon. In the interests of civic peace and social tranquility."

And we left proudly, the two most fearsome people in the Unified Kingdom, I in the Mantle of Death, and Shurf in the Garments of Truth—a veritable double-edged sword.

An hour later we returned, and Melifaro forced us to go over the whole thing again.

"Come on, what did you do to Loki-Lonki, Mr. Bad Dream?"

Poor Melifaro, the best investigator in all this World, kept on trying to get to the bottom of this unyielding mystery. I even started feeling sorry for him. It had been so long since I had had my own secrets, though. These days I was always trying to uncover the secrets of other people.

"I've told you the honest truth, friend. Shurf tried to wake me up, and I let him have it. Then I just about died with shame. But everything blew over, as you can see. Maybe my cursing worked like a spell."

"What exactly did you tell him?" Melifaro prodded incredulously.

"I don't remember. Ask him yourself. He took notes on my performance, and then demanded that I translate the meaning of some very colorful and exotic words."

"He took notes? Well, Max, you've put my mind at ease. It's not all that bad. Only good old Shurf is capable of writing down all the filth people say to him in good conscience. To broaden his horizons. Yes, that means everything is fine."

❦

Juffin was already waiting for me in the office by the time I returned to the House by the Bridge.

"Ta-da!" I exclaimed from the doorway. "I completely forgot! You asked me to bring you a souvenir from your homeland." I drew the crumpled parcel from the pocket of the Mantle of Death. "I decided to give you the thing that moved me more than all the other Kettarian wonders. Don't be offended."

"Offended? Why should I get offended, Max?" I noticed with astonishment that Juffin was sniffing the package and inhaling its unbearable stench with downright pleasure. "Oh, I understand. You know nothing about real delicacies, son!" Sir Juffin carefully unwrapped the parcel and bit off a piece in delight. "You wanted to laugh at the old man, didn't you? You can't imagine how happy you've made me!"

Deep down, I'm not such a scoundrel as I seem. I wasn't terribly disappointed. If Sir Juffin considers that to be a rare delicacy—well, so much the better.

"Excellent," I said, and smiled. "The greater are my chances of escaping alive from the clutches of the famous Kettarian Hunter."

"Well, if I were you, I wouldn't indulge in false modesty, nor would I get my hopes up. Didn't Mackie tell you that hope is a foolish sentiment?"

"So you were there with me, Juffin? I knew it, I just knew it!"

"Don't be silly, Max. I was right here in Echo, and I was engaged in much more important matters than—" He trailed off, but his smile was cunning.

"The next time you're on hand to observe my sensational adventures, if it's not too much trouble, will you please applaud my modest victories? I'd appreciate it."

And with enormous pleasure I demonstrated the famous Kettarian gesture, two gentle taps on the nose with the forefinger of the right had. Practice had made perfect—I did it almost automatically.

"Oh, Max!" Juffin said. "Sometimes you're really touching, do you know that? Fine. You'll be having a mug of kamra with Melamori soon. Sir Kofa will grab you tonight, there's no room for doubt there. And Lookfi won't fail to visit you at sundown, as soon as he puts the buriwoks to bed for the night, and before you leave for home. How do you like that for a busy schedule? You won't collapse in exhaustion?"

"I just might. And you, Juffin? Have you had enough for today?"

"Absolutely. I'm on my way home. Do as you wish, but I'm tired after the past few days. I'll just stop by Xolomi—one of the old-timers there took a notion to escape, can you imagine? Now the boys are trying to scrape his remains from the walls of his cell, and I'm required to be present, since someone there thinks it's a serious case. A 'serious case'!" Juffin said comically, and stood up. I plunked myself down in the chair he had just vacated.

Thereafter, everything happened strictly according to the schedule Sir Juffin Hully had devised. I even shared some kamra with Lady Melamori, as he had predicted—something I really hadn't counted on. But we chattered away like old friends, I won't deny it.

Things were falling into place in my life. I didn't dare count on more. For the time being, it was enough.

✳

It took me three days to realize that none of my colleagues liked cigars. Only Lady Melamori was daring enough to try one, but it was pure bravado. Her face didn't show a trace of pleasure, just undiluted determination. I stuffed the box in the desk drawer. I had one vague hope left—that General Boboota would recover.

He had to be good for something, that big meanie! He'd look great with a cigar stuck in his mouth. And these were the biggest worries I had, Magicians be praised!

"You're still not missing a dose of daily marvels?" Sir Juffin asked innocently on about the fourth day after my return.

"Not at all," I said. "Has something happened?"

"Well, the marvels have been missing you," Juffin said, with a grin. "I was just wondering whether you'd want to keep me company. I'm thinking of visiting Maba."

"What a question! Of course I do!"

This time Maba Kalox met us in the hall.

"I think today we might sit in another room," he remarked casually. "You have no objection to a little variety, do you?"

Wandering rather aimlessly through the corridors (I got the impression that Sir Maba himself wasn't entirely sure which door led to this 'other room'), we finally settled ourselves in a small chamber that resembled a bedroom more than a living room, though I didn't see a bed.

"Mackie's spoiling you, Max," our cordial host said, pulling out a tray with some strange dishes from under the small table. "He's sent you enough of those smoking sticks to last you the rest of your life. You've probably even stopped practicing."

"No, not at all," I said. "It's such a good way to economize on food. No need to spend money shopping—I just stick my hand somewhere, and presto! You're not the only one who loves money. Do you know how greedy I am?"

"I suspected you were," Sir Maba said. "Is this true, Juffin?"

"And how! You know what he sometimes eats? Some strange little sausage hidden inside a big bun. It's disgusting. And he enjoys it!"

"I've adored hot dogs my whole life." I was already tired of this subject. "The consequences of a deprived childhood, and all that. And look who's talking! That Kettarian 'delicacy' of yours . . ."

"I've got your numbers, boys," Maba said. "You're so much alike sometimes, it's just unbelievable. You know, Max, Juffin thinks that you've seen through his little trick, so . . . Well, so now you might be a bit angry with us."

"No way!" I exclaimed. "I'm already used to people making a fool of me, so don't worry!"

Sir Maba stood up and went over to the window.

"We're not worried. Come over here and take a look."

I went over to the window and froze. It didn't look out onto the garden at all, but onto a very familiar street. Dumbfounded, I stared at the yellow paving stones, then raised my eyes. A small fountain played merrily, sending its multihued spray into the sky.

"High Street?" I asked hoarsely. "Is it Kettari?"

"Well, at least it's not the border of the County Vook," Juffin replied cheerfully behind me.

"Only, don't tell your friend Old Mackie about this window. Agreed?"

Sir Maba Kalox winked at me.

"He doesn't have to worry. Fierce old Juffin isn't planning to climb through it." And Sir Maba lightly tapped his nose with the forefinger of his right hand.

Two good people can always come to an understanding. There's no denying it.